PENGUIN

THE PORTABLE EDITH WHARTON

EDITH WHARTON (1862–1937) was born Edith Newbold Jones. A
member of a distinguished New York family, she was educated privately in America and abroad. She spent long periods in Europe, and
from 1910 until her death made her home in France. She published
poetry and short stories in magazines and in volume form before her
novel *The House of Mirth* (1905) became a best-seller and established her as a writer of both distinction and popular appeal. During
her life, she published more than forty volumes: novels, stories,
verse, essays, travel books, and memoirs. *The House of Mirth, Ethan
Frome* (1911), *The Reef* (1912), *The Custom of the Country* (1913),
Summer (1917), and *The Age of Innocence* (1920; winner of the
Pulitzer Prize) are all available in Penguin Classics editions.

LINDA WAGNER-MARTIN is Frank Borden Hanes Professor of English at the University of North Carolina–Chapel Hill. The author of
books on William Faulkner, Ernest Hemingway, John Dos Passos,
Ellen Glasgow, Denise Levertov, William Carlos Williams, Edith
Wharton, and other American modernists, Wagner-Martin is the
biographer of both Sylvia Plath and Gertrude Stein. She is coeditor
of *The Oxford Companion to Women's Writing in the United States,*
and editor of the contemporary section of the *Heath Anthology of
American Literature.*

The Portable
Edith Wharton

Edited with an introduction by
LINDA WAGNER-MARTIN

PENGUIN BOOKS

PENGUIN BOOKS

Published by the Penguin Group
Penguin Group (USA) Inc., 375 Hudson Street, New York, New York 10014, U.S.A.
Penguin Books Ltd, 80 Strand, London WC2R 0RL, England
Penguin Books Australia Ltd, 250 Camberwell Road, Camberwell, Victoria 3124, Australia
Penguin Books Canada Ltd, 10 Alcorn Avenue, Toronto, Ontario, Canada M4V 3B2
Penguin Books India (P) Ltd, 11 Community Centre, Panchsheel Park, New Delhi–110 017, India
Penguin Books (N.Z.) Ltd, Cnr Rosedale and Airborne Roads, Albany, Auckland, New Zealand
Penguin Books (South Africa) (Pty) Ltd, 24 Sturdee Avenue, Rosebank, Johannesburg 2196, South Africa

Penguin Books Ltd, Registered Offices:
80 Strand, London WC2R 0RL, England

First published in Penguin Books 2003

3   5   7   9   10   8   6   4

Grateful acknowledgment is made for permission to reprint selections from *The Letters of Edith Wharton*
edited by R. W. B. Lewis and Nancy Lewis (Scribner, 1988). Reprinted by permission
of the Estate of Edith Wharton and the Watkins/Loomis Agency.

LIBRARY OF CONGRESS CATALOGING-IN-PUBLICATION DATA
Wharton, Edith, 1862–1937
[Selections. 2003]
The portable Edith Wharton / Edith Wharton ; edited with an introduction by Linda Wagner-Martin.
p.   cm.—(Penguin classics)
Includes bibliographical references.
ISBN 0-14-243758-1
I. Wagner-Martin, Linda. II. Title. III. Series.

PS3545.H16A6 2003
813'.52—dc21   2003045620

Printed in the United States of America
Set in Adobe Sabon

Contents

Introduction   ix

Chronology   xxiii

I. SHORT FICTION

Souls Belated   7

The Muse's Tragedy   34

Friends   48

The Choice   69

The Lady's Maid's Bell   84

The Other Two   105

The Hermit and the Wild Woman   125

His Father's Son   148

Afterward   164

The Eyes   194

The Letters   213

Autres Temps . . .   250

Xingu   280

Coming Home   304

Writing a War Story   336

II. NOVELS

Summer   357

FROM *The House of Mirth*

    Chapters I and II   497

FROM *The Reef*

    Chapters XXIII through XXVI   519

FROM *The Age of Innocence*

    Chapters XXX and XXXI   543

III. LETTERS

To Edward L. Burlingame, July 30, 1894   567

To Edward L. Burlingame, December 14, 1895   568

To Sara Norton, February 28, 1901   569

To Sara Norton, November 25, 1901   569

To Annie Adams Fields, Summer 1902   570

To William Crary Brownell, September 12, 1902   571

To Sara Norton, March 17, 1903   572

To Sara Norton, June 5, 1903   574

To William Crary Brownell, June 25, 1904   575

To Charles Scribner, November 11, 1905   577

To Dr. Morgan Dix, December 5, 1905   577

To W. Morton Fullerton, October 15, 1907   579

To Robert Grant, November 19, 1907   579

To W. Morton Fullerton, February 1908   581

To W. Morton Fullerton, March 1908   581

To W. Morton Fullerton, April 1908   582

To W. Morton Fullerton, May 20, 1908   583

To W. Morton Fullerton, June 19, 1908   584

To W. Morton Fullerton, August 26, 1908   585

To W. Morton Fullerton, June 19, 1912   588

To Sara Norton, September 2, 1914   589

To Henry James, March 11, 1915   591

To Bernard Berenson, September 4, 1917   594

IV. NONFICTION

FROM A Midsummer Week's Dream: August in Italy   601

FROM Paris to Poitiers   608

In Argonne   612

FROM In Lorraine and the Vosges   630

Explanatory Notes   639

Selected Bibliography   651

Introduction

From her modest beginning as a published writer of short stories, Edith Newbold Jones Wharton became one of the most esteemed American novelists of the twentieth century. She dominated the best-seller lists from the 1905 publication of *The House of Mirth* through her autobiography, *A Backward Glance* (1934). More important, her work is frequently taught today, and even more frequently bought and read by thousands of people who are not required to do so for classes.

Few writers have had such a continuous success story. In some ways, the longevity of Wharton's success could not have been predicted: her highly formal style, the slowly developing narrative, the method that depended on the inclusion of subtle details, the characterization that was, finally, more intimate than might have been fashionable were qualities that often seemed reminiscent of nineteenth-century fiction. Yet, given that the turn of the century was a time of cautious yet flamboyant exploration of mores, Wharton's place in the literary scene makes sense.

Alternatively subversive of accepted social values and yet insistent upon many of them, her fiction spun textures of ambivalence so dense that one reader could find the ending of *Summer* "happy" while another cried over Charity Royall's choice that brought the novel to a close. By the time Edith Wharton published *Summer* in 1917, she had already explored so many facets of American society—from both male points of view and female ones—that she was thinking of giving up the profession of novelist. She already had been a best-selling author for more than a dozen years; she had been introduced to writers she had long worshipped, and one of those masters, Henry James, had become a close friend. Yet she came to realize that, despite her publishing success, she was faced with the contradiction between being able to write memorably about life and being able to live it.

Edith Newbold Jones Wharton was not trained to be a writer. By today's standards, she was not trained to "be" anything. Edith was the daughter of the extremely well-placed Jones family of New York City (allegedly the Joneses of the phrase "keeping up with the Joneses"). Born in 1862 to parents whose families were themselves members of New York's socially elite "Four Hundred," she felt it a privilege even to be allowed to write. Writing was considered less an art than just plain "work." As the daughter and granddaughter of prominent families, she would not have been allowed to work, no matter how satisfying she may have found an intellectual interest. In the classic model of patriarchy, daughters and wives were to be protected by male providers; when a daughter was of marriageable age, having made her debut, she married and left her father's house, in order to be cared for by a husband her family had approved. Most likely, she would not have been allowed to go to a school or university. In this severely stratified society, middle-class families sent their children to college, but the children of wealthy families were educated at home, taught by private tutors. Daughters were taught differently than sons, with their instruction emphasizing art and music, French and Italian. Sons—in Edith's case, her two older brothers—were trained in logic, mathematics, and Latin.

Edith Jones's education was somewhat more erratic than might have been intended. The Jones family—like many other wealthy families in New York society—had lost money after the Civil War and found that they could live comfortably, and cheaply, in Europe while renting out their homes in the city and at Newport, Rhode Island. Between the ages of four and ten, then, Edith lived in Florence and Paris, as well as in locations in Germany and Spain. She learned languages easily, and was proficient, even fluent, in French, Italian, and German.

As a result of this childhood abroad, Edith Jones seldom felt at home in the States. She endured her society's emphasis on what one wore and whom one saw, but she tended to live in her imaginative "making up." As a young child who could not yet read, Edith would stand—book in hand—and tell detailed stories to whoever would listen. At first, her mother, Lucretia (famous as the best-dressed woman in New York), humored her daughter: she transcribed Edith's stories, and later she paid to have a collection of her daughter's poems privately published. But after Edith had completed a thirty-thousand-word novella (*Fast and Loose*) when she was only fourteen, Lucretia began to worry that her daughter might never find a suitable mate; accordingly, before her eighteenth birthday, Edith had her debut (to which she wore a startling black gown).

Before she was twenty-one, Edith Jones suffered two grave losses. The death of her father, George Jones, the man who remained in the background of the family's social life but who doted on his daughter and taught her to read at an early age, was a severe blow. But so, too, was the breaking of her first engagement, that to Henry Stevens, son of Mrs. Paran Stevens, a doyenne of society who did not find Edith a suitable match for her son. At Mrs. Stevens's insistence, the engagement was to be broken, though Edith was given the opportunity to end the liaison herself. After it was over, she traveled abroad with her mother.

The following summer, at Bar Harbor, Maine, Edith was sure she would become engaged to the young lawyer Walter Van Rensselaer Berry. Berry, however, did not propose. Later that season, Edith met Teddy Wharton, a wealthy Boston sportsman who was a friend of her older brother's; they married in the spring of 1885 at Trinity Chapel in New York City. Edith's name was omitted from the wedding invitation; perhaps her mother's haste to announce the wedding caused the error.

For the next five or six years, Teddy and Edith Wharton lived alternately in New York and in the Joneses' cottage, Pencraig, at Newport. After disastrous early sexual experiences, their relations became largely nonsexual. They traveled abroad (in 1888, the two spent a year's income, more than $10,000, on a four-month Aegean cruise) and Edith wrote poetry, some of which was published. Edith Wharton's health, however, was very poor; she was plagued with inexplicable fatigue and depression. In July of 1891, *Scribner's Magazine* published one of her short stories, though it rejected her important novella, *Bunner Sisters,* a text about one sister's sacrifice for another—a very long, complicated story of marriage.

The decade of the 1890s continued to be marred by health problems for both Whartons. Although Charles Scribner wanted to publish a collection of Edith's stories, she disappeared to Europe and did not correspond with the company for more than a year. The Whartons bought Land's End, a Newport estate on the Atlantic, which Edith and architect Ogden Codman decorated. Several years later, she and Codman wrote *The Decoration of Houses,* which was Wharton's first book. In recovery mode, she sought help at the S. Weir Mitchell clinic in Philadelphia. The usual practice there was to order bed rest and no intellectual activity for patients, but Wharton's physicians encouraged her to write. In 1899, her story collection *The Greater Inclination* was published by Scribner, followed in 1900 by a novella, *The Touchstone.*

The Whartons bought a large estate near Lenox, Massachusetts, and built The Mount. Edith planned and decorated the house and grounds, and continued to publish (a second book of stories, an historical novel *The Valley of Decision,* travel essays). Teddy had his first breakdown after they moved into The Mount; Edith's illness returned. Through an introduction by friends, Edith corresponded with Henry James, who encouraged her to continue writing but—in his words—to "Do New York!"

The publication history of Edith Wharton's writing—both short stories and novels—provides a kind of "how-to" list for aspiring writers. Its main ingredient is that Wharton *wrote.* Whether she was a studious teenager or a sought-after socialite, she spent a good share of her morning hours with pen in hand. Her imagination, and her personal interest, were devoted to writing. Even when she traveled abroad, which she sometimes did for months of each year, she wrote—travel essays, dozens of letters, stories, novels in progress.

Armed with Henry James's injunction that she write about her culture, her society, her New York, Wharton began the novel that was to place her work on the lists of best-sellers. *The House of Mirth,* the ultimately sad story of Lily Bart, the twenty-nine-year-old ex-debutante who has not yet decided to marry, made Wharton's reputation as it was serialized in *Scribner's Magazine* month

by month. Before the last installment of the novel, readers wrote
to Wharton, beseeching the author not to let Lily die.

As Edith Wharton had learned herself, any ambition except
marrying well made a woman a freak of nature: Lily has no abili-
ties except dressing well, playing bridge, and being a social leader.
Unfortunately, though she is from an excellent family, she has no
personal fortune, and once her maiden aunt decides to disinherit
Lily, her marriage prospects crumble. The story of Lily (a name
chosen in part because it was what Edith's family had called her
when she was a child) moves to its inevitable end—society can
make no room for a penniless upper-class woman, one untrained
to earn any kind of living, so Lily chooses to take an overdose of
sleeping potion. In short, despite readers' pleas, Lily dies.

Wharton's ironic distance from her protagonist is signaled in
the title. Fashionable society looks pleasant, but as myriad New
Yorkers know too well, there is no "house of mirth" that exists
apart from its layers of anxiety—anxiety about money (personi-
fied in the broken man who is Lily's father), about position (Lily's
mother with her class-bound ambition), about propriety (Lily's
aunt, whose own spinsterhood equips her to be disdainful of any human passion), and about the sham of appearances (Gus Trenor's
preying on Lily's innocence). *The House of Mirth* is not a comedy,
but despite Lily's death, there is nothing melodramatic about it.
Wharton incisively shows the pretension of both the upper-class
society and the hangers-on, people like Lawrence Selden, who
pretend to be above that society's mores. Unfortunately for Lily
Bart, she believes the protestations of a Selden—even though he
does nothing to help her once her social group has abandoned her.
Wharton's novel also shows clearly the prejudice that can mark
upper-class people's behavior: the character of the Jewish Simon
Rosedale is one of the strongest in the novel, and it is rendered
sympathetically. Wharton also attacks class snobbery by creating
the persona of Gerty Farish, a self-supporting young woman who
lives unfashionably so that she can do good work among the
poor.

With *The House of Mirth,* Wharton made her reputation as a
novelist of manners. In this category, she followed in the footsteps
not only of Henry James but also of Kate Chopin, George Eliot,

Theodore Dreiser, and Ellen Glasgow, writers of mixed reputa-
tions, fates, and sales. To emphasize the depiction of a culture as
being an author's primary concern might seem to undercut his or
her ability to draw character or to tell an interesting story. The
term "novelist of manners," however, created a kind of bridge for
readers who wanted all fiction to teach moralistic lessons. For
those who wanted to read wholesome books, the narrative of Lily
Bart's life of gambling, flirting, and being generally useless might
be repulsive. But if those same readers could see *The House of
Mirth* as an accurate picture of life in the upper echelons of New
York late in the nineteenth century, the novel was itself useful. As
a novel of manners of urban life decades ago, the book provided
a social commentary, rather than being only—or primarily—Lily
Bart's tragic story.

Wharton's next novel, *The Fruit of the Tree,* focuses on indus-
trial America and the economic role of factory owners. *Ethan
Frome* draws the picture of an educated man, trapped in his
provincial New England home and destroyed by an illicit love.
The Reef, one of Wharton's least-praised books, tells the story of
a man's infidelity and how it destroys the lives it has touched.
With *The Custom of the Country* in 1913, Wharton makes her
most definitive statement about the tragedy of the American
woman who follows her culture's punishing script: to be beautiful, to marry well, and marry well, and marry well again (using
marriage as a ladder to the finer things—i.e., wealth) is to succeed.
The most bitterly ironic of Wharton's novels, *The Custom of the
Country* places Undine Spragg squarely in the midst of the fashionable society that excluded Lily Bart, and leaves the reader
grappling with whether Undine is the protagonist of the novel or
the antagonist. (Interestingly, the suicide in this novel is that of
one of Undine's naïve former husbands.)

Woven throughout this tapestry of the publication of Wharton's novels are her many other books that readers avidly bought.
Even before *The House of Mirth* appeared in 1905, Wharton's
travel books, largely comprising essays reprinted from periodicals,
sold well: *Italian Villas and Their Gardens, Italian Backgrounds,*
and, later, *A Motor-Flight Through France* (the latter essays composed once Edith had purchased her own motorcar). But, more

important, Wharton's short stories—appearing first in *Scribner's Magazine* or other prestigious journals and then collected into books published by Charles Scribner—drew an immense readership. So integral were the stories to the rise of Wharton's reputation as a writer, in fact, that the author's development can be charted as well through the short stories as through her novels.

Thematically, Wharton's stories are much like her novels. They deal consistently with the difficulties of marriage, of first achieving it and then existing within its confines, or with heterosexuality in relation to friendship. One set of stories focuses on the problems of being an artist or a writer and continuing to belong to a social world: What does society do with the artist? How does a community respond to the work of an artist or a writer? What are the effects of belonging on the soul of the artist? Formal in structure, Wharton's stories—all eighty-six of them, many of novella length—turn repeatedly to what one might suppose was Wharton's personal dilemma: How to exist in the real world even while working as a woman who wrote, and, as a subcategory, how to be a normal, sentient woman.

The formality of the short story form in the late nineteenth century saved Wharton from readers seeing her life in her art. The stories published first in *Scribner's Magazine* were far from transparent, and they appeared anything but autobiographical. "A Cup of Cold Water," for instance, shows a disappointed man able to rescue a poor woman from her attempted suicide; rather than take his own life, he becomes useful to his society, and to the bereft woman. Because the protagonist is male, and the woman character so poor, few would read the story as autobiographical. "The Muse's Tragedy" and "Souls Belated," both from 1899, show different approaches to characters' making good marriages, and therefore living good lives. In "Souls Belated," the foolish avoidance of marriage—especially on Lydia's part—shows how dangerous any kind of romanticization of conventions, or the absence of them, can be. Gannett can only hope Lydia will come to realize that passion can live even within the marriage he so desires for them. "The Muse's Tragedy" is the story of Mrs. Anerton, whose life has been so often confused with its replication in art that she has known very little truth—or life—at all. It is the narrative of a woman sacrificed to become an artist's muse, the life of a human being turned into the life of art robbed of any immediacy or satisfaction.

"Friends" is a deft treatment of the impossibility of friendship between women—women here shown as needy and dependent on marriage—even if the characters' lives would have been enriched by it. "The Other Two" is a rare comic story, also from 1904, in which Wharton shows the aplomb of a thrice-married woman who serves tea to her present spouse in the company of her two former husbands. The relentless intrigue of heterosexual relationships, outside or within marriage, is here set against conventional society's expectations.

In Wharton's first three collections of stories—*The Greater Inclination* in 1899, *Crucial Instances* in 1901, and *The Descent of Man* in 1904—most of the protagonists are men, many of the settings are European, and the plot lines are intricate. These read as highly traditional stories, competently structured with main characters who are educated, intellectual, and given to meditating about their problems. Most of the protagonists are middle class rather than wealthy; most of them are heterosexual. Nearly all the stories could be said to have moralistic outcomes.

There are some exceptions to these generalizations, however. Wharton throughout her career wrote ghost stories, a genre popular in itself but one that recent feminist critics point out gave women authors the chance to write about subjects that might have been taboo or have gone unspoken in polite society—the sensual friendship, the knowledge of another's intimate life, the extraordinary power of sexuality. "The Lady's Maid's Bell," from Wharton's 1904 collection, for example, prompts the reader to wonder what the relationship between the crude Mr. Brympton and his wife really is. The occasional presence of the dead maidservant Emma Saxon, the ghost who appears when Alice Hartley's (the lady's maid's) bell rings, makes the narrative a ghost story, though it is never explained why Emma has died, or what her presence portends. (One intuits, however, that Mrs. Brympton is sexually abused by her spouse, and finds her true love only in the neighborly man who visits and reads to her. That Alice Hartley stays until Mrs. Brympton's death is a tribute to her steadfastness, her heart, and her sympathy with her quiet, withdrawn mistress.)

Another story from this time period, "The Choice," is Wharton's most overt presentation of a woman's loving someone other than her husband. Wharton makes clear in the story, a narrative of betrayal, that Isabel Stilling and her lover, Austin Wrayford, hope for the death of her spouse—but he outlives Wrayford and will continue to spend Isabel's fortune, as well as that of his mother, without a qualm. Cobham Stilling is one of Wharton's most objectionable male characters.

Wharton's short stories, if read autobiographically, help to complete the chronology of her life. Although Wharton was in her early forties when she found enormous success through the publication of *The House of Mirth,* she was still a woman hungry for both romance and sexual fulfillment. As we have seen, in "The Lady's Maid's Bell" and "The Choice" she dares to make sympathetic a wife who finds only misery in her marriage.

Unhappy as Edith Wharton was in her own marriage, her fictional portraits of these wives may have stemmed more logically from her hopeful interest in men other than Teddy Wharton: in other words, Edith Wharton seemed to believe she would yet have a choice. As early as 1889, she and Teddy had resumed her earlier friendship with Walter Berry, now a practicing lawyer in the Washington, D.C., area; in a subsequent year, they rented a house in Washington to see if they would enjoy that location. Edith's friendship with Berry continued to his death—and hers; in fact, she is buried beside him. Berry never married.

The more apparent choice that might have been hers was to leave her husband for Morton Fullerton, a younger journalist she had met in 1907 through her friendship with Henry James. As her letters to Fullerton reprinted here witness, theirs was a sexual affair, even if brief. The incongruity in Edith Wharton's being so passionately in love with a man already marked by his deceit about his poverty, his bisexuality, and his long history of flagrant liaisons, complete with blackmail and incestuous overtones, suggests her ability to cling to the notion of romance despite what she could understand to be facts. Wharton's 1912 novel *The Reef,* which she showed to Fullerton as she was writing it, is a relatively undisguised fiction about the heartbreak of the widowed Anna Leath as she learns about the character of the old beau she had

somehow promised to marry. The infidelities are George Darrow's, but the heartbreak remains Anna's.

Behind the façade of world-famous novelist, Edith Wharton led
a life that had little promise left in it: Teddy Wharton, who had
customarily handled the considerable income from Edith's writing,
had taken $50,000 of that income to spend on mistresses and their
living quarters. He, like Henry James, was undergoing a series of
breakdowns. Edith and Teddy planned to separate—several times.
She no longer heard from Fullerton. But she continued to write.

Some of her stories reflected the impasse of the romance plot, as
it had played out in her own life. "The Letters," for instance, is a
tongue-in-cheek admission that men lie, repeatedly; but in the
story, the newly wealthy young woman accepts her former em-
ployer, who has lied about getting her letters, and marries him.
The warmly comic tone makes this a story of reconciliation, not
recrimination. "His Father's Son" is Wharton's rare attempt to
create a male character who is as driven by passion as a woman—
in this case, same-sex passion. Some of Wharton's later ghost
stories—"The Eyes," "Afterward"—give the powers of pre-
science to a modest wife and an unassuming man: the hero in patriarchy is oftentimes not heroic in Wharton's fiction.

It isn't useful, or necessary, to compare all of Wharton's short
fiction with her novels, or to link all stories to her biography.
Wharton's oeuvre also includes classic stories that have no antecedent in the novels. "The Hermit and the Wild Woman" is one
rare and perfectly achieved narrative, the story for which Wharton titled her fifth collection of stories in 1908. Parabolic in its
form, "The Hermit and the Wild Woman" draws on the Edith
Wharton–Henry James friendship and, like many of their fictions,
plays a privately coded language game. A religious analogy in
some respects, the narrative focuses on the male *isolato,* the hermit,
whereas the energetic yet apparently misdirected "wild woman,"
one of James's terms of endearment for Wharton, seems to lead a
life oblique to the path of the hermit: both characters, however,
find the end they desire. The aestheticism of the artist, regardless
of that figure's sex, is the text and texture of this story. And in
"Xingu"—the title story of her 1916 collection—Wharton sends
up a feigned intellectualism so pervasive in the upper levels of cosmopolitan society.

When Edith Wharton's divorce from Teddy was final in 1913, she took France as her permanent residence and began living out her self-chosen expatriation—a kind of rarefied exile—which she had described so well in "Autre Temps . . ." The woman who chose her own path, whether society regarded her as a wild woman or a divorcée or a success, would seldom find either conventional romance or genuine love, no matter where on earth she turned. Perhaps it was fortunate for Wharton that she was then living abroad, because she was able to throw herself into war relief efforts. During 1914, the year World War I began, she raised more than $100,000 for refugee relief and the care and placement of war orphans. She also invested her time, will, and personal fortune in caring for these Belgian children, who numbered more than seven hundred, and in setting up and maintaining a sewing room for Frenchwomen who had no other incomes. In 1917, she was awarded both the Order of Leopold (Belgium) and the French Legion of Honor.

Wharton visited the Front four or five times during the intense fighting of 1915. Enabled by having her own car and chauffeur, and by being famous, she was allowed to take these trips when most civilians would have been turned back. She came to be more familiar with battle and with the constant atmosphere of fear than most women of her time—and she did what she was accustomed to doing with such knowledge: she wrote about it. In 1915, she published *Fighting France,* an admittedly propagandistic effort to encourage the United States to enter the war. (See "In Argonne" and the excerpt from "In Lorraine and the Vosges.") The next year, she edited *The Book of the Homeless,* a money-raising project for those refugees she was tending, and others. Fearing for her health, her doctors prescribed a hiatus in her involvement (Wharton was approaching her mid-fifties and in a culture in which people lived less long than they do at present, she was well past middle-age). So she wrote *Summer,* the story of Charity Royall's great passion for the upper-class man who disdained her love. Setting the novella among the poor villages of New England, a terrain not so different from the French villages she was learning to understand through her war work, Wharton revisited the setting she had used successfully in *Ethan Frome* (1911). But this time, the story was of passion explored and brought to literal fruition—not of passion frustrated.

Returning to the war as her subject, Wharton wrote an effective novel, *The Marne;* an anthropological study, *French Ways and Their Meaning* (a copy of which Ernest Hemingway kept in his personal library); and more stories. "Writing a War Story" is an ironic spoof of writers who assume they can put on the mantle of patriotism and earn publication because of the themes they treat, but "Coming Home" is a jarringly realistic fiction about the immensity of hatred a Frenchman feels for the German who has helped to destroy his own homeland, his own village. Later, Wharton published the very interesting *A Son at the Front,* a novel about a father's involvement with his son's sacrifice.

True to her consistent pattern of treating herself once her depression and malaise grew overwhelming, Wharton in 1918 bought Pavillon Colombe, an estate near Paris, and reclaimed it from the ravages of disuse. She continued to mourn the death of her beloved friend Henry James (in 1916), and that of one of her two brothers. But she threw most of her remaining energy into the novel that truly made her reputation for all time: *The Age of Innocence* (1920). In this novel, Wharton sidestepped the problem of appearing to criticize the American culture to which she legally belonged. She made the story of Newland Archer, May Welland, and the "foreign" cousin Ellen Olenska a retrospective one, giving readers the opportunity to be nostalgic about what New York and its upper classes would have been like fifty years earlier. That the social attitudes had changed little (and that World War I had drawn these well-established Americans even further back into conservatism, into a nativism that would eventually see the rise of many repressive political groups, among them the Ku Klux Klan) was not the point of Wharton's romance. The point was, once again, relinquishment. Newland Archer stays with his young and less-than-naïve wife rather than follow his emotion to join with Ellen. The crowning irony of Wharton's narrative is that even after May's death from natural causes, even with the blessing of his son, Archer will not resume his friendship with the lovely Ellen—who has lived these decades in a Paris apartment, an expatriate like Wharton, presumably waiting for Archer to return to her. Instead, Archer walks away from their arranged meeting.

Part of the unforgettable effect of Wharton's *The Age of Innocence* is the fusion of the writer's own emotional life with the events of the urban society she remembered as a child. The novel is a tribute to her friend Henry James, who had instructed her to "Do New York!" And so she did. *The Age of Innocence* won the Pulitzer Prize for fiction (the award was given first to Sinclair Lewis's novel *Main Street* and then taken back, on moral grounds). It was filmed (1934, 1993). It led to her receiving an honorary doctorate from Yale University (the first woman to do so, and she had never even attended college), and to making what was to be her last trip to the United States, in 1923. In 1926, she was elected to the National Institute of Arts and Letters. In the next two years, both Walter Berry and Teddy Wharton died, and Wharton's own health continued to fail.

But Wharton wrote, and wrote, and the later work does not represent any falling-away of her considerable talent. She lived until 1937.

Her hegira through her existence is itself a kind of metaphor for the life of the writer—that such an artist does live in her imagination, does find comfort in her aesthetic and in her product. The story of Edith Newbold Jones Wharton—known as "Mrs. Wharton" throughout her entire career, even long after she had divorced Teddy—is that of the writer who lives to "make up," to find ways of keeping one's balance through the exercise of the imagination, and of the sharp and not always comforting vision that the study of humankind makes essential. Edith Newbold Jones Wharton: writer not only for the age of innocence, but for our continuing times.

The Portable Edith Wharton has a double aim. Its primary task is to make accessible to today's readers (people of the twenty-first century) a great many Wharton stories that are now relatively unknown. Wharton's work is, of course, frequently anthologized— but the same two or three stories appear repeatedly. Wharton novels are often taught; but when complete novels are chosen, readers have no extra time to read her stories or novellas. While the contemporary reader may know *The House of Mirth* or *The Age of Innocence,* her parallel accomplishments in shorter forms are in danger of being forgotten. It is an irony of literary study, in a way, this forgetting, because the short story in its various lengths is a very American form. The immense popularity of the glossy magazine, which began during the nineteenth century, created a seemingly insatiable market for good short fiction: F. Scott Fitzgerald made his living for years from the high payments for his stories. It was a market that William Faulkner labored hard to break into (though he never received the kind of payment that Fitzgerald and Wharton did). The finesse of Wharton's stories of various lengths marks her as the craftsman James respected. Reading these stories enables the best kind of imaginative escape into other objects, other lives. At the short story, Wharton grew to earn her accolades.

That she also wrote nonfiction (for the same magazine market) and letters (by the thousands) is a fact sometimes forgotten in the immediate linking of her name with the novel (especially since the novels keep recurring in this culture as Hollywood films). This collection reprints both nonfiction excerpts and a few of the letters.

It also tries to give readers a sense of the immense accomplishment of Wharton's novels. By reprinting *Summer,* a book that has come into prominence during the last twenty years—partly as a result of feminist scholarship—this collection tries to pay homage to the author's sheer skill. But the segments of *The House of Mirth, The Reef,* and *The Age of Innocence* are intended to send readers back to these three remarkable fictions, all of which are readily available in paperback editions today.

The Portable's second aim is to focus on the years during which Wharton was becoming the astute and truly brilliant writer we have come to know. Although she lived another seventeen years after the last selection here published, and it is not true that her later novels are inferior works, the real drama in her development comes during the first twenty years of this past century. This collection provides, admittedly in brief, a description and an explanation of her work of those years of learning, and of maturing. It gives the reader a chance to see the passion of Edith Wharton at work, creating the writing that she knew would be her reason for existence.

LINDA WAGNER-MARTIN
University of North Carolina, Chapel Hill

Chronology

1862 Edith Newbold Jones, born January 24, at 14 West 23rd Street, New York City, third and last child of Lucretia Stevens Rhinelander and George Jones; her brothers are Frederic, born 1846, and Henry, born 1850.

1865 Receives gift of spitz puppy, starting her lifelong passion for dogs.

1866–1872 Travels abroad (Italy, England, Spain, France, Germany) with her family and her nurse Hannah Doyle ("Doyley") as a result of losses in her father's real estate investments after the Civil War. The family lives in Rome, Paris, Florence. Her childhood passion for "making up" and reciting stories and poems begins long before she can read; her father taught her to read. Her fluency in various languages in addition to English starts here.

1872–1879 After returning to the United States, the family spends winters in New York and summers at Pencraig in Newport, Rhode Island. Edith studies with Anna Bahlmann, who later becomes her governess. Less sociable than some of her family and friends, in 1876–1877 Edith writes her thirty-thousand-word novella *Fast and Loose*.

1879 With her mother as publisher, Edith collects her poems in a book titled *Verses*. William Dean Howells publishes one of the poems in *Atlantic Monthly*. Worried that Edith is becoming too intellectual, Lucretia brings her daughter into society a year earlier than her age would mandate; Edith wears black for her debut.

1880–1882 Edith publishes two poems in the New York *World*. Courted by Henry Leyden Stevens, son of the prominent Mrs. Paran Stevens, Edith goes to France with her family. The sojourn is an attempt to improve George Jones's failing health, but he dies in the spring of 1882. In August, Edith's engagement to Harry Stevens is announced, despite his mother's objections. In October, the engagement is broken. Edith travels with her mother to Paris.

1883 Edith meets the young lawyer Walter Van Rensselaer Berry at Bar Harbor, Maine, but he does not propose. Later in the season, she meets Edward Robbins ("Teddy") Wharton, a Boston friend of her older brother's. From her father, Edith has inherited a $20,000 trust fund; Teddy receives a $2,000 annuity from his family, with whom he lives.

1884 Edith hires Catherine Gross, Alsatian immigrant, as personal attendant, the beginning of a forty-year association.

1885 Marries Teddy Wharton April 29 at Trinity Chapel in New York City; the couple moves into Pencraig Cottage on Lucretia's Newport estate. They travel—mostly in Italy—for four months of every year. In July, Henry Stevens dies of tuberculosis.

1888 Edith and Teddy spend a year's income ($10,000) on a four-month Aegean cruise; she inherits $120,000 from her New York cousin Joshua Jones.

1889 The Whartons rent a small house on Madison Avenue in New York; Edith's poems appear in *Scribner's Magazine, Harper's Monthly,* and *Century Illustrated Monthly Magazine.*

1890–1892 Edith suffers from inexplicable nausea and fatigue. *Scribner's Magazine* publishes a short story July 1891, but rejects her novella *Bunner Sisters.*

1893 Buys Land's End, a Newport estate on the Atlantic, for $80,000 and works with architect Ogden Codman on its decoration. Three stories accepted by *Scribner's Magazine;* the publisher Scribner's suggests a book of her stories.

1894–1895 Travels in Italy and writes travel essays. Suffering nausea and melancholy, Wharton breaks off negotiations with Scribner's for sixteen months. Her mother moves to Paris (her brothers live in Europe).

1896–1897 With Ogden Codman, writes *The Decoration of Houses;* sales are good when the book appears in December 1897. Resumes friendship with Berry.

1898 Writes and revises seven stories, despite illness. Is treated in Philadelphia as an outpatient.

1899 Story collection *The Greater Inclination* published in March; Teddy and Edith live in Washington, D.C., for several months, then travel in Europe. In the fall, return to Land's End.

1900 Publishes *The Touchstone,* a novella, in April; travels abroad and considers buying land near Lenox, Massachusetts.

1901 Buys 113-acre property at Lenox and hires Francis V. L. Hoppin to design home, named "The Mount." *Crucial Instances,* second collection of stories, is published. Lucretia dies and leaves Edith's share of her estate in trust.

1902 Edith's *The Valley of Decision,* an historical novel, is published; works on translation of Hermann Sudermann's *Es Lebe das Leben.* Her illness returns. After moving into The Mount, Teddy suffers the first of his breakdowns.

1903 Travels in Europe; meets Henry James, with whom she has been corresponding. Publishes novella *Sanctuary* and begins writing *The House of Mirth.*

1904 Third story collection, *The Descent of Man,* published. *The House of Mirth* serialized in *Scribner's Magazine. Italian Villas and Their Gardens* (reprinted travel essays) published by the Century Company. Buys first auto, a Panhard-Levassor; travels through New England and abroad.

1905 *Italian Backgrounds* (reprinted essays) published by Scribner's. *The House of Mirth,* published in the fall, sells more than 140,000 copies by the end of the year. Henry James visits the Whartons; they also dine at the White House.

1906 *Madame de Treymes* is published. Edith's illness continues.

1907 *The Fruit of the Tree* is published. The Whartons with Henry James tour southern France; frequent visits between James and Edith. She meets journalist Morton Fullerton through James.

1908–1910 Short-lived affair with Fullerton. Teddy is plagued by depression and breakdown; admits taking $50,000 from Edith's accounts and establishing an apartment for his mistress. He repays the money. 1908, *The Hermit and the Wild Woman* (fourth collection of stories) and *A Motor-Flight Through France* published. 1909, *Artemis to Actaeon,* book of poems. 1910, *Tales of Men and Ghosts* published.

1911 Both Henry James and Teddy Wharton suffer breakdowns; Edith is not well. The Whartons consider separation but change their minds. Edith travels with Walter Berry. *Ethan Frome* serialized in *Scribner's* while Edith begins *The Reef*.

1912 *The Reef* published by Appleton, which had given her a large advance ($15,000); sales, however, are small. Her books subsequently are published by either Appleton (first serialized in *Pictorial Review*) or Scribner's (after being serialized in *Scribner's Magazine*).

1913 *The Custom of the Country* is serialized. Tries to raise gift of $5,000 for Henry James's seventieth birthday (plan dropped when James objects). Edith sues for divorce from Teddy on grounds of adultery; decree granted April 16. Scribner's sells sixty thousand copies of *The Custom of the Country* in the autumn.

1914 Much European travel before war is declared—Algiers with Percy Lubbock and Gaillard Lapsley; Majorca with Walter Berry. During the fall, Wharton raises more than $100,000 for refugee relief and the care and placement of orphans.

1915 Wharton visits the Front four or five times. She provides homes for more than 750 Belgian orphans. Her sewing room in Paris gives women occupation and food. *Fighting France* is published, to encourage the United States to enter the war.

1916 Wharton publishes *The Book of the Homeless,* and continues her many war relief activities. Henry James dies in England.

1917 Wharton is awarded the Order of Leopold, Belgium, and the French Legion of Honor. *Summer* is serialized in *McClure's* and published by Appleton; her story collection, *Xingu and Other Stories,* appears from Scribner's.

1918 Wharton buys Pavillon Colombe near Paris and publishes *The Marne.* Her brother Frederic dies, but the remaining brother, Henry, does not notify her.

1919 *French Ways and Their Meaning* is published; Appleton advances her $15,000 on *The Age of Innocence.*

1920 Wharton restores medieval monastery at Hyères on the Riviera for a summer home. Publishes *The Age of Innocence* (first serialized in *Pictorial Review*) and (with Scribner's) *In Morocco.*

1921 *The Age of Innocence* wins the Pulitzer Prize for fiction. The first of Wharton's New York tales, *The Old Maid,* is published.

1922 Wharton publishes another best-seller, *The Glimpses of the Moon* (first serialized in the *Pictorial Review,* then published by Appleton).

1923 The film version of *Glimpses,* with subtitles by F. Scott Fitzgerald. Wharton returns to the States to receive an honorary doctorate from Yale University (the first woman recipient). This is her last visit to America. Scribner's publishes her war novel *A Son at the Front.*

1924 Wharton receives the Gold Medal from the National Institute of Arts and Letters; *Old New York* is published by Scribner's.

1925 Scribner's publishes *The Writing of Fiction;* Appleton brings out *The Mother's Recompense* (after serialization in *Pictorial Review*).

1926 Wharton is elected to the National Institute of Arts and Letters. She publishes *Here and Beyond* (a story collection) and *Twelve Poems,* and takes an extensive yacht trip on the Aegean.

1927 Walter Berry dies. Appleton publishes *Twilight Sleep.*

1928 Teddy Wharton dies. *The Children* is published by Appleton (serialization in *Pictorial Review*).

1929 Though seriously ill, Wharton continues writing; Appleton publishes *Hudson River Bracketed.* Wharton receives the Gold Medal from the American Academy of Arts and Letters.

1930 Wharton is elected to the American Academy of Arts and Letters. Appleton publishes the story collection *Certain People.*

1932 Appleton publishes *The Gods Arrive.*

1933 Wharton's companion Catherine Gross dies; Appleton publishes the story collection *Human Nature.*

1934 Wharton's autobiography, *A Backward Glance,* is published after excerpts appear in the *Ladies' Home Journal.*

1935 Zoë Akins's dramatization of *The Old Maid* has a long run in New York; Wharton has a stroke.

1936 The dramatization of *Ethan Frome,* with proceeds from *The Old Maid,* brings Wharton income of $130,000. Appleton publishes the story collection *The World Over.*

1937 *Ghosts* (a story collection) published. Wharton dies August
    11, following a stroke, and is buried at Versailles next to the
    ashes of Walter Berry. Her papers are left to Yale University,
    with publication rights withheld until 1968.

1938 *The Buccaneers* (a novel) published.

PART I

SHORT FICTION

One of the most impressive qualities of Edith Wharton's short fiction (ranging from a moderate length to novella length) is its variety. Because so many critics have been interested primarily in her novels, serious attention to her short stories has of late been sparse—and may have led to the sense that she did capable but not innovative work within that form. Yet, in the number of stories she wrote, and in their range of theme and method, Wharton may be considered one of America's most versatile short-fiction writers.

It was certainly her short fiction that attracted the attention of the young male twentieth-century writers who, for many readers, embody America's modernist movement. F. Scott Fitzgerald, for example, credited both Wharton and Willa Cather with fiction that helped him write his own. Ernest Hemingway was characteristically reticent about discussing writers whose example had been useful to his work, including Wharton—except for the fact that a number of her books were among his personal holdings in his several libraries. Although Wharton was a good friend to Sinclair Lewis and many European modernist writers, it became fashionable to pretend that she was not a part of the modernist group. That critical stance was in some ways a means of undercutting her prominence on the international scene, but it was also unfair.

Wharton's short stories from the mid-1890s through the early 1920s show her almost constant attempts to change the pattern of what she tried, and usually accomplished, in her short fiction. Contrary to R. W. B. Lewis's assessment (in his introduction to the two-volume edition of Wharton's stories) that she didn't change the form much, close reading of her stories shows that her form is fluid: it depends on what the narrative of the story tries to induce the reader to do. If the essence of modernism was the concept of "organic form," of dispensing with any preconceived notion of the way the writer achieved an aim, then Wharton's short stories run the gamut of experimentation that effects the reader's immersion in both characters and plot.

Lewis also claims, accurately, that Wharton was a short story writer at the beginning of her career, and at its end. When she was almost thirty, *Scribner's Magazine* published her first story—and gave her, in 1891, the conviction that writing could be her métier. The market for her stories never diminished and, although she seldom needed money, she was reassured that her role as a well-published writer continued through whatever personal, and national, problems occurred.

Lewis considers "The Other Two" the best of Wharton's short stories. One of her more comic treatments of the problems of modern marriage and divorce, this story typifies the novelist-of-manners view of Edith Wharton: the outsider's glance at an inherently troubling situation, a woman surrounded by her present and past husbands and the vestiges of her lives with them. Wharton abandons her customary detailed—and intimate—presentation of the protagonist in order to achieve the narrative distance that Lewis admires. But most of her stories affect the reader with a greater sense of reality.

Wharton's way with dialogue is masterful. Whether she uses it sparingly, as in "The Lady's Maid's Bell," or—more rarely—to carry the weight of the story, her sense of timing is beyond the expert. So subtle is that use of dialogue that some readers might be hardly aware of it, or of its role in the story. Blocks of description and elaboration are more characteristic of the stories, but even in the midst of lengthy prose sections, a metaphor or a detail occurs that later connects with a key phrase or image. As Claire Preston has written (in *Soft Canons*, Karen L. Kilcup, ed., 1999), Wharton's best stories "are usually measured, almost architecturally patterned, entirely governed by their design, with scant room for extraneous detail or episode." Her stories must be read as wholes, and the final effect is integral to the whole of the structure.

Like most modernist works, Wharton's stories are often "open." While such openness needs no comment in her many ghost and/or mystery stories, because many of the happenings are themselves mysterious, to find that strategy in the story "The Choice"—at the end of which one hungers to know what the distraught wife, Isabel Stilling, will feel and do once her lover has drowned and her husband is left to speak his self-congratulatory dialogue—is to create a very different kind of nontraditional form.

As the pairing of several of these stories suggests, Wharton was able to take the same theme and give it very different impact as she changed narrative strategies. "The Other Two," for instance, treats the dilemma of a woman's several loves or marriages with humorous effect; "Autres Temps . . ." in contrast shows the painful isolation of a woman who chose to love a man who was not her husband, as well as her subsequent alienation from the respectable society—her and her daughter's only community.

Similarly, the change in tone between "Writing a War Story" and "Coming Home" makes the first a slight and ironic treatment, a story not even collected during Wharton's lifetime, whereas the second is one of the most authentically believable, and bitter, of her works.

SOULS BELATED

Their railway carriage had been full when the train left Bologna; but at the first station beyond Milan their only remaining companion—a courtly person who ate garlic out of a carpetbag—had left his crumb-strewn seat with a bow.

Lydia's eye regretfully followed the shiny broadcloth of his retreating back till it lost itself in the cloud of touts and cab drivers hanging about the station; then she glanced across at Gannett and caught the same regret in his look. They were both sorry to be alone.

"*Par-ten-za!*" shouted the guard. The train vibrated to a sudden slamming of doors; a waiter ran along the platform with a tray of fossilized sandwiches; a belated porter flung a bundle of shawls and bandboxes into a third-class carriage; the guard snapped out a brief *Partenza!* which indicated the purely ornamental nature of his first shout; and the train swung out of the station.

The direction of the road had changed, and a shaft of sunlight struck across the dusty red-velvet seats into Lydia's corner. Gannett did not notice it. He had returned to his *Revue de Paris,* and she had to rise and lower the shade of the farther window. Against the vast horizon of their leisure such incidents stood out sharply.

Having lowered the shade, Lydia sat down, leaving the length of the carriage between herself and Gannett. At length he missed her and looked up.

"I moved out of the sun," she hastily explained.

He looked at her curiously: the sun was beating on her through the shade.

"Very well," he said pleasantly; adding, "You don't mind?" as he drew a cigarette case from his pocket.

It was a refreshing touch, relieving the tension of her spirit with the suggestion that, after all, if he could *smoke*—! The relief was only momentary. Her experience of smokers was limited (her husband had disapproved of the use of tobacco) but she knew from hearsay that men sometimes smoked to get away from things; that a cigar might be the masculine equivalent of darkened windows and a headache. Gannett, after a puff or two, returned to his review.

It was just as she had foreseen; he feared to speak as much as she did. It was one of the misfortunes of their situation that they were never busy enough to necessitate, or even to justify, the postponement of unpleasant discussions. If they avoided a question it was obviously, unconcealably because the question was disagreeable. They had unlimited leisure and an accumulation of mental energy to devote to any subject that presented itself; new topics were in fact at a premium. Lydia sometimes had premonitions of a famine-stricken period when there would be nothing left to talk about, and she had already caught herself doling out piecemeal what, in the first prodigality of their confidences, she would have flung to him in a breath. Their silence therefore might simply mean that they had nothing to say; but it was another disadvantage of their position that it allowed infinite opportunity for the classification of minute differences. Lydia had learned to distinguish between real and factitious silences; and under Gannett's she now detected a hum of speech to which her own thoughts made breathless answer.

How could it be otherwise, with that thing between them? She glanced up at the rack overhead. The *thing* was there, in her dressing bag, symbolically suspended over her head and his. He was thinking of it now, just as she was; they had been thinking of it in unison ever since they had entered the train. While the carriage had held other travelers they had screened her from his thoughts; but now that he and she were alone she knew exactly what was passing through his mind; she could almost hear him asking himself what he should say to her.

The thing had come that morning, brought up to her in an innocent-looking envelope with the rest of their letters, as they were leaving the hotel at Bologna. As she tore it open, she and Gannett were laughing over some ineptitude of the local guidebook—they had been driven, of late, to make the most of such incidental humors of travel. Even when she had unfolded the document she took it for some unimportant business paper sent abroad for her signature, and her eye traveled inattentively over the curly *Whereases* of the preamble until a word arrested her: Divorce. There it stood, an impassable barrier, between her husband's name and hers.

She had been prepared for it, of course, as healthy people are said to be prepared for death, in the sense of knowing it must come without in the least expecting that it will. She had known from the first that Tillotson meant to divorce her—but what did it matter? Nothing mattered, in those first days of supreme deliverance, but the fact that she was free; and not so much (she had begun to be aware) that freedom had released her from Tillotson as that it had given her to Gannett. This discovery had not been agreeable to her self-esteem. She had preferred to think that Tillotson had himself embodied all her reasons for leaving him; and those he represented had seemed cogent enough to stand in no need of reinforcement. Yet she had not left him till she met Gannett. It was her love for Gannett that had made life with Tillotson so poor and incomplete a business. If she had never, from the first, regarded her marriage as a full canceling of her claims upon life, she had at least, for a number of years, accepted it as a provisional compensation,—she had made it "do." Existence in the commodious Tillotson mansion in Fifth Avenue— with Mrs. Tillotson senior commanding the approaches from the second-story front windows—had been reduced to a series of purely automatic acts. The moral atmosphere of the Tillotson interior was as carefully screened and curtained as the house itself: Mrs. Tillotson senior dreaded ideas as much as a draft in her back. Prudent people liked an even temperature; and to do anything unexpected was as foolish as going out in the rain. One of the chief advantages of being rich was that one need not be exposed to unforeseen contingencies: by the use of ordinary firmness and common sense one could make sure of doing exactly the same thing every day at the same hour. These doctrines, reverentially imbibed with his mother's milk, Tillotson (a model son who had never given his parents an hour's anxiety) complacently expounded to his wife, testifying to his sense of their importance by the regularity with which he wore galoshes on damp days, his

punctuality at meals, and his elaborate precautions against bur-
glars and contagious diseases. Lydia, coming from a smaller town,
and entering New York life through the portals of the Tillotson
mansion, had mechanically accepted this point of view as insepa-
rable from having a front pew in church and a parterre box at the
opera. All the people who came to the house revolved in the same
small circle of prejudices. It was the kind of society in which, after dinner, the ladies compared the exorbitant charges of their
children's teachers, and agreed that, even with the new duties on
French clothes, it was cheaper in the end to get everything from
Worth; while the husbands, over their cigars, lamented municipal
corruption, and decided that the men to start a reform were those
who had no private interests at stake.

To Lydia this view of life had become a matter of course, just as
lumbering about in her mother-in-law's landau had come to seem
the only possible means of locomotion, and listening every Sunday to a fashionable Presbyterian divine the inevitable atonement
for having thought oneself bored on the other six days of the
week. Before she met Gannett her life had seemed merely dull; his
coming made it appear like one of those dismal Cruikshank prints
in which the people are all ugly and all engaged in occupations
that are either vulgar or stupid.

It was natural that Tillotson should be the chief sufferer from
this readjustment of focus. Gannett's nearness had made her husband ridiculous, and a part of the ridicule had been reflected on
herself. Her tolerance laid her open to a suspicion of obtuseness
from which she must, at all costs, clear herself in Gannett's eyes.

She did not understand this until afterwards. At the time she
fancied that she had merely reached the limits of endurance. In so
large a charter of liberties as the mere act of leaving Tillotson
seemed to confer, the small question of divorce or no divorce did
not count. It was when she saw that she had left her husband only
to be with Gannett that she perceived the significance of anything
affecting their relations. Her husband, in casting her off, had virtually flung her at Gannett: it was thus that the world viewed it.
The measure of alacrity with which Gannett would receive her
would be the subject of curious speculation over afternoon tea tables and in club corners. She knew what would be said—she had
heard it so often of others! The recollection bathed her in misery.

The men would probably back Gannett to "do the decent thing"; but the ladies' eyebrows would emphasize the worthlessness of such enforced fidelity; and after all, they would be right. She had put herself in a position where Gannett "owed" her something; where, as a gentleman, he was bound to "stand the damage." The idea of accepting such compensation had never crossed her mind; the so-called rehabilitation of such a marriage had always seemed to her the only real disgrace. What she dreaded was the necessity of having to explain herself; of having to combat his arguments; of calculating, in spite of herself, the exact measure of insistence with which he pressed them. She knew not whether she most shrank from his insisting too much or too little. In such a case the nicest sense of proportion might be at fault; and how easily to fall into the error of taking her resistance for a test of his sincerity! Whichever way she turned, an ironical implication confronted her: she had the exasperated sense of having walked into the trap of some stupid practical joke.

Beneath all these preoccupations lurked the dread of what he was thinking. Sooner or later, of course, he would have to speak; but that, in the meantime, he should think, even for a moment, that there was any use in speaking, seemed to her simply unendurable. Her sensitiveness on this point was aggravated by another fear, as yet barely on the level of consciousness; the fear of unwillingly involving Gannett in the trammels of her dependence. To look upon him as the instrument of her liberation; to resist in herself the least tendency to a wifely taking possession of his future; had seemed to Lydia the one way of maintaining the dignity of their relation. Her view had not changed, but she was aware of a growing inability to keep her thought fixed on the essential point—the point of parting with Gannett. It was easy to face as long as she kept it sufficiently far off: but what was this act of mental postponement but a gradual encroachment on his future? What was needful was the courage to recognize the moment when, by some word or look, their voluntary fellowship should be transformed into a bondage the more wearing that it was based on none of those common obligations which make the most imperfect marriage in some sort a center of gravity.

When the porter, at the next station, threw the door open, Lydia drew back, making way for the hoped-for intruder; but none came, and the train took up its leisurely progress through the spring wheat fields and budding copses. She now began to hope that Gannett would speak before the next station. She watched him furtively, half-disposed to return to the seat opposite his, but there was an artificiality about his absorption that restrained her. She had never before seen him read with so conspicuous an air of warding off interruption. What could he be thinking of? Why should he be afraid to speak? Or was it her answer that he dreaded?

The train paused for the passing of an express, and he put down his book and leaned out of the window. Presently he turned to her with a smile.

"There's a jolly old villa out here," he said.

His easy tone relieved her, and she smiled back at him as she crossed over to his corner.

Beyond the embankment, through the opening in a mossy wall, she caught sight of the villa, with its broken balustrades, its stagnant fountains, and the stone satyr closing the perspective of a dusky grass walk.

"How should you like to live there?" he asked as the train moved on.

"There?"

"In some such place, I mean. One might do worse, don't you think so? There must be at least two centuries of solitude under those yew trees. Shouldn't you like it?"

"I—I don't know," she faltered. She knew now that he meant to speak.

He lit another cigarette. "We shall have to live somewhere, you know," he said as he bent above the match.

Lydia tried to speak carelessly, "*Je n'en vois pas la nécessité!*[1] Why not live everywhere, as we have been doing?"

"But we can't travel forever, can we?"

"Oh, forever's a long word," she objected, picking up the review he had thrown aside.

"For the rest of our lives then," he said, moving nearer.

She made a slight gesture which caused his hand to slip from hers.

"Why should we make plans? I thought you agreed with me that it's pleasanter to drift."

He looked at her hesitatingly. "It's been pleasant, certainly; but

I suppose I shall have to get at my work again some day. You know I haven't written a line since—all this time," he hastily amended.

She flamed with sympathy and self-reproach. "Oh, if you mean *that*—if you want to write—of course we must settle down. How stupid of me not to have thought of it sooner! Where shall we go? Where do you think you could work best? We oughtn't to lose any more time."

He hesitated again. "I had thought of a villa in these parts. It's quiet; we shouldn't be bothered. Should you like it?"

"Of course I should like it." She paused and looked away. "But I thought—I remember your telling me once that your best work had been done in a crowd—in big cities. Why should you shut yourself up in a desert?"

Gannett, for a moment, made no reply. At length he said, avoiding her eye as carefully as she avoided his: "It might be different now; I can't tell, of course, till I try. A writer ought not to be dependent on his *milieu;* it's a mistake to humor oneself in that way; and I thought that just at first you might prefer to be—"

She faced him. "To be what?"

"Well—quiet. I mean—"

"What do you mean by 'at first'?" she interrupted.

He paused again. "I mean after we are married."

She thrust up her chin and turned toward the window. "Thank you!" she tossed back at him.

"Lydia!" he exclaimed blankly; and she felt in every fiber of her averted person that he had made the inconceivable, the unpardonable mistake of anticipating her acquiescence.

The train rattled on and he groped for a third cigarette. Lydia remained silent.

"I haven't offended you?" he ventured at length, in the tone of a man who feels his way.

She shook her head with a sigh. "I thought you understood," she moaned. Their eyes met and she moved back to his side.

"Do you want to know how not to offend me? By taking it for granted, once and for all, that you've said your say on the odious question and that I've said mine, and that we stand just where we did this morning before that—that hateful paper came to spoil everything between us!"

"To spoil everything between us? What on earth do you mean? Aren't you glad to be free?"

"I was free before."

"Not to marry me," he suggested.

"But I don't *want* to marry you!" she cried.

She saw that he turned pale. "I'm obtuse, I suppose," he said slowly. "I confess I don't see what you're driving at. Are you tired of the whole business? Or was I simply a—an excuse for getting away? Perhaps you didn't care to travel alone? Was that it? And now you want to chuck me?" His voice had grown harsh. "You owe me a straight answer, you know; don't be tenderhearted!"

Her eyes swam as she leaned to him. "Don't you see it's because I care—because I care so much? Oh, Ralph! Can't you see how it would humiliate me? Try to feel it as a woman would! Don't you see the misery of being made your wife in this way? If I'd known you as a girl—that would have been a real marriage! But now—this vulgar fraud upon society—and upon a society we despised and laughed at—this sneaking back into a position that we've voluntarily forfeited: don't you see what a cheap compromise it is? We neither of us believe in the abstract 'sacredness' of marriage; we both know that no ceremony is needed to consecrate our love for each other; what object can we have in marrying, except the secret fear of each that the other may escape, or the secret longing to work our way back gradually—oh, very gradually—into the esteem of the people whose conventional morality we have always ridiculed and hated? And the very fact that, after a decent interval, these same people would come and dine with us—the women who talk about the indissolubility of marriage, and who would let me die in a gutter today because I am 'leading a life of sin'—doesn't that disgust you more than their turning their backs on us now? I can stand being cut by them, but I couldn't stand their coming to call and asking what I meant to do about visiting that unfortunate Mrs. So-and-so!"

She paused, and Gannett maintained a perplexed silence.

"You judge things too theoretically," he said at length, slowly. "Life is made up of compromises."

"The life we ran away from—yes! If we had been willing to accept them"—she flushed—"we might have gone on meeting each other at Mrs. Tillotson's dinners."

He smiled slightly. "I didn't know that we ran away to found a new system of ethics. I supposed it was because we loved each other."

"Life is complex, of course; isn't it the very recognition of that fact that separates us from the people who see it *tout d'une pièce?*[2] If *they* are right—if marriage is sacred in itself and the individual must always be sacrificed to the family—then there can be no real marriage between us, since our—our being together is a protest against the sacrifice of the individual to the family." She interrupted herself with a laugh. "You'll say now that I'm giving you a lecture on sociology! Of course one acts as one can—as one must, perhaps—pulled by all sorts of invisible threads; but at least one needn't pretend, for social advantages, to subscribe to a creed that ignores the complexity of human motives—that classifies people by arbitrary signs, and puts it in everybody's reach to be on Mrs. Tillotson's visiting list. It may be necessary that the world should be ruled by conventions—but if we believed in them, why did we break through them? And if we don't believe in them, is it honest to take advantage of the protection they afford?"

Gannett hesitated. "One may believe in them or not; but as long as they do rule the world it is only by taking advantage of their protection that one can find a *modus vivendi.*"

"Do outlaws need a *modus vivendi?*"

He looked at her hopelessly. Nothing is more perplexing to man than the mental process of a woman who reasons her emotions.

She thought she had scored a point and followed it up passionately. "You do understand, don't you? You see how the very thought of the thing humiliates me! We are together today because we choose to be—don't let us look any farther than that!" She caught his hands. "*Promise* me you'll never speak of it again; promise me you'll never *think* of it even," she implored, with a tearful prodigality of italics.

Through what followed—his protests, his arguments, his final unconvinced submission to her wishes—she had a sense of his but half-discerning all that, for her, had made the moment so tumultuous. They had reached that memorable point in every heart history when, for the first time, the man seems obtuse and the woman irrational. It was the abundance of his intentions that consoled her, on reflection, for what they lacked in quality. After all, it would have been worse, incalculably worse, to have detected any overreadiness to understand her.

II

When the train at nightfall brought them to their journey's end at the edge of one of the lakes, Lydia was glad that they were not, as usual, to pass from one solitude to another. Their wanderings during the year had indeed been like the flight of outlaws: through Sicily, Dalmatia, Transylvania and Southern Italy they had persisted in their tacit avoidance of their kind. Isolation, at first, had deepened the flavor of their happiness, as night intensifies the scent of certain flowers; but in the new phase on which they were entering, Lydia's chief wish was that they should be less abnormally exposed to the action of each other's thoughts.

She shrank, nevertheless, as the brightly-looming bulk of the fashionable Anglo-American hotel on the water's brink began to radiate toward their advancing boat its vivid suggestion of social order, visitors' lists, Church services, and the bland inquisition of the *table d'hôte*. The mere fact that in a moment or two she must take her place on the hotel register as Mrs. Gannett seemed to weaken the springs of her resistance.

They had meant to stay for a night only, on their way to a lofty village among the glaciers of Monte Rosa; but after the first plunge into publicity, when they entered the dining room, Lydia felt the relief of being lost in a crowd, of ceasing for a moment to be the center of Gannett's scrutiny; and in his face she caught the reflection of her feeling. After dinner, when she went upstairs, he strolled into the smoking room, and an hour or two later, sitting in the darkness of her window, she heard his voice below and saw him walking up and down the terrace with a companion cigar at his side. When he came up he told her he had been talking to the hotel chaplain—a very good sort of fellow.

"Queer little microcosms, these hotels! Most of these people live here all summer and then migrate to Italy or the Riviera. The English are the only people who can lead that kind of life with dignity—those soft-voiced old ladies in Shetland shawls somehow carry the British Empire under their caps. *Civis Romanus sum.*[3]

It's a curious study—there might be some good things to work up here."

He stood before her with the vivid preoccupied stare of the novelist on the trail of a "subject." With a relief that was half painful she noticed that, for the first time since they had been together, he was hardly aware of her presence.

"Do you think you could write here?"

"Here? I don't know." His stare dropped. "After being out of things so long one's first impressions are bound to be tremendously vivid, you know. I see a dozen threads already that one might follow—"

He broke off with a touch of embarrassment.

"Then follow them. We'll stay," she said with sudden decision.

"Stay here?" He glanced at her in surprise, and then, walking to the window, looked out upon the dusky slumber of the garden.

"Why not?" she said at length, in a tone of veiled irritation.

"The place is full of old cats in caps who gossip with the chaplain. Shall you like—I mean, it would be different if—"

She flamed up.

"Do you suppose I care? It's none of their business."

"Of course not; but you won't get them to think so."

"They may think what they please."

He looked at her doubtfully.

"It's for you to decide."

"We'll stay," she repeated.

Gannett, before they met, had made himself known as a successful writer of short stories and of a novel which had achieved the distinction of being widely discussed. The reviewers called him "promising," and Lydia now accused herself of having too long interfered with the fulfilment of his promise. There was a special irony in the fact, since his passionate assurances that only the stimulus of her companionship could bring out his latent faculty had almost given the dignity of a "vocation" to her course: there had been moments when she had felt unable to assume, before posterity, the responsibility of thwarting his career. And, after all, he had not written a line since they had been together: his first desire to write had come from renewed contact with the world! Was it all a mistake then? Must the most intelligent choice work more disastrously than the blundering combinations of chance?

Or was there a still more humiliating answer to her perplexities? His sudden impulse of activity so exactly coincided with her own wish to withdraw, for a time, from the range of his observation, that she wondered if he too were not seeking sanctuary from intolerable problems.

"You must begin tomorrow!" she cried, hiding a tremor under the laugh with which she added, "I wonder if there's any ink in the inkstand?"

Whatever else they had at the Hotel Bellosguardo, they had, as Miss Pinsent said, "a certain tone." It was to Lady Susan Condit that they owed this inestimable benefit: an advantage ranking in Miss Pinsent's opinion above even the lawn tennis courts and the resident chaplain. It was the fact of Lady Susan's annual visit that made the hotel what it was. Miss Pinsent was certainly the last to underrate such a privilege: "It's so important, my dear, forming as we do a little family, that there should be someone to give *the tone*; and no one could do it better than Lady Susan—an earl's daughter and a person of such determination. Dear Mrs. Ainger now—who really *ought*, you know, when Lady Susan's away— absolutely refuses to assert herself." Miss Pinsent sniffed derisively. "A bishop's niece!—my dear, I saw her once actually give in to some South Americans—and before us all. She gave up her seat at table to oblige them—such a lack of dignity! Lady Susan spoke to her very plainly about it afterwards."

Miss Pinsent glanced across the lake and adjusted her auburn front.

"But of course I don't deny that the stand Lady Susan takes is not always easy to live up to—for the rest of us, I mean. Monsieur Grossart, our good proprietor, finds it trying at times, I know—he has said as much, privately, to Mrs. Ainger and me. After all, the poor man is not to blame for wanting to fill his hotel, is he? And Lady Susan is so difficult—so very difficult—about new people. One might almost say that she disapproves of them beforehand, on principle. And yet she's had warnings—she very nearly made a dreadful mistake once with the Duchess of Levens, who dyed her hair and—well, swore and smoked. One would have thought that might have been a lesson to Lady Susan." Miss Pinsent resumed her knitting with a sigh. "There are exceptions, of course. She took at once to you and Mr. Gannett—it was quite remarkable, really. Oh, I don't mean that either—of course not! It was perfectly natural—we *all* thought you so charming and interesting from the first day—we knew at once that Mr. Gannett was intellectual, by the magazines you took in; but you know what I mean. Lady Susan is so very—well, I won't say prejudiced, as Mrs. Ainger does—but so prepared *not* to like new people, that her taking to you in that way was a surprise to us all, I confess."

Miss Pinsent sent a significant glance down the long laurustinus alley from the other end of which two people—a lady and a gentleman—were strolling toward them through the smiling neglect of the garden.

"In this case, of course, it's very different; that I'm willing to admit. Their looks are against them; but, as Mrs. Ainger says, one can't exactly tell them so."

"She's very handsome," Lydia ventured, with her eyes on the lady, who showed, under the dome of a vivid sunshade, the hourglass figure and superlative coloring of a Christmas chromo.

"That's the worst of it. She's too handsome."

"Well, after all, she can't help that."

"Other people manage to," said Miss Pinsent skeptically.

"But isn't it rather unfair of Lady Susan—considering that nothing is known about them?"

"But, my dear, that's the very thing that's against them. It's infinitely worse than any actual knowledge."

Lydia mentally agreed that, in the case of Mrs. Linton, it possibly might be.

"I wonder why they came here?" she mused.

"That's against them too. It's always a bad sign when loud people come to a quiet place. And they've brought van loads of boxes—her maid told Mrs. Ainger's that they meant to stop indefinitely."

"And Lady Susan actually turned her back on her in the salon?"

"My dear, she said it was for our sakes: that makes it so unanswerable! But poor Grossart *is* in a way! The Lintons have taken his most expensive suite, you know—the yellow damask drawing room above the portico—and they have champagne with every meal!"

They were silent as Mr. and Mrs. Linton sauntered by; the lady with tempestuous brows and challenging chin; the gentleman, a blond stripling, trailing after her, head downward, like a reluctant child dragged by his nurse.

"What does your husband think of them, my dear?" Miss Pinsent whispered as they passed out of earshot.

Lydia stooped to pick a violet in the border.

"He hasn't told me."

"Of your speaking to them, I mean. Would he approve of that? I know how very particular nice Americans are. I think your action might make a difference; it would certainly carry weight with Lady Susan."

"Dear Miss Pinsent, you flatter me!"

Lydia rose and gathered up her book and sunshade.

"Well, if you're asked for an opinion—if Lady Susan asks you for one—I think you ought to be prepared," Miss Pinsent admonished her as she moved away.

III

Lady Susan held her own. She ignored the Lintons, and her little family, as Miss Pinsent phrased it, followed suit. Even Mrs. Ainger agreed that it was obligatory. If Lady Susan owed it to the others not to speak to the Lintons, the others clearly owed it to Lady Susan to back her up. It was generally found expedient, at the Hotel Bellosguardo, to adopt this form of reasoning.

Whatever effect this combined action may have had upon the Lintons, it did not at least have that of driving them away. Monsieur Grossart, after a few days of suspense, had the satisfaction of seeing them settle down in his yellow damask *premier* with what looked like a permanent installation of palm trees and silk cushions, and a gratifying continuance in the consumption of champagne. Mrs. Linton trailed her Doucet draperies[4] up and down the garden with the same challenging air, while her husband, smoking innumerable cigarettes, dragged himself dejectedly in her wake; but neither of them, after the first encounter with Lady Susan, made any attempt to extend their acquaintance. They simply ignored their ignorers. As Miss Pinsent resentfully observed, they behaved exactly as though the hotel were empty.

It was therefore a matter of surprise, as well as of displeasure, to Lydia, to find, on glancing up one day from her seat in the garden, that the shadow which had fallen across her book was that of the enigmatic Mrs. Linton.

"I want to speak to you," that lady said, in a rich hard voice that seemed the audible expression of her gown and her complexion.

Lydia started. She certainly did not want to speak to Mrs. Linton.

"Shall I sit down here?" the latter continued, fixing her intensely-shaded eyes on Lydia's face, "or are you afraid of being seen with me?"

"Afraid?" Lydia colored. "Sit down, please. What is it that you wish to say?"

Mrs. Linton, with a smile, drew up a garden chair and crossed one openwork ankle above the other.

"I want you to tell me what my husband said to your husband last night."

Lydia turned pale.

"My husband—to yours?" she faltered, staring at the other.

"Didn't you know they were closeted together for hours in the smoking room after you went upstairs? My man didn't get to bed until nearly two o'clock and when he did I couldn't get a word out of him. When he wants to be aggravating I'll back him against anybody living!" Her teeth and eyes flashed persuasively upon Lydia. "But you'll tell me what they were talking about, won't you? I know I can trust you—you look so awfully kind. And it's for his own good. He's such a precious donkey and I'm so afraid he's got into some beastly scrape or other. If he'd only trust his own old woman! But they're always writing to him and setting him against me. And I've got nobody to turn to." She laid her hand on Lydia's with a rattle of bracelets. "You'll help me, won't you?"

Lydia drew back from the smiling fierceness of her brows.

"I'm sorry—but I don't think I understand. My husband has said nothing to me of—of yours."

The great black crescents above Mrs. Linton's eyes met angrily.

"I say—is that true?" she demanded.

Lydia rose from her seat.

"Oh, look here, I didn't mean that, you know—you mustn't take one up so! Can't you see how rattled I am?"

Lydia saw that, in fact, her beautiful mouth was quivering beneath softened eyes.

"I'm beside myself!" the splendid creature wailed, dropping into her seat.

"I'm so sorry," Lydia repeated, forcing herself to speak kindly; "but how can I help you?"

Mrs. Linton raised her head sharply.

"By finding out—there's a darling!"

"Finding what out?"

"What Trevenna told him."

"Trevenna—?" Lydia clapped her hand to her mouth.

"Oh, Lord—there, it's out! What a fool I am! But I supposed of course you knew; I supposed everybody knew." She dried her eyes and bridled. "Didn't you know that he's Lord Trevenna? I'm Mrs. Cope."

Lydia recognized the names. They had figured in a flamboyant elopement which had thrilled fashionable London some six months earlier.

"Now you see how it is—you understand, don't you?" Mrs. Cope continued on a note of appeal. "I knew you would—that's the reason I came to you. I suppose *he* felt the same thing about your husband; he's not spoken to another soul in the place." Her face grew anxious again. "He's awfully sensitive, generally—he feels our position, he says—as if it wasn't *my* place to feel that! But when he does get talking there's no knowing what he'll say. I know he's been brooding over something lately, and I *must* find out what it is—it's to his interest that I should. I always tell him that I think only of his interest; if he'd only trust me! But he's been so odd lately—I can't think what he's plotting. You will help me, dear?"

Lydia, who had remained standing, looked away uncomfortably.

"If you mean by finding out what Lord Trevenna has told my husband, I'm afraid it's impossible."

"Why impossible?"

"Because I infer that it was told in confidence."

Mrs. Cope stared incredulously.

"Well, what of that? Your husband looks such a dear—anyone can see he's awfully gone on you. What's to prevent your getting it out of him?"

Lydia flushed.

"I'm not a spy!" she exclaimed.

"A spy—a spy? How dare you?" Mrs. Cope flamed out. "Oh, I don't mean that either! Don't be angry with me—I'm so miserable." She essayed a softer note. "Do you call that spying—for one woman to help out another? I do need help so dreadfully! I'm at my wits' end with Trevenna, I am indeed. He's such a boy—a mere baby, you know; he's only two-and-twenty." She dropped her orbed lids. "He's younger than me—only fancy, a few months younger. I tell him he ought to listen to me as if I was his mother; oughtn't he now? But he won't, he won't! All his people are at him, you see—oh, I know *their* little game! Trying to get him away from me before I can get my divorce—that's what they're up to. At first he wouldn't listen to them; he used to toss their letters over to me to read; but now he reads them himself, and answers 'em too, I fancy; he's always shut up in his room, writing. If I only knew what his plan is I could stop him fast enough—he's such a simpleton. But he's dreadfully deep too—at times I can't make him out. But I know he's told your husband everything—I knew that last night the minute I laid eyes on him. And I *must* find out—you must help me—I've got no one else to turn to!"

She caught Lydia's fingers in a stormy pressure.

"Say you'll help me—you and your husband."

Lydia tried to free herself.

"What you ask is impossible; you must see that it is. No one could interfere in—in the way you ask."

Mrs. Cope's clutch tightened.

"You won't, then? You won't?"

"Certainly not. Let me go, please."

Mrs. Cope released her with a laugh.

"Oh, go by all means—pray don't let me detain you! Shall you go and tell Lady Susan Condit that there's a pair of us—or shall I save you the trouble of enlightening her?"

Lydia stood still in the middle of the path, seeing her antagonist through a mist of terror. Mrs. Cope was still laughing.

"Oh, I'm not spiteful by nature, my dear; but you're a little more than flesh and blood can stand! It's impossible, is it? Let you go, indeed! You're too good to be mixed up in my affairs, are you? Why, you little fool, the first day I laid eyes on you I saw that you and I were both in the same box—that's the reason I spoke to you."

She stepped nearer, her smile dilating on Lydia like a lamp through a fog.

"You can take your choice, you know; I always play fair. If you'll tell I'll promise not to. Now then, which is it to be?"

Lydia, involuntarily, had begun to move away from the pelting storm of words; but at this she turned and sat down again.

"You may go," she said simply. "I shall stay here."

IV

She stayed there for a long time, in the hypnotized contemplation, not of Mrs. Cope's present, but of her own past. Gannett, early that morning, had gone off on a long walk—he had fallen into the habit of taking these mountain tramps with various fellow lodgers; but even had he been within reach she could not have gone to him just then. She had to deal with herself first. She was surprised to find how, in the last months, she had lost the habit of introspection. Since their coming to the Hotel Bellosguardo she and Gannett had tacitly avoided themselves and each other.

She was aroused by the whistle of the three o'clock steamboat as it neared the landing just beyond the hotel gates. Three o'clock! Then Gannett would soon be back—he had told her to expect him before four. She rose hurriedly, her face averted from the inquisitorial façade of the hotel. She could not see him just yet; she could not go indoors. She slipped through one of the overgrown garden alleys and climbed a steep path to the hills.

It was dark when she opened their sitting-room door. Gannett was sitting on the window ledge smoking a cigarette. Cigarettes were now his chief resource: he had not written a line during the two months they had spent at the Hotel Bellosguardo. In that respect, it had turned out not to be the right *milieu* after all.

He started up at Lydia's entrance.

"Where have you been? I was getting anxious."

She sat down in a chair near the door.

"Up the mountain," she said wearily.

"Alone?"

"Yes."

Gannett threw away his cigarette: the sound of her voice made him want to see her face.

"Shall we have a little light?" he suggested.

She made no answer and he lifted the globe from the lamp and put a match to the wick. Then he looked at her.

"Anything wrong? You look done up."

She sat glancing vaguely about the little sitting room, dimly lit by the pallid-globed lamp, which left in twilight the outlines of the furniture, of his writing table heaped with books and papers, of the tea roses and jasmine drooping on the mantelpiece. How like home it had all grown—how like home!

"Lydia, what is wrong?" he repeated.

She moved away from him, feeling for her hatpins and turning to lay her hat and sunshade on the table.

Suddenly she said: "That woman has been talking to me."

Gannett stared.

"That woman? What woman?"

"Mrs. Linton—Mrs. Cope."

He gave a start of annoyance, still, as she perceived, not grasping the full import of her words.

"The deuce! She told you—?"

"She told me everything."

Gannett looked at her anxiously.

"What impudence! I'm so sorry that you should have been exposed to this, dear."

"Exposed!" Lydia laughed.

Gannett's brow clouded and they looked away from each other.

"Do you know *why* she told me? She had the best of reasons. The first time she laid eyes on me she saw that we were both in the same box."

"Lydia!"

"So it was natural, of course, that she should turn to me in a difficulty."

"What difficulty?"

"It seems she has reason to think that Lord Trevenna's people are trying to get him away from her before she gets her divorce—"

"Well?"

"And she fancied he had been consulting with you last night as to—as to the best way of escaping from her."

Gannett stood up with an angry forehead.

"Well—what concern of yours was all this dirty business? Why should she go to you?"

"Don't you see? It's so simple. I was to wheedle his secret out of you."

"To oblige that woman?"

"Yes; or, if I was unwilling to oblige her, then to protect myself."

"To protect yourself? Against whom?"

"Against her telling everyone in the hotel that she and I are in the same box."

"She threatened that?"

"She left me the choice of telling it myself or of doing it for me."

"The beast!"

There was a long silence. Lydia had seated herself on the sofa, beyond the radius of the lamp, and he leaned against the window. His next question surprised her.

"When did this happen? At what time, I mean?"

She looked at him vaguely.

"I don't know—after luncheon, I think. Yes, I remember; it must have been at about three o'clock."

He stepped into the middle of the room and as he approached the light she saw that his brow had cleared.

"Why do you ask?" she said.

"Because when I came in, at about half-past three, the mail was just being distributed, and Mrs. Cope was waiting as usual to pounce on her letters; you know she was always watching for the postman. She was standing so close to me that I couldn't help seeing a big official-looking envelope that was handed to her. She tore it open, gave one look at the inside, and rushed off upstairs like a whirlwind, with the director shouting after her that she had left all her other letters behind. I don't believe she ever thought of you again after that paper was put into her hand."

"Why?"

"Because she was too busy. I was sitting in the window, watching for you, when the five o'clock boat left, and who should go on board, bag and baggage, valet and maid, dressing bags and poodle, but Mrs. Cope and Trevenna. Just an hour and a half to pack up in! And you should have seen her when they started. She was radiant—shaking hands with everybody—waving her handkerchief from the deck—distributing bows and smiles like an empress. If ever a woman got what she wanted just in the nick of time that woman did. She'll be Lady Trevenna within a week, I'll wager."

"You think she has her divorce?"

"I'm sure of it. And she must have got it just after her talk with you."

Lydia was silent.

At length she said, with a kind of reluctance, "She was horribly angry when she left me. It wouldn't have taken long to tell Lady Susan Condit."

"Lady Susan Condit has not been told."

"How do you know?"

"Because when I went downstairs half an hour ago I met Lady Susan on the way—"

He stopped, half smiling.

"Well?"

"And she stopped to ask if I thought you would act as patroness to a charity concert she is getting up."

In spite of themselves they both broke into a laugh. Lydia's ended in sobs and she sank down with her face hidden. Gannett bent over her, seeking her hands.

"That vile woman—I ought to have warned you to keep away from her; I can't forgive myself! But he spoke to me in confidence; and I never dreamed—well, it's all over now."

Lydia lifted her head.

"Not for me. It's only just beginning."

"What do you mean?"

She put him gently aside and moved in her turn to the window. Then she went on, with her face turned toward the shimmering blackness of the lake, "You see of course that it might happen again at any moment."

"What?"

"This—this risk of being found out. And we could hardly count again on such a lucky combination of chances, could we?"

He sat down with a groan.

Still keeping her face toward the darkness, she said, "I want you to go and tell Lady Susan—and the others."

Gannett, who had moved towards her, paused a few feet off.

"Why do you wish me to do this?" he said at length, with less surprise in his voice than she had been prepared for.

"Because I've behaved basely, abominably, since we came here: letting these people believe we were married—lying with every breath I drew—"

"Yes, I've felt that too," Gannett exclaimed with sudden energy.

The words shook her like a tempest: all her thoughts seemed to fall about her in ruins.

"You—you've felt so?"

"Of course I have." He spoke with low-voiced vehemence. "Do you suppose I like playing the sneak any better than you do? It's damnable."

He had dropped on the arm of a chair, and they stared at each other like blind people who suddenly see.

"But you have liked it here," she faltered.

"Oh, I've liked it—I've liked it." He moved impatiently. "Haven't you?"

"Yes," she burst out; "that's the worst of it—that's what I can't bear. I fancied it was for your sake that I insisted on staying—because you thought you could write here; and perhaps just at first that really was the reason. But afterwards I wanted to stay myself—I loved it." She broke into a laugh. "Oh, do you see the full derision of it? These people—the very prototypes of the bores you took me away from, with the same fenced-in view of life, the same keep-off-the-grass morality, the same little cautious virtues and the same little frightened vices—well, I've clung to them, I've delighted in them, I've done my best to please them. I've toadied Lady Susan, I've gossiped with Miss Pinsent, I've pretended to be shocked with Mrs. Ainger. Respectability! It was the one thing in life that I was sure I didn't care about, and it's grown so precious to me that I've stolen it because I couldn't get it in any other way."

She moved across the room and returned to his side with another laugh.

"I who used to fancy myself unconventional! I must have been born with a cardcase in my hand. You should have seen me with that poor woman in the garden. She came to me for help, poor creature, because she fancied that, having 'sinned,' as they call it, I might feel some pity for others who had been tempted in the same way. Not I! She didn't know me. Lady Susan would have been kinder, because Lady Susan wouldn't have been afraid. I hated the woman—my one thought was not to be seen with her—I could have killed her for guessing my secret. The one thing that mattered to me at that moment was my standing with Lady Susan!"

Gannett did not speak.

"And you—you've felt it too!" she broke out accusingly. "You've enjoyed being with these people as much as I have; you've let the chaplain talk to you by the hour about The Reign of Law and Professor Drummond. When they asked you to hand the plate in church I was watching you—*you wanted to accept.*"

She stepped close, laying her hand on his arm.

"Do you know, I begin to see what marriage is for. It's to keep people away from each other. Sometimes I think that two people who love each other can be saved from madness only by the things that come between them—children, duties, visits, bores, relations—the things that protect married people from each other. We've been too close together—that has been our sin. We've seen the nakedness of each other's souls."

She sank again on the sofa, hiding her face in her hands.

Gannett stood above her perplexedly: he felt as though she were being swept away by some implacable current while he stood helpless on its bank.

At length he said, "Lydia, don't think me a brute—but don't you see yourself that it won't do?"

"Yes, I see it won't do," she said without raising her head.

His face cleared.

"Then we'll go tomorrow."

"Go—where?"

"To Paris; to be married."

For a long time she made no answer; then she asked slowly, "Would they have us here if we were married?"

"Have us here?"

"I mean Lady Susan—and the others."

"Have us here? Of course they would."

"Not if they knew—at least, not unless they could pretend not to know."

He made an impatient gesture.

"We shouldn't come back here, of course; and other people needn't know—no one need know."

She sighed. "Then it's only another form of deception and a meaner one. Don't you see that?"

"I see that we're not accountable to any Lady Susans on earth!"

"Then why are you ashamed of what we are doing here?"

"Because I'm sick of pretending that you're my wife when you're not—when you won't be."

She looked at him sadly.

"If I were your wife you'd have to go on pretending. You'd have to pretend that I'd never been—anything else. And our friends would have to pretend that they believed what you pretended."

Gannett pulled off the sofa tassel and flung it away.

"You're impossible," he groaned.

"It's not I—it's our being together that's impossible. I only want you to see that marriage won't help it."

"What will help it then?"

She raised her head.

"My leaving you."

"Your leaving me?" He sat motionless, staring at the tassel, which lay at the other end of the room. At length some impulse of retaliation for the pain she was inflicting made him say deliberately:

"And where would you go if you left me?"

"Oh!" she cried.

He was at her side in an instant.

"Lydia—Lydia—you know I didn't mean it; I couldn't mean it! But you've driven me out of my senses; I don't know what I'm saying. Can't you get out of this labyrinth of self-torture? It's destroying us both."

"That's why I must leave you."

"How easily you say it!" He drew her hands down and made her face him. "You're very scrupulous about yourself—and others. But have you thought of me? You have no right to leave me unless you've ceased to care—"

"It's because I care—"

"Then I have a right to be heard. If you love me you can't leave me."

Her eyes defied him.

"Why not?"

He dropped her hands and rose from her side.

"Can you?" he said sadly.

The hour was late and the lamp flickered and sank. She stood up with a shiver and turned toward the door of her room.

V

At daylight a sound in Lydia's room woke Gannett from a troubled sleep. He sat up and listened. She was moving about softly, as though fearful of disturbing him. He heard her push back one of the creaking shutters; then there was a moment's silence, which seemed to indicate that she was waiting to see if the noise had roused him.

Presently she began to move again. She had spent a sleepless night, probably, and was dressing to go down to the garden for a breath of air. Gannett rose also; but some undefinable instinct made his movements as cautious as hers. He stole to his window and looked out through the slats of the shutter.

It had rained in the night and the dawn was gray and lifeless. The cloud-muffled hills across the lake were reflected in its surface as in a tarnished mirror. In the garden, the birds were beginning to shake the drops from the motionless laurustinus boughs.

An immense pity for Lydia filled Gannett's soul. Her seeming intellectual independence had blinded him for a time to the feminine cast of her mind. He had never thought of her as a woman who wept and clung: there was a lucidity in her intuitions that made them appear to be the result of reasoning. Now he saw the cruelty he had committed in detaching her from the normal conditions of life; he felt, too, the insight with which she had hit upon the real cause of their suffering. Their life was "impossible," as she had said—and its worst penalty was that it had made any other life impossible for them. Even had his love lessened, he was bound to her now by a hundred ties of pity and self-reproach; and she, poor child, must turn back to him as Latude returned to his cell.[5]

A new sound startled him: it was the stealthy closing of Lydia's door. He crept to his own and heard her footsteps passing down the corridor. Then he went back to the window and looked out.

A minute or two later he saw her go down the steps of the porch and enter the garden. From his post of observation her face was invisible, but something about her appearance struck him. She wore a long traveling cloak and under its folds he detected the outline of a bag or bundle. He drew a deep breath and stood watching her.

She walked quickly down the laurustinus alley toward the gate; there she paused a moment, glancing about the little shady square. The stone benches under the trees were empty, and she seemed to gather resolution from the solitude about her, for she crossed the square to the steamboat landing, and he saw her pause before the ticket office at the head of the wharf. Now she was buying her ticket. Gannett turned his head a moment to look at the clock: the boat was due in five minutes. He had time to jump into his clothes and overtake her—

He made no attempt to move; an obscure reluctance restrained him. If any thought emerged from the tumult of his sensations, it was that he must let her go if she wished it. He had spoken last night of his rights: what were they? At the last issue, he and she were two separate beings, not made one by the miracle of common forbearances, duties, abnegations, but bound together in a *noyade*[6] of passion that left them resisting yet clinging as they went down.

After buying her ticket, Lydia had stood for a moment looking out across the lake; then he saw her seat herself on one of the benches near the landing. He and she, at that moment, were both listening for the same sound: the whistle of the boat as it rounded the nearest promontory. Gannett turned again to glance at the clock: the boat was due now.

Where would she go? What would her life be when she had left him? She had no near relations and few friends. There was money enough . . . but she asked so much of life, in ways so complex and immaterial. He thought of her as walking barefooted through a stony waste. No one would understand her—no one would pity her—and he, who did both, was powerless to come to her aid.

He saw that she had risen from the bench and walked toward the edge of the lake. She stood looking in the direction from which the steamboat was to come; then she turned to the ticket office, doubtless to ask the cause of the delay. After that she went back to the bench and sat down with bent head. What was she thinking of?

The whistle sounded; she started up, and Gannett involuntarily made a movement toward the door. But he turned back and continued to watch her. She stood motionless, her eyes on the trail of smoke that preceded the appearance of the boat. Then the little craft rounded the point, a dead white object on the leaden water: a minute later it was puffing and backing at the wharf.

The few passengers who were waiting—two or three peasants and a snuffy priest—were clustered near the ticket office. Lydia stood apart under the trees.

The boat lay alongside now; the gangplank was run out and the peasants went on board with their baskets of vegetables, followed by the priest. Still Lydia did not move. A bell began to ring querulously; there was a shriek of steam, and someone must have called to her that she would be late, for she started forward, as though in answer to a summons. She moved waveringly, and at the edge of the wharf she paused. Gannett saw a sailor beckon to her; the bell rang again and she stepped upon the gangplank.

Halfway down the short incline to the deck she stopped again; then she turned and ran back to the land. The gangplank was drawn in, the bell ceased to ring, and the boat backed out into the lake. Lydia, with slow steps, was walking toward the garden.

As she approached the hotel she looked up furtively and Gannett drew back into the room. He sat down beside a table; a Bradshaw[7] lay at his elbow, and mechanically, without knowing what he did, he began looking out the trains to Paris.

THE MUSE'S TRAGEDY

Danyers afterwards liked to fancy that he had recognized Mrs. Anerton at once; but that, of course, was absurd, since he had seen no portrait of her—she affected a strict anonymity, refusing even her photograph to the most privileged—and from Mrs. Memorall, whom he revered and cultivated as her friend, he had extracted but the one impressionist phrase: "Oh, well, she's like one of those old prints where the lines have the value of color."

He was almost certain, at all events, that he had been thinking of Mrs. Anerton as he sat over his breakfast in the empty hotel restaurant, and that, looking up on the approach of the lady who seated herself at the table near the window, he had said to himself, *"That might be she."*

Ever since his Harvard days—he was still young enough to think of them as immensely remote—Danyers had dreamed of Mrs. Anerton, the Silvia of Vincent Rendle's immortal sonnet cycle, the Mrs. A. of the *Life and Letters*. Her name was enshrined in some of the noblest English verse of the nineteenth century—and of all past or future centuries, as Danyers, from the standpoint of a maturer judgment, still believed. The first reading of certain poems—of the *Antinous,* the *Pia Tolomei,* the *Sonnets to Silvia*—had been epochs in Danyers' growth, and the verse seemed to gain in mellowness, in amplitude, in meaning as one brought to its interpretation more experience of life, a finer emotional sense. Where, in his boyhood, he had felt only the perfect, the almost austere beauty of form, the subtle interplay of vowel sounds, the rush and fullness of lyric emotion, he now thrilled to the close-packed significance of each line, the allusiveness of each word—his imagination lured hither and thither on fresh trails of thought, and perpetually spurred by the sense that, beyond what he had already discovered, more marvelous regions lay waiting to be explored. Danyers had written, at college, the prize essay on Rendle's poetry (it chanced to be the moment of the great man's death); he had fashioned the fugitive verse of his own Storm and Stress period on the forms which Rendle had first given to English meter, and when two years later the *Life and Letters* appeared, and the Silvia of the sonnets took substance as Mrs. A., he had included in his worship of Rendle the woman who had inspired not only such divine verse but such playful, tender, incomparable prose.

Danyers never forgot the day when Mrs. Memorall happened to mention that she knew Mrs. Anerton. He had known Mrs. Memorall for a year or more, and had somewhat contemptuously classified her as the kind of woman who runs cheap excursions to celebrities: when one afternoon she remarked, as she put a second lump of sugar in his tea:

"Is it right this time? You're almost as particular as Mary Anerton."

"Mary Anerton?"

"Yes, I never *can* remember how she likes her tea. Either it's lemon *with* sugar, or lemon without sugar, or cream without either, and whichever it is must be put into the cup before the tea is poured in; and if one hasn't remembered, one must begin all over again. I suppose it was Vincent Rendle's way of taking his tea and has become a sacred rite."

"Do you *know* Mrs. Anerton?" cried Danyers, disturbed by this careless familiarity with the habits of his divinity.

" 'And did I once see Shelley plain?'[1] Mercy, yes! She and I were at school together—she's an American, you know. We were at a *pension* near Tours for nearly a year; then she went back to New York, and I didn't see her again till after her marriage. She and Anerton spent a winter in Rome while my husband was attached to our Legation there, and she used to be with us a great deal." Mrs. Memorall smiled reminiscently. "It was *the* winter."

"The winter they first met?"

"Precisely—but unluckily I left Rome just before the meeting took place. Wasn't it too bad? I might have been in the *Life and Letters*. You know he mentions that stupid Madame Vodki, at whose house he first saw her."

"And did you see much of her after that?"

"Not during Rendle's life. You know she has lived in Europe almost entirely, and though I used to see her off and on when I went abroad, she was always so engrossed, so preoccupied, that one felt one wasn't wanted. The fact is, she cared only about his friends—she separated herself gradually from all her own people. Now, of course, it's different; she's desperately lonely; she's taken to writing to me now and then; and last year, when she heard I was going abroad, she asked me to meet her in Venice, and I spent a week with her there."

"And Rendle?"

Mrs. Memorall smiled and shook her head. "Oh, I never was allowed a peep at *him;* none of her old friends met him, except by accident. Ill-natured people say that was the reason she kept him so long. If one happened in while he was there, he was hustled into Anerton's study, and the husband mounted guard till the inopportune visitor had departed. Anerton, you know, was really much more ridiculous about it than his wife. Mary was too clever to lose her head, or at least to show she'd lost it—but Anerton couldn't conceal his pride in the conquest. I've seen Mary shiver when he spoke of Rendle as *our poet.* Rendle always had to have a certain seat at the dinner table, away from the draft and not too near the fire, and a box of cigars that no one else was allowed to touch, and a writing table of his own in Mary's sitting room—and Anerton was always telling one of the great man's idiosyncrasies: how he never would cut the ends of his cigars, though Anerton himself had given him a gold cutter set with a star sapphire, and how untidy his writing table was, and how the housemaid had orders always to bring the wastepaper basket to her mistress before emptying it, lest some immortal verse should be thrown into the dustbin."

"The Anertons never separated, did they?"

"Separated? Bless you, no. He never would have left Rendle! And besides, he was very fond of his wife."

"And she?"

"Oh, she saw he was the kind of man who was fated to make himself ridiculous, and she never interfered with his natural tendencies."

From Mrs. Memorall, Danyers further learned that Mrs. Anerton, whose husband had died some years before her poet, now divided her life between Rome, where she had a small apartment, and England, where she occasionally went to stay with those of her friends who had been Rendle's. She had been engaged, for some time after his death, in editing some juvenilia which he had bequeathed to her care; but that task being accomplished, she had been left without definite occupation, and Mrs. Memorall, on the occasion of their last meeting, had found her listless and out of spirits.

"She misses him too much—her life is too empty. I told her so— I told her she ought to marry."

"Oh!"

"Why not, pray? She's a young woman still—what many people would call young," Mrs. Memorall interjected, with a parenthetic glance at the mirror. "Why not accept the inevitable and begin over again? All the King's horses and all the King's men won't bring Rendle to life—and besides, she didn't marry *him* when she had the chance."

Danyers winced slightly at this rude fingering of his idol. Was it possible that Mrs. Memorall did not see what an anticlimax such a marriage would have been? Fancy Rendle "making an honest woman" of Silvia; for so society would have viewed it! How such a reparation would have vulgarized their past—it would have been like "restoring" a masterpiece; and how exquisite must have been the perceptions of the woman who, in defiance of appearances, and perhaps of her own secret inclination, chose to go down to posterity as Silvia rather than as Mrs. Vincent Rendle!

Mrs. Memorall, from this day forth, acquired an interest in Danyers' eyes. She was like a volume of unindexed and discursive memoirs, through which he patiently plodded in the hope of finding embedded amid layers of dusty twaddle some precious allusion to the subject of his thought. When, some months later, he brought out his first slim volume, in which the remodeled college essay on Rendle figured among a dozen somewhat overstudied "appreciations," he offered a copy to Mrs. Memorall; who surprised him, the next time they met, with the announcement that she had sent the book to Mrs. Anerton.

Mrs. Anerton in due time wrote to thank her friend. Danyers was privileged to read the few lines in which, in terms that suggested the habit of "acknowledging" similar tributes, she spoke of the author's "feeling and insight," and was "so glad of the oppor-

tunity," etc. He went away disappointed, without clearly knowing
what else he had expected.

The following spring, when he went abroad, Mrs. Memorall offered him letters to everybody, from the Archbishop of Canterbury
to Louise Michel. She did not include Mrs. Anerton, however, and
Danyers knew, from a previous conversation, that Silvia objected to
people who "brought letters." He knew also that she traveled during
the summer, and was unlikely to return to Rome before the term of
his holiday should be reached, and the hope of meeting her was not
included among his anticipations.

The lady whose entrance broke upon his solitary repast in the
restaurant of the Hotel Villa d'Este had seated herself in such a
way that her profile was detached against the window; and thus
viewed, her domed forehead, small arched nose, and fastidious lip
suggested a silhouette of Marie Antoinette. In the lady's dress and
movements—in the very turn of her wrist as she poured out her
coffee—Danyers thought he detected the same fastidiousness, the
same air of tacitly excluding the obvious and unexceptional. Here
was a woman who had been much bored and keenly interested.
The waiter brought her a *Secolo,* and as she bent above it Danyers noticed that the hair rolled back from her forehead was turning gray; but her figure was straight and slender, and she had the
invaluable gift of a girlish back.

The rush of Anglo-Saxon travel had not set toward the lakes,
and with the exception of an Italian family or two, and a hump-
backed youth and an *abbé,* Danyers and the lady had the marble
halls of the Villa d'Este to themselves.

When he returned from his morning ramble among the hills he
saw her sitting at one of the little tables at the edge of the lake. She
was writing, and a heap of books and newspapers lay on the table
at her side. That evening they met again in the garden. He had
strolled out to smoke a last cigarette before dinner, and under the
black vaulting of ilexes, near the steps leading down to the boat
landing, he found her leaning on the parapet above the lake. At
the sound of his approach she turned and looked at him. She had
thrown a black lace scarf over her head, and in this somber setting
her face seemed thin and unhappy. He remembered afterwards
that her eyes, as they met his, expressed not so much sorrow as
profound discontent.

To his surprise she stepped toward him with a detaining gesture.

"Mr. Lewis Danyers, I believe?"

He bowed.

"I am Mrs. Anerton. I saw your name on the visitors' list and wished to thank you for an essay on Mr. Rendle's poetry—or rather to tell you how much I appreciated it. The book was sent to me last winter by Mrs. Memorall."

She spoke in even melancholy tones, as though the habit of perfunctory utterance had robbed her voice of more spontaneous accents; but her smile was charming.

They sat down on a stone bench under the ilexes, and she told him how much pleasure his essay had given her. She thought it the best in the book—she was sure he had put more of himself into it than into any other; was she not right in conjecturing that he had been very deeply influenced by Mr. Rendle's poetry? *Pour comprendre il faut aimer,*[2] and it seemed to her that, in some ways, he had penetrated the poet's inner meaning more completely than any other critic. There were certain problems, of course, that he had left untouched; certain aspects of that many-sided mind that he had perhaps failed to seize—

"But then you are young," she concluded gently, "and one could not wish you, as yet, the experience that a fuller understanding would imply."

II

She stayed a month at Villa d'Este, and Danyers was with her daily. She showed an unaffected pleasure in his society; a pleasure so obviously founded on their common veneration of Rendle, that the young man could enjoy it without fear of fatuity. At first he was merely one more grain of frankincense on the altar of her insatiable divinity; but gradually a more personal note crept into their intercourse. If she still liked him only because he appreciated Rendle, she at least perceptibly distinguished him from the herd of Rendle's appreciators.

Her attitude toward the great man's memory struck Danyers as perfect. She neither proclaimed nor disavowed her identity. She was frankly Silvia to those who knew and cared; but there was no trace of the Egeria[3] in her pose. She spoke often of Rendle's books, but seldom of himself; there was no posthumous conjugality, no use of the possessive tense, in her abounding reminiscences. Of the master's intellectual life, of his habits of thought and work, she never wearied of talking. She knew the history of each poem; by what scene or episode each image had been evoked; how many times the words in a certain line had been transposed; how long a certain adjective had been sought, and what had at last suggested it; she could even explain that one impenetrable line, the torment of critics, the joy of detractors, the last line of *The Old Odysseus*.

Danyers felt that in talking of these things she was no mere echo of Rendle's thought. If her identity had appeared to be merged in his it was because they thought alike, not because he had thought for her. Posterity is apt to regard the women whom poets have sung as chance pegs on which they hung their garlands; but Mrs. Anerton's mind was like some fertile garden wherein, inevitably, Rendle's imagination had rooted itself and flowered. Danyers began to see how many threads of his complex mental tissue the poet had owed to the blending of her temperament with his; in a certain sense Silvia had herself created the *Sonnets to Silvia*.

To be the custodian of Rendle's inner self, the door, as it were, to the sanctuary, had at first seemed to Danyers so comprehensive a privilege that he had the sense, as his friendship with Mrs. Anerton advanced, of forcing his way into a life already crowded. What room was there, among such towering memories, for so small an actuality as his? Quite suddenly, after this, he discovered that Mrs. Memorall knew better: his fortunate friend was bored as well as lonely.

"You have had more than any other woman!" he had exclaimed to her one day: and her smile flashed a derisive light on his blunder. Fool that he was, not to have seen that she had not had enough! That she was young still—do years count?—tender, human, a woman; that the living have need of the living.

After that, when they climbed the alleys of the hanging park, resting in one of the little ruined temples, or watching, through a ripple of foliage, the remote blue flash of the lake, they did not always talk of Rendle or of literature. She encouraged Danyers to speak of himself; to confide his ambitions to her; she asked him the questions which are the wise woman's substitute for advice.

"You must write," she said, administering the most exquisite flattery that human lips could give.

Of course he meant to write—why not to do something great in his turn? His best, at least; with the resolve, at the outset, that his best should be *the* best. Nothing less seemed possible with that mandate in his ears. How she had divined him; lifted and disentangled his groping ambitions; laid the awakening touch on his spirit with her creative *Let there be light!*

It was his last day with her, and he was feeling very hopeless and happy.

"You ought to write a book about *him*," she went on gently.

Danyers started; he was beginning to dislike Rendle's way of walking in unannounced.

"You ought to do it," she insisted. "A complete interpretation—a summing up of his style, his purpose, the theory of life and art. No one else could do it as well."

He sat looking at her perplexedly. Suddenly—dared he guess?

"I couldn't do it without you," he faltered.

"I could help you—I would help you, of course."

They sat silent, both looking at the lake.

It was agreed, when they parted, that he should rejoin her six weeks later in Venice. There they were to talk about the book.

III

Lago d'Iseo, August 14th.

When I said good-bye to you yesterday I promised to come back to Venice in a week: I was to give you your answer then. I was not honest in saying that; I didn't mean to go back to Venice or to see you again. I was running away from you—and I mean to keep on running! If *you* won't, *I* must. Somebody must save you from marrying a disappointed woman of—well, you say years don't count, and why should they, after all, since you are not to marry me?

That is what I dare not go back to say. *You are not to marry me.*

We have had our month together in Venice (such a good month, was it not?) and now you are to go home and write a book—any book but the one we—didn't talk of!—and I am to stay here, attitudinizing among my memories like a sort of female Tithonus.[4] The dreariness of this enforced immortality!

But you shall know the truth. I care for you, or at least for your love, enough to owe you that.

You thought it was because Vincent Rendle had loved me that there was so little hope for you. I had had what I wanted to the full; wasn't that what you said? It is just when a man begins to think he understands a woman that he may be sure he doesn't! It is because Vincent Rendle *didn't love me* that there is no hope for you. I never had what I wanted, and never, never, never will I stoop to wanting anything else.

Do you begin to understand? It was all a sham then, you say? No, it was all real as far as it went. You are young—you haven't learned, as you will later, the thousand imperceptible signs by which one gropes one's way through the labyrinth of human nature; but didn't it strike you, sometimes, that I never told you any foolish little anecdotes about him? His trick, for instance, of twirling a paper knife round and round between his thumb and forefinger while he talked; his mania for saving the backs of notes; his greediness for wild strawberries, the little pungent Alpine ones; his childish delight in acrobats and jugglers; his way of always calling me *you—dear you,* every letter began—I never told you a word of all that, did I? Do you suppose I could have helped telling you, if he had loved me? These little things would have been mine, then, a part of my life—of our life—they would have slipped out in spite of me (it's only your unhappy woman who is always reticent and dignified). But there never was any "our life"; it was always "our lives" to the end. . . .

If you knew what a relief it is to tell someone at last, you would bear with me, you would let me hurt you! I shall never be quite so lonely again, now that someone knows.

Let me begin at the beginning. When I first met Vincent Rendle I was not twenty-five. That was twenty years ago. From that time until his death, five years ago, we were fast friends. He gave me fifteen years, perhaps the best fifteen years, of his life. The world, as you know, thinks that his greatest poems were written during those years; I am supposed to have "inspired" them, and in a sense I did. From the first, the intellectual sympathy between us was almost complete; my mind must have been to him (I fancy) like some perfectly tuned instrument on which he was never tired of playing. Someone told me of his once saying of me that I "always understood"; it is the only praise I ever heard of his giving me. I don't even know if he thought me pretty, though I hardly think my appearance could have been disagreeable to him, for he hated to be with ugly people. At all events he fell into the way of spending more and more of his time with me. He liked our house; our ways suited him. He was nervous, irritable; people bored him and yet he disliked solitude. He took sanctuary with us. When we traveled he went with us; in the winter he took rooms near us in Rome. In England or on the continent he was always with us for a good part of the year. In small ways I was able to help him in his work; he grew dependent on me. When we were apart he wrote to me continually—he liked to have me share in all he was doing or thinking; he was impatient for my criticism of every new book that interested him; I was a part of his intellectual life. The pity of it was that I wanted to be something more. I was a young woman and I was in love with him—not because he was Vincent Rendle, but just because he was himself!

People began to talk, of course—I was Vincent Rendle's Mrs. Anerton; when the *Sonnets to Silvia* appeared, it was whispered that I was Silvia. Wherever he went, I was invited; people made up to me in the hope of getting to know him; when I was in London my doorbell never stopped ringing. Elderly peeresses, aspiring hostesses, lovesick girls and struggling authors overwhelmed me with their assiduities. I hugged my success, for I knew what it meant—they thought that Rendle was in love with me! Do you know, at times, they almost made me think so too? Oh, there was no phase of folly I didn't go through. You can't imagine the excuses a woman will invent for a man's not telling her that he loves her—pitiable arguments that she would see through at a glance if any other woman used them! But all the while, deep down, I knew he had never cared. I should have known it if he had made love to me every day of his life. I could never guess whether he knew what people said about us—he listened so little to what people said; and cared still less, when he heard. He was always quite honest and straightforward with me; he treated me as one man treats another; and yet at times I felt he *must* see that with me it was different. If he did see, he made no sign. Perhaps he never noticed—I am sure he never meant to be cruel. He had never made love to me; it was no fault of his if I wanted more than he could give me. The *Sonnets to Silvia,* you say? But what are they? A cosmic philosophy, not a love poem; addressed to Woman, not to a woman!

But then, the letters? Ah, the letters! Well, I'll make a clean breast of it. You have noticed the breaks in the letters here and there, just as they seem to be on the point of growing a little—warmer? The critics, you may remember, praised the editor for his commendable delicacy and good taste (so rare in these days!) in omitting from the correspondence all personal allusions, all those *détails intimes* which should be kept sacred from the public gaze. They referred, of course, to the asterisks in the letters to Mrs. A. Those letters I myself prepared for publication; that is to say, I copied them out for the editor, and every now and then I put in a line of asterisks to make it appear that something had been left out. You understand? The asterisks were a sham—*there was nothing to leave out.*

No one but a woman could understand what I went through during those years—the moments of revolt, when I felt I must break away from it all, fling the truth in his face and never see him again; the inevitable reaction, when not to see him seemed the one unendurable thing, and I trembled lest a look or word of mine should disturb the poise of our friendship; the silly days when I hugged the delusion that he *must* love me, since everybody thought he did; the long periods of numbness, when I didn't seem to care whether he loved me or not. Between these wretched days came others when our intellectual accord was so perfect that I forgot everything else in the joy of feeling myself lifted up on the wings of his thought. Sometimes, then, the heavens seemed to be opened.

All this time he was so dear a friend! He had the genius of friendship, and he spent it all on me. Yes, you were right when you said that I have had more than any other woman. *Il faut de l'adresse pour aimer,*[5] Pascal says; and I was so quiet, so cheerful, so frankly affectionate with him, that in all those years I am almost sure I never bored him. Could I have hoped as much if he had loved me?

You mustn't think of him, though, as having been tied to my skirts. He came and went as he pleased, and so did his fancies. There was a girl once (I am telling you everything), a lovely being who called his poetry "deep" and gave him *Lucile*[6] on his birthday. He followed her to Switzerland one summer, and all the time that he was dangling after her (a little too conspicuously, I always thought, for a Great Man), he was writing to *me* about his theory of vowel combinations—or was it his experiments in English hexameter? The letters were dated from the very places where I knew they went and sat by waterfalls together and he thought out adjectives for her hair. He talked to me about it quite frankly afterwards. She was perfectly beautiful and it had been a pure delight to watch her; but she *would* talk, and her mind, he said, was "all elbows." And yet, the next year, when her marriage was announced, he went away alone, quite suddenly . . . and it was just afterwards that he published *Love's Viaticum*. Men are queer!

After my husband died—I am putting things crudely, you see—I had a return of hope. It was because he loved me, I argued, that he had never spoken; because he had always hoped someday to make me his wife; because he wanted to spare me the "reproach." Rubbish! I knew well enough, in my heart of hearts, that my one chance lay in the force of habit. He had grown used to me; he was no longer young; he dreaded new people and new ways; *il avait pris son pli.*[7] Would it not be easier to marry me?

I don't believe he ever thought of it. He wrote me what people call "a beautiful letter"; he was kind, considerate, decently commiserating; then, after a few weeks, he slipped into his old way of coming in every afternoon, and our interminable talks began again just where they had left off. I heard later that people thought I had shown "such good taste" in not marrying him.

So we jogged on for five years longer. Perhaps they were the best years, for I had given up hoping. Then he died.

After his death—this is curious—there came to me a kind of mirage of love. All the books and articles written about him, all the reviews of the *Life,* were full of discreet allusions to Silvia. I became again the Mrs. Anerton of the glorious days. Sentimental girls and dear lads like you turned pink when somebody whispered, "That was Silvia you were talking to." Idiots begged for my autograph—publishers urged me to write my reminiscences of him—critics consulted me about the reading of doubtful lines. And I knew that, to all these people, I was the woman Vincent Rendle had loved.

After a while that fire went out too and I was left alone with my past. Alone—quite alone; for he had never really been with me. The intellectual union counted for nothing now. It had been soul to soul, but never hand in hand, and there were no little things to remember him by.

Then there set in a kind of Arctic winter. I crawled into myself as into a snow hut. I hated my solitude and yet dreaded anyone who disturbed it. That phase, of course, passed like all the others. I took up life again, and began to read the papers and consider the cut of my gowns. But here was one question that I could not be rid of, that haunted me night and day. Why had he never loved me? Why had I been so much to him, and no more? Was I so ugly, so essentially unlovable, that though a man might cherish me as his mind's comrade, he could not care for me as a woman? I can't tell you how that question tortured me. It became an obsession.

My poor friend, do you begin to see? I had to find out what some other man thought of me. Don't be too hard on me! Listen first—consider. When I first met Vincent Rendle I was a young woman, who had married early and led the quietest kind of life; I had had no "experiences." From the hour of our first meeting to the day of his death I never looked at any other man, and never noticed whether any other man looked at me. When he died, five years ago, I knew the extent of my powers no more than a baby. Was it too late to find out? Should I never know *why*?

Forgive me—forgive me. You are so young; it will be an episode, a mere "document," to you so soon! And, besides, it wasn't as deliberate, as cold-blooded as those disjointed lines have made it appear. I didn't plan it, like a woman in a book. Life is so much more complex than any rendering of it can be. I liked you from the first—I was drawn to you (you must have seen that)—I wanted you to like me; it was not a mere psychological experiment. And yet in a sense it was that, too—I must be honest. I had to have an answer to that question; it was a ghost that had to be laid.

At first I was afraid—oh, so much afraid—that you cared for
me only because I was Silvia, that you loved me because you
thought Rendle had loved me. I began to think there was no escaping my destiny.

How happy I was when I discovered that you were growing
jealous of my past; that you actually hated Rendle! My heart beat
like a girl's when you told me you meant to follow me to Venice.

After our parting at Villa d'Este my old doubts reasserted themselves. What did I know of your feeling for me, after all? Were you
capable of analyzing it yourself? Was it not likely to be two-thirds
vanity and curiosity, and one-third literary sentimentality? You
might easily fancy that you cared for Mary Anerton when you
were really in love with Silvia—the heart is such a hypocrite! Or
you might be more calculating than I had supposed. Perhaps it
was you who had been flattering *my* vanity in the hope (the par-
donable hope!) of turning me, after a decent interval, into a pretty
little essay with a margin.

When you arrived in Venice and we met again—do you remember the music on the lagoon, that evening, from my balcony?—I
was so afraid you would begin to talk about the book—the book,
you remember, was your ostensible reason for coming. You never
spoke of it, and I soon saw your one fear was *I* might do so—
might remind you of your object in being with me. Then I knew
you cared for me! yes, at that moment really cared! We never
mentioned the book once, did we, during that month in Venice?

I have read my letter over; and now I wish that I had said this
to you instead of writing it. I could have felt my way then, watching your face and seeing if you understood. But, no, I could not go
back to Venice; and I could not tell you (though I tried) while we
were there together. I couldn't spoil that month—my one month.
It was so good, for once in my life, to get away from literature.

You will be angry with me at first—but, alas! not for long.
What I have done would have been cruel if I had been a younger
woman; as it is, the experiment will hurt no one but myself. And
it will hurt me horribly (as much as, in your first anger, you may
perhaps wish), because it has shown me, for the first time, all that
I have missed.

FRIENDS

Sailport is an ugly town. It makes, indeed, certain concessions to the eye in one or two streets on the hill, where there are elms, and houses set apart behind clipped hedges; but this favored quarter is a mere incident in the harsh progressiveness of a New England town seated on a capacious harbor and in touch with a widely radiating railway system.

The streets, too narrow for the present needs of the town, run between buildings of discordant character; the new brick warehouse, like a factory chimney with windows in it, looking down from its lean eminence on the low wooden "store" of a past generation, and the ambitious office building, with its astrologer's tower and rustications of sham granite, turning a contemptuous side wall on the recessed door and balustraded roof of the old dwelling house which had been adapted to commercial uses with the least possible outlay.

These streets, through which the electric cars rush with a rapidity dazing to the simple-minded and perilously fascinating to small boys on the way to school, are full of snow and mud in winter, of dust and garbage in summer. At each corner a narrow cross street leads the eye down to a glimpse of wooden wharves and a confusion of masts and smoke-stacks against a quiver of yellowish water. Nowhere is there the least peep of green, the smallest open space that spring may use as a signboard; even in the outlying districts, where cottages and tenements are being "run up" for the increasing population of laboring men and operatives, the patches of ground between the houses are not gardens, but waste spaces strewn with nameless refuse.

The inhabitants of Sailport would doubtless be surprised to hear their "city" (as they are careful to call it) thus characterized.

The greater number are probably of the opinion that handsome is as handsome does; and according to the national interpretation of the adage, Sailport is doing very handsomely, increasing in private and civic wealth, and multiplying with astonishing rapidity its telephone poles and electric wires, its car tracks and factory chimneys.

To Penelope Bent, now emerging from the railway station, her traveling bag in hand, Sailport had never appeared ugly; or only with the homely, lovable ugliness of a face that has bent above one's first awakenings; a face that has always been there; that one would not exchange for any Venus[1] of the museums.

She looked at it now, after her long journey, with an unexpected sense of relief, the consciousness of being once more in a place where Penelope Bent had an identity, where twenty friendly hearts would ache for her, if they but knew! She would have died rather than have them know. As she stepped from the station she shrank even from the scrutiny of the sunshine; yet she was not proof against the comfort of feeling that the sympathy she dreaded was within reach; and she almost smiled at the nod of the Irish apple woman who greeted her as she hurried down the steps.

Everything all these last days had been so unreal; she had journeyed far into such a strange world, passing through so endless a nightmare of unknown sights and sounds and names. Here all was peacefully, prosaically familiar; the streets deep in spring mud, the house fronts blotched with signboards, the hoardings with their flamboyant advertisements, the junction of car tracks and the peristyle of the Baptist Church opposite the station all formed a part of her earliest consciousness.

Although she returned to it all so heavily, although the mere fact of her return testified to a disaster too recent to tolerate the touch of thought, yet the spell of association was upon her before she had picked her way through the mud to the opposite sidewalk.

Miss Bent, in her neat traveling dress, her hat still protected from the contamination of the journey by the folds of a thick veil, did not look like a victim of Olympian ire.[2] She had passed well beyond thirty, in appearance if not in years, and her small, spare figure and pale face suggested the flatness and premature discoloration of a pressed flower. There was, however, nothing else about her in accordance with so tender a simile, her air of almost military precision rather implying a past devoted to the punctual accomplishment of didactic duties.

Her whole mien, in fact, savored of the educational. Her small features were as neatly balanced as a sentence of Lindley Murray's and her black hair assumed, in parting on her forehead, the exact curves of a pair of copybook parentheses. The eyes alone played traitor to this well-tutored mask, all that was feminine and inconsequent in their possessor lurking there under a spring of moisture, like Truth at the bottom of her well.

It was a bright April day, and the clock in the Gothic tower, which an unbridled fancy had recently appended to the classic façade of the city hall, struck twelve as Miss Bent passed beneath it. For a moment she paused, glancing down the main street, congested, as usual at that hour, by the pressure of traffic; then she hastened along the narrow sidewalk, drawing down her veil, and pressing close to the sides of the houses to escape the contact of hurrying shoulders.

She had washed her face and smoothed her dress in the toilet room of the sleeping car, and there seemed to be no reason why she should not stop and see Mr. Boutwell for a moment on her way home.

She walked on hurriedly without raising her eyes, till at last, reaching a certain side street, she paused to glance at a building which faced her—a large brick building with brownstone angles and a massive porch. It stood by itself at the end of the street, with an air of moral superiority that at once proclaimed it to be one of the public schools of Sailport.

Miss Bent's heart began to beat. There were *her* windows—the three with geraniums on the sill, at the left-hand corner of the second story. Would she be sitting behind them again, in a day or two at her desk on the raised platform, facing the double file of benches? Why not, indeed? Why even raise the question? What possible doubt could there be of the place having been kept for her?

The whole school board had assured her of it when, a month earlier, laughing and crying, she had taken, as she thought, a last leave of them. "Till the next general meeting we shall engage a temporary substitute. One word from you, and we'll put you back—remember that."

How she had smiled then at such idle toying with impossibilities! But she had smiled through tears of gratification. It was so pleasant to feel that they had liked her, that they had valued her services; to know that no teacher had ever left the school amid such a chorus of lamentations, that none had ever been so urgently entreated by the school board to reconsider her determination and come back to them!

"Why not persuade Mr. Dayton to sell out in Louisville and go into business here?" one commissioner had even laughingly suggested; and she, taken by the humor of it, had promised to submit the plan to Mr. Dayton. It seemed all a part then—the tears, the regrets, the little professional jokes—of the general cumulative pleasantness of life; now the wish of the school board remained the one reed she had to cling to, and she told herself how thankful she ought to be that it was so strong a one.

How many women, after resigning such a place as hers, could comfort themselves with the hope of being able to return to it? How many, whom she knew, had spent years in the vain effort to get into one of the schools!

There was her friend, Vexilla Thurber, for instance—poor Vexilla! How hard she had tried for a place in Penelope's school, how long it had been the unattainable ambition of her life! And she had never even had a hope of success. All of Miss Bent's efforts had been unavailing; the school board remained obdurate, retiring behind hazy generalities; but Mr. Boutwell, one of their number, confided to Miss Bent that her friend was not "smart enough."

In vain Miss Bent protested that Vexilla's apparent dullness was only timidity; in vain offered to answer for the sufficiency of her knowledge and for her untiring industry. The school board bowed in general acquiescence, but did not find Miss Thurber to their liking. In vain Miss Bent, letting her eyes speak, reminded them of her friend's difficult situation, with a helpless grandmother, a crippled brother and an idle sister to support; the board bowed again, implying that the public schools of Sailport were not asylums for the indigent.

And so, year after year, Miss Bent had to bear the same heavy news to her friend; and year after year Vexilla, smiling down her discomfiture, had to return to the underpaid toil of a few private lessons, combined with odd jobs in the way of bookkeeping and typewriting. At the recollection Miss Bent's eyes melted. Poor Vexilla—hers was the harder lot!

"Perhaps now, if they're *very* glad to get me back," Miss Bent murmured under her veil, "I may be able to do something for Vexilla." And she remembered with fresh thankfulness that her letter must have reached Mr. Boutwell three days before the meeting of the school board.

This fortifying thought hastened the step with which she sped along Main Street toward a shabby-looking building, with glass doors surmounted by an inscription declaring it to be the People's Library. Nothing in the interior of the library belied its outer shabbiness; the rooms, as she entered, emitted an odor of much-handled books that gave her a qualm after her draught of salt April air. At a desk near the door sat a young woman with a cold-veal complexion and taffy-colored hair who, in the absence of more pressing duties, was engaged in polishing her nails.

"Is Mr. Boutwell in?" Miss Bent asked.

"Guess he's in his office."

Miss Bent walked down the room between the lines of dingy books to a door at the farther end.

A prompt "Come in" answered her knock, and she entered a room almost filled by a large writing table, at which a man sat in an office chair, collating catalogues.

He raised a pale face, elongated in one direction by the baldness of his high forehead, in the other by the vague neutral tints of his beard, and the expression of distress wrinkling his neuralgic-looking brows seemed involuntarily to contradict the smile of welcome that lent a sudden blueness to his spectacled gray eyes.

"Miss Bent!"

She stood before him, fingering her bag in a spasm of nervousness that gripped her throat.

"O Mr. Boutwell," broke from her at last, as she dropped into the seat he pushed forward. It was so unlike her usual mode of address, she was so little given to feminine falterings and incoherencies, that, under the contagion of her emotion, he could only stammer, "I'm afraid you've had a trying time." And at once he doubted if the words were in good taste.

His perturbation increased when she drew from her pocket a

neatly folded handkerchief, and pushing back her veil, silently wiped her eyes.

She restored the handkerchief to her pocket and put her bag aside, keeping one wrist slipped through its handle, as, with the caution of the unaccustomed traveler, she had done during all the long hours of the journey. "You must excuse me," she said, "but I've been in the cars since yesterday afternoon, and I came right here from the station."

"You must be very tired!" he murmured.

"Oh no, not very, but I've been through a good deal."

She glanced vaguely about the little room, with its book-lined walls and the window looking out on a blind alley, full of rubbish.

"You didn't expect me back so soon, did you?" she added, with a sigh.

Boutwell had taken off his spectacles and was rubbing them with a bit of chamois skin. He coughed instead of replying.

"Isn't it a mercy I didn't take mother?" she went on in a tone of confidence that contrasted with her usual impersonal manner. "The long journey there and back would have been too awful for her. I've been so thankful ever since. It seemed to keep me from breaking down, and I needed something to do that. I've been through everything."

"I was afraid so," he answered, feeling now that she would not repudiate his sympathy. "I got your letter."

"Oh, my letter!" she exclaimed.

The blood rushed to her forehead. A few minutes ago, in passing the schoolhouse, she had felt very sure of the future; but now—Her hand slipped from the bag, rejoining the other which trembled on her knee. The librarian's brows were a projecting bunch of wrinkles.

"I got your letter, Miss Bent, but only yesterday."

"Only *yesterday!*"

"Yes, you unfortunately addressed it to me personally, instead of sending it to the school board, and—"

"I did that on purpose," she interposed, "to keep my—to keep it private. I didn't want to have everybody talking about my—my having broken off my engagement; mother doesn't even know yet; I couldn't bear to tell anybody but *you!*"

"I know, I know; I gathered that from what you wrote. But it was most unlucky that you wrote to me, for I've been away, up in Maine, for the last week with my wife's mother, who's been sick, and I only got back yesterday."

"Only yes-ter-day!" she repeated, dividing the words into syllables, as if they belonged to a foreign tongue which she did not perfectly understand. Then, suddenly lifting her head: "But my place—they must have filled my place?"

"It was filled three days ago at the general meeting. There was no help for it. No one could imagine—"

"No, no, of course—of course."

He had been afraid that she would cry again, but to his surprise she remained quite calm.

"Who has it?" she asked.

He hesitated a moment; the words seemed hard to say: "Your friend, Miss Thurber."

"Vexilla!"

The room swung round; her lips grew dry; she felt an inconsequent desire to laugh. "But Vexilla—Vexilla! You always said—why, not one of you would *look* at her—not even for the third primary—and now, my class! *My* class!"

She was bathed in a hot wave of anger. The whole air seemed thick with ingratitude and treachery, as if all these years she had walked in an atmosphere of lies. What did it mean? What could it mean? Perhaps, even while they were urging her to remain, imploring her to come back to them, they had been plotting her removal; possibly keeping Vexilla to fill this very place, while they glossed over with hypocritical excuses their refusal to give her a lesser one! And Vexilla herself—might not she, too, have had a hand in it? Who could tell, in a world that swarmed with such grinning incongruities?

"But Vexilla—Vexilla—" she repeated.

"I don't wonder at your surprise." Mr. Boutwell's familiar voice fell strangely on the tumult of her thoughts. "We've been unwilling to employ Miss Thurber for reasons with which you are perfectly familiar, and which you have often told me you thought inadequate. You remember how much you've talked with me about her; how often you've told me it was only shyness that made her appear so dull and hesitating; that she was really better educated than many of our present teachers." He paused, but Miss Bent made no answer.

"Well," he continued, "there were very few candidates for your place, and among them there was only one who appeared at all satisfactory to the board, and that was Miss Euphemia Staples. We had just decided to appoint her when she was called out West, to keep house for a brother who has lost his wife; and that left us without a single eligible applicant—for of course Miss Thurber was not among the applicants."

A low sound like a laugh escaped Miss Bent.

"At last somebody suggested Miss Thurber. It rather took us aback at first, but we hadn't much time to think the matter over, and there didn't seem to be anybody else. We recalled what you'd said about her—the board always thought a great deal of your opinion—and finally we sent for her. She was considerably over-come—she cried a good deal—and for a time it didn't seem as if we could get her to accept. She said she'd sooner have taken any other place in the school."

Miss Bent moved impatiently in her seat. Vexilla had evidently expressed all the proper sentiments; for once in her life she had not been tongue-tied; she seemed indeed to have surprised Mr. Boutwell by her eloquence. The supplanted teacher rose, feeling for her bag.

"I guess I'd better be going along," she murmured.

"Wait a minute, please; I haven't quite finished. I hope we shall see you back among us all the same, Miss Bent, for Miss Thurber accepted your place only on the condition that if by any chance you—you changed your mind and came back within the next few weeks, she should be permitted to resign. And I know she'll hold us to our agreement."

Miss Bent turned red, then pale. "Changed my mind? Changed my mind? How dare she?" Her anger dropped and she sank back into her chair. "Did she say that? Did she? Poor Vexilla! That she'd only accept on that condition? She made you promise? She made the whole board agree to it? Poor Vexilla—oh, poor Vexilla!"

"And what's more, she means it, too," Mr. Boutwell went on. "She's restless and worried at the idea of being in your place; says she can't get used to it; it don't seem natural to her. She's a devoted friend, Miss Bent."

"I know, I know."

"I met her only this morning on my way here, and she stopped to talk about you and tell me how she missed you. She said she'd give up her place in a minute to have you back here, and I believe she would, though from what I hear it means a good deal to her to be getting a regular salary. She's had a pretty hard time of it up to now, I guess."

"You met Vexilla this morning?" Miss Bent interrupted, without noticing his last words. "You didn't tell her—about me, did you, Mr. Boutwell?"

"I said nothing."

"Thank you—thank you. You always understand. I'm so confused myself; I don't yet know how I mean to act. Even mother doesn't suspect anything. She doesn't know I've come—she doesn't know but what I'm married!" She gave a constrained laugh and rose once more.

The laugh troubled Boutwell; it seemed to conceal some inaccessible disaster.

"Don't you think," he began, for the sake of saying something, "that it would have been wiser to let Mrs. Bent know? Won't she be considerably startled at seeing you?"

"I'm afraid she will; but I couldn't tell her in a letter; she'd have shown it to everybody. You know she just *has* to talk things over."

"I understand."

Miss Bent looked at him hesitatingly. "I guess I'll go now. I'm very grateful to you for not having spoken about my letter."

"Oh, that's all right," said the librarian, taking refuge again in the examination of his spectacles. "But, see here, Miss Bent, what are you going to do?"

"About what?"

"Why—the school."

"Oh, I don't know," she said slowly. "I'm so bewildered I can't think straight yet. I'll have to go home and quiet down a little. Only please don't let Vexilla know I'm here; don't tell anybody you've seen me; I'm so afraid she'll find out about it before I've seen her."

"Don't worry about that, Miss Bent."

"No; I know I can trust you."

Their hands met and she moved away, adding, as she reached the door, "I'll come in tomorrow and tell you what I've decided."

"Very well; but I'm sure Miss Thurber won't keep the place. I guess she's got a will of her own, and I don't believe you could make her stay if you tried."

Miss Bent turned back abruptly.

"O Mr. Boutwell, I don't know what you must think of me! I was perfectly hateful about Vexilla when you first told me—perfectly hateful! I don't see how I could behave so. As if she hadn't as much right to take my class as anybody else! But the fact is, I'm almost crazy. I don't seem to know what I'm doing—" Her eyes clung to Boutwell with a look of shipwrecked terror. "I must tell you—I must tell you! I can't endure it another minute by myself! What I wrote you wasn't true—about having broken off my engagement. There wasn't a word of truth in it. When I got to Louisville Mr. Dayton wasn't there. He'd gone off the day before, and nobody knew where he was. I had to get detectives—his partner helped me. It took us nearly a week to find him. He was away down in Texas—and he'd married another woman!"

Boutwell jumped up with a wrathful exclamation, but before it was out of his mouth the office door had closed on Miss Bent.

II

Late that afternoon Miss Bent, having unpacked her few possessions (she looked the other way as she slipped the gray cashmere with lace ruffles into a drawer by itself), sat in her little bedroom trying to think. The sense of familiarity which had soothed the first moments of her return to Sailport had given way to a profounder estrangement. As she glanced about the room, it seemed impossible that four walls which had held so much of her life should assume a look of such chill indifference. Every line of the furniture, every twist in the pattern of the wallpaper, seemed to repeat the same "I know thee not!" No, she was not the Penelope Bent who had lived there through so many happy, monotonous years; she was a stranger who had never been in the room before, and who knew as little of its history as it knew of hers.

The fanciful wanderings of her thoughts frightened her—she was not accustomed to such divagations; she felt herself on the brink of delirium. The interview with her mother had been terrible. She had told Mrs. Bent that her marriage was postponed, taking refuge in this euphuism under the merciless tenderness of the maternal gaze. It would have been so much easier to face indifference! Mrs. Bent's tremulous avoidance of surmises, her abruptly deflected questions, her unwonted acquiescences, seemed to intensify the vividness of the mute insight that lighted up every corner of her daughter's consciousness. The two women lived in that involuntary familiarity from which neither speech nor silence can give sanctuary.

Suddenly the solitude seemed to be full of her mother's eyes, and Miss Bent, starting up, moved toward the window. Twilight was falling, and a few steps in the open air might do her good. She put on her hat and veil, and unlocking her door, stepped into the cheerful sitting room beyond. Ivy and geranium throve on the sunny window sill, and a lump of coal had just been kindled in the grate.

Mrs. Bent, a small, withered woman, rooted to her seat by some obscure ailment, looked up at her daughter with shrinking, inquisitive eyes. Miss Bent drew up the shawl about her mother's knees, and absently broke a yellow leaf from one of the geranium plants.

"Seems to me the geraniums have had too much water this last week," she said.

"I'm afraid they have, Penelope. Nobody's got your knack with them."

Miss Bent stirred the soil in the pot. "It needs loosening." She drew on her gloves, avoiding her mother's eye.

"You're going out a little way, Penelope?"

"Yes, I'll be back soon." She hesitated. "If anybody comes in, mother, don't—don't—"

Mrs. Bent's eyelids trembled; the violence of her protest confessed her weakness. "Penelope Bent, how can you think—"

"Oh, that's all right!" the daughter said, resignedly.

Although it was growing dark indoors, the spring daylight still lingered, and Miss Bent, instinctively seeking for solitude, turned up a quiet side street, disturbed only by the calls of a few children at play. The air brought little ease to her head, and she was conscious of a growing inability to think. Yet she knew that in a few hours she must act; she could not continue to keep her presence in Sailport a secret; had she cherished any such design, her mother's tongue would have frustrated it. She must prepare to meet Vexilla Thurber the next day; before they met she must decide on some course of action, and as yet no conclusion had suggested itself.

Try as she might to examine the problem before her, she could see but one point of it—that she had lost her place at the school, that the greater part of her savings had been absorbed by the journey to Louisville and the preparations for her wedding, and that now she was left stranded, with heavy expenses to face and without means of meeting them. Although Miss Bent had only her mother to support, she had found her salary barely sufficient for her needs. Her own tastes were simple, but Mrs. Bent's ill health taxed her daughter's purse with demands that had every quality of unexpectedness except that of inevitable recurrence.

Under such conditions, the future looked disheartening enough. She remembered Boutwell's words: "Miss Thurber won't keep the place"; but the suggestion they conveyed was intolerable. Of course, if something else could be found for Vexilla—but she smiled at herself for trusting her hopes to this frail hypothesis. Had not she and all Vexilla's friends been searching for years for that delusive something? Yes, but Boutwell had said that Vexilla would insist on resigning, and he was right in thinking that Vexilla had a will of her own. If Vexilla meant to resign, the whole of Sailport could not stop her. And if she resigned, what was to prevent—

Miss Bent pulled herself together. She had a sudden vision of Vexilla's household, with the infirm grandmother, the crippled brother, helpless as a baby, who lay in his chair playing with tin soldiers, the handsome, slatternly sister, who drifted back from every "job" that Vexilla obtained for her into a languid permanence of novel reading and street corner flirtation. Vexilla had three to support; Miss Bent but one. Yes, but if Vexilla insisted on resigning?

Down the empty street a woman's figure was approaching. Even in the failing light there was no mistaking the thick-set figure, the oscillating walk that suggested a ship with her steering gear out of order, or the round face framed in meek drab hair. Miss Bent glanced about in the instinctive attempt to escape; but it was too late.

"Penelope!"

"Vexilla!"

The two women faced each other, Miss Bent silent, Vexilla Thurber emitting her astonishment in a series of soft cries:

"You, Penelope—*you!* Back in Sailport? Gracious mercy! But is it you, really? I feel as if it might be your ghost. Oh no, there's your cameo brooch! *Penelope*—why don't you say something?"

"You don't give me time, Vexilla; but I'm not a ghost—and I've come back."

"For mercy's sake! What in the world has happened? Penelope Bent, you've had some misfortune! You'd never have come back—has anything happened to *him?* I know something's happened—you look awful! What *is* it?"

Vexilla's agonized italics echoed through the silent street, and a woman on the opposite sidewalk slackened her pace to listen.

"I can't tell you here, Vexilla. Don't be so excited! I'll walk along with you a little way."

Her friend, clutching her arm, watched her with perturbed blue eyes.

"You needn't talk to *me*, Penelope—something has happened, or else you're sick; one or the other! You're as white as a sheet, and I can feel you trembling all over! Penelope—Penelope—you don't want me to go away and leave you? You aren't angry with me for—for meeting you?" Her apple face was wet with tears; they ran down unheeded, dabbling her fawn-colored dress.

"Nonsense, Vexilla! Why should I be angry with you for meeting me? I've only just got home, and I'm a little tired, that's all!"

"Oh, you poor soul, you're *dead* tired! I can see that. But, Penelope—" She drew closer, her voice sinking to a frightened whisper. "I don't quite understand—*are you married?*"

"No, I'm not married." Miss Bent glanced over her friend's shoulder and saw a group of people approaching. "But we can't stand here and talk, and I can't ask you to come and see me just now. Mother's in the parlor, and we couldn't talk before her."

"No, no; I know we couldn't," Miss Thurber emotionally acquiesced. "But why won't you come home with me for a few minutes? Do, Penelope! Lally will be getting supper for grandma and Phil, and we can have my room all to ourselves. Lally's getting real helpful, Penelope. She cares for grandma so nicely when I have to be out!"

Miss Bent hesitated. "Where were you going, Vexilla?"

"Me? I was only going to run down to Main Street for a minute to get some books. It's of no consequence——" She broke off suddenly and her color rose. The books of which she was in quest were probably the textbooks for her new class at the school. "Come with me, Penelope," she deprecatingly entreated.

"Very well," said Miss Bent, with sudden resolution; and they began to walk in the direction of Vexilla's home.

Vexilla, eased of her first agitation, respected her friend's reticence, and they moved on silently through the dusk, pricked here and there by the yellow points of the street lamps. At length they reached a house divided from the sidewalk by a strip of downtrodden earth enclosed with broken palings. Vexilla opened the door and led her friend through an entry smelling of boiled cabbage, and up a narrow staircase to the top of the house. On the upper landing she paused to say, with visible embarrassment, "You mustn't mind if Lally and Phil seem surprised to see you back. We've been talking so much about——"

"Yes, yes; I understand," Miss Bent hastily interposed.

Vexilla stepped into a low-ceilinged room which was almost in darkness.

"Why, Lally! Haven't you lighted the lamp? Haven't you got supper?"

Vexilla advanced into the room, leaving Miss Bent on the threshold.

"I can't see where I'm going! Where are the matches? Oh, here. It's a mercy I filled the lamp before I went out, anyway!"

She bent over a lamp which stood on the center table, and the room was presently revealed in all its shabby disorder. In an old bath chair near the window lay the paralyzed boy, his drawn face detached like a death's-head against the shawl thrust pillow-wise behind his head. Lally, the sister, dragging herself from the sofa on which she had been stretched, stepped listlessly into the lamplight, which illuminated the beauty of her heavy white face, helmeted with somber hair.

"Goodness!" she exclaimed. "That you, Miss Bent? Have you got married already? Vexilla never told us you were coming back!"

"Vexilla's got your place at school!" piped the paralyzed boy from the window.

Vexilla paid no heed. She had hurried toward her grandmother, a huge ruin of a woman with a face like a broken statue, who sat vaguely smiling in a rocking chair beside the stove.

"Gracious, Lally, you've left the stove door open, and there's a cinder right in grandma's lap!"

"Lally's been asleep!" the boy shrilly interposed. Vexilla smoothed the old woman's hair, straightened the knitted shawl about her shoulders, and closed the door of the stove. Lally had thrown herself back on the sofa, still gazing at Miss Bent under the projecting visor of her hair, while the boy began impatiently: "Vexilla, aren't you going to get supper?"

"No; Lally's going to." Vexilla turned to her friend. "Come this way, Penelope."

Miss Bent followed her down a passageway to a small room with two beds in it. Miss Thurber struck a match and lighted a lamp which stood on a desk piled with schoolbooks.

"Sit down and wait, please, Penelope. I'll be back in a minute."

She turned away, shutting the door after her, while Miss Bent sank into a chair. She longed to fly, to escape from the depressing influences of Vexilla's home to the orderly silence of her own little room. The cracked looking glass and threadbare carpet, the bed in which the helpless grandmother slept, all the evidences of Vexilla's hardships and privations, seemed to add their pressure to the weight upon her burdened nerves. Never before had life appeared so meaningless and cruel.

Vexilla returned, demonstrative and breathless, with a cup of steaming tea.

"Please drink it, Penelope, please do—you're regularly worn out. I can see you are. Just take a mouthful—I know it'll do you good!" Her blue eyes had the look of a dog begging to be noticed.

Miss Bent took the cup and leaned back, sipping the tea reluctantly, while Vexilla sat by in an ecstasy of mute contemplation.

"I do feel better," Miss Bent said at last, meeting her friend's gaze. "And now, Vexilla, we must talk."

She paused a moment, as if rallying her forces, and then began again: "I must tell you—"

Vexilla leaned forward. "Wait a minute, Penelope—there's something I must tell *you* first. I can't bear to have you speak a word before you know what's happened."

Miss Bent looked at her, half smiling. "I know," she said.

"You *know!* About the school?"

"Yes. I've seen Mr. Boutwell."

"Oh!" said Vexilla, in a long shudder of comprehension. For a moment or two both women were silent. Then Vexilla began to speak in quick, entreating tones.

"O Penelope, what *must* you have thought? It all happened so strangely! They sent for me, Penelope—of course I never would have dreamed of applying. Even if I'd been smart enough, I never would have applied for *your* place! And I always supposed they thought I was too stupid. You'd tried so often to get me into the schools that I didn't suppose there was any chance for me. When they sent for me I thought it must be a mistake. I couldn't believe it! And even when I found they really wanted me, I couldn't bear the idea, Penelope. I said if it had only been any other place but yours; but they said that was the only one that was vacant. And of course everybody said you'd never come back here—you were so positive you wouldn't, Penelope—" She paused, shrinking back from the unrevealed mystery of her friend's return. "And I've got so many to think of that it didn't seem as if I ought to refuse. But I said I'd only take it on one condition. I made them solemnly agree to that—that if you changed your mind and—and decided to come back to Sailport—"

"I know that, too," said Miss Bent, slowly. Bending forward, she kissed the wet cheek of her friend. Fresh tears rose to Vexilla's eyes; but the intensity of the resolve which animated her drove them back and subdued the quivering of her lips.

"I'm glad Mr. Boutwell told you, Penelope. I couldn't bear to have had you think, for one minute, even, that I'd have taken the place on any other terms."

"I knew you wouldn't, Vexilla!"

"O Penelope! How like you to say that!" In the rapture of being understood she ventured to lay one large hand on Miss Bent's. "There's nobody like you—nobody! Oh, it's so good to have you back!" Again she faltered, in fear of appearing to touch intentionally upon Penelope's enigmatic course.

Miss Bent did not speak. She sat motionless, her eyes fixed on a plush-framed photograph of herself that hung above Vexilla's desk. It was the only picture in the room.

"And there's another thing I want to tell you right off, Penelope! I know just what you are—always thinking of other people first and yourself last; and I don't want you to think it's any loss to me to—to give up that place. I don't want to keep it, Penelope! It's a relief to me to give it up. I never should have got used to it. I'm not half bright enough, anyway! I don't much believe they'd have kept me more than one term, even if—and it doesn't suit me, somehow! I'd rather go back to my old work. I—I think I'd have resigned, anyway. I'm sure I would, Penelope! The fact is, it ties me down too much—I'm more independent with my other work."

Miss Bent raised her eyes. "Your bookkeeping and typewriting, you mean? Where's your typewriter, by the way? It always used to stand on your desk."

In the faint candlelight she thought she saw Miss Thurber's color change.

"It's not here now."

"Where is it? What's become of it?"

"I—well, the fact is I sold it."

"You sold it? Why? Oh, because—I see." Miss Bent paused, struggling with a resentment that suddenly forced itself through her sympathy for her friend. She repressed the ungenerous impulse. What could be more natural than that Vexilla should sell her typewriter?

Miss Thurber went on precipitately "I guess I shan't have much time for typewriting, anyway. You see, it's going to be a great help to have had that appointment. I don't believe I'll have a bit of trouble getting private pupils now. Fact is, that's the real reason I was always so crazy to get into the schools. I never thought the work would really suit me—but it makes such a lot of difference if you can refer parents to the board! I guess I'll have more work than I can manage."

Miss Bent laughed, and rising from her seat, laid her hand on Vexilla's shoulder. "You're a goose, Vexilla! How do you know I'm going to stay in Sailport?"

"Penelope!"

Miss Thurber had also risen, and the two women stood facing each other.

"You don't know yet why I'm here," Miss Bent continued in the same bantering tone. "It seems to me you're taking a good deal for granted, aren't you?"

"O Penelope! I didn't mean—"

Miss Bent, withdrawing her hand, took a few hesitating steps across the room. Vexilla hung back, waiting for her to speak. "I'm going to tell you, Vexilla," she said at last.

"Yes," the other nodded.

There was another silence. Miss Bent seemed to find difficulty in choosing her words.

"My marriage isn't going to take place—just at present—that's all. When I got to Louisville I found—but I can't tell you all that now; it's too long. Perhaps tomorrow. I only got back this morning, and I had to explain it all to mother. Of course my coming back upset her a good deal."

"Don't say another word, Penelope! I can see how tired you are. Only tell me you're not in any trouble—"

Miss Bent met her gaze calmly.

"I'm not in any trouble, Vexilla. My marriage has been put off for reasons that—that are perfectly satisfactory to Mr. Dayton and myself. He's obliged to be away from Louisville a good deal just now—and I didn't want to stay out there alone—with mother here—"

"O Penelope—but couldn't he have let you know?" Vexilla cried, her sympathy outrunning her discretion.

"I'll explain all that another time. I only want to tell you that I've decided to leave Sailport with mother now, instead of waiting till—afterward. You know she was to have joined me in Louisville, and we've given up our rooms here, so we'd have to move on the first of May, anyhow." She now spoke without perceptible hesitation.

"But, Penelope, I don't understand!" Miss Thurber faltered. "Where are you going? You are not going back to Louisville right off?"

Miss Bent's face stiffened. "No; not there." She paused a moment. "I think we shall go to New York," she said at last. "Aunt Sarah Tillman, mother's younger sister, lives there, and I could get plenty to do in a big place like that. It's very easy, if you know some one who lives there. But it's not on my account; it's because of mother. She's a good deal upset by the change in my plans. She'd made up her mind to leave Sailport, and I'm afraid it would be hard for her to settle down again after making all her preparations to go. You know mother's very excitable."

"I know, but—"

"I've had a good many offers of work in New York," Miss Bent continued, ignoring the interruption. "My aunt's always writing to us to come and stay with her. She says she could get me half a dozen pupils right off. Her husband's related to a Presbyterian minister, with a large parish. And I don't know but what I should like the change, too. I feel rather restless myself."

Miss Thurber continued to gaze at her with a tender incredulity. "But New York—you've never been there—"

"Well, I don't know that it's too late to begin."

"No; but it's all so queer! Why, you've hardly ever been away from Sailport, Penelope! I can't think what you want to go to New York for."

Miss Bent rose again. Her lips were compressed and she forced the words through them with a certain precipitation. "New York is nearer Louisville, for one thing. You hadn't thought of that, I suppose?"

"No," Vexilla faltered.

"You know Mr. Dayton was never able to get as far east as this."

Miss Thurber colored. She felt that it was singularly obtuse of her not to have understood this. "To be sure," she murmured, "I never thought of it! You must excuse me, Penelope. I've asked you so many questions, and I know how tired you are! But I couldn't help it. It's all so sudden! I can't take it in yet—the idea of your going away again, just as I was so glad to have you back!"

Miss Bent was putting on her jacket and adjusting her brown veil. For a moment she did not speak, and some indefinable change in her face made Vexilla suddenly exclaim: "But *is* it true? Are you really going away?"

Miss Bent turned on her almost angrily. "I don't know what you mean! You talk as if I didn't know my own mind! I'm not in the habit of saying things I don't mean!"

"Oh, I know, but—" Vexilla's words ran into tears.

Miss Bent leaned forward and gently kissed her.

"Mother and I are going away in a few days, that's quite settled. My reason for telling you so at once is that I was afraid you might do something foolish about the school."

"O Penelope, Penelope!"

"And I want you to keep the class, Vexilla. I particularly want you to keep it! I was so glad when Mr. Boutwell told me they'd given it to you! I couldn't bear to think of a stranger in my class. You must write me about the girls, Vexilla, and perhaps I can help you sometimes with your work."

"O Penelope! It seems as if I couldn't bear it—*your* class!"

"You're a goose, Vexilla, and now good-bye! It's dark, and mother will be getting worried."

"Let me walk home with you, Penelope. I feel as if I wasn't ever going to see you again."

"You silly child! You'll see me tomorrow, I hope. Come in the afternoon, while mother's taking her nap."

"You won't let me walk back with you now?"

"Not now. I want to be alone."

She opened the door and stepped hurriedly along the passage-way ahead of Vexilla, passing, she hardly knew how, among the inmates of the living room, now gathered about an untidy supper table. On the landing Vexilla clung to her with another mute pressure, full of confused doubts and tremors; then she found herself on the staircase, and a moment later she was alone in the dim street.

For a while she stood irresolute, as if awaiting the subsidence of some strong wave of emotion; then, slowly, she began to move forward along the deserted sidewalk.

At the next corner, instead of turning homeward, she bent her steps toward Main Street, unconsciously quickening her pace as she advanced. She was in that curiously detached state when one's body seems like an inert mass, propelled from one point to another without conscious action of its own. In this condition she reached the corner where the brightly-lighted post-office windows pro-

jected their oblongs of yellow light across the shadows of Main
Street. She pushed open one of the doors, and, going to a small
window at the back of the office, asked for a sheet of paper and a
stamped envelope.

Having received them, she withdrew to one of the shelves lining
the wall, and dipped a ragged pen into the cup of grayish coagu-
lated matter which a paternal government provides for the convenience of the peripatetic letter writer. She wrote a few lines,
which she addressed to Mr. Boutwell, and having dropped the envelope into a letter box, she left the post office and turned toward
home.

Her step had lost all hesitancy. She seemed to be moving with
decision toward a definitely chosen goal. In the course of the past
hour her whole relation to life had changed. The experience of the
last weeks had flung her out of her orbit, whirling her through
dread spaces of moral darkness and bewilderment. She seemed to
have lost her connection with the general scheme of things, to
have no further part in the fulfilment of the laws that made life
comprehensible and duty a joyful impulse. Now the old sense of
security had returned. There still loomed before her, in tragic amplitude, the wreck of her individual hope; but she had escaped
from the falling ruins and stood safe, outside of herself, in touch
once more with the common troubles of her kind, enfranchised
forever from the bondage of a lonely grief.

THE CHOICE

Stilling, that night after dinner, had surpassed himself. He always did, Wrayford reflected, when the small fry from Highfield came to dine. He, Cobham Stilling, who had to find his bearings and keep to his level in the big heedless ironic world of New York, dilated and grew vast in the congenial medium of Highfield. The Red House was the biggest house of the Highfield summer colony, and Cobham Stilling was its biggest man. No one else within a radius of a hundred miles (on a conservative estimate) had as many horses, as many greenhouses, as many servants, and assuredly no one else had three motors and a motorboat for the lake.

The motorboat was Stilling's latest hobby, and he rode—or steered—it in and out of the conversation all the evening, to the obvious edification of everyone present save his wife and his visitor, Austin Wrayford. The interest of the latter two who, from opposite ends of the drawing room, exchanged a fleeting glance when Stilling again launched his craft on the thin current of the talk—the interest of Mrs. Stilling and Wrayford had already lost its edge by protracted contact with the subject.

But the dinner guests—the Rector, Mr. Swordsley, his wife Mrs. Swordsley, Lucy and Agnes Granger, their brother Addison, and young Jack Emmerton from Harvard—were all, for divers reasons, stirred to the proper pitch of feeling. Mr. Swordsley, no doubt, was saying to himself: "If my good parishioner here can afford to buy a motorboat, in addition to all the other expenditures which an establishment like this must entail, I certainly need not scruple to appeal to him again for a contribution for our Galahad Club." The Granger girls, meanwhile, were evoking visions of lakeside picnics, not unadorned with the presence of young Mr. Emmerton; while that youth himself speculated as to whether his

affable host would let him, when he came back on his next vaca-
tion, "learn to run the thing himself"; and Mr. Addison Granger,
the elderly bachelor brother of the volatile Lucy and Agnes, mentally formulated the precise phrase in which, in his next letter to
his cousin Professor Spildyke of the University of East Latmos, he
should allude to "our last delightful trip in my old friend Cobham
Stilling's ten thousand dollar motor launch"—for East Latmos
was still in that primitive stage of culture on which five figures im-
pinge.

   Isabel Stilling, sitting beside Mrs. Swordsley, her head slightly
bent above the needlework with which on these occasions it was
her old-fashioned habit to employ herself—Isabel also had doubtless her reflections to make. As Wrayford leaned back in his corner and looked at her across the wide flower-filled drawing room
he noted, first of all—for the how many hundredth time?—the
play of her hands above the embroidery frame, the shadow of
the thick dark hair on her forehead, the listless droops of the
lids over her somewhat full grey eyes. He noted all this with a
conscious deliberateness of enjoyment, taking in unconsciously,
at the same time, the particular quality in her attitude, in the fall
of her dress and the turn of her head, which had set her for him,
from the first day, in a separate world; then he said to himself:
"She is certainly thinking: 'Where on earth will Cobham get the
money to pay for it?'"

   Stilling, cigar in mouth and thumbs in his waistcoat pockets,
was impressively perorating from his usual dominant position on
the hearthrug.

   "I said: 'If I have the thing at all, I want the best that can be
got.' That's my way, you know, Swordsley; I suppose I'm what
you'd call fastidious. Always was, about everything, from cigars
to wom—" his eye met the apprehensive glance of Mrs. Swordsley, who looked like her husband with his clerical coat cut slightly
lower "—so I said: 'If I have the thing at all, I want the best that
can be got.' Nothing makeshift for me, no second best. I never
cared for the cheap and showy. I always say frankly to a man: 'If
you can't give me a first-rate cigar, for the Lord's sake let me
smoke my own.'" He paused to do so. "Well, if you have my standards, you can't buy a thing in a minute. You must look round,
compare, select. I found there were lots of motorboats on the

market, just as there's lots of stuff called champagne. But I said to myself: 'Ten to one there's only one fit to buy, just as there's only one champagne fit for a gentleman to drink.' Argued like a lawyer, eh, Austin?" He tossed this to Wrayford. "Take me for one of your own trade, wouldn't you? Well, I'm not such a fool as I look. I suppose you fellows who are tied to the treadmill—excuse me, Swordsley, but work's work, isn't it?—I suppose you think a man like me has nothing to do but take it easy: loll through life like a woman. By George, sir, I'd like either of you to see the time it takes—I won't say the *brains*—but just the time it takes to pick out a good motorboat. Why, I went—"

Mrs. Stilling set her embroidery frame noiselessly on the table at her side, and turned her head toward Wrayford. "Would you mind ringing for the tray?"

The interruption helped Mrs. Swordsley to waver to her feet. "I'm afraid we ought really to be going; my husband has an early service tomorrow."

Her host intervened with a genial protest. "Going already? Nothing of the sort! Why, the night's still young, as the poet says. Long way from here to the rectory? Nonsense! In our little twenty-horse car we do it in five minutes—don't we, Belle? Ah, you're walking, to be sure—" Stilling's indulgent gesture seemed to concede that, in such a case, allowances must be made, and that he was the last man not to make them. "Well, then, Swordsley—" He held out a thick red hand that seemed to exude beneficence, and the clergyman, pressing it, ventured to murmur a suggestion.

"What, that Galahad Club again? Why, I thought my wife—Isabel, didn't we—No? Well, it must have been my mother, then. Of course, you know, anything my good mother gives is—well—virtually—You haven't asked her? Sure? I could have sworn; I get so many of these appeals. And in these times, you know, we have to go cautiously. I'm sure you recognize that yourself, Swordsley. With my obligations—here now, to show you don't bear malice, have a brandy and soda before you go. Nonsense, man! This brandy isn't liquor, it's liqueur. I picked it up last year in London—last of a famous lot from Lord St. Oswyn's cellar. Laid down here, it stood me at—Eh?" he broke off as his wife moved toward him. "Ah, yes, of course. Miss Lucy, Miss Agnes—a drop of soda water? Look here, Addison, you won't refuse my tipple, I know. Well, take a cigar, at any rate, Swordsley. And, by the way, I'm afraid you'll have to go round the long way by the avenue tonight. Sorry, Mrs. Swordsley, but I forgot to tell them to leave the gate into the lane unlocked. Well, it's a jolly night, and I dare say you won't mind the extra turn along the lake. And, by Jove! if the moon's out, you'll have a glimpse of the motorboat. She's moored just out beyond our boathouse; and it's a privilege to look at her, I can tell you!"

The dispersal of his guests carried Stilling out into the hall, where his pleasantries reverberated under the oak rafters while the Granger girls were being muffled for the drive and the carriages summoned from the stables.

By a common impulse Mrs. Stilling and Wrayford had moved together toward the fireplace, which was hidden by a tall screen from the door into the hall. Wrayford leaned his elbow against the mantelpiece, and Mrs. Stilling stood beside him, her clasped hands hanging down before her.

"Have you anything more to talk over with him?" she asked.

"No. We wound it all up before dinner. He doesn't want to talk about it any more than he can help."

"It's so bad?"

"No; but this time he's got to pull up."

She stood silent, with lowered lids. He listened a moment, catching Stilling's farewell shout; then he moved a little nearer, and laid his hand on her arm.

"In an hour?"

She made an imperceptible motion of assent.

"I'll tell you about it then. The key's as usual?"

She signed another "Yes" and walked away with her long drifting step as her husband came in from the hall. He went up to the tray and poured himself out a tall glass of brandy and soda.

"The weather is turning queer—black as pitch. I hope the Swordsleys won't walk into the lake—involuntary immersion, eh? He'd come out a Baptist, I suppose. What'd the Bishop do in such a case? There's a problem for a lawyer, my boy!"

He clapped his hand on Wrayford's thin shoulder and then walked over to his wife, who was gathering up her embroidery silks and dropping them into her workbag. Stilling took her by the arms and swung her playfully about so that she faced the lamplight.

"What's the matter with you tonight?"

"The matter?" she echoed, coloring a little, and standing very straight in her desire not to appear to shrink from his touch.

"You never opened your lips. Left me the whole job of entertaining those blessed people. Didn't she, Austin?"

Wrayford laughed and lit a cigarette.

"There! You see even Austin noticed it. What's the matter, I say? Aren't they good enough for you? I don't say they're particularly exciting; but, hang it! I like to ask them here—I like to give people pleasure."

"I didn't mean to be dull," said Isabel.

"Well, you must learn to make an effort. Don't treat people as if they weren't in the room just because they don't happen to amuse you. Do you know what they'll think? They'll think it's because you've got a bigger house and more money than they have. Shall I tell you something? My mother said she'd noticed the same thing in you lately. She said she sometimes felt you looked down on her for living in a small house. Oh, she was half joking, of course; but you see you do give people that impression. I can't understand treating any one in that way. The more I have myself, the more I want to make other people happy."

Isabel gently freed herself and laid the workbag on her embroidery frame. "I have a headache; perhaps that made me stupid. I'm going to bed." She turned toward Wrayford and held out her hand. "Good night."

"Good night," he answered, opening the door for her.

When he turned back into the room, his host was pouring himself a third glass of brandy and soda.

"Here, have a nip, Austin? Gad, I need it badly, after the shaking up you gave me this afternoon." Stilling laughed and carried his glass to the hearth, where he took up his usual commanding position. "Why the deuce don't you drink something? You look as glum as Isabel. One would think you were the chap that had been hit by this business."

Wrayford threw himself into the chair from which Mrs. Stilling had lately risen. It was the one she usually sat in, and to his fancy a faint scent of her clung to it. He leaned back and looked up at Stilling.

"Want a cigar?" the latter continued. "Shall we go into the den and smoke?"

Wrayford hesitated. "If there's anything more you want to ask me about—"

"Gad, no! I had full measure and running over this afternoon. The deuce of it is, I don't see where the money's all gone to. Luckily I've got plenty of nerve; I'm not the kind of man to sit down and snivel because I've been touched in Wall Street."

Wrayford got to his feet again. "Then, if you don't want me, I think I'll go up to my room and put some finishing touches to a brief before I turn in. I must get back to town tomorrow afternoon."

"All right, then." Stilling set down his empty glass, and held out his hand with a tinge of alacrity. "Good night, old man."

They shook hands, and Wrayford moved toward the door.

"I say, Austin—stop a minute!" his host called after him. Wrayford turned, and the two men faced each other across the hearthrug. Stilling's eyes shifted uneasily.

"There's one thing more you can do for me before you leave. Tell Isabel about that loan; explain to her that she's got to sign a note for it."

Wrayford, in his turn, flushed slightly. "You want me to tell her?"

"Hang it! I'm softhearted—that's the worst of me." Stilling moved toward the tray, and lifted the brandy decanter. "And she'll take it better from you; she'll *have* to take it from you. She's proud. You can take her out for a row tomorrow morning—look here, take her out in the motor launch if you like. I meant to have a spin in it myself; but if you'll tell her—"

Wrayford hesitated. "All right, I'll tell her."

"Thanks a lot, my dear fellow. And you'll make her see it wasn't my fault, eh? Women are awfully vague about money, and she'll think it's all right if you back me up."

Wrayford nodded. "As you please."

"And, Austin—there's just one more thing. You needn't say anything to Isabel about the other business—I mean about my mother's securities."

"Ah?" said Wrayford, pausing.

Stilling shifted from one foot to the other. "I'd rather put that to the old lady myself. I can make it clear to her. She idolizes me, you know—and, hang it! I've got a good record. Up to now, I mean. My mother's been in clover since I married; I may say she's been my first thought. And I don't want her to hear of this beastly business from Isabel. Isabel's a little harsh at times—and of course this isn't going to make her any easier to live with."

"Very well," said Wrayford.

Stilling, with a look of relief, walked toward the window which opened on the terrace. "Gad! what a queer night! Hot as the kitchen range. Shouldn't wonder if we had a squall before morning. I wonder if that infernal skipper took in the launch's awnings before he went home."

Wrayford stopped with his hand on the door. "Yes, I saw him do it. She's shipshape for the night."

"Good! That saves me a run down to the shore."

"Good night, then," said Wrayford.

"Good night, old man. You'll tell her?"

"I'll tell her."

"And mum about my mother!" his host called after him.

II

The darkness had thinned a little when Wrayford scrambled down the steep path to the shore. Though the air was heavy the threat of a storm seemed to have vanished, and now and then the moon's edge showed above a torn slope of cloud.

But in the thick shrubbery about the boathouse the darkness was still dense, and Wrayford had to strike a match before he could find the lock and insert his key. He left the door unlatched, and groped his way in. How often he had crept into this warm pine-scented obscurity, guiding himself by the edge of the bench along the wall, and hearing the soft lap of water through the gaps in the flooring! He knew just where one had to duck one's head to avoid the two canoes swung from the rafters, and just where to put his hand on the latch of the farther door that led to the broad balcony above the lake.

The boathouse represented one of Stilling's abandoned whims. He had built it some seven years before, and for a time it had been the scene of incessant nautical exploits. Stilling had rowed, sailed, paddled indefatigably, and all Highfield had been impressed to bear him company, and to admire his versatility. Then motors had come in, and he had forsaken aquatic sports for the flying chariot. The canoes of birch bark and canvas had been hoisted to the roof, the sailboat had rotted at her moorings, and the movable floor of the boathouse, ingeniously contrived to slide back on noiseless runners, had laid undisturbed through several seasons. Even the key of the boathouse had been mislaid—by Isabel's fault, her husband said—and the locksmith had to be called in to make a new one when the purchase of the motorboat made the lake once more the center of Stilling's activity.

As Wrayford entered he noticed that a strange oily odor overpowered the usual scent of dry pine wood; and at the next step his foot struck an object that rolled noisily across the boards. He lighted another match, and found he had overturned a can of grease which the boatman had no doubt been using to oil the runners of the sliding floor.

Wrayford felt his way down the length of the boathouse, and softly opening the balcony door looked out on the lake. A few yards away, he saw the launch lying at anchor in the veiled moonlight; and just below him, on the black water, was the dim outline of the skiff which the boatman kept to paddle out to her. The silence was so intense that Wrayford fancied he heard a faint rustling in the shrubbery on the high bank behind the boathouse, and the crackle of gravel on the path descending to it.

He closed the door again and turned back into the darkness; and as he did so the other door, on the land side, swung inward, and he saw a figure in the dim opening. Just enough light entered through the round holes above the respective doors to reveal Mrs. Stilling's cloaked outline, and to guide her to him as he advanced. But before they met she stumbled and gave a little cry.

"What is it?" he exclaimed.

"My foot caught; the floor seemed to give way under me. Ah, of course"—she bent down in the darkness—"I saw the men oiling it this morning."

Wrayford caught her by the arm. "Do take care! It might be dangerous if it slid too easily. The water's deep under here."

"Yes; the water's very deep. I sometimes wish—" She leaned against him without finishing her sentence, and he put both arms about her.

"Hush!" he said, his lips to hers.

Suddenly she threw her head back and seemed to listen.

"What's the matter? What do you hear?"

"I don't know." He felt her trembling. "I'm not sure this place is as safe as it used to be—"

Wrayford held her to him reassuringly. "But the boatman sleeps down at the village; and who else should come here at this hour?"

"Cobham might. He thinks of nothing but the launch."

"He won't tonight. I told him I'd seen the skipper put her ship-shape, and that satisfied him."

"Ah—he did think of coming, then?"

"Only for a minute, when the sky looked so black half an hour ago, and he was afraid of a squall. It's clearing now, and there's no danger."

He drew her down on the bench, and they sat a moment or two in silence, her hands in his. Then she said: "You'd better tell me."

Wrayford gave a faint laugh. "Yes, I suppose I had. In fact, he asked me to."

"He asked you to?"

"Yes."

She uttered an exclamation of contempt. "He's afraid!"

Wrayford made no reply, and she went on: "I'm not. Tell me everything, please."

"Well, he's chucked away a pretty big sum again—"

"How?"

"He says he doesn't know. He's been speculating, I suppose. The madness of making him your trustee!"

She drew her hands away. "You know why I did it. When we married I didn't want to put him in the false position of the man who contributes nothing and accepts everything; I wanted people to think the money was partly his."

"I don't know what you've made people think; but you've been eminently successful in one respect. *He* thinks it's all his—and he loses it as if it were."

"There are worse things. What was it that he wished you to tell me?"

"That you've got to sign another promissory note—for fifty thousand this time."

"Is that all?"

Wrayford hesitated; then he said: "Yes—for the present."

She sat motionless, her head bent, her hand resting passively in his.

He leaned nearer. "What did you mean just now, by worse things?"

She hesitated. "Haven't you noticed that he's been drinking a great deal lately?"

"Yes; I've noticed."

They were both silent; then Wrayford broke out, with sudden vehemence: "And yet you won't—"

"Won't?"

"Put an end to it. Good God! Save what's left of your life."

She made no answer, and in the stillness the throb of the water underneath them sounded like the beat of a tormented heart.

"Isabel—" Wrayford murmured. He bent over to kiss her. "Isabel! I can't stand it! Listen—"

"No; no. I've thought of everything. There's the boy—the boy's fond of him. He's not a bad father."

"Except in the trifling matter of ruining his son."

"And there's his poor old mother. He's a good son, at any rate; he'd never hurt her. And I know her. If I left him, she'd never take a penny of my money. What she has of her own is not enough to live on; and how could he provide for her? If I put him out of doors, I should be putting his mother out too."

"You could arrange that—there are always ways."

"Not for her! She's proud. And then she believes in him. Lots of people believe in him, you know. It would kill her if she ever found out."

Wrayford made an impatient movement. "It will kill you if you stay with him to prevent her finding out."

She laid her other hand on his. "Not while I have you."

"Have me? In this way?"

"In any way."

"My poor girl—poor child!"

"Unless you grow tired—unless your patience gives out."

He was silent, and she went on insistently: "Don't you suppose I've thought of that too—foreseen it?"

"Well—and then?" he exclaimed.

"I've accepted that too."

He dropped her hands with a despairing gesture. "Then, indeed, I waste my breath!"

She made no answer, and for a time they sat silent again, a little between them. At length he asked: "You're not crying?"

"No."

"I can't see your face, it's grown so dark."

"Yes. The storm must be coming." She made a motion as if to rise.

He drew close and put his arm about her. "Don't leave me yet. You know I must go tomorrow." He broke off with a laugh. "I'm to break the news to you tomorrow morning, by the way; I'm to take you out in the motor launch and break it to you." He dropped her hands and stood up. "Good God! How can I go and leave you here with him?"

"You've done it often."

"Yes; but each time it's more damnable. And then I've always had a hope—"

She rose also. "Give it up! Give it up!"

"You've none, then, yourself?"

She was silent, drawing the folds of her cloak about her.

"None—none?" he insisted.

He had to bend his head to hear her answer. "Only one!"

"What, my dearest? What?"

"Don't touch me! That he may die!"

They drew apart again, hearing each other's quick breathing through the darkness.

"You wish that too?" he said.

"I wish it always—every day, every hour, every moment!" She paused, and then let the words break from her. "You'd better know it; you'd better know the worst of me. I'm not the saint you suppose; the duty I do is poisoned by the thoughts I think. Day by day, hour by hour, I wish him dead. When he goes out I pray for something to happen; when he comes back I say to myself: 'Are you here again?' When I hear of people being killed in accidents, I think: 'Why wasn't he there?' When I read the death notices in the paper I say: 'So-and-so was just his age.' When I see him tak-ing such care of his health and his diet—as he does, you know, ex-cept when he gets reckless and begins to drink too much—when I see him exercising and resting, and eating only certain things, and weighing himself, and feeling his muscles, and boasting that he hasn't gained a pound, I think of the men who die from overwork, or who throw their lives away for some great object, and I say to myself: 'What can kill a man who thinks only of himself?' And night after night I keep myself from going to sleep for fear I may dream that he's dead. When I dream that, and wake and find him there it's worse than ever—"

She broke off with a sob, and the loud lapping of the water un-der the floor was like the beat of a rebellious heart.

"There, you know the truth!" she said.

He answered after a pause: "People do die."

"Do they?" She laughed. "Yes—in happy marriages!"

They were silent again, and Isabel turned, feeling her way toward the door. As she did so, the profound stillness was broken by the sound of a man's voice trolling out unsteadily the refrain of a music-hall song.

The two in the boathouse darted toward each other with a si-multaneous movement, clutching hands as they met.

"He's coming!" Isabel said.

Wrayford disengaged his hands.

"He may only be out for a turn before he goes to bed. Wait a minute. I'll see." He felt his way to the bench, scrambled up on it, and stretching his body forward managed to bring his eyes in line with the opening above the door.

"It's as black as pitch. I can't see anything."

The refrain rang out nearer.

"Wait! I saw something twinkle. There it is again. It's his cigar. It's coming this way—down the path."

There was a long rattle of thunder through the stillness.

"It's the storm!" Isabel whispered. "He's coming to see about the launch."

Wrayford dropped noiselessly from the bench and she caught him by the arm.

"Isn't there time to get up the path and slip under the shrub-bery?"

"No, he's in the path now. He'll be here in two minutes. He'll find us."

He felt her hand tighten on his arm.

"You must go in the skiff, then. It's the only way."

"And let him find you? And hear my oars? Listen—there's something I must say."

She flung her arms about him and pressed her face to his.

"Isabel, just now I didn't tell you everything. He's ruined his mother—taken everything of hers too. And he's got to tell her; it can't be kept from her."

She uttered an incredulous exclamation and drew back.

"Is this the truth? Why didn't you tell me before?"

"He forbade me. You were not to know."

Close above them, in the shrubbery, Stilling warbled:

> "Nita, Juanita,
> Ask thy soul if we must part!"

Wrayford held her by both arms. "Understand this—if he comes in, he'll find us. And if there's a row you'll lose your boy."

She seemed not to hear him. "You—you—you—he'll kill you!" she exclaimed.

Wrayford laughed impatiently and released her, and she stood shrinking against the wall, her hands pressed to her breast. Wrayford straightened himself and she felt that he was listening intently. Then he dropped to his knees and laid his hands against the boards of the sliding floor. It yielded at once, as if with a kind of evil alacrity; and at their feet they saw, under the motionless solid night, another darker night that moved and shimmered. Wrayford threw himself back against the opposite wall, behind the door.

A key rattled in the lock, and after a moment's fumbling the door swung open. Wrayford and Isabel saw a man's black bulk against the obscurity. It moved a step, lurched forward, and vanished out of sight. From the depths beneath them there came a splash and a long cry.

"Go! go!" Wrayford cried out, feeling blindly for Isabel in the blackness.

"Oh—" she cried, wrenching herself away from him.

He stood still a moment, as if dazed; then she saw him suddenly plunge from her side, and heard another splash far down, and a tumult in the beaten water.

In the darkness she cowered close to the opening, pressing her face over the edge, and crying out the name of each of the two men in turn. Suddenly she began to see: the obscurity was less opaque, as if a faint moon pallor diluted it. Isabel vaguely discerned the two shapes struggling in the black pit below her; once she saw the gleam of a face. She glanced up desperately for some means of rescue, and caught sight of the oars ranged on brackets against the walls. She snatched the nearest, bent over the opening, and pushed the oar down into the blackness, crying out her husband's name.

The clouds had swallowed the moon again, and she could see nothing below her; but she still heard the tumult in the beaten water.

"Cobham! Cobham!" she screamed.

As if in answer, she felt a mighty clutch on the oar, a clutch that strained her arms to the breaking point as she tried to brace her knees against the runners on the sliding floor.

"Hold on! Hold on! Hold on!" a voice gasped out from below; and she held on, with racked muscles, with bleeding palms, with eyes straining from their sockets, and a heart that tugged at her as the weight was tugging at the oar.

Suddenly the weight relaxed, and the oar slipped up through her lacerated hands. She felt a wet body scrambling over the edge of the opening, and Stilling's voice, raucous and strange, groaned out, close to her: "God! I thought I was done for."

He staggered to his knees, coughing and sputtering, and the water dripped on her from his streaming clothes.

She flung herself down, again, straining over the pit. Not a sound came up from it.

"Austin! Austin! Quick! Another oar!" she shrieked.

Stilling gave a cry. "My God! Was it Austin? What in hell— Another oar? No, no; untie the skiff, I tell you. But it's no use. Nothing's any use. I felt him lose hold as I came up."

After that she was conscious of nothing till, hours later, as it appeared to her, she became dimly aware of her husband's voice, high, hysterical and important, haranguing a group of scared lantern-struck faces that had sprung up mysteriously about them in the night.

"Poor Austin! Poor Wrayford . . . terrible loss to me . . . mysterious dispensation. Yes, I do feel gratitude—miraculous escape—but I wish old Austin could have known that I was saved!"

THE LADY'S MAID'S BELL

It was the autumn after I had the typhoid. I'd been three months in hospital, and when I came out I looked so weak and tottery that the two or three ladies I applied to were afraid to engage me. Most of my money was gone, and after I'd boarded for two months, hanging about the employment agencies, and answering any advertisement that looked any way respectable, I pretty nearly lost heart, for fretting hadn't made me fatter, and I didn't see why my luck should ever turn. It did though—or I thought so at the time. A Mrs. Railton, a friend of the lady that first brought me out to the States, met me one day and stopped to speak to me: she was one that had always a friendly way with her. She asked me what ailed me to look so white, and when I told her, "Why, Hartley," says she, "I believe I've got the very place for you. Come in tomorrow and we'll talk about it."

The next day, when I called, she told me the lady she'd in mind was a niece of hers, a Mrs. Brympton, a youngish lady, but something of an invalid, who lived all the year round at her country place on the Hudson, owing to not being able to stand the fatigue of town life.

"Now, Hartley," Mrs. Railton said, in that cheery way that always made me feel things must be going to take a turn for the better—"now understand me; it's not a cheerful place I'm sending you to. The house is big and gloomy; my niece is nervous, vaporish; her husband—well, he's generally away; and the two children are dead. A year ago I would as soon have thought of shutting a rosy active girl like you into a vault; but you're not particularly brisk yourself just now, are you? and a quiet place, with country air and wholesome food and early hours, ought to be the very thing for you. Don't mistake me," she added, for I suppose I looked a trifle downcast; "you may find it dull but you won't be unhappy. My niece is an angel. Her former maid, who died last spring, had been with her twenty years and worshipped the ground she walked on. She's a kind mistress to all, and where the mistress is kind, as you know, the servants are generally good-humored, so you'll probably get on well enough with the rest of the household. And you're the very woman I want for my niece: quiet, well-mannered, and educated above your station. You read aloud well, I think? That's a good thing; my niece likes to be read to. She wants a maid that can be something of a companion: her last was, and I can't say how she misses her. It's a lonely life. . . . Well, have you decided?"

"Why, ma'am," I said, "I'm not afraid of solitude."

"Well, then, go; my niece will take you on my recommendation. I'll telegraph her at once and you can take the afternoon train. She has no one to wait on her at present, and I don't want you to lose any time."

I was ready enough to start, yet something in me hung back; and to gain time I asked, "And the gentleman, ma'am?"

"The gentleman's almost always away, I tell you," said Mrs. Railton, quicklike—"and when he's there," says she suddenly, "you've only to keep out of his way."

I took the afternoon train and got to the station at about four o'clock. A groom in a dogcart was waiting, and we drove off at a smart pace. It was a dull October day, with rain hanging close overhead, and by the time we turned into Brympton Place woods the daylight was almost gone. The drive wound through the woods for a mile or two, and came out on a gravel court shut in with thickets of tall black-looking shrubs. There were no lights in the windows, and the house *did* look a bit gloomy.

I had asked no questions of the groom, for I never was one to get my notion of new masters from their other servants: I prefer to wait and see for myself. But I could tell by the look of everything that I had got into the right kind of house, and that things were done handsomely. A pleasant-faced cook met me at the back door and called the housemaid to show me up to my room. "You'll see madam later," she said. "Mrs. Brympton has a visitor."

I hadn't fancied Mrs. Brympton was a lady to have many visitors, and somehow the words cheered me. I followed the house-

maid upstairs, and saw, through a door on the upper landing, that
the main part of the house seemed well furnished, with dark pan-
eling and a number of old portraits. Another flight of stairs led up
up to the servants' wing. It was almost dark now, and the housemaid excused herself for not having brought a light. "But there's
matches in your room," she said, "and if you go careful you'll be
all right. Mind the step at the end of the passage. Your room is
just beyond."

I looked ahead as she spoke, and halfway down the passage I
saw a woman standing. She drew back into a doorway as we
passed and the housemaid didn't appear to notice her. She was a
thin woman with a white face, and a dark gown and apron. I took
her for the housekeeper and thought it odd that she didn't speak,
but just gave me a long look as she went by. My room opened
into a square hall at the end of the passage. Facing my door was
another which stood open: the housemaid exclaimed when she
saw it:

"There—Mrs. Blinder's left that door open again!" said she,
closing it.

"Is Mrs. Blinder the housekeeper?"

"There's no housekeeper: Mrs. Blinder's the cook."

"And is that her room?"

"Laws, no," said the housemaid, crosslike. "That's nobody's
room. It's empty, I mean, and the door hadn't ought to be open.
Mrs. Brympton wants it kept locked."

She opened my door and led me into a neat room, nicely furnished, with a picture or two on the walls; and having lit a candle
she took leave, telling me that the servants' hall tea was at six, and
that Mrs. Brympton would see me afterward.

I found them a pleasant-spoken set in the servants' hall, and by
what they let fall I gathered that, as Mrs. Railton had said, Mrs.
Brympton was the kindest of ladies; but I didn't take much notice
of their talk, for I was watching to see the pale woman in the dark
gown come in. She didn't show herself, however, and I wondered
if she ate apart; but if she wasn't the housekeeper, why should
she? Suddenly it struck me that she might be a trained nurse, and
in that case her meals would of course be served in her room. If
Mrs. Brympton was an invalid it was likely enough she had a
nurse. The idea annoyed me, I own, for they're not always the eas-

iest to get on with, and if I'd known I shouldn't have taken the place. But there I was and there was no use pulling a long face over it; and not being one to ask questions I waited to see what would turn up.

When tea was over the housemaid said to the footman: "Has Mr. Ranford gone?" and when he said yes, she told me to come up with her to Mrs. Brympton.

Mrs. Brympton was lying down in her bedroom. Her lounge stood near the fire and beside it was a shaded lamp. She was a delicate-looking lady, but when she smiled I felt there was nothing I wouldn't do for her. She spoke very pleasantly, in a low voice, asking me my name and age and so on, and if I had everything I wanted, and if I wasn't afraid of feeling lonely in the country.

"Not with you I wouldn't be, madam," I said, and the words surprised me when I'd spoken them, for I'm not an impulsive person; but it was just as if I'd thought aloud.

She seemed pleased at that, and said she hoped I'd continue in the same mind; then she gave me a few directions about her toilet, and said Agnes the housemaid would show me next morning where things were kept.

"I am tired tonight, and shall dine upstairs," she said. "Agnes will bring me my tray, so that you may have time to unpack and settle yourself; and later you may come and undress me."

"Very well, ma'am," I said. "You'll ring, I suppose?"

I thought she looked odd.

"No—Agnes will fetch you," says she quickly, and took up her book again.

Well—that was certainly strange: a lady's maid having to be fetched by the housemaid whenever her lady wanted her! I wondered if there were no bells in the house; but the next day I satisfied myself that there was one in every room, and a special one ringing from my mistress's room to mine; and after that it did strike me as queer that, whenever Mrs. Brympton wanted anything, she rang for Agnes, who had to walk the whole length of the servants' wing to call me.

But that wasn't the only queer thing in the house. The very next day I found out that Mrs. Brympton had no nurse; and then I asked Agnes about the woman I had seen in the passage the afternoon before. Agnes said she had seen no one, and I saw that she thought I was dreaming. To be sure, it was dusk when we went down the passage, and she had excused herself for not bringing a light; but I had seen the woman plain enough to know her again if we should meet. I decided that she must have been a friend of the cook's, or of one of the other women servants; perhaps she had come down from town for a night's visit, and the servants wanted it kept secret. Some ladies are very stiff about having their servants' friends in the house overnight. At any rate, I made up my mind to ask no more questions.

In a day or two another odd thing happened. I was chatting one afternoon with Mrs. Blinder, who was a friendly-disposed woman, and had been longer in the house than the other servants, and she asked me if I was quite comfortable and had everything I needed. I said I had no fault to find with my place or with my mistress, but I thought it odd that in so large a house there was no sewing room for the lady's maid.

"Why," says she, "there *is* one: the room you're in is the old sewing room."

"Oh," said I; "and where did the other lady's maid sleep?"

At that she grew confused, and said hurriedly that the servants' rooms had all been changed about last year, and she didn't rightly remember.

That struck me as peculiar, but I went on as if I hadn't noticed: "Well, there's a vacant room opposite mine, and I mean to ask Mrs. Brympton if I mayn't use that as a sewing room."

To my astonishment, Mrs. Blinder went white, and gave my hand a kind of squeeze. "Don't do that, my dear," said she, trembling-like. "To tell you the truth, that was Emma Saxon's room, and my mistress has kept it closed ever since her death."

"And who was Emma Saxon?"

"Mrs. Brympton's former maid."

"The one that was with her so many years?" said I, remembering what Mrs. Railton had told me.

Mrs. Blinder nodded.

"What sort of woman was she?"

"No better walked the earth," said Mrs. Blinder. "My mistress loved her like a sister."

"But I mean—what did she look like?"

Mrs. Blinder got up and gave me a kind of angry stare. "I'm no great hand at describing," she said; "and I believe my pastry's rising." And she walked off into the kitchen and shut the door after her.

II

I had been near a week at Brympton before I saw my master. Word came that he was arriving one afternoon, and a change passed over the whole household. It was plain that nobody loved him below stairs. Mrs. Blinder took uncommon care with the dinner that night, but she snapped at the kitchenmaid in a way quite unusual with her; and Mr. Wace, the butler, a serious, slow-spoken man, went about his duties as if he'd been getting ready for a funeral. He was a great Bible reader, Mr. Wace was, and had a beautiful assortment of texts at his command; but that day he used such dreadful language, that I was about to leave the table, when he assured me it was all out of Isaiah; and I noticed that whenever the master came Mr. Wace took to the prophets.

About seven, Agnes called me to my mistress' room; and there I found Mr. Brympton. He was standing on the hearth; a big fair bull-necked man, with a red face and little bad-tempered blue eyes: the kind of man a young simpleton might have thought handsome, and would have been like to pay dear for thinking it.

He swung about when I came in, and looked me over in a trice. I knew what the look meant, from having experienced it once or twice in my former places. Then he turned his back on me, and went on talking to his wife; and I knew what *that* meant, too. I was not the kind of morsel he was after. The typhoid had served me well enough in one way: it kept that kind of gentleman at arm's length.

"This is my new maid, Hartley," says Mrs. Brympton in her kind voice; and he nodded and went on with what he was saying.

In a minute or two he went off, and left my mistress to dress for dinner, and I noticed as I waited on her that she was white, and chill to the touch.

Mr. Brympton took himself off the next morning, and the whole house drew a long breath when he drove away. As for my mistress, she put on her hat and furs (for it was a fine winter morning) and went out for a walk in the gardens, coming back quite fresh and rosy, so that for a minute, before her color faded, I could guess what a pretty young lady she must have been, and not so long ago, either.

She had met Mr. Ranford in the grounds, and the two came back together, I remember, smiling and talking as they walked along the terrace under my window. That was the first time I saw Mr. Ranford, though I had often heard his name mentioned in the hall. He was a neighbor, it appeared, living a mile or two beyond Brympton, at the end of the village; and as he was in the habit of spending his winters in the country he was almost the only company my mistress had at that season. He was a slight tall gentleman of about thirty, and I thought him rather melancholy looking till I saw his smile, which had a kind of surprise in it, like the first warm day of spring. He was a great reader, I heard, like my mistress, and the two were forever borrowing books of one another, and sometimes (Mr. Wace told me) he would read aloud to Mrs. Brympton by the hour, in the big dark library where she sat in the winter afternoons. The servants all liked him, and perhaps that's more of a compliment than the masters suspect. He had a friendly word for every one of us, and we were all glad to think that Mrs. Brympton had a pleasant companionable gentleman like that to keep her company when the master was away. Mr. Ranford seemed on excellent terms with Mr. Brympton too; though I couldn't but wonder that two gentlemen so unlike each other should be so friendly. But then I knew how the real quality can keep their feelings to themselves.

As for Mr. Brympton, he came and went, never staying more than a day or two, cursing the dullness and the solitude, grumbling at everything, and (as I soon found out) drinking a deal more than was good for him. After Mrs. Brympton left the table he would sit half the night over the old Brympton port and madeira, and once, as I was leaving my mistress's room rather later than usual, I met him coming up the stairs in such a state that I turned sick to think of what some ladies have to endure and hold their tongues about.

The servants said very little about their master; but from what they let drop I could see it had been an unhappy match from the beginning. Mr. Brympton was coarse, loud and pleasure-loving;

my mistress quiet, retiring, and perhaps a trifle cold. Not that she was not always pleasant-spoken to him: I thought her wonderfully forbearing; but to a gentleman as free as Mr. Brympton I dare say she seemed a little offish.

Well, things went on quietly for several weeks. My mistress was kind, my duties were light, and I got on well with the other servants. In short, I had nothing to complain of; yet there was always a weight on me. I can't say why it was so, but I know it was not the loneliness that I felt. I soon got used to that; and being still languid from the fever, I was thankful for the quiet and the good country air. Nevertheless, I was never quite easy in my mind. My mistress, knowing I had been ill, insisted that I should take my walk regularly, and often invented errands for me: a yard of ribbon to be fetched from the village, a letter posted, or a book returned to Mr. Ranford. As soon as I was out of doors my spirits rose, and I looked forward to my walks through the bare moist-smelling woods; but the moment I caught sight of the house again my heart dropped down like a stone in a well. It was not a gloomy house exactly, yet I never entered it but a feeling of gloom came over me.

Mrs. Brympton seldom went out in winter; only on the finest days did she walk an hour at noon on the south terrace. Excepting Mr. Ranford, we had no visitors but the doctor, who drove over from town about once a week. He sent for me once or twice to give me some trifling direction about my mistress, and though he never told me what her illness was, I thought, from a waxy look she had now and then of a morning, that it might be the heart that ailed her. The season was soft and unwholesome, and in January we had a long spell of rain. That was a sore trial to me, I own, for I couldn't go out, and sitting over my sewing all day, listening to the drip, drip of the eaves, I grew so nervous that the least sound made me jump. Somehow, the thought of that locked room across the passage began to weigh on me. Once or twice, in the long rainy nights, I fancied I heard noises there; but that was nonsense, of course, and the daylight drove such notions out of my head. Well, one morning Mrs. Brympton gave me quite a start of pleasure by telling me she wished me to go to town for some shopping. I hadn't known till then how low my spirits had fallen. I set off in high glee, and my first sight of the crowded streets and the cheerful-looking shops quite took me out of myself. Toward afternoon, however, the noise and confusion began to tire me, and I was actually looking forward to the quiet of Brympton, and thinking how I should enjoy the drive home through the dark woods, when I ran across an old acquaintance, a maid I had once been in service with. We had lost sight of each other for a number of years, and I had to stop and tell her what had happened to me in the interval. When I mentioned where I was living she rolled up her eyes and pulled a long face.

"What! The Mrs. Brympton that lives all the year at her place on the Hudson? My dear, you won't stay there three months."

"Oh, but I don't mind the country," says I, offended somehow at her tone. "Since the fever I'm glad to be quiet."

She shook her head. "It's not the country I'm thinking of. All I know is she's had four maids in the last six months, and the last one, who was a friend of mine, told me nobody could stay in the house."

"Did she say why?" I asked.

"No—she wouldn't give me her reason. But she says to me, 'Mrs. Ansey,' she says, 'if ever a young woman as you know of thinks of going there, you tell her it's not worth-while to unpack her boxes.'"

"Is she young and handsome?" said I, thinking of Mr. Brympton.

"Not her! She's the kind that mothers engage when they've gay young gentlemen at college."

Well, though I knew the woman was an idle gossip, the words stuck in my head, and my heart sank lower than ever as I drove up to Brympton in the dusk. There *was* something about the house— I was sure of it now. . . .

When I went in to tea I heard that Mr. Brympton had arrived, and I saw at a glance that there had been a disturbance of some kind. Mrs. Blinder's hand shook so that she could hardly pour the tea, and Mr. Wace quoted the most dreadful texts full of brimstone. Nobody said a word to me then, but when I went up to my room Mrs. Blinder followed me.

"Oh, my dear," says she, taking my hand, "I'm so glad and thankful you've come back to us!"

That struck me, as you may imagine. "Why," said I, "did you think I was leaving for good?"

"No, no, to be sure," said she, a little confused, "but I can't a-bear to have madam left alone for a day even." She pressed my hand hard, and "Oh, Miss Hartley," says she, "be good to your mistress, as you're a Christian woman." And with that she hurried away, and left me staring.

A moment later Agnes called me to Mrs. Brympton. Hearing Mr. Brympton's voice in her room, I went round by the dressing room, thinking I would lay out her dinner gown before going in. The dressing room is a large room with a window over the portico that looks toward the gardens. Mr. Brympton's apartments are beyond. When I went in, the door into the bedroom was ajar, and I heard Mr. Brympton saying angrily: "One would suppose he was the only person fit for you to talk to."

"I don't have many visitors in winter," Mrs. Brympton answered quietly.

"You have *me!*" he flung at her, sneeringly.

"You are here so seldom," said she.

"Well—whose fault is that? You make the place about as lively as the family vault."

With that I rattled the toilet things, to give my mistress warning, and she rose and called me in.

The two dined alone, as usual, and I knew by Mr. Wace's manner at supper that things must be going badly. He quoted the prophets something terrible, and worked on the kitchenmaid so that she declared she wouldn't go down alone to put the cold meat in the icebox. I felt nervous myself, and after I had put my mistress to bed I was half tempted to go down again and persuade Mrs. Blinder to sit up awhile over a game of cards. But I heard her door closing for the night and so I went on to my own room. The rain had begun again, and the drip, drip, drip seemed to be dropping into my brain. I lay awake listening to it, and turning over what my friend in town had said. What puzzled me was that it was always the maids who left. . . .

After a while I slept; but suddenly a loud noise wakened me. My bell had rung. I sat up, terrified by the unusual sound, which seemed to go on jangling through the darkness. My hands shook so that I couldn't find the matches. At length I struck a light and jumped out of bed. I began to think I must have been dreaming; but I looked at the bell against the wall, and there was the little hammer still quivering.

I was just beginning to huddle on my clothes when I heard another sound. This time it was the door of the locked room opposite mine softly opening and closing. I heard the sound distinctly, and it frightened me so that I stood stock still. Then I heard a footstep hurrying down the passage toward the main house. The floor being carpeted, the sound was very faint, but I was quite sure it was a woman's step. I turned cold with the thought of it, and for a minute or two I dursn't breathe or move. Then I came to my senses.

"Alice Hartley," says I to myself, "someone left that room just now and ran down the passage ahead of you. The idea isn't pleasant, but you may as well face it. Your mistress has rung for you, and to answer her bell you've got to go the way that other woman has gone."

Well—I did it. I never walked faster in my life, yet I thought I should never get to the end of the passage or reach Mrs. Brympton's room. On the way I heard nothing and saw nothing: all was dark and quiet as the grave. When I reached my mistress' door the silence was so deep that I began to think I must be dreaming, and was half minded to turn back. Then a panic seized me, and I knocked.

There was no answer, and I knocked again, loudly. To my astonishment the door was opened by Mr. Brympton. He started back when he saw me, and in the light of my candle his face looked red and savage.

"You?" he said, in a queer voice. *"How many of you are there, in God's name?"*

At that I felt the ground give under me; but I said to myself that he had been drinking, and answered as steadily as I could: "May I go in, sir? Mrs. Brympton has rung for me."

"You may all go in, for what I care," says he, and, pushing by me, walked down the hall to his own bedroom. I looked after him as he went, and to my surprise I saw that he walked as straight as a sober man.

I found my mistress lying very weak and still, but she forced a smile when she saw me, and signed to me to pour out some drops for her. After that she lay without speaking, her breath coming quick, and her eyes closed. Suddenly she groped out with her hand, and *"Emma,"* says she, faintly.

"It's Hartley, madam," I said. "Do you want anything?"

She opened her eyes wide and gave me a startled look.

"I was dreaming," she said. "You may go, now, Hartley, and thank you kindly. I'm quite well again, you see." And she turned her face away from me.

III

There was no more sleep for me that night, and I was thankful when daylight came.

Soon afterward, Agnes called me to Mrs. Brympton. I was afraid she was ill again, for she seldom sent for me before nine, but I found her sitting up in bed, pale and drawn-looking, but quite herself.

"Hartley," says she quickly, "will you put on your things at once and go down to the village for me? I want this prescription made up—" here she hesitated a minute and blushed "—and I should like you to be back again before Mr. Brympton is up."

"Certainly, madam," I said.

"And—stay a moment—" she called me back as if an idea had just struck her "—while you're waiting for the mixture, you'll have time to go on to Mr. Ranford's with this note."

It was a two mile walk to the village, and on my way I had time to turn things over in my mind. It struck me as peculiar that my mistress should wish the prescription made up without Mr. Brympton's knowledge; and, putting this together with the scene of the night before, and with much else that I had noticed and suspected, I began to wonder if the poor lady was weary of her life, and had come to the mad resolve of ending it. The idea took such hold on me that I reached the village on a run, and dropped breathless into a chair before the chemist's counter. The good man, who was just taking down his shutters, stared at me so hard that it brought me to myself.

"Mr. Limmel," I says, trying to speak indifferently, "will you run your eyes over this, and tell me if it's quite right?"

He put on his spectacles and studied the prescription.

"Why, it's one of Dr. Walton's," says he. "What should be wrong with it?"

"Well—is it dangerous to take?"

"Dangerous—how do you mean?"

I could have shaken the man for his stupidity.

"I mean—if a person was to take too much of it—by mistake of course—" says I, my heart in my throat.

"Lord bless you, no. It's only lime water. You might feed it to a baby by the bottleful."

I gave a great sigh of relief and hurried on to Mr. Ranford's. But on the way another thought struck me. If there was nothing to conceal about my visit to the chemist's, was it my other errand that Mrs. Brympton wished me to keep private? Somehow, that thought frightened me worse than the other. Yet the two gentlemen seemed fast friends, and I would have staked my head on my mistress' goodness. I felt ashamed of my suspicions, and concluded that I was still disturbed by the strange events of the night. I left the note at Mr. Ranford's, and hurrying back to Brympton, slipped in by a side door without being seen, as I thought.

An hour later, however, as I was carrying in my mistress's breakfast, I was stopped in the hall by Mr. Brympton.

"What were you doing out so early?" he says, looking hard at me.

"Early—me, sir?" I said, in a tremble.

"Come, come," he says, an angry red spot coming out on his forehead, "didn't I see you scuttling home through the shrubbery an hour or more ago?"

I'm a truthful woman by nature, but at that a lie popped out ready-made. "No, sir, you didn't," said I and looked straight back at him.

He shrugged his shoulders and gave a sullen laugh. "I suppose you think I was drunk last night?" he asked suddenly.

"No, sir, I don't," I answered, this time truthfully enough.

He turned away with another shrug. "A pretty notion my servants have of me!" I heard him mutter as he walked off.

Not till I had settled down to my afternoon's sewing did I realize how the events of the night had shaken me. I couldn't pass that locked door without a shiver. I knew I had heard someone come out of it, and walk down the passage ahead of me. I thought of speaking to Mrs. Blinder or to Mr. Wace, the only two in the house who appeared to have an inkling of what was going on, but I had a feeling that if I questioned them they would deny everything, and that I might learn more by holding my tongue and keeping my eyes open. The idea of spending another night opposite the locked room sickened me, and once I was seized with the notion of packing my trunk and taking the first train to town; but it wasn't in me to throw over a kind mistress in that manner, and I tried to go on with my sewing as if nothing had happened. I hadn't worked ten minutes before the sewing machine broke down. It was one I had found in the house, a good machine but a trifle out of order: Mrs. Blinder said it had never been used since Emma Saxon's death. I stopped to see what was wrong, and as I was working at the machine a drawer which I had never been able to open slid forward and a photograph fell out. I picked it up and sat looking at it in a maze. It was a woman's likeness, and I knew I had seen the face somewhere—the eyes had an asking look that I had felt on me before. And suddenly I remembered the pale woman in the passage.

I stood up, cold all over, and ran out of the room. My heart seemed to be thumping in the top of my head, and I felt as if I should never get away from the look in those eyes. I went straight to find Mrs. Blinder. She was taking her afternoon nap, and sat up with a jump when I came in.

"Mrs. Blinder," said I, "who is that?" And I held out the photograph.

She rubbed her eyes and stared.

"Why, Emma Saxon," says she. "Where did you find it?"

I looked hard at her for a minute. "Mrs. Blinder," I said, "I've seen that face before."

Mrs. Blinder got up and walked over to the looking glass. "Dear me! I must have been asleep," she says. "My front is all over one ear. And now do run along, Miss Hartley, dear, for I hear the clock striking four, and I must go down this very minute and put on the Virginia ham for Mr. Brympton's dinner."

IV

To all appearances, things went on as usual for a week or two. The only difference was that Mr. Brympton stayed on, instead of going off as he usually did, and that Mr. Ranford never showed himself. I heard Mr. Brympton remark on this one afternoon when he was sitting in my mistress' room before dinner:

"Where's Ranford?" says he. "He hasn't been near the house for a week. Does he keep away because I'm here?"

Mrs. Brympton spoke so low that I couldn't catch her answer.

"Well," he went on, "two's company and three's trumpery; I'm sorry to be in Ranford's way, and I suppose I shall have to take myself off again in a day or two and give him a show." And he laughed at his own joke.

The very next day, as it happened, Mr. Ranford called. The footman said the three were very merry over their tea in the library, and Mr. Brympton strolled down to the gate with Mr. Ranford when he left.

I have said that things went on as usual; and so they did with the rest of the household; but as for myself, I had never been the same since the night my bell had rung. Night after night I used to lie awake, listening for it to ring again, and for the door of the locked room to open stealthily. But the bell never rang, and I heard no sound across the passage. At last the silence began to be more dreadful to me than the most mysterious sounds. I felt that *someone* was cowering there, behind the locked door, watching and listening as I watched and listened, and I could almost have cried out, "Whoever you are, come out and let me see you face to face, but don't lurk there and spy on me in the darkness!"

Feeling as I did, you may wonder I didn't give warning. Once I very nearly did so; but at the last moment something held me back. Whether it was compassion for my mistress, who had grown more and more dependent on me, or unwillingness to try a new place, or some other feeling that I couldn't put a name to, I lingered on as if spellbound, though every night was dreadful to me, and the days but little better.

For one thing, I didn't like Mrs. Brympton's looks. She had never been the same since that night, no more than I had. I thought she would brighten up after Mr. Brympton left, but though she seemed easier in her mind, her spirits didn't revive, nor her strength either. She had grown attached to me, and seemed to like to have me about; and Agnes told me one day that, since Emma Saxon's death, I was the only maid her mistress had taken to. This gave me a warm feeling for the poor lady, though after all there was little I could do to help her.

After Mr. Brympton's departure, Mr. Ranford took to coming again, though less often than formerly. I met him once or twice in the grounds, or in the village, and I couldn't but think there was a change in him too; but I set it down to my disordered fancy.

The weeks passed, and Mr. Brympton had now been a month absent. We heard he was cruising with a friend in the West Indies, and Mr. Wace said that was a long way off, but though you had the wings of a dove and went to the uttermost parts of the earth, you couldn't get away from the Almighty. Agnes said that as long as he stayed away from Brympton the Almighty might have him and welcome; and this raised a laugh, though Mrs. Blinder tried to look shocked, and Mr. Wace said the bears would eat us.

We were all glad to hear that the West Indies were a long way off, and I remember that, in spite of Mr. Wace's solemn looks, we had a very merry dinner that day in the hall. I don't know if it was because of my being in better spirits, but I fancied Mrs. Brympton looked better too, and seemed more cheerful in her manner. She had been for a walk in the morning, and after luncheon she lay down in her room, and I read aloud to her. When she dismissed me I went to my own room feeling quite bright and happy, and for the first time in weeks walked past the locked door without thinking of it. As I sat down to my work I looked out and saw a few snowflakes falling. The sight was pleasanter than the eternal rain, and I pictured to myself how pretty the bare gardens would look in their white mantle. It seemed to me as if the snow would cover up all the dreariness, indoors as well as out.

The fancy had hardly crossed my mind when I heard a step at my side. I looked up, thinking it was Agnes.

"Well, Agnes—" said I, and the words froze on my tongue; for there, in the door, stood *Emma Saxon*.

I don't know how long she stood there. I only know I couldn't stir or take my eyes from her. Afterward I was terribly frightened,

but at the time it wasn't fear I felt, but something deeper and quieter. She looked at me long and hard, and her face was just one
dumb prayer to me—but how in the world was I to help her? Suddenly she turned, and I heard her walk down the passage. This
time I wasn't afraid to follow—I felt that I must know what she
wanted. I sprang up and ran out. She was at the other end of the
passage, and I expected her to take the turn toward my mistress'
room; but instead of that she pushed open the door that led to the
backstairs. I followed her down the stairs, and across the passageway to the back door. The kitchen and hall were empty at
that hour, the servants being off duty, except for the footman,
who was in the pantry. At the door she stood still a moment, with
another look at me; then she turned the handle, and stepped out.
For a minute I hesitated. Where was she leading me to? The door
had closed softly after her, and I opened it and looked out, half-
expecting to find that she had disappeared. But I saw her a few
yards off hurrying across the courtyard to the path through the
woods. Her figure looked black and lonely in the snow, and for a
second my heart failed me and I thought of turning back. But all
the while she was drawing me after her; and catching up an old
shawl of Mrs. Blinder's I ran out into the open.

Emma Saxon was in the wood path now. She walked on
steadily, and I followed her at the same pace, till we passed out of
the gates and reached the highroad. Then she struck across the
open fields to the village. By this time the ground was white, and
as she climbed the slope of a bare hill ahead of me I noticed that
she left no footsteps behind her. At sight of that my heart shriveled
up within me, and my knees were water. Somehow, it was worse
here than indoors. She made the whole countryside seem lonely as
the grave, with none but us two in it, and no help in the wide
world.

Once I tried to go back; but she turned and looked at me, and
it was as if she had dragged me with ropes. After that I followed
her like a dog. We came to the village and she led me through it,
past the church and the blacksmith's shop, and down the lane to
Mr. Ranford's. Mr. Ranford's house stands close to the road: a
plain old-fashioned building, with a flagged path leading to the
door between box borders. The lane was deserted, and as I turned
into it I saw Emma Saxon pause under the old elm by the gate.

And now another fear came over me. I saw that we had reached the end of our journey, and that it was my turn to act. All the way from Brympton I had been asking myself what she wanted of me, but I had followed in a trance, as it were, and not till I saw her stop at Mr. Ranford's gate did my brain begin to clear itself. I stood a little way off in the snow, my heart beating fit to strangle me, and my feet frozen to the ground; and she stood under the elm and watched me.

I knew well enough that she hadn't led me there for nothing. I felt there was something I ought to say or do—but how was I to guess what it was? I had never thought harm of my mistress and Mr. Ranford, but I was sure now that, from one cause or another, some dreadful thing hung over them. *She* knew what it was; she would tell me if she could; perhaps she would answer if I questioned her.

It turned me faint to think of speaking to her; but I plucked up heart and dragged myself across the few yards between us. As I did so, I heard the house door open and saw Mr. Ranford approaching. He looked handsome and cheerful, as my mistress had looked that morning, and at sight of him the blood began to flow again in my veins.

"Why, Hartley," said he, "what's the matter? I saw you coming down the lane just now, and came out so see if you had taken root in the snow." He stopped and stared at me. "What are you looking at?" he says.

I turned toward the elm as he spoke, and his eyes followed me; but there was no one there. The lane was empty as far as the eye could reach.

A sense of helplessness came over me. She was gone, and I had not been able to guess what she wanted. Her last look had pierced me to the marrow; and yet it had not told me! All at once, I felt more desolate than when she had stood there watching me. It seemed as if she had left me all alone to carry the weight of the secret I couldn't guess. The snow went round me in great circles, and the ground fell away from me. . . .

A drop of brandy and the warmth of Mr. Ranford's fire soon brought me to, and I insisted on being driven back at once to Brympton. It was nearly dark, and I was afraid my mistress might be wanting me. I explained to Mr. Ranford that I had been out for a walk and had been taken with a fit of giddiness as I passed his gate. This was true enough; yet I never felt more like a liar than when I said it.

When I dressed Mrs. Brympton for dinner she remarked on my pale looks and asked what ailed me. I told her I had a headache, and she said she would not require me again that evening, and advised me to go to bed.

It was a fact that I could scarcely keep on my feet; yet I had no fancy to spend a solitary evening in my room. I sat downstairs in the hall as long as I could hold my head up; but by nine I crept upstairs, too weary to care what happened if I could but get my head on a pillow. The rest of the household went to bed soon afterward; they kept early hours when the master was away, and before ten I heard Mrs. Blinder's door close, and Mr. Wace's soon after.

It was a very still night, earth and air all muffled in snow. Once in bed I felt easier, and lay quiet, listening to the strange noises that come out in a house after dark. Once I thought I heard a door open and close again below: it might have been the glass door that led to the gardens. I got up and peered out of the window; but it was in the dark of the moon, and nothing visible outside but the streaking of snow against the panes.

I went back to bed and must have dozed, for I jumped awake to the furious ringing of my bell. Before my head was clear I had sprung out of bed, and was dragging on my clothes. *It is going to happen now,* I heard myself saying; but what I meant I had no notion. My hands seemed to be covered with glue—I thought I should never get into my clothes. At last I opened my door and peered down the passage. As far as my candle flame carried, I could see nothing unusual ahead of me. I hurried on, breathless; but as I pushed open the baize door leading to the main hall my heart stood still, for there at the head of the stairs was Emma Saxon, peering dreadfully down into the darkness.

For a second I couldn't stir; but my hand slipped from the door, and as it swung shut the figure vanished. At the same instant there came another sound from below stairs—a stealthy mysterious sound, as of a latchkey turning in the house door. I ran to Mrs. Brympton's room and knocked.

There was no answer, and I knocked again. This time I heard

someone moving in the room; the bolt slipped back and my mistress stood before me. To my surprise I saw that she had not undressed for the night. She gave me a startled look.

"What is this, Hartley?" she says in a whisper. "Are you ill? What are you doing here at this hour?"

"I am not ill, madam; but my bell rang."

At that she turned pale, and seemed about to fall.

"You are mistaken," she said harshly; "I didn't ring. You must have been dreaming." I had never heard her speak in such a tone. "Go back to bed," she said, closing the door on me.

But as she spoke I heard sounds again in the hall below: a man's step this time; and the truth leaped out on me.

"Madam," I said, pushing past her, "there is someone in the house—"

"Someone—?"

"Mr. Brympton, I think—I hear his step below—"

A dreadful look came over her, and without a word, she dropped flat at my feet. I fell on my knees and tried to lift her: by the way she breathed I saw it was no common faint. But as I raised her head there came quick steps on the stairs and across the hall: the door was flung open, and there stood Mr. Brympton, in his traveling clothes, the snow dripping from him. He drew back with a start as he saw me kneeling by my mistress.

"What the devil is this?" he shouted. He was less high-colored than usual, and the red spot came out on his forehead.

"Mrs. Brympton has fainted, sir," said I.

He laughed unsteadily and pushed by me. "It's a pity she didn't choose a more convenient moment. I'm sorry to disturb her, but—"

I raised myself up aghast at the man's action.

"Sir," said I, "are you mad? What are you doing?"

"Going to meet a friend," said he, and seemed to make for the dressing room.

At that my heart turned over. I don't know what I thought or feared; but I sprang up and caught him by the sleeve.

"Sir, sir," said I, "for pity's sake look at your wife!"

He shook me off furiously.

"It seems that's done for me," says he, and caught hold of the dressing room door.

At that moment I heard a slight noise inside. Slight as it was, he

heard it too, and tore the door open; but as he did so he dropped
back. On the threshold stood Emma Saxon. All was dark behind
her, but I saw her plainly, and so did he. He threw up his hands as
if to hide his face from her; and when I looked again she was
gone.

He stood motionless, as if the strength had run out of him; and
in the stillness my mistress suddenly raised herself, and opening
her eyes fixed a look on him. Then she fell back, and I saw the
death flutter pass over her face. . . .

We buried her on the third day, in a driving snowstorm. There
were few people in the church, for it was bad weather to come
from town, and I've a notion my mistress was one that hadn't
many near friends. Mr. Ranford was among the last to come, just
before they carried her up the aisle. He was in black, of course,
being such a friend of the family, and I never saw a gentleman so
pale. As he passed me, I noticed that he leaned a trifle on a stick
he carried; and I fancy Mr. Brympton noticed it too, for the red
spot came out on his forehead, and all through the service he kept
staring across the church at Mr. Ranford, instead of following the
prayers as a mourner should.

When it was over and we went out to the graveyard, Mr. Ranford had disappeared, and as soon as my poor mistress's body was
underground, Mr. Brympton jumped into the carriage nearest the
gate and drove off without a word to any of us. I heard him call
out, "To the station," and we servants went back alone to the
house.

THE OTHER TWO

Waythorn, on the drawing-room hearth, waited for his wife to come down to dinner.

It was their first night under his own roof, and he was surprised at his thrill of boyish agitation. He was not so old, to be sure—his glass gave him little more than the five-and-thirty years to which his wife confessed—but he had fancied himself already in the temperate zone; yet here he was listening for her step with a tender sense of all it symbolized, with some old trail of verse about the garlanded nuptial doorposts floating through his enjoyment of the pleasant room and the good dinner just beyond it.

They had been hastily recalled from their honeymoon by the illness of Lily Haskett, the child of Mrs. Waythorn's first marriage. The little girl, at Waythorn's desire, had been transferred to his house on the day of her mother's wedding, and the doctor, on their arrival, broke the news that she was ill with typhoid, but declared that all the symptoms were favorable. Lily could show twelve years of unblemished health, and the case promised to be a light one. The nurse spoke as reassuringly, and after a moment of alarm Mrs. Waythorn had adjusted herself to the situation. She was very fond of Lily—her affection for the child had perhaps been her decisive charm in Waythorn's eyes—but she had the perfectly balanced nerves which her little girl had inherited, and no woman ever wasted less tissue in unproductive worry. Waythorn was therefore quite prepared to see her come in presently, a little late because of a last look at Lily, but as serene and well-appointed as if her good-night kiss had been laid on the brow of health. Her composure was restful to him; it acted as ballast to his somewhat unstable sensibilities. As he pictured her bending over the child's bed he thought how soothing her presence must be in illness: her very step would prognosticate recovery.

His own life had been a gray one, from temperament rather than circumstance, and he had been drawn to her by the unperturbed gaiety which kept her fresh and elastic at an age when most women's activities are growing either slack or febrile. He knew what was said about her; for, popular as she was, there had always been a faint undercurrent of detraction. When she had appeared in New York, nine or ten years earlier, as the pretty Mrs. Haskett whom Gus Varick had unearthed somewhere—was it in Pittsburg or Utica?—society, while promptly accepting her, had reserved the right to cast a doubt on its own indiscrimination. Inquiry, however, established her undoubted connection with a socially reigning family, and explained her recent divorce as the natural result of a runaway match at seventeen; and as nothing was known of Mr. Haskett it was easy to believe the worst of him.

Alice Haskett's remarriage with Gus Varick was a passport to the set whose recognition she coveted, and for a few years the Varicks were the most popular couple in town. Unfortunately the alliance was brief and stormy, and this time the husband had his champions. Still, even Varick's stanchest supporters admitted that he was not meant for matrimony, and Mrs. Varick's grievances were of a nature to bear the inspection of the New York courts. A New York divorce is in itself a diploma of virtue, and in the semi-widowhood of this second separation Mrs. Varick took on an air of sanctity, and was allowed to confide her wrongs to some of the most scrupulous ears in town. But when it was known that she was to marry Waythorn there was a momentary reaction. Her best friends would have preferred to see her remain in the role of the injured wife, which was as becoming to her as crepe to a rosy complexion. True, a decent time had elapsed, and it was not even suggested that Waythorn had supplanted his predecessor. People shook their heads over him, however, and one grudging friend, to whom he affirmed that he took the step with his eyes open, replied oracularly: "Yes—and with your ears shut."

Waythorn could afford to smile at these innuendoes. In the Wall Street phrase, he had "discounted" them. He knew that society has not yet adapted itself to the consequences of divorce, and that till the adaptation takes place every woman who uses the freedom the law accords her must be her own social justification. Waythorn had an amused confidence in his wife's ability to justify herself. His expectations were fulfilled, and before the wedding took place Alice Varick's group had rallied openly to her support. She took it all imperturbably: she had a way of surmounting obstacles without seeming to be aware of them, and Waythorn looked back with wonder at the trivialities over which he had worn his nerves thin. He had the sense of having found refuge in a richer, warmer nature than his own, and his satisfaction, at the moment, was humorously summed up in the thought that his wife, when she had done all she could for Lily, would not be ashamed to come down and enjoy a good dinner.

The anticipation of such enjoyment was not, however, the sentiment expressed by Mrs. Waythorn's charming face when she presently joined him. Though she had put on her most engaging tea gown she had neglected to assume the smile that went with it, and Waythorn thought he had never seen her look so nearly worried.

"What is it?" he asked. "Is anything wrong with Lily?"

"No; I've just been in and she's still sleeping." Mrs. Waythorn hesitated. "But something tiresome has happened."

He had taken her two hands, and now perceived that he was crushing a paper between them.

"This letter?"

"Yes—Mr. Haskett has written—I mean his lawyer has written."

Waythorn felt himself flush uncomfortably. He dropped his wife's hands.

"What about?"

"About seeing Lily. You know the courts—"

"Yes, yes," he interrupted nervously.

Nothing was known about Haskett in New York. He was vaguely supposed to have remained in the outer darkness from which his wife had been rescued, and Waythorn was one of the few who were aware that he had given up his business in Utica and followed her to New York in order to be near his little girl. In the days of his wooing, Waythorn had often met Lily on the doorstep, rosy and smiling, on her way "to see papa."

"I am so sorry," Mrs. Waythorn murmured.

He roused himself. "What does he want?"

"He wants to see her. You know she goes to him once a week."

"Well—he doesn't expect her to go to him now, does he?"

"No—he has heard of her illness; but he expects to come here."

"Here?"

Mrs. Waythorn reddened under his gaze. They looked away from each other.

"I'm afraid he has the right. . . . You'll see. . . ." She made a proffer of the letter.

Waythorn moved away with a gesture of refusal. He stood staring about the softly-lighted room, which a moment before had seemed so full of bridal intimacy.

"I'm so sorry," she repeated. "If Lily could have been moved—"

"That's out of the question," he returned impatiently.

"I suppose so."

Her lip was beginning to tremble, and he felt himself a brute.

"He must come, of course," he said. "When is—his day?"

"I'm afraid—tomorrow."

"Very well. Send a note in the morning."

The butler entered to announce dinner.

Waythorn turned to his wife. "Come—you must be tired. It's beastly, but try to forget about it," he said, drawing her hand through his arm.

"You're so good, dear. I'll try," she whispered back.

Her face cleared at once, and as she looked at him across the flowers, between the rosy candleshades, he saw her lips waver back into a smile.

"How pretty everything is!" she sighed luxuriously.

He turned to the butler. "The champagne at once, please. Mrs. Waythorn is tired."

In a moment or two their eyes met above the sparkling glasses. Her own were quite clear and untroubled: he saw that she had obeyed his injunction and forgotten.

II

Waythorn, the next morning, went downtown earlier than usual. Haskett was not likely to come till the afternoon, but the instinct of flight drove him forth. He meant to stay away all day—he had thoughts of dining at his club. As his door closed behind him he reflected that before he opened it again it would have admitted another man who had as much right to enter it as himself, and the thought filled him with a physical repugnance.

He caught the elevated at the employees' hour, and found himself crushed between two layers of pendulous humanity. At Eighth Street the man facing him wriggled out, and another took his place. Waythorn glanced up and saw that it was Gus Varick. The men were so close together that it was impossible to ignore the smile of recognition on Varick's handsome overblown face. And after all—why not? They had always been on good terms, and Varick had been divorced before Waythorn's attentions to his wife began. The two exchanged a word on the perennial grievance of the congested trains, and when a seat at their side was miraculously left empty the instinct of self-preservation made Waythorn slip into it after Varick.

The latter drew the stout man's breath of relief. "Lord—I was beginning to feel like a pressed flower." He leaned back, looking unconcernedly at Waythorn. "Sorry to hear that Sellers is knocked out again."

"Sellers?" echoed Waythorn, starting at his partner's name.

Varick looked surprised. "You didn't know he was laid up with the gout?"

"No. I've been away—I only got back last night." Waythorn felt himself reddening in anticipation of the other's smile.

"Ah—yes; to be sure. And Sellers' attack came on two days ago. I'm afraid he's pretty bad. Very awkward for me, as it happens, because he was just putting through a rather important thing for me."

"Ah?" Waythorn wondered vaguely since when Varick had been dealing in "important things." Hitherto he had dabbled only in the shallow pools of speculation, with which Waythorn's office did not usually concern itself.

It occurred to him that Varick might be talking at random, to relieve the strain of their propinquity. That strain was becoming momentarily more apparent to Waythorn, and when, at Cortlandt Street, he caught sight of an acquaintance and had a sudden vision of the picture he and Varick must present to an initiated eye, he jumped up with a muttered excuse.

"I hope you'll find Sellers better," said Varick civilly, and he stammered back: "If I can be of any use to you—" and let the departing crowd sweep him to the platform.

At his office he heard that Sellers was in fact ill with the gout, and would probably not be able to leave the house for some weeks.

"I'm sorry it should have happened so, Mr. Waythorn," the senior clerk said with affable significance. "Mr. Sellers was very much upset at the idea of giving you such a lot of extra work just now."

"Oh, that's no matter," said Waythorn hastily. He secretly welcomed the pressure of additional business, and was glad to think that, when the day's work was over, he would have to call at his partner's on the way home.

He was late for luncheon, and turned in at the nearest restaurant instead of going to his club. The place was full, and the waiter hurried him to the back of the room to capture the only vacant table. In the cloud of cigar smoke Waythorn did not at once distinguish his neighbors: but presently, looking about him, he saw Varick seated a few feet off. This time, luckily, they were too far apart for conversation, and Varick, who faced another way, had probably not even seen him; but there was an irony in their renewed nearness.

Varick was said to be fond of good living, and as Waythorn sat dispatching his hurried luncheon he looked across half enviously at the other's leisurely degustation of his meal. When Waythorn first saw him he had been helping himself with critical deliberation to a bit of Camembert at the ideal point of liquefaction, and now, the cheese removed, he was just pouring his *café double* from its little two-storied earthen pot. He poured slowly, his ruddy profile bent over the task, and one beringed white hand steadying the lid of the coffeepot; then he stretched his other hand to the decanter of cognac at his elbow, filled a liqueur glass, took a tentative sip, and poured the brandy into his coffee cup.

Waythorn watched him in a kind of fascination. What was he thinking of—only of the flavor of the coffee and the liqueur? Had the morning's meeting left no more trace in his thoughts than on his face? Had his wife so completely passed out of his life that even this odd encounter with her present husband, within a week after her remarriage, was no more than an incident in his day?

And as Waythorn mused, another idea struck him: had Haskett ever met Varick as Varick and he had just met? The recollection of Haskett perturbed him, and he rose and left the restaurant, taking a circuitous way out to escape the placid irony of Varick's nod.

It was after seven when Waythorn reached home. He thought the footman who opened the door looked at him oddly.

"How is Miss Lily?" he asked in haste.

"Doing very well, sir. A gentleman—"

"Tell Barlow to put off dinner for half an hour," Waythorn cut him off, hurrying upstairs.

He went straight to his room and dressed without seeing his wife. When he reached the drawing room she was there, fresh and radiant. Lily's day had been good; the doctor was not coming back that evening.

At dinner Waythorn told her of Seller's illness and of the resulting complications. She listened sympathetically, adjuring him not to let himself be overworked, and asking vague feminine questions about the routine of the office. Then she gave him the chronicle of Lily's day; quoted the nurse and doctor, and told him who had called to inquire. He had never seen her more serene and unruffled. It struck him, with a curious pang, that she was very happy in being with him, so happy that she found a childish pleasure in rehearsing the trivial incidents of her day.

After dinner they went to the library, and the servant put the coffee and liqueurs on a low table before her and left the room. She looked singularly soft and girlish in her rosy-pale dress, against the dark leather of one of his bachelor armchairs. A day earlier the contrast would have charmed him.

He turned away now, choosing a cigar with affected deliberation.

"Did Haskett come?" he asked, with his back to her.

"Oh, yes—he came."

"You didn't see him, of course?"

She hesitated a moment. "I let the nurse see him."

That was all. There was nothing more to ask. He swung round toward her, applying a match to his cigar. Well, the thing was over for a week, at any rate. He would try not to think of it. She looked up at him, a trifle rosier than usual, with a smile in her eyes.

"Ready for your coffee, dear?"

He leaned against the mantelpiece, watching her as she lifted the coffeepot. The lamplight struck a gleam from her bracelets and tipped her soft hair with brightness. How light and slender she was, and how each gesture flowed into the next! She seemed a creature all compact of harmonies. As the thought of Haskett receded, Waythorn felt himself yielding again to the joy of possessorship. They were his, those white hands with their flitting motions, his the light haze of hair, the lips and eyes. . . .

She set down the coffeepot, and reaching for the decanter of cognac, measured off a liqueur glass and poured it into his cup.

Waythorn uttered a sudden exclamation.

"What is the matter?" she said, startled.

"Nothing; only—I don't take cognac in my coffee."

"Oh, how stupid of me," she cried.

Their eyes met, and she blushed a sudden agonized red.

III

Ten days later, Mr. Sellers, still housebound, asked Waythorn to call on his way downtown.

The senior partner, with his swaddled foot propped up by the fire, greeted his associate with an air of embarrassment.

"I'm sorry, my dear fellow; I've got to ask you to do an awkward thing for me."

Waythorn waited, and the other went on, after a pause apparently given to the arrangement of his phrases: "The fact is, when I was knocked out I had just gone into a rather complicated piece of business for—Gus Varick."

"Well?" said Waythorn, with an attempt to put him at his ease.

"Well—it's this way: Varick came to me the day before my attack. He had evidently had an inside tip from somebody, and had made about a hundred thousand. He came to me for advice, and I suggested his going in with Vanderlyn."

"Oh, the deuce!" Waythorn exclaimed. He saw in a flash what had happened. The investment was an alluring one, but required negotiation. He listened quietly while Sellers put the case before him, and, the statement ended, he said: "You think I ought to see Varick?"

"I'm afraid I can't as yet. The doctor is obdurate. And this thing can't wait. I hate to ask you, but no one else in the office knows the ins and outs of it."

Waythorn stood silent. He did not care a farthing for the success of Varick's venture, but the honor of the office was to be considered, and he could hardly refuse to oblige his partner.

"Very well," he said, "I'll do it."

That afternoon, apprised by telephone, Varick called at the office. Waythorn, waiting in his private room, wondered what the others thought of it. The newspapers, at the time of Mrs. Waythorn's marriage, had acquainted their readers with every detail of her previous matrimonial ventures, and Waythorn could fancy the clerks smiling behind Varick's back as he was ushered in.

Varick bore himself admirably. He was easy without being undignified, and Waythorn was conscious of cutting a much less impressive figure. Varick had no experience in business, and the talk prolonged itself for nearly an hour while Waythorn set forth with scrupulous precision the details of the proposed transaction.

"I'm awfully obliged to you," Varick said as he rose. "The fact is I'm not used to having much money to look after, and I don't want to make an ass of myself—" He smiled, and Waythorn could not help noticing that there was something pleasant about his smile. "It feels uncommonly queer to have enough cash to pay one's bills. I'd have sold my soul for it a few years ago!"

Waythorn winced at the allusion. He had heard it rumored that a lack of funds had been one of the determining causes of the Varick separation, but it did not occur to him that Varick's words were intentional. It seemed more likely that the desire to keep clear of embarrassing topics had fatally drawn him into one. Waythorn did not wish to be outdone in civility.

"We'll do the best we can for you," he said. "I think this is a good thing you're in."

"Oh, I'm sure it's immense. It's awfully good of you—" Varick broke off, embarrassed. "I suppose the thing's settled now—but if—"

"If anything happens before Sellers is about, I'll see you again," said Waythorn quietly. He was glad, in the end, to appear the more self-possessed of the two.

———

The course of Lily's illness ran smooth, and as the days passed Waythorn grew used to the idea of Haskett's weekly visit. The first time the day came round, he stayed out late, and questioned his wife as to the visit on his return. She replied at once that Haskett had merely seen the nurse downstairs, as the doctor did not wish anyone in the child's sickroom till after the crisis.

The following week Waythorn was again conscious of the recurrence of the day, but had forgotten it by the time he came home to dinner. The crisis of the disease came a few days later, with a rapid decline of fever, and the little girl was pronounced out of danger. In the rejoicing which ensued the thought of Haskett passed out of Waythorn's mind, and one afternoon, letting himself into the house with a latchkey, he went straight to his library without noticing a shabby hat and umbrella in the hall.

In the library he found a small effaced-looking man with a thinnish gray beard sitting on the edge of a chair. The stranger might have been a piano tuner, or one of those mysteriously efficient persons who are summoned in emergencies to adjust some detail of the domestic machinery. He blinked at Waythorn through a pair of gold-rimmed spectacles and said mildly: "Mr. Waythorn, I presume? I am Lily's father."

Waythorn flushed. "Oh—" he stammered uncomfortably. He broke off, disliking to appear rude. Inwardly he was trying to adjust the actual Haskett to the image of him projected by his wife's reminiscences. Waythorn had been allowed to infer that Alice's first husband was a brute.

"I am sorry to intrude," said Haskett, with his over-the-counter politeness.

"Don't mention it," returned Waythorn, collecting himself. "I suppose the nurse has been told?"

"I presume so. I can wait," said Haskett. He had a resigned way of speaking, as though life had worn down his natural powers of resistance.

Waythorn stood on the threshold, nervously pulling off his gloves.

"I'm sorry you've been detained. I will send for the nurse," he said; and as he opened the door he added with an effort: "I'm glad we can give you a good report of Lily." He winced as the *we* slipped out, but Haskett seemed not to notice it.

"Thank you, Mr. Waythorn. It's been an anxious time for me."

"Ah, well, that's past. Soon she'll be able to go to you." Waythorn nodded and passed out.

In his own room he flung himself down with a groan. He hated the womanish sensibility which made him suffer so acutely from the grotesque chances of life. He had known when he married that his wife's former husbands were both living, and that amid the multiplied contacts of modern existence there were a thousand chances to one that he would run against one or the other, yet he found himself as much disturbed by his brief encounter with Haskett as though the law had not obligingly removed all difficulties in the way of their meeting.

Waythorn sprang up and began to pace the room nervously. He had not suffered half as much from his two meetings with Varick. It was Haskett's presence in his own house that made the situation so intolerable. He stood still, hearing steps in the passage.

"This way, please," he heard the nurse say. Haskett was being taken upstairs, then: not a corner of the house but was open to him. Waythorn dropped into another chair, staring vaguely ahead of him. On his dressing table stood a photograph of Alice, taken when he had first known her. She was Alice Varick then—how fine and exquisite he had thought her! Those were Varick's pearls about her neck. At Waythorn's instance they had been returned before her marriage. Had Haskett ever given her any trinkets—and what had become of them, Waythorn wondered? He realized suddenly that he knew very little of Haskett's past or present situation; but from the man's appearance and manner of speech he could reconstruct with curious precision the surroundings of Alice's first marriage. And it startled him to think that she had, in the background of her life, a phase of existence so different from anything with which he had connected her. Varick, whatever his faults, was a gentleman, in the conventional, traditional sense of the term: the sense which at that moment seemed, oddly enough, to have most meaning to Waythorn. He and Varick had the same social habits, spoke the same language, understood the same allusions. But this other man . . . it was grotesquely uppermost in Waythorn's mind that Haskett had worn a made-up tie attached with an elastic. Why should that ridiculous detail symbolize the whole man? Waythorn was exasperated by his own paltriness, but the fact of the tie expanded, forced itself on him, became as it were the key to Alice's past. He could see her, as Mrs. Haskett, sitting in a "front parlor" furnished in plush, with a pianola, and copy of *Ben Hur* on the center table. He could see her going to the theater with Haskett—or perhaps even to a "Church Sociable"—she in a "picture hat" and Haskett in a black frock coat, a little creased, with the made-up tie on an elastic. On the way home they would stop and look at the illuminated shop windows, lingering over the photographs of New York actresses. On Sunday afternoons Haskett would take her for a walk, pushing Lily ahead of them in a white enameled perambulator, and Waythorn had a vision of the people they would stop and talk to. He could fancy how pretty Alice must have looked, in a dress adroitly constructed from the hints of a New York fashion paper, and how she must have looked down on the other women, chafing at her life, and secretly feeling that she belonged in a bigger place.

For the moment his foremost thought was one of wonder at the way in which she had shed the phase of existence which her marriage with Haskett implied. It was as if her whole aspect, every gesture, every inflection, every allusion, were a studied negation of that period of her life. If she had denied being married to Haskett she could hardly have stood more convicted of duplicity than in this obliteration of the self which had been his wife.

Waythorn started up, checking himself in the analysis of her motives. What right had he to create a fantastic effigy of her and then pass judgment on it? She had spoken vaguely of her first marriage as unhappy, had hinted, with becoming reticence, that Haskett had wrought havoc among her young illusions. . . . It was a pity for Waythorn's peace of mind that Haskett's very inoffensiveness shed a new light on the nature of those illusions. A man would rather think that his wife has been brutalized by her first husband than that the process has been reversed.

IV

"Mr. Waythorn, I don't like that French governess of Lily's."

Haskett, subdued and apologetic, stood before Waythorn in the library, revolving his shabby hat in his hand.

Waythorn, surprised in his armchair over the evening paper, stared back perplexedly at his visitor.

"You'll excuse my asking to see you," Haskett continued. "But this is my last visit, and I thought if I could have a word with you it would be a better way than writing to Mrs. Waythorn's lawyer."

Waythorn rose uneasily. He did not like the French governess either; but that was irrelevant.

"I am not so sure of that," he returned stiffly; "but since you wish it I will give your message to—my wife." He always hesitated over the possessive pronoun in addressing Haskett.

The latter sighed. "I don't know as that will help much. She didn't like it when I spoke to her."

Waythorn turned red. "When did you see her?" he asked.

"Not since the first day I came to see Lily—right after she was taken sick. I remarked to her then that I didn't like the governess."

Waythorn made no answer. He remembered distinctly that, after that first visit, he had asked his wife if she had seen Haskett. She had lied to him then, but she had respected his wishes since; and the incident cast a curious light on her character. He was sure she would not have seen Haskett that first day if she had divined that Waythorn would object, and the fact that she did not divine it was almost as disagreeable to the latter as the discovery that she had lied to him.

"I don't like the woman," Haskett was repeating with mild persistency. "She ain't straight, Mr. Waythorn—she'll teach the child to be underhand. I've noticed a change in Lily—she's too anxious to please—and she don't always tell the truth. She used to be the straightest child, Mr. Waythorn—" He broke off, his voice a little thick. "Not but what I want her to have a stylish education," he ended.

Waythorn was touched. "I'm sorry, Mr. Haskett; but frankly, I don't quite see what I can do."

Haskett hesitated. Then he laid his hat on the table, and advanced to the hearthrug, on which Waythorn was standing. There was nothing aggressive in his manner, but he had the solemnity of a timid man resolved on a decisive measure.

"There's just one thing you can do, Mr. Waythorn," he said. "You can remind Mrs. Waythorn that, by the decree of the courts, I am entitled to have a voice in Lily's bringing-up." He paused, and went on more deprecatingly: "I'm not the kind to talk about enforcing my rights, Mr. Waythorn. I don't know as I think a man is entitled to rights he hasn't known how to hold on to; but this business of the child is different. I've never let go there—and I never mean to."

The scene left Waythorn deeply shaken. Shamefacedly, in indirect ways, he had been finding out about Haskett; and all that he had learned was favorable. The little man, in order to be near his daughter, had sold out his share in a profitable business in Utica, and accepted a modest clerkship in a New York manufacturing house. He boarded in a shabby street and had few acquaintances. His passion for Lily filled his life. Waythorn felt that his exploration of Haskett was like groping about with a dark lantern in his wife's past; but he saw now that there were recesses his lantern had not explored. He had never inquired into the exact circumstances of his wife's first matrimonial rupture. On the surface all had been fair. It was she who had obtained the divorce, and the court had given her the child. But Waythorn knew how many ambiguities such a verdict might cover. The mere fact that Haskett retained a right over his daughter implied an unsuspected compromise. Waythorn was an idealist. He always refused to recognize unpleasant contingencies till he found himself confronted with them, and then he saw them followed by a spectral train of consequences. His next days were thus haunted, and he determined to try to lay the ghosts by conjuring them up in his wife's presence.

When he repeated Haskett's request a flame of anger passed over her face; but she subdued it instantly and spoke with a slight quiver of outraged motherhood.

"It is very ungentlemanly of him," she said.

The word grated on Waythorn. "That is neither here nor there. It's a bare question of rights."

She murmured: "It's not as if he could ever be a help to Lily—"

Waythorn flushed. This was even less to his taste. "The question is," he repeated, "what authority has he over her?"

She looked downward, twisting herself a little in her seat. "I am willing to see him—I thought you objected," she faltered.

In a flash he understood that she knew the extent of Haskett's claims. Perhaps it was not the first time she had resisted them.

"My objecting has nothing to do with it," he said coldly; "if Haskett has a right to be consulted you must consult him."

She burst into tears, and he saw that she expected him to regard her as a victim.

Haskett did not abuse his rights. Waythorn had felt miserably sure that he would not. But the governess was dismissed, and from time to time the little man demanded an interview with Alice. After the first outburst she accepted the situation with her usual adaptability. Haskett had once reminded Waythorn of the piano tuner, and Mrs. Waythorn, after a month or two, appeared to class him with that domestic familiar. Waythorn could not but respect the father's tenacity. At first he had tried to cultivate the suspicion that Haskett might be "up to" something, that he had an object in securing a foothold in the house. But in his heart Waythorn was sure of Haskett's single-mindedness; he even guessed in the latter a mild contempt for such advantages as his relation with the Waythorns might offer. Haskett's sincerity of purpose made him invulnerable, and his successor had to accept him as a lien on the property.

Mr. Sellers was sent to Europe to recover from his gout, and Varick's affairs hung on Waythorn's hands. The negotiations were prolonged and complicated; they necessitated frequent conferences between the two men, and the interests of the firm forbade Waythorn's suggesting that his client should transfer his business to another office.

Varick appeared well in the transaction. In moments of relaxation his coarse streak appeared, and Waythorn dreaded his geniality; but in the office he was concise and clear-headed, with a flattering deference to Waythorn's judgment. Their business relations being so affably established, it would have been absurd for the two men to ignore each other in society. The first time they met in a drawing room, Varick took up their intercourse in the same easy key, and his hostess' grateful glance obliged Waythorn to respond to it. After that they ran across each other frequently, and one evening at a ball Waythorn, wandering through the remoter rooms, came upon Varick seated beside his wife. She colored a little, and faltered in what she was saying; but Varick nodded to Waythorn without rising, and the latter strolled on.

In the carriage, on the way home, he broke out nervously: "I didn't know you spoke to Varick."

Her voice trembled a little. "It's the first time—he happened to be standing near me; I didn't know what to do. It's so awkward, meeting everywhere—and he said you had been very kind about some business."

"That's different," said Waythorn.

She paused a moment. "I'll do just as you wish," she returned pliantly. "I thought it would be less awkward to speak to him when we meet."

Her pliancy was beginning to sicken him. Had she really no will of her own—no theory about her relation to these men? She had accepted Haskett—did she mean to accept Varick? It was "less awkward," as she had said, and her instinct was to evade difficulties or to circumvent them. With sudden vividness Waythorn saw how the instinct had developed. She was "as easy as an old shoe"—a shoe that too many feet had worn. Her elasticity was the result of tension in too many different directions. Alice Haskett—Alice Varick—Alice Waythorn—she had been each in turn, and had left hanging to each name a little of her privacy, a little of her personality, a little of the inmost self where the unknown god abides.

"Yes—it's better to speak to Varick," said Waythorn wearily.

V

The winter wore on, and society took advantage of the Waythorns' acceptance of Varick. Harassed hostesses were grateful to them for bridging over a social difficulty, and Mrs. Waythorn was held up as a miracle of good taste. Some experimental spirits could not resist the diversion of throwing Varick and his former wife together, and there were those who thought he found a zest in the propinquity. But Mrs. Waythorn's conduct remained irreproachable. She neither avoided Varick nor sought him out. Even

Waythorn could not but admit that she had discovered the solution of the newest social problem.

He had married her without giving much thought to that problem. He had fancied that a woman can shed her past like a man. But now he saw that Alice was bound to hers both by the circumstances which forced her into continued relation with it, and by the traces it had left on her nature. With grim irony Waythorn compared himself to a member of a syndicate. He held so many shares in his wife's personality and his predecessors were his partners in the business. If there had been any element of passion in the transaction he would have felt less deteriorated by it. The fact that Alice took her change of husbands like a change of weather reduced the situation to mediocrity. He could have forgiven her for blunders, for excesses; for resisting Haskett, for yielding to Varick; for anything but her acquiescence and her tact. She reminded him of a juggler tossing knives; but the knives were blunt and she knew they would never cut her.

And then, gradually, habit formed a protecting surface for his sensibilities. If he paid for each day's comfort with the small change of his illusions, he grew daily to value the comfort more and set less store upon the coin. He had drifted into a dulling propinquity with Haskett and Varick and he took refuge in the cheap revenge of satirizing the situation. He even began to reckon up the advantages which accrued from it, to ask himself if it were not better to own a third of a wife who knew how to make a man happy than a whole one who had lacked opportunity to acquire the art. For it *was* an art, and made up, like all others, of concessions, eliminations and embellishments; of lights judiciously thrown and shadows skillfully softened. His wife knew exactly how to manage the lights, and he knew exactly to what training she owed her skill. He even tried to trace the source of his obligations, to discriminate between the influences which had combined to produce his domestic happiness: he perceived that Haskett's commonness had made Alice worship good breeding, while Varick's liberal construction of the marriage bond had taught her to value the conjugal virtues; so that he was directly indebted to his predecessors for the devotion which made his life easy if not inspiring.

From this phase he passed into that of complete acceptance. He ceased to satirize himself because time dulled the irony of the situation and the joke lost its humor with its sting. Even the sight of Haskett's hat on the hall table had ceased to touch the springs of epigram. The hat was often seen there now, for it had been decided that it was better for Lily's father to visit her than for the little girl to go to his boardinghouse. Waythorn, having acquiesced in this arrangement, had been surprised to find how little difference it made. Haskett was never obtrusive, and the few visitors who met him on the stairs were unaware of his identity. Waythorn did not know how often he saw Alice, but with himself Haskett was seldom in contact.

One afternoon, however, he learned on entering that Lily's father was waiting to see him. In the library he found Haskett occupying a chair in his usual provisional way. Waythorn always felt grateful to him for not leaning back.

"I hope you'll excuse me, Mr. Waythorn," he said rising. "I wanted to see Mrs. Waythorn about Lily, and your man asked me to wait here till she came in."

"Of course," said Waythorn, remembering that a sudden leak had that morning given over the drawing room to the plumbers.

He opened his cigar case and held it out to his visitor, and Haskett's acceptance seemed to mark a fresh stage in their intercourse. The spring evening was chilly, and Waythorn invited his guest to draw up his chair to the fire. He meant to find an excuse to leave Haskett in a moment; but he was tired and cold, and after all the little man no longer jarred on him.

The two were enclosed in the intimacy of their blended cigar smoke when the door opened and Varick walked into the room. Waythorn rose abruptly. It was the first time that Varick had come to the house, and the surprise of seeing him, combined with the singular inopportuneness of his arrival, gave a new edge to Waythorn's blunted sensibilities. He stared at his visitor without speaking.

Varick seemed too preoccupied to notice his host's embarrassment.

"My dear fellow," he exclaimed in his most expansive tone, "I must apologize for tumbling in on you in this way, but I was too late to catch you downtown, and so I thought—"

He stopped short, catching sight of Haskett, and his sanguine color deepened to a flush which spread vividly under his scant blond hair. But in a moment he recovered himself and nodded slightly. Haskett returned the bow in silence, and Waythorn was still groping for speech when the footman came in carrying a tea table.

The intrusion offered a welcome vent to Waythorn's nerves. "What the deuce are you bringing this here for?" he said sharply.

"I beg your pardon, sir, but the plumbers are still in the drawing room, and Mrs. Waythorn said she would have tea in the library." The footman's perfectly respectful tone implied a reflection on Waythorn's reasonableness.

"Oh, very well," said the latter resignedly, and the footman proceeded to open the folding tea table and set out its complicated appointments. While this interminable process continued the three men stood motionless, watching it with a fascinated stare, till Waythorn, to break the silence, said to Varick, "Won't you have a cigar?"

He held out the case he had just tendered to Haskett, and Varick helped himself with a smile. Waythorn looked about for a match, and finding none, proffered a light from his own cigar. Haskett, in the background, held his ground mildly, examining his cigar tip now and then, and stepping forward at the right moment to knock its ashes into the fire.

The footman at last withdrew, and Varick immediately began: "If I could just say half a word to you about this business—"

"Certainly," stammered Waythorn; "in the dining room—"

But as he placed his hand on the door it opened from without, and his wife appeared on the threshold.

She came in fresh and smiling, in her street dress and hat, shedding a fragrance from the boa which she loosened in advancing.

"Shall we have tea in here, dear?" she began; and then she caught sight of Varick. Her smile deepened, veiling a slight tremor of surprise.

"Why, how do you do?" she said with a distinct note of pleasure.

As she shook hands with Varick she saw Haskett standing behind him. Her smile faded for a moment, but she recalled it quickly, with a scarcely perceptible side glance at Waythorn.

"How do you do, Mr. Haskett?" she said, and shook hands with him a shade less cordially.

The three men stood awkwardly before her, till Varick, always the most self-possessed, dashed into an explanatory phrase.

"We—I had to see Waythorn a moment on business," he stammered, brick-red from chin to nape.

Haskett stepped forward with his air of mild obstinacy. "I am sorry to intrude; but you appointed five o'clock—" he directed his resigned glance at the timepiece on the mantel.

She swept aside their embarrassment with a charming gesture of hospitality.

"I'm so sorry—I'm always late; but the afternoon was so lovely." She stood drawing off her gloves, propitiatory and graceful, diffusing about her a sense of ease and familiarity in which the situation lost its grotesqueness. "But before talking business," she added brightly, "I'm sure everyone wants a cup of tea."

She dropped into her low chair by the tea table, and the two visitors, as if drawn by her smile, advanced to receive the cups she held out.

She glanced about for Waythorn, and he took the third cup with a laugh.

THE HERMIT
AND THE WILD WOMAN

The Hermit lived in a cave in the hollow of a hill. Below him was a glen, with a stream in a coppice of oaks and alders, and across the valley, half a day's journey distant, another hill, steep and bristling, raised against the sky a little walled town with Ghibelline swallowtails.[1]

When the Hermit was a lad, and lived in the town, the crenellations of the walls had been square topped, and a Guelf lord had flown his standard from the keep. Then one day a steel-colored line of men-at-arms rode across the valley, wound up the hill and battered in the gates. Stones and Greek fire rained from the ramparts, shields clashed in the streets, blade sprang at blade in passages and stairways, pikes and lances dripped above huddled flesh, and all the still familiar place was a stew of dying bodies. The boy fled from it in horror. He had seen his father go forth and not come back, his mother drop dead from an arquebuse shot as she leaned from the platform of the tower, his little sister fall with a slit throat across the altar steps of the chapel—and he ran, ran for his life, through the slippery streets, over warm twitching bodies, between legs of soldiers carousing, out of the gates, past burning farms, trampled wheat fields, orchards stripped and broken, till the still woods received him and he fell face down on the unmutilated earth.

He had no wish to go back. His longing was to live hidden from life. Up the hillside he found a hollow rock, and built before it a porch of boughs bound with withies. He fed on nuts and roots, and on trout caught with his hands under the stones in the stream. He had always been a quiet boy, liking to sit at his mother's feet and watch the flowers grow under her needle, while the chaplain read the histories of the Desert Fathers[2] from a great silver-clasped volume. He would rather have been bred a clerk and scholar than a knight's son, and his happiest moments were when he served Mass for the chaplain in the early morning, and felt his heart flutter up and up like a lark, up and up till it was lost in infinite space and brightness. Almost as happy were the hours when he sat beside the foreign painter who came over the mountains to paint the chapel, and under whose brush celestial faces grew out of the wall as if he had sown some magic seed which flowered while you watched it. With the appearing of every gold-rimmed face the boy felt he had won another friend, a friend who would come and bend above him at night, keeping the ugly visions from his pillow—visions of the gnawing monsters about the church porch, evil-faced bats and dragons, giant worms and winged bristling hogs, a devil's flock that crept down from the stonework at night and hunted the souls of sinful children through the town. With the growth of the picture the bright-mailed angels thronged so close about the boy's bed that between their interwoven wings not a snout or a claw could force itself; and he would turn over sighing on his pillow, which felt as soft and warm as if it had been lined with down from those sheltering pinions.

All these thoughts came back to him in his cave on the cliffside. The stillness seemed to enclose him with wings, to fold him away from life and evil. He was never restless or discontented. He loved the long silent empty days, each one as like the other as pearls in a well-matched string. Above all he liked to have time to save his soul. He had been greatly troubled about his soul since a band of Flagellants had passed through the town, showing their gaunt scourged bodies and exhorting the people to turn from soft raiment and delicate fare, from marriage and money-getting and dancing and games, and think only how they might escape the devil's talons and the great red blaze of hell. For days that red blaze hung on the edge of the boy's thoughts like the light of a burning city across a plain. There seemed to be so many pitfalls to avoid—so many things were wicked which one might have supposed to be harmless. How could a child of his age tell? He dared not for a moment think of anything else. And the scene of sack and slaughter from which he had fled gave shape and distinctness to that blood-red vision. Hell was like that, only a million million times worse. Now be knew how flesh looked when devil's pincers tore it, how the shrieks of the damned sounded, and how roasting bodies smelled. How could a Christian spare one moment of his days and nights from the long, long struggle to keep safe from the wrath to come?

Gradually the horror faded, leaving only a tranquil pleasure in the minute performance of his religious duties. His mind was not naturally given to the contemplation of evil, and in the blessed solitude of his new life his thoughts dwelt more and more on the beauty of holiness. His desire was to be perfectly good, and to live in love and charity with his fellows; and how could one do this without fleeing from them?

At first his life was difficult, for in winter he was put to great straits to feed himself; and there were nights when the sky was like an iron vault, and a hoarse wind rattled the oak wood in the valley, and a fear came on him that was worse than any cold. But in time it became known to his townsfolk and to the peasants in the neighboring valleys that he had withdrawn to the wilderness to lead a godly life; and after that his worst hardships were over, for pious persons brought him gifts of oil and dried fruit, one good woman gave him seeds from her garden, another spun for him a hodden[3] gown, and others would have brought him all manner of food and clothing, had he not refused to accept anything but for his bare needs. The woman who had given him the seeds showed him also how to build a little garden on the southern ledge of his cliff, and all one summer the Hermit carried up soil from the stream side, and the next he carried up water to keep his garden green. After that the fear of solitude passed from him, for he was so busy all day that at night he had much ado to fight off the demon of sleep, which Saint Aresenius the Abbot has denounced as the chief foe of the solitary. His memory kept good store of prayers and litanies, besides long passages from the Mass and other offices, and he marked the hours of his day by different acts of devotion. On Sundays and feast days, when the wind was set his way, he could hear the church bells from his native town, and these helped him to follow the worship of the faithful, and to bear in mind the seasons of the liturgical year; and what with carrying up water from the river, digging in the garden, gathering fagots for his fire, observing his religious duties, and keeping his thoughts continually on the salvation of his soul, the Hermit knew not a moment's idleness.

At first, during his night vigils, he had felt a fear of the stars, which seemed to set a cruel watch on him, as though they spied out the frailty of his heart and took the measure of his littleness. But one day a wandering clerk, to whom he chanced to give a night's shelter, explained to him that, in the opinion of the most learned doctors in theology, the stars were inhabited by the spirits of the blessed, and this thought brought great solace to the Hermit. Even on winter nights, when the eagles screamed among the peaks, and he heard the long howl of wolves about the sheep cotes in the valley, he no longer felt any fear, but thought of those sounds as representing the evil voices of the world, and hugged himself in the seclusion of his cave. Sometimes, to keep himself awake, he composed lauds in honor of Christ and the saints, and they seemed to him so pleasant that he feared to forget them, so after much debate with himself he decided to ask a friendly priest, who sometimes visited him, to write them down; and the priest wrote them on comely sheepskin, which the Hermit dried and prepared with his own hands. When the Hermit saw them written they appeared to him so beautiful that he feared to commit the sin of vanity if he looked at them too often, so he hid them between two smooth stones in his cave, and vowed that he would take them out only once in the year, at Easter, when our Lord has risen and it is meet that Christians should rejoice. And this vow he faithfully kept; but, alas, when Easter drew near, he found he was looking forward to the blessed festival less because of our Lord's rising than because he should then be able to read his pleasant lauds written on fair sheepskin; and thereupon he took a vow that he would not look on the lauds till he lay dying.

So the Hermit, for many years, lived to the glory of God and in great peace of mind.

II

One day he resolved to set forth on a visit to the Saint of the Rock, who lived on the other side of the mountains. Travelers had brought the Hermit report of this solitary, how he lived in holiness and austerity in a desert place among the hills, where snow lay all winter, and in summer the sun beat down cruelly. The Saint, it appeared, had vowed that he would withdraw from the world to a spot where there was neither shade nor water, lest he should be tempted to take his ease and think less continually upon his Maker; but wherever he went he found a spreading tree or a gushing fountain, till at last he climbed to the bare heights where nothing grows, and where the only water comes from the melting of the snow in spring. Here he found a tall rock rising from the ground, and in it he scooped a hollow with his own hands, laboring for five years and wearing his fingers to the bone. Then he seated himself in the hollow which faced the west, so that in winter he should have small warmth of the sun and in summer be consumed by it; and there he had sat without moving for years beyond number.

The Hermit was greatly drawn by the tale of such austerities, which in his humility he did not dream of emulating, but desired, for his soul's good, to contemplate and praise; so one day he bound sandals to his feet, cut an alder staff from the stream, and set out to visit the Saint of the Rock.

It was the pleasant season when seeds are shooting and the bud is on the tree. The Hermit was troubled at the thought of leaving his plants without water, but he could not travel in winter by reason of the snows, and in summer he feared the garden would suffer even more from his absence. So he set out, praying that rain might fall while he was away, and hoping to return again in five days. The peasants in the fields left their work to ask his blessing; and they would even have followed him in great numbers had he not told them that he was bound on a pilgrimage to the Saint of the Rock, and that it behooved him to go alone, as one solitary seeking another. So they respected his wish, and he went on and entered the forest. In the forest he walked for two days and slept for two nights. He heard the wolves crying, and foxes rustling in the covert, and once, at twilight, a shaggy brown man peered at him through the leaves and galloped away with a soft padding of hoofs; but the Hermit feared neither wild beasts nor evil-doers, nor even the fauns and satyrs who linger in unhallowed forest depths where the Cross has not been raised; for he said: "if I die, I die to the glory of God, and if I live, it must be to the same end."

Only he felt a secret pang at the thought that he might die without seeing his lauds again. But the third day, without misadventure, he came out on another valley.

Then he began to climb the mountain, first through brown woods of beech and oak, then through pine and broom, and then across red stony ledges where only a pinched growth of lentiscus and briar spread over the bald rock. By this time he thought to have reached his goal, but for two more days he fared on through the same scene, the sky close over him and the green earth receding far below. Sometimes for hours he saw only the red glistering slopes tufted with thin bushes, and the hard blue heaven so close that it seemed his hand could touch it; then at a turn of the path the rocks rolled apart, the eye plunged down a long pine-clad defile, and beyond it the forest flowed away to a plain shining with cities and another mountain range many days' journey away. To some eyes this would have been a terrible spectacle, reminding the wayfarer of his remoteness from his kind, and of the perils which lurk in waste places and the weakness of man against them; but the Hermit was so mated to solitude, and felt such love for all created things, that to him the bare rocks sang of their Maker and the vast distance bore witness to His greatness. So His servant journeyed on unafraid.

But one morning, after a long climb over steep and difficult slopes, the wayfarer halted at a bend of the way; for below him was no plain shining with cities, but a bare expanse of shaken silver that reached to the rim of the world; and the Hermit knew it was the sea. Fear seized him then, for it was terrible to see that great plain move like a heaving bosom, and, as he looked on it, the earth seemed also to heave beneath him. But presently he remembered how Christ had walked the waves, and how even Saint Mary of Egypt, a great sinner, had crossed the waters of Jordan dry-shod to receive the Sacrament from the Abbot Zosimus;[4] and then the Hermit's heart grew still, and he sang as he went down the mountain: "The sea shall praise Thee, O Lord."

All day he kept seeing it and then losing it; but toward night he came to a cleft of the hills, and lay down in a pine wood to sleep. He had now been six days gone, and once and again he thought anxiously of his herbs; but he said to himself: "What though my garden perish, if I see a holy man face to face and praise God in his company?" So he was never long cast down.

Before daylight he was afoot under the stars: and leaving the wood where he had slept, began climbing the face of a tall cliff, where he had to clutch the jutting ledges with his hands, and with every step he gained, a rock seemed thrust forth to hurl him back. So, footsore and bleeding, he reached a high stony plain as the sun dropped to the sea: and in the red light he saw a hollow rock and the Saint sitting in the hollow.

The Hermit fell on his knees, praising God, then he rose and ran across the plain to the rock. As he drew near he saw that the Saint was a very old man, clad in goatskin, with a long white beard. He sat motionless, his hands on his knees, and two red eye sockets turned to the sunset. Near him was a young boy in skins who brushed the flies from his face; but they always came back and settled on the rheum from his eyes.

He did not appear to hear or see the approach of the Hermit, but sat quite still till the boy said: "Father, here is a pilgrim."

Then he lifted up his voice and asked angrily who was there and what the stranger sought.

The Hermit answered: "Father, the report of your holy practices came to me a long way off, and being myself a solitary, though not worthy to be named with you for godliness, it seemed fitting that I should cross the mountains to visit you that we might sit together and speak in praise of solitude."

The Saint replied: "You fool, how can two sit together and praise solitude, since by so doing they put an end to the thing they praise?"

The Hermit, at that, was sorely abashed, for he had thought his speech out on the way, reciting it many times over; and now it appeared to him vainer than the crackling of thorns under a pot.

Nevertheless he took heart and said: "True, Father; but may not two sinners sit together and praise Christ, who has taught them the blessings of solitude?"

But the other only answered: "If you had really learned the blessings of solitude you would not squander them in idle wandering." And, the Hermit not knowing how to reply, he said again: "If two sinners meet they can best praise Christ by going each his own way in silence."

After that he shut his lips and continued motionless while the boy brushed the flies from his eye sockets; but the Hermit's heart sank, and for the first time he felt the weariness of the way he had traveled, and the great distance dividing him from home.

He had meant to take counsel with the Saint concerning his lauds, and whether he ought to destroy them; but now he had no heart to say more, and turning away he began to go down the mountain. Presently he heard steps running at his back, and the boy came up and pressed a honeycomb on him.

"You have come a long way and must be hungry," he said; but before the Hermit could thank him he hastened back to his task. So the Hermit crept down the mountain till he reached the wood where he had slept before; and there he made his bed again, but he had no mind to eat before sleeping, for his heart hungered more than his body; and his tears made the honeycomb bitter.

III

On the fourteenth day he came to his own valley and saw the walls of his native town against the sky. He was footsore and heavy of heart, for his long pilgrimage had brought him only weariness and humiliation, and as no drop of rain had fallen he knew that his garden must have perished. So he climbed the cliff heavily and reached his cave at the angelus.

But there a wonder awaited him. For though the scant earth of the hillside was parched and crumbling, his garden soil shone with moisture, and his plants had shot up, fresh and glistening, to a height they had never attained. More wonderful still, the tendrils of the gourd had been trained about his door; and kneeling down he saw that the earth had been loosened between the rows of sprouting vegetables, and that every leaf dripped as though the rain had but newly ceased. Then it appeared to the Hermit that he beheld a miracle, but doubting his own deserts he refused to believe himself worthy, and went within doors to ponder on what had befallen him. And on his bed of rushes he saw a young woman sleeping, clad in an outlandish garment with strange amulets about her neck.

The sight was full of fear to the Hermit, for he recalled how of-

ten the demon, in tempting the Desert Fathers, had taken the form
of a woman; but he reflected that, since there was nothing pleas-
ing to him in the sight of this female, who was brown as a nut and
lean with wayfaring, he ran no great danger in looking at her. At
first he took her for a wandering Egyptian, but as he looked
he perceived, among the heathen charms, an Agnus Dei in her
bosom; and this so surprised him that he bent over and called on
her to wake.

She sprang up with a start, but seeing the Hermit's gown and
staff, and his face above her, lay quiet and said: "I have watered
your garden daily in return for the beans and oil that I took from
your store."

"Who are you, and how come you here?" asked the Hermit.

She said: "I am a wild woman and live in the woods."

And when he pressed her again to tell him why she had sought
shelter in his cave, she said that the land to the south, whence she
came, was full of armed companies and bands of marauders, and
that great license and bloodshed prevailed there; and this the Hermit knew to be true, for he had heard of it on his homeward journey. The Wild Woman went on to tell him that she had been
hunted through the woods like an animal by a band of drunken
men-at-arms, Landsknechts[5] from the north by their barbarous
dress and speech, and at length, starving and spent, had come on
his cave and hidden herself from her pursuers. "For," she said, "I
fear neither wild beasts nor the woodland people, charcoal burners, Egyptians, wandering minstrels or chapmen; even the highway robbers do not touch me, because I am poor and brown; but
these armed men flown with wine are more terrible than wolves
and tigers."

And the Hermit's heart melted, for he thought of his little sister
lying with her throat slit across the altar, and of the scenes of
blood and rapine from which he had fled into the wilderness. So
he said to the stranger that it was not fitting he should house her
in his cave, but that he would send a messenger to the town, and
beg a pious woman there to give her lodging and work in her
household. "For," said he, "I perceive by the blessed image about
your neck that you are not a heathen wilding, but a child of
Christ, though so far astray in the desert."

"Yes," she said, "I am a Christian, and know as many prayers as you; but I will never set foot in city walls again, lest I be caught and put back into the convent."

"What," cried the Hermit with a start, "you are a runagate nun?" And he crossed himself, and again thought of the demon.

She smiled and said: "It is true I was once a cloistered woman, but I will never willingly be one again. Now drive me forth if you like; but I cannot go far, for I have a wounded foot, which I got in climbing the cliff with water for your garden." And she pointed to a cut in her foot.

At that, for all his fear, the Hermit was moved to pity, and washed the cut and bound it up; and as he did so he bethought him that perhaps his strange visitor had been sent to him not for his soul's undoing but for her own salvation. And from that hour he yearned to save her.

But it was not fitting that she should remain in his cave; so, having given her water to drink and a handful of lentils, he raised her up, and putting his staff in her hand guided her to a hollow not far off in the face of the cliff. And while he was doing this he heard the sunset bells across the valley, and set about reciting the *Angelus Domini nuntiavit Mariae;*[6] and she joined in piously, her hands folded, not missing a word.

Nevertheless the thought of her wickedness weighed on him, and the next day when he went to carry her food he asked her to tell him how it came about that she had fallen into such abominable sin. And this is the story she told.

IV

I was born (said she) in the north country, where the winters are long and cold, where snow sometimes falls in the valleys, and the high mountains for months are white with it. My father's castle is in a tall green wood, where the winds always rustle, and a cold river runs down from the ice gorges. South of us was the wide plain, glowing with heat, but above us were stony passes where eagles nest and the storms howl; in winter fires roared in our chimneys, and even in summer there was always a cool air off the gorges. But when I was a child my mother went southward in the great Empress's train and I went with her. We traveled many days, across plains and mountains, and saw Rome, where the Pope lives in a golden palace, and many other cities, till we came to the great Emperor's court. There for two years or more we lived in pomp and merriment, for it was a wonderful court, full of mimes, magicians, philosophers and poets; and the Empress's ladies spent their days in mirth and music, dressed in light silken garments, walking in gardens of roses, and bathing in a cool marble tank, while the Emperor's eunuchs guarded the approach to the gardens. Oh, those baths in the marble tank, my Father! I used to lie awake through the whole hot southern night, and think of that plunge at sunrise under the last stars. For we were in a burning country, and I pined for the tall green woods and the cold stream of my father's valley; and when I had cooled my body in the tank I lay all day in the scant cypress shade and dreamed of my next bath.

My mother pined for the coolness till she died; then the Empress put me in a convent and I was forgotten. The convent was on the side of a bare yellow hill, where bees made a hot buzzing in the thyme. Below was the sea, blazing with a million shafts of light; and overhead a blinding sky, which reflected the sun's glitter like a huge baldric of steel. Now the convent was built on the site of an old pleasure house which a holy princess had given to our Order; and a part of the house was left standing, with its court and garden. The nuns had built all about the garden; but they left the cypresses in the middle, and the long marble tank where the Princess and her ladies had bathed. The tank, however, as you may conceive, was no longer used as a bath, for the washing of the body is an indulgence forbidden to cloistered virgins; and our Abbess, who was famed for her austerities, boasted that, like holy Sylvia the nun, she never touched water save to bathe her fingertips before receiving the Sacrament. With such an example before them, the nuns were obliged to conform to the same pious rule, and many, having been bred in the convent from infancy, regarded all ablutions with horror, and felt no temptation to cleanse the filth from their flesh; but I, who had bathed daily, had the freshness of water in my veins, and perished slowly for want of it, like your garden herbs in a drought.

My cell did not look on the garden, but on the steep mule path leading up the cliff, where all day long the sun beat as with flails of fire, and I saw the sweating peasants toil up and down behind their thirsty asses, and the beggars whining and scraping their sores. Oh, how I hated to look out on that burning world! I used to turn away from it, sick with disgust, and lying on my hard bed, stare up by the hour at the ceiling of my cell. But flies crawled in hundreds on the ceiling, and the hot noise they made was worse than the glare. Sometimes, at an hour when I knew myself unobserved, I tore off my stifling gown, and hung it over the grated window, that I might no longer see the shaft of sunlight lying across my cell, and the dust dancing in it like fat in the fire. But the darkness choked me, and I struggled for breath as though I lay at the bottom of a pit; so that at last I would spring up, and dragging down the dress, fling myself on my knees before the Cross, and entreat our Lord to give me the gift of holiness, that I might escape the everlasting fires of hell, of which this heat was a foretaste. For if I could not endure the scorching of a summer's day, with what constancy could I meet the thought of the flame that dieth not?

This longing to escape the heat of hell made me apply myself to a devouter way of living and I reflected that if my bodily distress were somewhat eased I should be able to throw myself with greater zeal into the practice of vigils and austerities. And at length, having set forth to the Abbess that the sultry air of my cell induced in me a grievous heaviness of sleep, I prevailed on her to lodge me in that part of the building which overlooked the garden.

For a few days I was happy, for instead of the dusty mountainside, and the sight of the sweating peasants and their asses, I looked out on dark cypresses and rows of budding vegetables. But presently I found I had not bettered myself. For with the approach of midsummer the garden, being all enclosed with buildings, grew as stifling as my cell. All the green things in it withered and dried off, leaving trenches of bare red earth, across which the cypresses cast strips of shade too narrow to cool the aching heads of the nuns; and I began to think sorrowfully of my former cell, where now and then there came a sea breeze, hot and languid, yet alive, and where at least I could look out on the sea. But this was not the worst; for when the dog days came I found that the sun, at a certain hour, cast on the ceiling of my cell the reflection of the ripples on the garden tank; and to say how I suffered from this sight is not within the power of speech. It was indeed agony to watch the

clear water rippling and washing above my head, yet feel no solace of it on my limbs: as though I had been a senseless brazen image lying at the bottom of a well. But the image, if it felt no
refreshment, would have suffered no torture; whereas every vein
of my body was a mouth of Dives praying for water.[7] Oh, Father,
how shall I tell you the grievous pains that I endured? Sometimes
I so feared the sight of the mocking ripples overhead that I hid my
eyes from their approach, lying face down on my bed till I knew
that they were gone; yet on cloudy days, when they did not come,
the heat was even worse to bear.

By day I hardly dared trust myself in the garden, for the nuns
walked there, and one fiery noon they found me hanging so close
above the tank that they snatched me away, crying out that I had
tried to destroy myself. The scandal of this reaching the Abbess,
she sent for me to know what demon had beset me; and when I
wept and said, the longing to bathe my burning body, she broke
into anger and cried out: "Do you not know that this is a sin well-
nigh as grave as the other, and condemned by all the greatest
saints? For a nun may be tempted to take her life through excess
of self-scrutiny and despair of her own worthiness; but this desire
to indulge the despicable body is one of the lusts of the flesh, to be
classed with concupiscence and adultery." And she ordered me to
sleep every night for a month in my heavy gown, with a veil upon
my face.

Now, Father, I believe it was this penance that drove me to sin.
For we were in the dog days, and it was more than flesh could
bear. And on the third night, after the portress had passed, and the
lights were out, I rose and flung off my veil and gown, and knelt
in my window fainting. There was no moon, but the sky was full
of stars. At first the garden was all blackness; but as I looked I saw
a faint twinkle between the cypress trunks, and I knew it was the
starlight on the tank. The water! The water! It was there close to
me—only a few bolts and bars were between us. . . .

The portress was a heavy sleeper, and I knew where she hung
her keys. I stole thither, seized the keys and crept barefoot down
the long corridor. The bolts of the cloister door were stiff and
heavy, and I dragged at them till my wrists were bursting. Then I
turned the key and it cried out in the ward. I stood still, my whole
body beating with fear lest the hinges too should have a voice—

but no one stirred, and I pushed open the door and slipped out.
The garden was as airless as a pit, but at least I could stretch my
arms in it; and, oh, my Father, the sweetness of the stars! Sharp
stones cut my feet as I ran, but I thought of the joy of bathing
them in the tank, and that made the wounds sweet to me. . . . My
Father, I have heard of the temptations which assailed the holy
Solitaries of the desert, flattering the reluctant flesh beyond resistance; but none, I think, could have surpassed in ecstasy that first
touch of the water on my limbs. To prolong the joy I let myself
slip in slowly, resting my hands on the edge of the tank, and smiling to see my body, as I lowered it, break up the shining black surface and shatter the star beams into splinters. And the water, my
Father, seemed to crave me as I craved it. Its ripples rose about
me, first in furtive touches, then in a long embrace that clung and
drew me down; till at length they lay like kisses on my lips. It was
no frank comrade like the mountain pools of my childhood, but a
secret playmate compassionating my pains and soothing them
with noiseless hands. From the first I thought of it as an accomplice—its whisper seemed to promise me secrecy if I would
promise it love. And I went back and back to it, my Father; all
day I lived in the thought of it; each night I stole to it with fresh
thirst. . . .

But at length the old portress died, and a young lay sister took her
place. She was a light sleeper, and keen-eared; and I knew the danger of venturing to her cell. I knew the danger, but when darkness
came I felt the water drawing me. The first night I fought and held
out; but the second I crept to her door. She made no motion when I
entered, but rose up secretly and stole after me; and the next night
she warned the Abbess, and the two came on me by the tank.

I was punished with terrible penances: fasting, scourging, im-
prisonment, and the privation of drinking water; for the Abbess
stood amazed at the obduracy of my sin, and was resolved to
make me an example. For a month I endured the pains of hell;
then one night the Saracen pirates fell on our convent. On a sudden the darkness was full of flames and blood; but while the other
nuns ran hither and thither, clinging to the Abbess or shrieking on
the steps of the altar, I slipped through an unwatched postern and
made my way to the hills. The next day the Emperor's soldiery descended on the carousing heathen, slew them and burned their

vessels on the beach; the Abbess and nuns were rescued, the convent walls rebuilt, and peace was restored to the holy precincts. All this I heard from a shepherdess of the hills, who found me in my hiding, and brought me honeycomb and water. In her simplicity she offered to lead me home to the convent; but while she slept I laid off my wimple and scapular, and stealing her cloak fled away. And since then I have wandered alone over the face of the world, living in woods and desert places, often hungry, often cold and sometimes fearful; yet resigned to any hardship, and with a front for any peril, if only I may sleep under the free heaven and wash the dust from my body in cool water.

V

The Hermit, as may be supposed, was much perturbed by this story, and dismayed that such sinfulness should cross his path. His first motion was to drive the woman forth, for he knew the heinousness of the craving for water, and how Saint Jerome, Saint Augustine and other holy doctors have taught that they who would purify the soul must not be distraught by the vain cares of bodily cleanliness; yet, remembering the desire that drew him to his lauds, he dared not judge his sister's fault too harshly.

Moreover he was moved by the Wild Woman's story of the hardships she had suffered, and the godless company she had been driven to keep—Egyptians, jugglers, outlaws and even sorcerers, who are masters of the pagan lore of the East, and still practice their rites among the simple folk of the hills. Yet she would not have him think wholly ill of this vagrant people, from whom she had often received food and comfort; and her worst danger, as he learned with shame, had come from the *girovaghi* or wandering monks, who are the scourge and shame of Christendom; carrying their ribald idleness from one monastery to another, and leaving on their way a trail of thieving, revelry and worse. Once or twice the Wild Woman had nearly fallen into their hands; but had been saved by her own quick wit and skill in woodcraft. Once, so she assured the Hermit, she had found refuge with a faun and his female, who fed and sheltered her in their cave, where she slept on a bed of leaves with their shaggy nurslings; and in this cave she had seen a stock or idol of wood, extremely seamed and ancient, before which the wood creatures, when they thought she slept, laid garlands and the wild bees' honeycomb.

She told him also of a hill village of weavers, where she lived many weeks, and learned to ply their trade in return for her lodging; and where wayfaring men in the guise of cobblers, charcoal burners or goatherds came at midnight and taught strange doctrines in the hovels. What they taught she could not clearly tell, save that they believed each soul could commune directly with its Maker, without need of priest or intercessor; and she had heard from some of their disciples that there are two Gods, one of good and one of evil, and that the God of evil has his throne in the Pope's palace in Rome. But in spite of these dark teachings they were a mild and merciful folk, full of loving kindness toward poor persons and wayfarers; so that she grieved for them when one day a Dominican monk appeared with a company of soldiers, seizing some of the weavers and dragging them to prison, while others, with their wives and babes, fled to the winter woods. She fled with them, fearing to be charged with their heresy, and for months they lay hid in desert places, the older and weaker, when they fell sick from want and exposure, being devoutly ministered to by their brethren, and dying in the sure faith of heaven.

All this she related modestly and simply, not as one who joys in a godless life, but as having been drawn into it through misadventure; and she told the Hermit that when she heard the sound of church bells she never failed to say an *Ave* or a *Pater;* and that often, as she lay in the darkness of the forest, she had hushed her fears by reciting the versicles from the Evening Hour:

> Keep us, O Lord, as the apple of the eye,
> Protect us under the shadow of Thy wings.

The wound in her foot healed slowly; and the Hermit, while it was mending, repaired daily to her cave, reasoning with her in love and charity, and exhorting her to return to the cloister. But this she still refused to do; and fearing, lest she attempt to fly before her foot was healed, and so expose herself to hunger and ill usage, he promised not to betray her presence, or to take any measures toward restoring her to her Order.

He began indeed to doubt whether she had any calling to the life enclosed; yet her innocency of mind made him feel that she might be won back to holy living if only her freedom were assured. So after many inward struggles (since his promise forbade his taking counsel with any concerning her) he resolved to let her stay in the cave till some light should come to him. And one day, visiting her about the hour of *Nones*[8] (for it became his pious habit to say the evening office with her), he found her engaged with a little goatherd, who in a sudden seizure had fallen from a rock above her cave, and lay senseless and full of blood at her feet. And the Hermit saw with wonder how skillfully she bound up his cuts and restored his senses, giving him to drink of a liquor she had distilled from the simples of the mountain; whereat the boy opened his eyes and praised God, as one restored by heaven. Now it was known that this lad was subject to possessions, and had more than once dropped lifeless while he heeded his flock; and the Hermit, knowing that only great saints or unclean necromancers can loosen devils, feared that the Wild Woman had exorcised the spirits by means of unholy spells. But she told him that the goatherd's sickness was caused only by the heat of the sun, and that, such seizures being common in the hot countries whence she came, she had learned from a wise woman how to stay them by a decoction of the *carduus benedictus*,[9] made in the third night of the waxing moon, but without the aid of magic.

"But," she continued, "you need not fear my bringing scandal on your holy retreat, for by the arts of the same wise woman my own wound is well-nigh healed, and tonight at sunset I set forth."

The Hermit's heart grew heavy as she spoke, and it seemed to him that her own look was sorrowful. And suddenly his perplexities were lifted from him, and he saw what was God's purpose with the Wild Woman.

"Why," said he, "do you fly from this place, where you are safe from molestation, and can look to the saving of your soul? Is it that your feet weary for the road, and your spirits are heavy for lack of worldly discourse?"

She replied that she had no wish to travel, and felt no repugnance to solitude. "But," she said, "I must go forth to beg my bread, since in this wilderness there is none but yourself to feed me; and moreover, when it is known that I have healed the goatherd, curious folk and scandalmongers may seek me out, and, learning whence I come, drag me back to the cloister."

Then the Hermit answered and said: "In the early days, when the faith of Christ was first preached, there were holy women who fled to the desert and lived there in solitude, to the glory of God and the edification of their sex. If you are minded to embrace so austere a life, contenting you with such sustenance as the wilderness yields, and wearing out your days in prayer and vigil, it may be that you shall make amends for the great sin you have committed, and live and die in the peace of the Lord Jesus."

He spoke thus, knowing that if she left him and returned to her roaming, hunger and fear might drive her to fresh sin; whereas in a life of penance and reclusion her eyes might be opened to her iniquity.

He saw that his words moved her, and she seemed about to consent, and embrace a life of holiness; but suddenly she fell silent, and looked down on the valley at their feet.

"A stream flows in the glen below us," she said. "Do you forbid me to bathe in it in the heat of summer?"

"It is not I that forbid you, my daughter, but the laws of God," said the Hermit; "yet see how miraculously heaven protects you— for in the hot season, when your lust is upon you, our stream runs dry, and temptation will be removed from you. Moreover, on these heights there is no excess of heat to madden the body, but always, before dawn and at the angelus, a cool breeze which refreshes it like water."

And after thinking long on this, and again receiving his promise not to betray her, the Wild Woman agreed to embrace a life of reclusion; and the Hermit fell on his knees, worshiping God and rejoicing to think that, if he saved his sister from sin, his own term of probation would be shortened.

VI

Thereafter for two years the Hermit and the Wild Woman lived side by side, meeting together to pray on the great feast days of the year, but on all other days dwelling apart, engaged in pious practices.

At first the Hermit, knowing the weakness of woman, and her little aptitude for the life apart, had feared that he might be disturbed by the nearness of his penitent; but she faithfully held to his commands, abstaining from all sight of him save on the Days of Obligation; and when they met, so modest and devout was her demeanor that she raised his soul to fresh fervency. And gradually it grew sweet to him to think that, nearby though unseen, was one who performed the same tasks at the same hours; so that, whether he tended his garden, or recited his chaplet, or rose under the stars to repeat the midnight office, he had a companion in all his labors and devotions.

Meanwhile the report had spread abroad that a holy woman who cast out devils had made her dwelling in the Hermit's cliff; and many sick persons from the valley sought her out, and went away restored by her. These poor pilgrims brought her oil and flour, and with her own hands she made a garden like the Hermit's, and planted it with corn and lentils; but she would never take a trout from the brook, or receive the gift of a snared wild fowl, for she said that in her vagrant life the wild creatures of the wood had befriended her, and as she had slept in peace among them, so now she would never suffer them to be molested.

In the third year came a plague, and death walked the cities, and many poor peasants fled to the hills to escape it. These the Hermit and his penitent faithfully tended, and so skillful were the Wild Woman's ministrations that the report of them reached the town across the valley, and a deputation of burgesses came with rich offerings, and besought her to descend and comfort their sick. The Hermit, seeing her depart on so dangerous a mission, would have accompanied her, but she bade him remain and tend those who fled to the hills; and for many days his heart was consumed in prayer for her, and he feared lest every fugitive should bring him word of her death.

But at length she returned, wearied out but whole, and covered with the blessings of the townsfolk; and thereafter her name for holiness spread as wide as the Hermit's.

Seeing how constant she remained in her chosen life, and what advance she had made in the way of perfection, the Hermit now felt that it behooved him to exhort her again to return to the convent; and more than once he resolved to speak with her, but his

heart hung back. At length he bethought him that by failing in this
duty he imperiled his own soul, and thereupon, on the next feast
day, when they met, he reminded her that in spite of her good
works she still lived in sin and excommunicate, and that, now she
had once more tasted the sweets of godliness, it was her duty to
confess her fault and give herself up to her superiors.

She heard him meekly, but when he had spoken she was silent
and her tears ran over; and looking at her he wept also, and said
no more. And they prayed together, and returned each to his cave.

It was not till late winter that the plague abated; and the spring
and early summer following were heavy with rains and great heat.
When the Hermit visited his penitent at the feast of Pentecost, she
appeared to him so weak and wasted that, when they had recited
the *Veni, sancte spiritus*,[10] and the proper psalms, he taxed her
with too great rigor of penitential practices; but she replied that
her weakness was not due to an excess of discipline, but that she
had brought back from her labors among the sick a heaviness of
body which the intemperance of the season no doubt increased.
The evil rains continued, falling chiefly at night, while by day the
land reeked with heat and vapors; so that lassitude fell on the
Hermit also, and he could hardly drag himself down to the spring
whence he drew his drinking water. Thus he fell into the habit of
going down to the glen before cockcrow, after he had recited
Matins; for at that hour the rain commonly ceased, and a faint air
was stirring. Now because of the wet season the stream had not
gone dry, and instead of replenishing his flagon slowly at the trick-
ling spring, the Hermit went down to the waterside to fill it; and
once, as he descended the steep slope of the glen, he heard the
covert rustle, and saw the leaves stir as though something moved
behind them. As the sound ceased the leaves grew still; but his
heart was shaken, for it seemed to him that what he had seen in
the dusk had a human semblance, such as the wood people wear.
And he was loath to think that such unhallowed beings haunted
the glen.

A few days passed, and again, descending to the stream, he saw
a figure flit through the covert, and this time a deeper fear entered
into him; but he put away the thought, and prayed fervently for
all souls in temptation. And when he spoke with the Wild Woman
again, on the feast of the Seven Maccabees, which falls on the first

day of August, he was smitten with fear to see her wasted looks, and besought her to cease from laboring and let him minister to her. But she denied him gently, and replied that all she asked of him was to keep her steadfastly in his prayers.

Before the feast of the Assumption the rains ceased, and the plague, which had begun to show itself, was stayed; but the ardency of the sun grew greater, and the Hermit's cliff was a fiery furnace. Never had such heat been known in those regions; but the people did not murmur, for with the cessation of the rain their crops were saved and the pestilence banished; and these mercies they ascribed in great part to the prayers and macerations of the two holy anchorets. Therefore on the eve of the Assumption they sent a messenger to the Hermit, saying that at daylight on the morrow the townspeople and all the dwellers in the valley would come forth, led by their Bishop, who bore the Pope's blessing to the two Solitaries, and who was minded to celebrate the Mass of the Assumption in the Hermit's cave in the cliffside. At the word the Hermit was well-nigh distraught with joy, for he felt this to be a sign from heaven that his prayers were heard, and that he had won the Wild Woman's grace as well as his own. And all night he prayed that on the morrow she might confess her fault and receive the Sacrament with him.

Before dawn he recited the psalms of the proper nocturn; then he girded on his gown and sandals, and went forth to meet the Bishop.

As he went downward daylight stood on the mountains, and he thought he had never seen so fair a dawn. It filled the farthest heaven with brightness, and penetrated even to the woody crevices of the glen, as the grace of God had entered into the obscurest folds of his heart. The morning airs were hushed, and he heard only the sound of his own footfall, and the murmur of the stream which, though diminished, still poured a swift current between the rocks; but as he reached the bottom of the glen a sound of chanting came to him, and he knew that the pilgrims were at hand. His heart leapt up and his feet hastened forward; but at the stream's edge they were suddenly stayed, for in a pool where the water was still deep he saw the shining of a woman's body—and on the bank lay the Wild Woman's gown and sandals.

Fear and rage possessed the Hermit's heart, and he stood as one

smitten dumb, covering his eyes from the shame. But the song of
the approaching pilgrims swelled louder and nearer, and he cried
angrily to the Wild Woman to come forth and hide herself from
the people.

She made no answer, but in the dusk he saw her limbs sway
with the swaying water, and her eyes were turned to him as if in
mockery. At the sight fury filled him, and clambering over the
rocks to the pool's edge he bent down and caught her by the
shoulder. At that moment he could have strangled her with his
hands, so abhorrent was the touch of her flesh; but as he cried out,
heaping her with cruel names, he saw that her eyes returned his
look without wavering; and suddenly it came to him that she was
dead. Then through all his anger and fear a great pang smote him;
for here was his work undone, and one he had loved in Christ laid
low in her sin, in spite of all his labors.

One moment pity possessed him; the next he thought how the
people would find him bending above the body of a naked
woman, whom he had held up to them as holy, but whom they
might now well take for the secret instrument of his undoing; and
seeing how at her touch all the slow edifice of his holiness was demolished, and his soul in mortal jeopardy, he felt the earth reel
round him and his eyes grew blind.

Already the head of the procession had appeared, and the glen
shook with the great sound of the *Salve Regina*.[11] When the Hermit opened his eyes once more the air shone with thronged candle
flames, which glittered on the gold of priestly vestments, and on
the blazing monstrance beneath its canopy; and close above him
he saw the Bishop's face.

The Hermit struggled to his knees.

"My Father in God," he cried, "behold, for my sins I have been
visited by a demon—" But as he spoke he perceived that those
about him no longer listened, and that the Bishop and all his
clergy had fallen on their knees beside the pool. Then the Hermit,
following their gaze, saw that the brown waters of the pool covered the Wild Woman's limbs as with a garment, and that about
her floating head a brightness floated; and to the utmost edges of
the throng a cry of praise went up, for many were there whom the
Wild Woman had healed and who read God's mercy in this wonder. But fresh fear fell on the Hermit, for he had cursed a dying

saint, and denounced her aloud to all the people; and this new anguish, coming so close on the other, smote down his enfeebled frame, so that his limbs failed him and again he sank to the ground.

The earth reeled, and the bending faces grew dim about him; but as he forced his weak voice once more to proclaim his sins he felt the touch of absolution, and the holy oils of the last voyage on his lips and eyes. Peace returned to him then, and with it the longing to look once more upon his lauds, as he had dreamed of doing at his death; but he was too far gone to make this longing known, and so tried to put it from his mind. Yet in his weakness it held him, and the tears ran down his face.

Then, as he lay there, feeling the earth slip from him, and the everlasting arms replace it, he heard a peal of voices that seemed to come down from the sky and mingle with the singing of the throng; and the words of the chant were the words of his own lauds, so long hidden in the secret of his breast, and now rejoicing above him through the spheres. And his soul rose on the chant, and soared with it to the seat of mercy.

HIS FATHER'S SON

After his wife's death Mason Grew took the momentous step of selling out his business and moving from Wingfield, Connecticut, to Brooklyn.

For years he had secretly nursed the hope of such a change, but had never dared to suggest it to Mrs. Grew, a woman of immutable habits. Mr. Grew himself was attached to Wingfield, where he had grown up, prospered, and become what the local press described as "prominent." He was attached to his brick house with sandstone trimmings and a cast-iron area railing neatly sanded to match; to the similar row of houses across the street, with trolley wires forming a kind of aerial pathway between, and to the vista closed by the sandstone steeple of the church which he and his wife had always attended, and where their only child had been baptised.

It was hard to snap all these threads of association, yet still harder, now that he was alone, to live so far from his boy. Ronald Grew was practicing law in New York, and there was no more chance of his returning to live at Wingfield than of a river's flowing inland from the sea. Therefore to be near him his father must move; and it was characteristic of Mr. Grew, and of the situation generally, that the translation, when it took place, was to Brooklyn, and not to New York.

"Why you bury yourself in that hole I can't think," had been Ronald's comment; and Mr. Grew simply replied that rents were lower in Brooklyn, and that he had heard of a house there that would suit him. In reality he had said to himself—being the only recipient of his own confidences—that if he went to New York he might be on the boy's mind; whereas, if he lived in Brooklyn, Ronald would always have a good excuse for not popping over to see him every other day. The sociological isolation of Brooklyn, combined with its geographical nearness, presented in fact the precise conditions that Mr. Grew sought. He wanted to be near enough to New York to go there often, to feel under his feet the same pavement that Ronald trod, to sit now and then in the same theaters, and find on his breakfast table the journals which, with increasing frequency, inserted Ronald's name in the sacred bounds of the society column. It had always been a trial to Mr. Grew to have to wait twenty-four hours to read that "among those present was Mr. Ronald Grew." Now he had it with his coffee, and left it on the breakfast table to the perusal of a hired girl cosmopolitan enough to do it justice. In such ways Brooklyn attested the advantages of its nearness to New York, while remaining, as regards Ronald's duty to his father, as remote and inaccessible as Wingfield.

It was not that Ronald shirked his filial obligations, but rather because of his heavy sense of them, that Mr. Grew so persistently sought to minimize and lighten them. It was he who insisted, to Ronald, on the immense difficulty of getting from New York to Brooklyn.

"Any way you look at it, it makes a big hole in the day; and there's not much use in the ragged rim left. You say you're dining out next Sunday? Then I forbid you to come over here to lunch. Do you understand me, sir? You disobey at the risk of your father's malediction! Where did you say you were dining? With the Waltham Bankshires again? Why, that's the second time in three weeks, ain't it? Big blow-out, I suppose? Gold plate and orchids—opera singers in afterward? Well, you'd be in a nice box if there was a fog on the river, and you got hung up halfway over. That'd be a handsome return for the attention Mrs. Bankshire has shown you—singling out a whipper-snapper like you twice in three weeks! (What's the daughter's name—Daisy?) No, sir—don't you come fooling round here next Sunday, or I'll set the dogs on you. And you wouldn't find me in anyhow, come to think of it. I'm lunching out myself, as it happens—yes, sir, *lunching out*. Is there anything especially comic in my lunching out? I don't often do it, you say? Well, that's no reason why I never should. Who with? Why, with—with old Dr. Bleaker: Dr. Eliphalet Bleaker. No, you wouldn't know about him—he's only an old friend of your mother's and mine."

Gradually Ronald's insistence became less difficult to over-come. With his customary sweetness and tact (as Mr. Grew put it) he began to "take the hint," to give in to "the old gentleman's" growing desire for solitude.

"I'm set in my ways, Ronny, that's about the size of it; I like to go tick-ticking along like a clock. I always did. And when you come bouncing in I never feel sure there's enough for dinner—or that I haven't sent Maria out for the evening. And I don't want the neighbors to see me opening my own door to my son. That's the kind of cringing snob I am. Don't give me away, will you? I want 'em to think I keep four or five powdered flunkeys in the hall day and night—same as the lobby of one of those Fifth Avenue hotels. And if you pop over when you're not expected how am I going to keep up the bluff?"

Ronald yielded after the proper amount of resistance—his intu-itive sense, in every social transaction, of the proper amount of force to be expended, was one of the qualities his father most ad-mired in him. Mr. Grew's perceptions in this line were probably more acute than his son suspected. The souls of short thick-set men, with chubby features, mutton chop whiskers, and pale eyes peering between folds of fat like almond kernels in half-split shells—souls thus encased do not reveal themselves to the casual scrutiny as delicate emotional instruments. But in spite of the disguise in which he walked Mr. Grew vibrated exquisitely in response to every imaginative appeal; and his son Ronald was always stimulating and feeding his imagination.

Ronald in fact constituted Mr. Grew's one escape from the ele-ment of mediocrity which had always hemmed him in. To a man so enamored of beauty, and so little qualified to add to its sum to-tal, it was a wonderful privilege to have bestowed on the world such a being. Ronald's resemblance to Mr. Grew's early concep-tion of what he himself would have liked to look might have put new life into the discredited theory of prenatal influences. At any rate, if the young man owed his beauty, his distinction and his winning manner to the dreams of one of his parents, it was cer-tainly to those of Mr. Grew, who, while outwardly devoting his life to the manufacture and dissemination of Grew's Secure Sus-pender Buckle, moved in an enchanted inward world peopled with all the figures of romance. In this company Mr. Grew cut as brilliant a figure as any of its noble phantoms; and to see his vision of himself projected on the outer world in the shape of a brilliant popular conquering son, seemed, in retrospect, to give to it a belated reality. There were even moments when, forgetting his face, Mr. Grew said to himself that if he'd had "half a chance" he might have done as well as Ronald; but this only fortified his resolve that Ronald should do infinitely better.

Ronald's ability to do well almost equaled his gift of looking well. Mr. Grew constantly affirmed to himself that the boy was "not a genius"; but, barring this slight deficiency, he had almost every gift that a parent could wish. Even at Harvard he had managed to be several desirable things at once—writing poetry in the college magazine, playing delightfully "by ear," acquitting himself creditably of his studies, and yet holding his own in the sporting set that formed, as it were, the gateway of the temple of Society. Mr. Grew's idealism did not preclude the frank desire that his son should pass through that gateway; but the wish was not prompted by material considerations. It was Mr. Grew's notion that, in the rough and hurrying current of a new civilization, the little pools of leisure and enjoyment must nurture delicate growths, material graces as well as moral refinements, likely to be uprooted and swept away by the rush of the main torrent. He based his theory on the fact that he had liked the few "society" people he had met—had found their manners simpler, their voices more agreeable, their views more consonant with his own, than those of the leading citizens of Wingfield. But then he had met very few.

Ronald's sympathies needed no urging in the same direction. He took naturally, dauntlessly, to all the high and exceptional things about which his father's imagination had so long ineffectually hovered—from the start he was what Mr. Grew had dreamed of being. And so precise, so detailed, was Mr. Grew's vision of his own imaginary career, that as Ronald grew up, and began to travel in a widening orbit, his father had an almost uncanny sense of the extent to which that career was enacting itself before him. At Harvard, Ronald had done exactly what the hypothetical Mason Grew would have done, had not his actual self, at the same age, been working his way up in old Slagden's button factory—the institution which was later to acquire fame, and even notoriety, as the birthplace of Grew's Secure Suspender Buckle. Afterward, at a period when the actual Grew had passed from the factory to the bookkeeper's desk, his invisible double had been reading law at Columbia—precisely again what Ronald did! But it was when the young man left the paths laid out for him by the parental hand, and cast himself boldly on the world, that his adventures began to bear the most astonishing resemblance to those of the unrealized Mason Grew. It was in New York that the scene of this hypothetical being's first exploits had always been laid; and it was in New York that Ronald was to achieve his first triumph. There was nothing small or timid about Mr. Grew's imagination; it had never stopped at anything between Wingfield and the metropolis. And the real Ronald had the same cosmic vision as his parent. He brushed aside with a contemptuous laugh his mother's entreaty that he should stay at Wingfield and continue the dynasty of the Grew Suspender Buckle. Mr. Grew knew that in reality Ronald winced at the Buckle, loathed it, blushed for his connection with it. Yet it was the Buckle that had seen him through Groton, Harvard and the Law School, and had permitted him to enter the office of a distinguished corporation lawyer, instead of being enslaved to some sordid business with quick returns. The Buckle had been Ronald's fairy godmother—yet his father did not blame him for abhorring and disowning it. Mr. Grew himself often bitterly regretted having attached his own name to the instrument of his material success, though, at the time, his doing so had been the natural expression of his romanticism. When he invented the Buckle, and took out his patent, he and his wife both felt that to bestow their name on it was like naming a battleship or a peak of the Andes.

Mrs. Grew had never learned to know better; but Mr. Grew had discovered his error before Ronald was out of school. He read it first in a black eye of his boy's. Ronald's symmetry had been marred by the insolent fist of a fourth former whom he had chastised for alluding to his father as "Old Buckles"; and when Mr. Grew heard the epithet he understood in a flash that the Buckle was a thing to blush for. It was too late then to dissociate his name from it, or to efface from the hoardings of the entire continent the picture of two gentlemen, one contorting himself in the abject effort to repair a broken brace, while the careless ease of the other's attitude proclaimed his trust in the Secure Suspender

Buckle. These records were indelible, but Ronald could at least be spared all direct connection with them; and that day Mr. Grew decided that the boy should not return to Wingfield.

"You'll see," he had said to Mrs. Grew, "he'll take right hold in New York. Ronald's got my knack for taking hold," he added, throwing out his chest.

"But the way you took hold was in business," objected Mrs. Grew, who was large and literal.

Mr. Grew's chest collapsed, and he became suddenly conscious of his comic face in its rim of sandy whisker. "That's not the only way," he said, with a touch of wistfulness which escaped his wife's analysis.

"Well, of course you could have written beautifully," she rejoined with admiring eyes.

"*Written?* Me!" Mr. Grew became sardonic.

"Why, those letters—weren't *they* beautiful, I'd like to know?"

The couple exchanged a glance, innocently allusive and amused on the wife's part, and charged with a sudden tragic significance on the husband's.

"Well, I've got to be going along to the office now," he merely said, dragging himself out of his chair.

This had happened while Ronald was still at school; and now Mrs. Grew slept in the Wingfield cemetery, under a lifesize theological virtue of her own choosing, and Mr. Grew's prognostications as to Ronald's ability to "take right hold" in New York were being more and more brilliantly fulfilled.

II

Ronald obeyed his father's injunction not to come to luncheon on the day of the Bankshires' dinner; but in the middle of the following week Mr. Grew was surprised by a telegram from his son.

"Want to see you important matter. Expect me tomorrow afternoon."

Mr. Grew received the telegram after breakfast. To peruse it he had lifted his eye from a paragraph of morning paper describing a fancy dress dinner which the Hamilton Gliddens had given the night before for the housewarming of their new Fifth Avenue palace.

"Among the couples who afterward danced in the Poets' Quadrille were Miss Daisy Bankshire, looking more than usually lovely as Laura,[1] and Mr. Ronald Grew as the young Petrarch."[2]

Petrarch and Laura! Well—if *anything* meant anything, Mr. Grew supposed he knew what that meant. For weeks past he had noticed how constantly the names of the young people were coupled in the society notes he so insatiably devoured. Even the soulless reporter was getting into the habit of uniting them in his lists. And this Laura and Petrarch business was almost an announcement. . . .

Mr. Grew dropped the telegram, wiped his eyeglasses, and reread the paragraph. "Miss Daisy Bankshire . . . more than usually lovely . . ." Yes; she *was* lovely. He had often seen her photograph in the papers—seen her represented in every attitude of the mundane game: fondling her prize bulldog, taking a fence on her thoroughbred, dancing a *gavotte,* all patches and plumes, or fingering a guitar, all tulle and lilies; and once he had caught a glimpse of her at the theater. Hearing that Ronald was going to a fashionable first night with the Bankshires, Mr. Grew had for once overcome his repugnance to following his son's movements, and had secured for himself, under the shadow of the balcony, a stall whence he could observe the Bankshire box without fear of detection. Ronald had never known of his father's presence; and for three blessed hours Mr. Grew had watched his boy's handsome dark head bent above the fair hair and averted shoulder that were all he could catch of Miss Bankshire's beauties.

He recalled the vision now; and with it came, as usual, its ghostly double: the vision of his young self bending above such a shoulder and such shining hair. Needless to say that the real Mason Grew had never found himself in so enviable a situation. The late Mrs. Grew had no more resembled Miss Daisy Bankshire than he had looked like the happy victorious Ronald. And the mystery was that from their dull faces, their dull endearments, the miracle of Ronald should have sprung. It was almost—fantastically—as if the boy had been a changeling, child of a Latmian night,[3] whom the divine companion of Mr. Grew's early reveries had secretly laid in the cradle of the Wingfield bedroom while Mr. and Mrs. Grew slept the sleep of conjugal indifference.

The young Mason Grew had not at first accepted this astral episode as the complete canceling of his claims on romance. He too had grasped at the high-hung glory; and, with his tendency to reach too far when he reached at all, had singled out the prettiest girl in Wingfield. When he recalled his stammered confession of love his face still tingled under her cool bright stare. His audacity had struck her dumb; and when she recovered her voice it was to fling a taunt at him.

"Don't be too discouraged, you know—have you ever thought of trying Addie Wicks?"

All Wingfield would have understood the gibe: Addie Wicks was the dullest girl in town. And a year later he had married Addie Wicks. . . .

He looked up from the perusal of Ronald's telegram with this memory in his mind. Now at last his dream was coming true! His boy would taste of the joys that had mocked his thwarted youth and his dull middle-age. And it was fitting that they should be realized in Ronald's destiny. Ronald was made to take happiness boldly by the hand and lead it home like a bride. He had the carriage, the confidence, the high faith in his fortune, that compel the wilful stars. And, thanks to the Buckle, he would also have the background of material elegance that became his conquering person. Since Mr. Grew had retired from business his investments had prospered, and he had been saving up his income for just such a purpose. His own wants were few: he had brought the Wingfield furniture to Brooklyn, and his sitting room was a replica of that in which the long years of his married life had been spent. Even the florid carpet on which Ronald's first footsteps had been taken was carefully matched when it became too threadbare. And on the marble center table, with its beaded cover and bunch of dyed pampas grass, lay the illustrated Longfellow and the copy of Ingersoll's lectures which represented literature to Mr. Grew when he had led home his bride. In the light of Ronald's romance, Mr. Grew found himself reliving, with mingled pain and tenderness, all the poor prosaic incidents of his own personal history. Curiously enough, with this new splendor on them they began to emit a faint ray of their own. His wife's armchair, in its usual place by the fire, recalled her placid unperceiving presence, seated opposite to him during the long drowsy years; and he felt her kindness, her equanimity, where formerly he had only ached at her obtuseness. And from the chair he glanced up at the discolored photograph on the wall above, with a withered laurel wreath suspended on a corner of the frame. The photograph represented a young man with a poetic necktie and untrammeled hair, leaning against a Gothic chair back, a roll of music in his hand; and beneath was scrawled a bar of Chopin, with the words: "*Adieu, Adèle.*"

The portrait was that of the great pianist, Fortuné Dolbrowski; and its presence on the wall of Mr. Grew's sitting room commemorated the only exquisite hour of his life save that of Ronald's birth. It was some time before the latter event, a few months only after Mr. Grew's marriage, that he had taken his wife to New York to hear the great Dolbrowski. Their evening had been magically beautiful, and even Addie, roused from her usual inexpressiveness, had waked into a momentary semblance of life. "I never—I never—" she gasped out when they had regained their hotel bedroom, and sat staring back entranced at the evening's vision. Her large face was pink and tremulous, and she sat with her hands on knees, forgetting to roll up her bonnet strings and prepare her curl papers.

"I'd like to *write* him just how I felt—I wish I knew how!" she burst out in a final effervescence of emotion.

Her husband lifted his head and looked at her.

"Would you? I feel that way too," he said with a sheepish laugh. And they continued to stare at each other through a transfiguring mist of sound.

The scene rose before Mr. Grew as he gazed up at the pianist's photograph. "Well, I owe her that anyhow—poor Addie!" he said, with a smile at the inconsequences of fate. With Ronald's telegram in his hand he was in a mood to count his mercies.

III

"A clear twenty-five thousand a year: that's what you can tell 'em with my compliments," said Mr. Grew, glancing complacently across the center table at his boy.

It struck him that Ronald's gift for looking his part in life had never so completely expressed itself. Other young men, at such a moment, would have been red, damp, tight about the collar; but Ronald's cheek was a shade paler, and the contrast made his dark eyes more expressive.

"A clear twenty-five thousand; yes, sir—that's what I always meant you to have."

Mr. Grew leaned carelessly back, his hands thrust in his pockets, as though to divert attention from the agitation of his features. He had often pictured himself rolling out that phrase to Ronald, and now that it was on his lips he could not control their tremor.

Ronald listened in silence, lifting a hand to his slight mustache, as though he, too, wished to hide some involuntary betrayal of emotion. At first Mr. Grew took his silence for an expression of gratified surprise; but as it prolonged itself it became less easy to interpret.

"I—see here, my boy; did you expect more? Isn't it enough?" Mr. Grew cleared his throat. "Do *they* expect more?" he asked nervously. He was hardly able to face the pain of inflicting a disappointment on Ronald at the very moment when he had counted on putting the final touch to his bliss.

Ronald moved uneasily in his chair and his eyes wandered upward to the laurel-wreathed photograph of the pianist.

"*Is* it the money, Ronald? Speak out, my boy. We'll see, we'll look round—I'll manage somehow."

"No, no," the young man interrupted, abruptly raising his hand as though to check his father.

Mr. Grew recovered his cheerfulness. "Well, what's the trouble then, if *she's* willing?"

Ronald shifted his position again and finally rose from his seat and wandered across the room.

"Father," he said, coming back, "there's something I've got to tell you. I can't take your money."

Mr. Grew sat speechless a moment, staring blankly at his son; then he emitted a laugh. "My money? What are you talking about? What's this about my money? Why, it ain't *mine*, Ronny; it's all yours—every cent of it!"

The young man met his tender look with a gesture of tragic refusal.

"No, no, it's not mine—not even in the sense you mean. Not in any sense. Can't you understand my feeling so?"

"Feeling so? I don't know how you're feeling. I don't know what you're talking about. Are you too proud to touch any money you haven't earned? Is that what you're trying to tell me?"

"No. It's not that. You must know—"

Mr. Grew flushed to the rim of his bristling whiskers. "Know? Know *what*? Can't you speak out?"

Ronald hesitated, and the two faced each other for a long strained moment, during which Mr. Grew's congested countenance grew gradually pale again.

"What's the meaning of this? Is it because you've done something . . . something you're ashamed of . . . ashamed to tell me?" he gasped; and walking around the table he laid his hand gently on his son's shoulder. "There's nothing you can't tell me, my boy."

"It's not that. Why do you make it so hard for me?" Ronald broke out with passion. "You must have known this was sure to happen sooner or later."

"Happen? What was sure to hap—?" Mr. Grew's question wavered on his lip and passed into a tremulous laugh. "Is it something I've done that you don't approve of? Is it—is it *the Buckle* you're ashamed of, Ronald Grew?"

Ronald laughed too, impatiently. "The Buckle? No, I'm not ashamed of the Buckle; not any more than you are," he returned with a flush. "But I'm ashamed of all I owe to it—all I owe to you—when—when—" He broke off and took a few distracted steps across the room. "You might make this easier for me," he protested, turning back to his father.

"Make what easier? I know less and less what you're driving at," Mr. Grew groaned.

Ronald's walk had once more brought him beneath the photograph on the wall. He lifted his head for a moment and looked at it; then he looked again at Mr. Grew.

"Do you suppose I haven't always known?"

"Known—?"

"Even before you gave me those letters at the time of my mother's death—even before that, I suspected. I don't know how it began . . . perhaps from little things you let drop . . . you and she . . . and resemblances that I couldn't help seeing . . . in myself . . . How on earth could you suppose I *shouldn't guess?* I always thought you gave me the letters as a way of telling me—"

Mr. Grew rose slowly from his chair. "The letters? Do you mean Dolbrowski's letters?"

Ronald nodded with white lips. "You must remember giving them to me the day after the funeral."

Mr. Grew nodded back. "Of course. I wanted you to have everything your mother valued."

"Well—how could I help knowing after that?"

"Knowing *what?*" Mr. Grew stood staring helplessly at his son. Suddenly his look caught at a clue that seemed to confront it with a deeper difficulty. "You thought—you thought those letters . . . Dolbrowski's letters . . . you thought they meant . . ."

"Oh, it wasn't only the letters. There were so many other signs. My love of music—my—all my feelings about life . . . and art . . . and when you gave me the letters I thought you must mean me to know."

Mr. Grew had grown quiet. His lips were firm, and his small eyes looked out steadily from their creased lids.

"To know that you were Fortuné Dolbrowski's son?"

Ronald made a mute sign of assent.

"I see. And what did you intend to do?"

"I meant to wait till I could earn my living, and then repay you . . . as far as I can ever repay you for what you'd spent on me . . . But now that there's a chance of my marrying . . . and that your generosity overwhelms me . . . I'm obliged to speak."

"I see," said Mr. Grew again. He let himself down into his chair, looking steadily and not unkindly at the young man. "Sit down too, Ronald. Let's talk."

Ronald made a protesting movement. "Is anything to be gained by it? You can't change me—change what I feel. The reading of those letters transformed my whole life—I was a boy till then: they made a man of me. From that moment I understood myself." He paused, and then looked up at Mr. Grew's face. "Don't imagine that I don't appreciate your kindness—your extraordinary generosity. But I can't go through life in disguise. And I want you to know that I have not won Daisy under false pretenses—"

Mr. Grew started up with the first expletive Ronald had ever heard on his lips.

"You damned young fool, you, you haven't *told* her—?"

Ronald raised his head with pride. "Oh, you don't know her, sir! She thinks no worse of me for knowing my secret. She is above and beyond all such conventional prejudices. She's *proud* of my parentage"—he straightened his slim young shoulders—"as I'm proud of it . . . yes, sir, proud of it . . ."

Mr. Grew sank back into his seat with a dry laugh. "Well, you ought to be. You come of good stock. And you're your father's son, every inch of you!" He laughed again, as though the humor of the situation grew on him with its closer contemplation.

"Yes, I've always felt that," Ronald murmured, gravely.

"Your father's son, and no mistake." Mr. Grew leaned forward. "You're the son of as big a fool as yourself. And here he sits, Ronald Grew!"

The young man's color deepened to crimson; but his reply was checked by Mr. Grew's decisive gesture. "Here he sits, with all your young nonsense still alive in him. Don't you begin to see the likeness? If you don't I'll tell you the story of those letters."

Ronald stared. "What do you mean? Don't they tell their own story?"

"I supposed they did when I gave them to you; but you've given it a twist that needs straightening out." Mr. Grew squared his elbows on the table, and looked at the young man across the gift books and dyed pampas grass. "I wrote all the letters that Dolbrowski answered."

Ronald gave back his look in frowning perplexity. "*You* wrote them? I don't understand. His letters are all addressed to my mother."

"Yes. And he thought he was corresponding with her."

"But my mother—what did she think?"

Mr. Grew hesitated, puckering his thick lids. "Well, I guess she kinder thought it was a joke. Your mother didn't think about things much."

Ronald continued to bend a puzzled frown on the question. "I don't understand," he reiterated.

Mr. Grew cleared his throat with a nervous laugh. "Well, I don't know as you ever will—*quite*. But this is the way it came about. I had a toughish time of it when I was young. Oh, I don't mean so much the fight I had to put up to make my way—there was always plenty of fight in me. But inside of myself it was kinder lonesome. And the outside didn't attract callers." He laughed again, with an apologetic gesture toward his broad blinking face. "When I went round with the other young fellows I was always the forlorn hope—the one that had to eat the drumsticks and dance with the leftovers. As sure as there was a blighter at a picnic I had to swing her, and feed her, and drive her home. And all the time I was mad after all the things you've got—poetry and music and all the joy-forever business. So there were the pair of us—my face and my imagination—chained together, and fighting, and hating each other like poison.

"Then your mother came along and took pity on me. It sets up a gawky fellow to find a girl who ain't ashamed to be seen walking with him Sundays. And I was grateful to your mother, and we got along first-rate. Only I couldn't say things to her—and she couldn't answer. Well—one day, a few months after we were married, Dolbrowski came to New York, and the whole place went wild about him. I'd never heard any good music, but I'd always had an inkling of what it must be like, though I couldn't tell you to this day how I knew. Well, your mother read about him in the papers too, and she thought it'd be the swagger thing to go to New York and hear him play—so we went. . . . I'll never forget that evening. Your mother wasn't easily stirred up—she never seemed to need to let off steam. But that night she seemed to understand the way I felt. And when we got back to the hotel she said to me: 'I'd like to tell him how I feel. I'd like to sit right down and write to him.'

" 'Would you?' I said. 'So would I.'

"There was paper and pens there before us, and I pulled a sheet toward me, and began to write. 'Is this what you'd like to say to him?' I asked her when the letter was done. And she got pink and said: 'I don't understand it, but it's lovely.' And she copied it out and signed her name to it, and sent it."

Mr. Grew paused, and Ronald sat silent, with lowered eyes.

"That's how it began; and that's where I thought it would end. But it didn't, because Dolbrowski answered. His first letter was dated January 10, 1872. I guess you'll find I'm correct. Well, I went back to hear him again, and I wrote him after the performance, and he answered again. And after that we kept it up for

six months. Your mother always copied the letters and signed
them. She seemed to think it was a kinder joke, and she was proud
of his answering my letters. But she never went back to New York
to hear him, though I saved up enough to give her the treat again.
She was too lazy, and she let me go without her. I heard him three
times in New York; and in the spring he came to Wingfield and
played once at the Academy. Your mother was sick and couldn't
go; so I went alone. After the performance I meant to get one of
the directors to take me in to see him; but when the time came, I
just went back home and wrote to him instead. And the month after, before he went back to Europe, he sent your mother a last little note, and that picture hanging up there. . . ."

Mr. Grew paused again, and both men lifted their eyes to the
photograph.

"Is that all?" Ronald slowly asked.

"That's all—every bit of it," said Mr. Grew.

"And my mother—my mother never even spoke to Dolbrowski?"

"Never. She never even saw him but that once in New York at
his concert."

The blood crept again to Ronald's face. "Are you sure of that,
sir?" he asked in a trembling voice.

"Sure as I am that I'm sitting here. Why, she was too lazy to
look at his letters after the first novelty wore off. She copied the
answers just to humor me—but she always said she couldn't understand what we wrote."

"But how could you go on with such a correspondence? It's incredible!"

Mr. Grew looked at his son thoughtfully. "I suppose it is, to
you. You've only had to put out your hand and get the things I
was starving for—music, and good talk, and ideas. Those letters
gave me all that. You've read them, and you know that Dolbrowski was not only a great musician but a great man. There
was nothing beautiful he didn't see, nothing fine he didn't feel. For
six months I breathed his air, and I've lived on it ever since. Do
you begin to understand a little now?"

"Yes—a little. But why write in my mother's name? Why make
it appear like a sentimental correspondence?"

Mr. Grew reddened to his bald temples. "Why, I tell you it began that way, as a kinder joke. And when I saw that the first letter pleased and interested him, I was afraid to tell him—I *couldn't* tell him. Do you suppose he'd gone on writing if he'd ever seen me, Ronny?"

Ronald suddenly looked at him with new eyes. "But he must have thought your letters very beautiful—to go on as he did," he broke out.

"Well—I did my best," said Mr. Grew modestly.

Ronald pursued his idea. "Where *are* all your letters, I wonder? Weren't they returned to you at his death?"

Mr. Grew laughed. "Lord, no. I guess he had trunks and trunks full of better ones. I guess Queens and Empresses wrote to him."

"I should have liked to see your letters," the young man insisted.

"Well, they weren't bad," said Mr. Grew drily. "But I'll tell you one thing, Ronny," he added. Ronald raised his head with a quick glance, and Mr. Grew continued: "I'll tell you where the best of those letters is—it's in *you*. If it hadn't been for that one look at life I couldn't have made you what you are. Oh, I know you've done a good deal of your own making—but I've been there behind you all the time. And you'll never know the work I've spared you and the time I've saved you. Fortuné Dolbrowski helped me do that. I never saw things little again after I'd looked at 'em with him. And I tried to give you the big view from the start. . . . So that's what became of my letters."

Mr. Grew paused, and for a long time Ronald sat motionless, his elbows on the table, his face dropped on his hands.

Suddenly Mr. Grew's touch fell on his shoulder.

"Look at here, Ronald Grew—do you want me to tell you how you're feeling at this minute? Just a mite let down, after all, at the idea that you ain't the romantic figure you'd got to think yourself. . . . Well, that's natural enough, too; but I'll tell you what it proves. It proves you're my son right enough, if any more proof was needed. For it's just the kind of fool nonsense I used to feel at your age—and if there's anybody here to laugh at it's myself, and not you. And you can laugh at me just as much as you like. . . ."

AFTERWARD

"Oh, there *is* one, of course, but you'll never know it."

The assertion, laughingly flung out six months earlier in a bright June garden, came back to Mary Boyne with a new perception of its significance as she stood, in the December dusk, waiting for the lamps to be brought into the library.

The words had been spoken by their friend Alida Stair, as they sat at tea on her lawn at Pangbourne, in reference to the very house of which the library in question was the central, the pivotal "feature." Mary Boyne and her husband, in quest of a country place in one of the southern or southwestern counties, had, on their arrival in England, carried their problem straight to Alida Stair, who had successfully solved it in her own case; but it was not until they had rejected, almost capriciously, several practical and judicious suggestions that she threw out: "Well, there's Lyng, in Dorsetshire. It belongs to Hugo's cousins, and you can get it for a song."

The reason she gave for its being obtainable on these terms—its remoteness from a station, its lack of electric light, hot water pipes, and other vulgar necessities—were exactly those pleading in its favor with two romantic Americans perversely in search of the economic drawbacks which were associated, in their tradition, with unusual architectural felicities.

"I should never believe I was living in an old house unless I was thoroughly uncomfortable," Ned Boyne, the more extravagant of the two, had jocosely insisted; "the least hint of convenience would make me think it had been bought out of an exhibition, with the pieces numbered, and set up again." And they had proceeded to enumerate, with humorous precision, their various doubts and demands, refusing to believe that the house their cousin recommended was *really* Tudor till they learned it had no heating system, or that the village church was literally in the grounds till she assured them of the deplorable uncertainty of the water supply.

"It's too uncomfortable to be true!" Edward Boyne had continued to exult as the avowal of each disadvantage was successively wrung from her; but he had cut short his rhapsody to ask, with a relapse to distrust: "And the ghost? You've been concealing from us the fact that there is no ghost!"

Mary, at the moment, had laughed with him, yet almost with her laugh, being possessed of several sets of independent perceptions, had been struck by a note of flatness in Alida's answering hilarity.

"Oh, Dorsetshire's full of ghosts, you know."

"Yes, yes; but that won't do. I don't want to have to drive ten miles to see somebody else's ghost. I want one of my own on the premises. *Is* there a ghost at Lyng?"

His rejoinder had made Alida laugh again, and it was then that she had flung back tantalizing: "Oh, there *is* one, of course, but you'll never know it."

"Never know it?" Boyne pulled her up. "But what in the world constitutes a ghost except the fact of its being known for one?"

"I can't say. But that's the story."

"That there's a ghost, but that nobody knows it's a ghost?"

"Well—not till afterward, at any rate."

"Till afterward?"

"Not till long long afterward."

"But if it's once been identified as an unearthly visitant, why hasn't its *signalement*[1] been handed down in the family? How has it managed to preserve its incognito?"

Alida could only shake her head. "Don't ask me. But it has."

"And then suddenly"—Mary spoke up as if from cavernous depths of divination—"suddenly, long afterward, one says to one's self 'That was it?'"

She was startled at the sepulchral sound with which her question fell on the banter of the other two, and she saw the shadow of the same surprise flit across Alida's pupils. "I suppose so. One just has to wait."

"Oh, hang waiting!" Ned broke in. "Life's too short for a ghost who can only be enjoyed in retrospect. Can't we do better than that, Mary?"

But it turned out that in the event they were not destined to, for within three months of their conversation with Mrs. Stair they were settled at Lyng, and the life they had yearned for, to the point of planning it in advance in all its daily details, had actually begun for them.

It was to sit, in the thick December dusk, by just such a wide-hooded fireplace, under just such black oak rafters, with the sense that beyond the mullioned panes the downs were darkened to a deeper solitude: it was for the ultimate indulgence of such sensations that Mary Boyne, abruptly exiled from New York by her husband's business, had endured for nearly fourteen years the soul-deadening ugliness of a Middle Western town, and that Boyne had ground on doggedly at his engineering till, with a suddenness that still made her blink, the prodigious windfall of the Blue Star Mine had put them at a stroke in possession of life and the leisure to taste it. They had never for a moment meant their new state to be one of idleness; but they meant to give themselves only to harmonious activities. She had her vision of painting and gardening (against a background of grey walls), he dreamed of the production of his long-planned book on the "Economic Basis of Culture"; and with such absorbing work ahead no existence could be too sequestered: they could not get far enough from the world, or plunge deep enough into the past.

Dorsetshire had attracted them from the first by an air of remoteness out of all proportion to its geographical position. But to the Boynes it was one of the ever-recurring wonders of the whole incredibly compressed island—a nest of counties, as they put it—that for the production of its effects so little of a given quality went so far: that so few miles made a distance, and so short a distance a difference.

"It's that," Ned had once enthusiastically explained, "that gives such depth to their effects, such relief to their contrasts. They've been able to lay the butter so thick on every delicious mouthful."

The butter had certainly been laid on thick at Lyng: the old house hidden under a shoulder of the downs had almost all the finer marks of commerce with a protracted past. The mere fact that it was neither large nor exceptional made it, to the Boynes, abound the more completely in its special charm—the charm of having been for centuries a deep dim reservoir of life. The life had probably not been of the most vivid order: for long periods, no doubt, it had fallen as noiselessly into the past as the quiet drizzle of autumn fell, hour after hour, into the fish pond between the yews; but these backwaters of existence sometimes breed, in their sluggish depths, strange acuities of emotion, and Mary Boyne had felt from the first the mysterious stir of intenser memories.

The feeling had never been stronger than on this particular afternoon when, waiting in the library for the lamps to come, she rose from her seat and stood among the shadows of the hearth. Her husband had gone off, after luncheon, for one of his long tramps on the downs. She had noticed of late that he preferred to go alone; and, in the tried security of their personal relations, had been driven to conclude that his book was bothering him, and that he needed the afternoons to turn over in solitude the problems left from the morning's work. Certainly the book was not going as smoothly as she had thought it would, and there were lines of perplexity between his eyes such as had never been there in his engineering days. He had often, then, looked fagged to the verge of illness, but the native demon of worry had never branded his brow. Yet the few pages he had so far read to her—the introduction, and a summary of the opening chapter—showed a firm hold on his subject, and an increasing confidence in his powers.

The fact threw her into deeper perplexity, since, now that he had done with business and its disturbing contingencies, the one other possible source of anxiety was eliminated. Unless it were his health, then? But physically he had gained since they had come to Dorsetshire, grown robuster, ruddier and fresher eyed. It was only within the last week that she had felt in him the undefinable change which made her restless in his absence, and as tongue-tied in his presence as though it were *she* who had a secret to keep from him!

The thought that there *was* a secret somewhere between them struck her with a sudden rap of wonder, and she looked about her down the long room.

"Can it be the house?" she mused.

The room itself might have been full of secrets. They seemed to be piling themselves up, as evening fell, like the layers and layers of velvet shadow dropping from the low ceiling, the rows of books, the smoke-blurred sculpture of the hearth.

"Why, of course—the house is haunted!" she reflected.

The ghost—Alida's imperceptible ghost—after figuring largely in the banter of their first month or two at Lyng, had been gradually left aside as too ineffectual for imaginative use. Mary had, indeed, as became the tenant of a haunted house, made the customary inquiries among her rural neighbors, but, beyond a vague "They dü say so, ma'am," the villagers had nothing to impart. The elusive specter had apparently never had sufficient identity for a legend to crystallize about it, and after a time the Boynes had set the matter down to their profit-and-loss account, agreeing that Lyng was one of the few houses good enough in itself to dispense with supernatural enhancements.

"And I suppose, poor ineffectual demon, that's why it beats its beautiful wings in vain in the void," Mary had laughingly concluded.

"Or, rather," Ned answered in the same strain, "why, amid so much that's ghostly, it can never affirm its separate existence as *the* ghost." And thereupon their invisible housemate had finally dropped out of their references, which were numerous enough to make them soon unaware of the loss.

Now, as she stood on the hearth, the subject of their earlier curiosity revived in her with a new sense of its meaning—a sense gradually acquired through daily contact with the scene of the lurking mystery. It was the house itself, of course, that possessed the ghost-seeing faculty, that communed visually but secretly with its own past; if one could only get into close enough communion with the house, one might surprise its secret, and acquire the ghost sight on one's own account. Perhaps, in his long hours in this very room, where she never trespassed till the afternoon, her husband *had* acquired it already, and was silently carrying about the weight of whatever it had revealed to him. Mary was too well versed in the code of the spectral world not to know that one could not talk about the ghosts one saw: to do so was almost as great a breach of taste as to name a lady in a club. But this explanation did not really satisfy her. "What, after all, except for the fun of the shudder," she reflected, "would he really care for any of their old ghosts?" And thence she was thrown back once more on the fundamental dilemma: the fact that one's greater or less susceptibility to spectral influences had no particular bearing on the case, since, when one *did* see a ghost at Lyng, one did not know it.

"Not till long afterward," Alida Stair had said. Well, supposing Ned *had* seen one when they first came, and had known only within the last week what had happened to him? More and more under the spell of the hour, she threw back her thoughts to the early days of their tenancy, but at first only to recall a lively confusion of unpacking, settling, arranging of books, and calling to each other from remote corners of the house as, treasure after treasure, it revealed itself to them. It was in this particular connection that she presently recalled a certain soft afternoon of the previous October, when, passing from the first rapturous flurry of exploration to a detailed inspection of the old house, she had pressed (like a novel heroine) a panel that opened on a flight of corkscrew stairs leading to a flat ledge of the roof—the roof which, from below, seemed to slope away on all sides too abruptly for any but practiced feet to scale.

The view from this hidden coign was enchanting, and she had flown down to snatch Ned from his papers and give him the freedom of her discovery. She remembered still how, standing at her side, he had passed his arm about her while their gaze flew to the long tossed horizon line of the downs, and then dropped contentedly back to trace the arabesque of yew hedges about the fish pond, and the shadow of the cedar on the lawn.

"And now the other way," he had said, turning her about within his arm; and closely pressed to him, she had absorbed, like some long satisfying draught, the picture of the grey-walled court, the squat lions on the gates, and the lime avenue reaching up to the highroad under the downs.

It was just then, while they gazed and held each other, that she had felt his arm relax, and heard a sharp "Hullo!" that made her turn to glance at him.

Distinctly, yes, she now recalled that she had seen, as she glanced, a shadow of anxiety, of perplexity, rather, fall across his face; and, following his eyes, had beheld the figure of a man—a man in loose greyish clothes, as it appeared to her—who was sauntering down the lime avenue to the court with the doubtful gait of a stranger who seeks his way. Her shortsighted eyes had given her but a blurred impression of slightness and greyishness, with something foreign, or at least unlocal, in the cut of the figure or its dress; but her husband had apparently seen more—seen enough to make him push past her with a hasty "Wait!" and dash down the stairs without pausing to give her a hand.

A slight tendency to dizziness obliged her, after a provisional clutch at the chimney against which they had been leaning, to follow him first more cautiously; and when she had reached the landing she paused again, for a less definite reason, leaning over the banister to strain her eyes through the silence of the brown sun-flecked depths. She lingered there till, somewhere in those depths, she heard the closing of a door; then, mechanically impelled, she went down the shallow flights of steps till she reached the lower hall.

The front door stood open on the sunlight of the court, and hall and court were empty. The library door was open, too, and after listening in vain for any sound of voices within, she crossed the threshold, and found her husband alone, vaguely fingering the papers on his desk.

He looked up, as if surprised at her entrance, but the shadow of anxiety had passed from his face, leaving it even, as she fancied, a little brighter and clearer than usual.

"What was it? Who was it?" she asked.

"Who?" he repeated, with the surprise still all on his side.

"The man we saw coming toward the house."

He seemed to reflect. "The man? Why, I thought I saw Peters; I dashed after him to say a word about the stable drains, but he had disappeared before I could get down."

"Disappeared? But he seemed to be walking so slowly when we saw him."

Boyne shrugged his shoulders. "So I thought; but he must have got up steam in the interval. What do you say to our trying to scramble up Meldon Steep before sunset?"

That was all. At the time the occurrence had been less than nothing, had, indeed, been immediately obliterated by the magic of their first vision from Meldon Steep, a height which they had dreamed of climbing ever since they had first seen its bare spine rising above the roof of Lyng. Doubtless it was the mere fact of the other incident's having occurred on the very day of the ascent to Meldon that had kept it stored away in the fold of memory from which it now emerged; for in itself it had no mark of the portentous. At the moment there could have been nothing more natural than that Ned should dash himself from the roof in the pursuit of dilatory tradesmen. It was the period when they were always on the watch for one or the other of the specialists employed about the place; always lying in wait for them, and rushing out at them with questions, reproaches or reminders. And certainly in the distance the grey figure had looked like Peters.

Yet now, as she reviewed the scene, she felt her husband's explanation of it to have been invalidated by the look of anxiety on his face. Why had the familiar appearance of Peters made him anxious? Why, above all, if it was of such prime necessity to confer with him on the subject of the stable drains, had the failure to find him produced such a look of relief? Mary could not say that any one of these questions had occurred to her at the time, yet, from the promptness with which they now marshalled themselves at her summons, she had a sense that they must all along have been there, waiting their hour.

II

Weary with her thoughts, she moved to the window. The library was now quite dark, and she was surprised to see how much faint light the outer world still held.

As she peered out into it across the court, a figure shaped itself far down the perspective of bare limes: it looked a mere blot of deeper grey in the greyness, and for an instant, as it moved toward her, her heart thumped to the thought "It's the ghost!"

She had time, in that long instant, to feel suddenly that the man of whom, two months earlier, she had had a distant vision from the roof, was now, at his predestined hour, about to reveal himself as *not* having been Peters; and her spirit sank under the impending fear of the disclosure. But almost with the next tick of the clock the figure, gaining substance and character, showed itself even to her weak sight as her husband's; and she turned to meet him, as he entered, with the confession of her folly.

"It's really too absurd," she laughed out, "but I never *can* remember!"

"Remember what?" Boyne questioned as they drew together.

"That when one sees the Lyng ghost one never knows it."

Her hand was on his sleeve, and he kept it there, but with no response in his gesture or in the lines of his preoccupied face.

"Did you think you'd seen it?" he asked, after an appreciable interval.

"Why, I actually took *you* for it, my dear, in my mad determination to spot it!"

"Me—just now?" His arm dropped away, and he turned from her with a faint echo of her laugh. "Really, dearest, you'd better give it up, if that's the best you can do."

"Oh, yes, I give it up. Have *you?*" she asked, turning round on him abruptly.

The parlormaid had entered with letters and a lamp, and the light struck up into Boyne's face as he bent above the tray she presented.

"Have *you?*" Mary perversely insisted, when the servant had disappeared on her errand of illumination.

"Have I what?" he rejoined absently, the light bringing out the sharp stamp of worry between his brows as he turned over the letters.

"Given up trying to see the ghost." Her heart beat a little at the experiment she was making.

Her husband, laying his letters aside, moved away into the shadow of the hearth.

"I never tried," he said, tearing open the wrapper of a newspaper.

"Well, of course," Mary persisted, "the exasperating thing is that there's no use trying, since one can't be sure till so long afterward."

He was unfolding the paper as if he had hardly heard her; but after a pause, during which the sheets rustled spasmodically between his hands, he looked up to ask, "Have you any idea *how long?*"

Mary had sunk into a low chair beside the fireplace. From her seat she glanced over, startled, at her husband's profile, which was projected against the circle of lamplight.

"No; none. Have *you?*" she retorted, repeating her former phrase with an added stress of intention.

Boyne crumpled the paper into a bunch, and then, inconsequently, turned back with it toward the lamp.

"Lord, no! I only meant," he exclaimed, with a faint tinge of impatience, "is there any legend, any tradition, as to that?"

"Not that I know of," she answered; but the impulse to add "What makes you ask?" was checked by the reappearance of the parlormaid, with tea and a second lamp.

With the dispersal of shadows, and the repetition of the daily domestic office, Mary Boyne felt herself less oppressed by the sense of something mutely imminent which had darkened her afternoon. For a few moments she gave herself to the details of her task, and when she looked up from it she was struck to the point of bewilderment by the change in her husband's face. He had seated himself near the farther lamp, and was absorbed in the perusal of his letters; but was it something he had found in them, or merely the shifting of her own point of view, that had restored his features to their normal aspect? The longer she looked the more definitely the change affirmed itself. The lines of tension had vanished, and such traces of fatigue as lingered were of the kind easily attributable to steady mental effort. He glanced up, as if drawn by her gaze, and met her eyes with a smile.

"I'm dying for my tea, you know; and here's a letter for you," he said.

She took the letter he held out in exchange for the cup she proffered him, and, returning to her seat, broke the seal with the languid gesture of the reader whose interests are all enclosed in the circle of one cherished presence.

Her next conscious motion was that of starting to her feet, the letter falling to them as she rose, while she held out to her husband a newspaper clipping.

"Ned! What's this? What does it mean?"

He had risen at the same instant, almost as if hearing her cry before she uttered it; and for a perceptible space of time he and she studied each other, like adversaries watching for an advantage, across the space between her chair and his desk.

"What's what? You fairly made me jump!" Boyne said at length, moving toward her with a sudden half-exasperated laugh. The shadow of apprehension was on his face again, not now a look of fixed foreboding, but a shifting vigilance of lips and eyes that gave her the sense of his feeling himself invisibly surrounded.

Her hand shook so that she could hardly give him the clipping.

"This article—from the *Waukesha Sentinel*—that a man named Elwell has brought suit against you—that there was something wrong about the Blue Star Mine. I can't understand more than half."

They continued to face each other as she spoke, and to her astonishment she saw that her words had the almost immediate effect of dissipating the strained watchfulness of his look.

"Oh, *that!*" He glanced down the printed slip, and then folded it with the gesture of one who handles something harmless and familiar. "What's the matter with you this afternoon, Mary? I thought you'd got bad news."

She stood there before him with her undefinable terror subsiding slowly under the reassurance of his tone.

"You knew about this, then—it's all right?"

"Certainly I knew about it; and it's all right."

"But what *is* it? I don't understand. What does this man accuse you of?"

"Pretty nearly every crime in the calendar." Boyne had tossed the clipping down, and thrown himself into an armchair near the fire. "Do you want to hear the story? It's not particularly interesting—just a squabble over interests in the Blue Star."

"But who is this Elwell? I don't know the name."

"Oh, he's a fellow I put into it—gave him a hand up. I told you all about him at the time."

"I dare say. I must have forgotten." Vainly she strained back among her memories. "But if you helped him, why does he make this return?"

"Probably some shyster lawyer got hold of him and talked him over. It's all rather technical and complicated. I thought that kind of thing bored you."

His wife felt a sting of compunction. Theoretically, she deprecated the American wife's detachment from her husband's professional interests, but in practice she had always found it difficult to

fix her attention on Boyne's report of the transactions in which his
varied interests involved him. Besides, she had felt during their
years of exile, that, in a community where the amenities of living
could be obtained only at the cost of efforts as arduous as her husband's professional labors, such brief leisure as he and she could
command should be used as an escape from immediate preoccupations, a flight to the life they always dreamed of living. Once or
twice, now that this new life had actually drawn its magic circle
about them, she had asked herself if she had done right; but hitherto such conjectures had been no more than the retrospective excursions of an active fancy. Now, for the first time, it startled her
a little to find how little she knew of the material foundation on
which her happiness was built.

She glanced at her husband, and was again reassured by the
composure of his face; yet she felt the need for more definite
grounds for her reassurance.

"But doesn't this suit worry you? Why have you never spoken
to me about it?"

He answered both questions at once. "I didn't speak of it at first
because it *did* worry me—annoyed me, rather. But it's all ancient
history now. Your correspondent must have got hold of a back
number of the *Sentinel*."

She felt a quick thrill of relief. "You mean it's over? He's lost his
case?"

There was a just perceptible delay in Boyne's reply. "The suit's
been withdrawn—that's all."

But she persisted, as if to exonerate herself from the inward
charge of being too easily put off. "Withdrawn it because he saw
he had no chance?"

"Oh, he had no chance," Boyne answered.

She was still struggling with a dimly felt perplexity at the back
of her thoughts.

"How long ago was it withdrawn?"

He paused, as if with a slight return to his former uncertainty.
"I've just had the news now; but I've been expecting it."

"Just now—in one of your letters?"

"Yes; in one of my letters."

She made no answer, and was aware only, after a short interval
of waiting, that he had risen, and strolling across the room, had

placed himself on the sofa at her side. She felt him, as he did so, pass an arm about her, she felt his hand seek hers and clasp it, and turning slowly, drawn by the warmth of his cheek, she met his smiling eyes.

"It's all right—it's all right?" she questioned, through the flood of her dissolving doubts; and "I give you my word it was never righter!" he laughed back at her, holding her close.

III

One of the strangest things she was afterward to recall out of all the next day's strangeness was the sudden and complete recovery of her sense of security.

It was in the air when she woke in her low-ceiled, dusky room; it went with her downstairs to the breakfast table, flashed out at her from the fire, and reduplicated itself from the flanks of the urn and the sturdy flutings of the Georgian teapot. It was as if in some roundabout way, all her diffused fears of the previous day, with their moment of sharp concentration about the newspaper article—as if this dim questioning of the future, and startled return upon the past, had between them liquidated the arrears of some haunting moral obligation. If she had indeed been careless of her husband's affairs, it was, her new state seemed to prove, because her faith in him instinctively justified such carelessness; and his right to her faith had now affirmed itself in the very face of menace and suspicion. She had never seen him more untroubled, more naturally and unconsciously himself, than after the cross-examination to which she had subjected him: it was almost as if he had been aware of her doubts, and had wanted the air cleared as much as she did.

It was as clear, thank heaven, as the bright outer light that surprised her almost with a touch of summer when she issued from the house for her daily round of the gardens. She had left Boyne at his desk, indulging herself, as she passed the library door, by a last peep at his quiet face, where he bent, pipe in mouth, above his papers; and now she had her own morning's task to perform. The task involved, on such charmed winter days, almost as much happy loitering about the different quarters of her domain as if

spring were already at work there. There were such endless possibilities still before her, such opportunities to bring out the latent
graces of the old place, without a single irreverent touch of alteration, that the winter was all too short to plan what spring and
autumn executed. And her recovered sense of safety gave, on this
particular morning, a peculiar zest to her progress through the
sweet still place. She went first to the kitchen garden, where the
espaliered pear trees drew complicated patterns on the walls, and
pigeons were fluttering and preening about the silvery-slated roof
on their cot. There was something wrong abut the piping of the
hothouse, and she was expecting an authority from Dorchester,
who was to drive out between trains and make a diagnosis of the
boiler. But when she dipped into the damp heat of the greenhouses, among the spiced scents and waxy pinks and reds of old-
fashioned exotics—even the flora of Lyng was in the note!—she
learned that the great man had not arrived, and, the day being too
rare to waste in an artificial atmosphere, she came out again and
paced along the springy turf of the bowling green to the gardens
behind the house. At their farther end rose a grass terrace, looking across the fish pond and yew hedges to the long house front
with its twisted chimney stacks and blue roof angles all drenched
in the pale gold moisture of the air.

Seen thus, across the level tracery of the gardens, it sent her,
from open windows and hospitably smoking chimneys, the look
of some warm human presence, of a mind slowly ripened on a
sunny wall of experience. She had never before had such a sense
of her intimacy with it, such a conviction that its secrets were all
beneficent, kept, as they said to children, "for one's good," such a
trust in its power to gather up her life and Ned's into the harmonious pattern of the long long story it sat there weaving in the sun.

She heard steps behind her, and turned, expecting to see the gardener accompanied by the engineer from Dorchester. But only one
figure was in sight, that of a youngish slightly built man, who, for
reasons she could not on the spot have given, did not remotely re-
semble her notion of an authority on hothouse boilers. The newcomer, on seeing her, lifted his hat, and paused with the air of a
gentleman—perhaps a traveler—who wishes to make it known
that his intrusion is involuntary. Lyng occasionally attracted the
more cultivated traveler, and Mary half expected to see the

stranger dissemble a camera, or justify his presence by producing it. But he made no gesture of any sort, and after a moment she asked, in a tone responding to the courteous hesitation of his attitude: "Is there anyone you wish to see?"

"I came to see Mr. Boyne," he answered. His intonation, rather than his accent, was faintly American, and Mary, at the note, looked at him more closely. The brim of his soft felt hat cast a shade on his face, which, thus obscured, wore to her shortsighted gaze a look of seriousness, as a person arriving on business, and civilly but firmly aware of his rights.

Past experience had made her equally sensible to such claims; but she was jealous of her husband's morning hours, and doubtful of his having given anyone the right to intrude on them.

"Have you an appointment with my husband?" she asked.

The visitor hesitated, as if unprepared for the question.

"I think he expects me," he replied.

It was Mary's turn to hesitate. "You see this is his time for work: he never sees anyone in the morning."

He looked at her a moment without answering; then, as if accepting her decision, he began to move away. As he turned, Mary saw him pause and glance up at the peaceful house front. Something in his air suggested weariness and disappointment, the dejection of the traveler who has come from far off and whose hours are limited by the timetable. It occurred to her that if this were the case her refusal might have made his errand vain, and a sense of compunction caused her to hasten after him.

"May I ask if you have come a long way?"

He gave her the same grave look. "Yes—I have come a long way."

"Then, if you'll go to the house, no doubt my husband will see you now. You'll find him in the library."

She did not know why she had added the last phrase, except from a vague impulse to atone for her previous inhospitality. The visitor seemed about to express his thanks, but her attention was distracted by the approach of the gardener with a companion who bore all the marks of being the expert from Dorchester.

"This way," she said, waving the stranger to the house; and an instant later she had forgotten him in the absorption of her meeting with the boiler maker.

The encounter led to such far-reaching results that the engineer ended by finding it expedient to ignore his train, and Mary was beguiled into spending the remainder of the morning in absorbed confabulation among the flower pots. When the colloquy ended, she was surprised to find that it was nearly luncheon time, and she half expected, as she hurried back to the house, to see her husband coming out to meet her. But she found no one in the court but an undergardener raking the gravel, and the hall, when she entered it, was so silent that she guessed Boyne to still be at work.

Not wishing to disturb him, she turned into the drawing room, and there, at her writing table, lost herself in renewed calculations of the outlay to which the morning's conference had pledged her. The fact that she could permit herself such follies had not yet lost its novelty; and somehow, in contrast to the vague fears of the previous days, it now seemed an element of her recovered security, of the sense that, as Ned had said, things in general had never been "righter."

She was still luxuriating in a lavish play of figures when the parlormaid, from the threshold, roused her with an inquiry as to the expediency of serving luncheon. It was one of their jokes that Trimmle announced luncheon as if she were divulging a state secret, and Mary, intent upon her papers, merely murmured an absent-minded assent.

She felt Trimmle wavering doubtfully on the threshold, as if in rebuke of such unconsidered assent; then her retreating steps sounded down the passage, and Mary, pushing away her papers, crossed the hall and went to the library door. It was still closed, and she wavered in her turn, disliking to disturb her husband, yet anxious that he should not exceed his usual measure of work. As she stood there, balancing her impulses, Trimmle returned with the announcement of luncheon, and Mary, thus impelled, opened the library door.

Boyne was not at his desk, and she peered about her, expecting to discover him before the bookshelves, somewhere down the length of the room; but her call brought no response, and gradually it became clear to her that he was not there.

She turned back to the parlormaid.

"Mr. Boyne must be upstairs. Please tell him that luncheon is ready."

Trimmle appeared to hesitate between the obvious duty of obedience and an equally obvious conviction of the foolishness of the
injunction laid on her. The struggle resulted in her saying: "If you
please, Madam, Mr. Boyne's not upstairs."

"Not in his room? Are you sure?"

"I'm sure, Madam."

Mary consulted the clock. "Where is he, then?"

"He's gone out," Trimmle announced, with a superior air of
one who has respectfully waited for the question that a well-
ordered mind would have put first.

Mary's conjecture had been right, then. Boyne must have gone
to the gardens to meet her, and since she had missed him, it was
clear that he had taken the shorter way by the south door, instead
of going round to the court. She crossed the hall to the French
window opening directly on the yew garden, but the parlormaid,
after another moment of inner conflict, decided to bring out:
"Please, Madam, Mr. Boyne didn't go that way."

Mary turned back. "Where *did* he go? And when?"

"He went out of the front door, up the drive, Madam." It was
a matter of principle with Trimmle never to answer more than one
question at a time.

"Up the drive? At this hour?" Mary went to the door herself,
and glanced across the court through the tunnel of bare limes. But
its perspective was as empty as when she had scanned it on entering.

"Did Mr. Boyne leave no message?"

Trimmle seemed to surrender herself to a last struggle with the
forces of chaos.

"No, Madam. He just went out with the gentleman."

"The gentleman? What gentleman?" Mary wheeled about, as if
to front this new factor.

"The gentleman who called, Madam," said Trimmle resignedly.

"When did a gentleman call? Do explain yourself, Trimmle!"

Only the fact that Mary was very hungry, and that she wanted
to consult her husband about the greenhouses, would have caused
her to lay so unusual an injunction on her attendant; and even
now she was detached enough to note in Trimmle's eye the dawning defiance of the respectful subordinate who has been pressed
too hard.

"I couldn't exactly say the hour, Madam, because I didn't let the gentleman in," she replied, with an air of discreetly ignoring the irregularity of her mistress's course.

"You didn't let him in?"

"No, Madam. When the bell rang I was dressing, and Agnes—"

"Go and ask Agnes, then," said Mary.

Trimmle still wore her look of patient magnanimity. "Agnes would not know, Madam, for she had unfortunately burnt her hand in trimming the wick of the new lamp from town"—Trimmle, as Mary was aware, had always been opposed to the new lamp—"and so Mrs. Dockett sent the kitchenmaid instead."

Mary looked again at the clock. "It's after two! Go and ask the kitchenmaid if Mr. Boyne left any word."

She went into luncheon without waiting, and Trimmle presently brought her there the kitchenmaid's statement that the gentleman had called about eleven o'clock, and that Mr. Boyne had gone out with him without leaving any message. The kitchenmaid did not even know the caller's name, for he had written it on a slip of paper, which he had folded and handed to her, with the injunction to deliver it at once to Mr. Boyne.

Mary finished her luncheon, still wondering, and when it was over, and Trimmle had brought the coffee to the drawing room, her wonder had deepened to a first faint tinge of disquietude. It was unlike Boyne to absent himself without explanation at so unwonted an hour, and the difficulty of identifying the visitor whose summons he had apparently obeyed made his disappearance the more unaccountable. Mary Boyne's experience as the wife of a busy engineer, subject to sudden calls and compelled to keep irregular hours, had trained her to the philosophic acceptance of surprises; but since Boyne's withdrawal from business he had adopted a Benedictine regularity of life. As if to make up for the dispersed and agitated years, with their "stand-up" lunches, and dinners rattled down to the joltings of the dining cars, he cultivated the last refinements of punctuality and monotony, discouraging his wife's fancy for the unexpected, and declaring that to a delicate taste there were indefinite gradations of pleasure in the recurrences of habit.

Still, since no life can completely defend itself from the unforeseen, it was evident that all Boyne's precautions would sooner or later prove unavailable, and Mary concluded that he had cut short a tiresome visit by walking with his caller to the station, or at least accompanying him for part of the way.

This conclusion relieved her from further preoccupation, and she went out herself to take up her conference with the gardener. Thence she walked to the village post office, a mile or so away; and when she turned toward home the early twilight was setting in.

She had taken a footpath across the downs, and as Boyne, meanwhile, had probably returned from the station by the high-road, there was little likelihood of their meeting. She felt sure, however, of his having reached the house before her; so sure that, when she entered it herself, without even pausing to inquire of Trimmle, she made directly for the library. But the library was still empty, and with an unwonted exactness of visual memory she observed that the papers on her husband's desk lay precisely as they had lain when she had gone in to call him to luncheon.

Then of a sudden she was seized by a vague dread of the unknown. She had closed the door behind her on entering, and as she stood alone in the long silent room, her dread seemed to take shape and sound, to be there breathing and lurking among the shadows. Her shortsighted eyes strained through them, half-discerning an actual presence, something aloof, that watched and knew; and in the recoil from that intangible presence she threw herself on the bell rope and gave it a sharp pull.

The sharp summons brought Trimmle in precipitately with a lamp, and Mary breathed again at this sobering reappearance of the usual.

"You may bring tea if Mr. Boyne is in," she said, to justify her ring.

"Very well, Madam. But Mr. Boyne is not in," said Trimmle, putting down the lamp.

"Not in? You mean he's come back and gone out again?"

"No, Madam. He's never been back."

The dread stirred again, and Mary knew that now it had her fast.

"Not since he went out with—the gentleman?"

"Not since he went out with the gentleman."

"But who *was* the gentleman?" Mary insisted, with the shrill note of someone trying to be heard through a confusion of noises.

"That I couldn't say, Madam." Trimmle, standing there by the lamp, seemed suddenly to grow less round and rosy, as though eclipsed by the same creeping shade of apprehension.

"But the kitchenmaid knows—wasn't it the kitchenmaid who let him in?"

"She doesn't know either, Madam, for he wrote his name on a folded paper."

Mary, through her agitation, was aware that they were both designating the unknown visitor by a vague pronoun, instead of the conventional formula which, till then, had kept their allusions within the bounds of conformity. And at the same moment her mind caught at the suggestion of the folded paper.

"But he must have a name! Where's the paper?"

She moved to the desk, and began to turn over the documents that littered it. The first that caught her eye was an unfinished letter in her husband's hand, with his pen lying across it, as though dropped there at a sudden summons.

"My dear Parvis"—who was Parvis?—"I have just received your letter announcing Elwell's death, and while I suppose there is now no further risk of trouble, it might be safer—"

She tossed the sheet aside, and continued her search; but no folded paper was discoverable among the letters and pages of manuscript which had been swept together in a heap, as if by a hurried or a startled gesture.

"But the kitchenmaid *saw* him. Send her here," she commanded, wondering at her dullness in not thinking sooner of so simple a solution.

Trimmle vanished in a flash, as if thankful to be out of the room, and when she reappeared, conducting the agitated underling, Mary had regained her self-possession, and had her questions ready.

The gentleman was a stranger, yes—that she understood. But what had he said? And, above all, what had he looked like? The first question was easily enough answered, for the disconcerting reason that he had said so little—had merely asked for Mr. Boyne, and scribbling something on a bit of paper, had requested that it should at once be carried in to him.

"Then you don't know what he wrote? You're not sure it *was* his name?"

The kitchenmaid was not sure, but supposed it was, since he had written it in answer to her inquiry as to whom she should announce.

"And when you carried that paper in to Mr. Boyne, what did he say?"

The kitchenmaid did not think that Mr. Boyne had said anything, but she could not be sure, for just as she had handed him the paper and he was opening it, she had become aware that the visitor had followed her into the library, and she had slipped out, leaving the two gentlemen together.

"But then, if you left them in the library, how do you know that they went out of the house?"

This question plunged the witness into momentary inarticulateness, from which she was rescued by Trimmle, who, by means of ingenious circumlocutions, elicited the statement that before she could cross the hall to the back passage she had heard the two gentlemen behind her, and had seen them go out of the front door together.

"Then, if you saw the strange gentleman twice, you must be able to tell me what he looked like."

But with this final challenge to her powers of expression it became clear that the limit of the kitchenmaid's endurance had been reached. The obligation of going to the front door to "show in" a visitor was in itself so subversive of the fundamental order of things that it had thrown her faculties into hopeless disarray, and she could only stammer out, after various panting efforts: "His hat, mum, was different-like, as you might say—"

"Different? How different?" Mary flashed out, her own mind, in the same instant, leaping back to an image left on it that morning, and then lost under layers of subsequent impressions.

"His hat had a wide brim, you mean, and his face was pale—a youngish face?" Mary pressed her, with a white-lipped intensity of interrogation. But if the kitchenmaid found any adequate answer to this challenge, it was swept away for her listener down the rushing current of her own convictions. The stranger—the stranger in the garden! Why had Mary not thought of him before? She needed no one now to tell her that it was he who had called for her husband and gone away with him. But who was he, and why had Boyne obeyed him?

IV

It leaped out at her suddenly, like a grin out of the dark, that they had often called England so little—"such a confoundedly hard place to get lost in."

A confoundedly hard place to get lost in! That had been her husband's phrase. And now, with the whole machinery of official investigation sweeping its flashlights from shore to shore, and across the dividing straits; now, with Boyne's name blazing from the walls of every town and village, his portrait (how that wrung her!) hawked up and down the country like the image of a hunted criminal; now the little compact populous island, so policed, surveyed and administered, revealed itself as a Sphinxlike guardian of abysmal mysteries, staring back into his wife's anguished eyes as if with the wicked joy of knowing something they would never know!

In the fortnight since Boyne's disappearance there had been no word of him, no trace of his movements. Even the usual misleading reports that raise expectancy in tortured bosoms had been few and fleeting. No one but the kitchenmaid had seen Boyne leave the house, and no one else had seen "the gentleman" who accompanied him. All inquiries in the neighborhood failed to elicit the memory of a stranger's presence that day in the neighborhood of Lyng. And no one had met Edward Boyne, either alone or in company, in any of the neighboring villages, or on the road across the downs, or at either of the local railway stations. The sunny English noon had swallowed him as completely as if he had gone out into Cimmerian night.

Mary, while every official means of investigation was working at its highest pressure, had ransacked her husband's papers for any trace of antecedent complications, of entanglements or obligations unknown to her, that might throw a ray into the darkness. But if any such had existed in the background of Boyne's life, they had vanished like the slip of paper on which the visitor had written his name. There remained no possible thread of guidance except—if it were indeed an exception—the letter which Boyne had apparently been in the art of writing when he received his mysterious summons. That letter, read and reread by his wife, and submitted by her to the police, yielded little enough to feed conjecture.

"I have just heard of Elwell's death, and while I suppose there is now no further risk of trouble, it might be safer—" That was all. The "risk of trouble" was easily explained by the newspaper clipping which had apprised Mary of the suit brought against her husband by one of his associates in the Blue Star enterprise. The only new information conveyed by the letter was the fact of its showing Boyne, when he wrote it, to be still apprehensive of the results of the suit, though he had told his wife that it had been withdrawn, and though the letter itself proved that the plaintiff was dead. It took several days of cabling to fix the identity of the "Parvis" to whom the fragment was addressed, but even after these inquiries had shown him to be a Waukesha lawyer, no new facts concerning the Elwell suit were elicited. He appeared to have had no direct concern in it, but to have been conversant with the facts merely as an acquaintance, and possible intermediary; and he declared himself unable to guess with what object Boyne intended to seek his assistance.

This negative information, sole fruit of the first fortnight's search, was not increased by a jot during the slow weeks that followed. Mary knew that the investigations were still being carried on, but she had a vague sense of their gradually slackening, as the actual march of time seemed to slacken. It was as though the days, flying horror-struck from the shrouded image of the one inscrutable day, gained assurance as the distance lengthened, till at last they fell back into their normal gait. And so with the human imaginations at work on the dark event. No doubt it occupied them still, but week by week and hour by hour it grew less absorbing, took up less space, was slowly but inevitably crowded out of the foreground of consciousness by the new problems perpetually bubbling up from the cloudy caldron of human experience.

Even Mary Boyne's consciousness gradually felt the same lowering of velocity. It still swayed with the incessant oscillations of conjecture; but they were slower, more rhythmical in their beat. There were even moments of weariness when, like the victim of some poison which leaves the brain clear, but holds the body motionless, she saw herself domesticated with the Horror, accepting its perpetual presence as one of the fixed conditions of life.

These moments lengthened into hours and days, till she passed into a phase of stolid acquiescence. She watched the routine of daily life with the incurious eye of a savage on whom the meaningless processes of civilization make but the faintest impression. She had come to regard herself as part of the routine, a spoke of the wheel, revolving with its motion; she felt almost like the furniture of the room in which she sat, an insensate object to be dusted and pushed about with the chairs and tables. And this deepening apathy held her fast at Lyng, in spite of the entreaties of friends and the usual medical recommendation of "change." Her friends supposed that her refusal to move was inspired by the belief that her husband would one day return to the spot from which he had vanished, and a beautiful legend grew up about this imaginary state of waiting. But in reality she had no such belief: the depths of anguish enclosing her were no longer lighted by flashes of hope. She was sure that Boyne would never come back, that he had gone out of her sight as completely as if Death itself had waited that day on the threshold. She had even renounced, one by one, the various theories as to his disappearance which had been advanced by the press, the police, and her own agonized imagination. In sheer lassitude her mind turned from these alternatives of horror, and sank back into the blank fact that he was gone.

No, she would never know what had become of him—no one would ever know. But the house *knew;* the library in which she spent her long lonely evenings knew. For it was here that the last scene had been enacted, here that the stranger had come, and spoken the word which had caused Boyne to rise and follow him. The floor she trod had felt his tread; the books on the shelves had seen his face; and there were moments when the intense consciousness of the old dusky walls seemed about to break out into some audible revelation of their secret. But the revelation never came, and she knew it would never come. Lyng was not one of the garrulous old houses that betray the secrets entrusted to them. Its very legend proved that it had always been the mute accomplice, the incorruptible custodian, of the mysteries it had surprised. And Mary Boyne, sitting face to face with its silence, felt the futility of seeking to break it by any human means.

V

"I don't say it *wasn't* straight, and yet I don't say it *was* straight. It was business."

Mary, at the words, lifted her head with a start, and looked intently at the speaker.

When, half an hour before, a card with "Mr. Parvis" on it had been brought up to her, she had been immediately aware that the name had been a part of her consciousness ever since she had read it at the head of Boyne's unfinished letter. In the library she had found awaiting her a small sallow man with a bald head and gold eyeglasses, and it sent a tremor through her to know that this was the person to whom her husband's last known thought had been directed.

Parvis, civilly, but without vain preamble—in the manner of a man who has his watch in his hand—had set forth the object of his visit. He had "run over" to England on business, and finding himself in the neighborhood of Dorchester, had not wished to leave it without paying his respects to Mrs. Boyne; and without asking her, if the occasion offered, what she meant to do about Bob Elwell's family.

The words touched the spring of some obscure dread in Mary's bosom. Did her visitor, after all, know what Boyne had meant by his unfinished phrase? She asked for an elucidation of his question, and noticed at once that he seemed surprised at her continued ignorance of the subject. Was it possible that she really knew as little as she said?

"I know nothing—you must tell me," she faltered out; and her visitor thereupon proceeded to unfold his story. It threw, even to her confused perceptions, and imperfectly initiated vision, a lurid glare on the whole hazy episode of the Blue Star Mine. Her husband had made his money in that brilliant speculation at the cost of "getting ahead" of someone less alert to seize the chance; and the victim of his ingenuity was young Robert Elwell, who had "put him on" to the Blue Star scheme.

Parvis, at Mary's first cry, had thrown her a sobering glance through his impartial glasses.

"Bob Elwell wasn't smart enough, that's all; if he had been, he might have turned round and served Boyne the same way. It's the kind of thing that happens every day in business. I guess it's what the scientists call the survival of the fittest—see?" said Mr. Parvis, evidently pleased with the aptness of his analogy.

Mary felt a physical shrinking from the next question she tried to frame: it was as though the words on her lips had a taste that nauseated her.

"But then—you accuse my husband of doing something dishonorable?"

Mr. Parvis surveyed the question dispassionately. "Oh, no, I don't. I don't even say it wasn't straight." He glanced up and down the long lines of books, as if one of them might have supplied him with the definition he sought. "I don't say it *wasn't* straight, and yet I don't say it *was* straight. It was business." After all, no definition in his category could be more comprehensive than that.

Mary sat staring at him with a look of terror. He seemed to her like the indifferent emissary of some evil power.

"But Mr. Elwell's lawyers apparently did not take your view, since I suppose the suit was withdrawn by their advice."

"Oh, yes; they knew he hadn't a leg to stand on, technically. It was when they advised him to withdraw the suit that he got desperate. You see, he'd borrowed most of the money he lost in the Blue Star, and he was up a tree. That's why he shot himself when they told him he had no show."

The horror was sweeping over Mary in great deafening waves.

"He shot himself? He killed himself because of *that*?"

"Well, he didn't kill himself, exactly. He dragged on two months before he died." Parvis emitted the statement as unemotionally as a gramophone grinding out its record.

"You mean that he tried to kill himself, and failed? And tried again?"

"Oh, he didn't have to *try* again," said Parvis grimly.

They sat opposite each other in silence, he swinging his eyeglasses thoughtfully about his finger, she, motionless, her arms stretched along her knees in an attitude of rigid tension.

"But if you knew all this," she began at length, hardly able to force her voice above a whisper, "how is it that when I wrote you at the time of my husband's disappearance you said you didn't understand his letter?"

Parvis received this without perceptible embarrassment: "Why, I didn't understand it—strictly speaking. And it wasn't the time to talk about it, if I had. The Elwell business was settled when the suit was withdrawn. Nothing I could have told you would have helped you to find your husband."

Mary continued to scrutinize him. "Then why are you telling me now?"

Still Parvis did not hesitate. "Well, to begin with, I supposed you knew more than you appear to—I mean about the circumstances of Elwell's death. And then people are talking of it now; the whole matter's been raked up again. And I thought if you didn't know you ought to."

She remained silent, and he continued: "You see, it's only come out lately what a bad state Elwell's affairs were in. His wife's a proud woman, and she fought on as long as she could, going out to work, and taking sewing at home when she got too sick— something with the heart, I believe. But she had his mother to look after, and the children, and she broke down under it, and finally had to ask for help. That called attention to the case, and the papers took it up, and a subscription was started. Everybody out there liked Bob Elwell, and most of the prominent names in the place are down on the list, and people began to wonder why—"

Parvis broke off to fumble in an inner pocket. "Here," he continued, "here's an account of the whole thing from the *Sentinel*—a little sensational, of course. But I guess you'd better look it over."

He held out a newspaper to Mary, who unfolded it slowly, remembering, as she did so, the evening when, in that same room, the perusal of a clipping from the *Sentinel* had first shaken the depths of her security.

As she opened the paper, her eyes, shrinking from the glaring headlines, "Widow of Boyne's Victim Forced to Appeal for Aid," ran down the column of text to two portraits inserted in it. The first was her husband's, taken from a photograph made the year they had come to England. It was the picture of him that she liked best, the one that stood on the writing table upstairs in her bedroom. As the eyes in the photograph met hers, she felt it would be impossible to read what was said of him, and closed her lids with the sharpness of the pain.

"I thought if you felt disposed to put your name down—" she heard Parvis continue.

She opened her eyes with an effort, and they fell on the other portrait. It was that of a youngish man, slightly built, with features somewhat blurred by the shadow of a projecting hat brim. Where had she seen that outline before? She stared at it confusedly, her heart hammering in her ears. Then she gave a cry.

"This is the man—the man who came for my husband!"

She heard Parvis start to his feet, and was dimly aware that she had slipped backward into the corner of the sofa, and that he was bending above her in alarm. She straightened herself, and reached out for the paper, which she had dropped.

"It's the man! I should know him anywhere!" she persisted in a voice that sounded to her own ears like a scream.

Parvis's answer seemed to come to her from far off, down endless fog-muffled windings.

"Mrs. Boyne, you're not very well. Shall I call somebody? Shall I get a glass of water?"

"No, no, no!" She threw herself toward him, her hand frantically clutching the newspaper. "I tell you, it's the man! I know him! He spoke to me in the garden!"

Parvis took the journal from her, directing his glasses to the portrait. "It can't be, Mrs. Boyne. It's Robert Elwell."

"Robert Elwell?" Her white stare seemed to travel into space. "Then it was Robert Elwell who came for him."

"Came for Boyne? The day he went away from here?" Parvis's voice dropped as hers rose. He bent over, laying a fraternal hand on her, as if to coax her gently back into her seat. "Why, Elwell was dead! Don't you remember?"

Mary sat with her eyes fixed on the picture, unconscious of what he was saying.

"Don't you remember Boyne's unfinished letter to me—the one you found on his desk that day? It was written just after he'd heard of Elwell's death." She noticed an odd shake in Parvis's unemotional voice. "Surely you remember!" he urged her.

Yes, she remembered: that was the profoundest horror of it. Elwell had died the day before her husband's disappearance; and this was Elwell's portrait; and it was the portrait of the man who had spoken to her in the garden. She lifted her head and looked slowly about the library. The library could have borne witness that it was also the portrait of the man who had come in that day to call Boyne from his unfinished letter. Through the misty surgings of her brain she heard the faint boom of half-forgotten words—words spoken by Alida Stair on the lawn at Pangbourne before Boyne and his wife had ever seen the house at Lyng, or had imagined that they might one day live there.

"This was the man who spoke to me," she repeated.

She looked again at Parvis. He was trying to conceal his disturbance under what he probably imagined to be an expression of indulgent commiseration; but the edges of his lips were blue. "He thinks me mad; but I'm not mad," she reflected; and suddenly there flashed upon her a way of justifying her strange affirmation.

She sat quiet, controlling the quiver of her lips, and waiting till she could trust her voice; then she said, looking straight at Parvis: "Will you answer me one question, please? When was it that Robert Elwell tried to kill himself?"

"When—when?" Parvis stammered.

"Yes; the date. Please try to remember."

She saw that he was growing still more afraid of her. "I have a reason," she insisted.

"Yes, yes. Only I can't remember. About two months before, I should say."

"I want the date," she repeated.

Parvis picked up the newspaper. "We might see here," he said, still humoring her. He ran his eyes down the page. "Here it is. Last October—the—"

She caught the words from him. "The 20th, wasn't it?" With a sharp look at her, he verified. "Yes, the 20th. Then you *did* know?"

"I know now." Her gaze continued to travel past him. "Sunday, the 20th—that was the day he came first."

Parvis's voice was almost inaudible. "Came *here* first?"

"Yes."

"You saw him twice, then?"

"Yes, twice." She just breathed it at him. "He came first on the 20th of October. I remember the date because it was the day we went up Meldon Steep for the first time." She felt a faint gasp of inward laughter at the thought that but for that she might have forgotten.

Parvis continued to scrutinize her, as if trying to intercept her gaze.

"We saw him from the roof," she went on. "He came down the lime avenue toward the house. He was dressed just as he is in that picture. My husband saw him first. He was frightened, and ran down ahead of me; but there was no one there. He had vanished."

"Elwell had vanished?" Parvis faltered.

"Yes." Their two whispers seemed to grope for each other. "I couldn't think what had happened. I see now. He *tried* to come then; but he wasn't dead enough—he couldn't reach us. He had to wait for two months to die; and then he came back again—and Ned went with him."

She nodded at Parvis with the look of triumph of a child who has worked out a difficult puzzle. But suddenly she lifted her hands with a desperate gesture, pressing them to her temples.

"Oh, my God! I sent him to Ned—I told him where to go! I sent him to this room!" she screamed.

She felt the walls of books rush toward her, like inward falling ruins; and she heard Parvis, a long way off, through the ruins, crying to her, and struggling to get at her. But she was numb to his touch, she did not know what he was saying. Through the tumult she heard but one clear note, the voice of Alida Stair, speaking on the lawn at Pangbourne.

"You won't know till afterward," it said. "You won't know till long, long afterward."

THE EYES

We had been put in the mood for ghosts, that evening, after an excellent dinner at our old friend Culwin's, by a tale of Fred Murchard's—the narrative of a strange personal visitation.

Seen through the haze of our cigars, and by the drowsy gleam of a coal fire, Culwin's library, with its oak walls and dark old bindings, made a good setting for such evocations; and ghostly experiences at first hand being, after Murchard's opening, the only kind acceptable to us, we proceeded to take stock of our group and tax each member for a contribution. There were eight of us, and seven contrived, in a manner more or less adequate, to fulfill the condition imposed. It surprised us all to find that we could muster such a show of supernatural impressions, for none of us, excepting Murchard himself and young Phil Frenham—whose story was the slightest of the lot—had the habit of sending our souls into the invisible. So that, on the whole, we had every reason to be proud of our seven "exhibits," and none of us would have dreamed of expecting an eighth from our host.

Our old friend, Mr. Andrew Culwin, who had sat back in his armchair, listening and blinking through the smoke circles with the cheerful tolerance of a wise old idol, was not the kind of man likely to be favored with such contacts, though he had imagination enough to enjoy, without envying, the superior privileges of his guests. By age and by education he belonged to the stout Positivist tradition, and his habit of thought had been formed in the days of the epic struggle between physics and metaphysics. But he had been, then and always, essentially a spectator, a humorous detached observer of the immense muddled variety show of life, slipping out of his seat now and then for a brief dip into the convivialities at the back of the house, but never, as far as one knew, showing the least desire to jump on the stage and do a "turn."

Among his contemporaries there lingered a vague tradition of his having, at a remote period, and in a romantic clime, been wounded in a duel; but this legend no more tallied with what we younger men knew of his character than my mother's assertion that he had once been "a charming little man with nice eyes" corresponded to any possible reconstitution of his physiognomy.

"He never can have looked like anything but a bundle of sticks," Murchard had once said of him. "Or a phosphorescent log, rather," someone else amended; and we recognized the happiness of this description of his small squat trunk, with the red blink of the eyes in a face like mottled bark. He had always been possessed of a leisure which he had nursed and protected, instead of squandering it in vain activities. His carefully guarded hours had been devoted to the cultivation of a fine intelligence and a few judiciously chosen habits; and none of the disturbances common to human experience seemed to have crossed his sky. Nevertheless, his dispassionate survey of the universe had not raised his opinion of that costly experiment, and his study of the human race seemed to have resulted in the conclusion that all men were superfluous, and women necessary only because someone had to do the cooking. On the importance of this point his convictions were absolute, and gastronomy was the only science which he revered as a dogma. It must be owned that his little dinners were a strong argument in favor of this view, besides being a reason—though not the main one—for the fidelity of his friends.

Mentally be exercised a hospitality less seductive but no less stimulating. His mind was like a forum, or some open meeting place for the exchange of ideas: somewhat cold and drafty, but light, spacious and orderly—a kind of academic grove from which all the leaves have fallen. In this privileged area a dozen of us were wont to stretch our muscles and expand our lungs; and, as if to prolong as much as possible the tradition of what we felt to be a vanishing institution, one or two neophytes were now and then added to our band.

Young Phil Frenham was the last, and the most interesting, of these recruits, and a good example of Murchard's somewhat morbid assertion that our old friend "liked 'em juicy." It was indeed a

fact that Culwin, for all his dryness, specially tasted the lyric qualities in youth. As he was far too good an Epicurean to nip the
flowers of soul which he gathered for his garden, his friendship
was not a disintegrating influence: on the contrary, it forced the
young idea to robuster bloom. And in Phil Frenham he had a
good subject for experimentation. The boy was really intelligent,
and the soundness of his nature was like the pure paste under a
fine glaze. Culwin had fished him out of a fog of family dullness,
and pulled him up to a peak in Darien; and the adventure hadn't
hurt him a bit. Indeed, the skill with which Culwin had contrived
to stimulate his curiosities without robbing them of their bloom
of awe seemed to me a sufficient answer to Murchard's ogreish
metaphor. There was nothing hectic in Frenham's efflorescence,
and his old friend had not laid even a finger tip on the sacred stu-
pidities. One wanted no better proof of that than the fact that
Frenham still reverenced them in Culwin.

"There's a side of him you fellows don't see. *I* believe that story
about the duel!" he declared; and it was of the very essence of this
belief that it should impel him—just as our little party was dis-
persing—to turn back to our host with the joking demand: "And
now you've got to tell us about *your* ghost!"

The outer door had closed on Murchard and the others; only
Frenham and I remained; and the devoted servant who presided
over Culwin's destinies, having brought a fresh supply of soda water, had been laconically ordered to bed.

Culwin's sociability was a night-blooming flower, and we knew
that he expected the nucleus of his group to tighten around him
after midnight. But Frenham's appeal seemed to disconcert him
comically, and he rose from the chair in which he had just reseated
himself after his farewells in the hall.

"*My* ghost? Do you suppose I'm fool enough to go to the expense of keeping one of my own, when there are so many charming ones in my friends' closets? Take another cigar," he said,
revolving toward me with a laugh.

Frenham laughed too, pulling up his slender height before the
chimney piece as he turned to face his short bristling friend.

"Oh," he said, "you'd never be content to share if you met one
you really liked."

Culwin had dropped back into his armchair, his shock head

embedded in the hollow of worn leather, his little eyes glimmering over a fresh cigar.

"Liked—*liked?* Good Lord!" he growled.

"Ah, you *have,* then!" Frenham pounced on him in the same instant, with a side glance of victory at me; but Culwin cowered gnomelike among his cushions, dissembling himself in a protective cloud of smoke.

"What's the use of denying it? You've seen everything, so of course you've seen a ghost!" his young friend persisted, talking intrepidly into the cloud. "Or, if you haven't seen one, it's only because you've seen two!"

The form of the challenge seemed to strike our host. He shot his head out of the mist with a queer tortoise-like motion he sometimes had, and blinked approvingly at Frenham.

"That's it," he flung at us on a shrill jerk of laughter; "it's only because I've seen two!"

The words were so unexpected that they dropped down and down into a deep silence, while we continued to stare at each other over Culwin's head, and Culwin stared at his ghosts. At length Frenham, without speaking, threw himself into the chair on the other side of the hearth, and leaned forward with his listening smile. . . .

II

"Oh, of course they're not show ghosts—a collector wouldn't think anything of them. . . . Don't let me raise your hopes . . . their one merit is their numerical strength: the exceptional fact of their being *two.* But, as against this, I'm bound to admit that at any moment I could probably have exorcised them both by asking my doctor for a prescription, or my oculist for a pair of spectacles. Only, as I never could make up my mind whether to go to the doctor or the oculist—whether I was afflicted by an optical or a digestive delusion—I left them to pursue their interesting double life, though at times they made mine exceedingly uncomfortable. . . .

"Yes—uncomfortable; and you know how I hate to be uncomfortable! But it was part of my stupid pride, when the thing began,

not to admit that I could be disturbed by the trifling matter of seeing two.

"And then I'd no reason, really, to suppose I was ill. As far as I
knew I was simply bored—horribly bored. But it was part of my
boredom—I remember—that I was feeling so uncommonly well,
and didn't know how on earth to work off my surplus energy. I
had come back from a long journey—down in South America and
Mexico—and had settled down for the winter near New York
with an old aunt who had known Washington Irving and corresponded with N. P. Willis. She lived, not far from Irvington, in a
damp Gothic villa overhung by Norway spruces and looking exactly like a memorial emblem done in hair. Her personal appearance was in keeping with this image, and her own hair—of which
there was little left—might have been sacrificed to the manufacture of the emblem.

"I had just reached the end of an agitated year, with considerable arrears to make up in money and emotion; and theoretically
it seemed as though my aunt's mild hospitality would be as bene-
ficial to my nerves as to my purse. But the deuce of it was that as
soon as I felt myself safe and sheltered my energy began to revive;
and how was I to work it off inside of a memorial emblem? I had,
at that time, the illusion that sustained intellectual effort could engage a man's whole activity; and I decided to write a great book—
I forget about what. My aunt, impressed by my plan, gave up to
me her Gothic library, filled with classics bound in black cloth and
daguerreotypes of faded celebrities; and I sat down at my desk to
win myself a place among their number. And to facilitate my task
she lent me a cousin to copy my manuscript.

"The cousin was a nice girl, and I had an idea that a nice girl
was just what I needed to restore my faith in human nature, and
principally in myself. She was neither beautiful nor intelligent—
poor Alice Nowell!—but it interested me to see any woman content to be so uninteresting, and I wanted to find out the secret of
her content. In doing this I handled it rather rashly, and put it out
of joint—oh, just for a moment! There's no fatuity in telling you
this, for the poor girl had never seen anyone but cousins. . . .

"Well, I was sorry for what I'd done, of course, and confoundedly bothered as to how I should put it straight. She was staying
in the house, and one evening, after my aunt had gone to bed, she

came down to the library to fetch a book she'd mislaid, like any artless heroine, on the shelves behind us. She was pink-nosed and flustered, and it suddenly occurred to me that her hair, though it was fairly thick and pretty, would look exactly like my aunt's when she grew older. I was glad I had noticed this, for it made it easier for me to decide to do what was right; and when I had found the book she hadn't lost I told her I was leaving for Europe that week.

"Europe was terribly far off in those days, and Alice knew at once what I meant. She didn't take it in the least as I'd expected— it would have been easier if she had. She held her book very tight, and turned away a moment to wind up the lamp on my desk—it had a ground-glass shade with vine leaves, and glass drops around the edge, I remember. Then she came back, held out her hand, and said: 'Good-bye.' And as she said it she looked straight at me and kissed me. I had never felt anything as fresh and shy and brave as her kiss. It was worse than any reproach, and it made me ashamed to deserve a reproach from her. I said to myself: 'I'll marry her, and when my aunt dies she'll leave us this house, and I'll sit here at the desk and go on with my book; and Alice will sit over there with her embroidery and look at me as she's looking now. And life will go on like that for any number of years.' The prospect frightened me a little, but at the time it didn't frighten me as much as doing anything to hurt her; and ten minutes later she had my seal ring on her finger, and my promise that when I went abroad she should go with me.

"You'll wonder why I'm enlarging on this incident. It's because the evening on which it took place was the very evening on which I first saw the queer sight I've spoken of. Being at that time an ardent believer in a necessary sequence between cause and effect, I naturally tried to trace some kind of link between what had just happened to me in my aunt's library, and what was to happen a few hours later on the same night; and so the coincidence between the two events always remained in my mind.

"I went up to bed with rather a heavy heart, for I was bowed under the weight of the first good action I had ever consciously committed; and young as I was, I saw the gravity of my situation. Don't imagine from this that I had hitherto been an instrument of destruction. I had been merely a harmless young man, who had followed his bent and declined all collaboration with Providence. Now I had suddenly undertaken to promote the moral order of the world, and I felt a good deal like the trustful spectator who has given his gold watch to the conjurer, and doesn't know in what shape he'll get it back when the trick is over. . . . Still, a glow of self-righteousness tempered my fears, and I said to myself as I undressed that when I'd got used to being good it probably wouldn't make me as nervous as it did at the start. And by the time I was in bed, and had blown out my candle, I felt that I really *was* getting used to it, and that, as far as I'd got, it was not unlike sinking down into one of my aunt's very softest wool mattresses.

"I closed my eyes on this image, and when I opened them it must have been a good deal later, for my room had grown cold, and intensely still. I was waked by the queer feeling we all know—the feeling that there was something in the room that hadn't been there when I fell asleep. I sat up and strained my eyes into the darkness. The room was pitch black, and at first I saw nothing; but gradually a vague glimmer at the foot of the bed turned into two eyes staring back at me. I couldn't distinguish the features attached to them, but as I looked the eyes grew more and more distinct: they gave out a light of their own.

"The sensation of being thus gazed at was far from pleasant, and you might suppose that my first impulse would have been to jump out of bed and hurl myself on the invisible figure attached to the eyes. But it wasn't—my impulse was simply to lie still. . . . I can't say whether this was due to an immediate sense of the uncanny nature of the apparition—to the certainty that if I did jump out of bed I should hurl myself on nothing—or merely to the benumbing effect of the eyes themselves. They were the very worst eyes I've ever seen: a man's eyes—but what a man! My first thought was that he must be frightfully old. The orbits were sunk, and the thick red-lined lids hung over the eyeballs like blinds of which the cords are broken. One lid drooped a little lower than the other, with the effect of a crooked leer; and between these folds of flesh, with their scant bristle of lashes, the eyes themselves, small glassy disks with an agatelike rim, looked like sea pebbles in the grip of a starfish.

"But the age of the eyes was not the most unpleasant thing about them. What turned me sick was their expression of vicious security. I don't know how else to describe the fact that they seemed to belong to a man who had done a lot of harm in his life, but had always kept just inside the danger lines. They were not the eyes of a coward, but of someone much too clever to take risks; and my gorge rose at their look of base astuteness. Yet even that wasn't the worst; for as we continued to scan each other I saw in them a tinge of derision, and felt myself to be its object.

"At that I was seized by an impulse of rage that jerked me to my feet and pitched me straight at the unseen figure. But of course there wasn't any figure there, and my fists struck at emptiness. Ashamed and cold, I groped about for a match and lit the candles. The room looked just as usual—as I had known it would; and I crawled back to bed, and blew out the lights.

"As soon as the room was dark again the eyes reappeared; and I now applied myself to explaining them on scientific principles. At first I thought the illusion might have been caused by the glow of the last embers in the chimney; but the fireplace was on the other side of my bed, and so placed that the fire could not be reflected in my toilet glass, which was the only mirror in the room. Then it struck me that I might have been tricked by the reflection of the embers in some polished bit of wood or metal; and though I couldn't discover any object of the sort in my line of vision, I got up again, groped my way to the hearth, and covered what was left of the fire. But as soon as I was back in bed the eyes were back at its foot.

"They were an hallucination, then: that was plain. But the fact that they were not due to any external dupery didn't make them a bit pleasanter. For if they were a projection of my inner consciousness, what the deuce was the matter with that organ? I had gone deeply enough into the mystery of morbid pathological states to picture the conditions under which an exploring mind might lay itself open to such a midnight admonition; but I couldn't fit it to my present case. I had never felt more normal, mentally and physically; and the only unusual fact in my situation—that of having assured the happiness of an amiable girl—did not seem of a kind to summon unclean spirits about my pillow. But there were the eyes still looking at me.

"I shut mine, and tried to evoke a vision of Alice Nowell's. They were not remarkable eyes, but they were as wholesome as fresh

water, and if she had had more imagination—or longer lashes—
their expression might have been interesting. As it was, they did
not prove very efficacious, and in a few moments I perceived that
they had mysteriously changed into the eyes at the foot of the bed.
It exasperated me more to feel these glaring at me through my
shut lids than to see them, and I opened my eyes again and looked
straight into their hateful stare. . . .

"And so it went on all night. I can't tell you what that night was
like, nor how long it lasted. Have you ever lain in bed, hopelessly
wide awake, and tried to keep your eyes shut, knowing that if you
opened 'em you'd see something you dreaded and loathed? It
sounds easy, but it's devilishly hard. Those eyes hung there and
drew me. I had the *vertige de l'abîme*,[1] and their red lids were the
edge of my abyss. . . . I had known nervous hours before: hours
when I'd felt the wind of danger in my neck; but never this kind
of strain. It wasn't that the eyes were awful; they hadn't the
majesty of the powers of darkness. But they had—how shall I
say?—a physical effect that was the equivalent of a bad smell:
their look left a smear like a snail's. And I didn't see what business
they had with me, anyhow—and I stared and stared, trying to find
out.

"I don't know what effect they were trying to produce; but the
effect they *did* produce was that of making me pack my portmanteau and bolt to town early the next morning. I left a note for my
aunt, explaining that I was ill and had gone to see my doctor; and
as a matter of fact I did feel uncommonly ill—the night seemed to
have pumped all the blood out of me. But when I reached town I
didn't go to the doctor's. I went to a friend's rooms, and threw
myself on a bed, and slept for ten heavenly hours. When I woke it
was the middle of the night, and I turned cold at the thought of
what might be waiting for me. I sat up, shaking, and stared into
the darkness; but there wasn't a break in its blessed surface, and
when I saw that the eyes were not there I dropped back into another long sleep.

"I had left no word for Alice when I fled, because I meant to go
back the next morning. But the next morning I was too exhausted
to stir. As the day went on the exhaustion increased, instead of
wearing off like the fatigue left by an ordinary night of insomnia:
the effect of the eyes seemed to be cumulative, and the thought of

seeing them again grew intolerable. For two days I fought my dread; and on the third evening I pulled myself together and decided to go back the next morning. I felt a good deal happier as soon as I'd decided, for I knew that my abrupt disappearance, and the strangeness of my not writing, must have been very distressing to poor Alice. I went to bed with an easy mind, and fell asleep at once; but in the middle of the night I woke, and there were the eyes. . . .

"Well, I simply couldn't face them; and instead of going back to my aunt's I bundled a few things into a trunk and jumped aboard the first steamer for England. I was so dead tired when I got on board that I crawled straight into my berth, and slept most of the way over; and I can't tell you the bliss it was to wake from those long dreamless stretches and look fearlessly into the dark, *knowing* that I shouldn't see the eyes. . . .

"I stayed abroad for a year, and then I stayed for another; and during that time I never had a glimpse of them. That was enough reason for prolonging my stay if I'd been on a desert island. Another was, of course, that I had perfectly come to see, on the voyage over, the complete impossibility of my marrying Alice Nowell. The fact that I had been so slow in making this discovery annoyed me, and made me want to avoid explanations. The bliss of escaping at one stroke from the eyes, and from this other embarrassment, gave my freedom an extraordinary zest; and the longer I savored it the better I liked its taste.

"The eyes had burned such a hole in my consciousness that for a long time I went on puzzling over the nature of the apparition, and wondering if it would ever come back. But as time passed I lost this dread, and retained only the precision of the image. Then that faded in its turn.

"The second year found me settled in Rome, where I was planning, I believe, to write another great book—a definitive work on Etruscan influences in Italian art. At any rate, I'd found some pretext of the kind for taking a sunny apartment in the Piazza di Spagna and dabbling about in the Forum; and there, one morning, a charming youth came to me. As he stood there in the warm light, slender and smooth and hyacinthine, he might have stepped from a ruined altar—one to Antinous, say; but he'd come instead from New York, with a letter from (of all people) Alice Nowell.

The letter—the first I'd had from her since our break—was simply a line introducing her young cousin, Gilbert Noyes, and appealing to me to befriend him. It appeared, poor lad, that he 'had talent,' and 'wanted to write'; and, an obdurate family having insisted that his calligraphy should take the form of double entry, Alice had intervened to win him six months' respite, during which he was to travel abroad on a meager pittance, and somehow prove his ability to increase it by his pen. The quaint conditions of the test struck me first: it seemed about as conclusive as a medieval 'ordeal.' Then I was touched by her having sent him to me. I had always wanted to do her some service, to justify myself in my own eyes rather than hers; and here was a beautiful occasion.

"I imagine it's safe to lay down the general principle that pre-destined geniuses don't, as a rule, appear before one in the spring sunshine of the Forum looking like one of its banished gods. At any rate, poor Noyes wasn't a predestined genius. But he *was* beautiful to see, and charming as a comrade. It was only when he began to talk literature that my heart failed me. I knew all the symptoms so well—the things he had 'in him,' and the things out-side him that impinged! There's the real test, after all. It was always—punctually, inevitably, with the inexorableness of a me-chanical law—it was *always* the wrong thing that struck him. I grew to find a certain fascination in deciding in advance exactly which wrong thing he'd select; and I acquired an astonishing skill at the game. . . .

"The worst of it was that his *bêtise*[2] wasn't of the too obvious sort. Ladies who met him at picnics thought him intellectual; and even at dinners he passed for clever. I, who had him under the mi-croscope, fancied now and then that he might develop some kind of a slim talent, something that he could make 'do' and be happy on; and wasn't that, after all, what I was concerned with? He was so charming—he continued to be so charming—that he called forth all my charity in support of this argument; and for the first few months I really believed there was a chance for him. . . .

"Those months were delightful. Noyes was constantly with me, and the more I saw of him the better I liked him. His stupidity was a natural grace—it was as beautiful, really, as his eyelashes. And he was so gay, so affectionate, and so happy with me, that telling him the truth would have been about as pleasant as slitting the throat of some gentle animal. At first I used to wonder what had put into that radiant head the detestable delusion that it held a brain. Then I began to see that it was simply protective mimicry—an instinctive ruse to get away from family life and an office desk. Not that Gilbert didn't—dear lad!—believe in himself. There wasn't a trace of hypocrisy in him. He was sure that his 'call' was irresistible, while to me it was the saving grace of his situation that it *wasn't,* and that a little money, a little leisure, a little pleasure would have turned him into an inoffensive idler. Unluckily, however, there was no hope of money, and with the alternative of the office desk before him he couldn't postpone his attempt at literature. The stuff he turned out was deplorable, and I see now that I knew it from the first. Still, the absurdity of deciding a man's whole future on a first trial seemed to justify me in withholding my verdict, and perhaps even in encouraging him a little, on the ground that the human plant generally needs warmth to flower.

"At any rate, I proceeded on that principle, and carried it to the point of getting his term of probation extended. When I left Rome he went with me, and we idled away a delicious summer between Capri and Venice. I said to myself: 'If he has anything in him, it will come out now,' and it *did*. He was never more enchanting and enchanted. There were moments of our pilgrimage when beauty born of murmuring sound seemed actually to pass into his face—but only to issue forth in a flood of the palest ink. . . .

"Well, the time came to turn off the tap; and I knew there was no hand but mine to do it. We were back in Rome, and I had taken him to stay with me, not wanting him to be alone in his *pension* when he had to face the necessity of renouncing his ambition. I hadn't, of course, relied solely on my own judgment in deciding to advise him to drop literature. I had sent his stuff to various people—editors and critics—and they had always sent it back with the same chilling lack of comment. Really there was nothing on earth to say.

"I confess I never felt more shabby than I did on the day when I decided to have it out with Gilbert. It was well enough to tell myself that it was my duty to knock the poor boy's hopes into splinters—but I'd like to know what act of gratuitous cruelty hasn't been justified on that plea? I've always shrunk from usurping the functions of Providence, and when I have to exercise them

I decidedly prefer that it shouldn't be on an errand of destruction. Besides, in the last issue, who was I to decide, even after a year's trial, if poor Gilbert had it in him or not?

"The more I looked at the part I'd resolved to play, the less I liked it; and I liked it still less when Gilbert sat opposite me, with his head thrown back in the lamplight, just as Phil's is now. . . . I'd been going over his last manuscript, and he knew it, and he knew that his future hung on my verdict—we'd tacitly agreed to that. The manuscript lay between us, on my table—a novel, his first novel, if you please!—and he reached over and laid his hand on it, and looked up at me with all his life in the look.

"I stood up and cleared my throat, trying to keep my eyes away from his face and on the manuscript.

"'The fact is, my dear Gilbert,' I began—

"I saw him turn pale, but he was up and facing me in an instant.

"'Oh, look here, don't take on so, my dear fellow! I'm not so awfully cut up as all that!' His hands were on my shoulders, and he was laughing down on me from his full height, with a kind of mortally stricken gaiety that drove the knife into my side.

"He was too beautifully brave for me to keep up any humbug about my duty. And it came over me suddenly how I should hurt others in hurting him; myself first, since sending him home meant losing him; but more particularly poor Alice Nowell, to whom I had so longed to prove my good faith and my desire to serve her. It really seemed like failing her twice to fail Gilbert.

"But my intuition was like one of those lightning flashes that encircle the whole horizon, and in the same instant I saw what I might be letting myself in for if I didn't tell the truth. I said to myself: 'I shall have him for life'—and I'd never yet seen anyone, man or woman, whom I was quite sure of wanting on those terms. Well, this impulse of egotism decided me. I was ashamed of it, and to get away from it I took a leap that landed me straight in Gilbert's arms.

"'The thing's all right, and you're all wrong!' I shouted up at him; and as he hugged me, and I laughed and shook in his clutch, I had for a minute the sense of self-complacency that is supposed to attend the footsteps of the just. Hang it all, making people happy *has* its charms.

"Gilbert, of course, was for celebrating his emancipation in some spectacular manner; but I sent him away alone to explode his emotions, and went to bed to sleep off mine. As I undressed I began to wonder what their aftertaste would be—so many of the finest don't keep! Still, I wasn't sorry, and I meant to empty the bottle, even if it *did* turn a trifle flat.

"After I got into bed I lay for a long time smiling at the memory of his eyes—his blissful eyes. . . . Then I fell asleep, and when I woke the room was deathly cold, and I sat up with a jerk—and there were *the other eyes*. . . .

"It was three years since I'd seen them, but I'd thought of them so often that I fancied they could never take me unawares again. Now, with their red sneer on me, I knew that I had never really believed they would come back, and that I was as defenceless as ever against them . . . As before, it was the insane irrelevance of their coming that made it so horrible. What the deuce were they after, to leap out at me at such a time? I had lived more or less carelessly in the years since I'd seen them, though my worst indiscretions were not dark enough to invite the searchings of their infernal glare; but at this particular moment I was really in what might have been called a state of grace; and I can't tell you how the fact added to their horror. . . .

"But it's not enough to say they were as bad as before: they were worse. Worse by just so much as I'd learned of life in the interval; by all the damnable implications my wider experience read into them. I saw now what I hadn't seen before: that they were eyes which had grown hideous gradually, which had built up their baseness coral-wise, bit by bit, out of a series of small turpitudes slowly accumulated through the industrious years. Yes—it came to me that what made them so bad was that they'd grown bad so slowly. . . .

"There they hung in the darkness, their swollen lids dropped across the little watery bulbs rolling loose in the orbits, and the puff of flesh making a muddy shadow underneath—and as their stare moved with my movements, there came over me a sense of their tacit complicity, of a deep hidden understanding between us that was worse than the first shock of their strangeness. Not that I understood them; but that they made it so clear that someday I should. . . . Yes, that was the worst part of it, decidedly; and it was the feeling that became stronger each time they came back. . . .

"For they got into the damnable habit of coming back. They reminded me of vampires with a taste for young flesh, they seemed so to gloat over the taste of a good conscience. Every night for a month they came to claim their morsel of mine: since I'd made Gilbert happy they simply wouldn't loosen their fangs. The coincidence almost made me hate him, poor lad, fortuitous as I felt it to be. I puzzled over it a good deal, but couldn't find any hint of an explanation except in the chance of his association with Alice Nowell. But then the eyes had let up on me the moment I had abandoned her, so they could hardly be the emissaries of a woman scorned, even if one could have pictured poor Alice charging such spirits to avenge her. That set me thinking, and I began to wonder if they would let up on me if I abandoned Gilbert. The temptation was insidious, and I had to stiffen myself against it; but really, dear boy! he was too charming to be sacrificed to such demons. And so, after all, I never found out what they wanted. . . ."

III

The fire crumbled, sending up a flash which threw into relief the narrator's gnarled face under its grey-black stubble. Pressed into the hollow of the chair back, it stood out an instant like an intaglio of yellowish red-veined stone, with spots of enamel for the eyes; then the fire sank and it became once more a dim Rembrandtish blur.

Phil Frenham, sitting in a low chair on the opposite side of the hearth, one long arm propped on the table behind him, one hand supporting his thrown-back head, and his eyes fixed on his old friend's face, had not moved since the tale began. He continued to maintain his silent immobility after Culwin had ceased to speak, and it was I who, with a vague sense of disappointment at the sudden drop of the story, finally asked: "But how long did you keep on seeing them?"

Culwin, so sunk into his chair that he seemed like a heap of his own empty clothes, stirred a little, as if in surprise at my question. He appeared to have half-forgotten what he had been telling us.

"How long? Oh, off and on all that winter. It was infernal. I never got used to them. I grew really ill."

Frenham shifted his attitude, and as he did so his elbow struck against a small mirror in a bronze frame standing on the table behind him. He turned and changed its angle slightly; then he resumed his former attitude, his dark head thrown back on his lifted palm, his eyes intent on Culwin's face. Something in his silent gaze embarrassed me, and as if to divert attention from it I pressed on with another question:

"And you never tried sacrificing Noyes?"

"Oh, no. The fact is I didn't have to. He did it for me, poor boy!"

"Did it for you? How do you mean?"

"He wore me out—wore everybody out. He kept on pouring out his lamentable twaddle, and hawking it up and down the place till be became a thing of terror. I tried to wean him from writing—oh, ever so gently, you understand, by throwing him with agreeable people, giving him a chance to make himself felt, to come to a sense of what he *really* had to give. I'd foreseen this solution from the beginning—felt sure that, once the first ardor of authorship was quenched, he'd drop into his place as a charming parasitic thing, the kind of chronic Cherubino[3] for whom, in old societies, there's always a seat at table, and a shelter behind the ladies' skirts. I saw him take his place as 'the poet': the poet who doesn't write. One knows the type in every drawing room. Living in that way doesn't cost much—I'd worked it all out in my mind, and felt sure that, with a little help, he could manage it for the next few years; and meanwhile he'd be sure to marry. I saw him married to a widow, rather older, with a good cook and a well-run house. And I actually had my eye on the widow. . . . Meanwhile I did everything to help the transition—lent him money to ease his conscience, introduced him to pretty women to make him forget his vows. But nothing would do him: he had but one idea in his beautiful obstinate head. He wanted the laurel and not the rose, and he kept on repeating Gautier's axiom,[4] and battering and filing at his limp prose till he'd spread it out over Lord knows how many hundred pages. Now and then he would send a barrelful to a publisher, and of course it would always come back.

"At first it didn't matter—he thought he was 'misunderstood.' He took the attitudes of genius, and whenever an opus came home he wrote another to keep it company. Then he had a reaction of despair, and accused me of deceiving him, and Lord knows what. I got angry at that, and told him it was he who had deceived himself. He'd come to me determined to write, and I'd done my best to help him. That was the extent of my offence, and I'd done it for his cousin's sake, not his.

"That seemed to strike home, and he didn't answer for a minute. Then he said: 'My time's up and my money's up. What do you think I'd better do?'

"'I think you'd better not be an ass,' I said.

"'What do you mean by being an ass?' he asked.

"I took a letter from my desk and held it out to him.

"'I mean refusing this offer of Mrs. Ellinger's: to be her secretary at a salary of five thousand dollars. There may be a lot more in it than that.'

"He flung out his hand with a violence that struck the letter from mine. 'Oh, I know well enough what's in it!' he said, red to the roots of his hair.

"'And what's the answer, if you know?' I asked.

"He made none at the minute, but turned away slowly to the door. There, with his hand on the threshold, he stopped to say, almost under his breath: 'Then you really think my stuff's no good?'

"I was tired and exasperated, and I laughed. I don't defend my laugh—it was in wretched taste. But I must plead in extenuation that the boy was a fool, and that I'd done my best for him—I really had.

"He went out of the room, shutting the door quietly after him. That afternoon I left for Frascati, where I'd promised to spend the Sunday with some friends. I was glad to escape from Gilbert, and by the same token, as I learned that night, I had also escaped from the eyes. I dropped into the same lethargic sleep that had come to me before when I left off seeing them; and when I woke the next morning in my peaceful room above the ilexes, I felt the utter weariness and deep relief that always followed on that sleep. I put in two blessed nights at Frascati, and when I got back to my rooms in Rome I found that Gilbert had gone. . . . Oh, nothing tragic had happened—the episode never rose to *that*. He'd simply packed his manuscripts and left for America—for his family and the Wall Street desk. He left a decent enough note to tell me of his decision, and behaved all together, in the circumstances, as little like a fool as it's possible for a fool to behave. . . ."

IV

Culwin paused again, and Frenham still sat motionless, the dusky contour of his young head reflected in the mirror at his back.

"And what became of Noyes afterward?" I finally asked, still disquieted by a sense of incompleteness, by the need of some connecting thread between the parallel lines of the tale.

Culwin twitched his shoulders. "Oh, nothing became of him— because he became nothing. There could be no question of 'becoming' about it. He vegetated in an office, I believe, and finally got a clerkship in a consulate, and married drearily in China. I saw him once in Hong Kong, years afterward. He was fat and hadn't shaved. I was told he drank. He didn't recognize me."

"And the eyes?" I asked, after another pause which Frenham's continued silence made oppressive.

Culwin, stroking his chin, blinked at me meditatively through the shadows. "I never saw them after my last talk with Gilbert. Put two and two together if you can. For my part, I haven't found the link."

He rose, his hands in his pockets, and walked stiffly over to the table on which reviving drinks had been set out.

"You must be parched after this dry tale. Here, help yourself, my dear fellow. Here, Phil—" He turned back to the hearth.

Frenham made no response to his host's hospitable summons. He still sat in his low chair without moving, but as Culwin advanced toward him, their eyes met in a long look; after which the young man, turning suddenly, flung his arms across the table behind him, and dropped his face upon them.

Culwin, at the unexpected gesture, stopped short, a flush on his face.

"Phil—what the deuce? Why, have the eyes scared *you?* My

dear boy—my dear fellow—I never had such a tribute to my literary ability, never!"

He broke into a chuckle at the thought, and halted on the hearth-rug, his hands still in his pockets, gazing down at the youth's bowed head. Then, as Frenham still made no answer, he moved a step or two nearer.

"Cheer up, my dear Phil! It's years since I've seen them— apparently I've done nothing lately bad enough to call them out of chaos. Unless my present evocation of them has made *you* see them; which would be their worst stroke yet!"

His bantering appeal quivered off into an uneasy laugh, and he moved still nearer, bending over Frenham, and laying his gouty hands on the lad's shoulders.

"Phil, my dear boy, really—what's the matter? Why don't you answer? *Have* you seen the eyes?"

Frenham's face was still hidden, and from where I stood behind Culwin I saw the latter, as if under the rebuff of this unaccountable attitude, draw back slowly from his friend. As he did so, the light of the lamp on the table fell full on his congested face, and I caught its reflection in the mirror behind Frenham's head.

Culwin saw the reflection also. He paused, his face level with the mirror, as if scarcely recognizing the countenance in it as his own. But as he looked his expression gradually changed, and for an appreciable space of time he and the image in the glass confronted each other with a glare of slowly gathering hate. Then Culwin let go on Frenham's shoulders, and drew back a step. . . .

Frenham, his face still hidden, did not stir.

THE LETTERS

Up the hill from the station at St. Cloud, Lizzie West climbed in the cold spring sunshine. As she breasted the incline, she noticed the first waves of wisteria over courtyard railings and the highlights of new foliage against the walls of ivy-matted gardens; and she thought again, as she had thought a hundred times before, that she had never seen so beautiful a spring.

She was on her way to the Deerings' house, in a street near the hilltop; and every step was dear and familiar to her. She went there five times a week to teach little Juliet Deering, the daughter of Mr. Vincent Deering, the distinguished American artist. Juliet had been her pupil for two years, and day after day, during that time, Lizzie West had mounted the hill in all weathers; sometimes with her umbrella bent against the rain, sometimes with her frail cotton parasol unfurled beneath a fiery sun, sometimes with the snow soaking through her boots or a bitter wind piercing her thin jacket, sometimes with the dust whirling about her and bleaching the flowers of the poor little hat that *had* to "carry her through" till next summer.

At first the ascent had seemed tedious enough, as dull as the trudge to her other lessons. Lizzie was not a heaven-sent teacher; she had no born zeal for her calling, and though she dealt kindly and dutifully with her pupils, she did not fly to them on winged feet. But one day something had happened to change the face of life, and since then the climb to the Deering house had seemed like a dream flight up a heavenly stairway.

Her heart beat faster as she remembered it—no longer in a tumult of fright and self-reproach, but softly, happily, as if brooding over a possession that none could take from her.

It was on a day of the previous October that she had stopped, after Juliet's lesson, to ask if she might speak to Juliet's papa. One had always to apply to Mr. Deering if there was anything to be said about the lessons. Mrs. Deering lay on her lounge upstairs, reading relays of dog-eared novels, the choice of which she left to the cook and the nurse, who were always fetching them for her from the *cabinet de lecture;*[1] and it was understood in the house that she was not to be "bothered" about Juliet. Mr. Deering's interest in his daughter was fitful rather than consecutive; but at least he was approachable, and listened sympathetically, if a little absently, stroking his long fair mustache, while Lizzie stated her difficulty or put in her plea for maps or copybooks.

"Yes, yes—of course—whatever you think right," he would always assent, sometimes drawing a five-franc piece from his pocket, and laying it carelessly on the table, or oftener saying, with his charming smile: "Get what you please, and just put it on your account, you know."

But this time Lizzie had not come to ask for maps or copybooks, or even to hint, in crimson misery—as once, poor soul, she had had to do—that Mr. Deering had overlooked her last little account—had probably not noticed that she had left it, some two months earlier, on a corner of his littered writing table. That hour had been bad enough, though he had done his best to carry it off gallantly and gaily; but this was infinitely worse. For she had come to complain of her pupil; to say that, much as she loved little Juliet, it was useless, unless Mr. Deering could "do something," to go on with the lessons.

"It wouldn't be honest—I should be robbing you; I'm not sure that I haven't already," she half laughed, through mounting tears, as she put her case. Little Juliet would not work, would not obey. Her poor little drifting existence floated aimlessly between the kitchen and the *lingerie,* and all the groping tendrils of her curiosity were fastened about the life of the backstairs.

It was the same kind of curiosity that Mrs. Deering, overhead in her drug-scented room, lavished on her dog-eared novels and on the "society notes" of the morning paper; but since Juliet's horizon was not yet wide enough to embrace these loftier objects, her interest was centered in the anecdotes that Céleste and Suzanne brought back from the market and the library. That these were not always of an edifying nature the child's artless prattle too often betrayed; but unhappily they occupied her fancy to the complete exclusion of such nourishing items as dates and dynasties, and the sources of the principal European rivers.

At length the crisis became so acute that poor Lizzie felt herself bound to resign her charge or ask Mr. Deering's intervention; and for Juliet's sake she chose the harder alternative. It *was* hard to speak to him not only because one hated to confess one's failure, and hated still more to ascribe it to such vulgar causes, but because one blushed to bring them to the notice of a spirit engaged with higher things. Mr. Deering was very busy at that moment: he had a new picture "on." And Lizzie entered the studio with the flutter of one profanely intruding on some sacred rite; she almost heard the rustle of retreating wings as she approached.

And then—and then—how differently it had all turned out! Perhaps it wouldn't have, if she hadn't been such a goose—she who so seldom cried, so prided herself on a stoic control of her little twittering cageful of "feelings." But if she had cried, it was because he had looked at her so kindly, and because she had nevertheless felt him so pained and shamed by what she said. The pain, of course, lay for both in the implication behind her words—in the one word she left unspoken. If little Juliet was as she was, it was because of the mother upstairs—the mother who had given the child her frivolous impulses, and grudged her the care that might have corrected them. The case so obviously revolved in its own vicious circle that when Mr. Deering had murmured, "Of course if my wife were not an invalid," they both turned with a spring to the flagrant "bad example" of Céleste and Suzanne, fastening on that with a mutual insistence that ended in his crying out: "All the more, then, how can you leave her to them?"

"But if I do her no good?" Lizzie wailed; and it was then that, when he took her hand and assured her gently, "But you do, you do!"—it was then that, in the traditional phrase, she "broke down," and her poor little protest quivered off into tears.

"You do *me* good, at any rate—you make the house seem less like a desert," she heard him say; and the next moment she felt herself drawn to him, and they kissed each other through her weeping.

They kissed each other—there was the new fact. One does not,

if one is a poor little teacher living in Mme. Clopin's Pension
Suisse at Passy, and if one has pretty brown hair and eyes that reach
out trustfully to other eyes—one does not, under these common
but defenceless conditions, arrive at the age of twenty-five without being now and then kissed—waylaid once by a noisy student
between two doors, surprised once by one's grey-bearded professor as one bent over the "theme" he was correcting—but these
episodes, if they tarnish the surface, do not reach the heart: it is
not the kiss endured, but the kiss returned, that lives. And Lizzie
West's first kiss was for Vincent Deering.

As she drew back from it, something new awoke in her—something deeper than the fright and the shame, and the penitent
thought of Mrs. Deering. A sleeping germ of life thrilled and unfolded, and started out to seek the sun.

She might have felt differently, perhaps—the shame and peni-
tence might have prevailed—had she not known him so kind and
tender, and guessed him so baffled, poor and disappointed. She
knew the failure of his married life, and she divined a corresponding failure in his artistic career. Lizzie, who had made her own
faltering snatch at the same laurels, brought her thwarted profi-
ciency to bear on the question of his pictures, which she judged to
be remarkable, but suspected of having somehow failed to affirm
their merit publicly. She understood that he had tasted an earlier
moment of success: a *mention*,[2] a medal, something official and
tangible; then the tide of publicity had somehow set the other
way, and left him stranded in a noble isolation. It was incredible
that any one so naturally eminent and exceptional should have
been subject to the same vulgar necessities that governed her own
life, should have known poverty and obscurity and indifference.
But she gathered that this had been the case, and felt that it
formed the miraculous link between them. For through what
medium less revealing than that of shared misfortune would he
ever have perceived so inconspicuous an object as herself? And
she recalled now how gently his eyes had rested on her from the
first—the grey eyes that might have seemed mocking if they had
not seemed so gentle.

She remembered how kindly he had met her the first day, when
Mrs. Deering's inevitable headache had prevented her receiving
the new teacher. Insensibly he had led Lizzie to talk of herself and

his questions had at once revealed his interest in the little stranded compatriot doomed to earn a precarious living so far from her native shore. Sweet as the moment of unburdening had been, she wondered afterward what had determined it: how she, so shy and sequestered, had found herself letting slip her whole poverty-stricken story, even to the avowal of the ineffectual "artistic" tendencies that had drawn her to Paris, and had then left her there to the dry task of tuition. She wondered at first, but she understood now; she understood everything after he had kissed her. It was simply because he was as kind as he was great.

She thought of this now as she mounted the hill in the spring sunshine, and she thought of all that had happened since. The intervening months, as she looked back at them, were merged in a vast golden haze, through which here and there rose the outline of a shining island. The haze was the general enveloping sense of his love, and the shining islands were the days they had spent together. They had never kissed again under his own roof. Lizzie's professional honor had a keen edge, but she had been spared the necessity of making him feel it. It was of the essence of her fatality that he always "understood" when his failing to do so might have imperiled his hold on her.

But her Thursdays and Sundays were free, and it soon became a habit to give them to him. She knew, for her peace of mind, only too much about pictures, and galleries and churches had been the one outlet from the greyness of her personal conditions. For poetry, too, and the other imaginative forms of literature, she had always felt more than she had hitherto had occasion to betray; and now all these folded sympathies shot out their tendrils to the light. Mr. Deering knew how to express with unmatched clearness the thoughts that trembled in her mind: to talk with him was to soar up into the azure on the outspread wings of his intelligence, and look down, dizzily yet clearly, on all the wonders and glories of the world. She was a little ashamed, sometimes, to find how few definite impressions she brought back from these flights; but that was doubtless because her heart beat so fast when he was near, and his smile made his words seem like a long quiver of light. Afterward, in quieter hours, fragments of their talk emerged in her memory with wonderous precision, every syllable as minutely chiseled as some of the delicate objects in crystal or ivory that he pointed out in the museums they frequented. It was always a puzzle to Lizzie that some of their hours should be so blurred and others so vivid.

She was reliving all these memories with unusual distinctness, because it was a fortnight since she had seen her friend. Mrs. Deering, some six weeks previously, had gone to visit a relative at St. Raphaël; and, after she had been a month absent, her husband and the little girl had joined her. Lizzie's adieux to Deering had been made on a rainy afternoon in the damp corridors of the Aquarium at the Trocadéro. She could not receive him at her own *pension*. That a teacher should be visited by the father of a pupil, especially when that father was still, as Madame Clopin said, *si bien,* was against that lady's austere Helvetian code. And from Deering's first tentative hint of another solution Lizzie had recoiled in a wild flurry of all her scruples. He took her "No, no, *no!*" as he took all her twists and turns of conscience, with eyes half tender and half mocking, and an instant acquiescence which was the finest homage to the "lady" she felt he divined and honored in her.

So they continued to meet in museums and galleries, or to extend, on fine days, their explorations to the suburbs, where now and then, in the solitude of grove or garden, the kiss renewed itself, fleeting, isolated, or prolonged in a shy pressure of the hand. But on the day of his leavetaking the rain kept them under cover; and as they threaded the subterranean windings of the Aquarium, and Lizzie gazed unseeingly at the grotesque faces glaring at her through walls of glass, she felt like a drowned wretch at the bottom of the sea, with all her sunlit memories rolling over her like the waves of its surface.

"You'll never see him again—never see him again," the waves boomed in her ears through his last words; and when she had said good-bye to him at the corner, and had scrambled, wet and shivering, into the Passy omnibus, its grinding wheels took up the derisive burden—"Never see him, never see him again."

All that was only two weeks ago, and here she was, as happy as a lark, mounting the hill to his door in the fresh spring sunshine! So weak a heart did not deserve such a radiant fate; and Lizzie said to herself that she would never again distrust her star.

II

The cracked bell tinkled sweetly through her heart as she stood listening for Juliet's feet. Juliet, anticipating the laggard Suzanne, almost always opened the door for her governess, not from any eagerness to hasten the hour of her studies, but from the irrepressible desire to see what was going on in the street. But doubtless on this occasion some unusually absorbing incident had detained the child belowstairs; for Lizzie, after vainly waiting for a step, had to give the bell a second twitch. Even a third produced no response, and Lizzie, full of dawning fears, drew back to look up at the house. She saw that the studio shutters stood wide, and then noticed, without surprise, that Mrs. Deering's were still unopened. No doubt Mrs. Deering was resting after the fatigue of the journey. Instinctively Lizzie's eyes turned again to the studio window; and as she looked, she saw Deering approach it. He caught sight of her, and an instant later was at the door. He looked paler than usual, and she noticed that he wore a black coat.

"I rang and rang—where is Juliet?" she asked.

He looked at her gravely; then, without answering, he led her down the passage to the studio, and closed the door when she had entered.

"My wife is dead—she died suddenly ten days ago. Didn't you see it in the papers?" he said.

Lizzie, with a cry, sank down on the rickety divan propped against the wall. She seldom saw a newspaper, since she could not afford one for her own perusal, and those supplied to the Pension Clopin were usually in the hands of its more privileged lodgers till long after the hour when she set out on her morning round.

"No; I didn't see it," she stammered.

Deering was silent. He stood twisting an unlit cigarette in his hand, and looking down at her with a gaze that was both constrained and hesitating.

She, too, felt the constraint of the situation, the impossibility of finding words which, after what had passed between them, should seem neither false nor heartless; and at last she exclaimed, standing up: "Poor little Juliet! Can't I go to her?"

"Juliet is not here. I left her at St. Raphaël with the relations with whom my wife was staying."

"Oh," Lizzie murmured, feeling vaguely that this added to the difficulty of the moment. How differently she had pictured their meeting!

"I'm so—so sorry for her!" she faltered.

Deering made no reply, but, turning on his heel, walked the length of the studio and halted before the picture on the easel. It was the landscape he had begun the previous autumn, with the intention of sending it to the Salon that spring. But it was still unfinished—seemed, indeed, hardly more advanced than on the fateful October day when Lizzie, standing before it for the first time, had confessed her inability to deal with Juliet. Perhaps the same thought struck its creator, for he broke into a dry laugh and turned from the easel with a shrug.

Under his protracted silence Lizzie roused herself to the fact that, since her pupil was absent, there was no reason for her remaining any longer; and as Deering approached her she rose and said with an effort: "I'll go, then. You'll send for me when she comes back?"

Deering still hesitated, tormenting the cigarette between his fingers.

"She's not coming back—not at present."

Lizzie heard him with a drop of the heart. Was everything to be changed in their lives? Of course; how could she have dreamed it would be otherwise? She could only stupidly repeat: "Not coming back? Not this spring?"

"Probably not, since our friends are so good as to keep her. The fact is, I've got to go to America. My wife left a little property, a few pennies, that I must go and see to—for the child."

Lizzie stood before him, a cold knife in her breast. "I see—I see," she reiterated, feeling all the while that she strained her eyes into utter blackness.

"It's a nuisance, have to pull up stakes," he went on, with a fretful glance about the studio.

She lifted her eyes to his face. "Shall you be gone long?" she took courage to ask.

"There again—I can't tell. It's all so mixed up." He met her look for an incredibly long strange moment. "I hate to go!" he murmured abruptly.

Lizzie felt a rush of moisture to her lashes, and the familiar wave of weakness at her heart. She raised her hand to her face with an instinctive gesture, and as she did so he held out his arms.

"Come here, Lizzie!" he said.

And she went—went with a sweet wild throb of liberation, with the sense that at last the house was his, that *she* was his, if he wanted her; that never again would that silent presence in the room above constrain and shame her rapture.

He pushed back her veil and covered her face with kisses. "Don't cry, you little goose!" he said.

III

That they must see each other before his departure, in some place less exposed than their usual haunts, was as clear to Lizzie as it appeared to be to Deering. His expressing the wish seemed, indeed, the sweetest testimony to the quality of his feeling, since, in the first weeks of the most perfunctory widowerhood, a man of his stamp is presumed to abstain from light adventures. If, then, he wished so much to be quietly and gravely with her, it could be only for reasons she did not call by name, but of which she felt the sacred tremor in her heart; and it would have seemed to her vain and vulgar to put forward, at such a moment, the conventional objections with which such little exposed existences defend the treasure of their freshness.

In such a mood as this one may descend from the Passy omnibus at the corner of the Pont de la Concorde (she had not let him fetch her in a cab) with a sense of dedication almost solemn, and may advance to meet one's fate, in the shape of a gentleman of melancholy elegance, with an auto taxi at his call, as one has advanced to the altar steps in some girlish bridal vision.

Even the experienced waiter ushering them into an upper room of the quiet restaurant on the Seine could hardly have supposed their quest for privacy to be based on the familiar motive, so soberly did Deering give his orders, while his companion sat small and grave at his side. She did not, indeed, mean to let her distress obscure their hour together: she was already learning that Deering shrank from sadness. He should see that she had courage and gaiety to face their coming separation, and yet give herself meanwhile to this completer nearness; but she waited, as always, for him to strike the opening note.

Looking back at it later, she wondered at the sweetness of the hour. Her heart was unversed in happiness, but he had found the tone to lull her fears, and make her trust her fate for any golden wonder. Deepest of all, he gave her the sense of something tacit and established between them, as if his tenderness were a habit of the heart hardly needing the support of outward proof.

Such proof as he offered came, therefore, as a kind of crowning luxury, the flowering of a profoundly rooted sentiment; and here again the instinctive reserves and defences would have seemed to vulgarize what his confidence ennobled. But if all the tender casuistries of her heart were at his service, he took no grave advantage of them. Even when they sat alone after dinner, with the lights of the river trembling through their one low window, and the rumor of Paris enclosing them in a heart of silence, he seemed, as much as herself, under the spell of hallowing influences. She felt it most of all as she yielded to the arm he presently put about her, to the long caress he laid on her lips and eyes: not a word or gesture missed the note of quiet understanding, or cast a doubt, in retrospect, on the pact they sealed with their last look.

That pact, as she reviewed it through a sleepless night, seemed to have consisted mainly, on his part, in pleadings for full and frequent news of her, on hers in the promise that it should be given as often as he wrote to ask it. She did not wish to show too much eagerness, too great a desire to affirm and define her hold on him. Her life had given her a certain acquaintance with the arts of defence: girls in her situation were supposed to know them all, and to use them as occasion called. But Lizzie's very need of them had intensified her disdain. Just because she was so poor, and had always, materially, so to count her change and calculate her margin, she would at least know the joy of emotional prodigality, and give her heart as recklessly as the rich their millions. She was sure now that Deering loved her, and if he had seized the occasion of their farewell to give her some definitely worded sign of his feeling—if, more plainly, he had asked her to marry him—his doing so would have seemed less a proof of his sincerity than of his suspecting in her the need of such a warrant. That he had abstained seemed to show that he trusted her as she trusted him, and that they were one most of all in this complete security of understanding.

She had tried to make him guess all this in the chariness of her promise to write. She would write; of course she would. But he would be busy, preoccupied, on the move: it was for him to let her know when he wished a word, to spare her the embarrassment of ill-timed intrusions.

"Intrusions?" He had smiled the word away. "You can't well intrude, my darling, on a heart where you're already established to the complete exclusion of other lodgers." And then, taking her hands, and looking up from them into her happy dizzy eyes: "You don't know much about being in love, do you, Lizzie?" he laughingly ended.

It seemed easy enough to reject this imputation in a kiss; but she wondered afterward if she had not deserved it. Was she really cold and conventional, and did other women give more richly and recklessly? She found that it was possible to turn about every one of her reserves and delicacies so that they looked like selfish scruples and petty pruderies, and at this game she came in time to exhaust all the resources of casuistry.

Meanwhile the first days after Deering's departure wore a soft refracted light like the radiance lingering after sunset. *He,* at any rate, was taxable with no reserves, no calculations, and his letters of farewell, from train and steamer, filled her with long murmurs and echoes of his presence. How he loved her, how he loved her— and how he knew how to tell her so!

She was not sure of possessing the same gift. Unused to the expression of personal emotion, she wavered between the impulse to pour out all she felt and the fear lest her extravagance should amuse or even bore him. She never lost the sense that what was to her the central crisis of experience must be a mere episode in a life so predestined as his to romantic incidents. All that she felt and said would be subjected to the test of comparison with what others had already given him: from all quarters of the globe she saw passionate missives winging their way toward Deering, for whom her poor little swallow flight of devotion could certainly not make a summer. But such moments were succeeded by others in which she raised her head and dared affirm her conviction that no woman had ever loved him just as she had, and that none, there-fore, had probably found just such things to say to him. And this conviction strengthened the other less solidly based belief that *he* also, for the same reason, had found new accents to express his tenderness, and that the three letters she wore all day in her shabby blouse, and hid all night beneath her pillow, not only sur-passed in beauty, but differed in quality from, all he had ever penned for other eyes.

They gave her, at any rate, during the weeks that she wore them on her heart, sensations more complex and delicate than Deering's actual presence had ever produced. To be with him was always like breasting a bright rough sea that blinded while it buoyed her; but his letters formed a still pool of contemplation, above which she could bend, and see the reflection of the sky, and the myriad movements of the life that flitted and gleamed below the surface. The wealth of this hidden life—that was what most surprised her! She had had no inkling of it, but had kept on along the narrow track of habit, like a traveler climbing a road in a fog, and sud-denly finding himself on a sunlit crag between leagues of sky and dizzy depths of valley. And the odd thing was that all the people about her—the whole world of the Passy pension—seemed plod-ding along the same dull path, preoccupied with the pebbles un-derfoot, and unaware of the glory beyond the fog!

There were hours of exultation, when she longed to cry out to them what one saw from the summit—and hours of abasement, when she asked herself why *her* feet had been guided there, while others, no doubt as worthy, stumbled and blundered in obscurity. She felt, in particular, an urgent pity for the two or three other girls at Mme. Clopin's—girls older, duller, less alive than she, and by that very token more thrown upon her sympathy. Would they ever know? Had they ever known? Those were the questions that haunted her as she crossed her companions on the stairs, faced them at the dinner table, and listened to their poor pining talk in the dimly-lit slippery-seated *salon*. One of the girls was Swiss, another English; a third, Andora Macy, was a young lady from the Southern States who was studying French with the ultimate object of im-parting it to the inmates of a girls' school at Macon, Georgia.

Andora Macy was pale, faded, immature. She had a drooping accent, and a manner which fluctuated between arch audacity and fits of panicky hauteur. She yearned to be admired, and feared to be insulted; and yet seemed wistfully conscious that she was destined to miss both these extremes of sensation, or to enjoy them only in the experiences of her more privileged friends.

It was perhaps for this reason that she took a tender interest in Lizzie, who had shrunk from her at first, as the depressing image of her own probable future, but to whom she now suddenly became an object of sentimental pity.

IV

Miss Macy's room was next to Miss West's, and the Southerner's knock often appealed to Lizzie's hospitality when Mme. Clopin's early curfew had driven her boarders from the *salon*. It sounded thus one evening, just as Lizzie, tired from an unusually long day of tuition, was in the act of removing her dress. She was in too indulgent a mood to withhold her "Come in," and as Miss Macy crossed the threshold, Lizzie felt that Vincent Deering's first letter—the letter from the train—had slipped from her bosom to the floor.

Miss Macy, as promptly aware, darted forward to recover it. Lizzie stooped also, instinctively jealous of her touch; but the visitor reached the letter first, and as she seized it, Lizzie knew that she had seen whence it fell, and was weaving round the incident a rapid web of romance.

Lizzie blushed with annoyance. "It's too stupid, having no pockets! If one gets a letter as one is going out in the morning, one has to carry it in one's blouse all day."

Miss Macy looked at her fondly. "It's warm from your heart!" she breathed, reluctantly yielding up the missive.

Lizzie laughed, for she knew it was the letter that had warmed her heart. Poor Andora Macy! *She* would never know. Her bleak bosom would never take fire from such a contact. Lizzie looked at her with kind eyes, chafing at the injustice of fate.

The next evening, on her return home, she found her friend hovering in the entrance hall.

"I thought you'd like me to put this in your own hand," Andora whispered significantly, pressing a letter upon Lizzie. "I couldn't *bear* to see it lying on the table with the others."

It was Deering's letter from the steamer. Lizzie blushed to the forehead, but without resenting Andora's divination. She could not have breathed a word of her bliss, but she was not sorry to have it guessed, and pity for Andora's destitution yielded to the pleasure of using it as a mirror for her own abundance.

Deering wrote again on reaching New York, a long fond dissatisfied letter, vague in its indication to his own projects, specific in the expression of his love. Lizzie brooded over every syllable till they formed the undercurrent of all her waking thoughts, and murmured through her midnight dreams; but she would have been happier if they had shed some definite light on the future.

That would come, no doubt, when he had had time to look about and get his bearings. She counted up the days that must elapse before she received his next letter, and stole down early to peep at the papers, and learn when the next American mail was due. At length the happy date arrived, and she hurried distractedly through the day's work, trying to conceal her impatience by the endearments she bestowed upon her pupils. It was easier, in her present mood, to kiss them than to keep them at their grammars.

That evening, on Mme. Clopin's threshold, her heart beat so wildly that she had to lean a moment against the doorpost before entering. But on the hall table, where the letters lay, there was none for her.

She went over them with an impatient hand, her heart dropping down and down, as she had sometimes fallen down an endless stairway in a dream—the very same stairway up which she had seemed to fly when she climbed the long hill to Deering's door. Then it struck her that Andora might have found and secreted her letter, and with a spring she was on the actual stairs, and rattling Miss Macy's door handle.

"You've a letter for me, haven't you?" she panted.

Miss Macy enclosed her in attenuated arms. "Oh, darling, did you expect another?"

"Do give it to me!" Lizzie pleaded with eager eyes.

"But I haven't any! There hasn't been a sign of a letter for you."

"I know there is. There *must* be," Lizzie cried, stamping her foot.

"But, dearest, I've *watched* for you, and there's been nothing."

Day after day, for the ensuing weeks, the same scene re-enacted itself with endless variations. Lizzie, after the first sharp spasm of disappointment, made no effort to conceal her anxiety from Miss Macy, and the fond Andora was charged to keep a vigilant eye upon the postman's coming, and to spy on the *bonne*[3] for possible negligence or perfidy. But these elaborate precautions remained fruitless, and no letter from Deering came.

During the first fortnight of silence, Lizzie exhausted all the ingenuities of explanation. She marveled afterward at the reasons she had found for Deering's silence: there were moments when she almost argued herself into thinking it more natural than his continuing to write. There was only one reason which her intelligence rejected; and that was the possibility that he had forgotten her, that the whole episode had faded from his mind like a breath from a mirror. From that she resolutely averted her thoughts, conscious that if she suffered herself to contemplate it, the motive power of life would fail, and she would no longer understand why she rose in the morning and lay down at night.

If she had had leisure to indulge her anguish she might have been unable to keep such speculations at bay. But she had to be up and working: the *blanchisseuse*[4] had to be paid, and Mme. Clopin's weekly bill, and all the little "extras" that even her frugal habits had to reckon with. And in the depths of her thought dwelt the dogging fear of illness and incapacity, goading her to work while she could. She hardly remembered the time when she had been without that fear; it was second nature now, and it kept her on her feet when other incentives might have failed. In the blankness of her misery she felt no dread of death; but the horror of being ill and "dependent" was in her blood.

In the first weeks of silence she wrote again and again to Deering, entreating him for a word, for a mere sign of life. From the first she had shrunk from seeming to assert any claim on his future, yet in her bewilderment she now charged herself with having been too possessive, too exacting in her tone. She told herself that his fastidiousness shrank from any but a "light touch," and that hers had not been light enough. She should have kept to the character of the "little friend," the artless consciousness in which tormented genius may find an escape from its complexities; and instead, she had dramatized their relation, exaggerated her own part in it, presumed, forsooth, to share the front of the stage with him, instead of being content to serve as scenery or chorus.

But though, to herself, she admitted, and even insisted on, the episodical nature of the experience, on the fact that for Deering it could be no more than an incident, she was still convinced that his sentiment for her, however fugitive, had been genuine.

His had not been the attitude of the unscrupulous male seeking a vulgar "advantage." For a moment he had really needed her, and if he was silent now, it was perhaps because he feared that she had mistaken the nature of the need, and built vain hopes on its possible duration.

It was of the essence of Lizzie's devotion that it sought, instinctively, the larger freedom of its object; she could not conceive of love under any form of exaction or compulsion. To make this clear to Deering became an overwhelming need, and in a last short letter she explicitly freed him from whatever sentimental obligation its predecessors might have seemed to impose. In this communication she playfully accused herself of having unwittingly sentimentalized their relation, affecting, in self-defence, a retrospective astuteness, a sense of the impermanence of the tenderer sentiments, that almost put Deering in the position of having mistaken coquetry for surrender. And she ended, gracefully, with a plea for the continuance of the friendly regard which she had "always understood" to be the basis of their sympathy. The document, when completed, seemed to her worthy of what she conceived to be Deering's conception of a woman of the world—and she found a spectral satisfaction in the thought of making her final appearance before him in this distinguished character. But she was never destined to learn what effect the appearance produced; for the letter, like those it sought to excuse, remained unanswered.

V

The fresh spring sunshine which had so often attended Lizzie West on her dusty climb up the hill of St. Cloud, beamed on her, some two years later in a scene and a situation of altered import.

Its rays, filtered through the horse chestnuts of the Champs Elysées, shone on the graveled circle about Laurent's restaurant; and Miss West, seated at a table within that privileged space, presented to the light a hat much better able to sustain its scrutiny than those which had shaded the brow of Juliet Deering's instructress.

Her dress was in keeping with the hat, and both belonged to a situation rife with such possibilities as the act of a leisurely luncheon at Laurent's in the opening week of the Salon. Her companions, of both sexes, confirmed this impression by an appropriateness of attire and an ease of manner implying the largest range of selection between the forms of Parisian idleness; and even Andora Macy, seated opposite, as in the place of co-hostess or companion, reflected, in coy greys and mauves, the festal note of the occasion.

This note reverberated persistently in the ears of a solitary gentleman straining for glimpses of the group from a table wedged in the remotest corner of the garden; but to Miss West herself the occurrence did not rise above the usual. For nearly a year she had been acquiring the habit of such situations, and the act of offering a luncheon at Laurent's to her cousins, the Harvey Mearses of Providence, and their friend Mr. Jackson Benn, produced in her no emotion beyond the languid glow which Mr. Benn's presence was beginning to impart to such scenes.

"It's frightful, the way you've got used to it," Andora Macy had wailed, in the first days of her friend's transfigured fortunes, when Lizzie West had waked one morning to find herself among the heirs of an ancient miserly cousin whose testamentary dispositions had formed, since her earliest childhood, the subject of pleasantry and conjecture in her own improvident family. Old Hezron Mears had never given any sign of life to the luckless Wests; had perhaps hardly been conscious of including them in the carefully drawn will which, following the old American convention, scrupulously divided his millions among his kin. It was by a mere genealogical accident that Lizzie, falling just within the golden circle, found herself possessed of a pittance sufficient to release her from the prospect of a long grey future in Mme. Clopin's *pension*.

The release had seemed wonderful at first; yet she presently found that it had destroyed her former world without giving her a new one. On the ruins of the old *pension* life bloomed the only flower that had ever sweetened her path; and beyond the sense of present ease, and the removal of anxiety for the future, her reconstructed existence blossomed with no compensating joys. She had hoped great things from the opportunity to rest, to travel, to look about her, above all, in various artful feminine ways, to be "nice" to the companions of her less privileged state; but such widenings of scope left her, as it were, but the more conscious of the empty margin of personal life beyond them. It was not till she woke to the leisure of her new days that she had the full sense of what was gone from them.

Their very emptiness made her strain to pack them with transient sensations: she was like the possessor of an unfurnished house, with random furniture and bric-a-brac perpetually pouring in "on approval." It was in this experimental character that Mr. Jackson Benn had fixed her attention, and the languid effort of her imagination to adjust him to her taste was seconded by the fond complicity of Andora, and by the smiling approval of her cousins. Lizzie did not discourage these attempts: she suffered serenely Andora's allusions to Mr. Benn's infatuation, and Mrs. Mears's boasts of his business standing. All the better if they could drape his narrow square-shouldered frame and round unwinking countenance in the trailing mists of sentiment: Lizzie looked and listened, not unhopeful of the miracle.

"I never saw anything like the way these Frenchmen stare! Doesn't it make you nervous, Lizzie?" Mrs. Mears broke out suddenly, ruffling her feather boa about an outraged bosom. Mrs. Mears was still in that stage of development when her countrywomen taste to the full the peril of being exposed to the gaze of the licentious Gaul.

Lizzie roused herself from the contemplation of Mr. Benn's round baby cheeks and the square blue jaw resting on his perpendicular collar. "Is someone staring at me?" she asked.

"Don't turn round, whatever you do! There—just over there, between the rhododendrons—the tall blond man alone at that table. Really, Harvey, I think you ought to speak to the head-waiter, or something; though I suppose in one of these places they'd only laugh at you," Mrs. Mears shudderingly concluded.

Her husband, as if inclining to this probability, continued the undisturbed dissection of his chicken wing, but Mr. Benn, perhaps conscious that his situation demanded a more punctilious attitude, sternly revolved upon the parapet of his high collar in the direction of Mrs. Mears's glance.

"What, that fellow all alone over there? Why, *he's* not French; he's an American," he then proclaimed with a perceptible relaxing of the muscles.

"Oh!" murmured Mrs. Mears, as perceptibly disappointed, and Mr. Benn continued: "He came over on the steamer with me. He's some kind of an artist—a fellow named Deering. He was staring at *me,* I guess: wondering whether I was going to remember him. Why, how d' 'e do? How are you? Why, yes of course; with pleasure—my friends, Mrs. Harvey Mears—Mr. Mears; my friends, Miss Macy and Miss West."

"I have the pleasure of knowing Miss West," said Vincent Deering with a smile.

VI

Even through his smile Lizzie had seen, in the first moment, how changed he was; and the impression of the change deepened to the point of pain when, a few days later, in reply to his brief note, she granted him a private hour.

That the first sight of his writing—the first answer to her letters—should have come, after three long years, in the shape of this impersonal line, too curt to be called humble, yet revealing a consciousness of the past in the studied avoidance of its language! As she read, her mind flashed back over what she had dreamed his letters would be, over the exquisite answers she had composed above his name. There was nothing exquisite in the lines before her; but dormant nerves began to throb again at the mere touch of the paper he had touched, and she threw the note into the fire before she dared to reply to it.

Now that he was actually before her again, he became, as usual, the one live spot in her consciousness. Once more her tormented self sank back passive and numb, but now with all its power of suffering mysteriously transferred to the presence, so known yet so unknown, at the opposite corner of her hearth. She was still Lizzie West, and he was still Vincent Deering; but the Styx rolled between them, and she saw his face through its fog. It was his face, really, rather than his words, that told her, as she furtively studied it, the tale of failure and discouragement which had so blurred its handsome lines. She kept, afterward, no precise memory of the details of his narrative: the pain it evidently cost him to impart it was so much the sharpest fact in her new vision of him. Confusedly, however, she gathered that on reaching America he had found his wife's small property gravely impaired; and that, while lingering on to secure what remained of it, he had contrived to sell a picture or two, and had even known a moment of success, during which he received orders and set up a studio. Then the tide had ebbed, his work had remained on his hands, and a tedious illness, with its miserable sequel of debt, soon wiped out his advantage. There followed a period of eclipse, during which she inferred that he had tried his hand at diverse means of livelihood, accepting employment from a fashionable house decorator, designing wallpapers, illustrating magazine articles, and acting for a time— she dimly understood—as the social tout of a new hotel desirous of advertising its restaurant. These disjointed facts were strung on a slender thread of personal allusions—references to friends who had been kind (jealously, she guessed them to be women), and to enemies who had schemed against him. But, true to his tradition of "correctness," he carefully avoided the mention of names, and left her imagination to grope dimly through a crowded world in which there seemed little room for her small shy presence.

As she listened, her private grievance vanished beneath the sense of his unhappiness. Nothing he had said explained or excused his conduct to her; but he had suffered, he had been lonely, had been humiliated, and she felt, with a fierce maternal rage, that there was no possible justification for any scheme of things in which such facts were possible. She could not have said why: she simply knew that it hurt too much to see him hurt.

Gradually it came to her that her absence of resentment was due to her having so definitely settled her own future. She was glad she had decided—as she now felt she had—to marry Jackson Benn, if only for the sense of detachment it gave her in dealing with Vincent Deering. Her personal safety insured her the requisite impartiality, and justified her in lingering as long as she chose over the last lines of a chapter to which her own act had fixed the close. Any lingering hesitations as to the finality of this decision were dispelled by the need of making it known to Deering; and when her visitor paused in his reminiscences to say, with a sigh, "But many things have happened to you too," the words did not so much evoke the sense of her altered fortunes as the image of the suitor to whom she was about to entrust them.

"Yes, many things; it's three years," she answered.

Deering sat leaning forward, in his sad exiled elegance, his eyes gently bent on hers; and at his side she saw the form of Mr. Jackson Benn, with shoulders preternaturally squared by the cut of his tight black coat, and a tall shiny collar sustaining his baby cheeks and hard blue chin. Then the vision faded as Deering began to speak.

"Three years," he repeated musingly. "I've so often wondered what they'd brought you."

She lifted her head with a blush, and the terrified wish that he should not—at the cost of all his notions of correctness—lapse into the blunder of becoming "personal."

"You've wondered?" she smiled back bravely.

"Do you suppose I haven't?" His look dwelt on her. "Yes, I dare say that *was* what you thought of me."

She had her answer pat—"Why, frankly, you know, I *didn't* think of you at all." But the mounting tide of her memories swept it indignantly away. If it was his correctness to ignore, it could never be hers to disavow!

"*Was* that what you thought of me?" she heard him repeat in a tone of sad insistence; and at that, with a lift of her head, she resolutely answered: "How could I know what to think? I had no word from you."

If she had expected, and perhaps almost hoped, that this answer would create difficulty for him, the gaze of quiet fortitude with which he met it proved that she had underestimated his resources.

"No, you had no word. I kept my vow," he said.

"Your vow?"

"That you *shouldn't* have a word—not a syllable. Oh, I kept it through everything!"

Lizzie's heart was sounding in her ears the old confused rumor of the sea of life, but through it she desperately tried to distinguish the still small voice of reason.

"What was your vow? Why shouldn't I have had a syllable from you?"

He sat motionless, still holding her with a look so gentle that it almost seemed forgiving.

Then, abruptly, he rose, and crossing the space between them, sat down in a chair at her side. The movement might have implied a forgetfulness of changed conditions, and Lizzie, as if thus viewing it, drew slightly back; but he appeared not to notice her recoil, and his eyes, at last leaving her face, slowly and approvingly made the round of the small bright drawing room. "This is charming. Yes, things *have* changed for you," he said.

A moment before, she had prayed that he might be spared the error of a vain return upon the past. It was as if all her retrospective tenderness, dreading to see him at such a disadvantage, rose up to protect him from it. But his evasiveness exasperated her, and suddenly she felt the desire to hold him fast, face to face with his own words.

Before she could repeat her question, however, he had met her with another.

"You *did* think of me, then? Why are you afraid to tell me that you did?"

The unexpectedness of the challenge wrung a cry from her. "Didn't my letters tell you so enough?"

"Ah—your letters—" Keeping her gaze on his with unrelenting fixity, she could detect in him no confusion, not the least quiver of a nerve. He only gazed back at her more sadly.

"They went everywhere with me—your letters," he said.

"Yet you never answered them." At last the accusation trembled to her lips.

"Yet I never answered them."

"Did you ever so much as read them, I wonder?"

All the demons of self-torture were up in her now, and she loosed them on him as if to escape from their rage.

Deering hardly seemed to hear her question. He merely shifted his attitude, leaning a little nearer to her, but without attempting, by the least gesture, to remind her of the privileges which such nearness had once implied.

"There were beautiful, wonderful things in them," he said, smiling.

She felt herself stiffen under his smile. "You've waited three years to tell me so!"

He looked at her with grave surprise. "And do you resent my telling you, even now?"

His parries were incredible. They left her with a sense of thrusting at emptiness, and a desperate, almost vindictive desire to drive him against the wall and pin him there.

"No. Only I wonder you should take the trouble to tell me, when at the time—"

And now, with a sudden turn, he gave her the final surprise of meeting her squarely on her own ground.

"When at the time I didn't? But how *could* I—at the time?"

"Why couldn't you? You've not yet told me."

He gave her again his look of disarming patience. "Do I need to? Hasn't my whole wretched story told you?"

"Told me why you never answered my letters?"

"Yes—since I could only answer them in one way: by protesting my love and my longing."

There was a pause, of resigned expectancy on his part, on hers of a wild, confused reconstruction of her shattered past. "You mean, then, that you didn't write because—"

"Because I found, when I reached America, that I was a pauper; that my wife's money was gone, and that what I could earn—I've so little gift that way!—was barely enough to keep Juliet clothed and educated. It was as if an iron door had been locked and barred between us."

Lizzie felt herself driven back, panting, on the last defences of her incredulity. "You might at least have told me—have explained. Do you think I shouldn't have understood?"

He did not hesitate. "You would have understood. It wasn't that."

"What was it then?" she quavered.

"It's wonderful you shouldn't see! Simply that I couldn't write you *that*. Anything else—not *that*!"

"And so you preferred to let me suffer?"

There was a shade of reproach in his eyes. "I suffered too," he said.

It was his first direct appeal to her compassion, and for a moment it nearly unsettled the delicate poise of her sympathies, and sent them trembling in the direction of scorn and irony. But even as the impulse rose it was stayed by another sensation. Once again, as so often in the past, she became aware of a fact which, in his absence, she always failed to reckon with; the fact of the deep irreducible difference between his image in her mind and his actual self—the mysterious alteration in her judgment produced by the inflections of his voice, the look of his eyes, the whole complex pressure of his personality. She had phrased it once, self-reproachfully, by saying to herself that she "never could remember him—" so completely did the sight of him supersede the counterfeit about which her fancy wove its perpetual wonders. Bright and breathing as that counterfeit was, it became a figment of the mind at the touch of his presence, and on this occasion the immediate result was to cause her to feel his possible unhappiness with an intensity beside which her private injury paled.

"I suffered horribly," he repeated, "and all the more that I couldn't make a sign, couldn't cry out my misery. There was only one escape from it all—to hold my tongue, and pray that you might hate me."

The blood rushed to Lizzie's forehead. "Hate you—you prayed that I might hate you?"

He rose from his seat, and moving closer, lifted her hand in his. "Yes; because your letters showed me that if you didn't, you'd be unhappier still."

Her hand lay motionless, with the warmth of his flowing through it, and her thoughts, too—her poor fluttering stormy thoughts—felt themselves suddenly penetrated by the same soft current of communion.

"And I meant to keep my resolve," he went on, slowly releasing his clasp. "I meant to keep it even after the random stream of things swept me back here, in your way; but when I saw you the other day I felt that what had been possible at a distance was impossible now that we were near each other. How could I see you, and let you hate me?"

He had moved away, but not to resume his seat. He merely paused at a little distance, his hand resting on a chair back, in the transient attitude that precedes departure.

Lizzie's heart contracted. He was going, then, and this was his farewell. He was going, and she could find no word to detain him but the senseless stammer: "I never hated you."

He considered her with a faint smile. "It's not necessary, at any rate, that you should do so now. Time and circumstances have made me so harmless—that's exactly why I've dared to venture back. And I wanted to tell you how I rejoice in your good fortune. It's the only obstacle between us that I can't bring myself to wish away."

Lizzie sat silent, spellbound, as she listened, by the sudden evocation of Mr. Jackson Benn. He stood there again, between herself and Deering, perpendicular and reproachful, but less solid and sharply outlined than before, with a look in his small hard eyes that desperately wailed for re-embodiment.

Deering was continuing his farewell speech. "You're rich now—you're free. You will marry." She saw him holding out his hand.

"It's not true that I'm engaged!" she broke out. They were the last words she had meant to utter; they were hardly related to her conscious thoughts; but she felt her whole will gathered up in the irrepressible impulse to repudiate and fling away from her forever the spectral claim of Mr. Jackson Benn.

VII

It was the firm conviction of Andora Macy that every object in the Vincent Deerings' charming little house at Neuilly had been expressly designed for the Deerings' son to play with.

The house was full of pretty things, some not obviously applicable to the purpose; but Miss Macy's casuistry was equal to the baby's appetite, and the baby's mother was no match for them in the art of defending her possessions. There were moments, in fact, when she almost fell in with Andora's summary division of her works of art into articles safe or unsafe for the baby to lick, or resisted it only to the extent of occasionally substituting some less precious, or less perishable, object for the particular fragility on which her son's desire was fixed. And it was with this intention that, on a certain spring morning—which wore the added luster of being the baby's second birthday—she had murmured, with her mouth in his curls, and one hand holding a bit of Chelsea above his clutch: "Wouldn't he rather have that beautiful shiny thing in Aunt Andora's hand?"

The two friends were together in Lizzie's morning room—the room she had chosen, on acquiring the house, because, when she sat there, she could hear Deering's step as he paced up and down before his easel in the studio she had built for him. His step had been less regularly audible than she had hoped, for, after three years of wedded bliss, he had somehow failed to settle down to the great work which was to result from that state; but even when she did not hear him she knew that he was there, above her head, stretched out on the old divan from St. Cloud, and smoking countless cigarettes while he skimmed the morning papers; and the sense of his nearness had not yet lost its first keen edge of wonder.

Lizzie herself, on the day in question, was engaged in a more arduous task than the study of the morning's news. She had never unlearned the habit of orderly activity, and the trait she least understood in her husband's character was his way of letting the loose ends of life hang as they would. She had been disposed to ascribe this to the chronic incoherence of his first *ménage*; but now she knew that, though he basked under her beneficent rule, he would never feel any impulse to further its work. He liked to see things fall into place about him at a wave of her wand; but his enjoyment of her household magic in no way diminished his smiling irresponsibility, and it was with one of its least amiable consequences that his wife and her friend were now dealing.

Before them stood two travel-worn trunks and a distended portmanteau, which had shed their heterogeneous contents over Lizzie's rosy carpet. They represented the hostages left by her husband on his somewhat precipitate departure from a New York boardinghouse, and redeemed by her on her learning, in a curt letter from his landlady, that the latter was not disposed to regard them as an equivalent for the arrears of Deering's board.

Lizzie had not been shocked by the discovery that her husband had left America in debt. She had too sad an acquaintance with the economic strain to see any humiliation in such accidents; but it offended her sense of order that he should not have liquidated his obligation in the three years since their marriage. He took her remonstrance with his usual good humor, and left her to forward the liberating draft, though her delicacy had provided him with a bank account which assured his personal independence. Lizzie had discharged the duty without repugnance, since she knew that his delegating it to her was the result of his indolence and not of any design on her exchequer. Deering was not dazzled by money; his altered fortunes had tempted him to no excesses: he was simply too lazy to draw the check, as he had been too lazy to remember the debt it canceled.

"No, dear! No!" Lizzie lifted the Chelsea higher. "Can you find something for him, Andora, among that rubbish over there? Where's the beaded bag you had in your hand? I don't think it could hurt him to lick that."

Miss Macy, bag in hand, rose from her knees, and stumbled across the room through the frayed garments and old studio properties. Before the group of mother and son she fell into a rapturous attitude.

"Do look at him reach for it, the tyrant! Isn't he just like the young Napoleon?"

Lizzie laughed and swung her son in air. "Dangle it before him, Andora. If you let him have it too quickly, he won't care for it. He's just like any man, I think."

Andora slowly lowered the bag till the heir of the Deerings closed his masterful fist upon it. "There—my Chelsea's safe!" Lizzie smiled, setting her boy on the floor, and watching him stagger away with his booty.

Andora stood beside her, watching too. "Do you know where that bag came from, Lizzie?"

Mrs. Deering, bent above a pile of discollared shirts, shook an inattentive head. "I never saw such wicked washing! There isn't one that's fit to mend. The bag? No; I've not the least idea."

Andora surveyed her incredulously. "Doesn't it make you utterly miserable to think that some woman may have made it for him?"

Lizzie, still bowed in scrutiny above the shirts, broke into a laugh. "Really, Andora, really! Six, seven, nine; no, there isn't even a dozen. There isn't a whole dozen of *anything*. I don't see how men live alone."

Andora broodingly pursued her theme. "Do you mean to tell me it doesn't make you jealous to handle these things of his that other women may have given him?"

Lizzie shook her head again, and, straightening herself with a smile, tossed a bundle in her friend's direction. "No, I don't feel jealous. Here, count these socks for me, like a darling."

Andora moaned "Don't you feel *anything at all?*" as the socks landed in her hollow bosom; but Lizzie, intent upon her task, tranquilly continued to unfold and sort. She felt a great deal as she did so, but her feelings were too deep and delicate for the simplifying processes of speech. She only knew that each article she drew from the trunks sent through her the long tremor of Deering's touch. It was part of her wonderful new life that everything belonging to him contained an infinitesimal fraction of himself— a fraction becoming visible in the warmth of her love as certain secret elements become visible in rare intensities of temperature. And in the case of the objects before her, poor shabby witnesses of his days of failure, what they gave out acquired a special poignancy from its contrast to his present cherished state. His shirts were all in round dozens now, and washed as carefully as old lace. As for his socks, she knew the pattern of every pair, and would have liked to see the washerwoman who dared to mislay one, or bring it home with the colors "run"! And in these homely tokens of his well-being she saw the symbol of what her tenderness had brought him. He was safe in it, encompassed by it, morally and materially, and she defied the embattled powers of malice to reach him through the armor of her love. Such feelings, however, were not communicable, even had one desired to express them: they were no more to be distinguished from the sense of life itself than bees from the lime blossoms in which they murmur.

"Oh, do *look* at him, Lizzie! He's found out how to open the bag!"

Lizzie lifted her head to look a moment at her son, throned on a heap of studio rubbish, with Andora before him on adoring knees. She thought vaguely "Poor Andora!" and then resumed the discouraged inspection of a buttonless white waistcoat. The next sound she was conscious of was an excited exclamation from her friend.

"Why, Lizzie, do you know what he used the bag for? To keep your letters in!"

Lizzie looked up more quickly. She was aware that Andora's pronoun had changed its object, and was now applied to Deering. And it struck her as odd, and slightly disagreeable, that a letter of hers should be found among the rubbish abandoned in her husband's New York lodgings.

"How funny! Give it to me, please."

"Give it to Aunt Andora, darling! Here—look inside, and see what else a big, big boy can find there! Yes, here's another! Why, why—"

Lizzie rose with a shade of impatience and crossed the floor to the romping group beside the other trunk.

"What is it? Give me the letters, please." As she spoke, she suddenly recalled the day when, in Mme. Clopin's *pension,* she had addressed a similar behest to Andora Macy.

Andora lifted to her a look of startled conjecture. "Why, this one's never been opened! Do you suppose that awful woman could have kept it from him?"

Lizzie laughed. Andora's imaginings were really puerile! "What awful woman? His landlady? Don't be such a goose, Andora. How can it have been kept back from him, when we've found it among his things?"

"Yes; but then why was it never opened?"

Andora held out the letter, and Lizzie took it. The writing was hers; the envelope bore the Passy postmark; and it was unopened. She looked at it with a sharp drop of the heart.

"Why, so are the others—all unopened!" Andora threw out on a rising note; but Lizzie, stooping over, checked her.

"Give them to me, please."

"Oh, Lizzie, Lizzie—" Andora, on her knees, held back the packet, her pale face paler with anger and compassion. "Lizzie, they're the letters I used to post for you—the letters he never answered! *Look!*"

"Give them back to me, please." Lizzie possessed herself of the letters.

The two women faced each other, Andora still kneeling, Lizzie motionless before her. The blood had rushed to her face, humming in her ears, and forcing itself into the veins of her temples. Then it ebbed, and she felt cold and weak.

"It must have been some plot—some conspiracy," Andora cried, so fired by the ecstasy of invention that for the moment she seemed lost to all but the aesthetic aspect of the case.

Lizzie averted her eyes with an effort, and they rested on the boy, who sat at her feet placidly sucking the tassels of the bag. His mother stooped and extracted them from his rosy mouth, which a cry of wrath immediately filled. She lifted him in her arms, and for the first time no current of life ran from his body into hers. He felt heavy and clumsy, like some other woman's child; and his screams annoyed her.

"Take him away, please, Andora."

"Oh, Lizzie, Lizzie!" Andora wailed.

Lizzie held out the child, and Andora, struggling to her feet, received him.

"I know just how you feel," she gasped, above the baby's head.

Lizzie, in some dark hollow of herself, heard the faint echo of a laugh. Andora always thought she knew how people felt!

"Tell Marthe to take him with her when she fetches Juliet home from school."

"Yes, yes." Andora gloated on her. "If you'd only give way, my darling!"

The baby, howling, dived over Andora's shoulder for the bag.

"Oh, *take* him!" his mother ordered.

Andora, from the door, cried out: "I'll be back at once. Remember, love, you're not alone!"

But Lizzie insisted, "Go with them—I wish you to go with them," in the tone to which Miss Macy had never learned the answer.

The door closed on her reproachful back, and Lizzie stood alone. She looked about the disordered room, which offered a dreary image of the havoc of her life. An hour or two ago, everything about her had been so exquisitely ordered, without and within: her thoughts and her emotions had all been outspread before her like jewels laid away symmetrically in a collector's cabinet. Now they had been tossed down helter-skelter among the rubbish there on the floor, and had themselves turned to rubbish like the rest. Yes, there lay her life at her feet, among all that tarnished trash.

She picked up her letters, ten in all, and examined the flaps of the envelopes. Not one had been opened—not one. As she looked, every word she had written fluttered to life, and every feeling prompting it sent a tremor through her. With vertiginous speed and microscopic distinctness of vision she was reliving that whole period of her life, stripping bare again the ruin over which the drift of three happy years had fallen.

She laughed at Andora's notion of a conspiracy—of the letters having been "kept back." She required no extraneous aid in deciphering the mystery: her three years' experience of Deering shed on it all the light she needed. And yet a moment before she had believed herself to be perfectly happy! Now it was the worst part of her pain that it did not really surprise her.

She knew so well how it must have happened. The letters had reached him when he was busy, occupied with something else, and had been put aside to be read at some future time—a time which never came. Perhaps on the steamer, even, he had met "someone else"—the "someone" who lurks, veiled and ominous, in the background of every woman's thoughts about her lover. Or perhaps he had been merely forgetful. She knew now that the sensations which he seemed to feel most intensely left no reverberations in his memory—that he did not relive either his pleasures or his pains. She needed no better proof than the lightness of his conduct toward his daughter. He seemed to have taken it for granted that Juliet would remain indefinitely with the friends who had received her after her mother's death, and it was at Lizzie's suggestion that the little girl was brought home and that they had established themselves at Neuilly to be near her school. But Juliet once with them, he became the model of a tender father, and Lizzie wondered that he had not felt the child's absence, since he seemed so affectionately aware of her presence.

Lizzie had noted all this in Juliet's case, but had taken for granted that her own was different; that she formed, for Deering, the exception which every woman secretly supposes herself to form in the experience of the man she loves. She had learned by this time that she could not modify his habits; but she imagined that she had deepened his sensibilities, had furnished him with an "ideal"—angelic function! And she now saw that the fact of her letters—her unanswered letters—having on his own assurance, "meant so much" to him, had been the basis on which this beautiful fabric was reared.

There they lay now, the letters, precisely as when they had left her hands. He had not had time to read them; and there had been a moment in her past when that discovery would have been to her the sharpest pang imaginable. She had traveled far beyond that point. She could have forgiven him now for having forgotten her; but she could never forgive him for having deceived her.

She sat down, and looked again about the room. Suddenly she heard his step overhead, and her heart contracted. She was afraid that he was coming down to her. She sprang up and bolted the door; then she dropped into the nearest chair, tremulous and exhausted, as if the act had required an immense effort. A moment later she heard him on the stairs, and her tremor broke into a fit of shaking. "I loathe you—I loathe you!" she cried.

She listened apprehensively for his touch on the handle of the door. He would come in, humming a tune, to ask some idle question and lay a caress on her hair. But no, the door was bolted; she was safe. She continued to listen, and the step passed on. He had not been coming to her, then. He must have gone downstairs to fetch something—another newspaper, perhaps. He seemed to read little else, and she sometimes wondered when he had found time to store the material that used to serve for their famous "literary" talks. The wonder shot through her again, barbed with a sneer. At that moment it seemed to her that everything he had ever done and been was a lie.

She heard the house door close, and started up. Was he going out? It was not his habit to leave the house in the morning.

She crossed the room to the window, and saw him walking, with a quick decided step, between the lilacs to the gate. What could have called him forth at that unusual hour? It was odd that he should not have told her. The fact that she thought it odd suddenly showed her how closely their lives were interwoven. She

had become a habit to him, and he was fond of his habits. But to
her it was as if a stranger had opened the gate and gone out. She
wondered what he would feel if he knew that she felt *that*.

"In an hour he will know," she said to herself, with a kind of
fierce exultation; and immediately she began to dramatize the
scene. As soon as he came in she meant to call him up to her room
and hand him the letters without a word. For a moment she
gloated on the picture; then her imagination recoiled. She was humiliated by the thought of humiliating him. She wanted to keep
his image intact; she would not see him.

He had lied to her about her letters—had lied to her when he
found it to his interest to regain her favor. Yes, there was the point
to hold fast. He had sought her out when he learned that she was
rich. Perhaps he had come back from America on purpose to
marry her; no doubt he had come back on purpose. It was incredible that she had not seen this at the time. She turned sick at the
thought of her fatuity and of the grossness of his arts. Well, the
event proved that they were all he needed. . . . But why had he
gone out at such an hour? She was irritated to find herself still preoccupied by his comings and goings.

Turning from the window, she sat down again. She wondered
what she meant to do next. . . . No, she would not show him the
letters; she would simply leave them on his table and go away. She
would leave the house with her boy and Andora. It was a relief to
feel a definite plan forming itself in her mind—something that her
uprooted thoughts could fasten on. She would go away, of course;
and meanwhile, in order not to see him, she would feign a headache and remain in her room till after luncheon. Then she and Andora would pack a few things, and fly with the child while he was
dawdling about upstairs in the studio. When one's house fell, one
fled from the ruins: nothing could be simpler, more inevitable.

Her thoughts were checked by the impossibility of picturing
what would happen next. Try as she would, she could not see herself and the child away from Deering. But that, of course, was because of her nervous weakness. She had youth, money, energy: all
the trumps were on her side. It was much more difficult to imagine what would become of Deering. He was so dependent on her,
and they had been so happy together! It struck her as illogical and

even immoral, and yet she knew he had been happy with her. It never happened like that in novels: happiness "built on a lie" always crumbled, burying the presumptuous architect beneath its ruins. According to the laws of fiction, Deering, having deceived her once, would inevitably have gone on deceiving her. Yet she knew he had not gone on deceiving her. . . .

She tried again to picture her new life. Her friends, of course, would rally about her. But the prospect left her cold; she did not want them to rally. She wanted only one thing—the life she had been living before she had given her baby the embroidered bag to play with. Oh, why had she given him the bag? She had been so happy, they had all been so happy! Every nerve in her clamored for her lost happiness, angrily, irrationally, as the boy had clamored for his bag! It was horrible to know too much; there was always blood in the foundations. Parents "kept things" from children—protected them from all the dark secrets of pain and evil. And was any life livable unless it were thus protected? Could anyone look in the Medusa's face and live?

But why should she leave the house, since it was hers? Here, with her boy and Andora, she could still make for herself the semblance of a life. It was Deering who would have to go; he would understand that as soon as he saw the letters.

She saw him going—leaving the house as he had left it just now. She saw the gate closing on him for the last time. Now her vision was acute enough: she saw him as distinctly as if he were in the room. Ah, he would not like returning to the old life of privations and expedients! And yet she knew he would not plead with her.

Suddenly a new thought seized her. What if Andora had rushed to him with the tale of the discovery of the letters—with the "Fly, you are discovered!" of romantic fiction? What if he *had* left her for good? It would not be unlike him, after all. For all his sweetness he was always evasive and inscrutable. He might have said to himself that he would forestall her action, and place himself at once on the defensive. It might be that she *had* seen him go out of the gate for the last time.

She looked about the room again, as if the thought had given it a new aspect. Yes, this alone could explain her husband's going out. It was past twelve o'clock, their usual luncheon hour, and he was scrupulously punctual at meals, and gently reproachful if she kept him waiting. Only some unwonted event could have caused him to leave the house at such an hour and with such marks of haste. Well, perhaps it was better that Andora should have spoken. She mistrusted her own courage; she almost hoped the deed had been done for her. Yet her next sensation was one of confused resentment. She said to herself, "Why has Andora interfered?" She felt baffled and angry, as though her prey had escaped her. If Deering had been in the house she would have gone to him instantly and overwhelmed him with her scorn. But he had gone out, and she did not know where he had gone, and oddly mingled with her anger against him was the latent instinct of vigilance, the solicitude of the woman accustomed to watch over the man she loves. It would be strange never to feel that solicitude again, never to hear him say, with his hand on her hair: "You foolish child, were you worried? Am I late?"

The sense of his touch was so real that she stiffened herself against it, flinging back her head as if to throw off his hand. The mere thought of his caress was hateful; yet she felt it in all her veins. Yes, she felt it, but with horror and repugnance. It was something she wanted to escape from, and the fact of struggling against it was what made its hold so strong. It was as though her mind were sounding her body to make sure of its allegiance, spying on it for any secret movement of revolt. . . .

To escape from the sensation, she rose and went again to the window. No one was in sight. But presently the gate began to swing back, and her heart gave a leap—she knew not whether up or down. A moment later the gate opened to admit a perambulator, propelled by the nurse and flanked by Juliet and Andora. Lizzie's eyes rested on the familiar group as if she had never seen it before, and she stood motionless, instead of flying down to meet the children.

Suddenly there was a step on the stairs, and she heard Andora's knock. She unbolted the door, and was strained to her friend's emaciated bosom.

"My darling!" Miss Macy cried. "Remember you have your child—and me!"

Lizzie loosened herself. She looked at Andora with a feeling of estrangement which she could not explain.

"Have you spoken to my husband?" she asked, drawing coldly back.

"Spoken to him? No." Andora stared at her, surprised.

"Then you haven't met him since he went out?"

"No, my love. Is he out? I haven't met him."

Lizzie sat down with a confused sense of relief, which welled up to her throat and made speech difficult.

Suddenly light seemed to come to Andora. "I understand, dearest. You don't feel able to see him yourself. You want me to go to him for you." She looked eagerly about her, scenting the battle. "You're right, darling. As soon as he comes in, I'll go to him. The sooner we get it over, the better."

She followed Lizzie, who had turned restlessly back to the window. As they stood there, the gate moved again, and Deering entered.

"There he is now!" Lizzie felt Andora's excited clutch upon her arm. "Where are the letters? I will go down at once. You allow me to speak for you? You trust my woman's heart? Oh, believe me, darling," Miss Macy panted, "I shall know exactly what to say to him!"

"What to say to him?" Lizzie absently repeated.

As her husband advanced up the path she had a sudden vision of their three years together. Those years were her whole life; everything before them had been colorless and unconscious, like the blind life of the plant before it reaches the surface of the soil. The years had not been exactly what she had dreamed; but if they had taken away certain illusions they had left richer realities in their stead. She understood now that she had gradually adjusted herself to the new image of her husband as he was, as he would always be. He was not the hero of her dreams, but he was the man she loved, and who had loved her. For she saw now, in this last wide flash of pity and initiation, that, as a comedy marble may be made out of worthless scraps of mortar, glass, and pebbles, so out of mean mixed substances may be fashioned a love that will bear the stress of life.

More urgently, she felt the pressure of Miss Macy's hand.

"I shall hand him the letters without a word. You may rely, love, on my sense of dignity. I know everything you're feeling at this moment!"

Deering had reached the doorstep. Lizzie watched him in silence till he disappeared under the projecting roof of the porch; then she turned and looked almost compassionately at her friend.

"Oh, poor Andora, you don't know anything—you don't know anything at all!" she said.

AUTRES TEMPS . . .

I

Mrs. Lidcote, as the huge menacing mass of New York defined itself far off across the waters, shrank back into her corner of the deck and sat listening with a kind of unreasoning terror to the steady onward drive of the screws.

She had set out on the voyage quietly enough—in what she called her "reasonable" mood—but the week at sea had given her too much time to think of things and had left her too long alone with the past.

When she was alone, it was always the past that occupied her. She couldn't get away from it, and she didn't any longer care to. During her long years of exile she had made her terms with it, had learned to accept the fact that it would always be there, huge, obstructing, encumbering, bigger and more dominant than anything the future could ever conjure up. And, at any rate, she was sure of it, she understood it, knew how to reckon with it; she had learned to screen and manage and protect it as one does an afflicted member of one's family.

There had never been any danger of her being allowed to forget the past. It looked out at her from the face of every acquaintance, it appeared suddenly in the eyes of strangers when a word enlightened them: "Yes, *the* Mrs. Lidcote, don't you know?" It had sprung at her the first day out, when, across the dining-room, from the captain's table, she had seen Mrs. Lorin Boulger's revolving eye-glass pause and the eye behind it grow as blank as a dropped blind. The next day, of course, the captain had asked: "You know your ambassadress, Mrs. Boulger?" and she had replied that, No, she seldom left Florence, and hadn't been to Rome for more than a day since the Boulgers had been sent to Italy. She was so used to these phrases that it cost her no effort to repeat them. And the captain had promptly changed the subject.

No, she didn't, as a rule, mind the past, because she was used to it and understood it. It was a great concrete act in her path that she had to walk around every time she moved in any direction. But now, in the light of the unhappy event that had summoned her from Italy—the sudden unanticipated news of her daughter's divorce from Horace Pursh and remarriage with Wilbour Barkley—the past, her own poor miserable past, started up at her with eyes of accusation, became, to her disordered fancy, like the afflicted relative suddenly breaking away from nurses and keepers and publicly parading the horror and misery she had, all the long years, so patiently screened and secluded.

Yes, there it had stood before her through the agitated weeks since the news had come—during her interminable journey from India, where Leila's letter had overtaken her, and the feverish halt in her apartment in Florence, where she had had to stop and gather up her possessions for a fresh start—there it had stood grinning at her with a new balefulness which seemed to say: "Oh, but you've got to look at me *now,* because I'm not only your own past but Leila's present."

Certainly it was a master-stroke of those arch-ironists of the shears and spindle to duplicate her own story in her daughter's. Mrs. Lidcote had always somewhat grimly fancied that, having so signally failed to be of use to Leila in other ways, she would at least serve her as a warning. She had even abstained from defending herself, from making the best of her case, had stoically refused to plead extenuating circumstances, lest Leila's impulsive sympathy should lead to deductions that might react disastrously on her own life. And now that very thing had happened, and Mrs. Lidcote could hear the whole of New York saying with one voice: "Yes, Leila's done just what her mother did. With such an example what could you expect?"

Yet if she had been an example, poor woman, she had been an awful one; she had been, she would have supposed, of more use as a deterrent than a hundred blameless mothers as incentives. For how could any one who had seen anything of her life in the last eighteen years have had the courage to repeat so disastrous an experiment?

Well, logic in such cases didn't count, example didn't count, nothing probably counted but having the same impulses in the blood; and that was the dark inheritance she had bestowed upon her daughter. Leila hadn't consciously copied her; she had simply "taken after" her, had been a projection of her own long-past rebellion.

Mrs. Lidcote had deplored, when she started, that the *Utopia* was a slow steamer, and would take eight full days to bring her to her unhappy daughter; but now, as the moment of reunion approached, she would willingly have turned the boat about and fled back to the high seas. It was not only because she felt still so unprepared to face what New York had in store for her, but because she needed more time to dispose of what the *Utopia* had already given her. The past was bad enough, but the present and future were worse, because they were less comprehensible, and because, as she grew older, surprises and inconsequences troubled her more than the worst certainties.

There was Mrs. Boulger, for instance. In the light, or rather the darkness, of new developments, it might really be that Mrs. Boulger had not meant to cut her, but had simply failed to recognize her. Mrs. Lidcote had arrived at this hypothesis simply by listening to the conversation of the persons sitting next to her on deck—two lively young women with the latest Paris hats on their heads and the latest New York ideas in them. These ladies, as to whom it would have been impossible for a person with Mrs. Lidcote's old-fashioned categories to determine whether they were married or unmarried, "nice" or "horrid," or any one or other of the definite things which young women, in her youth and her society, were conveniently assumed to be, had revealed a familiarity with the world of New York that, again according to Mrs. Lidcote's traditions, should have implied a recognized place in it. But in the present fluid state of manners what did anything imply except what their hats implied—that no one could tell what was coming next?

They seemed, at any rate, to frequent a group of idle and opulent people who executed the same gestures and revolved on the same pivots as Mrs. Lidcote's daughter and her friends: their

Coras, Matties and Mabels seemed at any moment likely to reveal familiar patronymics, and once one of the speakers, summing up a discussion of which Mrs. Lidcote had missed the beginning, had affirmed with headlong confidence: "Leila? Oh, *Leila's* all right."

Could it be *her* Leila, the mother had wondered, with a sharp thrill of apprehension? If only they would mention surnames! But their talk leaped elliptically from allusion to allusion, their unfinished sentences dangled over bottomless pits of conjecture, and they gave their bewildered hearer the impression not so much of talking only of their intimates, as of being intimate with every one alive.

Her old friend Franklin Ide could have told her, perhaps; but here was the last day of the voyage, and she hadn't yet found courage to ask him. Great as had been the joy of discovering his name on the passenger-list and seeing his friendly bearded face in the throng against the taffrail at Cherbourg, she had as yet said nothing to him except, when they had met: "Of course I'm going out to Leila."

She had said nothing to Franklin Ide because she had always instinctively shrunk from taking him into her confidence. She was sure he felt sorry for her, sorrier perhaps than any one had ever felt; but he had always paid her the supreme tribute of not showing it. His attitude allowed her to imagine that compassion was not the basis of his feeling for her, and it was part of her joy in his friendship that it was the one relation seemingly unconditioned by her state, the only one in which she could think and feel and behave like any other woman.

Now, however, as the problem of New York loomed nearer, she began to regret that she had not spoken, had not at least questioned him about the hints she had gathered on the way. He did not know the two ladies next to her, he did not even, as it chanced, know Mrs. Lorin Boulger; but he knew New York, and New York was the sphinx whose riddle she must read or perish.

Almost as the thought passed through her mind his stooping shoulders and grizzled head detached themselves against the blaze of light in the west, and he sauntered down the empty deck and dropped into the chair at her side.

"You're expecting the Barkleys to meet you, I suppose?" he asked.

It was the first time she had heard any one pronounce her daughter's new name, and it occurred to her that her friend, who was shy and inarticulate, had been trying to say it all the way over and had at last shot it out at her only because he felt it must be now or never.

"I don't know. I cabled, of course. But I believe she's at—they're at—*his* place somewhere."

"Oh, Barkley's; yes, near Lenox, isn't it? But she's sure to come to town to meet you."

He said it so easily and naturally that her own constraint was relieved, and suddenly, before she knew what she meant to do, she had burst out: "She may dislike the idea of seeing people."

Ide, whose absent short-sighted gaze had been fixed on the slowly gliding water, turned in his seat to stare at his companion.

"Who? Leila?" he said with an incredulous laugh.

Mrs. Lidcote flushed to her faded hair and grew pale again. "It took *me* a long time—to get used to it," she said.

His look grew gently commiserating. "I think you'll find"—he paused for a word—"that things are different now—altogether easier."

"That's what I've been wondering—ever since we started." She was determined now to speak. She moved nearer, so that their arms touched, and she could drop her voice to a murmur. "You see, it all came on me in a flash. My going off to India and Siam on that long trip kept me away from letters for weeks at a time; and she didn't want to tell me beforehand—oh, I understand *that*, poor child! You know how good she's always been to me; how she's tried to spare me. And she knew, of course, what a state of horror I'd be in. She knew I'd rush off to her at once and try to stop it. So she never gave me a hint of anything, and she even managed to muzzle Susy Suffern—you know Susy is the one of the family who keeps me informed about things at home. I don't yet see how she prevented Susy's telling me; but she did. And her first letter, the one I got up at Bangkok, simply said the thing was over—the divorce, I mean—and that the very next day she'd—well, I suppose there was no use waiting; and *he* seems to have behaved as well as possible, to have wanted to marry her as much as—"

"Who? Barkley?" he helped her out. "I should say so! Why

what do you suppose—" He interrupted himself. "He'll be devoted to her, I assure you."

"Oh, of course; I'm sure he will. He's written me—really beautifully. But it's a terrible strain on a man's devotion. I'm not sure that Leila realizes—"

Ide sounded again his little reassuring laugh. "I'm not sure that you realize. *They're* all right."

It was the very phrase that the young lady in the next seat had applied to the unknown "Leila," and its recurrence on Ide's lips flushed Mrs. Lidcote with fresh courage.

"I wish I knew just what you mean. The two young women next to me—the ones with the wonderful hats—have been talking in the same way."

"What? About Leila?"

"About *a* Leila; I fancied it might be mine. And about society in general. All their friends seem to be divorced; some of them seem to announce their engagements before they get their decree. One of them—*her* name was Mabel—as far as I could make out, her husband found out that she meant to divorce him by noticing that she wore a new engagement-ring."

"Well, you see Leila did everything 'regularly,' as the French say," Ide rejoined.

"Yes, but are these people in society? The people my neighbours talk about?"

He shrugged his shoulders. "It would take an arbitration commission a good many sittings to define the boundaries of society nowadays. But at any rate they're in New York; and I assure you you're *not;* farther and farther from it."

"But I've been back there several times to see Leila." She hesitated and looked away from him. Then she brought out slowly: "And I've never noticed—the least change—in—in my own case—"

"Oh," he sounded deprecatingly, and she trembled with the fear of having gone too far. But the hour was past when such scruples could restrain her. She must know where she was and where Leila was. "Mrs. Boulger still cuts me," she brought out with an embarrassed laugh.

"Are you sure? You've probably cut *her;* if not now, at least in the past. And in a cut if you're not first you're nowhere. That's what keeps up so many quarrels."

The word roused Mrs. Lidcote to a renewed sense of realities. "But the Purshes," she said—"the Purshes are so strong! There are so many of them, and they all back each other up, just as my husband's family did. I know what it means to have a clan against one. They're stronger than any number of separate friends. The Purshes will *never* forgive Leila for leaving Horace. Why, his mother opposed his marrying her because of—of me. She tried to get Leila to promise that she wouldn't see me when they went to Europe on their honeymoon. And now she'll say it was my example."

Her companion, vaguely stroking his beard, mused a moment upon this; then he asked, with seeming irrelevance, "What did Leila say when you wrote that you were coming?"

"She said it wasn't the least necessary, but that I'd better come, because it was the only way to convince me that it wasn't."

"Well, then, that proves she's not afraid of the Purshes."

She breathed a long sigh of remembrance. "Oh, just at first, you know—one never is."

He laid his hand on hers with a gesture of intelligence and pity. "You'll see, you'll see," he said.

A shadow lengthened down the deck before them, and a steward stood there, proffering a Marconigram.

"Oh, now I shall know!" she exclaimed.

She tore the message open, and then let it fall on her knees, dropping her hands on it in silence.

Ide's enquiry roused her: "It's all right?"

"Oh, quite right. Perfectly. She can't come; but she's sending Susy Suffern. She says Susy will explain." After another silence she added, with a sudden gush of bitterness: "As if I needed any explanation!"

She felt Ide's hesitating glance upon her. "She's in the country?"

"Yes. 'Prevented last moment. Longing for you, expecting you. Love from both.' Don't you *see*, the poor darling, that she couldn't face it?"

"No, I don't." He waited. "Do you mean to go to her immediately?"

"It will be too late to catch a train this evening; but I shall take the first to-morrow morning." She considered a moment. "Perhaps it's better. I need a talk with Susy first. She's to meet me at the dock, and I'll take her straight back to the hotel with me."

As she developed this plan, she had the sense that Ide was still thoughtfully, even gravely, considering her. When she ceased, he remained silent a moment; then he said almost ceremoniously: "If your talk with Miss Suffern doesn't last too late, may I come and see you when it's over? I shall be dining at my club, and I'll call you up at about ten, if I may. I'm off to Chicago on business to-morrow morning, and it would be a satisfaction to know, before I start, that your cousin's been able to reassure you, as I know she will."

He spoke with a shy deliberateness that, even to Mrs. Lidcote's troubled perceptions, sounded a long-silenced note of feeling. Perhaps the breaking down of the barrier of reticence between them had released unsuspected emotions in both. The tone of his appeal moved her curiously and loosened the tight strain of her fears.

"Oh, yes, come—do come," she said, rising. The huge threat of New York was imminent now, dwarfing, under long reaches of embattled masonry, the great deck she stood on and all the little specks of life it carried. One of them, drifting nearer, took the shape of her maid, followed by luggage-laden stewards, and signing to her that it was time to go below. As they descended to the main deck, the throng swept her against Mrs. Lorin Boulger's shoulder, and she heard the ambassadress call out to some one, over the vexed sea of hats: "So sorry! I should have been delighted, but I've promised to spend Sunday with some friends at Lenox."

II

Susy Suffern's explanation did not end till after ten o'clock, and she had just gone when Franklin Ide, who, complying with an old New York tradition, had caused himself to be preceded by a long white box of roses, was shown into Mrs. Lidcote's sitting-room.

He came forward with his shy half-humorous smile and, taking her hand, looked at her for a moment without speaking.

"It's all right," he then pronounced.

Mrs. Lidcote returned his smile. "It's extraordinary. Every-thing's changed. Even Susy has changed; and you know the extent to which Susy used to represent the old New York. There's no old New York left, it seems. She talked in the most amazing way. She snaps her fingers at the Purshes. She told me—*me*, that every woman had a right to happiness and that self-expression was the highest duty. She accused me of misunderstanding Leila; she said my point of view was conventional! She was bursting with pride at having been in the secret, and wearing a brooch that Wilbour Barkley'd given her!"

Franklin Ide had seated himself in the arm-chair she had pushed forward for him under the electric chandelier. He threw back his head and laughed. "What did I tell you?"

"Yes; but I can't believe that Susy's not mistaken. Poor dear, she has the habit of lost causes; and she may feel that, having stuck to me, she can do no less than stick to Leila."

"But she didn't—did she?—openly defy the world for you? She didn't snap her fingers at the Lidcotes?"

Mrs. Lidcote shook her head, still smiling. "No. It was enough to defy *my* family. It was doubtful at one time if they would toler-ate her seeing me, and she almost had to disinfect herself after each visit. I believe that at first my sister-in-law wouldn't let the girls come down when Susy dined with her."

"Well, isn't your cousin's present attitude the best possible proof that times have changed?"

"Yes, yes; I know." She leaned forward from her sofa-corner, fixing her eyes on his thin kindly face, which gleamed on her in-distinctly through her tears. "If it's true, it's—it's dazzling. She says Leila's perfectly happy. It's as if an angel had gone about lifting gravestones, and the buried people walked again, and the living didn't shrink from them."

"That's about it," he assented.

She drew a deep breath, and sat looking away from him down the long perspective of lamp-fringed streets over which her win-dows hung.

"I can understand how happy you must be," he began at length.

She turned to him impetuously. "Yes, yes; I'm happy. But I'm lonely, too—lonelier than ever. I didn't take up much room in the world before; but now—where is there a corner for me? Oh, since I've begun to confess myself, why shouldn't I go on? Telling you this lifts a gravestone from *me!* You see, before this, Leila needed me. She was unhappy, and I knew it, and though we hardly ever talked of it I felt that, in a way, the thought that I'd been through the same thing, and down to the dregs of it, helped her. And her needing me helped *me*. And when the news of her marriage came my first thought was that now she'd need me more than ever, that she'd have no one but me to turn to. Yes, under all my distress there was a fierce joy in that. It was so new and wonderful to feel again that there was one person who wouldn't be able to get on without me! And now what you and Susy tell me seems to have taken my child from me; and just at first that's all I can feel."

"Of course it's all you feel." He looked at her musingly. "Why didn't Leila come to meet you?"

"That was really my fault. You see, I'd cabled that I was not sure of being able to get off on the *Utopia,* and apparently my second cable was delayed, and when she received it she'd already asked some people over Sunday—one or two of her old friends, Susy says. I'm so glad they should have wanted to go to her at once; but naturally I'd rather have been alone with her."

"You still mean to go, then?"

"Oh, I must. Susy wanted to drag me off to Ridgefield with her over Sunday, and Leila sent me word that of course I might go if I wanted to, and that I was not to think of her; but I know how disappointed she would be. Susy said she was afraid I might be upset at her having people to stay, and that, if I minded, she wouldn't urge me to come. But if *they* don't mind, why should I? And of course, if they're willing to go to Leila it must mean—"

"Of course. I'm glad you recognize that," Franklin Ide exclaimed abruptly. He stood up and went over to her, taking her hand with one of his quick gestures. "There's something I want to say to you," he began—

The next morning, in the train, through all the other contending thoughts in Mrs. Lidcote's mind there ran the warm undercurrent of what Franklin Ide had wanted to say to her.

He had wanted, she knew, to say it once before, when, nearly eight years earlier, the hazard of meeting at the end of a rainy autumn in a deserted Swiss hotel had thrown them for a fortnight into unwonted propinquity. They had walked and talked together, borrowed each other's books and newspapers, spent the long chill evenings over the fire in the dim lamplight of her little pitch-pine sitting-room; and she had been wonderfully comforted by his presence, and hard frozen places in her had melted, and she had known that she would be desperately sorry when he went. And then, just at the end, in his odd indirect way, he had let her see that it rested with her to have him stay. She could still relive the sleepless night she had given to that discovery. It was preposterous, of course, to think of repaying his devotion by accepting such a sacrifice; but how find reasons to convince him? She could not bear to let him think her less touched, less inclined to him than she was: the generosity of his love deserved that she should repay it with the truth. Yet how let him see what she felt, and yet refuse what he offered? How confess to him what had been on her lips when he made the offer: "I've seen what it did to one man; and there must never, never be another"? The tacit ignoring of her past had been the element in which their friendship lived, and she could not suddenly, to him of all men, begin to talk of herself like a guilty woman in a play. Somehow, in the end, she had managed it, had averted a direct explanation, had made him understand that her life was over, that she existed only for her daughter, and that a more definite word from him would have been almost a breach of delicacy. She was so used to behaving as if her life were over! And, at any rate, he had taken her hint, and she had been able to spare her sensitiveness and his. The next year, when he came to Florence to see her, they met again in the old friendly way; and that till now had continued to be the tenor of their intimacy.

And now, suddenly and unexpectedly, he had brought up the question again, directly this time, and in such a form that she could not evade it: putting the renewal of his plea, after so long an interval, on the ground that, on her own showing, her chief argument against it no longer existed.

"You tell me Leila's happy. If she's happy, she doesn't need you—need you, that is, in the same way as before. You wanted, I know, to be always in reach, always free and available if she should suddenly call you to her or take refuge with you. I under-

stood that—I respected it. I didn't urge my case because I saw it
was useless. You couldn't, I understood well enough, have felt free
to take such happiness as life with me might give you while she
was unhappy, and, as you imagined, with no hope of release. Even
then I didn't feel as you did about it; I understood better the trend
of things here. But ten years ago the change hadn't really come;
and I had no way of convincing you that it was coming. Still, I always fancied that Leila might not think her case was closed, and
so I chose to think that ours wasn't either. Let me go on thinking
so, at any rate, till you've seen her, and confirmed with your own
eyes what Susy Suffern tells you."

III

All through what Susy Suffern told and retold during their four-
hours' flight to the hills this plea of Ide's kept coming back to Mrs.
Lidcote. She did not yet know what she felt as to its bearing on
her own fate, but it was something on which her confused
thoughts could stay themselves amid the welter of new impressions, and she was inexpressibly glad that he had said what he
had, and said it at that particular moment. It helped her to hold
fast to her identity in the rush of strange names and new categories that her cousin's talk poured out on her.

With the progress of the journey Miss Suffern's communications grew more and more amazing. She was like a cicerone
preparing the mind of an inexperienced traveller for the marvels
about to burst on it.

"You won't know Leila. She's had her pearls reset. Sargent's to
paint her. Oh, and I was to tell you that she hopes you won't mind
being the least bit squeezed over Sunday. The house was built by
Wilbour's father, you know, and it's rather old-fashioned—only
ten spare bedrooms. Of course that's small for what they mean to
do, and she'll show you the new plans they've had made. Their
idea is to keep the present house as a wing. She told me to
explain—she's so dreadfully sorry not to be able to give you a
sitting-room just at first. They're thinking of Egypt for next winter, unless, of course, Wilbour gets his appointment. Oh, didn't
she write you about that? Why, he wants Rome, you know—the

second secretaryship. Or, rather, he wanted England; but Leila insisted that if they went abroad she must be near you. You see Horace's uncle is in the Cabinet—one of the assistant secretaries—and I believe he has a good deal of pull—"

"Horace's uncle? You mean Wilbour's, I suppose," Mrs. Lidcote interjected, with a gasp of which a fraction was given to Miss Suffern's flippant use of the language.

"Wilbour's? No, I don't. I mean Horace's. There's no bad feeling between them, I assure you. Since Horace's engagement was announced—you didn't know Horace was engaged? Why, he's marrying one of Bishop Thorbury's girls: the red-haired one who wrote the novel that every one's talking about, 'This Flesh of Mine.' They're to be married in the cathedral. Of course Horace *can,* because it was Leila who—but, as I say, there's not the *least* feeling, and Horace wrote himself to his uncle about Wilbour."

Mrs. Lidcote's thoughts fled back to what she had said to Ide the day before on the deck of the *Utopia.* "I didn't take up much room before, but now where is there a corner for me?" Where indeed in this crowded, topsy-turvy world, with its headlong changes and helter-skelter readjustments, its new tolerances and indifferences and accommodations, was there room for a character fashioned by slower, sterner processes and a life broken under their inexorable pressure? And then, in a flash, she viewed the chaos from a new angle, and order seemed to move upon the void. If the old processes were changed, her case was changed with them; she, too, was a part of the general readjustment, a tiny fragment of the new pattern worked out in bolder freer harmonies. Since her daughter had no penalty to pay, was not she herself released by the same stroke? The rich arrears of youth and joy were gone; but was there not time enough left to accumulate new stores of happiness? That, of course, was what Franklin Ide had felt and had meant her to feel. He had seen at once what the change in her daughter's situation would make in her view of her own. It was almost—wondrously enough!—as if Leila's folly had been the means of vindicating hers.

Everything else for the moment faded for Mrs. Lidcote in the glow of her daughter's embrace. It was unnatural, it was almost terrifying, to find herself standing on a strange threshold, under an unknown roof, in a big hall full of pictures, flowers, firelight, and hurrying servants, and in this spacious unfamiliar confusion to discover Leila, bareheaded, laughing, authoritative, with a strange young man jovially echoing her welcome and transmitting her orders; but once Mrs. Lidcote had her child on her breast, and her child's "It's all right, you old darling!" in her ears, every other feeling was lost in the deep sense of well-being that only Leila's hug could give.

The sense was still with her, warming her veins and pleasantly fluttering her heart, as she went up to her room after luncheon. A little constrained by the presence of visitors, and not altogether sorry to defer for a few hours the "long talk" with her daughter for which she somehow felt herself tremulously unready, she had withdrawn, on the plea of fatigue, to the bright luxurious bedroom into which Leila had again and again apologized for having been obliged to squeeze her. The room was bigger and finer than any in her small apartment in Florence; but it was not the standard of affluence implied in her daughter's tone about it that chiefly struck her, nor yet the finish and complexity of its appointments. It was the look it shared with the rest of the house, and with the perspective of the gardens beneath its windows, of being part of an "establishment"—of something solid, avowed, founded on sacraments and precedents and principles. There was nothing about the place, or about Leila and Wilbour, that suggested either passion or peril: their relation seemed as comfortable as their furniture and as respectable as their balance at the bank.

This was, in the whole confusing experience, the thing that confused Mrs. Lidcote most, that gave her at once the deepest feeling of security for Leila and the strongest sense of apprehension for herself. Yes, there was something oppressive in the completeness and compactness of Leila's well-being. Ide had been right: her daughter did not need her. Leila, with her first embrace, had unconsciously attested the fact in the same phrase as Ide himself and as the two young women with the hats. "It's all right, you old darling!" she had said: and her mother sat alone, trying to fit herself in the new scheme of things which such a certainty betokened.

Her first distinct feeling was one of irrational resentment. If such a change was to come, why had it not come sooner? Here was she, a woman not yet old, who had paid with the best years of her life for the theft of the happiness that her daughter's contemporaries were taking as their due. There was no sense, no sequence, in it. She had had what she wanted, but she had had to pay too much for it. She had had to pay the last bitterest price of learning that love has a price: that it is worth so much and no more. She had known the anguish of watching the man she loved discover this first, and of reading the discovery in his eyes. It was a part of her history that she had not trusted herself to think of for a long time past: she always took a big turn about that haunted corner. But now, at the sight of the young man downstairs, so openly and jovially Leila's, she was overwhelmed at the senseless waste of her own adventure, and wrung with the irony of perceiving that the success or failure of the deepest human experiences may hang on a matter of chronology.

Then gradually the thought of Ide returned to her. "I chose to think that our case wasn't closed," he had said. She had been deeply touched by that. To everyone else her case had been closed so long! *Finis* was scrawled all over her. But here was one man who had believed and waited, and what if what he believed in and waited for were coming true? If Leila's "all right" should really foreshadow hers?

As yet, of course, it was impossible to tell. She had fancied, indeed, when she entered the drawing-room before luncheon, that a too-sudden hush had fallen on the assembled group of Leila's friends, on the slender vociferous young women and the lounging golf-stockinged young men. They had all received her politely, with the kind of petrified politeness that may be either a tribute to age or a protest at laxity; but to them, of course, she must be an old woman because she was Leila's mother, and in a society so dominated by youth the mere presence of maturity was a constraint.

One of the young girls, however, had presently emerged from the group, and, attaching herself to Mrs. Lidcote, had listened to her with a blue gaze of admiration which gave the older woman a sudden happy consciousness of her long-forgotten social graces. It was agreeable to find herself attracting this young Charlotte Wynn, whose mother had been among her closest friends, and in whom something of the soberness and softness of the earlier manners had survived. But the little colloquy, broken up by the announcement of luncheon, could of course result in nothing more definite than this reminiscent emotion.

No, she could not yet tell how her own case was to be fitted into the new order of things; but there were more people—"older people" Leila had put it—arriving by the afternoon train, and that evening at dinner she would doubtless be able to judge. She began to wonder nervously who the new-comers might be. Probably she would be spared the embarrassment of finding old acquaintances among them; but it was odd that her daughter had mentioned no names.

Leila had proposed that, later in the afternoon, Wilbour should take her mother for a drive: she said she wanted them to have a "nice, quiet talk." But Mrs. Lidcote wished her talk with Leila to come first, and had, moreover, at luncheon, caught stray allusions to an impending tennis-match in which her son-in-law was engaged. Her fatigue had been a sufficient pretext for declining the drive, and she had begged Leila to think of her as peacefully resting in her room till such time as they could snatch their quiet moment.

"Before tea, then, you duck!" Leila with a last kiss had decided; and presently Mrs. Lidcote, through her open window, had heard the fresh loud voices of her daughter's visitors chiming across the gardens from the tennis-court.

IV

Leila had come and gone, and they had had their talk. It had not lasted as long as Mrs. Lidcote wished, for in the middle of it Leila had been summoned to the telephone to receive an important message from town, and had sent word to her mother that she couldn't come back just then, as one of the young ladies had been called away unexpectedly and arrangements had to be made for her departure. But the mother and daughter had had almost an hour together, and Mrs. Lidcote was happy. She had never seen Leila so tender, so solicitous. The only thing that troubled her was the very excess of this solicitude, the exaggerated expression of her daughter's annoyance that their first moments together should have been marred by the presence of strangers.

"Not strangers to me, darling, since they're friends of yours," her mother had assured her.

"Yes; but I know your feeling, you queer wild mother. I know how you've always hated people." (*Hated people!* Had Leila forgotten why?) "And that's why I told Susy that if you preferred to go with her to Ridgefield on Sunday I should perfectly understand, and patiently wait for our good hug. But you didn't really mind them at luncheon, did you, dearest?"

Mrs. Lidcote, at that, had suddenly thrown a startled look at her daughter. "I don't mind things of that kind any longer," she had simply answered.

"But that doesn't console me for having exposed you to the bother of it, for having let you come here when I ought to have *ordered* you off to Ridgefield with Susy. If Susy hadn't been stupid she'd have made you go there with her. I hate to think of you up here all alone."

Again Mrs. Lidcote tried to read something more than a rather obtuse devotion in her daughter's radiant gaze. "I'm glad to have had a rest this afternoon, dear; and later—"

"Oh, yes, later, when all this fuss is over, we'll more than make up for it, sha'n't we, you precious darling?" And at this point Leila had been summoned to the telephone, leaving Mrs. Lidcote to her conjectures.

These were still floating before her in cloudy uncertainty when Miss Suffern tapped at the door.

"You've come to take me down to tea? I'd forgotten how late it was," Mrs. Lidcote exclaimed.

Miss Suffern, a plump peering little woman, with prim hair and a conciliatory smile, nervously adjusted the pendent bugles of her elaborate black dress. Miss Suffern was always in mourning, and always commemorating the demise of distant relatives by wearing the discarded wardrobe of their next of kin. "It isn't *exactly* mourning," she would say; "but it's the only stitch of black poor Julia had—and of course George was only my mother's step-cousin."

As she came forward Mrs. Lidcote found herself humorously

wondering whether she were mourning Horace Pursh's divorce in one of his mother's old black satins.

"Oh, *did* you mean to go down for tea?" Susy Suffern peered at her, a little fluttered. "Leila sent me up to keep you company. She thought it would be cozier for you to stay here. She was afraid you were feeling rather tired."

"I was; but I've had the whole afternoon to rest in. And this wonderful sofa to help me."

"Leila told me to tell you that she'd rush up for a minute before dinner, after everybody had arrived; but the train is always dreadfully late. She's in despair at not giving you a sitting-room; she wanted to know if I thought you really minded."

"Of course I don't mind. It's not like Leila to think I should." Mrs. Lidcote drew aside to make way for the housemaid, who appeared in the doorway bearing a table spread with a bewildering variety of tea-cakes.

"Leila saw to it herself," Miss Suffern murmured as the door closed. "Her one idea is that you should feel happy here."

It struck Mrs. Lidcote as one more mark of the subverted state of things that her daughter's solicitude should find expression in the multiplicity of sandwiches and the piping-hotness of muffins; but then everything that had happened since her arrival seemed to increase her confusion.

The note of a motor-horn down the drive gave another turn to her thoughts. "Are those the new arrivals already?" she asked.

"Oh, dear, no; they won't be here till after seven." Miss Suffern craned her head from the window to catch a glimpse of the motor. "It must be Charlotte leaving."

"Was it the little Wynn girl who was called away in a hurry? I hope it's not on account of illness."

"Oh, no; I believe there was some mistake about dates. Her mother telephoned her that she was expected at the Stepleys', at Fishkill, and she had to be rushed over to Albany to catch a train."

Mrs. Lidcote meditated. "I'm sorry. She's a charming young thing. I hoped I should have another talk with her this evening after dinner."

"Yes, it's too bad." Miss Suffern's gaze grew vague. "You *do* look tired, you know," she continued, seating herself at the tea-table and preparing to dispense its delicacies. "You must go straight back to your sofa and let me wait on you. The excitement has told on you more than you think, and you mustn't fight against it any longer. Just stay quietly up here and let yourself go. You'll have Leila to yourself on Monday."

Mrs. Lidcote received the tea-cup which her cousin proffered, but showed no other disposition to obey her injunctions. For a moment she stirred her tea in silence; then she asked: "Is it your idea that I should stay quietly up here till Monday?"

Miss Suffern set down her cup with a gesture so sudden that it endangered an adjacent plate of scones. When she had assured herself of the safety of the scones she looked up with a fluttered laugh. "Perhaps, dear, by to-morrow you'll be feeling differently. The air here, you know—"

"Yes, I know." Mrs. Lidcote bent forward to help herself to a scone. "Who's arriving this evening?" she asked.

Miss Suffern frowned and peered. "You know my wretched head for names. Leila told me—but there are so many—"

"So many? She didn't tell me she expected a big party."

"Oh, not big: but rather outside of her little group. And of course, as it's the first time, she's a little excited at having the older set."

"The older set? Our contemporaries, you mean?"

"Why—yes." Miss Suffern paused as if to gather herself up for a leap. "The Ashton Gileses," she brought out.

"The Ashton Gileses? Really? I shall be glad to see Mary Giles again. It must be eighteen years," said Mrs. Lidcote steadily.

"Yes," Miss Suffern gasped, precipitately refilling her cup.

"The Ashton Gileses; and who else?"

"Well, the Sam Fresbies. But the most important person, of course, is Mrs. Lorin Boulger."

"Mrs. Boulger? Leila didn't tell me she was coming."

"Didn't she? I suppose she forgot everything when she saw you. But the party was got up for Mrs. Boulger. You see, it's very important that she should—well, take a fancy to Leila and Wilbour; his being appointed to Rome virtually depends on it. And you know Leila insists on Rome in order to be near you. So she asked Mary Giles, who's intimate with the Boulgers, if the visit couldn't possibly be arranged; and Mary's cable caught Mrs. Boulger at

Cherbourg. She's to be only a fortnight in America; and getting her to come directly here was rather a triumph."

"Yes; I see it was," said Mrs. Lidcote.

"You know, she's rather—rather fussy; and Mary was a little doubtful if—"

"If she would, on account of Leila?" Mrs. Lidcote murmured.

"Well, yes. In her official position. But luckily she's a friend of the Barkleys. And finding the Gileses and Fresbies here will make it all right. The times have changed!" Susy Suffern indulgently summed up.

Mrs. Lidcote smiled. "Yes; a few years ago it would have seemed improbable that I should ever again be dining with Mary Giles and Harriet Fresbie and Mrs. Lorin Boulger."

Miss Suffern did not at the moment seem disposed to enlarge upon this theme; and after an interval of silence Mrs. Lidcote suddenly resumed: "Do they know I'm here, by the way?"

The effect of her question was to produce in Miss Suffern an exaggerated access of peering and frowning. She twitched the tea-things about, fingered her bugles, and, looking at the clock, exclaimed amazedly: "Mercy! Is it seven already?"

"Not that it can make any difference, I suppose," Mrs. Lidcote continued. "But did Leila tell them I was coming?"

Miss Suffern looked at her with pain. "Why, you don't suppose, dearest, that Leila would do anything—"

Mrs. Lidcote went on: "For, of course, it's of the first importance, as you say, that Mrs. Lorin Boulger should be favorably impressed, in order that Wilbour may have the best possible chance of getting to Rome."

"I *told* Leila you'd feel that, dear. You see, it's actually on *your* account—so that they may get a post near you—that Leila invited Mrs. Boulger."

"Yes, I see that." Mrs. Lidcote, abruptly rising from her seat, turned her eyes to the clock. "But, as you say, it's getting late. Oughtn't we to dress for dinner?"

Miss Suffern, at the suggestion, stood up also, an agitated hand among her bugles. "I do wish I could persuade you to stay up here this evening. I'm sure Leila'd be happier if you would. Really, you're much too tired to come down."

"What nonsense, Susy!" Mrs. Lidcote spoke with sudden

sharpness, her hand stretched to the bell. "When do we dine? At half-past eight? Then I must really send you packing. At my age it takes time to dress."

Miss Suffern, thus projected toward the threshold, lingered there to repeat: "Leila'll never forgive herself if you make an effort you're not up to." But Mrs. Lidcote smiled on her without answering, and the icy light-wave propelled her through the door.

V

Mrs. Lidcote, though she had made the gesture of ringing for her maid, had not done so.

When the door closed, she continued to stand motionless in the middle of her soft, spacious room. The fire which had been kindled at twilight danced on the brightness of silver and mirrors and sober gilding; and the sofa toward which she had been urged by Miss Suffern heaped up its cushions in inviting proximity to a table laden with new books and papers. She could not recall having ever been more luxuriously housed, or having ever had so strange a sense of being out alone, under the night, in a wind-beaten plain. She sat down by the fire and thought.

A knock on the door made her lift her head, and she saw her daughter on the threshold. The intricate ordering of Leila's fair hair and the flying folds of her dressing-gown showed that she had interrupted her dressing to hasten to her mother; but once in the room she paused a moment, smiling uncertainly, as though she had forgotten the object of her haste.

Mrs. Lidcote rose to her feet. "Time to dress, dearest? Don't scold, I sha'n't be late."

"To dress?" Leila stood before her with a puzzled look. "Why, I thought, dear—I mean, I hoped you'd decided just to stay here quietly and rest."

Her mother smiled. "But I've been resting all the afternoon!"

"Yes, but—you know you *do* look tired. And when Susy told me just now that you meant to make the effort—"

"You came to stop me?"

"I came to tell you that you needn't feel in the least obliged—"

"Of course. I understand that."

There was a pause during which Leila, vaguely averting herself from her mother's scrutiny, drifted toward the dressing-table and began to disturb the symmetry of the brushes and bottles laid out on it.

"Do your visitors know that I'm here?" Mrs. Lidcote suddenly went on.

"Do they—Of course—why, naturally," Leila rejoined, absorbed in trying to turn the stopper of a salts-bottle.

"Then won't they think it odd if I don't appear?"

"Oh, not in the least, dearest. I assure you they'll *all* understand." Leila laid down the bottle and turned back to her mother, her face alight with reassurance.

Mrs. Lidcote stood motionless, her head erect, her smiling eyes on her daughter's. "Will they think it odd if I *do?*"

Leila stopped short, her lips half parted to reply. As she paused, the colour stole over her bare neck, swept up to her throat, and burst into flame in her cheeks. Thence it sent its devastating crimson up to her very temples, to the lobes of her ears, to the edges of her eye-lids, beating all over her in fiery waves, as if fanned by some imperceptible wind.

Mrs. Lidcote silently watched the conflagration; then she turned away her eyes with a slight laugh. "I only meant that I was afraid it might upset the arrangement of your dinner-table if I didn't come down. If you can assure me that it won't, I believe I'll take you at your word and go back to this irresistible sofa." She paused, as if waiting for her daughter to speak; then she held out her arms. "Run off and dress, dearest; and don't have me on your mind." She clasped Leila close, pressing a long kiss on the last afterglow of her subsiding blush. "I do feel the least bit overdone, and if it won't inconvenience you to have me drop out of things, I believe I'll basely take to my bed and stay there till your party scatters. And now run off, or you'll be late; and make my excuses to them all."

VI

The Barkleys' visitors had dispersed, and Mrs. Lidcote, completely restored by her two days' rest, found herself, on the following Monday alone with her children and Miss Suffern.

There was a note of jubilation in the air, for the party had "gone off" so extraordinarily well, and so completely, as it appeared, to the satisfaction of Mrs. Lorin Boulger, that Wilbour's early appointment to Rome was almost to be counted on. So certain did this seem that the prospect of a prompt reunion mitigated the distress with which Leila learned of her mother's decision to return almost immediately to Italy. No one understood this decision; it seemed to Leila absolutely unintelligible that Mrs. Lidcote should not stay on with them till their own fate was fixed, and Wilbour echoed her astonishment.

"Why shouldn't you, as Leila says, wait here till we can all pack up and go together?"

Mrs. Lidcote smiled her gratitude with her refusal. "After all, it's not yet sure that you'll be packing up."

"Oh, you ought to have seen Wilbour with Mrs. Boulger," Leila triumphed.

"No, you ought to have seen Leila with her," Leila's husband exulted.

Miss Suffern enthusiastically appended: "I *do* think inviting Harriet Fresbie was a stroke of genius!"

"Oh, we'll be with you soon," Leila laughed. "So soon that it's really foolish to separate."

But Mrs. Lidcote held out with the quiet firmness which her daughter knew it was useless to oppose. After her long months in India, it was really imperative, she declared, that she should get back to Florence and see what was happening to her little place there; and she had been so comfortable on the *Utopia* that she had a fancy to return by the same ship. There was nothing for it, therefore, but to acquiesce in her decision and keep her with them till the afternoon before the day of the *Utopia's* sailing. This arrangement fitted in with certain projects which, during her two days' seclusion, Mrs. Lidcote had silently matured. It had become to her of the first importance to get away as soon as she could, and the little place in Florence, which held her past in every fold of its curtains and between every page of its books, seemed now to her the one spot where that past would be endurable to look upon.

She was not unhappy during the intervening days. The sight of Leila's well-being, the sense of Leila's tenderness, were, after all, what she had come for; and of these she had had full measure.

Leila had never been happier or more tender; and the contemplation of her bliss, and the enjoyment of her affection, were an absorbing occupation for her mother. But they were also a sharp strain on certain overtightened chords, and Mrs. Lidcote, when at last she found herself alone in the New York hotel to which she had returned the night before embarking, had the feeling that she had just escaped with her life from the clutch of a giant hand.

She had refused to let her daughter come to town with her; she had even rejected Susy Suffern's company. She wanted no viaticum but that of her own thoughts; and she let these come to her without shrinking from them as she sat in the same high-hung sitting-room in which, just a week before, she and Franklin Ide had had their memorable talk.

She had promised her friend to let him hear from her, but she had not kept her promise. She knew that he had probably come back from Chicago, and that if he learned of her sudden decision to return to Italy it would be impossible for her not to see him before sailing; and as she wished above all things not to see him she had kept silent, intending to send him a letter from the steamer.

There was no reason why she should wait till then to write it. The actual moment was more favorable, and the task, though not agreeable, would at least bridge over an hour of her lonely evening. She went up to the writing-table, drew out a sheet of paper and began to write his name. And as she did so, the door opened and he came in.

The words she met him with were the last she could have imagined herself saying when they had parted. "How in the world did you know that I was here?"

He caught her meaning in a flash. "You didn't want me to, then?" He stood looking at her. "Suppose I ought to have taken your silence as meaning that. But I happened to meet Mrs. Wynn, who is stopping here, and she asked me to dine with her and Charlotte, and Charlotte's young man. They told me they'd seen you arriving this afternoon, and I couldn't help coming up."

There was a pause between them, which Mrs. Lidcote at last surprisingly broke with the exclamation: "Ah, she *did* recognize me, then!"

"Recognize you?" He stated. "Why—"

"Oh, I saw she did, though she never moved an eyelid. I saw it by Charlotte's blush. The child has the prettiest blush. I saw that her mother wouldn't let her speak to me."

Ide put down his hat with an impatient laugh. "Hasn't Leila cured you of your delusions?"

She looked at him intently. "Then you don't think Margaret Wynn meant to cut me?"

"I think your ideas are absurd."

She paused for a perceptible moment without taking this up; then she said, at a tangent: "I'm sailing tomorrow early. I meant to write to you—there's the letter I'd begun."

Ide followed her gesture, and then turned his eyes back to her face. "You didn't mean to see me, then, or even to let me know that you were going till you'd left?"

"I felt it would be easier to explain to you in a letter—"

"What in God's name is there to explain?" She made no reply, and he pressed on: "It can't be that you're worried about Leila, for Charlotte Wynn told me she'd been there last week, and there was a big party arriving when she left: Fresbies and Gileses, and Mrs. Lorin Boulger—all the board of examiners! If Leila has passed *that,* she's got her degree."

Mrs. Lidcote had dropped down into a corner of the sofa where she had sat during their talk of the week before. "I was stupid," she began abruptly. "I ought to have gone to Ridgefield with Susy. I didn't see till afterward that I was expected to."

"You were expected to?"

"Yes. Oh, it wasn't Leila's fault. She suffered—poor darling; she was distracted. But she'd asked her party before she knew I was arriving."

"Oh, as to that—" Ide drew a deep breath of relief. "I can understand that it must have been a disappointment not to have you to herself just at first. But, after all, you were among old friends or their children: the Gileses and Fresbies—and little Charlotte Wynn." He paused a moment before the last name, and scrutinized her hesitatingly. "Even if they came at the wrong time, you must have been glad to see them all at Leila's."

She gave him back his look with a faint smile. "I didn't see them."

"You didn't see them?"

"No. That is, excepting little Charlotte Wynn. That child is exquisite. We had a talk before luncheon the day I arrived. But when her mother found out that I was staying in the house she telephoned her to leave immediately, and so I didn't see her again."

The colour rushed to Ide's sallow face. "I don't know where you get such ideas!"

She pursued, as if she had not heard him: "Oh, and I saw Mary Giles for a minute too. Susy Suffern brought her up to my room the last evening, after dinner, when all the others were at bridge. She meant it kindly—but it wasn't much use."

"But what were you doing in your room in the evening after dinner?"

"Why, you see, when I found out my mistake in coming—how embarrassing it was for Leila, I mean—I simply told her I was very tired, and preferred to stay upstairs till the party was over."

Ide, with a groan, struck his hand against the arm of the chair. "I wonder how much of all this you simply imagined!"

"I didn't imagine the fact of Harriet Fresbie's not even asking if she might see me when she knew I was in the house. Nor of Mary Giles's getting Susy, at the eleventh hour, to smuggle her up to my room when the others wouldn't know where she'd gone; nor poor Leila's ghastly fear lest Mrs. Lorin Boulger, for whom the party was given, should guess I was in the house, and prevent her husband's giving Wilbour the second secretaryship because she'd been obliged to spend a night under the same roof with his mother-in-law!"

Ide continued to drum on his chair-arm with exasperated fingers. "You don't *know* that any of the acts you describe are due to the causes you suppose."

Mrs. Lidcote paused before replying, as if honestly trying to measure the weight of this argument. Then she said in a low tone: "I know that Leila was in an agony lest I should come down to dinner the first night. And it was for me she was afraid, not for herself. Leila is never afraid for herself."

"But the conclusions you draw are simply preposterous. There are narrow-minded women everywhere, but the women who were at Leila's knew perfectly well that their going there would give her a sort of social sanction, and if they were willing that she should have it, why on earth should they want to withhold it from you?"

"That's what I told myself a week ago, in this very room after my first talk with Susy Suffern." She lifted a misty smile to his anxious eyes. "That's why I listened to what you said to me the same evening, and why your arguments half convinced me, and made me think that what had been possible for Leila might not be impossible for me. If the new dispensation had come, why not for me as well as for the others? I can't tell you the flight my imagination took!"

Franklin Ide rose from his seat and crossed the room to a chair near her sofa-corner. "All I cared about was that it seemed—for the moment—to be carrying you toward me," he said.

"I cared about that, too. That's why I meant to go away without seeing you." They gave each other grave look for look. "Because, you see, I was mistaken," she went on. "We were both mistaken. You say it's preposterous that the women who didn't object to accepting Leila's hospitality should have objected to meeting me under her roof. And so it is; but I begin to understand why. It's simply that society is much too busy to revise its own judgments. Probably no one in the house with me stopped to consider that my case and Leila's were identical. They only remembered that I'd done something which, at the time I did it, was condemned by society. My case has been passed on and classified: I'm the woman who has been cut for nearly twenty years. The older people have half forgotten why, and the younger ones have never really known: it's simply become a tradition to cut me. And traditions that have lost their meaning are the hardest of all to destroy."

Ide sat motionless while she spoke. As she ended, he stood up with a short laugh and walked across the room to the window. Outside, the immense black prospect of New York, strung with its myriad lines of light, stretched away into the smoky edges of the night. He showed it to her with a gesture.

"What do you suppose such words as you've been using—'society,' 'tradition,' and the rest—mean to all the life out there?"

She came and stood by him in the window. "Less than nothing, of course. But you and I are not out there. We're shut up in a little tight round of habit and association, just as we're shut up in this room. Remember, I thought I'd got out of it once; but what really happened was that the other people went out, and left me in the same little room. The only difference was that I was there alone. Oh, I've made it habitable now, I'm used to it; but I've lost any illusions I may have had as to an angel's opening the door."

Ide again laughed impatiently. "Well, if the door won't open, why not let another prisoner in? At least it would be less of a solitude—"

She turned from the dark window back into the vividly lighted room.

"It would be more of a prison. You forget that I know all about that. We're all imprisoned, of course—all of us middling people, who don't carry our freedom in our brains. But we've accommodated ourselves to our different cells, and if we're moved suddenly into new ones we're likely to find a stone wall where we thought there was thin air, and to knock ourselves senseless against it. I saw a man do that once."

Ide, leaning with folded arms against the window-frame, watched her in silence as she moved restlessly about the room, gathering together some scattered books and tossing a handful of torn letters into the paper-basket. When she ceased, he rejoined: "All you say is based on preconceived theories. Why didn't you put them to the test by coming down to meet your old friends? Don't you see the inference they would naturally draw from your hiding yourself when they arrived? It looked as though you were afraid of them—or as though you hadn't forgiven them. Either way, you put them in the wrong instead of waiting to let them put you in the right. If Leila had buried herself in a desert do you suppose society would have gone to fetch her out? You say you were afraid for Leila and that she was afraid for you. Don't you see what all these complications of feeling mean? Simply that you were too nervous at the moment to let things happen naturally, just as you're too nervous now to judge them rationally." He paused and turned his eyes to her face. "Don't try to just yet. Give yourself a little more time. Give *me* a little more time. I've always known it would take time."

He moved nearer, and she let him have her hand. With the grave kindness of his face so close above her she felt like a child roused out of frightened dreams and finding a light in the room.

"Perhaps you're right—" she heard herself begin; then something within her clutched her back, and her hand fell away from him.

"I know I'm right: trust me," he urged. "We'll talk of this in Florence soon."

She stood before him, feeling with despair his kindness, his patience and his unreality. Everything he said seemed like a painted gauze let down between herself and the real facts of life; and a sudden desire seized her to tear the gauze into shreds.

She drew back and looked at him with a smile of superficial reassurance. "You *are* right—about not talking any longer now. I'm nervous and tired, and it would do no good. I brood over things too much. As you say, I must try not to shrink from people." She turned away and glanced at the clock. "Why, it's only ten! If I send you off I shall begin to brood again; and if you stay we shall go on talking about the same thing. Why shouldn't we go down and see Margaret Wynn for half an hour?"

She spoke lightly and rapidly, her brilliant eyes on his face. As she watched him, she saw it change, as if her smile had thrown a too vivid light upon it.

"Oh, no—not to-night!" he exclaimed.

"Not to-night? Why, what other night have I, when I'm off at dawn? Besides, I want to show you at once that I mean to be more sensible—that I'm not going to be afraid of people any more. And I should really like another glimpse of little Charlotte." He stood before her, his hand in his beard, with the gesture he had in moments of perplexity. "Come!" she ordered him gaily, turning to the door.

He followed her and laid his hand on her arm. "Don't you think—hadn't you better let me go first and see? They told me they'd had a tiring day at the dressmaker's. I daresay they have gone to bed."

"But you said they'd a young man of Charlotte's dining with them. Surely he wouldn't have left by ten? At any rate, I'll go down with you and see. It takes so long if one sends a servant first." She put him gently aside, and then paused as a new thought struck her. "Or wait; my maid's in the next room. I'll tell her to go and ask if Margaret will receive me. Yes, that's much the best way."

She turned back and went toward the door that led to her bedroom; but before she could open it she felt Ide's quick touch again.

"I believe—I remember now—Charlotte's young man was suggesting that they should all go out—to a music-hall or something of the sort. I'm sure—I'm positively sure that you won't find them."

Her hand dropped from the door, his dropped from her arm, and as they drew back and faced each other she saw the blood rise slowly through his sallow skin, redden his neck and ears, encroach upon the edges of his beard, and settle in dull patches under his kind troubled eyes. She had seen the same blush on another face, and the same impulse of compassion she had then felt made her turn her gaze away again.

A knock on the door broke the silence, and a porter put his head into the room.

"It's only just to know how many pieces there'll be to go down to the steamer in the morning."

With the words she felt that the veil of painted gauze was torn in tatters, and that she was moving again among the grim edges of reality.

"Oh, dear," she exclaimed. "I never *can* remember! Wait a minute; I shall have to ask my maid."

She opened her bedroom door and called out: "Annette!"

XINGU

Mrs. Ballinger is one of the ladies who pursue Culture in bands, as though it were dangerous to meet alone. To this end she had founded the Lunch Club, an association composed of herself and several other indomitable huntresses of erudition. The Lunch Club, after three or four winters of lunching and debate, had acquired such local distinction that the entertainment of distinguished strangers became one of its accepted functions; in recognition of which it duly extended to the celebrated Osric Dane, on the day of her arrival in Hillbridge, an invitation to be present at the next meeting.

The club was to meet at Mrs. Ballinger's. The other members, behind her back, were of one voice in deploring her unwillingness to cede her rights in favor of Mrs. Plinth, whose house made a more impressive setting for the entertainment of celebrities; while, as Mrs. Leveret observed, there was always the picture gallery to fall back on.

Mrs. Plinth made no secret of sharing this view. She had always regarded it as one of her obligations to entertain the Lunch Club's distinguished guests. Mrs. Plinth was almost as proud of her obligations as she was of her picture gallery; she was in fact fond of implying that the one possession implied the other, and that only a woman of her wealth could afford to live up to a standard as high as that which she had set herself. An all-round sense of duty, roughly adaptable to various ends, was, in her opinion, all that Providence exacted of the more humbly stationed; but the power which had predestined Mrs. Plinth to keep a footman clearly intended her to maintain an equally specialized staff of responsibilities. It was the more to be regretted that Mrs. Ballinger, whose obligations to society were bounded by the narrow scope of two

parlormaids, should have been so tenacious of the right to entertain Osric Dane.

The question of that lady's reception had for a month past profoundly moved the members of the Lunch Club. It was not that
they felt themselves unequal to the task, but that their sense of the
opportunity plunged them into the agreeable uncertainty of the
lady who weighs the alternatives of a well-stocked wardrobe. If
such subsidiary members as Mrs. Leveret were fluttered by the
thought of exchanging ideas with the author of *The Wings of
Death,* no forebodings disturbed the conscious adequacy of Mrs.
Plinth, Mrs. Ballinger and Miss Van Vluyck. *The Wings of Death*
had, in fact, at Miss Van Vluyck's suggestion, been chosen as the
subject of discussion at the last club meeting, and each member
had thus been enabled to express her own opinion or to appropriate whatever sounded well in the comments of the others.

Mrs. Roby alone had abstained from profiting by the opportunity but it was now openly recognized that, as a member of the
Lunch Club, Mrs. Roby was a failure. "It all comes," as Miss Van
Vluyck put it, "of accepting a woman on a man's estimation."
Mrs. Roby, returning to Hillbridge from a prolonged sojourn in
exotic lands—the other ladies no longer took the trouble to remember where—had been heralded by the distinguished biologist,
Professor Foreland, as the most agreeable woman he had ever met;
and the members of the Lunch Club, impressed by an encomium
that carried the weight of a diploma, and rashly assuming that the
Professor's social sympathies would follow the line of his professional bent, had seized the chance of annexing a biological member. Their disillusionment was complete. At Miss Van Vluyck's first
offhand mention of the pterodactyl Mrs. Roby had confusedly
murmured: "I know so little about meters—" and after that painful betrayal of incompetence she had prudently withdrawn from
further participation in the mental gymnastics of the club.

"I suppose she flattered him," Miss Van Vluyck summed up—
"or else it's the way she does her hair."

The dimensions of Miss Van Vluyck's dining room having restricted the membership of the club to six, the nonconductiveness
of one member was a serious obstacle to the exchange of ideas,
and some wonder had already been expressed that Mrs. Roby
should care to live, as it were, on the intellectual bounty of the

others. This feeling was increased by the discovery that she had not yet read *The Wings of Death*. She owned to having heard the name of Osric Dane; but that—incredible as it appeared—was the extent of her acquaintance with the celebrated novelist. The ladies could not conceal their surprise; but Mrs. Ballinger, whose pride in the club made her wish to put even Mrs. Roby in the best possible light, gently insinuated that, though she had not had time to acquaint herself with *The Wings of Death,* she must at least be familiar with its equally remarkable predecessor, *The Supreme Instant.*

Mrs. Roby wrinkled her sunny brows in a conscientious effort of memory, as a result of which she recalled that, oh, yes, she *had* seen the book at her brother's, when she was staying with him in Brazil, and had even carried it off to read one day on a boating party; but they had all got to shying things at each other in the boat, and the book had gone overboard, so she had never had the chance—

The picture evoked by this anecdote did not increase Mrs. Roby's credit with the club, and there was a painful pause, which was broken by Mrs. Plinth's remarking: "I can understand that, with all your other pursuits, you should not find much time for reading; but I should have thought you might at least have *got up The Wings of Death* before Osric Dane's arrival."

Mrs. Roby took this rebuke good-humoredly. She had meant, she owned, to glance through the book; but she had been so absorbed in a novel of Trollope's that—

"No one reads Trollope now," Mrs. Ballinger interrupted.

Mrs. Roby looked pained. "I'm only just beginning," she confessed.

"And does he interest you?" Mrs. Plinth inquired.

"He amuses me."

"Amusement," said Mrs. Plinth, "is hardly what I look for in my choice of books."

"Oh, certainly, *The Wings of Death* is not amusing," ventured Mrs. Leveret, whose manner of putting forth an opinion was like that of an obliging salesman with a variety of other styles to submit if his first selection does not suit.

"Was it *meant* to be?" inquired Mrs. Plinth, who was fond of asking questions that she permitted no one but herself to answer. "Assuredly not."

"Assuredly not—that is what I was going to say," assented Mrs. Leveret, hastily rolling up her opinion and reaching for another. "It was meant to—to elevate."

Miss Van Vluyck adjusted her spectacles as though they were the black cap of condemnation. "I hardly see," she interposed, "how a book steeped in the bitterest pessimism can be said to elevate, however much it may instruct."

"I meant, of course, to instruct," said Mrs. Leveret, flurried by the unexpected distinction between two terms which she had supposed to be synonymous. Mrs. Leveret's enjoyment of the Lunch Club was frequently marred by such surprises; and not knowing her own value to the other ladies as a mirror for their mental complacency she was sometimes troubled by a doubt of her worthiness to join in their debates. It was only the fact of having a dull sister who thought her clever that saved her from a sense of hopeless inferiority.

"Do they get married in the end?" Mrs. Roby interposed.

"They—who?" the Lunch Club collectively exclaimed.

"Why, the girl and man. It's a novel, isn't it? I always think that's the one thing that matters. If they're parted it spoils my dinner."

Mrs. Plinth and Mrs. Ballinger exchanged scandalized glances, and the latter said: "I should hardly advise you to read *The Wings of Death* in that spirit. For my part, when there are so many books one *has* to read, I wonder how any one can find time for those that are merely amusing."

"The beautiful part of it," Laura Glyde murmured, "is surely just this—that no one can tell *how The Wings of Death* ends. Osric Dane, overcome by the awful significance of her own meaning, has mercifully veiled it—perhaps even from herself—as Apelles, in representing the sacrifice of Iphigenia, veiled the face of Agamemnon."

"What's that? Is it poetry?" whispered Mrs. Leveret to Mrs. Plinth, who, disdaining a definite reply, said coldly: "You should look it up. I always make it a point to look things up." Her tone added—"Though I might easily have it done for me by the footman."

"I was about to say," Miss Van Vluyck resumed, "that it must always be a question whether a book *can* instruct unless it elevates."

"Oh—" murmured Mrs. Leveret, now feeling herself hopelessly astray.

"I don't know," said Mrs. Ballinger, scenting in Miss Van Vluyck's tone a tendency to depreciate the coveted distinction of entertaining Osric Dane; "I don't know that such a question can seriously be raised as to a book which has attracted more attention among thoughtful people than any novel since *Robert Elsmere*."[1]

"Oh, but don't you see," exclaimed Laura Glyde, "that it's just the dark hopelessness of it all—the wonderful tone scheme of black on black—that makes it such an artistic achievement? It reminded me when I read it of Prince Rupert's *manière noire*[2] . . . the book is etched, not painted, yet one feels the color values so intensely. . . ."

"Who is *he?*" Mrs. Leveret whispered to her neighbor. "Someone she's met abroad?"

"The wonderful part of the book," Mrs. Ballinger conceded, "is that it may be looked at from so many points of view. I hear that as a study of determinism Professor Lupton ranks it with *The Data of Ethics*."[3]

"I'm told that Osric Dane spent ten years in preparatory studies before beginning to write it," said Mrs. Plinth. "She looks up everything—verifies everything. It has always been my principle, as you know. Nothing would induce me, now, to put aside a book before I'd finished it, just because I can buy as many more as I want."

"And what do *you* think of *The Wings of Death?*" Mrs. Roby abruptly asked her.

It was the kind of question that might be termed out of order, and the ladies glanced at each other as though disclaiming any share in such a breach of discipline. They all knew there was nothing Mrs. Plinth so much disliked as being asked her opinion of a book. Books were written to read; if one read them what more could be expected? To be questioned in detail regarding the contents of a volume seemed to her as great an outrage as being searched for smuggled laces at the Custom House. The club had always respected this idiosyncrasy of Mrs. Plinth's. Such opinions as she had were imposing and substantial: her mind, like her house, was furnished with monumental "pieces" that were not meant to be disarranged; and it was one of the unwritten rules of the Lunch Club that, within her own province, each member's habits of thought should be respected. The meeting therefore closed with an increased sense, on the part of the other ladies, of Mrs. Roby's hopeless unfitness to be one of them.

II

Mrs. Leveret, on the eventful day, arrived early at Mrs. Ballinger's, her volume of *Appropriate Allusions* in her pocket.

It always flustered Mrs. Leveret to be late at the Lunch Club: she liked to collect her thoughts and gather a hint, as the others assembled, of the turn the conversation was likely to take. Today, however, she felt herself completely at a loss; and even the familiar contact of *Appropriate Allusions,* which stuck into her as she sat down, failed to give her any reassurance. It was an admirable little volume, compiled to meet all the social emergencies; so that, whether on the occasion of Anniversaries, joyful or melancholy (as the classification ran), of Banquets, social or municipal, or of Baptisms, Church of England or sectarian, its student need never be at a loss for a pertinent reference. Mrs. Leveret, though she had for years devoutly conned its pages, valued it, however, rather for its moral support than for its practical services; for though in the privacy of her own room she commanded an army of quotations, these invariably deserted her at the critical moment, and the only phrase she retained—*Canst thou draw out leviathan with a hook?*[4]—was one she had never yet found occasion to apply.

Today she felt that even the complete mastery of the volume would hardly have insured her self-possession; for she thought it probable that, even if she *did*, in some miraculous way, remember an Allusion, it would be only to find that Osric Dane used a different volume (Mrs. Leveret was convinced that literary people always carried them), and would consequently not recognize her quotations.

Mrs. Leveret's sense of being adrift was intensified by the appearance of Mrs. Ballinger's drawing room. To a careless eye its aspect was unchanged; but those acquainted with Mrs. Ballinger's way of arranging her books would instantly have detected the marks of recent perturbation. Mrs. Ballinger's province, as a member of the Lunch Club, was the Book of the Day. On that, whatever it was, from a novel to a treatise on experimental psychology, she was confidently, authoritatively "up." What became of last year's books, or last week's even; what she did with the "subjects" she had previously professed with equal authority; no one had ever yet discovered. Her mind was an hotel where facts came and went like transient lodgers, without leaving their address behind, and frequently without paying for their board. It was Mrs. Ballinger's boast that she was "abreast with the Thought of the Day," and her pride that this advanced position should be expressed by the books on her table. These volumes, frequently renewed, and almost always damp from the press, bore names generally unfamiliar to Mrs. Leveret, and giving her, as she furtively scanned them, a disheartening glimpse of new fields of knowledge to be breathlessly traversed in Mrs. Ballinger's wake. But today a number of maturer-looking volumes were adroitly mingled with the *primeurs* of the press—Karl Marx[5] jostled Professor Bergson,[6] and the *Confessions of St. Augustine*[7] lay beside the last work on "Mendelism";[8] so that even to Mrs. Leveret's fluttered perceptions it was clear that Mrs. Ballinger didn't in the least know what Osric Dane was likely to talk about, and had taken measures to be prepared for anything. Mrs. Leveret felt like a passenger on an ocean steamer who is told that there is no immediate danger, but that she had better put on her lifebelt.

It was a relief to be roused from these forebodings by Miss Van Vluyck's arrival.

"Well, my dear," the newcomer briskly asked her hostess, "what subjects are we to discuss today?"

Mrs. Ballinger was furtively replacing a volume of Wordsworth[9] by a copy of Verlaine.[10] "I hardly know," she said, somewhat nervously. "Perhaps we had better leave that to circumstances."

"Circumstances?" said Miss Van Vluyck drily. "That means, I suppose, that Laura Glyde will take the floor as usual, and we shall be deluged with literature."

Philanthropy and statistics were Miss Van Vluyck's province, and she resented any tendency to divert their guest's attention from these topics.

Mrs. Plinth at this moment appeared.

"Literature?" she protested in a tone of remonstrance. "But this is perfectly unexpected. I understood we were to talk of Osric Dane's novel."

Mrs. Ballinger winced at the discrimination, but let it pass. "We can hardly make that our chief subject—at least not *too* intentionally," she suggested. "Of course we can let our talk *drift* in that direction; but we ought to have some other topic as an introduction, and that is what I wanted to consult you about. The fact is, we know so little of Osric Dane's tastes and interests that it is difficult to make any special preparation."

"It may be difficult," said Mrs. Plinth with decision, "but it is necessary. I know what that happy-go-lucky principle leads to. As I told one of my nieces the other day, there are certain emergencies for which a lady should always be prepared. It's in shocking taste to wear colors when one pays a visit of condolence, or a last year's dress when there are reports that one's husband is on the wrong side of the market; and so it is with conversation. All I ask is that I should know beforehand what is to be talked about; then I feel sure of being able to say the proper thing."

"I quite agree with you," Mrs. Ballinger assented; "but—"

And at that instant, heralded by the fluttered parlormaid, Osric Dane appeared upon the threshold.

Mrs. Leveret told her sister afterward that she had known at a glance what was coming. She saw that Osric Dane was not going to meet them halfway. That distinguished personage had indeed entered with an air of compulsion not calculated to promote the easy exercise of hospitality. She looked as though she were about to be photographed for a new edition of her books.

The desire to propitiate a divinity is generally in inverse ratio to its responsiveness, and the sense of discouragement produced by Osric Dane's entrance visibly increased the Lunch Club's eagerness to please her. Any lingering idea that she might consider herself under an obligation to her entertainers was at once dispelled by her manner: as Mrs. Leveret said afterward to her sister, she had a way of looking at you that made you feel as if there was something wrong with your hat. This evidence of greatness produced such an immediate impression on the ladies that a shudder of awe ran through them when Mrs. Roby, as their hostess led the great personage into the dining room, turned back to whisper to the others: "What a brute she is!"

The hour about the table did not tend to revise this verdict. It was passed by Osric Dane in the silent deglutition of Mrs. Ballinger's menu, and by the members of the club in the emission of tentative platitudes which their guest seemed to swallow as perfunctorily as the successive courses of the luncheon.

Mrs. Ballinger's reluctance to fix a topic had thrown the club into a mental disarray which increased with the return to the drawing room, where the actual business of discussion was to open. Each lady waited for the other to speak; and there was a general shock of disappointment when their hostess opened the conversation by the painfully commonplace inquiry: "Is this your first visit to Hillbridge?"

Even Mrs. Leveret was conscious that this was a bad beginning; and a vague impulse of deprecation made Miss Glyde interject: "It is a very small place indeed."

Mrs. Plinth bristled. "We have a great many representative people," she said, in the tone of one who speaks for her order.

Osric Dane turned to her. "What do they represent?" she asked.

Mrs. Plinth's constitutional dislike to being questioned was intensified by her sense of unpreparedness; and her reproachful glance passed the question on to Mrs. Ballinger.

"Why," said that lady, glancing in turn at the other members, "as a community I hope it is not too much to say that we stand for culture."

"For art—" Miss Glyde interjected.

"For art and literature," Mrs. Ballinger amended.

"And for sociology, I trust," snapped Miss Van Vluyck.

"We have a standard," said Mrs. Plinth, feeling herself suddenly secure on the vast expanse of a generalization; and Mrs. Leveret, thinking there must be room for more than one on so broad a statement, took courage to murmur: "Oh, certainly; we have a standard."

"The object of our little club," Mrs. Ballinger continued, "is to concentrate the highest tendencies of Hillbridge—to centralize and focus its intellectual effort."

This was felt to be so happy that the ladies drew an almost audible breath of relief.

"We aspire," the President went on, "to be in touch with whatever is highest in art, literature and ethics."

Osric Dane again turned to her. "What ethics?" she asked.

A tremor of apprehension encircled the room. None of the ladies required any preparation to pronounce on a question of morals; but when they were called ethics it was different. The club, when fresh from the *Encyclopedia Britannica,* the *Reader's Handbook* or Smith's *Classical Dictionary,* could deal confidently with any subject; but when taken unawares it had been known to define agnosticism as a heresy of the Early Church and Professor Froude as a distinguished histologist; and such minor members as Mrs. Leveret still secretly regarded ethics as something vaguely pagan.

Even to Mrs. Ballinger, Osric Dane's question was unsettling, and there was a general sense of gratitude when Laura Glyde leaned forward to say, with her most sympathetic accent: "You must excuse us, Mrs. Dane, for not being able, just at present, to talk of anything but *The Wings of Death.*"

"Yes," said Miss Van Vluyck, with a sudden resolve to carry the war into the enemy's camp. "We are so anxious to know the exact purpose you had in mind in writing your wonderful book."

"You will find," Mrs. Plinth interposed, "that we are not superficial readers."

"We are eager to hear from you," Miss Van Vluyck continued, "if the pessimistic tendency of the book is an expression of your own convictions or—"

"Or merely," Miss Glyde thrust in, "a somber background brushed in to throw your figures into more vivid relief. *Are* you not primarily plastic?"

"*I* have always maintained," Mrs. Ballinger interposed, "that you represent the purely objective method—"

Osric Dane helped herself critically to coffee. "How do you define objective?" she then inquired.

There was a flurried pause before Laura Glyde intensely murmured: "In reading *you* we don't define, we feel."

Osric Dane smiled. "The cerebellum," she remarked, "is not infrequently the seat of the literary emotions." And she took a second lump of sugar.

The sting that this remark was vaguely felt to conceal was almost neutralized by the satisfaction of being addressed in such technical language.

"Ah, the cerebellum," said Miss Van Vluyck complacently. "The club took a course in psychology last winter."

"Which psychology?" asked Osric Dane.

There was an agonizing pause, during which each member of the club secretly deplored the distressing inefficiency of the others. Only Mrs. Roby went on placidly sipping her chartreuse. At last Mrs. Ballinger said, with an attempt at a high tone: "Well, really, you know, it was last year that we took psychology, and this winter we have been so absorbed in—"

She broke off, nervously trying to recall some of the club's discussions; but her faculties seemed to be paralyzed by the petrifying stare of Osric Dane. What *had* the club been absorbed in? Mrs. Ballinger, with a vague purpose of gaining time, repeated slowly: "We've been so intensely absorbed in—"

Mrs. Roby put down her liqueur glass and drew near the group with a smile.

"In Xingu?" she gently prompted.

A thrill ran through the other members. They exchanged confused glances, and then, with one accord, turned a gaze of mingled relief and interrogation on their rescuer. The expression of each denoted a different phase of the same emotion. Mrs. Plinth was the first to compose her features to an air of reassurance: after a moment's hasty adjustment her look almost implied that it was she who had given the word to Mrs. Ballinger.

"Xingu, of course!" exclaimed the latter with her accustomed promptness, while Miss Van Vluyck and Laura Glyde seemed to be plumbing the depths of memory, and Mrs. Leveret, feeling apprehensively for *Appropriate Allusions,* was somehow reassured by the uncomfortable pressure of its bulk against her person.

Osric Dane's change of countenance was no less striking than that of her entertainers. She too put down her coffee cup, but with a look of distinct annoyance; she too wore, for a brief moment, what Mrs. Roby afterward described as the look of feeling for something in the back of her head; and before she could dissemble these momentary signs of weakness, Mrs. Roby, turning to her with a deferential smile, had said: "And we've been so hoping that today you would tell us just what you think of it."

Osric Dane received the homage of the smile as a matter of course; but the accompanying question obviously embarrassed her, and it became clear to her observers that she was not quick at shifting her facial scenery. It was as though her countenance had so long been set in an expression of unchallenged superiority that the muscles had stiffened, and refused to obey her orders.

"Xingu—" she said, as if seeking in her turn to gain time.

Mrs. Roby continued to press her. "Knowing how engrossing the subject is, you will understand how it happens that the club has let everything else go to the wall for the moment. Since we took up Xingu I might almost say—were it not for your books—that nothing else seems to us worth remembering."

Osric Dane's stern features were darkened rather than lit up by an uneasy smile. "I am glad to hear that you make one exception," she gave out between narrowed lips.

"Oh, of course," Mrs. Roby said prettily; "but as you have shown us that—so very naturally!—you don't care to talk of your own things, we really can't let you off from telling us exactly what you think about Xingu; especially," she added, with a still more persuasive smile, "as some people say that one of your last books was saturated with it."

It was an *it*, then—the assurance sped like fire through the parched minds of the other members. In their eagerness to gain the least little clue to Xingu they almost forgot the joy of assisting at the discomfiture of Mrs. Dane.

The latter reddened nervously under her antagonist's challenge. "May I ask," she faltered out, "to which of my books you refer?"

Mrs. Roby did not falter. "That's just what I want you to tell us; because, though I was present, I didn't actually take part."

"Present at what?" Mrs. Dane took her up; and for an instant the trembling members of the Lunch Club thought that the champion Providence had raised up for them had lost a point. But Mrs. Roby explained herself gaily: "At the discussion, of course. And so we're dreadfully anxious to know just how it was that you went into the Xingu."

There was a portentous pause, a silence so big with incalculable dangers that the members with one accord checked the words on their lips, like soldiers dropping their arms to watch a single combat between their leaders. Then Mrs. Dane gave expression to their inmost dread by saying sharply: "Ah—you say *the* Xingu, do you?"

Mrs. Roby smiled undauntedly. "It *is* a shade pedantic, isn't it? Personally, I always drop the article: but I don't know how the other members feel about it."

The other members looked as though they would willingly have dispensed with this appeal to their opinion, and Mrs. Roby, after a bright glance about the group, went on: "They probably think, as I do, that nothing really matters except the thing itself—except Xingu."

No immediate reply seemed to occur to Mrs. Dane, and Mrs. Ballinger gathered courage to say: "Surely everyone must feel that about Xingu."

Mrs. Plinth came to her support with a heavy murmur of assent, and Laura Glyde sighed out emotionally: "I have known cases where it has changed a whole life."

"It has done me worlds of good," Mrs. Leveret interjected, seeming to herself to remember that she had either taken it or read it the winter before.

"Of course," Mrs. Roby admitted, "the difficulty is that one must give up so much time to it. It's very long."

"I can't imagine," said Miss Van Vluyck, "grudging the time given to such a subject."

"And deep in places," Mrs. Roby pursued; (so then it was a book!) "And it isn't easy to skip."

"I never skip," said Mrs. Plinth dogmatically.

"Ah, it's dangerous to, in Xingu. Even at the start there are places where one can't. One must just wade through."

"I should hardly call it *wading*," said Mrs. Ballinger sarcastically.

Mrs. Roby sent her a look of interest. "Ah—you always found it went swimmingly?"

Mrs. Ballinger hesitated. "Of course there are difficult passages," she conceded.

"Yes; some are not at all clear—even," Mrs. Roby added, "if one is familiar with the original."

"As I suppose you are?" Osric Dane interposed, suddenly fixing her with a look of challenge.

Mrs. Roby met it by a deprecating gesture. "Oh, it's really not difficult up to a certain point; though some of the branches are very little known, and it's almost impossible to get at the source."

"Have you ever tried?" Mrs. Plinth inquired, still distrustful of Mrs. Roby's thoroughness.

Mrs. Roby was silent for a moment; then she replied with low-ered lids: "No—but a friend of mine did; a very brilliant man; and he told me it was best for women—not to. . . ."

A shudder ran around the room. Mrs. Leveret coughed so that the parlormaid, who was handing the cigarettes, should not hear; Miss Van Vluyck's face took on a nauseated expression, and Mrs. Plinth looked as if she were passing someone she did not care to bow to. But the most remarkable result of Mrs. Roby's words was the effect they produced on the Lunch Club's distinguished guest. Osric Dane's impassive features suddenly softened to an expression of the warmest human sympathy, and edging her chair toward Mrs. Roby's she asked: "Did you really? And—did you find he was right?"

Mrs. Ballinger, in whom annoyance at Mrs. Roby's unwonted assumption of prominence was beginning to displace gratitude for the aid she had rendered, could not consent to her being allowed, by such dubious means, to monopolize the attention of their guest. If Osric Dane had not enough self-respect to resent Mrs. Roby's flippancy, at least the Lunch Club would do so in the person of its President.

Mrs. Ballinger laid her hand on Mrs. Roby's arm. "We must not forget," she said with a frigid amiability, "that absorbing as Xingu is to *us*, it may be less interesting to—"

"Oh, no, on the contrary, I assure you," Osric Dane intervened.

"—to others," Mrs. Ballinger finished firmly; "and we must not allow our little meeting to end without persuading Mrs. Dane to say a few words to us on a subject which, today, is much more present in all our thoughts. I refer, of course, to *The Wings of Death*."

The other members, animated by various degrees of the same sentiment, and encouraged by the humanized mien of their redoubtable guest, repeated after Mrs. Ballinger: "Oh, yes, you really *must* talk to us a little about your book."

Osric Dane's expression became as bored, though not as haughty, as when her work had been previously mentioned. But before she could respond to Mrs. Ballinger's request, Mrs. Roby had risen from her seat, and was pulling down her veil over her frivolous nose.

"I'm so sorry," she said, advancing toward her hostess with outstretched hand, "but before Mrs. Dane begins I think I'd better run away. Unluckily, as you know, I haven't read her books, so I should be at a terrible disadvantage among you all, and besides, I've an engagement to play bridge."

If Mrs. Roby had simply pleaded her ignorance of Osric Dane's works as a reason for withdrawing, the Lunch Club, in view of her recent prowess, might have approved such evidence of discretion; but to couple this excuse with the brazen announcement that she was foregoing the privilege for the purpose of joining a bridge party was only one more instance of her deplorable lack of discrimination.

The ladies were disposed, however, to feel that her departure—now that she had performed the sole service she was ever likely to render them—would probably make for greater order and dignity in the impending discussion, besides relieving them of the sense of self-distrust which her presence always mysteriously produced. Mrs. Ballinger therefore restricted herself to a formal murmur of regret, and the other members were just grouping themselves comfortably about Osric Dane when the latter, to their dismay, started up from the sofa on which she had been seated.

"Oh wait—do wait, and I'll go with you!" she called out to Mrs. Roby; and, seizing the hands of the disconcerted members, she administered a series of farewell pressures with the mechanical haste of a railway conductor punching tickets.

"I'm so sorry—I'd quite forgotten—" she flung back at them from the threshold; and as she joined Mrs. Roby, who had turned in surprise at her appeal, the other ladies had the mortification of hearing her say, in a voice which she did not take the pains to lower: "If you'll let me walk a little way with you, I should so like to ask you a few more questions about Xingu. . . ."

III

The incident had been so rapid that the door closed on the departing pair before the other members had time to understand what was happening. Then a sense of the indignity put upon them by Osric Dane's unceremonious desertion began to contend with the confused feeling that they had been cheated out of their due without exactly knowing how or why.

There was a silence, during which Mrs. Ballinger, with a perfunctory hand, rearranged the skillfully grouped literature at which her distinguished guest had not so much as glanced; then Miss Van Vluyck tartly pronounced: "Well, I can't say that I consider Osric Dane's departure a great loss."

This confession crystallized the resentment of the other members, and Mrs. Leveret exclaimed: "I do believe she came on purpose to be nasty!"

It was Mrs. Plinth's private opinion that Osric Dane's attitude toward the Lunch Club might have been very different had it welcomed her in the majestic setting of the Plinth drawing rooms; but not liking to reflect on the inadequacy of Mrs. Ballinger's establishment she sought a roundabout satisfaction in deprecating her lack of foresight.

"I said from the first that we ought to have had a subject ready. It's what always happens when you're unprepared. Now if we'd only got up Xingu—"

The slowness of Mrs. Plinth's mental processes was always allowed for by the club; but this instance of it was too much for Mrs. Ballinger's equanimity.

"Xingu!" she scoffed. "Why, it was the fact of our knowing so much more about it than she did—unprepared though we were—that made Osric Dane so furious. I should have thought that was plain enough to everybody!"

This retort impressed even Mrs. Plinth, and Laura Glyde, moved by an impulse of generosity, said: "Yes, we really ought to be grateful to Mrs. Roby for introducing the topic. It may have made Osric Dane furious, but at least it made her civil."

"I am glad we were able to show her," added Miss Van Vluyck, "that a broad and up-to-date culture is not confined to the great intellectual centers."

This increased the satisfaction of the other members, and they began to forget their wrath against Osric Dane in the pleasure of having contributed to her discomfiture.

Miss Van Vluyck thoughtfully rubbed her spectacles. "What surprised me most," she continued, "was that Fanny Roby should be so up on Xingu."

This remark threw a slight chill on the company, but Mrs. Ballinger said with an air of indulgent irony: "Mrs. Roby always has the knack of making a little go a long way; still, we certainly owe her a debt for happening to remember that she'd heard of Xingu." And this was felt by the other members to be a graceful way of canceling once and for all the club's obligation to Mrs. Roby.

Even Mrs. Leveret took courage to speed a timid shaft of irony. "I fancy Osric Dane hardly expected to take a lesson in Xingu at Hillbridge!"

Mrs. Ballinger smiled. "When she asked me what we represented—do you remember?—I wish I'd simply said we represented Xingu!"

All the ladies laughed appreciatively at this sally, except Mrs. Plinth, who said, after a moment's deliberation: "I'm not sure it would have been wise to do so."

Mrs. Ballinger, who was already beginning to feel as if she had launched at Osric Dane the retort which had just occurred to her, turned ironically on Mrs. Plinth. "May I ask why?" she inquired.

Mrs. Plinth looked grave. "Surely," she said, "I understood from Mrs. Roby herself that the subject was one it was as well not to go into too deeply?"

Miss Van Vluyck rejoined with precision: "I think that applied only to an investigation of the origin of the—of the—"; and suddenly she found that her usually accurate memory had failed her. "It's a part of the subject I never studied myself," she concluded.

"Nor I," said Mrs. Ballinger.

Laura Glyde bent toward them with widened eyes. "And yet it seems—doesn't it—the part that is fullest of an esoteric fascination?"

"I don't know on what you base that," said Miss Van Vluyck argumentatively.

"Well, didn't you notice how intensely interested Osric Dane became as soon as she heard what the brilliant foreigner—he *was* a foreigner, wasn't he—had told Mrs. Roby about the origin—the origin of the rite—or whatever you call it?"

Mrs. Plinth looked disapproving, and Mrs. Ballinger visibly wavered. Then she said: "It may not be desirable to touch on the—on that part of the subject in general conversation; but, from the importance it evidently has to a woman of Osric Dane's distinction, I feel as if we ought not to be afraid to discuss it among ourselves—without gloves—though with closed doors, if necessary."

"I'm quite of your opinion," Miss Van Vluyck came briskly to her support; "on condition, that is, that all grossness of language is avoided."

"Oh, I'm sure we shall understand without that," Mrs. Leveret tittered; and Laura Glyde added significantly: "I fancy we can read between the lines," while Mrs. Ballinger rose to assure herself that the doors were really closed.

Mrs. Plinth had not yet given her adhesion. "I hardly see," she began, "what benefit is to be derived from investigating such peculiar customs—"

But Mrs. Ballinger's patience had reached the extreme limit of tension. "This at least," she returned; "that we shall not be placed again in the humiliating position of finding ourselves less up on our own subjects than Fanny Roby!"

Even to Mrs. Plinth this argument was conclusive. She peered furtively about the room and lowered her commanding tones to ask: "Have you got a copy?"

"A—a copy?" stammered Mrs. Ballinger. She was aware that the other members were looking at her expectantly, and that this answer was inadequate, so she supported it by asking another question. "A copy of what?"

Her companions bent their expectant gaze on Mrs. Plinth, who, in turn, appeared less sure of herself than usual. "Why, of—of—the book," she explained.

"What book?" snapped Miss Van Vluyck, almost as sharply as Osric Dane.

Mrs. Ballinger looked at Laura Glyde, whose eyes were interrogatively fixed on Mrs. Leveret. The fact of being deferred to was so new to the latter that it filled her with an insane temerity. "Why, Xingu, of course!" she exclaimed.

A profound silence followed this challenge to the resources of Mrs. Ballinger's library, and the latter, after glancing nervously toward the Books of the Day, returned with dignity: "It's not a thing one cares to leave about."

"I should think *not!*" exclaimed Mrs. Plinth.

"It *is* a book, then?" said Miss Van Vluyck.

This again threw the company into disarray, and Mrs. Ballinger, with an impatient sigh, rejoined: "Why—there *is* a book—naturally. . . ."

"Then why did Miss Glyde call it a religion?"

Laura Glyde started up. "A religion? I never—"

"Yes, you did," Miss Van Vluyck insisted; "you spoke of rites; and Mrs. Plinth said it was a custom."

Miss Glyde was evidently making a desperate effort to recall her statement; but accuracy of detail was not her strongest point. At length she began in a deep murmur: "Surely they used to do something of the kind at the Eleusinian mysteries—"

"Oh—" said Miss Van Vluyck, on the verge of disapproval; and Mrs. Plinth protested: "I understood there was to be no indelicacy!"

Mrs. Ballinger could not control her irritation. "Really, it is too bad that we should not be able to talk the matter over quietly among ourselves. Personally, I think that if one goes into Xingu at all—"

"Oh, so do I!" cried Miss Glyde.

"And I don't see how one can avoid doing so, if one wishes to keep up with the Thought of the Day—"

Mrs. Leveret uttered an exclamation of relief. "There—that's it!" she interposed.

"What's it?" the President took her up.

"Why—it's a—a Thought: I mean a philosophy."

This seemed to bring a certain relief to Mrs. Ballinger and Laura Glyde, but Miss Van Vluyck said: "Excuse me if I tell you that you're all mistaken. Xingu happens to be a language."

"A language!" the Lunch Club cried.

"Certainly. Don't you remember Fanny Roby's saying that

there were several branches, and that some were hard to trace? What could that apply to but dialects?"

Mrs. Ballinger could no longer restrain a contemptuous laugh. "Really, if the Lunch Club has reached such a pass that it has to go to Fanny Roby for instruction on a subject like Xingu, it had almost better cease to exist!"

"It's really her fault for not being clearer," Laura Glyde put in.

"Oh, clearness and Fanny Roby!" Mrs. Ballinger shrugged. "I dare say we shall find she was mistaken on almost every point."

"Why not look it up?" said Mrs. Plinth.

As a rule this recurrent suggestion of Mrs. Plinth's was ignored in the heat of discussion, and only resorted to afterward in the privacy of each member's home. But on the present occasion the desire to ascribe their own confusion of thought to the vague and contradictory nature of Mrs. Roby's statements caused the members of the Lunch Club to utter a collective demand for a book of reference.

At this point the production of her treasured volume gave Mrs. Leveret, for a moment, the unusual experience of occupying the center front; but she was not able to hold it long, for *Appropriate Allusions* contained no mention of Xingu.

"Oh, that's not the kind of thing we want!" exclaimed Miss Van Vluyck. She cast a disparaging glance over Mrs. Ballinger's assortment of literature, and added impatiently: "Haven't you any useful books?"

"Of course I have," replied Mrs. Ballinger indignantly; "I keep them in my husband's dressing room."

From this region, after some difficulty and delay, the parlormaid produced the W–Z volume of an *Encyclopedia* and, in deference to the fact that the demand for it had come from Miss Van Vluyck, laid the ponderous tome before her.

There was a moment of painful suspense while Miss Van Vluyck rubbed her spectacles, adjusted them, and turned to Z; and a murmur of surprise when she said: "It isn't here."

"I suppose," said Mrs. Plinth, "it's not fit to be put in a book of reference."

"Oh, nonsense!" exclaimed Mrs. Ballinger. "Try X."

Miss Van Vluyck turned back through the volume, peering

short-sightedly up and down the pages, till she came to a stop and remained motionless, like a dog on a point.

"Well, have you found it?" Mrs. Ballinger inquired after a considerable delay.

"Yes. I've found it," said Miss Van Vluyck in a queer voice.

Mrs. Plinth hastily interposed: "I beg you won't read it aloud if there's anything offensive."

Miss Van Vluyck, without answering, continued her silent scrutiny.

"Well, what *is* it?" exclaimed Laura Glyde excitedly.

"*Do* tell us!" urged Mrs. Leveret, feeling that she would have something awful to tell her sister.

Miss Van Vluyck pushed the volume aside and turned slowly toward the expectant group.

"It's a river."

"A *river?*"

"Yes: in Brazil. Isn't that where she's been living?"

"Who? Fanny Roby? Oh, but you must be mistaken. You've been reading the wrong thing," Mrs. Ballinger exclaimed, leaning over her to seize the volume.

"It's the only Xingu in the *Encyclopedia;* and she *has* been living in Brazil," Miss Van Vluyck persisted.

"Yes: her brother has a consulship there," Mrs. Leveret interposed.

"But it's too ridiculous! I—we—why we *all* remember studying Xingu last year—or the year before last," Mrs. Ballinger stammered.

"I thought I did when *you* said so," Laura Glyde avowed.

"*I* said so?" cried Mrs. Ballinger.

"Yes. You said it had crowded everything else out of your mind."

"Well *you* said it had changed your whole life!"

"For that matter Miss Van Vluyck said she had never grudged the time she'd given it."

Mrs. Plinth interposed: "I made it clear that I knew nothing whatever of the original."

Mrs. Ballinger broke off the dispute with a groan. "Oh, what does it all matter if she's been making fools of us? I believe Miss Van Vluyck's right—she was talking of the river all the while!"

"How could she? It's too preposterous," Miss Glyde exclaimed.

"Listen." Miss Van Vluyck had repossessed herself of the *Encyclopedia,* and restored her spectacles to a nose reddened by excitement. " 'The Xingu, one of the principal rivers of Brazil, rises on the plateau of Mato Grosso, and flows in a northerly direction for a length of no less than one-thousand one-hundred and eighteen miles, entering the Amazon near the mouth of the latter river. The upper course of the Xingu is auriferous and fed by numerous branches. Its source was first discovered in 1884 by the German explorer von den Steinen, after a difficult and dangerous expedition through a region inhabited by tribes still in the Stone Age of culture.' "

The ladies received this communication in a state of stupefied silence from which Mrs. Leveret was the first to rally. "She certainly *did* speak of its having branches."

The word seemed to snap the last thread of their incredulity. "And of its great length," gasped Mrs. Ballinger.

"She said it was awfully deep, and you couldn't skip—you just had to wade through," Miss Glyde added.

The idea worked its way more slowly through Mrs. Plinth's compact resistances. "How could there be anything improper about a river?" she inquired.

"Improper?"

"Why, what she said about the source—that it was corrupt?"

"Not corrupt, but hard to get at," Laura Glyde corrected. "Someone who'd been there had told her so. I dare say it was the explorer himself—doesn't it say the expedition was dangerous?"

" 'Difficult and dangerous,' " read Miss Van Vluyck.

Mrs. Ballinger pressed her hands to her throbbing temples. "There's nothing she said that wouldn't apply to a river—to this river!" She swung about excitedly to the other members. "Why, do you remember her telling us that she hadn't read *The Supreme Instant* because she'd taken it on a boating party while she was staying with her brother, and someone had 'shied' it overboard—'shied' of course was her own expression."

The ladiess breathlessly signified that the expression had not escaped them.

"Well—and then didn't she tell Osric Dane that one of her books was simply saturated with Xingu? Of course it was, if one of Mrs. Roby's rowdy friends had thrown it into the river!"

This surprising reconstruction of the scene in which they had just participated left the members of the Lunch Club inarticulate. At length, Mrs. Plinth, after visibly laboring with the problem, said in a heavy tone: "Osric Dane was taken in too."

Mrs. Leveret took courage at this. "Perhaps that's what Mrs. Roby did it for. She said Osric Dane was a brute, and she may have wanted to give her a lesson."

Miss Van Vluyck frowned. "It was hardly worth-while to do it at our expense."

"At least," said Miss Glyde with a touch of bitterness, "she succeeded in interesting her, which was more than we did."

"What chance had we?" rejoined Mrs. Ballinger. "Mrs. Roby monopolized her from the first. And *that,* I've no doubt, was her purpose—to give Osric Dane a false impression of her own standing in the club. She would hesitate at nothing to attract attention: we all know how she took in poor Professor Foreland."

"She actually makes him give bridge teas every Thursday," Mrs. Leveret piped up.

Laura Glyde struck her hands together. "Why, this is Thursday, and it's *there* she's gone, of course; and taken Osric with her!"

"And they're shrieking over us at this moment," said Mrs. Ballinger between her teeth.

This possibility seemed too preposterous to be admitted. "She would hardly dare," said Miss Van Vluyck, "confess the imposture to Osric Dane."

"I'm not so sure: I thought I saw her make a sign as she left. If she hadn't made a sign, why should Osric Dane have rushed out after her?"

"Well, you know, we'd all been telling her how wonderful Xingu was, and she said she wanted to find out more about it," Mrs. Leveret said, with a tardy impulse of justice to the absent.

This reminder, far from mitigating the wrath of the other members, gave it a stronger impetus.

"Yes—and that's exactly what they're both laughing over now," said Laura Glyde ironically.

Mrs. Plinth stood up and gathered her expensive furs about her monumental form. "I have no wish to criticize," she said; "but unless the Lunch Club can protect its members against the recurrence of such—such unbecoming scenes, I for one—"

"Oh, so do I!" agreed Miss Glyde, rising also.

Miss Van Vluyck closed the *Encyclopedia* and proceeded to button herself into her jacket. "My time is really too valuable—" she began.

"I fancy we are all of one mind," said Mrs. Ballinger, looking searchingly at Mrs. Leveret, who looked at the others.

"I always deprecate anything like a scandal—" Mrs. Plinth continued.

"She has been the cause of one today!" exclaimed Miss Glyde.

Mrs. Leveret moaned: "I don't see how she *could!*" and Miss Van Vluyck said, picking up her notebook: "Some women stop at nothing."

"—But if," Mrs. Plinth took up her argument impressively, "anything of the kind had happened in *my* house" (it never would have, her tone implied), "I should have felt that I owed it to myself either to ask for Mrs. Roby's resignation—or to offer mine."

"Oh, Mrs. Plinth—" gasped the Lunch Club.

"Fortunately for me," Mrs. Plinth continued with an awful magnanimity, "the matter was taken out of my hands by our President's decision that the right to entertain distinguished guests was a privilege vested in her office; and I think the other members will agree that, as she was alone in this opinion, she ought to be alone in deciding on the best way of effacing its—its really deplorable consequences."

A deep silence followed this outbreak of Mrs. Plinth's long-stored resentment.

"I don't see why *I* should be expected to ask her to resign—" Mrs. Ballinger at length began; but Laura Glyde turned back to remind her: "You know she made you say that you'd got on swimmingly in Xingu."

An ill-timed giggle escaped from Mrs. Leveret, and Mrs. Ballinger energetically continued "—But you needn't think for a moment that I'm afraid to!"

The door of the drawing room closed on the retreating backs of the Lunch Club, and the President of that distinguished association, seating herself at her writing table, and pushing away a copy of *The Wings of Death* to make room for her elbow, drew forth a sheet of the club's note-paper, on which she began to write: "My dear Mrs. Roby—"

COMING HOME

The young men of our American Relief Corps are beginning to come back from the front with stories.

There was no time to pick them up during the first months—the whole business was too wild and grim. The horror has not decreased, but nerves and sight are beginning to be disciplined to it. In the earlier days, moreover, such fragments of experience as one got were torn from their setting like bits of flesh scattered by shrapnel. Now things that seemed disjointed are beginning to link themselves together, and the broken bones of history are rising from the battlefields.

I can't say that, in this respect, all the members of the Relief Corps have made the most of their opportunity. Some are unobservant, or perhaps simply inarticulate; others, when going beyond the bald statistics of their job, tend to drop into sentiment and cinema scenes; and none but H. Macy Greer has the gift of making the thing told seem as true as if one had seen it. So it is on H. Macy Greer that I depend, and when his motor dashes him back to Paris for supplies I never fail to hunt him down and coax him to my rooms for dinner and a long cigar.

Greer is a small hard-muscled youth, with pleasant manners, a sallow face, straight hemp-colored hair and grey eyes of unexpected inwardness. He has a voice like thick soup, and speaks with the slovenly drawl of the new generation of Americans, dragging his words along like reluctant dogs on a string, and depriving his narrative of every shade of expression that intelligent intonation gives. But his eyes see so much that they make one see even what his foggy voice obscures.

Some of his tales are dark and dreadful, some are unutterably sad, and some end in a huge laugh of irony. I am not sure how I ought to classify the one I have written down here.

II

On my first dash to the Northern fighting line—Greer told me the other night—I carried supplies to an ambulance where the surgeon asked me to have a talk with an officer who was badly wounded and fretting for news of his people in the east of France.

He was a young Frenchman, a cavalry lieutenant, trim and slim, with a pleasant smile and obstinate blue eyes that I liked. He looked as if he could hold on tight when it was worth his while. He had had a leg smashed, poor devil, in the first fighting in Flanders, and had been dragging on for weeks in the squalid camp hospital where I found him. He didn't waste any words on himself, but began at once about his family. They were living, when the war broke out, at their country place in the Vosges; his father and mother, his sister, just eighteen, and his brother Alain, two years younger. His father, the Comte de Réchamp, had married late in life, and was over seventy: his mother, a good deal younger, was crippled with rheumatism; and there was, besides—to round off the group—a helpless but intensely alive and domineering old grandmother about whom all the others revolved. You know how French families hang together, and throw out branches that make new roots but keep hold of the central trunk, like that tree—what's it called?—that they give pictures of in books about the East.

Jean de Réchamp—that was my lieutenant's name—told me his family was a typical case. "We're very *province*," he said. "My people live at Réchamp all the year. We have a house at Nancy—rather a fine old hotel—but my parents go there only once in two or three years, for a few weeks. That's our 'season.' . . . Imagine the point of view! Or rather don't, because you couldn't. . . ." (He had been about the world a good deal, and known something of other angles of vision.)

Well, of this helpless exposed little knot of people he had had no word—simply nothing—since the first of August. He was at home, staying with them at Réchamp, when war broke out. He was mobilized the first day, and had only time to throw his traps into a cart and dash to the station. His depot was on the other side of France, and communications with the east by mail and telegraph were completely interrupted during the first weeks. His regiment was sent at once to the fighting line, and the first news he got came to him in October, from a communiqué in a Paris paper a month old, saying: "The enemy yesterday retook Réchamp." After that, dead silence: and the poor devil left in the trenches to digest that *"retook"*!

There are thousands and thousands of just such cases; and men bearing them, and cracking jokes, and hitting out as hard as they can. Jean de Réchamp knew this, and tried to crack jokes too—but he got his leg smashed just afterward, and ever since he'd been lying on a straw pallet under a horse blanket, saying to himself: *"Réchamp retaken."*

"Of course," he explained with a weary smile, "as long as you can tot up your daily bag in the trenches it's a sort of satisfaction—though I don't quite know why; anyhow, you're so deadbeat at night that no dreams come. But lying here staring at the ceiling one goes through the whole business once an hour, at the least: the attack, the slaughter, the ruins . . . and worse. . . . Haven't I seen and heard things enough on *this* side to know what's been happening on the other? Don't try to sugar the dose. I *like* it bitter."

I was three days in the neighborhood, and I went back every day to see him. He liked to talk to me because he had a faint hope of my getting news of his family when I returned to Paris. I hadn't much myself, but there was no use telling him so. Besides, things change from day to day, and when we parted I promised to get word to him as soon as I could find out anything. We both knew, of course, that that would not be till Réchamp was taken a third time—by his own troops; and perhaps soon after that, I should be able to get there, or near there, and make inquiries myself. To make sure that I should forget nothing, he drew the family photographs from under his pillow, and handed them over: the little witch-grandmother, with a face like a withered walnut, the father, a fine broken-looking old boy with a Roman nose and a weak chin, the mother, in crepe, simple, serious and provincial, the little sister ditto, and Alain, the young brother—just the age the brutes have been carrying off to German prisons—an over-grown thread-paper boy with too much forehead and eyes, and not a muscle in his body. A charming-looking family, distinguished and amiable; but all, except the grandmother, rather usual. The kind of people who come in sets.

As I pocketed the photographs I noticed that another lay face down by his pillow. "Is that for me too?" I asked.

He colored and shook his head, and I felt I had blundered. But after a moment he turned the photograph over and held it out.

"It's the young girl I am engaged to. She was at Réchamp visiting my parents when war was declared; but she was to leave the day after I did. . . ." He hesitated. "There may have been some difficulty about her going. . . . I should like to be sure she got away. . . . Her name is Yvonne Malo."

He did not offer me the photograph, and I did not need it. That girl had a face of her own! Dark and keen and splendid: a type so different from the others that I found myself staring. If he had not said "ma fiancée" I should have understood better. After another pause he went on: "I will give you her address in Paris. She has no family: she lives alone—she is a musician. Perhaps you may find her there." His color deepened again as he added: "But I know nothing—I have had no news of her either."

To ease the silence that followed I suggested: "But if she has no family, wouldn't she have been likely to stay with your people, and wouldn't that be the reason of your not hearing from her?"

"Oh, no—I don't think she stayed." He seemed about to add: "If she could help it," but shut his lips and slid the picture out of sight.

As soon as I got back to Paris I made inquiries, but without result. The Germans had been pushed back from that particular spot after a fortnight's intermittent occupation; but their lines were close by, across the valley, and Réchamp was still in a net of trenches. No one could get to it, and apparently no news could come from it. For the moment, at any rate, I found it impossible to get in touch with the place.

My inquiries about Mlle. Malo were equally unfruitful. I went to the address Réchamp had given me, somewhere off in Passy, among gardens, in what they called a "Square," no doubt because it's oblong: a kind of long narrow court with aesthetic-looking studio buildings round it. Mlle. Malo lived in one of them, on the top floor, the concierge said, and I looked up and saw a big studio window, and a roof terrace with dead gourds dangling from a pergola. But she wasn't there, she hadn't been there, and they had no news of her. I wrote to Réchamp of my double failure, he sent me back a line of thanks; and after that for a long while I heard no more of him.

By the beginning of November the enemy's hold had begun to loosen in the Argonne and along the Vosges, and one day we were sent off to the east with a couple of ambulances. Of course we had to have military chauffeurs, and the one attached to my ambulance happened to be a fellow I knew. The day before we started, in talking over our route with him, I said: "I suppose we can manage to get to Réchamp now?" He looked puzzled—it was such a little place that he'd forgotten the name. "Why do you want to get there?" he wondered. I told him, and he gave an exclamation. "Good God! Of course—but how extraordinary! Jean de Réchamp's here now, in Paris, too lame for the front, and driving a motor." We stared at each other, and he went on: "He must take my place—he must go with you. I don't know how it can be done; but done it shall be."

Done it was, and the next morning at daylight I found Jean de Réchamp at the wheel of my car. He looked another fellow from the wreck I had left in the Flemish hospital; all made over, and burning with activity, but older, and with lines about his eyes. He had had news from his people in the interval, and had learned that they were still at Réchamp, and well. What was more surprising was that Mlle. Malo was with them—had never left. Alain had been got away to England, where he remained; but none of the others had budged. They had fitted up an ambulance in the chateau, and Mlle. Malo and the little sister were nursing the wounded. There were not many details in the letters, and they had been a long time on the way; but their tone was so reassuring that Jean could give himself up to unclouded anticipation. You may fancy if he was grateful for the chance I was giving him; for of course he couldn't have seen his people in any other way.

Our permits, as you know, don't as a rule let us into the firing line: we only take supplies to second-line ambulances, and carry back the badly wounded in need of delicate operations. So I wasn't in the least sure we should be allowed to go to Réchamp—though I had made up my mind to get there, anyhow.

We were about a fortnight on the way, coming and going in Champagne and the Argonne, and that gave us time to get to know each other. It was bitter cold, and after our long runs over the lonely frozen hills we used to crawl into the café of the inn—if there was one—and talk and talk. We put up in fairly rough places, generally in a farmhouse or a cottage packed with soldiers; for the villages have all remained empty since the autumn, except when troops are quartered in them. Usually, to keep warm, we had to go up after supper to the room we shared, and get under the blankets with our clothes on. Once some jolly Sisters of Charity took us in at their Hospice, and we slept two nights in an ice-cold whitewashed cell—but what tales we heard around their kitchen fire! The Sisters had stayed alone to face the Germans, had seen the town burn, and had made the Teutons turn the hose on the singed roof of their Hospice and beat the fire back from it. It's a pity those Sisters of Charity can't marry. . . .

Réchamp told me a lot in those days. I don't believe he was talkative before the war, but his long weeks in hospital, starving for news, had unstrung him. And then he was mad with excitement at getting back to his own place. In the interval he'd heard how other people caught in their country houses had fared—you know the stories we all refused to believe at first, and that we now prefer not to think about. . . . Well, he'd been thinking about those stories pretty steadily for some months; and he kept repeating: "My people say they're all right—but they give no details."

"You see," he explained, "there never were such helpless beings. Even if there had been time to leave, they couldn't have done it. My mother had been having one of her worst attacks of rheumatism—she was in bed, helpless, when I left. And my grandmother, who is a demon of activity in the house, won't stir out of it. We haven't been able to coax her into the garden for years. She says it's drafty; and you know how we all feel about drafts! As for my father, he hasn't had to decide anything since the Comte de Chambord refused to adopt the tricolor. My father decided that he was right, and since then there has been nothing particular for him to take a stand about. But I know how he behaved just as well as if I'd been there—he kept saying: 'One must act—one must act!' and sitting in his chair and doing nothing. Oh, I'm not disrespectful: they were *like* that in his generation! Besides—it's better to laugh at things, isn't it?" And suddenly his face would darken. . . .

On the whole, however, his spirits were good till we began to traverse the line of ruined towns between Sainte Menehould and Bar-le-Duc. "This is the way the devils came," he kept saying to me; and I saw he was hard at work picturing the work they must have done in his own neighborhood.

"But since your sister writes that your people are safe!"

"They may have made her write that to reassure me. They'd heard I was badly wounded. And, mind you, there's never been a line from my mother."

"But you say your mother's hands are so lame that she can't hold a pen. And wouldn't Mlle. Malo have written you the truth?"

At that his frown would lift. "Oh, yes. She would despise any attempt at concealment."

"Well, then—what the deuce is the matter?"

"It's when I see these devils' traces—" he could only mutter.

One day, when we had passed through a particularly devastated little place, and had got from the curé some more than usually abominable details of things done there, Réchamp broke out to me over the kitchen fire of our night's lodging. "When I hear things like that I don't believe anybody who tells me my people are all right!"

"But you know well enough," I insisted, "that the Germans are not all alike—that it all depends on the particular officer. . . ."

"Yes, yes, I know," he assented, with a visible effort at impartiality. "Only, you see—as one gets nearer. . . ." He went on to say that, when he had been sent from the ambulance at the front to a hospital at Moulins, he had been for a day or two in a ward next to some wounded German soldiers—bad cases, they were—and had heard them talking. They didn't know he knew German, and he had heard things. . . . There was one name always coming back in their talk, von Scharlach, Oberst von Scharlach. One of them, a young fellow, said: "I wish now I'd cut my hand off rather than do what he told us to that night. . . . Every time the fever comes I see it all again. I wish I'd been struck dead first." They all said "Scharlach" with a kind of terror in their voices, as if he might hear them even there, and come down on them horribly. Réchamp had asked where their regiment came from, and had been told: From the Vosges. That had set his brain working, and whenever he saw a ruined village, or heard a tale of savagery, the Scharlach nerve began to quiver. At such times it was no use reminding him that the Germans had had at least three-hundred thousand men in the East in August. He simply didn't listen. . . .

III

The day before we started for Réchamp his spirits flew up again, and that night he became confidential. "You've been such a friend to me that there are certain things—seeing what's ahead of us— that I should like to explain"; and, noticing my surprise, he went on: "I mean about my people. The state of mind in my *milieu* must be so remote from anything you're used to in your happy country. . . . But perhaps I can make you understand. . . ."

I saw that what he wanted was to talk to me of the girl he was engaged to. Mlle. Malo, left an orphan at ten, had been the ward of a neighbor of the Réchamps', a chap with an old name and a starred chateau, who had lost almost everything else at baccarat before he was forty, and had repented, had the gout and studied agriculture for the rest of his life. The girl's father was a rather brilliant painter, who died young, and her mother, who followed him in a year or two, was a Pole: you may fancy that, with such antecedents, the girl was just the mixture to shake down quietly into French country life with a gouty and repentant guardian. The Marquis de Corvenaire—that was his name—brought her down to his place, got an old-maid sister to come and stay, and really, as far as one knows, brought his ward up rather decently. Now and then she used to be driven over to play with the young Réchamps, and Jean remembered her as an ugly little girl in a plaid frock, who used to invent wonderful games and get tired of playing them just as other children were beginning to learn how. But her domineering ways and searching questions did not meet with his mother's approval, and her visits were not encouraged. When she was seventeen her guardian died and left her a little money. The maiden sister had gone dotty, there was nobody to look after Yvonne, and she went to Paris, to an aunt, broke loose from the aunt when she came of age, set up her studio, traveled, painted, played the violin, knew lots of people; and never laid eyes on Jean de Réchamp till about a year before the war, when her guardian's place was sold, and she had to go down there to see about her interest in the property.

The old Réchamps heard she was coming, but didn't ask her to stay. Jean drove over to the shut-up chateau, however, and found Mlle. Malo lunching on a corner of the kitchen table. She exclaimed: "My little Jean!" flew to him with a kiss for each cheek, and made him sit down and share her omelet. . . . The ugly little girl had shed her chrysalis—and you may fancy if he went back once or twice!

Mlle. Malo was staying at the chateau all alone, with the farmer's wife to come in and cook her dinner: not a soul in the house at night but herself and her brindled sheep dog. She had to be there a week, and Jean suggested to his people to ask her to Réchamp. But at Réchamp they hesitated, coughed, looked away, said the spare rooms were all upside down, and the valet-de-chambre laid up with the mumps, and the cook shorthanded—till finally the irrepressible grandmother broke out: "A young girl who chooses to live alone—probably prefers to live alone!"

There was a deadly silence, and Jean did not raise the question again; but I can imagine his blue eyes getting obstinate.

Soon after Mlle. Malo's return to Paris he followed her and began to frequent the Passy studio. The life there was unlike anything he had ever seen—or conceived as possible, short of the prairies. He had sampled the usual varieties of French womankind, and explored most of the social layers; but he had missed the newest, that of the artistic-emancipated. I don't know much about that set myself, but from his descriptions I should say they were a good deal like intelligent Americans, except that they don't seem to keep art and life in such watertight compartments. But his great discovery was the new girl. Apparently he had never before known any but the traditional type, which predominates in the provinces, and still persists, he tells me, in the last fastnesses of the Faubourg St. Germain. The girl who comes and goes as she pleases, reads what she likes, has opinions about what she reads, who talks, looks, behaves with the independence of a married woman—and yet has kept the Diana-freshness—think how she must have shaken up such a man's inherited view of things! Mlle. Malo did far more than make Réchamp fall in love with her: she turned his world topsy-turvy, and prevented his ever again squeezing himself into his little old pigeonhole of prejudices.

Before long they confessed their love—just like any young couple of Anglo-Saxons—and Jean went down to Réchamp to ask permission to marry her. Neither you nor I can quite enter into the state of mind of a young man of twenty-seven who has knocked about all over the globe, and been in and out of the usual sentimental coils—and who has to ask his parents' leave to get married! Don't let us try: it's no use. We should only end by picturing him as an incorrigible ninny. But there isn't a man in France who wouldn't feel it his duty to take that step, as Jean de Réchamp did. All we can do is to accept the premise and pass on.

Well—Jean went down and asked his father and his mother and his old grandmother if they would permit him to marry Mlle. Malo; and they all with one voice said they wouldn't. There was an uproar, in fact; and the old grandmother contributed the most piercing note to the concert. Marry Mlle. Malo! A young girl who lived alone! Traveled! Spent her time with foreigners—with musicians and painters! *A young girl!* Of course, if she had been a married woman—that is, a widow—much as they would have preferred a young girl for Jean, or even, if widow it had to be, a widow of another type—still, it was conceivable that, out of affection for him, they might have resigned themselves to his choice. But a young girl—bring such a young girl to Réchamp! Ask them to receive her under the same roof with their little Simone, their innocent Alain. . . .

He had a bad hour of it; but he held his own, keeping silent while they screamed, and stiffening as they began to wobble from exhaustion. Finally he took his mother apart, and tried to reason with her. His arguments were not much use, but his resolution impressed her, and he saw it. As for his father, nobody was afraid of Monsieur de Réchamp. When he said: "Never—never while I live, and there is a roof on Réchamp!" they all knew he had collapsed inside. But the grandmother was terrible. She was terrible because she was so old, and so clever at taking advantage of it.

She could bring on a valvular heart attack by just sitting still and holding her breath, as Jean and his mother had long since found out; and she always treated them to one when things weren't going as she liked. Madame de Réchamp promised Jean that she would intercede with her mother-in-law; but she hadn't much faith in the result, and when she came out of the old lady's room she whispered: "She's just sitting there holding her breath."

The next day Jean himself advanced to the attack. His grandmother was the most intelligent member of the family, and she knew he knew it, and liked him for having found it out; so when he had her alone she listened to him without resorting to any valvular tricks. "Of course," he explained, "you're much too clever not to understand that the times have changed, and manners with them, and that what a woman was criticized for doing yesterday she is ridiculed for not doing today. Nearly all the old social thou-shalt-nots have gone: intelligent people nowadays don't give a fig for them, and that simple fact has abolished them. They only existed as long as there was someone left for them to scare." His grandmother listened with a sparkle of admiration in her ancient eyes. "And of course," Jean pursued, "that can't be the real reason for your opposing my marriage—a marriage with a young girl you've always known, who has been received here—"

"Ah, that's it—we've always known her!" the old lady snapped him up.

"What of that? I don't see—"

"Of course you don't. You're here so little: you don't hear things. . . ."

"What things?"

"Things in the air . . . that blow about. . . . You were doing your military service at the time. . . ."

"At what time?"

She leaned forward and laid a warning hand on his arm. "Why did Corvenaire leave her all that money—*why?*"

"But why not—why shouldn't he?" Jean stammered, indignant. Then she unpacked her bag—a heap of vague insinuations, baseless conjectures, village tattle, all, at the last analysis, based, as he succeeded in proving, and making her own, on a word launched at random by a discharged maidservant who had retailed her grievance to the curé's housekeeper. "Oh, she does what she likes

with Monsieur le Marquis, the young miss! *She* knows how. . . ."
On that single phrase the neighborhood had raised a slander built
of adamant.

Well, I'll give you an idea of what a determined fellow Réchamp
is, when I tell you he pulled it down—or thought he did. He kept
his temper, hunted up the servant's record, proved her a liar and
dishonest, cast grave doubts on the discretion of the curé's housekeeper, and poured such a flood of ridicule over the whole flimsy
fable, and those who had believed in it, that in sheer shamefaced-
ness at having based her objection on such grounds, his grandmother gave way, and brought his parents toppling down with her.

All this happened a few weeks before the war, and soon afterward Mlle. Malo came down to Réchamp. Jean had insisted on
her coming: he wanted her presence there, as his betrothed, to be
known to the neighborhood. As for her, she seemed delighted to
come. I could see from Réchamp's tone, when he reached this part
of his story, that he rather thought I should expect its heroine to
have shown a becoming reluctance—to have stood on her dignity.
He was distinctly relieved when he found I expected no such
thing.

"She's simplicity itself—it's her great quality. Vain complications don't exist for her, because she doesn't see them . . . that's
what my people can't be made to understand. . . ."

I gathered from the last phrase that the visit had not been a
complete success, and this explained his having let out, when he
first told me of his fears for his family, that he was sure Mlle.
Malo would not have remained at Réchamp if she could help it.
Oh, no, decidedly, the visit was not a success. . . .

"You see," he explained with a half-embarrassed smile, "it was
partly her fault. Other girls as clever, but less—how shall I say?—
less proud, would have adapted themselves, arranged things,
avoided startling allusions. She wouldn't stoop to that; she talked
to my family as naturally as she did to me. You can imagine for instance, the effect of her saying: 'One night, after a supper at
Montmartre, I was walking home with two or three pals'— It was
her way of affirming her convictions, and I adored her for it—but
I wished she wouldn't!"

And he depicted, to my joy, the neighbors rumbling over to call
in heraldic barouches (the mothers alone—with embarrassed ex-

cuses for not bringing their daughters), and the agony of not
knowing, till they were in the room, if Yvonne would receive them
with lowered lids and folded hands, sitting by in a *pose de fiancée*
while the elders talked; or if she would take the opportunity to air
her views on the separation of Church and State, or the necessity
of making divorce easier. "It's not," he explained, "that she really
takes much interest in such questions: she's much more absorbed
in her music and painting. But anything her eye lights on sets her
mind dancing—as she said to me once: 'It's your mother's friends'
bonnets that make me stand up for divorce!'" He broke off abruptly
to add: "Good God, how far off all that nonsense seems!"

IV

The next day we started for Réchamp, not sure if we could get
through, but bound to, anyhow! It was the coldest day we'd had,
the sky steel, the earth iron, and a snow-wind howling down on
us from the north. The Vosges are splendid in winter. In summer
they are just plump puddingy hills; when the wind strips them
they turn to mountains. And we seemed to have the whole country to ourselves—the black firs, the blue shadows, the beech-
woods cracking and groaning like rigging, the bursts of snowy
sunlight from cold clouds. Not a soul in sight except the sentinels
guarding the railways, muffled to the eyes, or peering out of their
huts of pine boughs at the crossroads. Every now and then we
passed a long string of seventy-fives, or a train of supply wagons
or army ambulances, and at intervals a cavalryman cantered by,
his cloak bellied out by the gale; but of ordinary people about the
common jobs of life, not a sign.

The sense of loneliness and remoteness that the absence of the
civil population produces everywhere in eastern France is increased by the fact that all the names and distances on the mile-
stones have been scratched out and the signposts at the crossroads
thrown down. It was done, presumably, to throw the enemy off
the track in September: and the signs have never been put back.
The result is that one is forever losing one's way, for the soldiers
quartered in the district know only the names of their particular
villages, and those on the march can tell you nothing about the

places they are passing through. We had got badly off our road several times during the trip, but on the last day's run Réchamp was in his own country, and knew every yard of the way—or thought he did. We had turned off the main road, and were running along between rather featureless fields and woods, crossed by a good many wood roads with nothing to distinguish them; but he continued to push ahead, saying: "We don't turn till we get to a manor house on a stream, with a big paper-mill across the road." He went on to tell me that the mill owners lived in the manor, and were old friends of his people: good old local stock, who had lived there for generations and done a lot for the neighborhood.

"It's queer I don't see their village steeple from this rise. The village is just beyond the house. How the devil could I have missed the turn?" We ran on a little farther, and suddenly he stopped the motor with a jerk. We were at a crossroad, with a stream running under the bank on our right. The place looked like an abandoned stoneyard. I never saw completer ruin. To the left, a fortified gate gaped on emptiness; to the right, a mill wheel hung in the stream. Everything else was as flat as your dinner-table.

"Was this what you were trying to see from that rise?" I asked; and I saw a tear or two running down his face.

"They were the kindest people: their only son got himself shot the first month in Champagne—"

He had jumped out of the car and was standing staring at the level waste. "The house was there—there was a splendid lime in the court. I used to sit under it and have a glass of *vin gris de Lorraine* with the old people. . . . Over there, where that cinder heap is, all their children are buried." He walked across to the graveyard under a blackened wall—a bit of the apse of the vanished church—and sat down on a gravestone. "If the devils have done this *here*—so close to us," he burst out, and covered his face.

An old woman walked toward us down the road. Réchamp jumped up and ran to meet her. "Why, Marie-Jeanne, what are you doing in these ruins?" The old woman looked at him with unastonished eyes. She seemed incapable of any surprise. "They left my house standing. I'm glad to see Monsieur," she simply said. We followed her to the one house left in the waste of stones. It was a two-roomed cottage, propped against a cow stable, but

fairly decent, with a curtain in the window and a cat on the sill.
Réchamp caught me by the arm and pointed to the door panel.
"Oberst von Scharlach" was scrawled on it. He turned as white as
your tablecloth, and hung on to me a minute; then he spoke to the
old woman. "The officers were quartered here: that was the reason they spared your house?"

She nodded. "Yes: I was lucky. But the gentlemen must come in
and have a mouthful."

Réchamp's finger was on the name. "And this one—this was
their commanding officer?"

"I suppose so. Is it somebody's name?" She had evidently never
speculated on the meaning of the scrawl that had saved her.

"You remember him—their captain? Was his name Scharlach?"
Réchamp persisted.

Under its rich weathering the old woman's face grew as pale as
his. "Yes, that was his name—I heard it often enough."

"Describe him, then. What was he like? Tall and fair? They're
all that—but what else? What in particular?"

She hesitated, and then said: "This one wasn't fair. He was
dark, and had a scar that drew up the left corner of his mouth."

Réchamp turned to me. "It's the same. I heard the men describing him at Moulins."

We followed the old woman into the house, and while she gave
us some bread and wine she told us about the wrecking of the
village and the factory. It was one of the most damnable stories
I've heard yet. Put together the worst of the typical horrors and
you'll have a fair idea of it. Murder, outrage, torture: Scharlach's
program seemed to be fairly comprehensive. She ended off by
saying: "His orderly showed me a silver-mounted flute he always
traveled with, and a beautiful paintbox mounted in silver too.
Before he left he sat down on my doorstep and made a painting of
the ruins. . . ."

Soon after leaving this place of death we got to the second lines
and our troubles began. We had to do a lot of talking to get through
the lines, but what Réchamp had just seen had made him eloquent.
Luckily, too, the ambulance doctor, a charming fellow, was short of
tetanus serum, and I had some left; and while I went over with
him to the pine-branch hut where he hid his wounded I explained

Réchamp's case, and implored him to get us through. Finally it was settled that we should leave the ambulance there—for in the lines the ban against motors is absolute—and drive the remaining twelve miles. A sergeant fished out of a farmhouse a toothless old woman with a furry horse harnessed to a two-wheeled trap, and we started off by roundabout wood tracks. The horse was in no hurry, nor the old lady either; for there were bits of road that were pretty steadily currycombed by shell, and it was to everybody's interest not to cross them before twilight. Jean de Réchamp's excitement seemed to have dropped: he sat beside me dumb as a fish, staring straight ahead of him. I didn't feel talkative either, for a word the doctor had let drop had left me thinking. "That poor old granny mind the shells? Not she!" he had said when our crazy chariot drove up. "She doesn't know them from snowflakes any more. Nothing matters to her now, except trying to outwit a German. They're all like that where Scharlach's been—you've heard of him? She had only one boy—half-witted: he cocked a broom handle at them, and they burnt him. Oh, she'll take you to Réchamp safe enough."

"Where Scharlach's been"—so he had been so close as this to Réchamp! I was wondering if Jean knew it, and if that had sealed his lips and given him that flinty profile. The old horse's woolly flanks jogged on under the bare branches and the old woman's bent back jogged in time with it. She never once spoke or looked around at us. "It isn't the noise we make that'll give us away," I said at last; and just then the old woman turned her head and pointed silently with the osier-twig she used as a whip. Just ahead of us lay a heap of ruins: the wreck, apparently, of a great chateau and its dependencies. "Lermont!" Réchamp explained, turning white. He made a motion to jump out and then dropped back into the seat. "What's the use?" he muttered. He leaned forward and touched the old woman's shoulder.

"I hadn't heard of this—when did it happen?"

"In September."

"*They* did it?"

"Yes. Our wounded were there. It's like this everywhere in our country."

I saw Jean stiffening himself for the next question. "At Réchamp, too?"

She relapsed into indifference. "I haven't been as far as Réchamp."

"But you must have seen people who'd been there—you must have heard."

"I've heard the masters were still there—so there must be something standing. Maybe though," she reflected, "they're in the cellars. . . ."

We continued to jog on through the dusk.

V

"There's the steeple!" Réchamp burst out.

Through the dimness I couldn't tell which way to look; but I suppose in the thickest midnight he would have known where he was. He jumped from the trap and took the old horse by the bridle. I made out that he was guiding us into a long village street edged by houses in which every light was extinguished. The snow on the ground sent up a pale reflection, and I began to see the gabled outline of the houses and the steeple at the head of the street. The place seemed as calm and unchanged as if the sound of war had never reached it. In the open space at the end of the village Réchamp checked the horse.

"The elm—there's the old elm in front of the church!" he shouted in a voice like a boy's. He ran back and caught me by both hands. "It was true, then—nothing's touched!" The old woman asked: "Is this Réchamp?" and he went back to the horse's head and turned the trap toward a tall gate between park walls. The gate was barred and padlocked, and not a gleam showed through the shutters of the porter's lodge; but Réchamp, after listening a minute or two, gave a low call twice repeated, and presently the lodge door opened, and an old man peered out. Well—I leave you to brush in the rest. Old family servant, tears and hugs and so on. I know you affect to scorn the cinema, and this was it, tremolo and all. Hang it! This war's going to teach us not to be afraid of the obvious.

We piled into the trap and drove down a long avenue to the house. Black as the grave, of course; but in another minute the door opened, and there, in the hall, was another servant, screening a light—and then more doors opened on another cinema scene: fine old drawing room with family portraits, shaded lamp, domestic group about the fire. They evidently thought it was the servant coming to announce dinner, and not a head turned at our approach. I could see them all over Jean's shoulder: a grey-haired lady knitting with stiff fingers, an old gentleman with a high nose and a weak chin sitting in a big carved armchair and looking more like a portrait than the portraits; a pretty girl at his feet, with a dog's head in her lap, and another girl, who had a Red Cross on her sleeve, at the table with a book. She had been reading aloud in a rich veiled voice, and broke off her last phrase to say: "Dinner. . . ." Then she looked up and saw Jean. Her dark face remained perfectly calm, but she lifted her hand in a just perceptible gesture of warning, and instantly understanding he drew back and pushed the servant forward in his place.

"Madame la Comtesse—it is someone outside asking for Mademoiselle."

The dark girl jumped up and ran out into the hall. I remember wondering: "Is it because she wants to have him to herself first—or because she's afraid of their being startled?" I wished myself out of the way, but she took no notice of me, and going straight to Jean flung her arms about him. I was behind him and could see her hands about his neck, and her brown fingers tightly locked. There wasn't much doubt about those two. . . .

The next minute she caught sight of me, and I was being rapidly tested by a pair of the finest eyes I ever saw—I don't apply the term to their setting, though that was fine too, but to the look itself, a look at once warm and resolute, all-promising and all-penetrating. I really can't do with fewer adjectives. . . .

Réchamp explained me, and she was full of thanks and welcome; not excessive, but—well, I don't know—eloquent! She gave every intonation all it could carry, and without the least emphasis: that's the wonder.

She went back to "prepare" the parents, as they say in melodrama; and in a minute or two we followed. What struck me first was that these insignificant and inadequate people had the command of the grand gesture—had *la ligne*. The mother had laid aside her knitting—*not* dropped it—and stood waiting with open arms. But even in clasping her son she seemed to include me in her

welcome. I don't know how to describe it; but they never let me
feel I was in the way. I suppose that's part of what you call distinction; knowing instinctively how to deal with unusual moments.

All the while, I was looking about me at the fine secure old
room, in which nothing seemed altered or disturbed, the portraits
smiling from the walls, the servants beaming in the doorway—
and wondering how such things could have survived in the trail of
death and havoc we had been following.

The same thought had evidently struck Jean, for he dropped his
sister's hand and turned to gaze about him too.

"Then nothing's touched—*nothing*? I don't understand," he
stammered.

Monsieur de Réchamp raised himself majestically from his
chair, crossed the room and lifted Yvonne Malo's hand to his lips.
"Nothing is touched—thanks to this hand and this brain."

Madame de Réchamp was shining on her son through tears.
"Ah, yes—we owe it all to Yvonne."

"All, all! Grandmamma will tell you!" Simone chimed in; and
Yvonne, brushing aside their praise with a half-impatient laugh,
said to her betrothed: "But your grandmother! You must go up to
her at once."

A wonderful specimen, that grandmother: I was taken to see
her after dinner. She sat by the fire in a bare paneled bedroom,
bolt upright in an armchair with ears, a knitting table at her elbow with a shaded candle on it. She was even more withered and
ancient than she looked in her photograph, and I judge she'd
never been pretty; but she somehow made me feel as if I'd got
through with prettiness. I don't know exactly what she reminded
me of: a dried bouquet, or something rich and clovy that had
turned brittle through long keeping in a sandalwood box. I suppose her sandalwood box had been Good Society. Well, I had a
rare evening with her. Jean and his parents were called down to
see the curé, who had hurried over to the chateau when he heard
of the young man's arrival; and the old lady asked me to stay on
and chat with her. She related their experiences with uncanny detachment, seeming chiefly to resent the indignity of having been
made to descend into the cellar—"to avoid French shells, if you'll
believe it: the Germans had the decency not to bombard us," she

observed impartially. I was so struck by the absence of rancor in her tone that finally, out of sheer curiosity, I made an allusion to the horror of having the enemy under one's roof. "Oh, I might almost say I didn't see them," she returned. "I never go downstairs any longer; and they didn't do me the honor of coming beyond my door. A glance sufficed them—an old woman like me!" she added with a phosphorescent gleam of coquetry.

"But they searched the chateau, surely?"

"Oh, a mere form; they were very decent—very decent," she almost snapped at me. "There was a first moment, of course, when we feared it might be hard to get Monsieur de Réchamp away with my young grandson; but Mlle. Malo managed that very cleverly. They slipped off while the officers were dining." She looked at me with the smile of some arch old lady in a Louis XV pastel. "My grandson Jean's fiancée is a very clever young woman: in my time no young girl would have been so sure of herself, so cool and quick. After all, there is something to be said for the new way of bringing up girls. My poor daughter-in-law, at Yvonne's age, was a bleating baby: she is so still, at times. The convent doesn't develop character. I'm glad Yvonne was not brought up in a convent." And this champion of tradition smiled on me more intensely.

Little by little I got from her the story of the German approach: the distracted fugitives pouring in from the villages north of Réchamp, the sound of distant cannonading, and suddenly, the next afternoon, after a reassuring lull, the sight of a single spiked helmet at the end of the drive. In a few minutes a dozen followed: mostly officers; then all at once the place hummed with them. There were supply wagons and motors in the court, bundles of hay, stacks of rifles, artillerymen unharnessing and rubbing down their horses. The crowd was hot and thirsty, and in a moment the old lady, to her amazement, saw wine and cider being handed about by the Réchamp servants. "Or so at least I was told," she added, correcting herself, "for it's not my habit to look out of the window. I simply sat here and waited." Her seat, as she spoke, might have been a curule chair.

Downstairs, it appeared, Mlle. Malo had instantly taken her measures. *She* didn't sit and wait. Surprised in the garden with Simone, she had made the girl walk quietly back to the house and

receive the officers with her on the doorstep. The officer in command—captain, or whatever he was—had arrived in a bad temper, cursing and swearing, and growling out menaces about spies.
The day was intensely hot, and possibly he had had too much
wine. At any rate Mlle. Malo had known how to "put him in his
place"; and when he and the other officers entered they found the
dining table set out with refreshing drinks and cigars, melons,
strawberries and iced coffee. "The clever creature! She even remembered that they liked whipped cream with their coffee!"

The effect had been miraculous. The captain—what was his
name? Yes, Charlot, Charlot—Captain Charlot had been especially complimentary on the subject of the whipped cream and the
cigars. Then he asked to see the other members of the family, and
Mlle. Malo told him there were only two—two old women! "He
made a face at that, and said all the same he should like to meet
them; and she answered: 'One is your hostess, the Comtesse de
Réchamp, who is ill in bed'—for my poor daughter-in-law was
lying in bed paralyzed with rheumatism—'and the other her
mother-in-law, a very old lady who never leaves her room.'"

"But aren't there any men in the family?" he had then asked;
and she had said: "Oh yes—two. The Comte de Réchamp and his
son."

"And where are they?"

"In England. Monsieur de Réchamp went a month ago to take
his son on a trip."

The officer said: "I was told they were here today"; and Mlle.
Malo replied: "You had better have the house searched and satisfy
yourself."

He laughed and said: "The idea *had* occurred to me." She
laughed also, and sitting down at the piano struck a few chords.
Captain Charlot, who had his foot on the threshold, turned
back—Simone had described the scene to her grandmother afterward. "Some of the brutes, it seems, are musical," the old lady
explained; "and this was one of them. While he was listening,
some soldiers appeared in the court carrying another who seemed
to be wounded. It turned out afterward that he'd been climbing a
garden wall after fruit, and cut himself on the broken glass at the
top; but the blood was enough—they raised the usual dreadful
outcry about an ambush, and a lieutenant clattered into the room

where Mlle. Malo sat playing Stravinsky." The old lady paused for her effect, and I was conscious of giving her all she wanted.

"Well—?"

"Will you believe it? It seems she looked at her watch bracelet and said: 'Do you gentlemen dress for dinner? *I* do—but we've still time for a little Moussorgsky'—or whatever wild names they call themselves—'if you'll make those people outside hold their tongues.' Our captain looked at her again, laughed, gave an order that sent the lieutenant right about, and sat down beside her at the piano. Imagine my stupor, dear sir: the drawing room is directly under this room, and in a moment I heard two voices coming up to me. Well, I won't conceal from you that his was the finest. But then I always adored a baritone." She folded her shriveled hands among their laces. "After that, the Germans were *très bien—très bien*. They stayed two days, and there was nothing to complain of. Indeed, when the second detachment came, a week later, they never even entered the gates. Orders had been left that they should be quartered elsewhere. Of course we were lucky in happening on a man of the world like Captain Charlot."

"Yes, very lucky. It's odd, though, his having a French name."

"Very. It probably accounts for his breeding," she answered placidly; and left me marveling at the happy remoteness of old age.

VI

The next morning early Jean de Réchamp came to my room. I was struck at once by the change in him: he had lost his first glow, and seemed nervous and hesitating. I knew what he had come for: to ask me to postpone our departure for another twenty-four hours. By rights we should have been off that morning; but there had been a sharp brush a few kilometers away, and a couple of poor devils had been brought to the chateau whom it would have been death to carry farther that day and criminal not to hurry to a base hospital the next morning. "We've simply *got* to stay till tomorrow: you're in luck," I said laughing.

He laughed back, but with a frown that made me feel I had been a brute to speak in that way of a respite due to such a cause.

"The men will pull through, you know—trust Mlle. Malo for that!" I said.

His frown did not lift. He went to the window and drummed on the pane.

"Do you see that breach in the wall, down there behind the trees? It's the only scratch the place has got. And think of Lermont! It's incredible—simply incredible!"

"But it's like that everywhere, isn't it? Everything depends on the officer in command."

"Yes: that's it, I suppose. I haven't had time to get a consecutive account of what happened: they're all too excited. Mlle. Malo is the only person who can tell me exactly how things went." He swung about on me. "Look here, it sounds absurd, what I'm asking; but try to get me an hour alone with her, will you?"

I stared at the request, and he went on, still half laughing: "You see, they all hang on me; my father and mother, Simone, the curé, the servants. The whole village is coming up presently: they want to stuff their eyes full of me. It's natural enough, after living here all these long months cut off from everything. But the result is I haven't said two words to her yet."

"Well, you shall," I declared; and with an easier smile he turned to hurry down to a mass of thanksgiving which the curé was to celebrate in the private chapel. "My parents wanted it," he explained; "and after that the whole village will be upon us. But later—"

"Later I'll effect a diversion; I swear I will," I assured him.

By daylight, decidedly, Mlle. Malo was less handsome than in the evening. It was my first thought as she came toward me, that afternoon, under the limes. Jean was still indoors, with his people, receiving the village; I rather wondered she hadn't stayed there with him. Theoretically, her place was at his side; but I knew she was a young woman who didn't live by rule, and she had already struck me as having a distaste for superfluous expenditures of feeling.

Yes, she was less effective by day. She looked older for one thing; her face was pinched, and a little sallow and for the first time I noticed that her cheekbones were too high. Her eyes, too, had lost their velvet depth: fine eyes still, but not unfathomable.

But the smile with which she greeted me was charming: it ran over her tired face like a lamplighter kindling flames as he runs.

"I was looking for you," she said. "Shall we have a little talk? The reception is sure to last another hour: every one of the villagers is going to tell just what happened to him or her when the Germans came."

"And you've run away from the ceremony?"

"I'm a trifle tired of hearing the same adventures retold," she said, still smiling.

"But I thought there *were* no adventures—that that was the wonder of it?"

She shrugged. "It makes their stories a little dull, at any rate; we've not a hero or a martyr to show." She had strolled farther from the house as we talked, leading me in the direction of a bare horse-chestnut walk that led toward the park.

"Of course Jean's got to listen to it all, poor boy; but *I* needn't," she explained.

I didn't know exactly what to answer and we walked on a little way in silence; then she said: "If you'd carried him off this morning he would have escaped all this fuss." After a pause she added slowly: "On the whole, it might have been as well."

"To carry him off?"

"Yes." She stopped and looked at me. "I wish you *would*."

"Would?—Now?"

"Yes, now: as soon as you can. He's really not strong yet—he's drawn and nervous." ("So are you," I thought.) "And the excitement is greater than you can perhaps imagine—"

I gave her back her look. "Why, I think I *can* imagine. . . ."

She colored up through her sallow skin and then laughed away her blush. "Oh, I don't mean the excitement of seeing *me!* But his parents, his grandmother, the curé, all the old associations—"

I considered for a moment; then I said: "As a matter of fact, you're about the only person he *hasn't* seen."

She checked a quick answer on her lips, and for a moment or two we faced each other silently. A sudden sense of intimacy, of complicity almost, came over me. What was it that the girl's silence was crying out to me?

"If I take him away now he won't have seen you at all," I continued.

She stood under the bare trees, keeping her eyes on me. "Then take him away now!" she retorted; and as she spoke I saw her face change, decompose into deadly apprehension and as quickly regain its usual calm. From where she stood she faced the courtyard, and glancing in the same direction I saw the throng of villagers coming out of the chateau. "Take him way—take him away at once!" she passionately commanded; and the next minute Jean de Réchamp detached himself from the group and began to limp down the walk in our direction.

What was I to do? I can't exaggerate the sense of urgency Mlle. Malo's appeal gave me, or my faith in her sincerity. No one who had seen her meeting with Réchamp the night before could have doubted her feeling for him: if she wanted him away it was not because she did not delight in his presence. Even now, as he approached, I saw her face veiled by a faint mist of emotion: it was like watching a fruit ripen under a midsummer sun. But she turned sharply from the house and began to walk on.

"Can't you give me a hint of your reason?" I suggested as I followed.

"My reason? I've given it!" I suppose I looked incredulous, for she added in a lower voice: "I don't want him to hear—yet—about all the horrors."

"The horrors? I thought there had been none here."

"All around us—" Her voice became a whisper. "Our friends . . . our neighbors . . . every one. . . ."

"He can hardly avoid hearing of that, can he? And besides, since you're all safe and happy. . . . Look here," I broke off, "he's coming after us. Don't we look as if we were running away?"

She turned around, suddenly paler; and in a stride or two Réchamp was at our side. He was pale too; and before I could find a pretext for slipping away he had begun to speak. But I saw at once that he didn't know or care if I was there.

"What was the name of the officer in command who was quartered here?" he asked, looking straight at the girl.

She raised her eyebrows slightly. "Do you mean to say that after listening for three hours to every inhabitant of Réchamp you haven't found that out?"

"They all call him something different. My grandmother says he had a French name: she calls him Charlot."

"Your grandmother was never taught German: his name was Oberst von Scharlach." She did not remember my presence either: the two were still looking straight in each other's eyes.

Réchamp had grown white to the lips: he was rigid with the effort to control himself.

"Why didn't you tell me it was Scharlach who was here?" he brought out at last in a low voice.

She turned her eyes in my direction. "I was just explaining to Mr. Greer—"

"To Mr. Greer?" He looked at me too, half angrily.

"I know the stories that are about," she continued quietly; "and I was saying to your friend that, since we had been so happy as to be spared, it seemed useless to dwell on what has happened elsewhere."

"Damn what happened elsewhere! I don't yet know what happened here."

I put a hand on his arm. Mlle. Malo was looking hard at me, but I wouldn't let her see I knew it. "I'm going to leave you to hear the whole story now," I said to Réchamp.

"But there isn't any story for him to hear!" she broke in. She pointed at the serene front of the chateau, looking out across its gardens to the unscarred fields. "We're safe; the place is untouched. Why brood on other horrors—horrors we were powerless to help?"

Réchamp held his ground doggedly. "But the man's name is a curse and an abomination. Wherever he went he spread ruin."

"So they say. Mayn't there be a mistake? Legends grow up so quickly in these dreadful times. Here—" she looked about her again at the peaceful scene—"here he behaved as you see. For heaven's sake be content with that!"

"Content?" He passed his hand across his forehead. "I'm blind with joy . . . or should be, if only. . . ."

She looked at me entreatingly, almost desperately, and I took hold of Réchamp's arm with a warning pressure. "My dear fellow, don't you see that Mlle. Malo has been under a great strain? *La joie fait peur*[1]—that's the trouble with both of you!"

He lowered his head. "Yes, I suppose it is." He took her hand and kissed it. "I beg your pardon. Greer's right: we're both on edge."

"Yes: I'll leave you for a little while, if you and Mr. Greer will excuse me." She included us both in a quiet look that seemed to me extremely noble, and walked slowly away toward the chateau. Réchamp stood gazing after her for a moment; then he dropped down on one of the benches at the edge of the path. He covered his face with his hands. "Scharlach—Scharlach!" I heard him repeat.

We sat there side by side for ten minutes or more without speaking. Finally I said: "Look here, Réchamp—she's right and you're wrong. I shall be sorry I brought you here if you don't see it before it's too late."

His face was still hidden; but presently he dropped his hands and answered me. "I do see. She's saved everything for me—my people and my house, and the ground we're standing on. And I worship it because she walks on it!"

"And so do your people: the war's done that for you, anyhow," I reminded him.

VII

The morning after we were off before dawn. Our time allowance was up, and it was thought advisable, on account of our wounded, to slip across the exposed bit of road in the dark.

Mlle. Malo was downstairs when we started, pale in her white dress, but calm and active. We had borrowed a farmer's cart in which our two men could be laid on a mattress, and she had stocked our trap with food and remedies. Nothing seemed to have been forgotten. While I was settling the men I suppose Réchamp turned back into the hall to bid her good-bye; anyhow, when she followed him out a moment later he looked quieter and less strained. He had taken leave of his parents and his sister upstairs, and Yvonne Malo stood alone in the dark doorway, watching us as we drove away.

There was not much talk between us during our slow drive back to the lines. We had to go at a snail's pace, for the roads were rough; and there was time for meditation. I knew well enough what my companion was thinking about and my own thoughts ran on the same lines. Though the story of the German occupa-

tion of Réchamp had been retold to us a dozen times the main
facts did not vary. There were little discrepancies of detail, and
gaps in the narrative here and there; but all the household, from
the astute ancestress to the last bewildered pantry boy, were at
one in saying that Mlle. Malo's coolness and courage had saved
the chateau and the village. The officer in command had arrived
full of threats and insolence: Mlle. Malo had placated and disarmed him, turned his suspicions to ridicule, entertained him and
his comrades at dinner, and contrived during that time—or rather
while they were making music afterward (which they did for half
the night, it seemed)—that Monsieur de Réchamp and Alain
should slip out of the cellar in which they had been hidden, gain
the end of the gardens through an old hidden passage, and get off
in the darkness. Meanwhile Simone had been safe upstairs with
her mother and grandmother, and none of the officers lodged in
the chateau had—after a first hasty inspection—set foot in any
part of the house but the wing assigned to them. On the third
morning they had left, and Scharlach, before going, had put in
Mlle. Malo's hands a letter requesting whatever officer should follow him to show every consideration to the family of the Comte
de Réchamp, and if possible—owing to the grave illness of the
Countess—avoid taking up quarters in the chateau: a request
which had been scrupulously observed.

Such were the amazing but undisputed facts over which
Réchamp and I, in our different ways, were now pondering. He
hardly spoke, and when he did it was only to make some casual
reference to the road or to our wounded soldiers; but all the while
I sat at his side I kept hearing the echo of the question he was inwardly asking himself, and hoping to God he wouldn't put it
to me. . . .

It was nearly noon when we finally reached the lines, and the
men had to have a rest before we could start again; but a couple
of hours later we landed them safely at the base hospital. From
there we had intended to go back to Paris; but as we were starting
there came an unexpected summons to another point of the front,
where there had been a successful night attack, and a lot of Germans taken in a blown-up trench. The place was fifty miles away,
and off my beat, but the number of wounded on both sides was
exceptionally heavy, and all the available ambulances had already

started. An urgent call had come for more, and there was nothing for it but to go; so we went.

We found things in a bad mess at the second-line shanty hospital where they were dumping the wounded as fast as they could bring them in. At first we were told that none were fit to be carried farther that night; and after we had done what we could we went off to hunt up a shakedown in the village. But a few minutes later an orderly overtook us with a message from the surgeon. There was a German with an abdominal wound who was in a bad way, but might be saved by an operation if he could be got back to the base before midnight. Would we take him at once and then come back for others?

There is only one answer to such requests, and a few minutes later we were back at the hospital, and the wounded man was being carried out on a stretcher. In the shaky lantern gleam I caught a glimpse of a livid face and a torn uniform, and saw that he was an officer, and nearly done for. Réchamp had climbed to the box, and seemed not to be noticing what was going on at the back of the motor. I understood that he loathed the job, and wanted not to see the face of the man we were carrying; so when we had got him settled I jumped into the ambulance beside him and called out to Réchamp that we were ready. A second later an *infirmier* ran up with a little packet and pushed it into my hand. "His papers," he explained. I pocketed them and pulled the door shut, and we were off.

The man lay motionless on his back, conscious, but desperately weak. Once I turned my pocket lamp on him and saw that he was young—about thirty—with damp dark hair and a thin face. He had received a flesh wound above the eyes, and his forehead was bandaged, but the rest of the face uncovered. As the light fell on him he lifted his eyelids and looked at me: his look was inscrutable.

For half an hour or so I sat there in the dark, the sense of that face pressing close on me. It was a damnable face—meanly handsome, basely proud. In my one glimpse of it I had seen that the man was suffering atrociously, but as we slid along through the night he made no sound. At length the motor stopped with a violent jerk that drew a single moan from him. I turned the light on him, but he lay perfectly still, lips and lids shut, making no sign;

and I jumped out and ran round to the front to see what had happened.

The motor had stopped for lack of gasoline and was stock-still in the deep mud. Réchamp muttered something about a leak in his tank. As he bent over it, the lantern flame struck up into his face, which was set and businesslike. It struck me vaguely that he showed no particular surprise.

"What's to be done?" I asked.

"I think I can tinker it up; but we've got to have more essence to go on with."

I stared at him in despair: it was a good hour's walk back to the lines, and we weren't so sure of getting any gasoline when we got there! But there was no help for it; and as Réchamp was dead lame, no alternative but for me to go.

I opened the ambulance door, gave another look at the motionless man inside and took out a remedy which I handed over to Réchamp with a word of explanation. "You know how to give a hypo? Keep a close eye on him and pop this in if you see a change—not otherwise."

He nodded. "Do you suppose he'll die?" he asked below his breath.

"No, I don't. If we get him to the hospital before morning I think he'll pull through."

"Oh, all right." He unhooked one of the motor lanterns and handed it over to me. "I'll do my best," he said as I turned away.

Getting back to the lines through that pitch black forest, and finding somebody to bring the gasoline back for me was about the weariest job I ever tackled. I couldn't imagine why it wasn't daylight when we finally got to the place where I had left the motor. It seemed to me as if I had been gone twelve hours when I finally caught sight of the grey bulk of the car through the thinning darkness.

Réchamp came forward to meet us, and took hold of my arm as I was opening the door of the car. "The man's dead," he said.

I had lifted up my pocket lamp, and its light fell on Réchamp's face, which was perfectly composed, and seemed less gaunt and drawn than at any time since we had started on our trip.

"Dead? Why—how? What happened? Did you give him the hypodermic?" I stammered, taken aback.

"No time to. He died in a minute."

"How do you know he did? Were you with him?"

"Of course I was with him," Réchamp retorted, with a sudden harshness which made me aware that I had grown harsh myself. But I had been almost sure the man wasn't anywhere near death when I left him. I opened the door of the ambulance and climbed in with my lantern. He didn't appear to have moved, but he was dead sure enough—had been for two or three hours, by the feel of him. It must have happened not long after I left. . . . Well, I'm not a doctor, anyhow. . . .

I don't think Réchamp and I exchanged a word during the rest of that run. But it was my fault and not his if we didn't. By the mere rub of his sleeve against mine as we sat side by side on the motor I knew he was conscious of no bar between us: he had somehow got back, in the night's interval, to a state of wholesome stolidity, while I, on the contrary, was tingling all over with exposed nerves.

I was glad enough when we got back to the base at last, and the grim load we carried was lifted out and taken into the hospital. Réchamp waited in the courtyard beside his car, lighting a cigarette in the cold early sunlight; but I followed the bearers and the surgeon into the whitewashed room where the dead man was laid out to be undressed. I had a burning spot at the pit of my stomach while his clothes were ripped off him and the bandages undone: I couldn't take my eyes from the surgeon's face. But the surgeon, with a big batch of wounded on his hands, was probably thinking more of the living than the dead; and besides, we were near the front, and the body before him was an enemy's.

He finished his examination and scribbled something in a notebook. "Death must have taken place nearly five hours ago," he merely remarked: it was the conclusion I had already come to myself.

"And how about the papers?" the surgeon continued. "You have them, I suppose? This way, please."

We left the half-stripped body on the bloodstained oilcloth, and he led me into an office where a functionary sat behind a littered desk.

"The papers? Thank you. You haven't examined them? Let us see, then."

I handed over the leather notecase I had thrust into my pocket the evening before, and saw for the first time its silver-edged corners and the coronet in one of them. The official took out the papers and spread them on the desk between us. I watched him absently while he did so.

Suddenly he uttered an exclamation. "Ah—that's a haul!" he said, and pushed a bit of paper toward me. On it was engraved the name: Oberst Graf Benno von Scharlach. . . .

"A good riddance," said the surgeon over my shoulder.

I went back to the courtyard and saw Réchamp still smoking his cigarette in the cold sunlight. I don't suppose I'd been in the hospital ten minutes; but I felt as old as Methuselah.

My friend greeted me with a smile. "Ready for breakfast?" he said, and a little chill ran down my spine. . . . But I said: "Oh, all right—come along. . . ."

For, after all, I *knew* there wasn't a paper of any sort on that man when he was lifted into my ambulance the night before: the French officials attend to their business too carefully for me not to have been sure of that. And there wasn't the least shred of evidence to prove that he hadn't died of his wounds during the unlucky delay in the forest; or that Réchamp had known his tank was leaking when we started out from the lines.

"I could do with a *café complet*,[2] couldn't you?" Réchamp suggested, looking straight at me with his good blue eyes; and arm in arm we started off to hunt for the inn. . . .

WRITING A WAR STORY

Miss Ivy Spang of Cornwall-on-Hudson had published a little volume of verse before the war.

It was called "Vibrations," and was preceded by a Foreword in which the author stated that she had yielded to the urgent request of friends in exposing her first-born to the public gaze. The public had not gazed very hard or very long, but the Cornwall-on-Hudson *News-Dispatch* had a flattering notice by the wife of the Rector of St. Dunstan's (signed "Asterisk"), in which, while the somewhat unconventional sentiment of the poems was gently deprecated, a graceful and ladylike tribute was paid to the "brilliant daughter of one of our most prominent and influential citizens, who has voluntarily abandoned *the primrose way of pleasure* to scale *the rugged heights of Parnassus*."

Also, after sitting one evening next to him at a bohemian dinner in New York, Miss Spang was honored by an article by the editor of *Zigzag,* the new "Weekly Journal of Defiance," in which that gentleman hinted that there was more than she knew in Ivy Spang's poems, and that their esoteric significance showed that she was a *vers-librist* in thought as well as in technique. He added that they would "gain incommensurably in meaning" when she abandoned the superannuated habit of beginning each line with a capital letter.

The editor sent a heavily-marked copy to Miss Spang, who was immensely flattered, and felt that at last she had been understood. But nobody she knew read *Zigzag,* and nobody who read *Zigzag* seemed to care to know her. So nothing in particular resulted from this tribute to her genius.

Then the war came, and she forgot all about writing poetry.

The war was two years old, and she had been pouring tea once a week for a whole winter in a big Anglo-American hospital in Paris, when one day, as she was passing through the flower-edged court on her way to her ward, she heard one of the doctors say to a pale gentleman in civilian clothes and spectacles, "But I believe that pretty Miss Spang writes. If you want an American contributor, why not ask her?" And the next moment the pale gentleman had been introduced and, beaming anxiously at her through his spectacles, was urging her to contribute a rattling war story to *The Man-at-Arms,* a monthly publication that was to bring joy to the wounded and disabled in British hospitals.

"A good rousing story, Miss Spang; a dash of sentiment, of course, but nothing to depress or discourage. I'm sure you catch my meaning? A tragedy with a happy ending—that's about the idea. But I leave it to you; with your large experience of hospital work of course you know just what hits the poor fellows' taste. Do you think you could have it ready for our first number? And have you a portrait—if possible in nurse's dress—to publish with it? The Queen of Norromania has promised us a poem, with a picture of herself giving the baby Crown Prince his morning tub. We want the first number to be an 'actuality,' as the French say; all the articles written by people who've done the thing themselves, or seen it done. You've been at the front, I suppose? As far as Rheims, once? That's capital! Give us a good stirring trench story, with a Coming-Home scene to close with . . . a Christmas scene, if you can manage it, as we hope to be out in November. Yes—that's the very thing; and I'll try to get Sargent to do us the wounded V. C. coming back to the old home on Christmas Eve—snow effect."

It was lucky that Ivy Spang's leave was due about that time, for, devoted though she was to her patients, the tea she poured for them might have suffered from her absorption in her new task.

Was it any wonder that she took it seriously?

She, Ivy Spang, of Cornwall-on-Hudson, had been asked to write a war story for the opening number of *The Man-at-Arms,* to which Queens and Archbishops and Field Marshals were to contribute poetry and photographs and patriotic sentiment in autograph! And her full-length photograph in nurse's dress was to precede her prose; in the table of contents she was to figure as "Ivy Spang, author of *Vibrations: A Book of Verse.*

She was dizzy with triumph, and went off to hide her exultation in a quiet corner of Brittany, where she happened to have an old governess, who took her in and promised to defend at all costs the sacredness of her mornings—for Ivy knew that the morning hours of great authors were always "sacred."

She shut herself up in her room with a ream of mauve paper and began to think.

At first the process was less exhilarating than she had expected. She knew so much about the war that she hardly knew where to begin; she found herself suffering from a plethora of impressions.

Moreover, the more she thought of the matter, the less she seemed to understand how a war story—or any story, for that matter—was written. Why did stories ever begin, and why did they ever leave off? Life didn't—it just went on and on.

This unforeseen problem troubled her exceedingly, and on the second morning she stealthily broke from her seclusion and slipped out for a walk on the beach. She had been ashamed to make known her projected escapade, and went alone, leaving her faithful governess to mount guard on her threshold while she sneaked out by a back way.

There were plenty of people on the beach, and among them some whom she knew; but she dared not join them lest they should frighten away her Inspiration. She knew that Inspirations were fussy and contrarious, and she felt rather as if she were dragging along a reluctant dog on a string.

"If you wanted to stay indoors, why didn't you say so?" she grumbled to it. But the Inspiration continued to sulk.

She wandered about under the cliff till she came to an empty bench, where she sat down and gazed at the sea. After a while her eyes were dazzled by the light, and she turned them toward the bench and saw lying on it a battered magazine—the midsummer "All Story" number of *Fact and Fiction*. Ivy pounced on it.

She had heard a good deal about not allowing one's self to be "influenced," about jealously guarding one's originality, and so forth; the editor of *Zigzag* had been particularly strong on that theme. But her story had to be written, and she didn't know how to begin it, so she decided just to glance casually at a few beginnings.

The first tale in the magazine was signed by a name great in fiction, one of the most famous names of the past generation of novelists. The opening sentence ran: "In the month of October, 1914—" and Ivy turned the page impatiently. She may not have known much about story writing, but she did know that *that* kind of a beginning was played out. She turned to the next.

"'My God!' roared the engineer, tightening his grasp on the lever, while the white, sneering face under the red lamp . . ."

No; that was beginning to be out of date, too.

"They sat there and stared at it in silence. Neither spoke; but the woman's heart ticked like a watch."

That was better but best of all she liked, "Lee Lorimer leaned to him across the flowers. She had always known that this was coming . . ." Ivy could imagine tying a story on to *that*.

But she had promised to write a war story; and in a war story the flowers must be at the end and not at the beginning.

At any rate, there was one clear conclusion to be drawn from the successive study of all these opening paragraphs; and that was that you must begin in the middle, and take for granted that your reader knew what you were talking about.

Yes; but where was the middle, and how could your reader know what you were talking about when you didn't know yourself?

After some reflection, and more furtive scrutiny of *Fact and Fiction,* the puzzled authoress decided that perhaps, if you pretended hard enough that you knew what your story was about, you might end by finding out toward the last page. "After all, if the reader can pretend, the author ought to be able to," she reflected. And she decided (after a cautious glance over her shoulder) to steal the magazine and take it home with her for private dissection.

On the threshold she met her governess, who beamed on her tenderly.

"Chérie, I saw you slip off, but I didn't follow. I knew you wanted to be alone with your Inspiration." Mademoiselle lowered her voice to add: "Have you found your plot?"

Ivy tapped her gently on the wrinkled cheek. "Dear old Madsy! People don't bother with plots nowadays."

"Oh, don't they, darling? Then it must be very much easier," said Mademoiselle. But Ivy was not so sure—

After a day's brooding over *Fact and Fiction,* she decided to begin on the empiric system. ("It's sure to come to me as I go along," she thought.) So she sat down before the mauve paper and wrote "A shot rang out—"

But just as she was appealing to her Inspiration to suggest the next phrase a horrible doubt assailed her, and she got up and turned to *Fact and Fiction.* Yes, it was just as she had feared, the last story in *Fact and Fiction* began: "A shot rang out—"

Its place on the list showed what the editor and his public thought of that kind of an opening, and her contempt for it was increased by reading the author's name. The story was signed "Edda Clubber Hump." Poor thing!

Ivy sat down and gazed at the page which she had polluted with that silly sentence.

And now (as they often said in *Fact and Fiction*) a strange thing happened. The sentence was there—she had written it—it was the first sentence on the first page of her story, it *was* the first sentence of her story. It was there, it had gone out of her, got away from her, and she seemed to have no further control of it. She could imagine no other way of beginning, now that she had made the effort of beginning in that way.

She supposed that was what authors meant when they talked about being "mastered by their Inspiration." She began to hate her Inspiration.

On the fifth day an abased and dejected Ivy confided to her old governess that she didn't believe she knew how to write a short story.

"If they'd only asked me for poetry!" she wailed.

She wrote to the editor of *The Man-at-Arms,* begging for permission to substitute a sonnet; but he replied firmly, if flatteringly, that they counted on a story, and had measured their space accordingly—adding that they already had rather more poetry than the first number could hold. He concluded by reminding her that he counted on receiving her contribution not later than September first; and it was now the tenth of August.

"It's all so sudden," she murmured to Mademoiselle, as if she were announcing her engagement.

"Of course, dearest—of course! I quite understand. How could the editor expect you to be tied to a date? But so few people know what the artistic temperament is; they seem to think one can dash off a story as easily as one makes an omelet."

Ivy smiled in spite of herself, "Dear Madsy, what an unlucky simile! So few people make good omelets."

"Not in France," said Mademoiselle firmly.

Her former pupil reflected. "In France a good many people have written good short stories, too—but I'm sure they were given more than three weeks to learn how. Oh, what shall I do?" she groaned.

The two pondered long and anxiously; and at last the governess modestly suggested: "Supposing you were to begin by thinking of a subject?"

"Oh, my dear, the subject's nothing!" exclaimed Ivy, remembering some contemptuous statement to that effect by the editor of *Zigzag*.

"Still—in writing a story, one has to have a subject. Of course I know it's only the treatment that really matters; but the treatment, naturally, would be yours, quite yours. . . ."

The authoress lifted a troubled gaze upon her Mentor. "What are you driving at, Madsy?"

"Only that during my year's work in the hospital here I picked up a good many stories—pathetic, thrilling, moving stories of our poor poilus; and in the evening, sometimes, I used to jot them down, just as the soldier told them to me—oh, without any art at all . . . simply for myself, you understand. . . ."

Ivy was on her feet in an instant. Since even Mademoiselle admitted that "only the treatment really mattered," why should she not seize on one of these artless tales and transform it into Literature? The more she considered the idea, the more it appealed to her; she remembered Shakespeare and Molière, and said gayly to her governess: "You darling Madsy! Do lend me your book to look over—and we'll be collaborators!"

"Oh—collaborators!" blushed the governess, overcome. But she finally yielded to her charge's affectionate insistence and brought out her shabby copybook, which began with lecture notes on Mr.

Bergson's[1] course at the Sorbonne in 1913, and suddenly switched off to "Military Hospital No. 13. November, 1914. Long talk with the Chasseur Alpin Emile Durand, wounded through the knee and the left lung at the Hautes Chaumes. I have decided to write down his story. . . ."

Ivy carried the little book off to bed with her, inwardly smiling at the fact that the narrative, written in a close, tremulous hand, covered each side of the page, and poured on and on without a paragraph—a good deal like life. Decidedly, poor Mademoiselle did not even know the rudiments of literature!

The story, not without effort, gradually built itself up about the adventures of Emile Durand. Notwithstanding her protests, Mademoiselle, after a day or two, found herself called upon in an advisory capacity and finally as a collaborator. She gave the tale a certain consecutiveness, and kept Ivy to the main point when her pupil showed a tendency to wander; but she carefully revised and polished the rustic speech in which she had originally transcribed the tale, so that it finally issued forth in the language that a young lady writing a composition on the Battle of Hastings would have used in Mademoiselle's school days.

Ivy decided to add a touch of sentiment to the anecdote, which was purely military, both because she knew the reader was entitled to a certain proportion of "heart interest," and because she wished to make the subject her own by this original addition. The revisions and transpositions which these changes necessitated made the work one of uncommon difficulty; and one day, in a fit of discouragement, Ivy privately decided to notify the editor of *The Man-at-Arms* that she was ill and could not fulfill her engagement.

But that very afternoon the "artistic" photographer to whom she had posed for her portrait sent home the proofs; and she saw herself, exceedingly long, narrow and sinuous, robed in white and monastically veiled, holding out a refreshing beverage to an invisible sufferer with a gesture halfway between Mélisande lowering her braid over the balcony[2] and Florence Nightingale[3] advancing with the lamp.

The photograph was really too charming to be wasted and Ivy, feeling herself forced onward by an inexorable fate, sat down again to battle with the art of fiction. Her perseverance was rewarded, and after a while the fellow authors (though Mademoiselle disclaimed any right to the honors of literary partnership) arrived at what seemed to both a satisfactory result.

"You've written a very beautiful story, my dear," Mademoiselle sighed with moist eyes; and Ivy modestly agreed that she had.

The task was finished on the last day of her leave; and the next morning she traveled back to Paris, clutching the manuscript to her bosom, and forgetting to keep an eye on the bag that contained her passport and money, in her terror lest the precious pages should be stolen.

As soon as the tale was typed she did it up in a heavily-sealed envelope (she knew that only silly girls used blue ribbon for the purpose), and dispatched it to the pale gentleman in spectacles, accompanied by the Mélisande-Nightingale photograph. The receipt of both was acknowledged by a courteous note (she had secretly hoped for more enthusiasm), and thereafter life became a desert waste of suspense. The very globe seemed to cease to turn on its axis while she waited for *The Man-at-Arms* to appear.

Finally one day a thick packet bearing an English publisher's name was brought to her. She undid it with trembling fingers, and there, beautifully printed on the large rough pages, her story stood out before her.

At first, in that heavy text, on those heavy pages, it seemed to her a pitifully small thing, hopelessly insignificant and yet pitilessly conspicuous. It was as though words meant to be murmured to sympathetic friends were being megaphoned into the ear of a heedless universe.

Then she began to turn the pages of the review; she analyzed the poems, she read the Queen of Norromania's domestic confidences, and she looked at the portraits of the authors. The latter experience was peculiarly comforting. The Queen was rather good-looking—for a Queen—but her hair was drawn back from the temples as if it were wound round a windlass, and struck out over her forehead in the good old-fashioned Royal Highness fuzz; and her prose was oddly built out of London drawing-room phrases grafted onto German genitives and datives. It was evident

that neither Ivy's portrait nor her story would suffer by comparison with the royal contribution.

But most of all was she comforted by the poems. They were
nearly all written on Kipling rhythms that broke down after two or
three wheezy attempts to "carry on" and their knowing mixture of
slang and pathos seemed oddly old-fashioned to the author of "Vibrations." Altogether, it struck her that *The Man-at-Arms* was
made up in equal parts of tired compositions by people who knew
how to write, and artless prattle by people who didn't. Against
such a background, "His Letter Home" began to loom up rather
large.

At any rate, it took such a place in her consciousness for the
next day or two that it was bewildering to find that no one about
her seemed to have heard of it. "The Man-at-Arms" was conspicuously shown in the windows of the principal English and American bookshops but she failed to see it lying on her friends' tables
and finally, when her tea-pouring day came round, she bought a
dozen copies and took them up to the English ward of her hospital, which happened to be full at the time.

It was not long before Christmas and the men and officers were
rather busy with home correspondence and the undoing and do-
ing-up of seasonable parcels but they all received *The Man-at-
Arms* with an appreciative smile, and were most awfully pleased
to know that Miss Spang had written something in it. After the
distribution of her tale, Miss Spang became suddenly hot and shy,
and slipped away before they had begun to read her.

The intervening week seemed long; and it was marked only by
the appearance of a review of *The Man-at-Arms* in the *Times*—a
long and laudatory article—in which, by some odd accident, "His
Letter Home" and its author were not so much as mentioned.
Abridged versions of this notice appeared in the English and
American newspapers published in Paris; and one anecdotic and
intimate article in a French journal celebrated the maternal graces
and literary art of the Queen of Norromania. It was signed
"Fleur-de-Lys," and described a banquet at the Court of Norromania at which the writer hinted that she had assisted.

The following week, Ivy re-entered her ward with a beating

heart. On the threshold one of the nurses detained her with a smile.

"Do be a dear and make yourself specially nice to the new officer in Number 5; he's only been here two days and he's rather down on his luck. Oh, by the way—he's a novelist. Harold Harbard; you know, the man who wrote the book they made such a fuss about."

Harold Harbard—the book they made such a fuss about! What a poor fool the woman was—not even to remember the title of *Broken Wings!* Ivy's heart stood still with the shock of the discovery. She remembered that she had left a copy of *The Man-at-Arms* in Number 5, and the blood coursed through her veins and flooded her to the forehead at the idea that Harold Harbard might at that very moment be reading "His Letter Home."

To collect herself, she decided to remain a while in the ward, serving tea to the soldiers and N. C. O.'s, before venturing into Number 5, which the previous week had been occupied only by a polo player drowsy with chloroform and uninterested in anything but his specialty. Think of Harold Harbard lying in the bed next to that man!

Ivy passed into the ward, and as she glanced down the long line of beds she saw several copies of *The Man-at-Arms* lying on them, and one special favorite of hers, a young lance-corporal, deep in its pages.

She walked down the ward, distributing tea and greetings; and she saw that her patients were all very glad to see her. They always were; but this time there was a certain unmistakable emphasis in their gladness; and she fancied they wanted her to notice it.

"Why," she cried gayly, "how uncommonly cheerful you all look!"

She was handing his tea to the young lance-corporal, who was usually the spokesman of the ward on momentous occasions. He lifted his eyes from the absorbed perusal of *The Man-at-Arms,* and as he did so she saw that it was open to the first page of her story.

"I say, you know," he said, "it's simply topping—and we're so awfully obliged to you for letting us see it."

She laughed, but would not affect incomprehension.

"That?" She laid a light finger on the review. "Oh, I'm glad—

I'm awfully pleased, of course—you *do* really like it?" she stammered.

"Rather—all of us—most tremendously—!" came a chorus from the long line of beds.

Ivy tasted her highest moment of triumph. She drew a deep breath and shone on them with glowing cheeks.

"There couldn't be higher praise . . . there couldn't be better judges. . . . You think it's really like, do you?"

"Really like? Rather! It's just topping," rang out the unanimous response.

She choked with emotion. "Coming from you—from all of you—it makes me most awfully glad."

They all laughed together shyly, and then the lance-corporal spoke up.

"We admire it so much that we're going to ask you a most tremendous favor—"

"Oh, yes," came from the other beds.

"A favor—?"

"Yes; if it's not too much." The lance-corporal became eloquent. "To remember you by, and all your kindness; we want to know if you won't give one to each of us—"

("Why, of course, of course," Ivy glowed.)

"—to frame and take away with us," the lance-corporal continued sentimentally. "There's a chap here who makes rather jolly frames out of Vichy corks."

"Oh—" said Ivy, with a protracted gasp.

"You see, in your nurse's dress, it'll always be such a jolly reminder," said the lance-corporal, concluding his lesson.

"I never saw a jollier photo," spoke up a bold spirit.

"Oh, do say yes, nurse," the shyest of the patients softly whispered; and Ivy, bewildered between tears and laughter, said, "Yes."

It was evident that not one of them had read her story.

She stopped on the threshold of Number 5, her heart beating uncomfortably.

She had already recovered from her passing mortification; it was absurd to have imagined that the inmates of the ward, dear, gallant young fellows, would feel the subtle meaning of a story like "His Letter Home." But with Harold Harbard it was different. Now, indeed, she was to be face to face with a critic.

She stopped on the threshold, and as she did so she heard a burst of hearty, healthy laughter from within. It was not the voice of the polo player; could it be that of the novelist?

She opened the door resolutely and walked in with her tray. The polo player's bed was empty, and the face on the pillow of the adjoining cot was the brown, ugly, tumultuous-locked head of Harold Harbard, well-known to her from frequent photographs in the literary weeklies. He looked up as she came in, and said in a voice that seemed to continue his laugh: "Tea? Come, that's something like!" And he began to laugh again.

It was evident that he was still carrying on the thread of his joke, and as she approached with the tea she saw that a copy of *The Man-at-Arms* lay on the bed at his side, and that he had his hand between the open pages.

Her heart gave an apprehensive twitch, but she determined to carry off the situation with a high hand.

"How do you do, Captain Harbard? I suppose you're laughing at the way the Queen of Norromania's hair is done."

He met her glance with a humorous look, and shook his head, while the laughter still rippled the muscles of his throat.

"No—no; I've finished laughing at that. It was the next thing; what's it called? 'His Letter Home,' by—" The review dropped abruptly from his hands, his brown cheek paled, and he fixed her with a stricken stare.

"Good lord," he stammered out, "but it's *you!*"

She blushed all colors, and dropped into a seat at his side. "After all," she faltered, half laughing too, "at least you read the story instead of looking at my photograph."

He continued to scrutinize her with a reviving eye. "Why—do you mean that everybody else—"

"All the ward over there," she assented, nodding in the direction of the door.

"They all forgot to read the story for gazing at its author?"

"Apparently." There was a painful pause. The review dropped from his lax hand.

"Your tea—?" she suggested, stiffly.

"Oh, yes; to be sure. . . . Thanks."

There was another silence, during which the act of pouring out the milk, and the dropping of the sugar into the cup, seemed to assume enormous magnitude, and make an echoing noise. At length Ivy said, with an effort at lightness, "Since I know who you are, Mr. Harbard—would you mind telling me what you were laughing at in my story?"

He leaned back against the pillows and wrinkled his forehead anxiously.

"My dear Miss Spang, not in the least—if I *could*."

"If you could?"

"Yes; I mean in any understandable way."

"In other words, you think it so silly that you don't dare to tell me anything more?"

He shook his head. "No; but it's queer—it's puzzling. You've got hold of a wonderfully good subject; and that's the main thing, of course—"

Ivy interrupted him eagerly. "The subject is the main thing?"

"Why, naturally; it's only the people without invention who tell you it isn't."

"Oh," she gasped, trying to readjust her carefully acquired theory of aesthetics.

"You've got hold of an awfully good subject," Harbard continued; "but you've rather mauled it, haven't you?"

She sat before him with her head drooping and the blood running back from her pale cheeks. Two tears had gathered on her lashes.

"There!" the novelist cried out irritably, "I knew that as soon as I was frank you'd resent it! What was the earthly use of asking me?"

She made no answer, and he added, lowering his voice a little, "Are you very angry with me, really?"

"No, of course not," she declared with a stony gaiety.

"I'm so glad you're not; because I do want most awfully to ask you for one of these photographs," he concluded.

She rose abruptly from her seat. To save her life she could not conceal her disappointment. But she picked up the tray with feverish animation.

"A photograph? Of course—with pleasure. And now, if you've quite finished, I'm afraid I must run back to my teapot."

Harold Harbard lay on the bed and looked at her. As she reached the door he said, "Miss Spang!"

"Yes?" she rejoined, pausing reluctantly.

"You were angry just now because I didn't admire your story; and now you're angrier still because I do admire your photograph. Do you wonder that we novelists find such an inexhaustible field in Woman?"

PART II

NOVELS

Edith Wharton's 1917 novel, *Summer,* appears here in its entirety. Called by Cynthia Griffin Wolff Wharton's "most balanced novel," the book is something of an anomaly within the Wharton oeuvre. Like the earlier *Ethan Frome, Summer* is set in the small village culture of provincial western Massachusetts. Even though Wharton had lived at The Mount near Lenox for some years, she was never a part of the rural life that dominated that locale. *Ethan Frome* was a story she had learned from a resident, and her creation of Charity Royall similarly drew on oral sources.

Another factor that distinguishes *Summer* stems from her liaison with Morton Fullerton—according to her journals and letters, she had herself experienced the kind of relentless passion, the physical yearning, that draws Charity to Lucius Harney. Notably absent in her first novels, such as *The House of Mirth* and *The Fruit of the Tree,* physical sexual desire here is fully drawn, and undisguised. The scene in which Charity watches Lucius through his bedroom window is a remarkable depiction of her as yet unexpressed longing. And, further, Wharton makes clear in the novel that Charity is not a bad woman because she has loved Lucius so completely: in fact, the guardian father figure, lawyer Royall, became the object of readers' criticism, even though he tries to rescue Charity by marrying her.

Summer is one of the earliest American abortion novels. In creating the small town and its community, Wharton gives the reader the chance to know the proper (and often unmarried) older women who condemn anything sexual; Julia Hawes, the sister of the town's seamstress, has become a prostitute in order to support herself since, having both lost her virginity and had an abortion, she can no longer return home. Julia's sexual taste makes her a surrogate for Charity, and the aftermath of what happens to Julia—including what appears to be her relationship with lawyer Royall—helps the reader understand the ending of *Summer*. Even as Charity decides she will return to the Mountain, and find solace and a home with her mother's people, the reader knows she will be unable to do this: realistically, she has few choices, and one of those involves explaining to Lucius that she is pregnant.

Summer is as much a novel about class as about women's sexuality. The fact that Charity knows she can never tell Lucius that she is carrying his child—like the fact that she must wear his fiancée's discarded shoes—depends on her place in the class hierarchy. It is bad enough that she lives as an orphan with the lawyer (renamed "Charity" once she was brought down from the Mountain so that she will never forget the kindness of the Royalls); what is worse is the fact that she came from the Mountain in the first place, that her father was jailed, and that her mother did not care that Charity was taken from her. The number of cardinal sins—a criminal for a father, a mother who cared only for her own sinful behavior, a community that was apparently completely lawless—mark Charity as a girl who will never fit in. Her background also provides the rationale for Miss Hatchard's allowing her to live in the Royall house after Mrs. Royall's death. The value of a poor child like Charity is questionable.

As in many of her stories, Wharton gives *Summer* a comparatively open ending. Working with the strands of narrative that encompass the blue brooch, unwritten letters, and the sexual rights of lawyer Royall as husband, the novel resonates with questions—How happy will Charity be? How able to forget the great passion of her life? How willing to become the dutiful wife of the aging, and alcoholic, guardian? Even though they share the exchange of the word "good" in the closing scene of the book, the reader has little confidence that Wharton intended this to be a happy ending. At least not for Charity.

The opening chapter of Wharton's first best-seller, *The House of Mirth*, appears here for its mastery of presenting a powerless woman's place in a proper society. Beautiful and well cared for, Lily Bart, too, has the strain of independence that suggests Charity's strong will. But in this novel, Lily already belongs to that elusive upper class; her challenge—and her duty—is to marry the right person so that she can remain in the class that she thinks of as hers.

Wharton presents the psychological conflict from the start: Lawrence Selden gives Lily Bart reason to question her expected role, that of becoming the wife of a wealthy (if boring) citizen. He encourages her to question her life's goals, always sounding intellectual, humane, somehow above the crowd that she normally lives amid. Lily goes to his home—easily, unchaperoned—and then lies about her presence there. By such slim errors, her respectability begins to crumble.

Lily's meeting with Percy Gryce is set up to be a great contrast. She likes Selden; she finds Gryce a monumental dullard. Yet she must continue her plan to catch Gryce, even if doing so means lying about her habits (playing bridge, smoking) as well as her intimate identity. Wharton's finesse in setting up these relationships, and exploring so deftly the society Lily commands, has seldom been bettered.

Wharton was a consummate craftsperson with beginnings, but her novels seldom lagged wherever a reader opened the book. In this middle section of *The Reef*, for instance, the novel Henry James thought was Wharton's best, the plot is already well in progress. George Darrow has proposed to his long-lost earlier love, Anna Leath, now that she is widowed and living in her French home, Givré, along with her stepson, Owen; her daughter, Effie; and Effie's governess, Sophy Viner. En route to visit Anna the previous spring, Darrow has had an impulsive affair with the beautiful young, gauche American, who now turns out to be both Effie's governess and Owen's betrothed. The intrigue of both Sophy and Darrow pretending they have never met occupies a large part of the book, as a foreshadowing of Anna Leath's premonition—and then her realization—of Darrow's duplicity. In this novel, too, Wharton redeems Sophy Viner through an understanding of her complex love for Darrow.

The excerpt from Wharton's Pulitzer Prize–winning *The Age of Innocence* focuses on the dilemma Newland Archer faces as he realizes he cannot relinquish his passion for Ellen Olenska, the cousin of his wife who has fled Europe (and her immoral husband). In these scenes, Wharton shows the unstated torment of both Archer and his young wife, May Welland, a woman who knows too well what is going on between her husband and her cousin.

These excerpts, alongside the full text of *Summer*, demonstrate the multilayered characterization that Wharton achieved: there are few authors more adept with a few lines of dialogue, or with the tremolo in May Welland's smile as she raises her face for her husband's kiss. Wharton's large themes—the difference between appearance and reality, the difficulty of believing in any kind of love, the coercive power of a social structure careful to protect its own—are frequently expressed through just such details.

SUMMER

I

A girl came out of lawyer Royall's house, at the end of the one street of North Dormer, and stood on the doorstep.

It was the beginning of a June afternoon. The springlike transparent sky shed a rain of silver sunshine on the roofs of the village, and on the pastures and larchwoods surrounding it. A little wind moved among the round white clouds on the shoulders of the hills, driving their shadows across the fields and down the grassy road that takes the name of street when it passes through North Dormer. The place lies high and in the open, and lacks the lavish shade of the more protected New England villages. The clump of weeping-willows about the duck pond, and the Norway spruces in front of the Hatchard gate, cast almost the only roadside shadow between lawyer Royall's house and the point where, at the other end of the village, the road rises above the church and skirts the black hemlock wall enclosing the cemetery.

The little June wind, frisking down the street, shook the doleful fringes of the Hatchard spruces, caught the straw hat of a young man just passing under them, and spun it clean across the road into the duck-pond.

As he ran to fish it out the girl on lawyer Royall's doorstep noticed that he was a stranger, that he wore city clothes, and that he was laughing with all his teeth, as the young and careless laugh at such mishaps.

Her heart contracted a little, and the shrinking that sometimes came over her when she saw people with holiday faces made her draw back into the house and pretend to look for the key that she knew she had already put into her pocket. A narrow greenish mirror with a gilt eagle over it hung on the passage wall, and she looked critically at her reflection, wished for the thousandth time that she had blue eyes like Annabel Balch, the girl who sometimes came from Springfield to spend a week with old Miss Hatchard, straightened the sunburnt hat over her small swarthy face, and turned out again into the sunshine.

"How I hate everything!" she murmured.

The young man had passed through the Hatchard gate, and she had the street to herself. North Dormer is at all times an empty place, and at three o'clock on a June afternoon its few able-bodied men are off in the fields or woods, and the women indoors, engaged in languid household drudgery.

The girl walked along, swinging her key on a finger, and looking about her with the heightened attention produced by the presence of a stranger in a familiar place. What, she wondered, did North Dormer look like to people from other parts of the world? She herself had lived there since the age of five, and had long supposed it to be a place of some importance. But about a year before, Mr. Miles, the new Episcopal clergyman at Hepburn, who drove over every other Sunday—when the roads were not ploughed up by hauling—to hold a service in the North Dormer church, had proposed, in a fit of missionary zeal, to take the young people down to Nettleton to hear an illustrated lecture on the Holy Land; and the dozen girls and boys who represented the future of North Dormer had been piled into a farm-waggon, driven over the hills to Hepburn, put into a way-train[1] and carried to Nettleton. In the course of that incredible day Charity Royall had, for the first and only time, experienced railway-travel, looked into shops with plate-glass fronts, tasted cocoanut pie, sat in a theatre, and listened to a gentleman saying unintelligible things before pictures that she would have enjoyed looking at if his explanations had not prevented her from understanding them. This initiation had shown her that North Dormer was a small place, and developed in her a thirst for information that her position as custodian of the village library had previously failed to excite. For a month or two she dipped feverishly and disconnectedly into the dusty volumes of the Hatchard Memorial Library; then the impression of Nettleton began to fade, and she found it easier to take North Dormer as the norm of the universe than to go on reading.

The sight of the stranger once more revived memories of Nettleton, and North Dormer shrank to its real size. As she looked up and down it, from lawyer Royall's faded red house at one end to the white church at the other, she pitilessly took its measure. There it lay, a weather-beaten sunburnt village of the hills, abandoned of men, left apart by railway, trolley, telegraph, and all the forces that link life to life in modern communities. It had no shops, no theatres, no lectures, no "business block"; only a church that was opened every other Sunday if the state of the roads permitted, and a library for which no new books had been bought for twenty years, and where the old ones mouldered undisturbed on the damp shelves. Yet Charity Royall had always been told that she ought to consider it a privilege that her lot had been cast in North Dormer. She knew that, compared to the place she had come from, North Dormer represented all the blessings of the most refined civilization. Everyone in the village had told her so ever since she had been brought there as a child. Even old Miss Hatchard had said to her, on a terrible occasion in her life: "My child, you must never cease to remember that it was Mr. Royall who brought you down from the Mountain."

She had been "brought down from the Mountain"; from the scarred cliff that lifted its sullen wall above the lesser slopes of Eagle Range, making a perpetual background of gloom to the lonely valley. The Mountain was a good fifteen miles away, but it rose so abruptly from the lower hills that it seemed almost to cast its shadow over North Dormer. And it was like a great magnet drawing the clouds and scattering them in storm across the valley. If ever, in the purest summer sky, there trailed a thread of vapour over North Dormer, it drifted to the Mountain as a ship drifts to a whirlpool, and was caught among the rocks, torn up and multiplied, to sweep back over the village in rain and darkness.

Charity was not very clear about the Mountain; but she knew it was a bad place, and a shame to have come from, and that, whatever befell her in North Dormer, she ought, as Miss Hatchard had once reminded her, to remember that she had been brought down from there, and hold her tongue and be thankful. She looked up at the Mountain, thinking of these things, and tried as usual to be thankful. But the sight of the young man turning in at Miss Hatchard's gate had brought back the vision of the glittering streets of Nettleton, and she felt ashamed of her old sun-hat, and sick of North Dormer, and jealously aware of Annabel Balch of Springfield, opening her blue eyes somewhere far off on glories greater than the glories of Nettleton.

"How I hate everything!" she said again.

Half way down the street she stopped at a weak-hinged gate. Passing through it, she walked down a brick path to a queer little brick temple with white wooden columns supporting a pediment on which was inscribed in tarnished gold letters: "The Honorius Hatchard Memorial Library, 1832."

Honorius Hatchard had been old Miss Hatchard's great-uncle; though she would undoubtedly have reversed the phrase, and put forward, as her only claim to distinction, the fact that she was his great-niece. For Honorius Hatchard, in the early years of the nineteenth century, had enjoyed a modest celebrity. As the marble tablet in the interior of the library informed its infrequent visitors, he had possessed marked literary gifts, written a series of papers called "The Recluse of Eagle Range," enjoyed the acquaintance of Washington Irving[2] and Fitz-Greene Halleck,[3] and been cut off in his flower by a fever contracted in Italy. Such had been the sole link between North Dormer and literature, a link piously commemorated by the erection of the monument where Charity Royall, every Tuesday and Thursday afternoon, sat at her desk under a freckled steel engraving of the deceased author, and wondered if he felt any deader in his grave than she did in his library.

Entering her prison-house with a listless step she took off her hat, hung it on a plaster bust of Minerva,[4] opened the shutters, leaned out to see if there were any eggs in the swallow's nest above one of the windows, and finally, seating herself behind the desk, drew out a roll of cotton lace and a steel crochet hook. She was not an expert workwoman, and it had taken her many weeks to make the half-yard of narrow lace which she kept wound about the buckram back of a disintegrated copy of "The Lamplighter."[5] But there was no other way of getting any lace to trim her summer blouse, and since Ally Hawes, the poorest girl in the village, had shown herself in church with enviable transparencies about the shoulders, Charity's hook had travelled faster. She unrolled the lace, dug the hook into a loop, and bent to the task with furrowed brows.

Suddenly the door opened, and before she had raised her eyes she knew that the young man she had seen going in at the Hatchard gate had entered the library.

Without taking any notice of her he began to move slowly about the long vault-like room, his hands behind his back, his short-sighted eyes peering up and down the rows of rusty bindings. At length he reached the desk and stood before her.

"Have you a card-catalogue?" he asked in a pleasant abrupt voice; and the oddness of the question caused her to drop her work.

"A *what?*"

"Why, you know—" He broke off, and she became conscious that he was looking at her for the first time, having apparently, on his entrance, included her in his general short-sighted survey as part of the furniture of the library.

The fact that, in discovering her, he lost the thread of his remark, did not escape her attention, and she looked down and smiled. He smiled also.

"No, I don't suppose you *do* know," he corrected himself. "In fact, it would be almost a pity—"

She thought she detected a slight condescension in his tone, and asked sharply: "Why?"

"Because it's so much pleasanter, in a small library like this, to poke about by one's self—with the help of the librarian."

He added the last phrase so respectfully that she was mollified, and rejoined with a sigh: "I'm afraid I can't help you much."

"Why?" he questioned in his turn; and she replied that there weren't many books anyhow, and that she'd hardly read any of them. "The worms are getting at them," she added gloomily.

"Are they? That's a pity, for I see there are some good ones." He seemed to have lost interest in their conversation, and strolled away again, apparently forgetting her. His indifference nettled her, and she picked up her work, resolved not to offer him the least assistance. Apparently he did not need it, for he spent a long time with his back to her, lifting down, one after another, the tall cobwebby volumes from a distant shelf.

"Oh, I say!" he exclaimed; and looking up she saw that he had drawn out his handkerchief and was carefully wiping the edges of the book in his hand. The action struck her as an unwarranted criticism on her care of the books, and she said irritably: "It's not my fault if they're dirty."

He turned around and looked at her with reviving interest. "Ah—then you're not the librarian?"

"Of course I am; but I can't dust all these books. Besides, nobody ever looks at them, now Miss Hatchard's too lame to come round."

"No, I suppose not." He laid down the book he had been wiping, and stood considering her in silence. She wondered if Miss Hatchard had sent him round to pry into the way the library was looked after, and the suspicion increased her resentment. "I saw you going into her house just now, didn't I?" she asked, with the New England avoidance of the proper name. She was determined to find out why he was poking about among her books.

"Miss Hatchard's house? Yes—she's my cousin and I'm staying there," the young man answered; adding, as if to disarm a visible distrust: "My name is Harney—Lucius Harney. She may have spoken of me."

"No, she hasn't," said Charity, wishing she could have said: "Yes, she has."

"Oh, well—" said Miss Hatchard's cousin with a laugh; and after another pause, during which it occurred to Charity that her answer had not been encouraging, he remarked: "You don't seem strong on architecture."

Her bewilderment was complete: the more she wished to appear to understand him the more unintelligible his remarks became. He reminded her of the gentleman who had "explained" the pictures at Nettleton, and the weight of her ignorance settled down on her again like a pall.

"I mean, I can't see that you have any books on the old houses about here. I suppose, for that matter, this part of the country hasn't been much explored. They all go on doing Plymouth and Salem. So stupid. My cousin's house, now, is remarkable. This place must have had a past—it must have been more of a place once." He stopped short, with the blush of a shy man who overhears himself, and fears he has been voluble. "I'm an architect, you see, and I'm hunting up old houses in these parts."

She stared. "Old houses? Everything's old in North Dormer, isn't it? The folks are, anyhow."

He laughed, and wandered away again.

"Haven't you any kind of a history of the place? I think there was one written about 1840: a book or pamphlet about its first settlement," he presently said from the farther end of the room.

She pressed her crochet hook against her lip and pondered. There was such a work, she knew: "North Dormer and the Early Townships of Eagle County." She had a special grudge against it because it was a limp weakly book that was always either falling off the shelf or slipping back and disappearing if one squeezed it in between sustaining volumes. She remembered, the last time she had picked it up, wondering how anyone could have taken the trouble to write a book about North Dormer and its neighbours: Dormer, Hamblin, Creston and Creston River. She knew them all, mere lost clusters of houses in the folds of the desolate ridges: Dormer, where North Dormer went for its apples; Creston River, where there used to be a paper-mill, and its grey walls stood decaying by the stream; and Hamblin, where the first snow always fell. Such were their titles to fame.

She got up and began to move about vaguely before the shelves. But she had no idea where she had last put the book, and something told her that it was going to play her its usual trick and remain invisible. It was not one of her lucky days.

"I guess it's somewhere," she said, to prove her zeal; but she spoke without conviction, and felt that her words conveyed none.

"Oh, well—" he said again. She knew he was going, and wished more than ever to find the book.

"It will be for next time," he added; and picking up the volume he had laid on the desk he handed it to her. "By the way, a little air and sun would do this good; it's rather valuable."

He gave her a nod and smile, and passed out.

II

The hours of the Hatchard Memorial librarian were from three to five; and Charity Royall's sense of duty usually kept her at her desk until nearly half-past four.

But she had never perceived that any practical advantage thereby accrued either to North Dormer or to herself; and she had no scruple in decreeing, when it suited her, that the library should close an hour earlier. A few minutes after Mr. Harney's departure she formed this decision, put away her lace, fastened the shutters, and turned the key in the door of the temple of knowledge.

The street upon which she emerged was still empty: and after glancing up and down it she began to walk toward her house. But instead of entering she passed on, turned into a field-path and mounted to a pasture on the hillside. She let down the bars of the gate, followed a trail along the crumbling wall of the pasture, and walked on till she reached a knoll where a clump of larches shook out their fresh tassels to the wind. There she lay down on the slope, tossed off her hat and hid her face in the grass.

She was blind and insensible to many things, and dimly knew it; but to all that was light and air, perfume and colour, every drop of blood in her responded. She loved the roughness of the dry mountain grass under her palms, the smell of the thyme into which she crushed her face, the fingering of the wind in her hair and through her cotton blouse, and the creak of the larches as they swayed to it.

She often climbed up the hill and lay there alone for the mere pleasure of feeling the wind and of rubbing her cheeks in the grass. Generally at such times she did not think of anything, but lay immersed in an inarticulate well-being. Today the sense of well-being was intensified by her joy at escaping from the library. She liked well enough to have a friend drop in and talk to her when she was on duty, but she hated to be bothered about books. How could she remember where they were, when they were so seldom asked for? Orma Fry occasionally took out a novel, and her brother Ben was fond of what he called "jography," and of books relating to trade and bookkeeping; but no one else asked for anything except, at intervals, "Uncle Tom's Cabin,"[6] or "Opening a Chestnut Burr,"[7] or Longfellow.[8] She had these under her hand, and could have found them in the dark; but unexpected demands came so rarely that they exasperated her like an injustice. . . .

She had liked the young man's looks, and his short-sighted eyes, and his odd way of speaking, that was abrupt yet soft, just as his hands were sunburnt and sinewy, yet with smooth nails like a woman's. His hair was sunburnt-looking too, or rather the colour of bracken after frost; his eyes grey, with the appealing look of the short-sighted, his smile shy yet confident, as if he knew lots of things she had never dreamed of, and yet wouldn't for the world have had her feel his superiority. But she did feel it, and liked the feeling; for it was new to her. Poor and ignorant as she was, and knew herself to be—humblest of the humble even in North Dormer, where to come from the Mountain was the worst disgrace—yet in her narrow world she had always ruled. It was partly, of course, owing to the fact that lawyer Royall was "the biggest man in North Dormer"; so much too big for it, in fact, that outsiders, who didn't know, always wondered how it held him. In spite of everything—and in spite even of Miss Hatchard—lawyer Royall ruled in North Dormer; and Charity ruled in lawyer Royall's house. She had never put it to herself in those terms; but she knew her power, knew what it was made of, and hated it. Confusedly, the young man in the library had made her feel for the first time what might be the sweetness of dependence.

She sat up, brushed the bits of grass from her hair, and looked down on the house where she held sway. It stood just below her, cheerless and untended, its faded red front divided from the road by a "yard" with a path bordered by gooseberry bushes, a stone well overgrown with traveller's joy, and a sickly Crimson Rambler[9] tied to a fan-shaped support, which Mr. Royall had once brought up from Hepburn to please her. Behind the house a bit of uneven ground with clothes-lines strung across it stretched up to a dry wall, and beyond the wall a patch of corn and a few rows of potatoes strayed vaguely into the adjoining wilderness of rock and fern.

Charity could not recall her first sight of the house. She had been told that she was ill of a fever when she was brought down from the Mountain; and she could only remember waking one day in a cot at the foot of Mrs. Royall's bed, and opening her eyes on the cold neatness of the room that was afterward to be hers.

Mrs. Royall died seven or eight years later; and by that time Charity had taken the measure of most things about her. She knew that Mrs. Royall was sad and timid and weak; she knew that lawyer Royall was harsh and violent, and still weaker. She knew that she had been christened Charity (in the white church at

the other end of the village) to commemorate Mr. Royall's disin-
terestedness in "bringing her down," and to keep alive in her a becoming sense of her dependence; she knew that Mr. Royall was
her guardian, but that he had not legally adopted her, though
everybody spoke of her as Charity Royall; and she knew why he
had come back to live at North Dormer, instead of practising at
Nettleton, where he had begun his legal career.

After Mrs. Royall's death there was some talk of sending her to
a boarding-school. Miss Hatchard suggested it, and had a long
conference with Mr. Royall, who, in pursuance of her plan, departed one day for Starkfield to visit the institution she recommended. He came back the next night with a black face; worse,
Charity observed, than she had ever seen him; and by that time
she had had some experience.

When she asked him how soon she was to start he answered
shortly, "You ain't going," and shut himself up in the room he
called his office; and the next day the lady who kept the school at
Starkfield wrote that "under the circumstances" she was afraid
she could not make room just then for another pupil.

Charity was disappointed; but she understood. It wasn't the
temptations of Starkfield that had been Mr. Royall's undoing; it
was the thought of losing her. He was a dreadfully "lonesome"
man; she had made that out because she was so "lonesome" herself. He and she, face to face in that sad house, had sounded the
depths of isolation; and though she felt no particular affection for
him, and not the slightest gratitude, she pitied him because she
was conscious that he was superior to the people about him, and
that she was the only being between him and solitude. Therefore,
when Miss Hatchard sent for her a day or two later, to talk of a
school at Nettleton, and to say that this time a friend of hers
would "make the necessary arrangements," Charity cut her short
with the announcement that she had decided not to leave North
Dormer.

Miss Hatchard reasoned with her kindly, but to no purpose; she
simply repeated: "I guess Mr. Royall's too lonesome."

Miss Hatchard blinked perplexedly behind her eye-glasses. Her
long frail face was full of puzzled wrinkles, and she leant forward,
resting her hands on the arms of her mahogany armchair, with the
evident desire to say something that ought to be said.

"The feeling does you credit, my dear."

She looked about the pale walls of her sitting-room, seeking counsel of ancestral daguerreotypes and didactic samplers; but they seemed to make utterance more difficult.

"The fact is, it's not only—not only because of the advantages. There are other reasons. You're too young to understand——"

"Oh, no, I ain't," said Charity harshly; and Miss Hatchard blushed to the roots of her blonde cap. But she must have felt a vague relief at having her explanation cut short, for she concluded, again invoking the daguerreotypes: "Of course I shall always do what I can for you; and in case . . . in case . . . you know you can always come to me. . . ."

Lawyer Royall was waiting for Charity in the porch when she returned from this visit. He had shaved, and brushed his black coat, and looked a magnificent monument of a man; at such moments she really admired him.

"Well," he said, "is it settled?"

"Yes, it's settled. I ain't going."

"Not to the Nettleton school?"

"Not anywhere."

He cleared his throat and asked sternly: "Why?"

"I'd rather not," she said, swinging past him on her way to her room. It was the following week that he brought her up the Crimson Rambler and its fan from Hepburn. He had never given her anything before.

The next outstanding incident of her life had happened two years later, when she was seventeen. Lawyer Royall, who hated to go to Nettleton, had been called there in connection with a case. He still exercised his profession, though litigation languished in North Dormer and its outlying hamlets; and for once he had had an opportunity that he could not afford to refuse. He spent three days in Nettleton, won his case, and came back in high good-humour. It was a rare mood with him, and manifested itself on this occasion by his talking impressively at the supper-table of the "rousing welcome" his old friends had given him. He wound up confidentially: "I was a damn fool ever to leave Nettleton. It was Mrs. Royall that made me do it."

Charity immediately perceived that something bitter had happened to him, and that he was trying to talk down the recollection. She went up to bed early, leaving him seated in moody thought, his elbows propped on the worn oilcloth of the supper table. On the way up she had extracted from his overcoat pocket the key of the cupboard where the bottle of whiskey was kept.

She was awakened by a rattling at her door and jumped out of bed. She heard Mr. Royall's voice, low and peremptory, and opened the door, fearing an accident. No other thought had occurred to her; but when she saw him in the doorway, a ray from the autumn moon falling on his discomposed face, she understood.

For a moment they looked at each other in silence; then, as he put his foot across the threshold, she stretched out her arm and stopped him.

"You go right back from here," she said, in a shrill voice that startled her; "you ain't going to have that key tonight."

"Charity, let me in. I don't want the key. I'm a lonesome man," he began, in the deep voice that sometimes moved her.

Her heart gave a startled plunge, but she continued to hold him back contemptuously. "Well, I guess you made a mistake, then. This ain't your wife's room any longer."

She was not frightened, she simply felt a deep disgust; and perhaps he divined it or read it in her face, for after staring at her a moment he drew back and turned slowly away from the door. With her ear to her keyhole she heard him feel his way down the dark stairs, and toward the kitchen; and she listened for the crash of the cupboard panel. But instead she heard him, after an interval, unlock the door of the house, and his heavy steps came to her through the silence as he walked down the path. She crept to the window and saw his bent figure striding up the road in the moonlight. Then a belated sense of fear came to her with the consciousness of victory, and she slipped into bed, cold to the bone.

A day or two later poor Eudora Skeff, who for twenty years had been the custodian of the Hatchard library, died suddenly of pneumonia; and the day after the funeral Charity went to see Miss Hatchard, and asked to be appointed librarian. The request seemed to surprise Miss Hatchard: she evidently questioned the new candidate's qualifications.

"Why, I don't know, my dear. Aren't you rather too young?" she hesitated.

"I want to earn some money," Charity merely answered.

"Doesn't Mr. Royall give you all you require? No one is rich in North Dormer."

"I want to earn money enough to get away."

"To get away?" Miss Hatchard's puzzled wrinkles deepened, and there was a distressful pause. "You want to leave Mr. Royall?"

"Yes: or I want another woman in the house with me," said Charity resolutely.

Miss Hatchard clasped her nervous hands about the arms of her chair. Her eyes invoked the faded countenances on the wall, and after a faint cough of indecision she brought out: "The . . . the housework's too hard for you, I suppose?"

Charity's heart grew cold. She understood that Miss Hatchard had no help to give her and that she would have to fight her way out of her difficulty alone. A deeper sense of isolation overcame her; she felt incalculably old. "She's got to be talked to like a baby," she thought, with a feeling of compassion for Miss Hatchard's long immaturity. "Yes, that's it," she said aloud. "The housework's too hard for me: I've been coughing a good deal this fall."

She noted the immediate effect of this suggestion. Miss Hatchard paled at the memory of poor Eudora's taking-off, and promised to do what she could. But of course there were people she must consult: the clergyman, the selectmen of North Dormer, and a distant Hatchard relative at Springfield. "If you'd only gone to school!" she sighed. She followed Charity to the door, and there, in the security of the threshold, said with a glance of evasive appeal: "I know Mr. Royall is . . . trying at times; but his wife bore with him; and you must always remember, Charity, that it was Mr. Royall who brought you down from the Mountain."

Charity went home and opened the door of Mr. Royall's "office." He was sitting there by the stove reading Daniel Webster's[10] speeches. They had met at meals during the five days that had elapsed since he had come to her door, and she had walked at his side at Eudora's funeral; but they had not spoken a word to each other.

He glanced up in surprise as she entered, and she noticed that he was unshaved, and that he looked unusually old; but as she had always thought of him as an old man the change in his appearance did not move her. She told him she had been to see Miss Hatchard, and with what object. She saw that he was astonished; but he made no comment.

"I told her the housework was too hard for me, and I wanted to earn the money to pay for a hired girl. But I ain't going to pay for her: you've got to. I want to have some money of my own."

Mr. Royall's bushy black eyebrows were drawn together in a frown, and he sat drumming with ink-stained nails on the edge of his desk.

"What do you want to earn money for?" he asked.

"So's to get away when I want to."

"Why do you want to get away?"

Her contempt flashed out. "Do you suppose anybody'd stay at North Dormer if they could help it? You wouldn't, folks say!"

With lowered head he asked: "Where'd you go to?"

"Anywhere where I can earn my living. I'll try here first, and if I can't do it here I'll go somewhere else. I'll go up the Mountain if I have to." She paused on this threat, and saw that it had taken effect. "I want you should get Miss Hatchard and the selectmen to take me at the library: and I want a woman here in the house with me," she repeated.

Mr. Royall had grown exceedingly pale. When she ended he stood up ponderously, leaning against the desk; and for a second or two they looked at each other.

"See here," he said at length, as though utterance were difficult, "there's something I've been wanting to say to you; I'd ought to have said it before. I want you to marry me."

The girl still stared at him without moving. "I want you to marry me," he repeated, clearing his throat. "The minister'll be up here next Sunday and we can fix it up then. Or I'll drive you down to Hepburn to the Justice, and get it done there. I'll do whatever you say." His eyes fell under the merciless stare she continued to fix on him, and he shifted his weight uneasily from one foot to the other. As he stood there before her, unwieldy, shabby, disordered, the purple veins distorting the hands he pressed against the desk, and his long orator's jaw trembling with the effort of his avowal, he seemed like a hideous parody of the fatherly old man she had always known.

"Marry you? Me?" she burst out with a scornful laugh. "Was

that what you came to ask me the other night? What's come over you, I wonder? How long is it since you've looked at yourself in the glass?" She straightened herself, insolently conscious of her youth and strength. "I suppose you think it would be cheaper to marry me than to keep a hired girl. Everybody knows you're the closest man in Eagle County; but I guess you're not going to get your mending done for you that way twice."

Mr. Royall did not move while she spoke. His face was ash-coloured and his black eyebrows quivered as though the blaze of her scorn had blinded him. When she ceased he held up his hand.

"That'll do—that'll about do," he said. He turned to the door and took his hat from the hat-peg. On the threshold he paused. "People ain't been fair to me—from the first they ain't been fair to me," he said. Then he went out.

A few days later North Dormer learned with surprise that Charity had been appointed librarian of the Hatchard Memorial at a salary of eight dollars a month, and that old Verena Marsh, from the Creston Almshouse,[11] was coming to live at lawyer Royall's and do the cooking.

III

It was not in the room known at the red house as Mr. Royall's "office" that he received his infrequent clients. Professional dignity and masculine independence made it necessary that he should have a real office, under a different roof; and his standing as the only lawyer of North Dormer required that the roof should be the same as that which sheltered the Town Hall and the post-office.

It was his habit to walk to this office twice a day, morning and afternoon. It was on the ground floor of the building, with a separate entrance, and a weathered name-plate on the door. Before going in he stepped in to the post-office for his mail—usually an empty ceremony—said a word or two to the town-clerk, who sat across the passage in idle state, and then went over to the store on the opposite corner, where Carrick Fry, the storekeeper, always kept a chair for him, and where he was sure to find one or two selectmen leaning on the long counter, in an atmosphere of rope, leather, tar and coffee-beans. Mr. Royall, though monosyllabic at home, was not averse, in certain moods, to imparting his views to his fellow-townsmen; perhaps, also, he was unwilling that his rare clients should surprise him sitting, clerkless and unoccupied, in his dusty office. At any rate, his hours there were not much longer or more regular than Charity's at the library; the rest of the time he spent either at the store or in driving about the country on business connected with the insurance companies that he represented, or in sitting at home reading Bancroft's History of the United States[12] and the speeches of Daniel Webster.

Since the day when Charity had told him that she wished to succeed to Eudora Skeff's post their relations had undefinably but definitely changed. Lawyer Royall had kept his word. He had obtained the place for her at the cost of considerable manœuvering, as she guessed from the number of rival candidates, and from the acerbity with which two of them, Orma Fry and the eldest Targatt girl, treated her for nearly a year afterward. And he had engaged Verena Marsh to come up from Creston and do the cooking. Verena was a poor old widow, doddering and shiftless: Charity suspected that she came for her keep. Mr. Royall was too close a man to give a dollar a day to a smart girl when he could get a deaf pauper for nothing. But at any rate, Verena was there, in the attic just over Charity, and the fact that she was deaf did not greatly trouble the young girl.

Charity knew that what had happened on that hateful night would not happen again. She understood that, profoundly as she had despised Mr. Royall ever since, he despised himself still more profoundly. If she had asked for a woman in the house it was far less for her own defense than for his humiliation. She needed no one to defend her: his humbled pride was her surest protection. He had never spoken a word of excuse or extenuation; the incident was as if it had never been. Yet its consequences were latent in every word that he and she exchanged, in every glance they instinctively turned from each other. Nothing now would ever shake her rule in the red house.

On the night of her meeting with Miss Hatchard's cousin Charity lay in bed, her bare arms clasped under her rough head, and continued to think of him. She supposed that he meant to spend some time in North Dormer. He had said he was looking up the old houses in the neighbourhood; and though she was not very clear as to his purpose, or as to why anyone should look for old houses, when they lay in wait for one on every roadside, she understood that he needed the help of books, and resolved to hunt up the next day the volume she had failed to find, and any others that seemed related to the subject.

Never had her ignorance of life and literature so weighed on her as in reliving the short scene of her discomfiture. "It's no use trying to be anything in this place," she muttered to her pillow; and she shrivelled at the vision of vague metropolises, shining super-Nettletons, where girls in better clothes than Belle Balch's talked fluently of architecture to young men with hands like Lucius Harney's. Then she remembered his sudden pause when he had come close to the desk and had his first look at her. The sight had made him forget what he was going to say; she recalled the change in his face, and jumping up she ran over the bare boards to her wash-stand, found the matches, lit a candle, and lifted it to the square of looking-glass on the white-washed wall. Her small face, usually so darkly pale, glowed like a rose in the faint orb of light, and under her rumpled hair her eyes seemed deeper and larger than by day. Perhaps after all it was a mistake to wish they were blue. A clumsy band and button fastened her unbleached night-gown about the throat. She undid it, freed her thin shoulders, and saw herself a bride in low-necked satin, walking down an aisle with Lucius Harney. He would kiss her as they left the church. . . . She put down the candle and covered her face with her hands as if to imprison the kiss. At that moment she heard Mr. Royall's step as he came up the stairs to bed, and a fierce revulsion of feeling swept over her. Until then she had merely despised him; now deep hatred of him filled her heart. He became to her a horrible old man. . . .

The next day, when Mr. Royall came back to dinner, they faced each other in silence as usual. Verena's presence at the table was an excuse for their not talking, though her deafness would have permitted the freest interchange of confidences. But when the meal was over, and Mr. Royall rose from the table, he looked back at Charity, who had stayed to help the old woman clear away the dishes.

"I want to speak to you a minute," he said; and she followed him across the passage, wondering.

He seated himself in his black horse-hair armchair, and she leaned against the window, indifferently. She was impatient to be gone to the library, to hunt for the book on North Dormer.

"See here," he said, "why ain't you at the library the days you're supposed to be there?"

The question, breaking in on her mood of blissful abstraction, deprived her of speech, and she stared at him for a moment without answering.

"Who says I ain't?"

"There's been some complaints made, it appears. Miss Hatchard sent for me this morning——"

Charity's smouldering resentment broke into a blaze. "I know! Orma Fry, and that toad of a Targatt girl—and Ben Fry, like as not. He's going round with her. The low-down sneaks—I always knew they'd try to have me out! As if anybody ever came to the library, anyhow!"

"Somebody did yesterday, and you weren't there."

"Yesterday?" she laughed at her happy recollection. "At what time wasn't I there yesterday, I'd like to know?"

"Round about four o'clock."

Charity was silent. She had been so steeped in the dreamy remembrance of young Harney's visit that she had forgotten having deserted her post as soon as he had left the library.

"Who came at four o'clock?"

"Miss Hatchard did."

"Miss Hatchard? Why, she ain't ever been near the place since she's been lame. She couldn't get up the steps if she tried."

"She can be helped up, I guess. She was yesterday, anyhow, by the young fellow that's staying with her. He found you there, I understand, earlier in the afternoon; and he went back and told Miss Hatchard the books were in bad shape and needed attending to. She got excited, and had herself wheeled straight round; and when she got there the place was locked. So she sent for me, and told me about that, and about the other complaints. She claims you've neglected things, and that she's going to get a trained librarian."

Charity had not moved while he spoke. She stood with her head thrown back against the window-frame, her arms hanging against her sides, and her hands so tightly clenched that she felt, without knowing what hurt her, the sharp edge of her nails against her palms.

Of all Mr. Royall had said she had retained only the phrase: "He told Miss Hatchard the books were in bad shape." What did she care for the other charges against her? Malice or truth, she despised them as she despised her detractors. But that the stranger to whom she had felt herself so mysteriously drawn should have betrayed her! That at the very moment when she had fled up the hillside to think of him more deliciously he should have been hastening home to denounce her shortcomings! She remembered how, in the darkness of her room, she had covered her face to press his imagined kiss closer; and her heart raged against him for the liberty he had not taken.

"Well, I'll go," she said suddenly. "I'll go right off."

"Go where?" She heard the startled note in Mr. Royall's voice.

"Why, out of their old library: straight out, and never set foot in it again. They needn't think I'm going to wait round and let them say they've discharged me!"

"Charity—Charity Royall, you listen——" he began, getting heavily out of his chair; but she waved him aside, and walked out of the room.

Upstairs she took the library key from the place where she always hid it under her pincushion—who said she wasn't careful?—put on her hat, and swept down again and out into the street. If Mr. Royall heard her go he made no motion to detain her: his sudden rages probably made him understand the uselessness of reasoning with hers.

She reached the brick temple, unlocked the door and entered into the glacial twilight. "I'm glad I'll never have to sit in this old vault again when other folks are out in the sun!" she said aloud as the familiar chill took her. She looked with abhorrence at the long dingy rows of books, the sheep-nosed Minerva on her black pedestal, and the mild-faced young man in a high stock[13] whose effigy pined above her desk. She meant to take out of the drawer her roll of lace and the library register, and go straight to Miss Hatchard to announce her resignation. But suddenly a great desolation overcame her, and she sat down and laid her face against the desk. Her heart was ravaged by life's cruellest discovery: the first creature who had come toward her out of the wilderness had brought her anguish instead of joy. She did not cry; tears came hard to her, and the storms of her heart spent themselves inwardly. But as she sat there in her dumb woe she felt her life to be too desolate, too ugly and intolerable.

"What have I ever done to it, that it should hurt me so?" she groaned, and pressed her fists against her lids, which were beginning to swell with weeping.

"I won't—I won't go there looking like a horror!" she muttered, springing up and pushing back her hair as if it stifled her. She opened the drawer, dragged out the register, and turned toward the door. As she did so it opened, and the young man from Miss Hatchard's came in whistling.

IV

He stopped and lifted his hat with a shy smile. "I beg your pardon," he said. "I thought there was no one here."

Charity stood before him, barring his way. "You can't come in. The library ain't open to the public Wednesdays."

"I know it's not; but my cousin gave me her key."

"Miss Hatchard's got no right to give her key to other folks, any more'n I have. I'm the librarian and I know the by-laws. This is my library."

The young man looked profoundly surprised.

"Why, I know it is; I'm so sorry if you mind my coming."

"I suppose you came to see what more you could say to set her against me? But you needn't trouble: it's my library today, but it won't be this time tomorrow. I'm on the way now to take her back the key and the register."

Young Harney's face grew grave, but without betraying the consciousness of guilt she had looked for.

"I don't understand," he said. "There must be some mistake. Why should I say things against you to Miss Hatchard—or to anyone?"

The apparent evasiveness of the reply caused Charity's indignation to overflow. "I don't know why you should. I could understand Orma Fry's doing it, because she's always wanted to get me out of here ever since the first day. I can't see why, when she's got her own home, and her father to work for her; nor Ida Targatt, neither, when she got a legacy from her step-brother on'y last year. But anyway we all live in the same place, and when it's a place like North Dormer it's enough to make people hate each other just to have to walk down the same street every day. But you don't live here, and you don't know anything about any of us, so what did you have to meddle for? Do you suppose the other girls'd have kept the books any better'n I did? Why, Orma Fry don't hardly know a book from a flat-iron! And what if I don't always sit round here doing nothing till it strikes five up at the church? Who cares if the library's open or shut? Do you suppose anybody ever comes here for books? What they'd like to come for is to meet the fellows they're going with—if I'd let 'em. But I wouldn't let Bill Sollas from over the hill hang round here waiting for the youngest Targatt girl, because I know him . . . that's all . . . even if I don't know about books all I ought to. . . ."

She stopped with a choking in her throat. Tremors of rage were running through her, and she steadied herself against the edge of the desk lest he should see her weakness.

What he saw seemed to affect him deeply, for he grew red under his sunburn, and stammered out: "But, Miss Royall, I assure you . . . I assure you . . ."

His distress inflamed her anger, and she regained her voice to fling back: "If I was you I'd have the nerve to stick to what I said!"

The taunt seemed to restore his presence of mind. "I hope I should if I knew; but I don't. Apparently something disagreeable has happened, for which you think I'm to blame. But I don't know what it is, because I've been up on Eagle Ridge ever since the early morning."

"I don't know where you've been this morning, but I know you were here in this library yesterday; and it was you that went home and told your cousin the books were in bad shape, and brought her round to see how I'd neglected them."

Young Harney looked sincerely concerned. "Was that what you were told? I don't wonder you're angry. The books *are* in bad shape, and as some are interesting it's a pity. I told Miss Hatchard they were suffering from dampness and lack of air; and I brought her here to show her how easily the place could be ventilated. I also told her you ought to have some one to help you do the dusting and airing. If you were given a wrong version of what I said I'm sorry; but I'm so fond of old books that I'd rather see them made into a bonfire than left to moulder away like these."

Charity felt her sobs rising and tried to stifle them in words. "I don't care what you say you told her. All I know is she thinks it's all my fault, and I'm going to lose my job, and I wanted it more'n anyone in the village, because I haven't got anybody belonging to me, the way other folks have. All I wanted was to put aside money enough to get away from here sometime. D'you suppose if it hadn't been for that I'd have kept on sitting day after day in this old vault?"

Of this appeal her hearer took up only the last question. "It *is* an old vault; but need it be? That's the point. And it's my putting the question to my cousin that seems to have been the cause of the trouble." His glance explored the melancholy penumbra of the long narrow room, resting on the blotched walls, the discoloured rows of books, and the stern rosewood desk surmounted by the portrait of the young Honorius. "Of course it's a bad job to do anything with a building jammed against a hill like this ridiculous mausoleum: you couldn't get a good draught through it without blowing a hole in the mountain. But it can be ventilated after a fashion, and the sun can be let in: I'll show you how if you like. . . ." The architect's passion for improvement had already made him lose sight of her grievance, and he lifted his stick instructively toward the cornice. But her silence seemed to tell him that she took no interest in the ventilation of the library, and turning back to her abruptly he held out both hands. "Look here—you don't mean what you said? You don't really think I'd do anything to hurt you?"

A new note in his voice disarmed her: no one had ever spoken to her in that tone.

"Oh, what *did* you do it for then?" she wailed. He had her hands in his, and she was feeling the smooth touch that she had imagined the day before on the hillside.

He pressed her hands lightly and let them go. "Why, to make things pleasanter for you here; and better for the books. I'm sorry if my cousin twisted around what I said. She's excitable, and she lives on trifles: I ought to have remembered that. Don't punish me by letting her think you take her seriously."

It was wonderful to hear him speak of Miss Hatchard as if she were a querulous baby: in spite of his shyness he had the air of power that the experience of cities probably gave. It was the fact of having lived in Nettleton that made lawyer Royall, in spite of his infirmities, the strongest man in North Dormer; and Charity was sure that this young man had lived in bigger places than Nettleton.

She felt that if she kept up her denunciatory tone he would secretly class her with Miss Hatchard; and the thought made her suddenly simple.

"It don't matter to Miss Hatchard how I take her. Mr. Royall says she's going to get a trained librarian; and I'd sooner resign than have the village say she sent me away."

"Naturally you would. But I'm sure she doesn't mean to send you away. At any rate, won't you give me the chance to find out first and let you know? It will be time enough to resign if I'm mistaken."

Her pride flamed into her cheeks at the suggestion of his intervening. "I don't want anybody should coax her to keep me if I don't suit."

He coloured too. "I give you my word I won't do that. Only wait till tomorrow, will you?" He looked straight into her eyes with his shy grey glance. "You can trust me, you know—you really can."

All the old frozen woes seemed to melt in her, and she murmured awkwardly, looking away from him: "Oh, I'll wait."

V

There had never been such a June in Eagle County. Usually it was a month of moods, with abrupt alternations of belated frost and midsummer heat; this year, day followed day in a sequence of temperate beauty. Every morning a breeze blew steadily from the hills. Toward noon it built up great canopies of white cloud that threw a cool shadow over fields and woods; then before sunset the clouds dissolved again, and the western light rained its unobstructed brightness on the valley.

On such an afternoon Charity Royall lay on a ridge above a sunlit hollow, her face pressed to the earth and the warm currents of the grass running through her. Directly in her line of vision a blackberry branch laid its frail white flowers and blue-green leaves against the sky. Just beyond, a tuft of sweet-fern uncurled between the beaded shoots of the grass, and a small yellow butterfly vibrated over them like a fleck of sunshine. This was all she saw; but she felt, above her and about her, the strong growth of the beeches clothing the ridge, the rounding of pale green cones on countless spruce-branches, the push of myriads of sweet-fern fronds in the cracks of the stony slope below the wood, and the crowding shoots of meadowsweet and yellow flags in the pasture beyond. All this bubbling of sap and slipping of sheaths and bursting of calyxes was carried to her on mingled currents of fragrance. Every leaf and bud and blade seemed to contribute its exhalation to the pervading sweetness in which the pungency of pine-sap prevailed over the spice of thyme and the subtle perfume of fern, and all were merged in a moist earth-smell that was like the breath of some huge sun-warmed animal.

Charity had lain there a long time, passive and sun-warmed as the slope on which she lay, when there came between her eyes and the dancing butterfly the sight of a man's foot in a large worn boot covered with red mud.

"Oh, don't!" she exclaimed, raising herself on her elbow and stretching out a warning hand.

"Don't what?" a hoarse voice asked above her head.

"Don't stamp on those bramble flowers, you dolt!" she retorted, springing to her knees. The foot paused and then descended clumsily on the frail branch, and raising her eyes she saw above her the bewildered face of a slouching man with a thin sunburnt beard, and white arms showing through his ragged shirt.

"Don't you ever *see* anything, Liff Hyatt?" she assailed him, as he stood before her with the look of a man who has stirred up a wasp's nest.

He grinned. "I seen you! That's what I come down for."

"Down from where?" she questioned, stooping to gather up the petals his foot had scattered.

He jerked his thumb toward the heights. "Been cutting down trees for Dan Targatt."

Charity sank back on her heels and looked at him musingly. She was not in the least afraid of poor Liff Hyatt, though he "came from the Mountain," and some of the girls ran when they saw him. Among the more reasonable he passed for a harmless creature, a sort of link between the mountain and civilized folk, who occasionally came down and did a little wood-cutting for a farmer when hands were short. Besides, she knew the Mountain people would never hurt her: Liff himself had told her so once when she was a little girl, and had met him one day at the edge of lawyer Royall's pasture. "They won't any of 'em touch you up there, f'ever you was to come up. . . . But I don't s'pose you will," he had added philosophically, looking at her new shoes, and at the red ribbon that Mrs. Royall had tied in her hair.

Charity had, in truth, never felt any desire to visit her birthplace. She did not care to have it known that she was of the Mountain, and was shy of being seen in talk with Liff Hyatt. But today she was not sorry to have him appear. A great many things had happened to her since the day when young Lucius Harney had entered the doors of the Hatchard Memorial, but none, perhaps, so unforeseen as the fact of her suddenly finding it a convenience to be on good terms with Liff Hyatt. She continued to look up curiously at his freckled weather-beaten face, with feverish hollows below the cheekbones and the pale yellow eyes of a harmless animal. "I wonder if he's related to me?" she thought, with a shiver of disdain.

"Is there any folks living in the brown house by the swamp, up under Porcupine?" she presently asked in an indifferent tone.

Liff Hyatt, for a while, considered her with surprise; then he scratched his head and shifted his weight from one tattered sole to the other.

"There's always the same folks in the brown house," he said with his vague grin.

"They're from up your way, ain't they?"

"Their name's the same as mine," he rejoined uncertainly.

Charity still held him with resolute eyes. "See here, I want to go there some day and take a gentleman with me that's boarding with us. He's up in these parts drawing pictures."

She did not offer to explain this statement. It was too far beyond Liff Hyatt's limitations for the attempt to be worth making.

"He wants to see the brown house, and go all over it," she pursued.

Liff was still running his fingers perplexedly through his shock of straw-colored hair. "Is it a fellow from the city?" he asked.

"Yes. He draws pictures of things. He's down there now drawing the Bonner house." She pointed to a chimney just visible over the dip of the pasture below the wood.

"The Bonner house?" Liff echoed incredulously.

"Yes. You won't understand—and it don't matter. All I say is: he's going to the Hyatts' in a day or two."

Liff looked more and more perplexed. "Bash is ugly sometimes in the afternoons."

"I know. But I guess he won't trouble me." She threw her head back, her eyes full on Hyatt's. "I'm coming too: you tell him."

"They won't none of them trouble you, the Hyatts won't. What d'you want a take a stranger with you, though?"

"I've told you, haven't I? You've got to tell Bash Hyatt."

He looked away at the blue mountains on the horizon; then his gaze dropped to the chimney-top below the pasture.

"He's down there now?"

"Yes."

He shifted his weight again, crossed his arms, and continued to survey the distant landscape. "Well, so long," he said at last, inconclusively; and turning away he shambled up the hillside. From the ledge above her, he paused to call down: "I wouldn't go there a Sunday"; then he clambered on till the trees closed in on him. Presently, from high overhead, Charity heard the ring of his axe.

She lay on the warm ridge, thinking of many things that the woodsman's appearance had stirred up in her. She knew nothing of her early life, and had never felt any curiosity about it: only a sullen reluctance to explore the corner of her memory where certain blurred images lingered. But all that had happened to her within the last few weeks had stirred her to the sleeping depths. She had become absorbingly interesting to herself, and everything that had to do with her past was illuminated by this sudden curiosity.

She hated more than ever the fact of coming from the Mountain; but it was no longer indifferent to her. Everything that in any way affected her was alive and vivid: even the hateful things had grown interesting because they were a part of herself.

"I wonder if Liff Hyatt knows who my mother was?" she mused; and it filled her with a tremor of surprise to think that some woman who was once young and slight, with quick motions of the blood like hers, had carried her in her breast, and watched her sleeping. She had always thought of her mother as so long dead as to be no more than a nameless pinch of earth; but now it occurred to her that the once-young woman might be alive, and wrinkled and elf-locked like the woman she had sometimes seen in the door of the brown house that Lucius Harney wanted to draw.

The thought brought her back to the central point in her mind, and she strayed away from the conjectures roused by Liff Hyatt's presence. Speculations concerning the past could not hold her long when the present was so rich, the future so rosy, and when Lucius Harney, a stone's throw away, was bending over his sketch-book, frowning, calculating, measuring, and then throwing his head back with the sudden smile that had shed its brightness over everything.

She scrambled to her feet, but as she did so she saw him coming up the pasture and dropped down on the grass to wait. When he was drawing and measuring one of "his houses," as she called them, she often strayed away by herself into the woods or up the hillside. It was partly from shyness that she did so: from a sense of inadequacy that came to her most painfully when her companion, absorbed in his job, forgot her ignorance and her inability to follow his least allusion, and plunged into a monologue on art and life. To avoid the awkwardness of listening with a blank face, and also to escape the surprised stare of the inhabitants of the houses before which he would abruptly pull up their horse and open his sketch-book, she slipped away to some spot from which, without being seen, she could watch him at work, or at least look down on the house he was drawing. She had not been displeased, at first, to have it known to North Dormer and the neighborhood that she was driving Miss Hatchard's cousin about the country in the buggy he had hired of lawyer Royall. She had always kept to herself, contemptuously aloof from village love-making, without exactly knowing whether her fierce pride was due to the sense of her tainted origin, or whether she was reserving herself for a more brilliant fate. Sometimes she envied the other girls their sentimental preoccupations, their long hours of inarticulate philandering with one of the few youths who still lingered in the village; but when she pictured herself curling her hair or putting a new ribbon on her hat for Ben Fry or one of the Sollas boys the fever dropped and she relapsed into indifference.

Now she knew the meaning of her disdains and reluctances. She had learned what she was worth when Lucius Harney, looking at her for the first time, had lost the thread of his speech, and leaned reddening on the edge of her desk. But another kind of shyness had been born in her: a terror of exposing to vulgar perils the sacred treasure of her happiness. She was not sorry to have the neighbors suspect her of "going with" a young man from the city; but she did not want it known to all the countryside how many hours of the long June days she spent with him. What she most feared was that the inevitable comments should reach Mr. Royall. Charity was instinctively aware that few things concerning her escaped the eyes of the silent man under whose roof she lived; and in spite of the latitude which North Dormer accorded to courting couples she had always felt that, on the day when she showed too open a preference, Mr. Royall might, as she phrased it, make her "pay for it." How, she did not know; and her fear was the greater because it was undefinable. If she had been accepting the attentions of one of the village youths she would have been less apprehensive: Mr. Royall could not prevent her marrying when she chose to. But everybody knew that "going with a city fellow" was a different and less straightforward affair: almost every village could show a victim of the perilous venture. And her dread of Mr. Royall's intervention gave a sharpened joy to the hours she spent with young Harney, and made her, at the same time, shy of being too generally seen with him.

As he approached she rose to her knees, stretching her arms above her head with the indolent gesture that was her way of expressing a profound well-being.

"I'm going to take you to that house up under Porcupine," she announced.

"What house? Oh, yes; that ramshackle place near the swamp, with the gipsy-looking people hanging about. It's curious that a house with traces of real architecture should have been built in such a place. But the people were a sulky-looking lot—do you suppose they'll let us in?"

"They'll do whatever I tell them," she said with assurance.

He threw himself down beside her. "Will they?" he rejoined with a smile. "Well, I should like to see what's left inside the house. And I should like to have a talk with the people. Who was it who was telling me the other day that they had come down from the Mountain?"

Charity shot a sideward look at him. It was the first time he had spoken of the Mountain except as a feature of the landscape. What else did he know about it, and about her relation to it? Her heart began to beat with the fierce impulse of resistance which she instinctively opposed to every imagined slight.

"The Mountain? I ain't afraid of the Mountain!"

Her tone of defiance seemed to escape him. He lay breast-down on the grass, breaking off sprigs of thyme and pressing them against his lips. Far off, above the folds of the nearer hills, the Mountain thrust itself up menacingly against a yellow sunset.

"I must go up there some day: I want to see it," he continued.

Her heart-beats slackened and she turned again to examine his profile. It was innocent of all unfriendly intention.

"What'd you want to go up the Mountain for?"

"Why, it must be rather a curious place. There's a queer colony up there, you know: sort of outlaws, a little independent kingdom. Of course you've heard them spoken of; but I'm told they have nothing to do with the people in the valleys—rather look down on them, in fact. I suppose they're rough customers; but they must have a good deal of character."

She did not quite know what he meant by having a good deal of character; but his tone was expressive of admiration, and deepened her dawning curiosity. It struck her now as strange that she knew so little about the Mountain. She had never asked, and no one had ever offered to enlighten her. North Dormer took the Mountain for granted, and implied its disparagement by an intonation rather than by explicit criticism.

"It's queer, you know," he continued, "that, just over there, on top of that hill, there should be a handful of people who don't give a damn for anybody."

The words thrilled her. They seemed the clue to her own revolts and defiances, and she longed to have him tell her more.

"I don't know much about them. Have they always been there?"

"Nobody seems to know exactly how long. Down at Creston they told me that the first colonists are supposed to have been men who worked on the railway that was built forty or fifty years ago between Springfield and Nettleton. Some of them took to drink, or got into trouble with the police, and went off—disappeared into the woods. A year or two later there was a report that they were living up on the Mountain. Then I suppose others joined them—and children were born. Now they say there are over a hundred people up there. They seem to be quite outside the jurisdiction of the valleys. No school, no church—and no sheriff ever goes up to see what they're about. But don't people ever talk of them at North Dormer?"

"I don't know. They say they're bad."

He laughed. "Do they? We'll go and see, shall we?"

She flushed at the suggestion, and turned her face to his. "You never heard, I suppose—I come from there. They brought me down when I was little."

"You?" He raised himself on his elbow, looking at her with sudden interest. "You're from the Mountain? How curious! I suppose that's why you're so different. . . ."

Her happy blood bathed her to the forehead. He was praising her—and praising her because she came from the Mountain!

"Am I . . . different?" she triumphed, with affected wonder.

"Oh, awfully!" He picked up her hand and laid a kiss on the sunburnt knuckles.

"Come," he said, "let's be off." He stood up and shook the grass from his loose grey clothes. "What a good day! Where are you going to take me tomorrow?"

VI

That evening after supper Charity sat alone in the kitchen and listened to Mr. Royall and young Harney talking in the porch.

She had remained indoors after the table had been cleared and old Verena had hobbled up to bed. The kitchen window was open, and Charity seated herself near it, her idle hands on her knee. The evening was cool and still. Beyond the black hills an amber west passed into pale green, and then to a deep blue in which a great star hung. The soft hoot of a little owl came through the dusk, and between its calls the men's voices rose and fell.

Mr. Royall's was full of a sonorous satisfaction. It was a long time since he had had anyone of Lucius Harney's quality to talk to: Charity divined that the young man symbolized all his ruined and unforgotten past. When Miss Hatchard had been called to Springfield by the illness of a widowed sister, and young Harney, by that time seriously embarked on his task of drawing and measuring all the old houses between Nettleton and the New Hampshire border, had suggested the possibility of boarding at the red house in his cousin's absence, Charity had trembled lest Mr. Royall should refuse. There had been no question of lodging the young man: there was no room for him. But it appeared that he could still live at Miss Hatchard's if Mr. Royall would let him take his meals at the red house; and after a day's deliberation Mr. Royall consented.

Charity suspected him of being glad of the chance to make a little money. He had the reputation of being an avaricious man; but she was beginning to think he was probably poorer than people knew. His practice had become little more than a vague legend, revived only at lengthening intervals by a summons to Hepburn or Nettleton; and he appeared to depend for his living mainly on the scant produce of his farm, and on the commissions received from the few insurance agencies that he represented in the neighbourhood. At any rate, he had been prompt in accepting Harney's offer to hire the buggy at a dollar and a half a day; and his satisfaction with the bargain had manifested itself, unexpectedly enough, at the end of the first week, by his tossing a ten-dollar bill into Charity's lap as she sat one day retrimming her old hat.

"Here—go get yourself a Sunday bonnet that'll make all the other girls mad," he said, looking at her with a sheepish twinkle in his deep-set eyes; and she immediately guessed that the unwonted present—the only gift of money she had ever received from him—represented Harney's first payment.

But the young man's coming had brought Mr. Royall other than pecuniary benefit. It gave him, for the first time in years, a man's companionship. Charity had only a dim understanding of her guardian's needs; but she knew he felt himself above the people among whom he lived, and she saw that Lucius Harney thought him so. She was surprised to find how well he seemed to talk now that he had a listener who understood him; and she was equally struck by young Harney's friendly deference.

Their conversation was mostly about politics, and beyond her range; but tonight it had a peculiar interest for her, for they had begun to speak of the Mountain. She drew back a little, lest they should see she was in hearing.

"The Mountain? The Mountain?" she heard Mr. Royall say. "Why, the Mountain's a blot—that's what it is, sir, a blot. That scum up there ought to have been run in long ago—and would have, if the people down here hadn't been clean scared of them. The Mountain belongs to this township, and it's North Dormer's fault if there's a gang of thieves and outlaws living over there, in sight of us, defying the laws of their country. Why, there ain't a sheriff or a tax-collector or a coroner'd durst go up there. When they hear of trouble on the Mountain the selectmen look the other way, and pass an appropriation to beautify the town pump. The only man that ever goes up is the minister, and he goes because they send down and get him whenever there's any of them dies. They think a lot of Christian burial on the Mountain—but I never heard of their having the minister up to marry them. And they never trouble the Justice of the Peace either. They just herd together like the heathen."

He went on, explaining in somewhat technical language how the little colony of squatters had contrived to keep the law at bay, and Charity, with burning eagerness, awaited young Harney's comment; but the young man seemed more concerned to hear Mr. Royall's views than to express his own.

"I suppose you've never been up there yourself?" he presently asked.

"Yes, I have," said Mr. Royall with a contemptuous laugh. "The wiseacres down here told me I'd be done for before I got back; but nobody lifted a finger to hurt me. And I'd just had one of their gang sent up for seven years too."

"You went up after that?"

"Yes, sir: right after it. The fellow came down to Nettleton and ran amuck, the way they sometimes do. After they've done a wood-cutting job they come down and blow the money in; and this man ended up with manslaughter. I got him convicted, though they were scared of the Mountain even at Nettleton; and then a queer thing happened. The fellow sent for me to go and see him in gaol. I went, and this is what he says: 'The fool that defended me is a chicken-livered son of a——and all the rest of it,' he says. 'I've got a job to be done for me up on the Mountain, and you're the only man I seen in court that looks as if he'd do it.' He told me he had a child up there—or thought he had—a little girl; and he wanted her brought down and reared like a Christian. I was sorry for the fellow, so I went up and got the child." He paused, and Charity listened with a throbbing heart. "That's the only time I ever went up the Mountain," he concluded.

There was a moment's silence; then Harney spoke. "And the child—had she no mother?"

"Oh, yes: there was a mother. But she was glad enough to have her go. She'd have given her to anybody. They ain't half human up there. I guess the mother's dead by now, with the life she was leading. Anyhow, I've never heard of her from that day to this."

"My God, how ghastly," Harney murmured; and Charity, choking with humiliation, sprang to her feet and ran upstairs. She knew at last: knew that she was the child of a drunken convict and of a mother who wasn't "half human," and was glad to have her go; and she had heard this history of her origin related to the one being in whose eyes she longed to appear superior to the people about her! She had noticed that Mr. Royall had not named her, had even avoided any allusion that might identify her with the child he had brought down from the Mountain; and she knew it was out of regard for her that he had kept silent. But of what use was his discretion, since only that afternoon, misled by Harney's interest in the outlaw colony, she had boasted to him of coming from the Mountain? Now every word that had been spoken showed her how such an origin must widen the distance between them.

During his ten days' sojourn at North Dormer Lucius Harney had not spoken a word of love to her. He had intervened in her behalf with his cousin, and had convinced Miss Hatchard of her merits as a librarian; but that was a simple act of justice, since it

was by his own fault that those merits had been questioned. He
had asked her to drive him about the country when he hired
lawyer Royall's buggy to go on his sketching expeditions; but that
too was natural enough, since he was unfamiliar with the region.
Lastly, when his cousin was called to Springfield, he had begged
Mr. Royall to receive him as a boarder; but where else in North
Dormer could he have boarded? Not with Carrick Fry, whose
wife was paralysed, and whose large family crowded his table to
overflowing; not with the Targatts, who lived a mile up the road,
nor with poor old Mrs. Hawes, who, since her eldest daughter
had deserted her, barely had the strength to cook her own meals
while Ally picked up her living as a seamstress. Mr. Royall's was
the only house where the young man could have been offered a
decent hospitality. There had been nothing, therefore, in the outward course of events to raise in Charity's breast the hopes with
which it trembled. But beneath the visible incidents resulting from
Lucius Harney's arrival there ran an undercurrent as mysterious
and potent as the influence that makes the forest break into leaf
before the ice is off the pools.

The business on which Harney had come was authentic; Charity had seen the letter from a New York publisher commissioning
him to make a study of the eighteenth century houses in the less
familiar districts of New England. But incomprehensible as the
whole affair was to her, and hard as she found it to understand
why he paused enchanted before certain neglected and paintless
houses, while others, refurbished and "improved" by the local
builder, did not arrest a glance, she could not but suspect that Eagle County was less rich in architecture than he averred, and that
the duration of his stay (which he had fixed at a month) was not
unconnected with the look in his eyes when he had first paused
before her in the library. Everything that had followed seemed to
have grown out of that look: his way of speaking to her, his quick-
ness in catching her meaning, his evident eagerness to prolong
their excursions and to seize on every chance of being with her.

The signs of his liking were manifest enough; but it was hard to
guess how much they meant, because his manner was so different
from anything North Dormer had ever shown her. He was at once
simpler and more deferential than any one she had known; and
sometimes it was just when he was simplest that she most felt the

distance between them. Education and opportunity had divided them by a width that no effort of hers could bridge, and even when his youth and his admiration brought him nearest, some chance word, some unconscious allusion, seemed to thrust her back across the gulf.

Never had it yawned so wide as when she fled up to her room carrying with her the echo of Mr. Royall's tale. Her first confused thought was the prayer that she might never see young Harney again. It was too bitter to picture him as the detached impartial listener to such a story. "I wish he'd go away: I wish he'd go tomorrow, and never come back!" she moaned to her pillow; and far into the night she lay there, in the disordered dress she had forgotten to take off, her whole soul a tossing misery on which her hopes and dreams spun about like drowning straws.

Of all this tumult only a vague heart-soreness was left when she opened her eyes the next morning. Her first thought was of the weather, for Harney had asked her to take him to the brown house under Porcupine, and then around by Hamblin; and as the trip was a long one they were to start at nine. The sun rose without a cloud, and earlier than usual she was in the kitchen, making cheese sandwiches, decanting buttermilk into a bottle, wrapping up slices of apple pie, and accusing Verena of having given away a basket she needed, which had always hung on a hook in the passage. When she came out into the porch, in her pink calico, which had run a little in the washing, but was still bright enough to set off her dark tints, she had such a triumphant sense of being a part of the sunlight and the morning that the last trace of her misery vanished. What did it matter where she came from, or whose child she was, when love was dancing in her veins, and down the road she saw young Harney coming toward her?

Mr. Royall was in the porch too. He had said nothing at breakfast, but when she came out in her pink dress, the basket in her hand, he looked at her with surprise. "Where you going to?" he asked.

"Why—Mr. Harney's starting earlier than usual today," she answered.

"Mr. Harney, Mr. Harney? Ain't Mr. Harney learned how to drive a horse yet?"

She made no answer, and he sat tilted back in his chair, drumming on the rail of the porch. It was the first time he had ever spoken of the young man in that tone, and Charity felt a faint chill of apprehension. After a moment he stood up and walked away toward the bit of ground behind the house, where the hired man was hoeing.

The air was cool and clear, with the autumnal sparkle that a north wind brings to the hills in early summer, and the night had been so still that the dew hung on everything, not as a lingering moisture, but in separate beads that glittered like diamonds on the ferns and grasses. It was a long drive to the foot of Porcupine: first across the valley, with blue hills bounding the open slopes; then down into the beech-woods, following the course of the Creston, a brown brook leaping over velvet ledges; then out again onto the farm-lands about Creston Lake, and gradually up the ridges of the Eagle Range. At last they reached the yoke of the hills, and before them opened another valley, green and wild, and beyond it more blue heights eddying away to the sky like the waves of a receding tide.

Harney tied the horse to a tree-stump, and they unpacked their basket under an aged walnut with a riven trunk out of which bumblebees darted. The sun had grown hot, and behind them was the noonday murmur of the forest. Summer insects danced on the air, and a flock of white butterflies fanned the mobile tips of the crimson fireweed. In the valley below not a house was visible; it seemed as if Charity Royall and young Harney were the only living beings in the great hollow of earth and sky.

Charity's spirits flagged and disquieting thoughts stole back on her. Young Harney had grown silent, and as he lay beside her, his arms under his head, his eyes on the network of leaves above him, she wondered if he were musing on what Mr. Royall had told him, and if it had really debased her in his thoughts. She wished he had not asked her to take him that day to the brown house; she did not want him to see the people she came from while the story of her birth was fresh in his mind. More than once she had been on the point of suggesting that they should follow the ridge and drive straight to Hamblin, where there was a little deserted house he wanted to see; but shyness and pride held her back. "He'd better know what kind of folks I belong to," she said to herself, with a somewhat forced defiance; for in reality it was shame that kept her silent.

Suddenly she lifted her hand and pointed to the sky. "There's a storm coming up."

He followed her glance and smiled. "Is it that scrap of cloud among the pines that frightens you?"

"It's over the Mountain; and a cloud over the Mountain always means trouble."

"Oh, I don't believe half the bad things you all say of the Mountain! But anyhow, we'll get down to the brown house before the rain comes."

He was not far wrong, for only a few isolated drops had fallen when they turned into the road under the shaggy flank of Porcupine, and came upon the brown house. It stood alone beside a swamp bordered with alder thickets and tall bulrushes. Not another dwelling was in sight, and it was hard to guess what motive could have actuated the early settler who had made his home in so unfriendly a spot.

Charity had picked up enough of her companion's erudition to understand what had attracted him to the house. She noticed the fan-shaped tracery of the broken light above the door, the flutings of the paintless pilasters at the corners, and the round window set in the gable; and she knew that, for reasons that still escaped her, these were things to be admired and recorded. Still, they had seen other houses far more "typical" (the word was Harney's); and as he threw the reins on the horse's neck he said with a slight shiver of repugnance: "We won't stay long."

Against the restless alders turning their white lining to the storm the house looked singularly desolate. The paint was almost gone from the clapboards, the window-panes were broken and patched with rags, and the garden was a poisonous tangle of nettles, burdocks and tall swamp-weeds over which big blue-bottles hummed.

At the sound of wheels a child with a tow-head and pale eyes like Liff Hyatt's peered over the fence and then slipped away behind an out-house. Harney jumped down and helped Charity out; and as he did so the rain broke on them. It came slantwise, on a furious gale, laying shrubs and young trees flat, tearing off their leaves like an autumn storm, turning the road into a river, and making hissing pools of every hollow. Thunder rolled incessantly through the roar of the rain, and a strange glitter of light ran along the ground under the increasing blackness.

"Lucky we're here after all," Harney laughed. He fastened the horse under a half-roofless shed, and wrapping Charity in his coat ran with her to the house. The boy had not reappeared, and as there was no response to their knocks Harney turned the door-handle and they went in.

There were three people in the kitchen to which the door admitted them. An old woman with a handkerchief over her head was sitting by the window. She held a sickly-looking kitten on her knees, and whenever it jumped down and tried to limp away she stooped and lifted it back without any change of her aged, un-noticing face. Another woman, the unkempt creature that Charity had once noticed in driving by, stood leaning against the window-frame and stared at them; and near the stove an unshaved man in a tattered shirt sat on a barrel asleep.

The place was bare and miserable and the air heavy with the smell of dirt and stale tobacco. Charity's heart sank. Old derided tales of the Mountain people came back to her, and the woman's stare was so disconcerting, and the face of the sleeping man so sodden and bestial, that her disgust was tinged with a vague dread. She was not afraid for herself; she knew the Hyatts would not be likely to trouble her; but she was not sure how they would treat a "city fellow."

Lucius Harney would certainly have laughed at her fears. He glanced about the room, uttered a general "How are you?" to which no one responded, and then asked the younger woman if they might take shelter till the storm was over.

She turned her eyes away from him and looked at Charity.

"You're the girl from Royall's, ain't you?"

The colour rose in Charity's face. "I'm Charity Royall," she said, as if asserting her right to the name in the very place where it might have been most open to question.

The woman did not seem to notice. "You kin stay," she merely said; then she turned away and stooped over a dish in which she was stirring something.

Harney and Charity sat down on a bench made of a board resting on two starch boxes. They faced a door hanging on a broken hinge, and through the crack they saw the eyes of the tow-headed boy and of a pale little girl with a scar across her cheek. Charity smiled, and signed to the children to come in; but as soon as they saw they were discovered they slipped away on bare feet. It occurred to her that they were afraid of rousing the sleeping man; and probably the woman shared their fear, for she moved about as noiselessly and avoided going near the stove.

The rain continued to beat against the house, and in one or two places it sent a stream through the patched panes and ran into pools on the floor. Every now and then the kitten mewed and struggled down, and the old woman stooped and caught it, holding it tight in her bony hands; and once or twice the man on the barrel half woke, changed his position and dozed again, his head falling forward on his hairy breast. As the minutes passed, and the rain still streamed against the windows, a loathing of the place and the people came over Charity. The sight of the weak-minded old woman, of the cowed children, and the ragged man sleeping off his liquor, made the setting of her own life seem a vision of peace and plenty. She thought of the kitchen at Mr. Royall's, with its scrubbed floor and dresser full of china, and the peculiar smell of yeast and coffee and soft-soap that she had always hated, but that now seemed the very symbol of household order. She saw Mr. Royall's room, with the high-backed horsehair chair, the faded rag carpet, the row of books on a shelf, the engraving of "The Surrender of Burgoyne"[14] over the stove, and the mat with a brown and white spaniel in a moss-green border. And then her mind travelled to Miss Hatchard's house, where all was freshness, purity and fragrance, and compared to which the red house had always seemed so poor and plain.

"This is where I belong—this is where I belong," she kept repeating to herself; but the words had no meaning for her. Every instinct and habit made her a stranger among these poor swamp-people living like vermin in their lair. With all her soul she wished she had not yielded to Harney's curiosity, and brought him there.

The rain had drenched her, and she began to shiver under the thin folds of her dress. The younger woman must have noticed it, for she went out of the room and came back with a broken teacup which she offered to Charity. It was half full of whiskey, and Charity shook her head; but Harney took the cup and put his lips to it. When he had set it down Charity saw him feel in his pocket and draw out a dollar; he hesitated a moment, and then put it back, and she guessed that he did not wish her to see him offering money to people she had spoken of as being her kin.

The sleeping man stirred, lifted his head and opened his eyes. They rested vacantly for a moment on Charity and Harney, and then closed again, and his head drooped; but a look of anxiety came into the woman's face. She glanced out of the window and then came up to Harney. "I guess you better go along now," she said. The young man understood and got to his feet. "Thank you," he said, holding out his hand. She seemed not to notice the gesture, and turned away as they opened the door.

The rain was still coming down, but they hardly noticed it: the pure air was like balm in their faces. The clouds were rising and breaking, and between their edges the light streamed down from remote blue hollows. Harney untied the horse, and they drove off through the diminishing rain, which was already beaded with sunlight.

For a while Charity was silent, and her companion did not speak. She looked timidly at his profile: it was graver than usual, as though he too were oppressed by what they had seen. Then she broke out abruptly: "Those people back there are the kind of folks I come from. They may be my relations, for all I know." She did not want him to think that she regretted having told him her story.

"Poor creatures," he rejoined. "I wonder why they came down to that fever-hole."

She laughed ironically. "To better themselves! It's worse up on the Mountain. Bash Hyatt married the daughter of the farmer that used to own the brown house. That was him by the stove, I suppose."

Harney seemed to find nothing to say and she went on: "I saw you take out a dollar to give to that poor woman. Why did you put it back?"

He reddened, and leaned forward to flick a swamp-fly from the horse's neck. "I wasn't sure——"

"Was it because you knew they were my folks, and thought I'd be ashamed to see you give them money?"

He turned to her with eyes full of reproach. "Oh, Charity——"

It was the first time he had ever called her by her name. Her misery welled over.

"I ain't—I ain't ashamed. They're my people, and I ain't ashamed of them," she sobbed.

"My dear . . ." he murmured, putting his arm about her; and she leaned against him and wept out her pain.

It was too late to go around to Hamblin, and all the stars were out in a clear sky when they reached the North Dormer valley and drove up to the red house.

VII

Since her reinstatement in Miss Hatchard's favour Charity had not dared to curtail by a moment her hours of attendance at the library. She even made a point of arriving before the time, and showed a laudable indignation when the youngest Targatt girl, who had been engaged to help in the cleaning and rearranging of the books, came trailing in late and neglected her task to peer through the window at the Sollas boy. Nevertheless, "library days" seemed more than ever irksome to Charity after her vivid hours of liberty; and she would have found it hard to set a good example to her subordinate if Lucius Harney had not been commissioned, before Miss Hatchard's departure, to examine with the local carpenter the best means of ventilating the "Memorial."

He was careful to prosecute this inquiry on the days when the library was open to the public; and Charity was therefore sure of spending part of the afternoon in his company. The Targatt girl's presence, and the risk of being interrupted by some passer-by suddenly smitten with a thirst for letters, restricted their intercourse to the exchange of commonplaces; but there was a fascination to Charity in the contrast between these public civilities and their secret intimacy.

The day after their drive to the brown house was "library day," and she sat at her desk working at the revised catalogue, while the Targatt girl, one eye on the window, chanted out the titles of a pile of books. Charity's thoughts were far away, in the dismal house by the swamp, and under the twilight sky during the long drive home, when Lucius Harney had consoled her with endearing

words. That day, for the first time since he had been boarding
with them, he had failed to appear as usual at the midday meal.
No message had come to explain his absence, and Mr. Royall,
who was more than usually taciturn, had betrayed no surprise,
and made no comment. In itself this indifference was not particularly significant, for Mr. Royall, in common with most of his
fellow-citizens, had a way of accepting events passively, as if he
had long since come to the conclusion that no one who lived in
North Dormer could hope to modify them. But to Charity, in the
reaction from her mood of passionate exaltation, there was something disquieting in his silence. It was almost as if Lucius Harney
had never had a part in their lives: Mr. Royall's imperturbable indifference seemed to relegate him to the domain of unreality.

As she sat at work, she tried to shake off her disappointment at
Harney's non-appearing. Some trifling incident had probably kept
him from joining them at midday; but she was sure he must be eager to see her again, and that he would not want to wait till they
met at supper, between Mr. Royall and Verena. She was wondering what his first words would be, and trying to devise a way of
getting rid of the Targatt girl before he came, when she heard
steps outside, and he walked up the path with Mr. Miles.

The clergyman from Hepburn seldom came to North Dormer
except when he drove over to officiate at the old white church
which, by an unusual chance, happened to belong to the Episcopal communion. He was a brisk affable man, eager to make the
most of the fact that a little nucleus of "church-people" had survived in the sectarian wilderness, and resolved to undermine the
influence of the ginger-bread-coloured Baptist chapel at the other
end of the village; but he was kept busy by parochial work at
Hepburn, where there were paper-mills and saloons, and it was
not often that he could spare time for North Dormer.

Charity, who went to the white church (like all the best people
in North Dormer), admired Mr. Miles, and had even, during the
memorable trip to Nettleton, imagined herself married to a man
who had such a straight nose and such a beautiful way of speaking, and who lived in a brown-stone rectory covered with Virginia
creeper. It had been a shock to discover that the privilege was already enjoyed by a lady with crimped hair and a large baby; but

the arrival of Lucius Harney had long since banished Mr. Miles
from Charity's dreams, and as he walked up the path at Harney's
side she saw him as he really was: a fat middle-aged man with a
baldness showing under his clerical hat, and spectacles on his Grecian nose. She wondered what had called him to North Dormer
on a weekday, and felt a little hurt that Harney should have
brought him to the library.

It presently appeared that his presence there was due to Miss
Hatchard. He had been spending a few days at Springfield, to fill a
friend's pulpit, and had been consulted by Miss Hatchard as to
young Harney's plan for ventilating the "Memorial." To lay hands
on the Hatchard ark was a grave matter, and Miss Hatchard, always
full of scruples, and of scruples about her scruples (it was Harney's
phrase), wished to have Mr. Miles's opinion before deciding.

"I couldn't," Mr. Miles explained, "quite make out from your
cousin what changes you wanted to make, and as the other
trustees did not understand either I thought I had better drive over
and take a look—though I'm sure," he added, turning his friendly
spectacles on the young man, "that no one could be more compe-
tent—but of course this spot has its peculiar sanctity!"

"I hope a little fresh air won't desecrate it," Harney laughingly
rejoined; and they walked to the other end of the library while he
set forth his idea to the Rector.

Mr. Miles had greeted the two girls with his usual friendliness,
but Charity saw that he was occupied with other things, and she
presently became aware, by the scraps of conversation drifting
over to her, that he was still under the charm of his visit to Springfield, which appeared to have been full of agreeable incidents.

"Ah, the Coopersons . . . yes, you know them, of course," she
heard. "That's a fine old house! And Ned Cooperson has collected
some really remarkable impressionist pictures. . . ." The names he
cited were unknown to Charity. "Yes; yes; the Schaefer quartette
played at Lyric Hall on Saturday evening; and on Monday I had
the privilege of hearing them again at the Towers. Beautifully
done . . . Bach and Beethoven . . . a lawn-party first . . . I saw
Miss Balch several times, by the way . . . looking extremely handsome. . . ."

Charity dropped her pencil and forgot to listen to the Targatt girl's sing-song. Why had Mr. Miles suddenly brought up Annabel Balch's name?

"Oh, really?" she heard Harney rejoin; and, raising his stick, he pursued: "You see, my plan is to move these shelves away, and open a round window in this wall, on the axis of the one under the pediment."

"I suppose she'll be coming up here later to stay with Miss Hatchard?" Mr. Miles went on, following on his train of thought; then, spinning about and tilting his head back: "Yes, yes, I see—I understand: that will give a draught without materially altering the look of things. I can see no objection."

The discussion went on for some minutes, and gradually the two men moved back toward the desk. Mr. Miles stopped again and looked thoughtfully at Charity. "Aren't you a little pale, my dear? Not overworking? Mr. Harney tells me you and Mamie are giving the library a thorough overhauling." He was always careful to remember his parishioners' Christian names, and at the right moment he bent his benignant spectacles on the Targatt girl.

Then he turned to Charity. "Don't take things hard, my dear; don't take things hard. Come down and see Mrs. Miles and me some day at Hepburn," he said, pressing her hand and waving a farewell to Mamie Targatt. He went out of the library, and Harney followed him.

Charity thought she detected a look of constraint in Harney's eyes. She fancied he did not want to be alone with her; and with a sudden pang she wondered if he repented the tender things he had said to her the night before. His words had been more fraternal than lover-like; but she had lost their exact sense in the caressing warmth of his voice. He had made her feel that the fact of her being a waif from the Mountain was only another reason for holding her close and soothing her with consolatory murmurs; and when the drive was over, and she got out of the buggy, tired, cold, and aching with emotion, she stepped as if the ground were a sunlit wave and she the spray on its crest.

Why, then, had his manner suddenly changed, and why did he leave the library with Mr. Miles? Her restless imagination fastened on the name of Annabel Balch: from the moment it had been mentioned she fancied that Harney's expression had altered. Annabel Balch at a garden-party at Springfield, looking "extremely handsome". . . perhaps Mr. Miles had seen her there at the very moment when Charity and Harney were sitting in the Hyatts' hovel, between a drunkard and a half-witted old woman! Charity did not know exactly what a garden-party was, but her glimpse of the flower-edged lawns of Nettleton helped her to visualize the scene, and envious recollections of the "old things" which Miss Balch avowedly "wore out" when she came to North Dormer made it only too easy to picture her in her splendour. Charity understood what associations the name must have called up, and felt the uselessness of struggling against the unseen influences in Harney's life.

When she came down from her room for supper he was not there; and while she waited in the porch she recalled the tone in which Mr. Royall had commented the day before on their early start. Mr. Royall sat at her side, his chair tilted back, his broad black boots with side-elastics resting against the lower bar of the railings. His rumpled grey hair stood up above his forehead like the crest of an angry bird, and the leather-brown of his veined cheeks was blotched with red. Charity knew that those red spots were the signs of a coming explosion.

Suddenly he said: "Where's supper? Has Verena Marsh slipped up again on her soda-biscuits?"

Charity threw a startled glance at him. "I presume she's waiting for Mr. Harney."

"Mr. Harney, is she? She'd better dish up, then. He ain't coming." He stood up, walked to the door, and called out, in the pitch necessary to penetrate the old woman's tympanum: "Get along with the supper, Verena."

Charity was trembling with apprehension. Something had happened—she was sure of it now—and Mr. Royall knew what it was. But not for the world would she have gratified him by showing her anxiety. She took her usual place, and he seated himself opposite, and poured out a strong cup of tea before passing her the tea-pot. Verena brought some scrambled eggs, and he piled his plate with them. "Ain't you going to take any?" he asked. Charity roused herself and began to eat.

The tone with which Mr. Royall had said "He's not coming" seemed to her full of an ominous satisfaction. She saw that he had suddenly begun to hate Lucius Harney, and guessed herself to be the cause of this change of feeling. But she had no means of finding out whether some act of hostility on his part had made the young man stay away, or whether he simply wished to avoid seeing her again after their drive back from the brown house. She ate her supper with a studied show of indifference, but she knew that Mr. Royall was watching her and that her agitation did not escape him.

After supper she went up to her room. She heard Mr. Royall cross the passage, and presently the sounds below her window showed that he had returned to the porch. She seated herself on her bed and began to struggle against the desire to go down and ask him what had happened. "I'd rather die than do it," she muttered to herself. With a word he could have relieved her uncertainty: but never would she gratify him by saying it.

She rose and leaned out of the window. The twilight had deepened into night, and she watched the frail curve of the young moon dropping to the edge of the hills. Through the darkness she saw one or two figures moving down the road; but the evening was too cold for loitering, and presently the strollers disappeared. Lamps were beginning to show here and there in the windows. A bar of light brought out the whiteness of a clump of lilies in the Hawes's yard: and farther down the street Carrick Fry's Rochester lamp cast its bold illumination on the rustic flower-tub in the middle of his grass-plot.

For a long time she continued to lean in the window. But a fever of unrest consumed her, and finally she went downstairs, took her hat from its hook, and swung out of the house. Mr. Royall sat in the porch, Verena beside him, her old hands crossed on her patched skirt. As Charity went down the steps Mr. Royall called after her: "Where you going?" She could easily have answered: "To Orma's," or "Down to the Targatts'"; and either answer might have been true, for she had no purpose. But she swept on in silence, determined not to recognize his right to question her.

At the gate she paused and looked up and down the road. The darkness drew her, and she thought of climbing the hill and plunging into the depths of the larch-wood above the pasture. Then she glanced irresolutely along the street, and as she did so a gleam appeared through the spruces at Miss Hatchard's gate. Lucius Harney was there, then—he had not gone down to Hepburn with Mr.

Miles, as she had at first imagined. But where had he taken his evening meal, and what had caused him to stay away from Mr. Royall's? The light was positive proof of his presence, for Miss Hatchard's servants were away on a holiday, and her farmer's wife came only in the mornings, to make the young man's bed and prepare his coffee. Beside that lamp he was doubtless sitting at this moment. To know the truth Charity had only to walk half the length of the village, and knock at the lighted window. She hesitated a minute or two longer, and then turned toward Miss Hatchard's.

She walked quickly, straining her eyes to detect anyone who might be coming along the street; and before reaching the Frys' she crossed over to avoid the light from their window. Whenever she was unhappy she felt herself at bay against a pitiless world, and a kind of animal secretiveness possessed her. But the street was empty, and she passed unnoticed through the gate and up the path to the house. Its white front glimmered indistinctly through the trees, showing only one oblong of light on the lower floor. She had supposed that the lamp was in Miss Hatchard's sitting-room; but she now saw that it shone through a window at the farther corner of the house. She did not know the room to which this window belonged, and she paused under the trees, checked by a sense of strangeness. Then she moved on, treading softly on the short grass, and keeping so close to the house that whoever was in the room, even if roused by her approach, would not be able to see her.

The window opened on a narrow verandah with a trellised arch. She leaned close to the trellis, and parting the sprays of clematis that covered it looked into a corner of the room. She saw the foot of a mahogany bed, an engraving on the wall, a washstand on which a towel had been tossed, and one end of the green-covered table which held the lamp. Half of the lamp-shade projected into her field of vision, and just under it two smooth sunburnt hands, one holding a pencil and the other a ruler, were moving to and fro over a drawing-board.

Her heart jumped and then stood still. He was there, a few feet away; and while her soul was tossing on seas of woe he had been quietly sitting at his drawing-board. The sight of those two hands, moving with their usual skill and precision, woke her out of her dream. Her eyes were opened to the disproportion between what she had felt and the cause of her agitation; and she was turning away from the window when one hand abruptly pushed aside the drawing-board and the other flung down the pencil.

Charity had often noticed Harney's loving care of his drawings, and the neatness and method with which he carried on and concluded each task. The impatient sweeping aside of the drawing-board seemed to reveal a new mood. The gesture suggested sudden discouragement, or distaste for his work, and she wondered if he too were agitated by secret perplexities. Her impulse of flight was checked; she stepped up on the verandah and looked into the room.

Harney had put his elbows on the table and was resting his chin on his locked hands. He had taken off his coat and waistcoat, and unbuttoned the low collar of his flannel shirt; she saw the vigorous lines of his young throat, and the root of the muscles where they joined the chest. He sat staring straight ahead of him, a look of weariness and self-disgust on his face: it was almost as if he had been gazing at a distorted reflection of his own features. For a moment Charity looked at him with a kind of terror, as if he had been a stranger under familiar lineaments; then she glanced past him and saw on the floor an open portmanteau half full of clothes. She understood that he was preparing to leave, and that he had probably decided to go without seeing her. She saw that the decision, from whatever cause it was taken, had disturbed him deeply; and she immediately concluded that his change of plan was due to some surreptitious interference of Mr. Royall's. All her old resentments and rebellions flamed up, confusedly mingled with the yearning roused by Harney's nearness. Only a few hours earlier she had felt secure in his comprehending pity; now she was flung back on herself, doubly alone after that moment of communion.

Harney was still unaware of her presence. He sat without moving, moodily staring before him at the same spot in the wall-paper. He had not even had the energy to finish his packing, and his clothes and papers lay on the floor about the portmanteau. Presently he unlocked his clasped hands and stood up; and Charity, drawing back hastily, sank down on the step of the verandah. The night was so dark that there was not much chance of his seeing her unless he opened the window, and before that she would have time to slip away and be lost in the shadow of the trees. He

stood for a minute or two looking around the room with the same
expression of self-disgust, as if he hated himself and everything
about him; then he sat down again at the table, drew a few more
strokes, and threw his pencil aside. Finally he walked across the
floor, kicking the portmanteau out of his way, and lay down on the
bed, folding his arms under his head, and staring up morosely at
the ceiling. Just so, Charity had seen him at her side, on the grass
or the pine-needles, his eyes fixed on the sky, and pleasure flashing
over his face like the flickers of sun the branches shed on it. But
now the face was so changed that she hardly knew it; and grief at
his grief gathered in her throat, rose to her eyes and ran over.

She continued to crouch on the steps, holding her breath and
stiffening herself into complete immobility. One motion of her
hand, one tap on the pane, and she could picture the sudden
change in his face. In every pulse of her rigid body she was aware
of the welcome his eyes and lips would give her; but something
kept her from moving. It was not the fear of any sanction, human
or heavenly; she had never in her life been afraid. It was simply
that she had suddenly understood what would happen if she went
in. It was the thing that *did* happen between young men and girls,
and that North Dormer ignored in public and snickered over on
the sly. It was what Miss Hatchard was still ignorant of, but every
girl of Charity's class knew about before she left school. It was
what had happened to Ally Hawes's sister Julia, and had ended in
her going to Nettleton, and in people's never mentioning her name.

It did not, of course, always end so sensationally; nor, perhaps,
on the whole, so untragically. Charity had always suspected that
the shunned Julia's fate might have its compensations. There were
other worse endings that the village knew of, mean, miserable,
unconfessed; other lives that went on drearily, without visible
change, in the same cramped setting of hypocrisy. But these were
not the reasons that held her back. Since the day before, she had
known exactly what she would feel if Harney should take her in
his arms: the melting of palm into palm and mouth on mouth, and
the long flame burning her from head to foot. But mixed with this
feeling was another: the wondering pride in his liking for her, the
startled softness that his sympathy had put into her heart. Sometimes, when her youth flushed up in her, she had imagined yield-

ing like other girls to furtive caresses in the twilight; but she could not so cheapen herself to Harney. She did not know why he was going; but since he was going she felt she must do nothing to deface the image of her that he carried away. If he wanted her he must seek her: he must not be surprised into taking her as girls like Julia Hawes were taken. . . .

No sound came from the sleeping village, and in the deep darkness of the garden she heard now and then a secret rustle of branches, as though some night-bird brushed them. Once a footfall passed the gate, and she shrank back into her corner; but the steps died away and left a profounder quiet. Her eyes were still on Harney's tormented face: she felt she could not move till he moved. But she was beginning to grow numb from her constrained position, and at times her thoughts were so indistinct that she seemed to be held there only by a vague weight of weariness.

A long time passed in this strange vigil. Harney still lay on the bed, motionless and with fixed eyes, as though following his vision to its bitter end. At last he stirred and changed his attitude slightly, and Charity's heart began to tremble. But he only flung out his arms and sank back into his former position. With a deep sigh he tossed the hair from his forehead; then his whole body relaxed, his head turned sideways on the pillow, and she saw that he had fallen asleep. The sweet expression came back to his lips, and the haggardness faded from his face, leaving it as fresh as a boy's.

She rose and crept away.

VIII

She had lost the sense of time, and did not know how late it was till she came out into the street and saw that all the windows were dark between Miss Hatchard's and the Royall house.

As she passed from under the black pall of the Norway spruces she fancied she saw two figures in the shade about the duck-pond. She drew back and watched; but nothing moved, and she had stared so long into the lamp-lit room that the darkness confused her, and she thought she must have been mistaken.

She walked on, wondering whether Mr. Royall was still in the porch. In her exalted mood she did not greatly care whether he was waiting for her or not: she seemed to be floating high over life, on a great cloud of misery beneath which everyday realities had dwindled to mere specks in space. But the porch was empty, Mr. Royall's hat hung on its peg in the passage, and the kitchen lamp had been left to light her to bed. She took it and went up.

The morning hours of the next day dragged by without incident. Charity had imagined that, in some way or other, she would learn whether Harney had already left; but Verena's deafness prevented her being a source of news, and no one came to the house who could bring enlightenment.

Mr. Royall went out early, and did not return till Verena had set the table for the midday meal. When he came in he went straight to the kitchen and shouted to the old woman: "Ready for dinner——" then he turned into the dining-room, where Charity was already seated. Harney's plate was in its usual place, but Mr. Royall offered no explanation of his absence, and Charity asked none. The feverish exaltation of the night before had dropped, and she said to herself that he had gone away, indifferently, almost callously, and that now her life would lapse again into the narrow rut out of which he had lifted it. For a moment she was inclined to sneer at herself for not having used the arts that might have kept him.

She sat at table till the meal was over, lest Mr. Royall should remark on her leaving; but when he stood up she rose also, without waiting to help Verena. She had her foot on the stairs when he called to her to come back.

"I've got a headache. I'm going up to lie down."

"I want you should come in here first; I've got something to say to you."

She was sure from his tone that in a moment she would learn what every nerve in her ached to know; but as she turned back she made a last effort of indifference.

Mr. Royall stood in the middle of the office, his thick eyebrows beetling, his lower jaw trembling a little. At first she thought he had been drinking; then she saw that he was sober, but stirred by a deep and stern emotion totally unlike his usual transient angers. And suddenly she understood that, until then, she had never really noticed him or thought about him. Except on the occasion of his one offense he had been to her merely the person who is always there, the unquestioned central fact of life, as inevitable but as uninteresting as North Dormer itself, or any of the other conditions fate had laid on her. Even then she had regarded him only in relation to herself, and had never speculated as to his own feelings, beyond instinctively concluding that he would not trouble her again in the same way. But now she began to wonder what he was really like.

He had grasped the back of his chair with both hands, and stood looking hard at her. At length he said: "Charity, for once let's you and me talk together like friends."

Instantly she felt that something had happened, and that he held her in his hand.

"Where is Mr. Harney? Why hasn't he come back? Have you sent him away?" she broke out, without knowing what she was saying.

The change in Mr. Royall frightened her. All the blood seemed to leave his veins and against his swarthy pallor the deep lines in his face looked black.

"Didn't he have time to answer some of those questions last night? You was with him long enough!" he said.

Charity stood speechless. The taunt was so unrelated to what had been happening in her soul that she hardly understood it. But the instinct of self-defense awoke in her.

"Who says I was with him last night?"

"The whole place is saying it by now."

"Then it was you that put the lie into their mouths.—Oh, how I've always hated you!" she cried.

She had expected a retort in kind, and it startled her to hear her exclamation sounding on through silence.

"Yes, I know," Mr. Royall said slowly. "But that ain't going to help us much now."

"It helps me not to care a straw what lies you tell about me!"

"If they're lies, they're not my lies: my Bible oath on that, Charity. I didn't know where you were: I wasn't out of this house last night."

She made no answer and he went on: "Is it a lie that you were seen coming out of Miss Hatchard's nigh onto midnight?"

She straightened herself with a laugh, all her reckless insolence recovered. "I didn't look to see what time it was."

"You lost girl . . . you . . . you . . . Oh, my God, why did you tell me?" he broke out, dropping into his chair, his head bowed down like an old man's.

Charity's self-possession had returned with the sense of her danger. "Do you suppose I'd take the trouble to lie to *you*? Who are you, anyhow, to ask me where I go to when I go out at night?"

Mr. Royall lifted his head and looked at her. His face had grown quiet and almost gentle, as she remembered seeing it sometimes when she was a little girl, before Mrs. Royall died.

"Don't let's go on like this, Charity. It can't do any good to either of us. You were seen going into that fellow's house . . . you were seen coming out of it. . . . I've watched this thing coming, and I've tried to stop it. As God sees me, I have. . . ."

"Ah, it *was* you, then? I knew it was you that sent him away!"

He looked at her in surprise. "Didn't he tell you so? I thought he understood." He spoke slowly, with difficult pauses, "I didn't name you to him: I'd have cut my hand off sooner. I just told him I couldn't spare the horse any longer; and that the cooking was getting too heavy for Verena. I guess he's the kind that's heard the same thing before. Anyhow, he took it quietly enough. He said his job here was about done, anyhow; and there didn't another word pass between us. . . . If he told you otherwise he told you an untruth."

Charity listened in a cold trance of anger. It was nothing to her what the village said . . . but all this fingering of her dreams!

"I've told you he didn't tell me anything. I didn't speak with him last night."

"You didn't speak with him?"

"No. . . . It's not that I care what any of you say . . . but you may as well know. Things ain't between us the way you think . . . and the other people in this place. He was kind to me; he was my friend; and all of a sudden he stopped coming, and I knew it was you that done it—*you!*" All her unreconciled memory of the past flamed out at him. "So I went there last night to find out what you'd said to him: that's all."

Mr. Royall drew a heavy breath. "But, then—if he wasn't there, what were you doing there all that time?—Charity, for pity's sake, tell me. I've got to know, to stop their talking."

This pathetic abdication of all authority over her did not move her: she could feel only the outrage of his interference.

"Can't you see that I don't care what anybody says? It's true I went there to see him; and he was in his room, and I stood outside for ever so long and watched him; but I dursn't go in for fear he'd think I'd come after him. . . ." She felt her voice breaking, and gathered it up in a last defiance. "As long as I live I'll never forgive you!" she cried.

Mr. Royall made no answer. He sat and pondered with sunken head, his veined hands clasped about the arms of his chair. Age seemed to have come down on him as winter comes on the hills after a storm. At length he looked up.

"Charity, you say you don't care; but you're the proudest girl I know, and the last to want people to talk against you. You know there's always eyes watching you: you're handsomer and smarter than the rest, and that's enough. But till lately you've never given them a chance. Now they've got it, and they're going to use it. I believe what you say, but they won't. . . . It was Mrs. Tom Fry seen you going in . . . and two or three of them watched for you to come out again. . . . You've been with the fellow all day long every day since he come here . . . and I'm a lawyer, and I know how hard slander dies." He paused, but she stood motionless, without giving him any sign of acquiescence or even of attention. "He's a pleasant fellow to talk to—I liked having him here myself. The young men up here ain't had his chances. But there's one thing as old as the hills and as plain as daylight: if he'd wanted you the right way he'd have said so."

Charity did not speak. It seemed to her that nothing could exceed the bitterness of hearing such words from such lips.

Mr. Royall rose from his seat. "See here, Charity Royall: I had a shameful thought once, and you've made me pay for it. Isn't that score pretty near wiped out? . . . There's a streak in me I ain't always master of; but I've always acted straight to you but that once. And you've known I would—you've trusted me. For all your sneers and your mockery you've always known I loved you the way a man loves a decent woman. I'm a good many years older than you, but I'm head and shoulders above this place and everybody in it, and you know that too. I slipped up once, but that's no reason for not starting again. If you'll come with me I'll do it. If you'll marry me we'll leave here and settle in some big town, where there's men, and business, and things doing. It's not too late for me to find an opening. . . . I can see it by the way folks treat me when I go down to Hepburn or Nettleton. . . ."

Charity made no movement. Nothing in his appeal reached her heart, and she thought only of words to wound and wither. But a growing lassitude restrained her. What did anything matter that he was saying? She saw the old life closing in on her, and hardly heeded his fanciful picture of renewal.

"Charity—Charity—say you'll do it," she heard him urge, all his lost years and wasted passion in his voice.

"Oh, what's the use of all this? When I leave here it won't be with you."

She moved toward the door as she spoke, and he stood up and placed himself between her and the threshold. He seemed suddenly tall and strong, as though the extremity of his humiliation had given him new vigour.

"That's all, is it? It's not much." He leaned against the door, so towering and powerful that he seemed to fill the narrow room. "Well, then—look here. . . . You're right: I've no claim on you— why should you look at a broken man like me? You want the other fellow . . . and I don't blame you. You picked out the best when you seen it . . . well, that was always my way." He fixed his stern eyes on her, and she had the sense that the struggle within him was at its highest. "Do you want him to marry you?" he asked.

They stood and looked at each other for a long moment, eye to eye, with the terrible equality of courage that sometimes made her feel as if she had his blood in her veins.

"Do you want him to—say? I'll have him here in an hour if you do. I ain't been in the law thirty years for nothing. He's hired Carrick Fry's team to take him to Hepburn, but he ain't going to start for another hour. And I can put things to him so he won't be long deciding. . . . He's soft: I could see that. I don't say you won't be sorry afterward—but, by God, I'll give you the chance to be, if you say so."

She heard him out in silence, too remote from all he was feeling and saying for any sally of scorn to relieve her. As she listened, there flitted through her mind the vision of Liff Hyatt's muddy boot coming down on the white bramble-flowers. The same thing had happened now; something transient and exquisite had flowered in her, and she had stood by and seen it trampled to earth. While the thought passed through her she was aware of Mr. Royall, still leaning against the door, but crestfallen, diminished, as though her silence were the answer he most dreaded.

"I don't want any chance you can give me: I'm glad he's going away," she said.

He kept his place a moment longer, his hand on the doorknob. "Charity!" he pleaded. She made no answer, and he turned the knob and went out. She heard him fumble with the latch of the front door, and saw him walk down the steps. He passed out of the gate, and his figure, stooping and heavy, receded slowly up the street.

For a while she remained where he had left her. She was still trembling with the humiliation of his last words, which rang so loud in her ears that it seemed as though they must echo through the village, proclaiming her a creature to lend herself to such vile suggestions. Her shame weighed on her like a physical oppression: the roof and walls seemed to be closing in on her, and she was seized by the impulse to get away, under the open sky, where there would be room to breathe. She went to the front door, and as she did so Lucius Harney opened it.

He looked graver and less confident than usual, and for a moment or two neither of them spoke. Then he held out his hand. "Are you going out?" he asked. "May I come in?"

Her heart was beating so violently that she was afraid to speak, and stood looking at him with tear-dilated eyes; then she became aware of what her silence must betray, and said quickly: "Yes: come in."

She led the way into the dining-room, and they sat down on opposite sides of the table, the cruet-stand and japanned bread-basket between them. Harney had laid his straw hat on the table, and as he sat there, in his easy-looking summer clothes, a brown tie knotted under his flannel collar, and his smooth brown hair brushed back from his forehead, she pictured him as she had seen him the night before, lying on his bed, with the tossed locks falling into his eyes, and his bare throat rising out of his unbuttoned shirt. He had never seemed so remote as at the moment when that vision flashed through her mind.

"I'm so sorry it's good-bye: I suppose you know I'm leaving,"

he began, abruptly and awkwardly; she guessed that he was wondering how much she knew of his reasons for going.

"I presume you found your work was over quicker than what
you expected," she said.

"Well, yes—that is, no: there are plenty of things I should have
liked to do. But my holiday's limited; and now that Mr. Royall
needs the horse for himself it's rather difficult to find means of getting about."

"There ain't any too many teams for hire around here," she acquiesced; and there was another silence.

"These days here have been—awfully pleasant: I wanted to
thank you for making them so," he continued, his colour rising.

She could not think of any reply, and he went on: "You've been
wonderfully kind to me, and I wanted to tell you. . . . I wish I
could think of you as happier, less lonely. . . . Things are sure to
change for you by and by. . . ."

"Things don't change at North Dormer: people just get used to
them."

The answer seemed to break up the order of his prearranged
consolations, and he sat looking at her uncertainly. Then he said,
with his sweet smile: "That's not true of you. It can't be."

The smile was like a knife-thrust through her heart: everything
in her began to tremble and break loose. She felt her tears run
over, and stood up.

"Well, good-bye," she said.

She was aware of his taking her hand, and of feeling that his
touch was lifeless.

"Good-bye." He turned away, and stopped on the threshold.
"You'll say good-bye for me to Verena?"

She heard the closing of the outer door and the sound of his
quick tread along the path. The latch of the gate clicked after him.

The next morning when she arose in the cold dawn and opened
her shutters she saw a freckled boy standing on the other side of
the road and looking up at her. He was a boy from a farm three or
four miles down the Creston road, and she wondered what he was
doing there at that hour, and why he looked so hard at her window. When he saw her he crossed over and leaned against the gate
unconcernedly. There was no one stirring in the house, and she
threw a shawl over her night-gown and ran down and let herself

out. By the time she reached the gate the boy was sauntering down the road, whistling carelessly; but she saw that a letter had been thrust between the slats and the crossbar of the gate. She took it out and hastened back to her room.

The envelope bore her name, and inside was a leaf torn from a pocket-diary.

DEAR CHARITY:

   I can't go away like this. I am staying for a few days at Creston River. Will you come down and meet me at Creston pool? I will wait for you till evening.

IX

Charity sat before the mirror trying on a hat which Ally Hawes, with much secrecy, had trimmed for her. It was of white straw, with a drooping brim and a cherry-coloured lining that made her face glow like the inside of the shell on the parlour mantelpiece.

She propped the square of looking-glass against Mr. Royall's black leather Bible, steadying it in front with a white stone on which a view of the Brooklyn Bridge was painted; and she sat before her reflection, bending the brim this way and that, while Ally Hawes's pale face looked over her shoulder like the ghost of wasted opportunities.

"I look awful, don't I?" she said at last with a happy sigh.

Ally smiled and took back the hat. "I'll stitch the roses on right here, so's you can put it away at once."

Charity laughed, and ran her fingers through her rough dark hair. She knew that Harney liked to see its reddish edges ruffled about her forehead and breaking into little rings at the nape. She sat down on her bed and watched Ally stoop over the hat with a careful frown.

"Don't you ever feel like going down to Nettleton for a day?" she asked.

Ally shook her head without looking up. "No, I always remember that awful time I went down with Julia—to that doctor's."

"Oh, Ally——"

"I can't help it. The house is on the corner of Wing Street and

Lake Avenue. The trolley from the station goes right by it, and the day the minister took us down to see those pictures I recognized it right off, and couldn't seem to see anything else. There's a big black sign with gold letters all across the front—'Private Consultations.' She came as near as anything to dying. . . ."

"Poor Julia!" Charity sighed from the height of her purity and her security. She had a friend whom she trusted and who respected her. She was going with him to spend the next day—the Fourth of July—at Nettleton. Whose business was it but hers, and what was the harm? The pity of it was that girls like Julia did not know how to choose, and to keep bad fellows at a distance. . . . Charity slipped down from the bed, and stretched out her hands.

"Is it sewed? Let me try it on again." She put the hat on, and smiled at her image. The thought of Julia had vanished. . . .

The next morning she was up before dawn, and saw the yellow sunrise broaden behind the hills, and the silvery lustre preceding a hot day tremble across the sleeping fields.

Her plans had been made with great care. She had announced that she was going down to the Band of Hope picnic, at Hepburn, and as no one else from North Dormer intended to venture so far it was not likely that her absence from the festivity would be reported. Besides, if it were she would not greatly care. She was determined to assert her independence, and if she stooped to fib about the Hepburn picnic it was chiefly from the secretive instinct that made her dread the profanation of her happiness. Whenever she was with Lucius Harney she would have liked some impenetrable mountain mist to hide her.

It was arranged that she should walk to a point of the Creston road where Harney was to pick her up and drive her across the hills to Hepburn in time for the nine-thirty train to Nettleton. Harney at first had been rather lukewarm about the trip. He declared himself ready to take her to Nettleton, but urged her not to go on the Fourth of July, on account of the crowds, the probable lateness of the trains, the difficulty of her getting back before night; but her evident disappointment caused him to give way, and even to affect a faint enthusiasm for the adventure. She understood why he was not more eager: he must have seen sights beside which even a Fourth of July at Nettleton would seem tame.

But she had never seen anything; and a great longing possessed her to walk the streets of a big town on a holiday, clinging to his arm and jostled by idle crowds in their best clothes. The only cloud on the prospect was the fact that the shops would be closed; but she hoped he would take her back another day, when they were open.

She started out unnoticed in the early sunlight, slipping through the kitchen while Verena bent above the stove. To avoid attracting notice, she carried her new hat carefully wrapped up, and had thrown a long grey veil of Mrs. Royall's over the new white muslin dress which Ally's clever fingers had made for her. All of the ten dollars Mr. Royall had given her, and a part of her own savings as well, had been spent on renewing her wardrobe; and when Harney jumped out of the buggy to meet her she read her reward in his eyes.

The freckled boy who had brought her the note two weeks earlier was to wait with the buggy at Hepburn till their return. He perched at Charity's feet, his legs dangling between the wheels, and they could not say much because of his presence. But it did not greatly matter, for their past was now rich enough to have given them a private language; and with the long day stretching before them like the blue distance beyond the hills there was a delicate pleasure in postponement.

When Charity, in response to Harney's message, had gone to meet him at the Creston pool her heart had been so full of mortification and anger that his first words might easily have estranged her. But it happened that he had found the right word, which was one of simple friendship. His tone had instantly justified her, and put her guardian in the wrong. He had made no allusion to what had passed between Mr. Royall and himself, but had simply let it appear that he had left because means of conveyance were hard to find at North Dormer, and because Creston River was a more convenient centre. He told her that he had hired by the week the buggy of the freckled boy's father, who served as livery-stable keeper to one or two melancholy summer boarding-houses on Creston Lake, and had discovered, within driving distance, a number of houses worthy of his pencil; and he said that he could not, while he was in the neighbourhood, give up the pleasure of seeing her as often as possible.

When they took leave of each other she promised to continue to be his guide; and during the fortnight which followed they roamed the hills in happy comradeship. In most of the village friendships between youths and maidens lack of conversation was made up for by tentative fondling; but Harney, except when he had tried to comfort her in her trouble on their way back from the Hyatts', had never put his arm about her, or sought to betray her into any sudden caress. It seemed to be enough for him to breathe her nearness like a flower's; and since his pleasure at being with her, and his sense of her youth and her grace, perpetually shone in his eyes and softened the inflections of his voice, his reserve did not suggest coldness, but the deference due to a girl of his own class.

The buggy was drawn by an old trotter who whirled them along so briskly that the pace created a little breeze; but when they reached Hepburn the full heat of the airless morning descended on them. At the railway station the platform was packed with a sweltering throng, and they took refuge in the waiting-room, where there was another throng, already dejected by the heat and the long waiting for retarded trains. Pale mothers were struggling with fretful babies, or trying to keep their older offspring from the fascination of the track; girls and their "fellows" were giggling and shoving, and passing about candy in sticky bags, and older men, collarless and perspiring, were shifting heavy children from one arm to the other, and keeping a haggard eye on the scattered members of their families.

At last the train rumbled in, and engulfed the waiting multitude. Harney swept Charity up on to the first car and they captured a bench for two, and sat in happy isolation while the train swayed and roared along through rich fields and languid tree-clumps. The haze of the morning had become a sort of clear tremor over everything, like the colourless vibration about a flame; and the opulent landscape seemed to droop under it. But to Charity the heat was a stimulant: it enveloped the whole world in the same glow that burned at her heart. Now and then a lurch of the train flung her against Harney, and through her thin muslin she felt the touch of his sleeve. She steadied herself, their eyes met, and the flaming breath of the day seemed to enclose them.

The train roared into the Nettleton station, the descending mob caught them on its tide, and they were swept out into a vague dusty square thronged with seedy "hacks" and long curtained omnibuses drawn by horses with tasselled fly-nets over their withers, who stood swinging their depressed heads drearily from side to side.

A mob of 'bus and hack drivers were shouting "To the Eagle House," "To the Washington House," "This way to the Lake," "Just starting for Greytop;" and through their yells came the popping of fire-crackers, the explosion of torpedoes,[15] the banging of toy-guns, and the crash of a firemen's band trying to play the Merry Widow[16] while they were being packed into a waggonette streaming with bunting.

The ramshackle wooden hotels about the square were all hung with flags and paper lanterns, and as Harney and Charity turned into the main street, with its brick and granite business blocks crowding out the old low-storied shops, and its towering poles strung with innumerable wires that seemed to tremble and buzz in the heat, they saw the double line of flags and lanterns tapering away gaily to the park at the other end of the perspective. The noise and colour of this holiday vision seemed to transform Nettleton into a metropolis. Charity could not believe that Springfield or even Boston had anything grander to show, and she wondered if, at this very moment, Annabel Balch, on the arm of as brilliant a young man, were threading her way through scenes as resplendent.

"Where shall we go first?" Harney asked; but as she turned her happy eyes on him he guessed the answer and said: "We'll take a look round, shall we?"

The street swarmed with their fellow-travellers, with other excursionists arriving from other directions, with Nettleton's own population, and with the mill-hands trooping in from the factories on the Creston. The shops were closed, but one would scarcely have noticed it, so numerous were the glass doors swinging open on saloons, on restaurants, on drug-stores gushing from every soda-water tap, on fruit and confectionery shops stacked with strawberry-cake, cocoanut drops, trays of glistening molasses candy, boxes of caramels and chewing-gum, baskets of sodden strawberries, and dangling branches of bananas. Outside of some of the doors were trestles with banked-up oranges and apples, spotted pears and dusty raspberries; and the air reeked with the smell of fruit and stale coffee, beer and sarsaparilla and fried potatoes.

Even the shops that were closed offered, through wide expanses of plate-glass, hints of hidden riches. In some, waves of silk and ribbon broke over shores of imitation moss from which ravishing hats rose like tropical orchids. In others, the pink throats of gramophones opened their giant convolutions in a soundless chorus; or bicycles shining in neat ranks seemed to await the signal of an invisible starter; or tiers of fancy-goods in leatherette and paste and celluloid dangled their insidious graces; and, in one vast bay that seemed to project them into exciting contact with the public, wax ladies in daring dresses chatted elegantly, or, with gestures intimate yet blameless, pointed to their pink corsets and transparent hosiery.

Presently Harney found that his watch had stopped, and turned in at a small jeweller's shop which chanced to be still open. While the watch was being examined Charity leaned over the glass counter where, on a background of dark blue velvet, pins, rings and brooches glittered like the moon and stars. She had never seen jewellery so near by, and she longed to lift the glass lid and plunge her hand among the shining treasures. But already Harney's watch was repaired, and he laid his hand on her arm and drew her from her dream.

"Which do you like best?" he asked leaning over the counter at her side.

"I don't know. . . ." She pointed to a gold lily-of-the-valley with white flowers.

"Don't you think the blue pin's better?" he suggested, and immediately she saw that the lily of the valley was mere trumpery compared to the small round stone, blue as a mountain lake, with little sparks of light all round it. She coloured at her want of discrimination.

"It's so lovely I guess I was afraid to look at it," she said.

He laughed, and they went out of the shop; but a few steps away he exclaimed: "Oh, by Jove, I forgot something," and turned back and left her in the crowd. She stood staring down a row of pink gramophone throats till he rejoined her and slipped his arm through hers.

"You mustn't be afraid of looking at the blue pin any longer, because it belongs to you," he said; and she felt a little box being pressed into her hand. Her heart gave a leap of joy, but it reached her lips only in a shy stammer. She remembered other girls whom she had heard planning to extract presents from their fellows, and was seized with a sudden dread lest Harney should have imagined that she had leaned over the pretty things in the glass case in the hope of having one given to her. . . .

A little farther down the street they turned in at a glass door-way opening on a shining hall with a mahogany staircase, and brass cages in its corners. "We must have something to eat," Har-ney said; and the next moment Charity found herself in a dressing-room all looking-glass and lustrous surfaces, where a party of showy-looking girls were dabbing on powder and straightening immense plumed hats. When they had gone she took courage to bathe her hot face in one of the marble basins, and to straighten her own hat-brim, which the parasols of the crowd had indented. The dresses in the shops had so impressed her that she scarcely dared look at her reflection; but when she did so, the glow of her face under her cherry-coloured hat, and the curve of her young shoulders through the transparent muslin, restored her courage; and when she had taken the blue brooch from its box and pinned it on her bosom she walked toward the restaurant with her head high, as if she had always strolled through tessellated halls beside young men in flannels.

Her spirit sank a little at the sight of the slim-waisted waitresses in black, with bewitching mob-caps on their haughty heads, who were moving disdainfully between the tables. "Not f'r another hour," one of them dropped to Harney in passing; and he stood doubtfully glancing about him.

"Oh, well, we can't stay sweltering here," he decided; "let's try somewhere else—" and with a sense of relief Charity followed him from that scene of inhospitable splendour.

The "somewhere else" turned out—after more hot tramping, and several failures—to be, of all things, a little open-air place in a back street that called itself a French restaurant, and consisted in two or three rickety tables under a scarlet-runner, between a patch of zinnias and petunias and a big elm bending over from the next yard. Here they lunched on queerly flavoured things, while Harney, leaning back in a crippled rocking-chair, smoked ciga-

rettes between the courses and poured into Charity's glass a pale
yellow wine which he said was the very same one drank in just
such jolly places in France.

Charity did not think the wine as good as sarsaparilla, but she
sipped a mouthful for the pleasure of doing what he did, and of
fancying herself alone with him in foreign countries. The illusion
was increased by their being served by a deep-bosomed woman
with smooth hair and a pleasant laugh, who talked to Harney in
unintelligible words,[17] and seemed amazed and overjoyed at his
answering her in kind. At the other tables other people sat, mill-
hands probably, homely but pleasant looking, who spoke the
same shrill jargon, and looked at Harney and Charity with friendly
eyes; and between the table-legs a poodle with bald patches and
pink eyes nosed about for scraps, and sat up on his hind legs ab-
surdly.

Harney showed no inclination to move, for hot as their corner
was, it was at least shaded and quiet; and, from the main thor-
oughfares came the clanging of trolleys, the incessant popping of
torpedoes, the jingle of street-organs, the bawling of megaphone
men and the loud murmur of increasing crowds. He leaned back,
smoking his cigar, patting the dog, and stirring the coffee that
steamed in their chipped cups. "It's the real thing, you know," he
explained; and Charity hastily revised her previous conception of
the beverage.

They had made no plans for the rest of the day, and when Harney asked her what she wanted to do next she was too bewildered
by rich possibilities to find an answer. Finally she confessed that
she longed to go to the Lake, where she had not been taken on her
former visit, and when he answered, "Oh, there's time for that—
it will be pleasanter later," she suggested seeing some pictures like
the ones Mr. Miles had taken her to. She thought Harney looked
a little disconcerted; but he passed his fine handkerchief over his
warm brow, said gaily "Come along, then," and rose with a last
pat for the pink-eyed dog.

Mr. Miles's pictures had been shown in an austere Y.M.C.A.
hall, with white walls and an organ; but Harney led Charity to a
glittering place—everything she saw seemed to glitter—where
they passed, between immense pictures of yellow-haired beauties
stabbing villains in evening dress, into a velvet-curtained audito-

rium packed with spectators to the last limit of compression. After that, for a while, everything was merged in her brain in swimming circles of heat and blinding alternations of light and darkness. All the world has to show seemed to pass before her in a chaos of palms and minarets, charging cavalry regiments, roaring lions, comic policemen and scowling murderers; and the crowd around her, the hundreds of hot sallow candy-munching faces, young, old, middle-aged, but all kindled with the same contagious excitement, became part of the spectacle, and danced on the screen with the rest.

Presently the thought of the cool trolley-run to the Lake grew irresistible, and they struggled out of the theatre. As they stood on the pavement, Harney pale with the heat, and even Charity a little confused by it, a young man drove by in an electric run-about with a calico band bearing the words: "Ten dollars to take you round the Lake." Before Charity knew what was happening, Harney had waved a hand, and they were climbing in. "Say, for twenny-five I'll run you out first to see the ball-game and back," the driver proposed with an insinuating grin; but Charity said quickly: "Oh, I'd rather go rowing on the Lake." The street was so thronged that progress was slow; but the glory of sitting in the little carriage while it wriggled its way between laden omnibuses and trolleys made the moments seem too short. "Next turn is Lake Avenue," the young man called out over his shoulder; and as they paused in the wake of a big omnibus groaning with Knights of Pythias[18] in cocked hats and swords, Charity looked and saw on the corner a brick house with a conspicuous black and gold sign across its front. "Dr. Merkle; Private Consultations at all hours. Lady Attendants," she read; and suddenly she remembered Ally Hawes's words: "The house was at the corner of Wing Street and Lake Avenue. . . . there's a big black sign across the front. . . ." Through all the heat and the rapture a shiver of cold ran over her.

X

The Lake at last—a sheet of shining metal brooded over by drooping trees. Charity and Harney had secured a boat and, getting away from the wharves and the refreshment-booths, they drifted idly along, hugging the shadow of the shore. Where the sun struck the water its shafts flamed back blindingly at the heat-veiled sky; and the least shade was black by contrast. The Lake was so smooth that the reflection of the trees on its edge seemed enamelled on a solid surface; but gradually, as the sun declined, the water grew transparent, and Charity, leaning over, plunged her fascinated gaze into depths so clear that she saw the inverted tree-tops interwoven with the green growths of the bottom.

They rounded a point at the farther end of the Lake, and entering an inlet pushed their bow against a protruding tree-trunk. A green veil of willows overhung them. Beyond the trees, wheatfields sparkled in the sun; and all along the horizon the clear hills throbbed with light. Charity leaned back in the stern, and Harney unshipped the oars and lay in the bottom of the boat without speaking.

Ever since their meeting at the Creston pool he had been subject to these brooding silences, which were as different as possible from the pauses when they ceased to speak because words were needless. At such times his face wore the expression she had seen on it when she had looked in at him from the darkness, and again there came over her a sense of the mysterious distance between them; but usually his fits of abstraction were followed by bursts of gaiety that chased away the shadow before it chilled her.

She was still thinking of the ten dollars he had handed to the driver of the run-about. It had given them twenty minutes of pleasure, and it seemed unimaginable that anyone should be able to buy amusement at that rate. With ten dollars he might have bought her an engagement ring; she knew that Mrs. Tom Fry's, which came from Springfield, and had a diamond in it, had cost only eight seventy-five. But she did not know why the thought had occurred to her. Harney would never buy her an engagement ring: they were friends and comrades, but no more. He had been perfectly fair to her: he had never said a word to mislead her. She wondered what the girl was like whose hand was waiting for his ring. . . .

Boats were beginning to thicken on the Lake and the clang of incessantly arriving trolleys announced the return of the crowds from the ball-field. The shadows lengthened across the pearl-grey water and two white clouds near the sun were turning golden. On the opposite shore men were hammering hastily at a wooden scaffolding in a field. Charity asked what it was for.

"Why, the fireworks. I suppose there'll be a big show." Harney looked at her and a smile crept into his moody eyes. "Have you never seen any good fireworks?"

"Miss Hatchard always sends up lovely rockets on the Fourth," she answered doubtfully.

"Oh——" his contempt was unbounded. "I mean a big performance like this: illuminated boats, and all the rest."

She flushed at the picture. "Do they send them up from the Lake, too?"

"Rather. Didn't you notice that big raft we passed? It's wonderful to see the rockets completing their orbits down under one's feet." She said nothing, and he put the oars into the rowlocks. "If we stay we'd better go and pick up something to eat."

"But how can we get back afterward?" she ventured, feeling it would break her heart if she missed it.

He consulted a time-table, found a ten o'clock train and reassured her. "The moon rises so late that it will be dark by eight, and we'll have over an hour of it."

Twilight fell, and lights began to show along the shore. The trolleys roaring out from Nettleton became great luminous serpents coiling in and out among the trees. The wooden eating-houses at the Lake's edge danced with lanterns, and the dusk echoed with laughter and shouts and the clumsy splashing of oars.

Harney and Charity had found a table in the corner of a balcony built over the Lake, and were patiently awaiting an unattainable chowder. Close under them the water lapped the piles, agitated by the evolutions of a little white steamboat trellised with coloured globes which was to run passengers up and down the Lake. It was already black with them as it sheered off on its first trip.

Suddenly Charity heard a woman's laugh behind her. The sound was familiar, and she turned to look. A band of showily dressed girls and dapper young men wearing badges of secret societies, with new straw hats tilted far back on their square-clipped hair, had invaded the balcony and were loudly clamouring for a table. The girl in the lead was the one who had laughed. She wore a large hat with a long white feather, and from under its brim her painted eyes looked at Charity with amused recognition.

"Say! if this ain't like Old Home Week," she remarked to the girl at her elbow; and giggles and glances passed between them. Charity knew at once that the girl with the white feather was Julia Hawes. She had lost her freshness, and the paint under her eyes made her face seem thinner; but her lips had the same lovely curve, and the same cold mocking smile, as if there were some secret absurdity in the person she was looking at, and she had instantly detected it.

Charity flushed to the forehead and looked away. She felt herself humiliated by Julia's sneer, and vexed that the mockery of such a creature should affect her. She trembled lest Harney should notice that the noisy troop had recognized her; but they found no table free, and passed on tumultuously.

Presently there was a soft rush through the air and a shower of silver fell from the blue evening sky. In another direction, pale Roman candles shot up singly through the trees, and a fire-haired rocket swept the horizon like a portent. Between these intermittent flashes the velvet curtains of the darkness were descending, and in the intervals of eclipse the voices of the crowds seemed to sink to smothered murmurs.

Charity and Harney, dispossessed by newcomers, were at length obliged to give up their table and struggle through the throng about the boat-landings. For a while there seemed no escape from the tide of late arrivals; but finally Harney secured the last two places on the stand from which the more privileged were to see the fireworks. The seats were at the end of a row, one above the other. Charity had taken off her hat to have an uninterrupted view; and whenever she leaned back to follow the curve of some dishevelled rocket she could feel Harney's knees against her head.

After a while the scattered fireworks ceased. A longer interval of darkness followed, and then the whole night broke into flower. From every point of the horizon, gold and silver arches sprang up and crossed each other, sky-orchards broke into blossom, shed their flaming petals and hung their branches with golden fruit; and all the while the air was filled with a soft supernatural hum, as though great birds were building their nests in those invisible tree-tops.

Now and then there came a lull, and a wave of moonlight swept the Lake. In a flash it revealed hundreds of boats, steel-dark against lustrous ripples; then it withdrew as if with a furling of vast translucent wings. Charity's heart throbbed with delight. It was as if all the latent beauty of things had been unveiled to her. She could not imagine that the world held anything more wonderful; but near her she heard someone say, "You wait till you see the set piece," and instantly her hopes took a fresh flight. At last, just as it was beginning to seem as though the whole arch of the sky were one great lid pressed against her dazzled eye-balls, and striking out of them continuous jets of jewelled light, the velvet darkness settled down again, and a murmur of expectation ran through the crowd.

"Now—now!" the same voice said excitedly; and Charity, grasping the hat on her knee, crushed it tight in the effort to restrain her rapture.

For a moment the night seemed to grow more impenetrably black; then a great picture stood out against it like a constellation. It was surmounted by a golden scroll bearing the inscription, "Washington crossing the Delaware," and across a flood of motionless golden ripples the National Hero passed, erect, solemn and gigantic, standing with folded arms in the stern of a slowly moving golden boat.

A long "Oh-h-h" burst from the spectators: the stand creaked and shook with their blissful trepidations. "Oh-h-h," Charity gasped: she had forgotten where she was, had at last forgotten even Harney's nearness. She seemed to have been caught up into the stars. . . .

The picture vanished and darkness came down. In the obscurity she felt her head clasped by two hands: her face was drawn backward, and Harney's lips were pressed on hers. With sudden vehemence he wound his arms about her, holding her head against his breast while she gave him back his kisses. An unknown Harney had revealed himself, a Harney who dominated her and yet over whom she felt herself possessed of a new mysterious power.

But the crowd was beginning to move, and he had to release her. "Come," he said in a confused voice. He scrambled over the side of the stand, and holding up his arm caught her as she sprang to the ground. He passed his arm about her waist, steadying her against the descending rush of people; and she clung to him, speechless, exultant, as if all the crowding and confusion about them were a mere vain stirring of the air.

"Come," he repeated, "we must try to make the trolley." He drew her along, and she followed, still in her dream. They walked as if they were one, so isolated in ecstasy that the people jostling them on every side seemed impalpable. But when they reached the terminus the illuminated trolley was already clanging on its way, its platforms black with passengers. The cars waiting behind it were as thickly packed; and the throng about the terminus was so dense that it seemed hopeless to struggle for a place.

"Last trip up the Lake," a megaphone bellowed from the wharf; and the lights of the little steamboat came dancing out of the darkness.

"No use waiting here; shall we run up the Lake?" Harney suggested.

They pushed their way back to the edge of the water just as the gang-plank was lowered from the white side of the boat. The electric light at the end of the wharf flashed full on the descending passengers, and among them Charity caught sight of Julia Hawes, her white feather askew, and the face under it flushed with coarse laughter. As she stepped from the gang-plank she stopped short, her dark-ringed eyes darting malice.

"Hullo, Charity Royall!" she called out; and then, looking back over her shoulder: "Didn't I tell you it was a family party? Here's grandpa's little darling come to take him home!"

A snigger ran through the group; and then, towering above them, and steadying himself by the hand-rail in a desperate effort at erectness, Mr. Royall stepped stiffly ashore. Like the young men of the party, he wore a secret society emblem in the buttonhole of his black frock-coat. His head was covered by a new Panama hat, and his narrow black tie, half undone, dangled down on his rumpled shirt-front. His face, a livid brown, with red blotches of anger and lips sunken in like an old man's, was a lamentable ruin in the searching glare.

He was just behind Julia Hawes, and had one hand on her arm; but as he left the gang-plank he freed himself, and moved a step or two away from his companions. He had seen Charity at once, and his glance passed slowly from her to Harney, whose arm was still about her. He stood staring at them, and trying to master the senile quiver of his lips; then he drew himself up with the tremulous majesty of drunkenness, and stretched out his arm.

"You whore—you damn—bare-headed whore, you!" he enunciated slowly.

There was a scream of tipsy laughter from the party, and Charity involuntarily put her hands to her head. She remembered that her hat had fallen from her lap when she jumped up to leave the stand; and suddenly she had a vision of herself, hatless, dishevelled, with a man's arm about her, confronting that drunken crew, headed by her guardian's pitiable figure. The picture filled her with shame. She had known since childhood about Mr. Royall's "habits": had seen him, as she went up to bed, sitting morosely in his office, a bottle at his elbow; or coming home, heavy and quarrelsome, from his business expeditions to Hepburn or Springfield; but the idea of his associating himself publicly with a band of disreputable girls and bar-room loafers was new and dreadful to her.

"Oh——" she said in a gasp of misery; and releasing herself from Harney's arm she went straight up to Mr. Royall.

"You come home with me—you come right home with me," she said in a low stern voice, as if she had not heard his apostrophe; and one of the girls called out: "Say, how many fellers does she want?"

There was another laugh, followed by a pause of curiosity, during which Mr. Royall continued to glare at Charity. At length his twitching lips parted. "I said, 'You—damn—whore!'" he repeated with precision, steadying himself on Julia's shoulder.

Laughs and jeers were beginning to spring up from the circle of people beyond their group; and a voice called out from the gangway: "Now, then, step lively there—all *aboard!*" The pressure of approaching and departing passengers forced the actors in the rapid scene apart, and pushed them back into the throng. Charity found herself clinging to Harney's arm and sobbing desperately. Mr. Royall had disappeared, and in the distance she heard the receding sound of Julia's laugh.

The boat, laden to the taffrail, was puffing away on her last trip.

XI

At two o'clock in the morning the freckled boy from Creston stopped his sleepy horse at the door of the red house, and Charity got out. Harney had taken leave of her at Creston River, charging the boy to drive her home. Her mind was still in a fog of misery, and she did not remember very clearly what had happened, or what they had said to each other, during the interminable interval since their departure from Nettleton; but the secretive instinct of the animal in pain was so strong in her that she had a sense of relief when Harney got out and she drove on alone.

The full moon hung over North Dormer, whitening the mist that filled the hollows between the hills and floated transparently above the fields. Charity stood a moment at the gate, looking out into the waning night. She watched the boy drive off, his horse's head wagging heavily to and fro; then she went around to the kitchen door and felt under the mat for the key. She found it, unlocked the door and went in. The kitchen was dark, but she discovered a box of matches, lit a candle and went upstairs. Mr. Royall's door, opposite hers, stood open on his unlit room; evidently he had not come back. She went into her room, bolted her door and began slowly to untie the ribbon about her waist, and to take off her dress. Under the bed she saw the paper bag in which she had hidden her new hat from inquisitive eyes. . . .

She lay for a long time sleepless on her bed, staring up at the moonlight on the low ceiling; dawn was in the sky when she fell asleep, and when she woke the sun was on her face.

She dressed and went down to the kitchen. Verena was there alone: she glanced at Charity tranquilly, with her old deaf-looking eyes. There was no sign of Mr. Royall about the house and the hours passed without his reappearing. Charity had gone up to her room, and sat there listlessly, her hands on her lap. Puffs of sultry air fanned her dimity window curtains and flies buzzed stiflingly against the bluish panes.

At one o'clock Verena hobbled up to see if she were not coming down to dinner; but she shook her head, and the old woman went away, saying: "I'll cover up, then."

The sun turned and left her room, and Charity seated herself in the window, gazing down the village street through the half-opened shutters. Not a thought was in her mind; it was just a dark whirlpool of crowding images; and she watched the people passing along the street, Dan Targatt's team hauling a load of pine-trunks down to Hepburn, the sexton's old white horse grazing on the bank across the way, as if she looked at these familiar sights from the other side of the grave.

She was roused from her apathy by seeing Ally Hawes come out of the Frys' gate and walk slowly toward the red house with her uneven limping step. At the sight Charity recovered her severed contact with reality. She divined that Ally was coming to hear about her day: no one else was in on the secret of the trip to Nettleton, and it had flattered Ally profoundly to be allowed to know of it.

At the thought of having to see her, of having to meet her eyes and answer or evade her questions, the whole horror of the previous night's adventure rushed back upon Charity. What had been a feverish nightmare became a cold and unescapable fact. Poor Ally, at that moment, represented North Dormer, with all its mean curiosities, its furtive malice, its sham unconsciousness of evil. Charity knew that, although all relations with Julia were supposed to be severed, the tender-hearted Ally still secretly communicated with her; and no doubt Julia would exult in the chance of retailing the scandal of the wharf. The story, exaggerated and distorted, was probably already on its way to North Dormer.

Ally's dragging pace had not carried her far from the Frys' gate when she was stopped by old Mrs. Sollas, who was a great talker, and spoke very slowly because she had never been able to get used to her new teeth from Hepburn. Still, even this respite would not last long; in another ten minutes Ally would be at the door, and Charity would hear her greeting Verena in the kitchen, and then calling up from the foot of the stairs.

Suddenly it became clear that flight, and instant flight, was the only thing conceivable. The longing to escape, to get away from familiar faces, from places where she was known, had always been strong in her in moments of distress. She had a childish belief in the miraculous power of strange scenes and new faces to transform her life and wipe out bitter memories. But such impulses were mere fleeting whims compared to the cold resolve which now possessed her. She felt she could not remain an hour longer under the roof of the man who had publicly dishonoured her, and face to face with the people who would presently be gloating over all the details of her humiliation.

Her passing pity for Mr. Royall had been swallowed up in loathing: everything in her recoiled from the disgraceful spectacle of the drunken old man apostrophizing her in the presence of a band of loafers and street-walkers. Suddenly, vividly, she relived again the horrible moment when he had tried to force himself into her room, and what she had before supposed to be a mad aberration now appeared to her as a vulgar incident in a debauched and degraded life.

While these thoughts were hurrying through her she had dragged out her old canvas school-bag, and was thrusting into it a few articles of clothing and the little packet of letters she had received from Harney. From under her pincushion she took the library key, and laid it in full view; then she felt at the back of a drawer for the blue brooch that Harney had given her. She would not have dared to wear it openly at North Dormer, but now she fastened it on her bosom as if it were a talisman to protect her in her flight. These preparations had taken but a few minutes, and when they were finished Ally Hawes was still at the Frys' corner talking to old Mrs. Sollas. . . .

She had said to herself, as she always said in moments of revolt: "I'll go to the Mountain—I'll go back to my own folks." She had never really meant it before; but now, as she considered her case, no other course seemed open. She had never learned any trade that would have given her independence in a strange place, and she knew no one in the big towns of the valley, where she might have hoped to find employment. Miss Hatchard was still away; but even had she been at North Dormer she was the last person to whom Charity would have turned, since one of the motives urging her to flight was the wish not to see Lucius Harney. Travelling back from Nettleton, in the crowded brightly-lit train, all exchange of confidence between them had been impossible; but during their drive from Hepburn to Creston River she had gathered from Harney's snatches of consolatory talk—again hampered by the freckled boy's presence—that he intended to see her the next day. At the moment she had found a vague comfort in the assurance; but in the desolate lucidity of the hours that followed she had come to see the impossibility of meeting him again. Her dream of comradeship was over; and the scene on the wharf—vile and disgraceful as it had been—had after all shed the light of truth on her minute of madness. It was as if her guardian's words had stripped her bare in the face of the grinning crowd and proclaimed to the world the secret admonitions of her conscience.

She did not think these things out clearly; she simply followed the blind propulsion of her wretchedness. She did not want, ever again, to see anyone she had known; above all, she did not want to see Harney. . . .

She climbed the hill-path behind the house and struck through the woods by a short-cut leading to the Creston road. A lead-coloured sky hung heavily over the fields, and in the forest the motionless air was stifling; but she pushed on, impatient to reach the road which was the shortest way to the Mountain.

To do so, she had to follow the Creston road for a mile or two, and go within half a mile of the village; and she walked quickly, fearing to meet Harney. But there was no sign of him, and she had almost reached the branch road when she saw the flanks of a large white tent projecting through the trees by the roadside. She supposed that it sheltered a travelling circus which had come there for the Fourth; but as she drew nearer she saw, over the folded-back flap, a large sign bearing the inscription, "Gospel Tent." The interior seemed to be empty; but a young man in a black alpaca coat, his lank hair parted over a round white face, stepped from under the flap and advanced toward her with a smile.

"Sister, your Saviour knows everything. Won't you come in and lay your guilt before Him?" he asked insinuatingly, putting his hand on her arm.

Charity started back and flushed. For a moment she thought the evangelist must have heard a report of the scene at Nettleton; then she saw the absurdity of the supposition.

"I on'y wish't I had any to lay!" she retorted, with one of her fierce flashes of self-derision; and the young man murmured, aghast: "Oh, Sister, don't speak blasphemy. . . ."

But she had jerked her arm out of his hold, and was running up the branch road, trembling with the fear of meeting a familiar face. Presently she was out of sight of the village, and climbing into the heart of the forest. She could not hope to do the fifteen miles to the Mountain that afternoon; but she knew of a place half-way to Hamblin where she could sleep, and where no one would think of looking for her. It was a little deserted house on a slope in one of the lonely rifts of the hills. She had seen it once, years before, when she had gone on a nutting expedition to the grove of walnuts below it. The party had taken refuge in the house from a sudden mountain storm, and she remembered that Ben Sollas, who liked frightening girls, had told them that it was said to be haunted.

She was growing faint and tired, for she had eaten nothing since morning, and was not used to walking so far. Her head felt light and she sat down for a moment by the roadside. As she sat there she heard the click of a bicycle-bell, and started up to plunge back into the forest; but before she could move the bicycle had swept around the curve of the road, and Harney, jumping off, was approaching her with outstretched arms.

"Charity! What on earth are you doing here?"

She stared as if he were a vision, so startled by the unexpectedness of his being there that no words came to her.

"Where were you going? Had you forgotten that I was coming?" he continued, trying to draw her to him; but she shrank from his embrace.

"I was going away—I don't want to see you—I want you should leave me alone," she broke out wildly.

He looked at her and his face grew grave, as though the shadow of a premonition brushed it.

"Going away—from me, Charity?"

"From everybody. I want you should leave me."

He stood glancing doubtfully up and down the lonely forest road that stretched away into sun-flecked distances.

"Where were you going?"

"Home."

"Home—this way?"

She threw her head back defiantly. "To my home—up yonder: to the Mountain."

As she spoke she became aware of a change in his face. He was no longer listening to her, he was only looking at her, with the passionate absorbed expression she had seen in his eyes after they had kissed on the stand at Nettleton. He was the new Harney again, the Harney abruptly revealed in that embrace, who seemed so penetrated with the joy of her presence that he was utterly careless of what she was thinking or feeling.

He caught her hands with a laugh. "How do you suppose I found you?" he said gaily. He drew out the little packet of his letters and flourished them before her bewildered eyes.

"You dropped them, you imprudent young person—dropped them in the middle of the road, not far from here; and the young man who is running the Gospel tent picked them up just as I was riding by." He drew back, holding her at arm's length, and scrutinizing her troubled face with the minute searching gaze of his short-sighted eyes.

"Did you really think you could run away from me? You see you weren't meant to," he said; and before she could answer he had kissed her again, not vehemently, but tenderly, almost fraternally, as if he had guessed her confused pain, and wanted her to know he understood it. He wound his fingers through hers.

"Come—let's walk a little. I want to talk to you. There's so much to say!"

He spoke with a boy's gaiety, carelessly and confidently, as if nothing had happened that could shame or embarrass them; and for a moment, in the sudden relief of her release from lonely pain, she felt herself yielding to his mood. But he had turned, and was drawing her back along the road by which she had come. She stiffened herself and stopped short.

"I won't go back," she said.

They looked at each other a moment in silence; then he answered gently: "Very well: let's go the other way, then."

She remained motionless, gazing silently at the ground, and he went on: "Isn't there a house up here somewhere—a little abandoned house—you meant to show me some day?" Still she made no answer, and he continued, in the same tone of tender reassurance: "Let us go there now and sit down and talk quietly." He took one of the hands that hung by her side and pressed his lips to the palm. "Do you suppose I'm going to let you send me away? Do you suppose I don't understand?"

———

The little old house—its wooden walls sun-bleached to a ghostly grey—stood in an orchard above the road. The garden palings had fallen, but the broken gate dangled between its posts, and the path to the house was marked by rose-bushes run wild and hanging their small pale blossoms above the crowding grasses. Slender pilasters and an intricate fan-light framed the opening where the door had hung; and the door itself lay rotting in the grass, with an old apple-tree fallen across it.

Inside, also, wind and weather had blanched everything to the same wan silvery tint: the house was as dry and pure as the interior of a long-empty shell. But it must have been exceptionally well built, for the little rooms had kept something of their human aspect: the wooden mantels with their neat classic ornaments were in place, and the corners of one ceiling retained a light film of plaster tracery.

Harney had found an old bench at the back door and dragged it into the house. Charity sat on it, leaning her head against the wall in a state of drowsy lassitude. He had guessed that she was hungry and thirsty, and had brought her some tablets of chocolate from his bicycle-bag, and filled his drinking-cup from a spring in the orchard; and now he sat at her feet, smoking a cigarette, and looking up at her without speaking. Outside, the afternoon shadows were lengthening across the grass, and through the empty window-frame that faced her she saw the Mountain thrusting its dark mass against a sultry sunset. It was time to go.

She stood up, and he sprang to his feet also, and passed his arm through hers with an air of authority. "Now, Charity, you're coming back with me."

She looked at him and shook her head. "I ain't ever going back. You don't know."

"What don't I know?" She was silent, and he continued: "What happened on the wharf was horrible—it's natural you should feel as you do. But it doesn't make any real difference: you can't be hurt by such things. You must try to forget. And you must try to understand that men . . . men sometimes . . ."

"I know about men. That's why."

He coloured a little at the retort, as though it had touched him in a way she did not suspect.

"Well, then . . . you must know one has to make allowances. . . . He'd been drinking. . . ."

"I know all that, too. I've seen him so before. But he wouldn't have dared speak to me that way if he hadn't . . ."

"Hadn't what? What do you mean?"

"Hadn't wanted me to be like those other girls. . . ." She lowered her voice and looked away from him. "So's 't he wouldn't have to go out. . . ."

Harney stared at her. For a moment he did not seem to seize her meaning; then his face grew dark. "The damned hound! The villainous low hound!" His wrath blazed up, crimsoning him to the temples. "I never dreamed—good God, it's too vile," he broke off, as if his thoughts recoiled from the discovery.

"I won't never go back there," she repeated doggedly.

"No——" he assented.

There was a long interval of silence, during which she imagined that he was searching her face for more light on what she had revealed to him; and a flush of shame swept over her.

"I know the way you must feel about me," she broke out, ". . . telling you such things. . . ."

But once more, as she spoke, she became aware that he was no longer listening. He came close and caught her to him as if he were snatching her from some imminent peril: his impetuous eyes were in hers, and she could feel the hard beat of his heart as he held her against it.

"Kiss me again—like last night," he said, pushing her hair back as if to draw her whole face up into his kiss.

XII

One afternoon toward the end of August a group of girls sat in a room at Miss Hatchard's in a gay confusion of flags, turkey-red, blue and white paper muslin, harvest sheaves and illuminated scrolls.

North Dormer was preparing for its Old Home Week. That form of sentimental decentralization was still in its early stages, and, precedents being few, and the desire to set an example contagious, the matter had become a subject of prolonged and passionate discussion under Miss Hatchard's roof. The incentive to the celebration had come rather from those who had left North

Dormer than from those who had been obliged to stay there, and there was some difficulty in rousing the village to the proper state of enthusiasm. But Miss Hatchard's pale prim drawing-room was the centre of constant comings and goings from Hepburn, Nettleton, Springfield and even more distant cities; and whenever a visitor arrived he was led across the hall, and treated to a glimpse of the group of girls deep in their pretty preparations.

"All the old names . . . all the old names. . . ." Miss Hatchard would be heard, tapping across the hall on her crutches. "Targatt . . . Sollas . . . Fry: this is Miss Orma Fry sewing the stars on the drapery for the organ-loft. Don't move, girls . . . and this is Miss Ally Hawes, our cleverest needle-woman . . . and Miss Charity Royall making our garlands of evergreen. . . . I like the idea of its all being homemade, don't you? We haven't had to call in any foreign talent: my young cousin Lucius Harney, the architect—you know he's up here preparing a book on Colonial houses—he's taken the whole thing in hand so cleverly; but you must come and see his sketch for the stage we're going to put up in the Town Hall."

One of the first results of the Old Home Week agitation had, in fact, been the reappearance of Lucius Harney in the village street. He had been vaguely spoken of as being not far off, but for some weeks past no one had seen him at North Dormer, and there was a recent report of his having left Creston River, where he was said to have been staying, and gone away from the neighbourhood for good. Soon after Miss Hatchard's return, however, he came back to his old quarters in her house, and began to take a leading part in the planning of the festivities. He threw himself into the idea with extraordinary good-humour, and was so prodigal of sketches, and so inexhaustible in devices, that he gave an immediate impetus to the rather languid movement, and infected the whole village with his enthusiasm.

"Lucius has such a feeling for the past that he has roused us all to a sense of our privileges," Miss Hatchard would say, lingering on the last word, which was a favourite one. And before leading her visitor back to the drawing-room she would repeat, for the hundredth time, that she supposed he thought it very bold of little North Dormer to start up and have a Home Week of its own, when so many bigger places hadn't thought of it yet; but that, after all, Associations counted more than the size of the population, didn't they? And of course North Dormer was so full of Associations . . . historic, literary (here a filial sigh for Honorius) and ecclesiastical . . . he knew about the old pewter communion service imported from England in 1769, she supposed? And it was so important, in a wealthy materialistic age, to set the example of reverting to the old ideals, the family and the homestead, and so on. This peroration usually carried her half-way back across the hall, leaving the girls to return to their interrupted activities.

The day on which Charity Royall was weaving hemlock garlands for the procession was the last before the celebration. When Miss Hatchard called upon the North Dormer maidenhood to collaborate in the festal preparations Charity had at first held aloof; but it had been made clear to her that her non-appearance might excite conjecture, and, reluctantly, she had joined the other workers. The girls, at first shy and embarrassed, and puzzled as to the exact nature of the projected commemoration, had soon become interested in the amusing details of their task, and excited by the notice they received. They would not for the world have missed their afternoons at Miss Hatchard's, and, while they cut out and sewed and draped and pasted, their tongues kept up such an accompaniment to the sewing-machine that Charity's silence sheltered itself unperceived under their chatter.

In spirit she was still almost unconscious of the pleasant stir about her. Since her return to the red house, on the evening of the day when Harney had overtaken her on her way to the Mountain, she had lived at North Dormer as if she were suspended in the void. She had come back there because Harney, after appearing to agree to the impossibility of her doing so, had ended by persuading her that any other course would be madness. She had nothing further to fear from Mr. Royall. Of this she had declared herself sure, though she had failed to add, in his exoneration, that he had twice offered to make her his wife. Her hatred of him made it impossible, at the moment, for her to say anything that might partly excuse him in Harney's eyes.

Harney, however, once satisfied of her security, had found plenty of reasons for urging her to return. The first, and the most unanswerable, was that she had nowhere else to go. But the one on which he laid the greatest stress was that flight would be equivalent to avowal. If—as was almost inevitable—rumours of the scandalous scene at Nettleton should reach North Dormer, how else would her disappearance be interpreted? Her guardian had publicly taken away her character, and she immediately vanished from his house. Seekers after motives could hardly fail to draw an unkind conclusion. But if she came back at once, and was seen leading her usual life, the incident was reduced to its true proportions, as the outbreak of a drunken old man furious at being surprised in disreputable company. People would say that Mr. Royall had insulted his ward to justify himself, and the sordid tale would fall into its place in the chronicle of his obscure debaucheries.

Charity saw the force of the argument; but if she acquiesced it was not so much because of that as because it was Harney's wish. Since that evening in the deserted house she could imagine no reason for doing or not doing anything except the fact that Harney wished or did not wish it. All her tossing contradictory impulses were merged in a fatalistic acceptance of his will. It was not that she felt in him any ascendency of character—there were moments already when she knew she was the stronger—but that all the rest of life had become a mere cloudy rim about the central glory of their passion. Whenever she stopped thinking about that for a moment she felt as she sometimes did after lying on the grass and staring up too long at the sky; her eyes were so full of light that everything about her was a blur.

Each time that Miss Hatchard, in the course of her periodical incursions into the work-room, dropped an allusion to her young cousin, the architect, the effect was the same on Charity. The hemlock garland she was wearing fell to her knees and she sat in a kind of trance. It was so manifestly absurd that Miss Hatchard should talk of Harney in that familiar possessive way, as if she had any claim on him, or knew anything about him. She, Charity Royall, was the only being on earth who really knew him, knew him from the soles of his feet to the rumpled crest of his hair, knew the shifting lights in his eyes, and the inflexions of his voice, and the things he liked and disliked, and everything there was to know about him, as minutely and yet unconsciously as a child knows the walls of the room it wakes up in every morning. It was this fact, which nobody about her guessed, or would have understood, that made her life something apart and inviolable, as if nothing had any power to hurt or disturb her as long as her secret was safe.

The room in which the girls sat was the one which had been Harney's bedroom. He had been sent upstairs, to make room for the Home Week workers; but the furniture had not been moved, and as Charity sat there she had perpetually before her the vision she had looked in on from the midnight garden. The table at which Harney had sat was the one about which the girls were gathered; and her own seat was near the bed on which she had seen him lying. Sometimes, when the others were not looking, she bent over as if to pick up something, and laid her cheek for a moment against the pillow.

Toward sunset the girls disbanded. Their work was done, and the next morning at daylight the draperies and garlands were to be nailed up, and the illuminated scrolls put in place in the Town Hall. The first guests were to drive over from Hepburn in time for the midday banquet under a tent in Miss Hatchard's field; and after that the ceremonies were to begin. Miss Hatchard, pale with fatigue and excitement, thanked her young assistants, and stood in the porch, leaning on her crutches and waving a farewell as she watched them troop away down the street.

Charity had slipped off among the first; but at the gate she heard Ally Hawes calling after her, and reluctantly turned.

"Will you come over now and try on your dress?" Ally asked, looking at her with wistful admiration. "I want to be sure the sleeves don't ruck up the same as they did yesterday."

Charity gazed at her with dazzled eyes. "Oh, it's lovely," she said, and hastened away without listening to Ally's protest. She wanted her dress to be as pretty as the other girls'—wanted it, in fact, to outshine the rest, since she was to take part in the "exercises"—but she had no time just then to fix her mind on such matters. . . .

She sped up the street to the library, of which she had the key about her neck. From the passage at the back she dragged forth a bicycle, and guided it to the edge of the street. She looked about to see if any of the girls were approaching; but they had drifted away together toward the Town Hall, and she sprang into the saddle and turned toward the Creston road. There was an almost continual descent to Creston, and with her feet against the pedals she floated through the still evening air like one of the hawks she had often watched slanting downward on motionless wings. Twenty minutes from the time when she had left Miss Hatchard's door she was turning up the wood-road on which Harney had overtaken her on the day of her flight; and a few minutes afterward she had jumped from her bicycle at the gate of the deserted house.

In the gold-powdered sunset it looked more than ever like some frail shell dried and washed by many seasons; but at the back, whither Charity advanced, drawing her bicycle after her, there were signs of recent habitation. A rough door made of boards hung in the kitchen doorway, and pushing it open she entered a room furnished in primitive camping fashion. In the window was a table, also made of boards, with an earthenware jar holding a big bunch of wild asters. Two canvas chairs stood near by, and in one corner was a mattress with a Mexican blanket over it.

The room was empty, and leaning her bicycle against the house Charity clambered up the slope and sat down on a rock under an old apple-tree. The air was perfectly still, and from where she sat she would be able to hear the tinkle of a bicycle-bell a long way down the road. . . .

She was always glad when she got to the little house before Harney. She liked to have time to take in every detail of its secret sweetness—the shadows of the apple-trees swaying on the grass, the old walnuts rounding their domes below the road, the meadows sloping westward in the afternoon light—before his first kiss blotted it all out. Everything unrelated to the hours spent in that tranquil place was as faint as the remembrance of a dream. The only reality was the wondrous unfolding of her new self, the reaching out to the light of all her contracted tendrils. She had lived all her life among people whose sensibilities seemed to have withered for lack of use; and more wonderful, at first, than Harney's endearments were the words that were a part of them. She had always thought of love as something confused and furtive, and he made it as bright and open as the summer air.

On the morrow of the day when she had shown him the way to the deserted house he had packed up and left Creston River for Boston; but at the first station he had jumped off the train with a hand-bag and scrambled up into the hills. For two golden rainless August weeks he had camped in the house, getting eggs and milk from the solitary farm in the valley, where no one knew him, and doing his cooking over a spirit-lamp. He got up every day with the sun, took a plunge in a brown pool he knew of, and spent long hours lying in the scented hemlock-woods above the house, or wandering along the yoke of the Eagle Ridge, far above the misty blue valleys that swept away east and west between the endless hills. And in the afternoon Charity came to him.

With part of what was left of her savings she had hired a bicycle for a month, and every day after dinner, as soon as her guardian started to his office, she hurried to the library, got out her bicycle, and flew down the Creston road. She knew that Mr. Royall, like everyone else in North Dormer, was perfectly aware of her acquisition: possibly he, as well as the rest of the village, knew what use she made of it. She did not care: she felt him to be so powerless that if he had questioned her she would probably have told him the truth. But they had never spoken to each other since the night on the wharf at Nettleton. He had returned to North Dormer only on the third day after that encounter, arriving just as Charity and Verena were sitting down to supper. He had drawn up his chair, taken his napkin from the side-board drawer, pulled it out of its ring, and seated himself as unconcernedly as if he had come in from his usual afternoon session at Carrick Fry's; and the long habit of the household made it seem almost natural that Charity should not so much as raise her eyes when he entered. She had simply let him understand that her silence was not accidental by leaving the table while he was still eating, and going up without a word to shut herself into her room. After that he formed the habit of talking loudly and genially to Verena whenever Charity was in the room; but otherwise there was no apparent change in their relations.

She did not think connectedly of these things while she sat waiting for Harney, but they remained in her mind as a sullen background against which her short hours with him flamed out like forest fires. Nothing else mattered, neither the good nor the bad, or what might have seemed so before she knew him. He had caught her up and carried her away into a new world, from which, at stated hours, the ghost of her came back to perform certain customary acts, but all so thinly and insubstantially that she sometimes wondered that the people she went about among could see her. . . .

Behind the swarthy Mountain the sun had gone down in waveless gold. From a pasture up the slope a tinkle of cow-bells sounded; a puff of smoke hung over the farm in the valley, trailed on the pure air and was gone. For a few minutes, in the clear light that is all shadow, fields and woods were outlined with an unreal precision; then the twilight blotted them out, and the little house turned grey and spectral under its wizened apple-branches.

Charity's heart contracted. The first fall of night after a day of radiance often gave her a sense of hidden menace: it was like looking out over the world as it would be when love had gone from it. She wondered if some day she would sit in that same place and watch in vain for her lover. . . .

His bicycle-bell sounded down the lane, and in a minute she was at the gate and his eyes were laughing in hers. They walked back through the long grass, and pushed open the door behind the house. The room at first seemed quite dark and they had to grope their way in hand in hand. Through the window-frame the sky looked light by contrast, and above the black mass of asters in the earthern jar one white star glimmered like a moth.

"There was such a lot to do at the last minute," Harney was explaining, "and I had to drive down to Creston to meet someone who has come to stay with my cousin for the show."

He had his arms about her, and his kisses were in her hair and on her lips. Under his touch things deep down in her struggled to the light and sprang up like flowers in sunshine. She twisted her fingers into his, and they sat down side by side on the improvised couch. She hardly heard his excuses for being late: in his absence a thousand doubts tormented her, but as soon as he appeared she ceased to wonder where he had come from, what had delayed him, who had kept him from her. It seemed as if the places he had been in, and the people he had been with, must cease to exist when he left them, just as her own life was suspended in his absence.

He continued, now, to talk to her volubly and gaily, deploring his lateness, grumbling at the demands on his time, and good-humouredly mimicking Miss Hatchard's benevolent agitation. "She hurried off Miles to ask Mr. Royall to speak at the Town Hall to-morrow: I didn't know till it was done." Charity was silent, and he added: "After all, perhaps it's just as well. No one else could have done it."

Charity made no answer: she did not care what part her guardian played in the morrow's ceremonies. Like all the other figures peopling her meagre world he had grown nonexistent to her. She had even put off hating him.

"Tomorrow I shall only see you from far off," Harney continued. "But in the evening there'll be the dance in the Town Hall. Do you want me to promise not to dance with any other girl?"

Any other girl? Were there any others? She had forgotten even that peril, so enclosed did he and she seem in their secret world. Her heart gave a frightened jerk.

"Yes, promise."

He laughed and took her in his arms. "You goose—not even if they're hideous?"

He pushed the hair from her forehead, bending her face back, as his way was, and leaning over so that his head loomed black between her eyes and the paleness of the sky, in which the white star floated . . .

Side by side they sped back along dark wood-road to the village. A late moon was rising, full orbed and fiery, turning the mountain ranges from fluid grey to a massive blackness, and making the upper sky so light that the stars looked as faint as their own reflections in water. At the edge of the wood, half a mile from North Dormer, Harney jumped from his bicycle, took Charity in his arms for a last kiss, and then waited while she went on alone.

They were later than usual, and instead of taking the bicycle to the library she propped it against the back of the wood-shed and entered the kitchen of the red house. Verena sat there alone; when Charity came in she looked at her with mild impenetrable eyes and then took a plate and a glass of milk from the shelf and set them silently on the table. Charity nodded her thanks, and sitting down fell hungrily upon her piece of pie and emptied the glass. Her face burned with her quick flight through the night, and her eyes were dazzled by the twinkle of the kitchen lamp. She felt like a night-bird suddenly caught and caged.

"He ain't come back since supper," Verena said. "He's down to the Hall."

Charity took no notice. Her soul was still winging through the forest. She washed her plate and tumbler, and then felt her way up the dark stairs. When she opened her door a wonder arrested her. Before going out she had closed her shutters against the afternoon heat, but they had swung partly open, and a bar of moonlight, crossing the room, rested on her bed and showed a dress of China silk laid out on it in virgin whiteness. Charity had spent more than she could afford on the dress, which was to surpass those of all the other girls; she had wanted to let North Dormer see that she was worthy of Harney's admiration. Above the dress, folded on the pillow, was the white veil which the young women who took part in the exercises were to wear under a wreath of asters; and beside the veil a pair of slim white satin shoes that Ally had produced from an old trunk in which she stored mysterious treasures.

Charity stood gazing at all the outspread whiteness. It recalled a vision that had come to her in the night after her first meeting with Harney. She no longer had such visions . . . warmer splendours had displaced them . . . but it was stupid of Ally to have paraded all those white things on her bed, exactly as Hattie Targatt's wedding dress from Springfield had been spread out for the neighbours to see when she married Tom Fry. . . .

Charity took up the satin shoes and looked at them curiously. By day, no doubt, they would appear a little worn, but in the moonlight they seemed carved of ivory. She sat down on the floor to try them on, and they fitted her perfectly, though when she stood up she lurched a little on the high heels. She looked down at her feet, which the graceful mould of the slippers had marvellously arched and narrowed. She had never seen such shoes before, even in the shop-windows at Nettleton . . . never, except . . . yes, once, she had noticed a pair of the same shape on Annabel Balch.

A blush of mortification swept over her. Ally sometimes sewed for Miss Balch when that brilliant being descended on North Dormer, and no doubt she picked up presents of cast-off clothing: the treasures in the mysterious trunk all came from the people she worked for. There could be no doubt that the white slippers were Annabel Balch's. . . .

As she stood there, staring down moodily at her feet, she heard the triple click-click-click of a bicycle-bell under her window. It was Harney's secret signal as he passed on his way home. She stumbled to the window on her high heels, flung open the shutters and leaned out. He waved to her and sped by, his black shadow dancing merrily ahead of him down the empty moonlit road; and she leaned there watching him till he vanished under the Hatchard spruces.

XIII

The Town Hall was crowded and exceedingly hot. As Charity marched into it, third in the white muslin file headed by Orma Fry, she was conscious mainly of the brilliant effect of the wreathed columns framing the green-carpeted stage toward which she was moving and of the unfamiliar faces turning from the front rows to watch the advance of the procession.

But it was all a bewildering blur of eyes and colours till she found herself standing at the back of the stage, her great bunch of asters and goldenrod held well in front of her, and answering the nervous glance of Lambert Sollas, the organist from Mr. Miles's church, who had come up from Nettleton to play the harmonium, and sat behind it, running his conductor's eye over the fluttered girls.

A moment later Mr. Miles, pink and twinkling, emerged from the background, as if buoyed up on his broad white gown, and briskly dominated the bowed heads in the front rows. He prayed energetically and briefly and then retired, and a fierce nod from Lambert Sollas warned the girls they were to follow at once with "Home, Sweet Home."[19] It was a joy to Charity to sing: it seemed as though, for the first time, her secret rapture might burst from her and flash its defiance at the world. All the glow in her blood, the breath of the summer earth, the rustle of the forest, the fresh call of birds at sunrise, and the brooding midday languors, seemed to pass into her untrained voice, lifted and led by the sustaining chorus.

And then suddenly the song was over, and after an uncertain pause, during which Miss Hatchard's pearl-grey gloves started a furtive signalling down the hall, Mr. Royall, emerging in turn, ascended the steps of the stage and appeared behind the flower-wreathed desk. He passed close to Charity, and she noticed that his gravely set face wore the look of majesty that used to awe and fascinate her childhood. His frock-coat had been carefully brushed and ironed, and the ends of his narrow black tie were so nearly even that the tying must have cost him a protracted struggle. His appearance struck her all the more because it was the first time she had looked him full in the face since the night at Nettleton, and nothing in his grave and impressive demeanour revealed a trace of the lamentable figure on the wharf.

He stood a moment behind the desk, resting his finger-tips against it, and bending slightly toward his audience; then he straightened himself and began.

At first she paid no heed to what he was saying: only fragments of sentences, sonorous quotations, allusions to illustrious men, including the obligatory tribute to Honorius Hatchard, drifted past her inattentive ears. She was trying to discover Harney among the notable people in the front row; but he was nowhere near Miss Hatchard, who, crowned by a pearl-grey hat that matched her gloves, sat just below the desk, supported by Mrs. Miles and an important-looking unknown lady. Charity was near one end of the stage, and from where she sat the other end of the first row of seats was cut off by the screen of foliage masking the harmonium. The effort to see Harney around the corner of the screen, or through its interstices, made her unconscious of everything else; but the effort was unsuccessful, and gradually she found her attention arrested by her guardian's discourse.

She had never heard him speak in public before, but she was familiar with the rolling music of his voice when he read aloud, or held forth to the selectmen about the stove at Carrick Fry's. Today his inflections were richer and graver than she had ever known them: he spoke slowly, with pauses that seemed to invite his hearers to silent participation in his thought; and Charity perceived a light of response in their faces.

He was nearing the end of his address . . . "Most of you," he said, "most of you who have returned here today, to take contact with this little place for a brief hour, have come only on a pious pilgrimage, and will go back presently to busy cities and lives full of larger duties. But that is not the only way of coming back to North Dormer. Some of us, who went out from here in our youth . . . went out, like you, to busy cities and larger duties . . . have come back in another way—come back for good. I am one of those, as many of you know. . . ." He paused, and there was a sense of suspense in the listening hall. "My history is without interest, but it has its lesson: not so much for those of you who have already made your lives in other places, as for the young men who are perhaps planning even now to leave these quiet hills and go down into the struggle. Things they cannot foresee may send some of those young men back some day to the little township and the old homestead: they may come back for good. . . ." He looked about him, and repeated gravely: "For *good*. There's the point I want to make . . . North Dormer is a poor little place, almost lost in a mighty landscape: perhaps, by this time, it might have been a bigger place, and more in scale with the landscape, if those who had to come back had come with that feeling in their minds—that they wanted to come back for *good* . . . and not for bad . . . or just for indifference. . . .

"Gentlemen, let us look at things as they are. Some of us have come back to our native town because we'd failed to get on elsewhere. One way or other, things had gone wrong with us . . . what we'd dreamed of hadn't come true. But the fact that we had failed elsewhere is no reason why we should fail here. Our very experiments in larger places, even if they were unsuccessful, ought to have helped us to make North Dormer a larger place . . . and you young men who are preparing even now to follow the call of ambition, and turn your back on the old homes—well, let me say this to you, that if ever you do come back to them it's worth while to come back to them for their good. . . . And to do that, you must keep on loving them while you're away from them; and even if you come back against your will—and thinking it's all a bitter mistake of Fate or Providence—you must try to make the best of it, and to make the best of your old town; and after a while—well, ladies and gentlemen, I give you my recipe for what it's worth; after a while, I believe you'll be able to say, as I can say today: 'I'm glad I'm here.' Believe me, all of you, the best way to help the places we live in is to be glad we live there."

He stopped, and a murmur of emotion and surprise ran through the audience. It was not in the least what they had expected, but it moved them more than what they had expected would have moved them. "Hear, hear!" a voice cried out in the middle of the hall. An outburst of cheers caught up the cry, and as they subsided Charity heard Mr. Miles saying to someone near him: "That was a *man* talking——" He wiped his spectacles.

Mr. Royall had stepped back from the desk, and taken his seat in the row of chairs in front of the harmonium. A dapper white-haired gentleman—a distant Hatchard—succeeded him behind the goldenrod, and began to say beautiful things about the old oaken bucket, patient white-haired mothers, and where the boys used to go nutting . . . and Charity began again to search for Harney. . . .

Suddenly Mr. Royall pushed back his seat, and one of the maple branches in front of the harmonium collapsed with a crash. It uncovered the end of the first row and in one of the seats Charity saw Harney, and in the next a lady whose face was turned toward him, and almost hidden by the brim of her drooping hat. Charity did not need to see the face. She knew at a glance the slim figure, the fair hair heaped up under the hat-brim, the long pale wrinkled gloves with bracelets slipping over them. At the fall of the branch Miss Balch turned her head toward the stage, and in her pretty thin-lipped smile there lingered the reflection of something her neighbour had been whispering to her. . . .

Someone came forward to replace the fallen branch, and Miss Balch and Harney were once more hidden. But to Charity the vision of their two faces had blotted out everything. In a flash they had shown her the bare reality of her situation. Behind the frail screen of her lover's caresses was the whole inscrutable mystery of his life: his relations with other people—with other women—his opinions, his prejudices, his principles, the net of influences and interests and ambitions in which every man's life is entangled. Of all these she knew nothing, except what he had told her of his architectural aspirations. She had always dimly guessed him to be in touch with important people, involved in complicated relations—but she felt it all to be so far beyond her understanding that the whole subject hung like a luminous mist on the farthest verge of her thoughts. In the foreground, hiding all else, there was the glow of his presence, the light and shadow of his face, the way his short-sighted eyes, at her approach, widened and deepened as if to draw her down into them; and, above all, the flush of youth and tenderness in which his words enclosed her.

Now she saw him detached from her, drawn back into the unknown, and whispering to another girl things that provoked the same smile of mischievous complicity he had so often called to her own lips. The feeling possessing her was not one of jealousy: she was too sure of his love. It was rather a terror of the unknown, of all the mysterious attractions that must even now be dragging him away from her, and of her own powerlessness to contend with them.

She had given him all she had—but what was it compared to the other gifts life held for him? She understood now the case of girls like herself to whom this kind of thing happened. They gave all they had, but their all was not enough: it could not buy more than a few moments. . . .

The heat had grown suffocating—she felt it descend on her in smothering waves, and the faces in the crowded hall began to dance like the pictures flashed on the screen at Nettleton. For an instant Mr. Royall's countenance detached itself from the general blur. He had resumed his place in front of the harmonium, and sat close to her, his eyes on her face; and his look seemed to pierce to the very centre of her confused sensations. . . . A feeling of physical sickness rushed over her—and then deadly apprehension. The light of the fiery hours in the little house swept back on her in a glare of fear. . . .

She forced herself to look away from her guardian, and became aware that the oratory of the Hatchard cousin had ceased, and that Mr. Miles was again flapping his wings. Fragments of his peroration floated through her bewildered brain. . . ."A rich harvest of hallowed memories. . . . A sanctified hour to which, in moments of trial, your thoughts will prayerfully return. . . . And now, O Lord, let us humbly and fervently give thanks for this blessed day of reunion, here in the old home to which we have come back from so far. Preserve it to us, O Lord, in times to come, in all its homely sweetness—in the kindliness and wisdom of its old people, in the courage and industry of its young men, in the

piety and purity of this group of innocent girls——" He flapped a
white wing in their direction, and at the same moment Lambert
Sollas, with his fierce nod, struck the opening bars of "Auld Lang
Syne."[20] . . . Charity stared straight ahead of her and then, dropping her flowers, fell face downward at Mr. Royall's feet.

XIV

North Dormer's celebration naturally included the villages attached to its township, and the festivities were to radiate over the
whole group, from Dormer and the two Crestons to Hamblin, the
lonely hamlet on the north slope of the Mountain where the first
snow always fell. On the third day there were speeches and ceremonies at Creston and Creston River; on the fourth the principal
performers were to be driven in buck-boards to Dormer and
Hamblin.

It was on the fourth day that Charity returned for the first time
to the little house. She had not seen Harney alone since they had
parted at the wood's edge the night before the celebrations began.
In the interval she had passed through many moods, but for the
moment the terror which had seized her in the Town Hall had
faded to the edge of consciousness. She had fainted because the
hall was stiflingly hot, and because the speakers had gone on
and on. . . . Several other people had been affected by the heat,
and had had to leave before the exercises were over. There had
been thunder in the air all the afternoon, and everyone said afterward that something ought to have been done to ventilate the
hall. . . .

At the dance that evening—where she had gone reluctantly, and
only because she feared to stay away, she had sprung back into instant reassurance. As soon as she entered she had seen Harney
waiting for her, and he had come up with kind gay eyes, and
swept her off in a waltz. Her feet were full of music, and though
her only training had been with the village youths she had no difficulty in tuning her steps to his. As they circled about the floor all
her vain fears dropped from her, and she even forgot that she was
probably dancing in Annabel Balch's slippers.

When the waltz was over Harney, with a last hand-clasp, left

her to meet Miss Hatchard and Miss Balch, who were just entering. Charity had a moment of anguish as Miss Balch appeared;
but it did not last. The triumphant fact of her own greater beauty,
and of Harney's sense of it, swept her apprehensions aside. Miss
Balch, in an unbecoming dress, looked sallow and pinched,
and Charity fancied there was a worried expression in her pale-
lashed eyes. She took a seat near Miss Hatchard and it was
presently apparent that she did not mean to dance. Charity did
not dance often either. Harney explained to her that Miss
Hatchard had begged him to give each of the other girls a turn;
but he went through the form of asking Charity's permission each
time he led one out, and that gave her a sense of secret triumph
even completer than when she was whirling about the room with
him. . . .

    She was thinking of all this as she waited for him in the deserted
house. The late afternoon was sultry, and she had tossed aside her
hat and stretched herself at full length on the Mexican blanket because it was cooler indoors than under the trees. She lay with her
arms folded beneath her head, gazing out at the shaggy shoulder
of the Mountain. The sky behind it was full of the splintered glories of the descending sun, and before long she expected to hear
Harney's bicycle-bell in the lane. He had bicycled to Hamblin, instead of driving there with his cousin and her friends, so that he
might be able to make his escape earlier and stop on the way back
at the deserted house, which was on the road to Hamblin. They
had smiled together at the joke of hearing the crowded buck-
boards roll by on the return, while they lay close in their hiding
above the road. Such childish triumphs still gave her a sense of
reckless security.

    Nevertheless she had not wholly forgotten the vision of fear
that had opened before her in the Town Hall. The sense of last-
ingness was gone from her and every moment with Harney would
now be ringed with doubt.

    The Mountain was turning purple against a fiery sunset from
which it seemed to be divided by a knife-edge of quivering light;
and above this wall of flame the whole sky was a pure pale green,
like some cold mountain lake in shadow. Charity lay gazing up at
it, and watching for the first white star. . . .

Her eyes were still fixed on the upper reaches of the sky when she became aware that a shadow had flitted across the glory-flooded room: it must have been Harney passing the window against the sunset. . . . She half raised herself, and then dropped back on her folded arms. The combs had slipped from her hair, and it trailed in a rough dark rope across her breast. She lay quite still, a sleepy smile on her lips, her indolent lids half shut. There was a fumbling at the padlock and she called out: "Have you slipped the chain?" The door opened, and Mr. Royall walked into the room.

She started up, sitting back against the cushions, and they looked at each other without speaking. Then Mr. Royall closed the door-latch and advanced a few steps.

Charity jumped to her feet. "What have you come for?" she stammered.

The last glare of the sunset was on her guardian's face, which looked ash-coloured in the yellow radiance.

"Because I knew you were here," he answered simply.

She had become conscious of the hair hanging loose across her breast, and it seemed as though she could not speak to him till she had set herself in order. She groped for her combs, and tried to fasten up the coil. Mr. Royall silently watched her.

"Charity," he said, "he'll be here in a minute. Let me talk to you first."

"You've got no right to talk to me. I can do what I please."

"Yes. What is it you mean to do?"

"I needn't answer that, or anything else."

He had glanced away, and stood looking curiously about the illuminated room. Purple asters and red maple-leaves filled the jar on the table; on a shelf against the wall stood a lamp, the kettle, a little pile of cups and saucers. The canvas chairs were grouped about the table.

"So this is where you meet," he said.

His tone was quiet and controlled, and the fact disconcerted her. She had been ready to give him violence for violence, but this calm acceptance of things as they were left her without a weapon.

"See here, Charity—you're always telling me I've got no rights over you. There might be two ways of looking at that—but I ain't going to argue it. All I know is I raised you as good as I could, and meant fairly by you always—except once, for a bad half-hour. There's no justice in weighing that half-hour against the rest, and you know it. If you hadn't, you wouldn't have gone on living under my roof. Seems to me the fact of your doing that gives me some sort of a right; the right to try and keep you out of trouble. I'm not asking you to consider any other."

She listened in silence, and then gave a slight laugh. "Better wait till I'm in trouble," she said.

He paused a moment, as if weighing her words. "Is that all your answer?"

"Yes, that's all."

"Well—I'll wait."

He turned away slowly, but as he did so the thing she had been waiting for happened; the door opened again and Harney entered.

He stopped short with a face of astonishment, and then, quickly controlling himself, went up to Mr. Royall with a frank look.

"Have you come to see me, sir?" he said coolly, throwing his cap on the table with an air of proprietorship.

Mr. Royall again looked slowly about the room; then his eyes turned to the young man.

"Is this your house?" he inquired.

Harney laughed: "Well—as much as it's anybody's. I come here to sketch occasionally."

"And to receive Miss Royall's visits?"

"When she does me the honour——"

"Is this the home you propose to bring her to when you get married?"

There was an immense and oppressive silence. Charity, quivering with anger, started forward, and then stood silent, too humbled for speech. Harney's eyes had dropped under the old man's gaze; but he raised them presently, and looking steadily at Mr. Royall, said: "Miss Royall is not a child. Isn't it rather absurd to talk of her as if she were? I believe she considers herself free to come and go as she pleases, without any questions from anyone." He paused and added: "I'm ready to answer any she wishes to ask me."

Mr. Royall turned to her. "Ask him when he's going to marry you, then——" There was another silence, and he laughed in his turn—a broken laugh, with a scraping sound in it. "You darsn't!" he shouted out with sudden passion. He went close up to Charity, his right arm lifted, not in menace but in tragic exhortation.

"You darsn't, and you know it—and you know why!" He swung back again upon the young man. "And you know why you ain't asked her to marry you, and why you don't mean to. It's because you hadn't need to; nor any other man either. I'm the only one that was fool enough not to know that; and I guess nobody'll repeat my mistake—not in Eagle County, anyhow. They all know what she is, and what she came from. They all know her mother was a woman of the town from Nettleton, that followed one of those Mountain fellows up to his place and lived there with him like a heathen. I saw her there sixteen years ago, when I went to bring this child down. I went to save her from the kind of life her mother was leading—but I'd better have left her in the kennel she came from. . . ." He paused and stared darkly at the two young people, and out beyond them, at the menacing Mountain with its rim of fire; then he sat down beside the table on which they had so often spread their rustic supper, and covered his face with his hands. Harney leaned in the window, a frown on his face: he was twirling between his fingers a small package that dangled from a loop of string. . . . Charity heard Mr. Royall draw a hard breath or two, and his shoulders shook a little. Presently he stood up and walked across the room. He did not look again at the young people: they saw him feel his way to the door and fumble for the latch; and then he went out into the darkness.

After he had gone there was a long silence. Charity waited for Harney to speak; but he seemed at first not to find anything to say. At length he broke out irrelevantly: "I wonder how he found out?"

She made no answer and he tossed down the package he had been holding, and went up to her.

"I'm so sorry, dear . . . that this should have happened. . . ."

She threw her head back proudly. "I ain't ever been sorry—not a minute!"

"No."

She waited to be caught into his arms, but he turned away from her irresolutely. The last glow was gone from behind the Mountain. Everything in the room had turned grey and indistinct, and an autumnal dampness crept up from the hollow below the orchard, laying its cold touch on their flushed faces. Harney walked the length of the room, and then turned back and sat down at the table.

"Come," he said imperiously.

She sat down beside him, and he untied the string about the package and spread out a pile of sandwiches.

"I stole them from the love-feast at Hamblin," he said with a laugh, pushing them over to her. She laughed too, and took one, and began to eat.

"Didn't you make the tea?"

"No," she said. "I forgot——"

"Oh, well—it's too late to boil the water now." He said nothing more, and sitting opposite to each other they went on silently eating the sandwiches. Darkness had descended in the little room, and Harney's face was a dim blur to Charity. Suddenly he leaned across the table and laid his hand on hers.

"I shall have to go off for a while—a month or two, perhaps—to arrange some things; and then I'll come back . . . and we'll get married."

His voice seemed like a stranger's: nothing was left in it of the vibrations she knew. Her hand lay inertly under his, and she left it there, and raised her head, trying to answer him. But the words died in her throat. They sat motionless, in their attitude of confident endearment, as if some strange death had surprised them. At length Harney sprang to his feet with a slight shiver. "God! it's damp—we couldn't have come here much longer." He went to the shelf, took down a tin candle-stick and lit the candle; then he propped an unhinged shutter against the empty window-frame and put the candle on the table. It threw up a queer shadow on his frowning forehead, and made the smile on his lips a grimace.

"But it's been good, though, hasn't it, Charity? . . . What's the matter—why do you stand there staring at me? Haven't the days here been good?" He went up to her and caught her to his breast. "And there'll be others—lots of others . . . jollier . . . even jollier . . . won't there, darling?"

He turned her head back, feeling for the curve of her throat below the ear, and kissing her there, and on the hair and eyes and lips. She clung to him desperately, and as he drew her to his knees on the couch she felt as if they were being sucked down together into some bottomless abyss.

XV

That night, as usual, they said good-bye at the wood's edge.

Harney was to leave the next morning early. He asked Charity to say nothing of their plans till his return, and, strangely even to herself, she was glad of the postponement. A leaden weight of shame hung on her, benumbing every other sensation, and she bade him good-bye with hardly a sign of emotion. His reiterated promises to return seemed almost wounding. She had no doubt that he intended to come back; her doubts were far deeper and less definable.

Since the fanciful vision of the future that had flitted through her imagination at their first meeting she had hardly ever thought of his marrying her. She had not had to put the thought from her mind; it had not been there. If ever she looked ahead she felt instinctively that the gulf between them was too deep, and that the bridge their passion had flung across it was as insubstantial as a rainbow. But she seldom looked ahead; each day was so rich that it absorbed her. . . . Now her first feeling was that everything would be different, and that she herself would be a different being to Harney. Instead of remaining separate and absolute, she would be compared with other people, and unknown things would be expected of her. She was too proud to be afraid, but the freedom of her spirit drooped. . . .

Harney had not fixed any date for his return; he had said he would have to look about first, and settle things. He had promised to write as soon as there was anything definite to say, and had left her his address, and asked her to write also. But the address frightened her. It was in New York, at a club with a long name in Fifth Avenue: it seemed to raise an insurmountable barrier between them. Once or twice, in the first days, she got out a sheet of paper, and sat looking at it, and trying to think what to say; but she had the feeling that her letter would never reach its destination. She had never written to anyone farther away than Hepburn.

Harney's first letter came after he had been gone about ten days. It was tender but grave, and bore no resemblance to the gay little notes he had sent her by the freckled boy from Creston River. He spoke positively of his intention of coming back, but named no date, and reminded Charity of their agreement that their plans should not be divulged till he had had time to "settle things." When that would be he could not yet foresee; but she could count on his returning as soon as the way was clear.

She read the letter with a strange sense of its coming from immeasurable distances and having lost most of its meaning on the way; and in reply she sent him a coloured post-card of Creston Falls, on which she wrote: "With love from Charity." She felt the pitiful inadequacy of this, and understood, with a sense of despair, that in her inability to express herself she must give him an impression of coldness and reluctance; but she could not help it. She could not forget that he had never spoken to her of marriage till Mr. Royall had forced the word from his lips; though she had not had the strength to shake off the spell that bound her to him she had lost all spontaneity of feeling, and seemed to herself to be passively awaiting a fate she could not avert.

She had not seen Mr. Royall on her return to the red house. The morning after her parting from Harney, when she came down from her room, Verena told her that her guardian had gone off to Worcester and Portland. It was the time of year when he usually reported to the insurance agencies he represented, and there was nothing unusual in his departure except its suddenness. She thought little about him, except to be glad he was not there. . . .

She kept to herself for the first days, while North Dormer was recovering from its brief plunge into publicity, and the subsiding agitation left her unnoticed. But the faithful Ally could not be long avoided. For the first few days after the close of the Old Home Week festivities Charity escaped her by roaming the hills all day when she was not at her post in the library; but after that a period of rain set in, and one pouring afternoon Ally, sure that she would find her friend indoors, came around to the red house with her sewing.

The two girls sat upstairs in Charity's room. Charity, her idle hands in her lap, was sunk in a kind of leaden dream, through which she was only half-conscious of Ally, who sat opposite her in a low rush-bottomed chair, her work pinned to her knee, and her thin lips pursed up as she bent above it.

"It was my idea running a ribbon through the gauging," she said proudly, drawing back to contemplate the blouse she was trimming. "It's for Miss Balch: she was awfully pleased." She paused and then added, with a queer tremor in her piping voice: "I darsn't have told her I got the idea from one I saw on Julia."

Charity raised her eyes listlessly. "Do you still see Julia sometimes?"

Ally reddened, as if the allusion had escaped her unintentionally. "Oh, it was a long time ago I seen her with those gaugings. . . ."

Silence fell again, and Ally presently continued: "Miss Balch left me a whole lot of things to do over this time."

"Why—has she gone?" Charity inquired with an inner start of apprehension.

"Didn't you know? She went off the morning after they had the celebration at Hamblin. I seen her drive by early with Mr. Harney."

There was another silence, measured by the steady tick of the rain against the window, and, at intervals, by the snipping sound of Ally's scissors.

Ally gave a meditative laugh. "Do you know what she told me before she went away? She told me she was going to send for me to come over to Springfield and make some things for her wedding."

Charity again lifted her heavy lids and stared at Ally's pale pointed face, which moved to and fro above her moving fingers.

"Is she going to get married?"

Ally let the blouse sink to her knee, and sat gazing at it. Her lips seemed suddenly dry, and she moistened them a little with her tongue.

"Why, I presume so . . . from what she said. . . . Didn't you know?"

"Why should I know?"

Ally did not answer. She bent above the blouse, and began picking out a basting thread with the point of the scissors.

"Why should I know?" Charity repeated harshly.

"I didn't know but what . . . folks here say she's engaged to Mr. Harney."

Charity stood up with a laugh, and stretched her arms lazily above her head.

"If all the people got married that folks say are going to you'd have your time full making wedding-dresses," she said ironically.

"Why—don't you believe it?" Ally ventured.

"It wouldn't make it true if I did—nor prevent it if I didn't."

"That's so. . . . I only know I seen her crying the night of the party because her dress didn't set right. That was why she wouldn't dance any. . . ."

Charity stood absently gazing down at the lacy garment on Ally's knee. Abruptly she stooped and snatched it up.

"Well, I guess she won't dance in this either," she said with sudden violence; and grasping the blouse in her strong young hands she tore it in two and flung the tattered bits to the floor.

"Oh, Charity——" Ally cried, springing up. For a long interval the two girls faced each other across the ruined garment. Ally burst into tears.

"Oh, what'll I say to her? What'll I do? It was real lace!" she wailed between her piping sobs.

Charity glared at her unrelentingly. "You'd oughtn't to have brought it here," she said, breathing quickly. "I hate other people's clothes—it's just as if they was there themselves." The two stared at each other again over this avowal, till Charity brought out, in a gasp of anguish: "Oh, go—go—go—or I'll hate you too. . . ."

When Ally left her, she fell sobbing across her bed.

The long storm was followed by a north-west gale, and when it was over the hills took on their first umber tints, the sky grew more densely blue, and the big white clouds lay against the hills like snow-banks. The first crisp maple-leaves began to spin across Miss Hatchard's lawn, and the Virginia creeper on the Memorial splashed the white porch with scarlet. It was a golden triumphant September. Day by day the flame of the Virginia creeper spread to the hillsides in wider waves of carmine and crimson, the larches glowed like the thin yellow halo about a fire, the maples blazed and smouldered, and the black hemlocks turned to indigo against the incandescence of the forest.

The nights were cold, with a dry glitter of stars so high up that they seemed smaller and more vivid. Sometimes, as Charity lay sleepless on her bed through the long hours, she felt as though she were bound to those wheeling fires and swinging with them around the great black vault. At night she planned many things . . . it was then she wrote to Harney. But the letters were never put on paper, for she did not know how to express what she wanted to tell him. So she waited. Since her talk with Ally she had felt sure that Harney was engaged to Annabel Balch, and that the process of "settling things" would involve the breaking of this tie. Her first rage of jealousy over, she felt no fear on this score. She was still sure that Harney would come back, and she was equally sure that, for the moment at least, it was she whom he loved and not Miss Balch. Yet the girl, no less, remained a rival, since she represented all the things that Charity felt herself most incapable of understanding or achieving. Annabel Balch was, if not the girl Harney ought to marry, at least the kind of girl it would be natural for him to marry. Charity had never been able to picture herself as his wife; had never been able to arrest the vision and follow it out in its daily consequences; but she could perfectly imagine Annabel Balch in that relation to him.

The more she thought of these things the more the sense of fatality weighed on her: she felt the uselessness of struggling against the circumstances. She had never known how to adapt herself; she could only break and tear and destroy. The scene with Ally had left her stricken with shame at her own childish savagery. What would Harney have thought if he had witnessed it? But when she turned the incident over in her puzzled mind she could not imagine what a civilized person would have done in her place. She felt herself too unequally pitted against unknown forces. . . .

At length this feeling moved her to sudden action. She took a sheet of letter paper from Mr. Royall's office, and sitting by the kitchen lamp, one night after Verena had gone to bed, began her first letter to Harney. It was very short:

I want you should marry Annabel Balch if you promised to. I think maybe you were afraid I'd feel too bad about it. I feel I'd rather you acted right.

Your loving
CHARITY

She posted the letter early the next morning, and for a few days her heart felt strangely light. Then she began to wonder why she received no answer.

One day as she sat alone in the library pondering these things the walls of books began to spin around her, and the rosewood desk to rock under her elbows. The dizziness was followed by a wave of nausea like that she had felt on the day of the exercises in the Town Hall. But the Town Hall had been crowded and stiflingly hot, and the library was empty, and so chilly that she had kept on her jacket. Five minutes before she had felt perfectly well; and now it seemed as if she were going to die. The bit of lace at which she still languidly worked dropped from her fingers, and the steel crochet hook clattered to the floor. She pressed her temples hard between her damp hands, steadying herself against the desk while the wave of sickness swept over her. Little by little it subsided, and after a few minutes she stood up, shaken and terrified, groped for her hat, and stumbled out into the air. But the whole sunlit autumn world reeled and roared around her as she dragged herself along the interminable length of the road home.

As she approached the red house she saw a buggy standing at the door, and her heart gave a leap. But it was only Mr. Royall who got out, his travelling-bag in hand. He saw her coming, and waited in the porch. She was conscious that he was looking at her intently, as if there was something strange in her appearance, and she threw back her head with a desperate effort at ease. Their eyes met, and she said: "You back?" as if nothing had happened, and he answered: "Yes, I'm back," and walked in ahead of her, pushing open the door of his office. She climbed to her room, every step of the stairs holding her fast as if her feet were lined with glue.

Two days later, she descended from the train at Nettleton, and walked out of the station into the dusty square. The brief interval of cold weather was over, and the day was as soft, and almost as hot, as when she and Harney had emerged on the same scene on the Fourth of July. In the square the same broken-down hacks and carry-alls stood drawn up in a despondent line, and the lank horses with fly-nets over their withers swayed their heads drearily to and fro. She recognized the staring signs over the eating-houses and billiard saloons, and the long lines of wires on lofty poles tapering down the main street to the park at its other end. Taking the way the wires pointed, she went on hastily, with bent head, till she reached a wide transverse street with a brick building at the corner. She crossed this street and glanced furtively up at the front of the brick building; then she returned, and entered a door opening on a flight of steep brass-rimmed stairs. On the second landing she rang a bell, and a mulatto girl with a bushy head and a frilled apron let her into a hall where a stuffed fox on his hind legs proffered a brass card-tray to visitors. At the back of the hall was a glazed door marked: "Office." After waiting a few minutes in a handsomely furnished room, with plush sofas surmounted by large gold-framed photographs of showy young women, Charity was shown into the office. . . .

When she came out of the glazed door Dr. Merkle followed, and led her into another room, smaller, and still more crowded with plush and gold frames. Dr. Merkle was a plump woman with small bright eyes, an immense mass of black hair coming down low on her forehead, and unnaturally white and even teeth. She wore a rich black dress, with gold chains and charms hanging from her bosom. Her hands were large and smooth, and quick in all their movements; and she smelt of musk and carbolic acid.

She smiled on Charity with all her faultless teeth. "Sit down, my dear. Wouldn't you like a little drop of something to pick you up? . . . No. . . . Well, just lay back a minute then. . . . There's nothing to be done just yet; but in about a month, if you'll step round again . . . I could take you right into my own house for two or three days, and there wouldn't be a mite of trouble. Mercy me! The next time you'll know better'n to fret like this. . . ."

Charity gazed at her with widening eyes. This woman with the false hair, the false teeth, the false murderous smile—what was she offering her but immunity from some unthinkable crime? Charity, till then, had been conscious only of a vague self-disgust and a frightening physical distress; now, of a sudden, there came to her the grave surprise of motherhood. She had come to this dreadful place because she knew of no other way of making sure that she was not mistaken about her state; and the woman had taken her for a miserable creature like Julia. . . . The thought was so horrible that she sprang up, white and shaking, one of her great rushes of anger sweeping over her.

Dr. Merkle, still smiling, also rose. "Why do you run off in such a hurry? You can stretch out right here on my sofa. . . ." She paused, and her smile grew more motherly. "Afterwards—if there's been any talk at home, and you want to get away for a while . . . I have a lady friend in Boston who's looking for a companion . . . you're the very one to suit her, my dear. . . ."

Charity had reached the door. "I don't want to stay. I don't want to come back here," she stammered, her hand on the knob; but with a swift movement Dr. Merkle edged her from the threshold.

"Oh, very well. Five dollars, please."

Charity looked helplessly at the doctor's tight lips and rigid face. Her last savings had gone in repaying Ally for the cost of Miss Balch's ruined blouse, and she had had to borrow four dollars from her friend to pay for her railway ticket and cover the doctor's fee. It had never occurred to her that medical advice could cost more than two dollars.

"I didn't know . . . I haven't got that much . . ." she faltered, bursting into tears.

Dr. Merkle gave a short laugh which did not show her teeth, and inquired with concision if Charity supposed she ran the establishment for her own amusement? She leaned her firm shoulders against the door as she spoke, like a grim gaoler making terms with her captive.

"You say you'll come round and settle later? I've heard that pretty often too. Give me your address, and if you can't pay me I'll send the bill to your folks. . . . What? I can't understand what you say. . . . That don't suit you either? My, you're pretty particular for a girl that ain't got enough to settle her own bills. . . ." She paused, and fixed her eyes on the brooch with a blue stone that Charity had pinned to her blouse.

"Ain't you ashamed to talk that way to a lady that's got to earn her living, when you go about with jewellery like that on you? . . . It ain't in my line, and I do it only as a favour . . . but if you're a mind to leave that brooch as a pledge, I don't say no. . . . Yes, of course, you can get it back when you bring me my money. . . ."

On the way home, she felt an immense and unexpected quietude. It had been horrible to have to leave Harney's gift in the woman's hands, but even at that price the news she brought away had not been too dearly bought. She sat with half-closed eyes as the train rushed through the familiar landscape; and now the memories of her former journey, instead of flying before her like dead leaves, seemed to be ripening in her blood like sleeping grain. She would never again know what it was to feel herself alone. Everything seemed to have grown suddenly clear and simple. She no longer had any difficulty in picturing herself as Harney's wife now that she was the mother of his child; and compared to her sovereign right Annabel Balch's claim seemed no more than a girl's sentimental fancy.

That evening, at the gate of the red house, she found Ally waiting in the dusk. "I was down at the post-office just as they were closing up, and Will Targatt said there was a letter for you, so I brought it."

Ally held out the letter, looking at Charity with piercing sympathy. Since the scene of the torn blouse there had been a new and fearful admiration in the eyes she bent on her friend.

Charity snatched the letter with a laugh. "Oh, thank you—good-night," she called out over her shoulder as she ran up the path. If she had lingered a moment she knew she would have had Ally at her heels.

She hurried upstairs and felt her way into her dark room. Her hands trembled as she groped for the matches and lit her candle, and the flap of the envelope was so closely stuck that she had to find her scissors and slit it open. At length she read:

DEAR CHARITY:

I have your letter, and it touches me more than I can say. Won't you trust me, in return, to do my best? There are things it is hard to explain, much less to justify; but your generosity makes everything

easier. All I can do now is to thank you from my soul for understanding. Your telling me that you wanted me to do right has helped
me beyond expression. If ever there is a hope of realizing what we
dreamed of you will see me back on the instant; and I haven't yet lost
that hope.

She read the letter with a rush; then she went over and over it,
each time more slowly and painstakingly. It was so beautifully expressed that she found it almost as difficult to understand as the
gentleman's explanation of the Bible pictures at Nettleton; but
gradually she became aware that the gist of its meaning lay in the
last few words. "If ever there is a hope of realizing what we
dreamed of . . ."

But then he wasn't even sure of that? She understood now that
every word and every reticence was an avowal of Annabel Balch's
prior claim. It was true that he was engaged to her, and that he
had not yet found a way of breaking his engagement.

As she read the letter over Charity understood what it must
have cost him to write it. He was not trying to evade an importu-
nate claim; he was honestly and contritely struggling between opposing duties. She did not even reproach him in her thoughts for
having concealed from her that he was not free: she could not see
anything more reprehensible in his conduct than in her own.
From the first she had needed him more than he had wanted her,
and the power that had swept them together had been as far beyond resistance as a great gale loosening the leaves of the forest. . . . Only, there stood between them, fixed and upright in the
general upheaval, the indestructible figure of Annabel Balch. . . .

Face to face with his admission of the fact, she sat staring at the
letter. A cold tremor ran over her, and the hard sobs struggled up
into her throat and shook her from head to foot. For a while she
was caught and tossed on great waves of anguish that left her
hardly conscious of anything but the blind struggle against their
assaults. Then, little by little, she began to relive, with a dreadful
poignancy, each separate stage of her poor romance. Foolish
things she had said came back to her, gay answers Harney had
made, his first kiss in the darkness between the fireworks, their
choosing the blue brooch together, the way he had teased her
about the letters she had dropped in her flight from the evangelist.

All these memories, and a thousand others, hummed through her brain till his nearness grew so vivid that she felt his fingers in her hair, and his warm breath on her cheek as he bent her head back like a flower. These things were hers; they had passed into her blood, and become a part of her, they were building the child in her womb; it was impossible to tear asunder strands of life so interwoven.

The conviction gradually strengthened her, and she began to form in her mind the first words of the letter she meant to write to Harney. She wanted to write it at once, and with feverish hands she began to rummage in her drawer for a sheet of letter paper. But there was none left; she must go downstairs to get it. She had a superstitious feeling that the letter must be written on the instant, that setting down her secret in words would bring her reassurance and safety; and taking up her candle she went down to Mr. Royall's office.

At that hour she was not likely to find him there: he had probably had his supper and walked over to Carrick Fry's. She pushed open the door of the unlit room, and the light of her lifted candle fell on his figure, seated in the darkness in his high-backed chair. His arms lay along the arms of the chair, and his head was bent a little; but he lifted it quickly as Charity entered. She started back as their eyes met, remembering that her own were red with weeping, and that her face was livid with the fatigue and emotion of her journey. But it was too late to escape, and she stood and looked at him in silence.

He had risen from his chair, and came toward her with outstretched hands. The gesture was so unexpected that she let him take her hands in his, and they stood thus, without speaking, till Mr. Royall said gravely: "Charity—was you looking for me?"

She freed herself abruptly and fell back. "Me? No——" She set down the candle on his desk. "I wanted some letter-paper, that's all."

His face contracted, and the bushy brows jutted forward over his eyes. Without answering he opened the drawer of the desk, took out a sheet of paper and an envelope, and pushed them toward her. "Do you want a stamp too?" he asked.

She nodded, and he gave her the stamp. As he did so she felt that he was looking at her intently, and she knew that the candle light flickering up on her white face must be distorting her swollen features and exaggerating the dark rings about her eyes. She snatched up the paper, her reassurance dissolving under his pitiless gaze, in which she seemed to read the grim perception of her state, and the ironic recollection of the day when, in that very room, he had offered to compel Harney to marry her. His look seemed to say that he knew she had taken the paper to write to her lover, who had left her as he had warned her she would be left. She remembered the scorn with which she had turned from him that day, and knew, if he guessed the truth, what a list of old scores it must settle. She turned and fled upstairs; but when she got back to her room all the words that had been waiting had vanished. . . .

If she could have gone to Harney it would have been different; she would only have had to show herself to let his memories speak for her. But she had no money left, and there was no one from whom she could have borrowed enough for such a journey. There was nothing to do but to write, and await his reply. For a long time she sat bent above the blank page; but she found nothing to say that really expressed what she was feeling. . . .

Harney had written that she had made it easier for him, and she was glad it was so; she did not want to make things hard. She knew she had it in her power to do that; she held his fate in her hands. All she had to do was to tell him the truth; but that was the very fact that held her back. . . . Her five minutes face to face with Mr. Royall had stripped her of her last illusion, and brought her back to North Dormer's point of view. Distinctly and pitilessly there rose before her the fate of the girl who was married "to make things right." She had seen too many village love-stories end in that way. Poor Rose Coles's miserable marriage was of the number; and what good had come of it for her or for Halston Skeff? They had hated each other from the day the minister married them; and whenever old Mrs. Skeff had a fancy to humiliate her daughter-in-law she had only to say: "Who'd ever think the baby's only two? And for a seven months' child—ain't it a wonder what a size he is?" North Dormer had treasures of indulgence for brands in the burning, but only derision for those who succeeded in getting snatched from it; and Charity had always understood Julia Hawes's refusal to be snatched. . . .

Only—was there no alternative but Julia's? Her soul recoiled from the vision of the white-faced woman among the plush sofas and gilt frames. In the established order of things as she knew them she saw no place for her individual adventure. . . .

She sat in her chair without undressing till faint grey streaks began to divide the black slats of the shutters. Then she stood up and pushed them open, letting in the light. The coming of a new day brought a sharper consciousness of ineluctable reality, and with it a sense of the need of action. She looked at herself in the glass, and saw her face, white in the autumn dawn, with pinched cheeks and dark-ringed eyes, and all the marks of her state that she herself would never have noticed, but that Dr. Merkle's diagnosis had made plain to her. She could not hope that those signs would escape the watchful village; even before her figure lost its shape she knew her face would betray her.

Leaning from her window she looked out on the dark and empty scene; the ashen houses with shuttered windows, the grey road climbing the slope to the hemlock belt above the cemetery, and the heavy mass of the Mountain black against a rainy sky. To the east a space of light was broadening above the forest; but over that also the clouds hung. Slowly her gaze travelled across the fields to the rugged curve of the hills. She had looked out so often on that lifeless circle, and wondered if anything could ever happen to anyone who was enclosed in it. . . .

Almost without conscious thought her decision had been reached; as her eyes had followed the circle of the hills her mind had also travelled the old round. She supposed it was something in her blood that made the Mountain the only answer to her questioning, the inevitable escape from all that hemmed her in and beset her. At any rate it began to loom in her now as it loomed against the rainy dawn; and the longer she looked at it the more clearly she understood that now at last she was really going there.

XVI

The rain held off, and an hour later, when she started, wild gleams of sunlight were blowing across the fields.

After Harney's departure she had returned her bicycle to its

owner at Creston, and she was not sure of being able to walk all
the way to the Mountain. The deserted house was on the road;
but the idea of spending the night there was unendurable, and she
meant to try to push on to Hamblin, where she could sleep under
a wood-shed if her strength should fail her. Her preparations had
been made with quiet forethought. Before starting she had forced
herself to swallow a glass of milk and eat a piece of bread; and she
had put in her canvas satchel a little packet of the chocolate that
Harney always carried in his bicycle bag. She wanted above all to
keep up her strength, and reach her destination without attracting
notice. . . .

Mile by mile she retraced the road over which she had so often
flown to her lover. When she reached the turn where the wood-
road branched off from the Creston highway she remembered the
Gospel tent—long since folded up and transplanted—and her
start of involuntary terror when the fat evangelist had said: "Your
Saviour knows everything. Come and confess your guilt." There
was no sense of guilt in her now, but only a desperate desire to defend her secret from irreverent eyes, and begin life again among
people to whom the harsh code of the village was unknown. The
impulse did not shape itself in thought: she only knew she must
save her baby, and hide herself with it somewhere where no one
would ever come to trouble them.

She walked on and on, growing more heavy-footed as the day
advanced. It seemed a cruel chance that compelled her to retrace
every step of the way to the deserted house; and when she came in
sight of the orchard, and the silver-grey roof slanting crookedly
through the laden branches, her strength failed her and she sat
down by the roadside. She sat there a long time, trying to gather
the courage to start again, and walk past the broken gate and the
untrimmed rose-bushes strung with scarlet hips. A few drops of
rain were falling, and she thought of the warm evenings when she
and Harney had sat embraced in the shadowy room, and the noise
of summer showers on the roof had rustled through their kisses.
At length she understood that if she stayed any longer the rain
might compel her to take shelter in the house overnight, and she
got up and walked on, averting her eyes as she came abreast of the
white gate and the tangled garden.

The hours wore on, and she walked more and more slowly,

pausing now and then to rest, and to eat a little bread and an apple picked up from the roadside. Her body seemed to grow heavier with every yard of the way, and she wondered how she would be able to carry her child later, if already he laid such a burden on her. . . . A fresh wind had sprung up, scattering the rain and blowing down keenly from the mountain. Presently the clouds lowered again, and a few white darts struck her in the face: it was the first snow falling over Hamblin. The roofs of the lonely village were only half a mile ahead, and she was resolved to push beyond it, and try to reach the Mountain that night. She had no clear plan of action, except that, once in the settlement, she meant to look for Liff Hyatt, and get him to take her to her mother. She herself had been born as her own baby was going to be born; and whatever her mother's subsequent life had been, she could hardly help remembering the past, and receiving a daughter who was facing the trouble she had known.

Suddenly the deadly faintness came over her once more and she sat down on the bank and leaned her head against a tree-trunk. The long road and the cloudy landscape vanished from her eyes, and for a time she seemed to be circling about in some terrible wheeling darkness. Then that too faded.

She opened her eyes, and saw a buggy drawn up beside her, and a man who had jumped down from it and was gazing at her with a puzzled face. Slowly consciousness came back, and she saw that the man was Liff Hyatt.

She was dimly aware that he was asking her something, and she looked at him in silence, trying to find strength to speak. At length her voice stirred in her throat, and she said in a whisper: "I'm going up the Mountain."

"Up the Mountain?" he repeated, drawing aside a little; and as he moved she saw behind him, in the buggy, a heavily coated figure with a familiar pink face and gold spectacles on the bridge of a Grecian nose.

"Charity! What on earth are you doing here?" Mr. Miles exclaimed, throwing the reins on the horse's back and scrambling down from the buggy.

She lifted her heavy eyes to his. "I'm going to see my mother."

The two men glanced at each other, and for a moment neither of them spoke.

Then Mr. Miles said: "You look ill, my dear, and it's a long way. Do you think it's wise?"

Charity stood up. "I've got to go to her."

A vague mirthless grin contracted Liff Hyatt's face, and Mr. Miles again spoke uncertainly. "You know, then—you'd been told?"

She stared at him. "I don't know what you mean. I want to go to her."

Mr. Miles was examining her thoughtfully. She fancied she saw a change in his expression, and the blood rushed to her forehead. "I just want to go to her," she repeated.

He laid his hand on her arm. "My child, your mother is dying. Liff Hyatt came down to fetch me. . . . Get in and come with us."

He helped her up to the seat at his side, Liff Hyatt clambered in at the back, and they drove off toward Hamblin. At first Charity had hardly grasped what Mr. Miles was saying; the physical relief of finding herself seated in the buggy, and securely on her road to the Mountain, effaced the impression of his words. But as her head cleared she began to understand. She knew the Mountain had but the most infrequent intercourse with the valleys; she had often enough heard it said that no one ever went up there except the minister, when someone was dying. And now it was her mother who was dying . . . and she would find herself as much alone on the Mountain as anywhere else in the world. The sense of unescapable isolation was all she could feel for the moment; then she began to wonder at the strangeness of its being Mr. Miles who had undertaken to perform this grim errand. He did not seem in the least like the kind of man who would care to go up the Mountain. But here he was at her side, guiding the horse with a firm hand, and bending on her the kindly gleam of his spectacles, as if there were nothing unusual in their being together in such circumstances.

For a while she found it impossible to speak, and he seemed to understand this, and made no attempt to question her. But presently she felt her tears rise and flow down over her drawn cheeks; and he must have seen them too, for he laid his hand on hers, and said in a low voice: "Won't you tell me what is troubling you?"

She shook her head, and he did not insist: but after a while he said, in the same low tone, so that they should not be overheard: "Charity, what do you know of your childhood, before you came down to North Dormer?"

She controlled herself, and answered: "Nothing, only what I heard Mr. Royall say one day. He said he brought me down because my father went to prison."

"And you've never been up there since?"

"Never."

Mr. Miles was silent again, then he said: "I'm glad you're coming with me now. Perhaps we may find your mother alive, and she may know that you have come."

They had reached Hamblin, where the snow-flurry had left white patches in the rough grass on the roadside, and in the angles of the roofs facing north. It was a poor bleak village under the granite flank of the Mountain, and as soon as they left it they began to climb. The road was steep and full of ruts, and the horse settled down to a walk while they mounted and mounted, the world dropping away below them in great mottled stretches of forest and field, and stormy dark blue distances.

Charity had often had visions of this ascent of the Mountain but she had not known it would reveal so wide a country, and the sight of those strange lands reaching away on every side gave her a new sense of Harney's remoteness. She knew he must be miles and miles beyond the last range of hills that seemed to be the outmost verge of things, and she wondered how she had ever dreamed of going to New York to find him. . . .

As the road mounted the country grew bleaker, and they drove across fields of faded mountain grass bleached by long months beneath the snow. In the hollows a few white birches trembled, or a mountain ash lit its scarlet clusters; but only a scant growth of pines darkened the granite ledges. The wind was blowing fiercely across the open slopes; the horse faced it with bent head and straining flanks, and now and then the buggy swayed so that Charity had to clutch its side.

Mr. Miles had not spoken again; he seemed to understand that she wanted to be left alone. After a while the track they were following forked, and he pulled up the horse, as if uncertain of the way. Liff Hyatt craned his head around from the back, and shouted against the wind: "Left——" and they turned into a stunted pine-wood and began to drive down the other side of the Mountain.

A mile or two farther on they came out on a clearing where two or three low houses lay in stony fields, crouching among the rocks as if to brace themselves against the wind. They were hardly more than sheds, built of logs and rough boards, with tin stove-pipes sticking out of their roofs. The sun was setting, and dusk had already fallen on the lower world, but a yellow glare still lay on the lonely hillside and the crouching houses. The next moment it faded and left the landscape in dark autumn twilight.

"Over there," Liff called out, stretching his long arm over Mr. Miles's shoulder. The clergyman turned to the left, across a bit of bare ground overgrown with docks and nettles, and stopped before the most ruinous of the sheds. A stove-pipe reached its crooked arm out of one window, and the broken panes of the other were stuffed with rags and paper. In contrast to such a dwelling the brown house in the swamp might have stood for the home of plenty.

As the buggy drew up two or three mongrel dogs jumped out of the twilight with a great barking, and a young man slouched to the door and stood there staring. In the twilight Charity saw that his face had the same sodden look as Bash Hyatt's, the day she had seen him sleeping by the stove. He made no effort to silence the dogs, but leaned in the door, as if roused from a drunken lethargy, while Mr. Miles got out of the buggy.

"Is it here?" the clergyman asked Liff in a low voice; and Liff nodded.

Mr. Miles turned to Charity. "Just hold the horse a minute, my dear: I'll go in first," he said, putting the reins in her hands. She took them passively, and sat staring straight ahead of her at the darkening scene while Mr. Miles and Liff Hyatt went up to the house. They stood a few minutes talking with the man in the door, and then Mr. Miles came back. As he came close, Charity saw that his smooth pink face wore a frightened solemn look.

"Your mother is dead, Charity; you'd better come with me," he said.

She got down and followed him while Liff led the horse away. As she approached the door she said to herself: "This is where I was born . . . this is where I belong. . . ." She had said it to herself often enough as she looked across the sunlit valleys at the Mountain; but it had meant nothing then, and now it had become a reality. Mr. Miles took her gently by the arm, and they entered what appeared to be the only room in the house. It was so dark that she could just discern a group of a dozen people sitting or sprawling about a table made of boards laid across two barrels. They looked up listlessly as Mr. Miles and Charity came in, and a woman's thick voice said: "Here's the preacher." But no one moved.

Mr. Miles paused and looked about him; then he turned to the young man who had met them at the door.

"Is the body here?" he asked.

The young man, instead of answering, turned his head toward the group. "Where's the candle? I tole yer to bring a candle," he said with sudden harshness to a girl who was lolling against the table. She did not answer, but another man got up and took from some corner a candle stuck into a bottle.

"How'll I light it? The stove's out," the girl grumbled.

Mr. Miles fumbled under his heavy wrappings and drew out a match-box. He held a match to the candle, and in a moment or two a faint circle of light fell on the pale aguish heads that started out of the shadow like the heads of nocturnal animals.

"Mary's over there," someone said; and Mr. Miles, taking the bottle in his hand, passed behind the table. Charity followed him, and they stood before a mattress on the floor in a corner of the room. A woman lay on it, but she did not look like a dead woman; she seemed to have fallen across her squalid bed in a drunken sleep, and to have been left lying where she fell, in her ragged disordered clothes. One arm was flung above her head, one leg drawn up under a torn skirt that left the other bare to the knee: a swollen glistening leg with a ragged stocking rolled down about the ankle. The woman lay on her back, her eyes staring up unblinkingly at the candle that trembled in Mr. Miles's hand.

"She jus' dropped off," a woman said, over the shoulder of the others; and the young man added: "I jus' come in and found her."

An elderly man with lank hair and a feeble grin pushed between them. "It was like this: I says to her on'y the night before: if you don't take and quit, I says to her . . ."

Someone pulled him back and sent him reeling against a bench along the wall, where he dropped down muttering his unheeded narrative.

There was a silence; then the young woman who had been lolling against the table suddenly parted the group, and stood in front of Charity. She was healthier and robuster looking than the others, and her weather-beaten face had a certain sullen beauty.

"Who's the girl? Who brought her here?" she said, fixing her eyes mistrustfully on the young man who had rebuked her for not having a candle ready.

Mr. Miles spoke. "I brought her; she is Mary Hyatt's daughter."

"What? Her too?" the girl sneered; and the young man turned on her with an oath. "Shut your mouth, damn you, or get out of here," he said; then he relapsed into his former apathy, and dropped down on the bench, leaning his head against the wall.

Mr. Miles had set the candle on the floor and taken off his heavy coat. He turned to Charity. "Come and help me," he said.

He knelt down by the mattress, and pressed the lids over the dead woman's eyes. Charity, trembling and sick, knelt beside him, and tried to compose her mother's body. She drew the stocking over the dreadful glistening leg, and pulled the skirt down to the battered upturned boots. As she did so, she looked at her mother's face, thin yet swollen, with lips parted in a frozen gasp above the broken teeth. There was no sign in it of anything human: she lay there like a dead dog in a ditch. Charity's hands grew cold as they touched her.

Mr. Miles drew the woman's arms across her breast and laid his coat over her. Then he covered her face with his handkerchief, and placed the bottle with the candle in it at her head. Having done this he stood up.

"Is there no coffin?" he asked, turning to the group behind him.

There was a moment of bewildered silence; then the fierce girl spoke up. "You'd oughter brought it with you. Where'd we get one here, I'd like ter know?"

Mr. Miles, looking at the others, repeated: "Is it possible you have no coffin ready?"

"That's what I say: them that has it sleeps better," an old woman murmured. "But then she never had no bed. . . ."

"And the stove warn't hers," said the lank-haired man, on the defensive.

Mr. Miles turned away from them and moved a few steps apart. He had drawn a book from his pocket, and after a pause he opened it and began to read, holding the book at arm's length and low down, so that the pages caught the feeble light. Charity had remained on her knees by the mattress: now that her mother's face was covered it was easier to stay near her, and avoid the sight of the living faces which too horribly showed by what stages hers had lapsed into death.

"I am the Resurrection and the Life," Mr. Miles began; "he that believeth in me, though he were dead, yet shall he live. . . . Though after my skin worms destroy my body, yet in my flesh shall I see God. . . ."

In my flesh shall I see God! Charity thought of the gaping mouth and stony eyes under the handkerchief, and of the glistening leg over which she had drawn the stocking. . . .

"We brought nothing into this world and we shall take nothing out of it——"

There was a sudden muttering and a scuffle at the back of the group. "I brought the stove," said the elderly man with lank hair, pushing his way between the others. "I wen' down to Creston'n bought it . . . n' I got a right to take it outer here . . . n' I'll lick any feller says I ain't. . . ."

"Sit down, damn you!" shouted the tall youth who had been drowsing on the bench against the wall.

"For man walketh in a vain shadow, and disquieteth himself in vain; he heapeth up riches and cannot tell who shall gather them . . ."

"Well, it *are* his," a woman in the background interjected in a frightened whine.

The tall youth staggered to his feet. "If you don't hold your mouths I'll turn you all out o' here, the whole lot of you," he cried with many oaths. "G'wan, minister . . . don't let 'em faze you. . . ."

"Now is Christ risen from the dead and become the first-fruits of them that slept. . . . Behold, I show you a mystery. We shall not all sleep, but we shall all be changed, in a moment, in the twinkling of an eye, at the last trump. . . . For this corruptible must put on incorruption and this mortal must put on immortality. So when this corruption shall have put on incorruption, and when this mortal shall have put on immortality, then shall be brought to pass the saying that is written, Death is swallowed up in Victory. . . ."

One by one the mighty words fell on Charity's bowed head, soothing the horror, subduing the tumult, mastering her as they mastered the drink-dazed creatures at her back. Mr. Miles read to the last word, and then closed the book.

"Is the grave ready?" he asked.

Liff Hyatt, who had come in while he was reading, nodded a "Yes," and pushed forward to the side of the mattress. The young man on the bench, who seemed to assert some sort of right of kinship with the dead woman, got to his feet again, and the proprietor of the stove joined him. Between them they raised up the mattress; but their movements were unsteady, and the coat slipped to the floor, revealing the poor body in its helpless misery. Charity, picking up the coat, covered her mother once more. Liff had brought a lantern, and the old woman who had already spoken took it up, and opened the door to let the little procession pass out. The wind had dropped, and the night was very dark and bitterly cold. The old woman walked ahead, the lantern shaking in her hand and spreading out before her a pale patch of dead grass and coarse-leaved weeds enclosed in an immensity of blackness.

Mr. Miles took Charity by the arm, and side by side they walked behind the mattress. At length the old woman with the lantern stopped, and Charity saw the light fall on the stooping shoulders of the bearers and on a ridge of upheaved earth over which they were bending. Mr. Miles released her arm and approached the hollow on the other side of the ridge; and while the men stooped down, lowering the mattress into the grave, he began to speak again.

"Man that is born of woman hath but a short time to live and is full of misery. . . . He cometh up and is cut down . . . he fleeth as it were a shadow. . . . Yet, O Lord God most holy, O Lord most mighty, O holy and merciful Saviour, deliver us not into the bitter pains of eternal death . . ."

"Easy there . . . is she down?" piped the claimant to the stove; and the young man called over his shoulder: "Lift the light there, can't you?"

There was a pause, during which the light floated uncertainly over the open grave. Someone bent over and pulled out Mr. Miles's coat—("No, no—leave the handkerchief," he interposed)—and then Liff Hyatt, coming forward with a spade, began to shovel in the earth.

"Forasmuch as it hath pleased Almighty God of His great mercy to take unto Himself the soul of our dear sister here departed, we therefore commit her body to the ground; earth to earth, ashes to ashes, dust to dust . . ." Liff's gaunt shoulders rose and bent in the lantern light as he dashed the clods of earth into the grave. "God—it's froze a'ready," he muttered, spitting into his palm and passing his ragged shirt-sleeve across his perspiring face.

"Through our Lord Jesus Christ, who shall change our vile body that it may be like unto His glorious body, according to the mighty working, whereby He is able to subdue all things unto Himself . . ." The last spadeful of earth fell on the vile body of Mary Hyatt, and Liff rested on his spade, his shoulder blades still heaving with the effort.

"Lord, have mercy upon us, Christ have mercy upon us, Lord have mercy upon us. . . ."

Mr. Miles took the lantern from the old woman's hand and swept its light across the circle of bleared faces. "Now kneel down, all of you," he commanded, in a voice of authority that Charity had never heard. She knelt down at the edge of the grave, and the others, stiffly and hesitatingly, got to their knees beside her. Mr. Miles knelt, too. "And now pray with me—you know this prayer," he said, and he began: "Our Father which art in Heaven . . ." One or two of the women falteringly took the words up, and when he ended, the lank-haired man flung himself on the neck of the tall youth. "It was this way," he said. "I tole her the night before, I says to her . . ." The reminiscence ended in a sob.

Mr. Miles had been getting into his coat again. He came up to Charity, who had remained passively kneeling by the rough mound of earth.

"My child, you must come. It's very late."

She lifted her eyes to his face: he seemed to speak out of another world.

"I ain't coming: I'm going to stay here."

"Here? Where? What do you mean?"

"These are my folks. I'm going to stay with them."

Mr. Miles lowered his voice. "But it's not possible—you don't know what you are doing. You can't stay among these people: you must come with me."

She shook her head and rose from her knees. The group about the grave had scattered in the darkness, but the old woman with the lantern stood waiting. Her mournful withered face was not unkind, and Charity went up to her.

"Have you got a place where I can lie down for the night?" she asked. Liff came up, leading the buggy out of the night. He looked from one to the other with his feeble smile. "She's my mother. She'll take you home," he said; and he added, raising his voice to speak to the old woman: "It's the girl from lawyer Royall's—Mary's girl . . . you remember. . . ."

The woman nodded and raised her sad old eyes to Charity's. When Mr. Miles and Liff clambered into the buggy she went ahead with the lantern to show them the track they were to follow; then she turned back, and in silence she and Charity walked away together through the night.

XVII

Charity lay on the floor on a mattress, as her dead mother's body had lain. The room in which she lay was cold and dark and low-ceilinged, and even poorer and barer than the scene of Mary Hyatt's earthly pilgrimage. On the other side of the fireless stove Liff Hyatt's mother slept on a blanket, with two children—her grandchildren, she said—rolled up against her like sleeping puppies. They had their thin clothes spread over them, having given the only other blanket to their guest.

Through the small square of glass in the opposite wall Charity saw a deep funnel of sky, so black, so remote, so palpitating with frosty stars that her very soul seemed to be sucked up into it. Up there somewhere, she supposed, the God whom Mr. Miles had invoked was waiting for Mary Hyatt to appear. What a long flight it was! And what would she have to say when she reached Him?

Charity's bewildered brain laboured with the attempt to picture her mother's past, and to relate it in any way to the designs of a just but merciful God; but it was impossible to imagine any link between them. She herself felt as remote from the poor creature she had seen lowered into her hastily dug grave as if the height of the heavens had divided them. She had seen poverty and misfortune in her life; but in a community where poor thrifty Mrs. Hawes and the industrious Ally represented the nearest approach to destitution there was nothing to suggest the savage misery of the Mountain farmers.

As she lay there, half-stunned by her tragic initiation, Charity vainly tried to think herself into the life about her. But she could not even make out what relationship these people bore to each other, or to her dead mother; they seemed to be herded together in a sort of passive promiscuity in which their common misery was the strongest link. She tried to picture to herself what her life would have been if she had grown up on the Mountain, running wild in rags, sleeping on the floor curled up against her mother, like the pale-faced children huddled against old Mrs. Hyatt, and turning into a fierce bewildered creature like the girl who had apostrophized her in such strange words. She was frightened by the secret affinity she had felt with this girl, and by the light it threw on her own beginnings. Then she remembered what Mr. Royall had said in telling her story to Lucius Harney: "Yes, there was a mother; but she was glad to have the child go. She'd have given her to anybody. . . ."

Well! after all, was her mother so much to blame? Charity, since that day, had always thought of her as destitute of all human feeling; now she seemed merely pitiful. What mother would not want to save her child from such a life? Charity thought of the future of her own child, and tears welled into her aching eyes, and ran down over her face. If she had been less exhausted, less burdened with his weight, she would have sprung up then and there and fled away. . . .

The grim hours of the night dragged themselves slowly by, and at last the sky paled and dawn threw a cold blue beam into the room. She lay in her corner staring at the dirty floor, the clothes-line hung with decaying rags, the old woman huddled against the cold stove, and the light gradually spreading across the wintry world, and bringing with it a new day in which she would have to live, to choose, to act, to make herself a place among these people—or to go back to the life she had left. A mortal lassitude weighed on her. There were moments when she felt that all she asked was to go on lying there unnoticed; then her mind revolted at the thought of becoming one of the miserable herd from which she sprang, and it seemed as though, to save her child from such a fate, she would find strength to travel any distance, and bear any burden life might put on her.

Vague thoughts of Nettleton flitted through her mind. She said to herself that she would find some quiet place where she could bear her child, and give it to decent people to keep; and then she would go out like Julia Hawes and earn its living and hers. She knew that girls of that kind sometimes made enough to have their children nicely cared for; and every other consideration disappeared in the vision of her baby, cleaned and combed and rosy, and hidden away somewhere where she could run in and kiss it, and bring it pretty things to wear. Anything, anything was better than to add another life to the nest of misery on the Mountain. . . .

The old woman and the children were still sleeping when Charity rose from her mattress. Her body was stiff with cold and fatigue, and she moved slowly lest her heavy steps should rouse them. She was faint with hunger, and had nothing left in her satchel; but on the table she saw the half of a stale loaf. No doubt it was to serve as the breakfast of old Mrs. Hyatt and the children; but Charity did not care; she had her own baby to think of. She broke off a piece of the bread and ate it greedily; then her glance fell on the thin faces of the sleeping children, and filled with compunction she rummaged in her satchel for something with which to pay for what she had taken. She found one of the pretty chemises that Ally had made for her, with a blue ribbon run through its edging. It was one of the dainty things on which she had squandered her savings, and as she looked at it the blood rushed to her forehead. She laid the chemise on the table, and stealing across the floor lifted the latch and went out. . . .

The morning was icy cold and a pale sun was just rising above

the eastern shoulder of the Mountain. The houses scattered on the
hillside lay cold and smokeless under the sun-flecked clouds, and
not a human being was in sight. Charity paused on the threshold
and tried to discover the road by which she had come the night
before. Across the field surrounding Mrs. Hyatt's shanty she saw
the tumble-down house in which she supposed the funeral service
had taken place. The trail ran across the ground between the
two houses and disappeared in the pine-wood on the flank of
the Mountain; and a little way to the right, under a wind-beaten
thorn, a mound of fresh earth made a dark spot on the fawn-
coloured stubble. Charity walked across the field to the mound.
As she approached it she heard a bird's note in the still air, and
looking up she saw a brown song-sparrow perched in an upper
branch of the thorn above the grave. She stood a minute listening
to his small solitary song; then she rejoined the trail and began to
mount the hill to the pine-wood.

Thus far she had been impelled by the blind instinct of flight;
but each step seemed to bring her nearer to the realities of which
her feverish vigil had given only a shadowy image. Now that she
walked again in a daylight world, on the way back to familiar
things, her imagination moved more soberly. On one point she
was still decided: she could not remain at North Dormer, and the
sooner she got away from it the better. But everything beyond was
darkness.

As she continued to climb the air grew keener, and when she
passed from the shelter of the pines to the open grassy roof of
the Mountain the cold wind of the night before sprang out on her.
She bent her shoulders and struggled on against it for a while;
but presently her breath failed, and she sat down under a ledge of
rock overhung by shivering birches. From where she sat she saw
the trail wandering across the bleached grass in the direction of
Hamblin, and the granite wall of the Mountain falling away to
infinite distances. On that side of the ridge the valleys still lay in
wintry shadow; but in the plain beyond the sun was touching village roofs and steeples, and gilding the haze of smoke over far-off
invisible towns.

Charity felt herself a mere speck in the lonely circle of the sky.
The events of the last two days seemed to have divided her forever
from her short dream of bliss. Even Harney's image had been

blurred by that crushing experience: she thought of him as so remote from her that he seemed hardly more than a memory. In her
fagged and floating mind only one sensation had the weight of reality; it was the bodily burden of her child. But for it she would
have felt as rootless as the whiffs of thistledown the wind blew
past her. Her child was like a load that held her down, and yet like
a hand that pulled her to her feet. She said to herself that she must
get up and struggle on. . . .

Her eyes turned back to the trail across the top of the Mountain, and in the distance she saw a buggy against the sky. She
knew its antique outline, and the gaunt build of the old horse
pressing forward with lowered head; and after a moment she recognized the heavy bulk of the man who held the reins. The buggy
was following the trail and making straight for the pine-wood
through which she had climbed; and she knew at once that the
driver was in search of her. Her first impulse was to crouch down
under the ledge till he had passed; but the instinct of concealment
was overruled by the relief of feeling that someone was near her in
the awful emptiness. She stood up and walked toward the buggy.

Mr. Royall saw her, and touched the horse with the whip. A
minute or two later he was abreast of Charity; their eyes met, and
without speaking he leaned over and helped her up into the buggy.
She tried to speak, to stammer out some explanation, but no
words came to her; and as he drew the cover over her knees he
simply said: "The minister told me he'd left you up here, so I come
up for you."

He turned the horse's head, and they began to jog back toward
Hamblin. Charity sat speechless, staring straight ahead of her, and
Mr. Royall occasionally uttered a word of encouragement to the
horse: "Get along there, Dan. . . . I gave him a rest at Hamblin;
but I brought him along pretty quick, and it's a stiff pull up here
against the wind."

As he spoke it occurred to her for the first time that to reach the
top of the Mountain so early he must have left North Dormer at
the coldest hour of the night, and have travelled steadily but for the
halt at Hamblin; and she felt a softness at her heart which no act of
his had ever produced since he had brought her the Crimson Rambler because she had given up boarding-school to stay with him.

After an interval he began again: "It was a day just like this,

only spitting snow, when I come up here for you the first time."
Then, as if fearing that she might take his remark as a reminder of
past benefits, he added quickly: "I dunno's you think it was such
a good job, either."

"Yes, I do," she murmured, looking straight ahead of her.

"Well," he said "I tried——"

He did not finish the sentence, and she could think of nothing
more to say.

"Ho, there, Dan, step out," he muttered, jerking the bridle.
"We ain't home yet.—You cold?" he asked abruptly.

She shook her head, but he drew the cover higher up, and
stooped to tuck it in about the ankles. She continued to look
straight ahead. Tears of weariness and weakness were dimming
her eyes and beginning to run over, but she dared not wipe them
away lest he should observe the gesture.

They drove in silence, following the long loops of the descent
upon Hamblin, and Mr. Royall did not speak again till they
reached the outskirts of the village. Then he let the reins droop on
the dashboard and drew out his watch.

"Charity," he said, "you look fair done up, and North Dormer's a goodish way off. I've figured out that we'd do better to
stop here long enough for you to get a mouthful of breakfast and
then drive down to Creston and take the train."

She roused herself from her apathetic musing. "The train—
what train?"

Mr. Royall, without answering, let the horse jog on till they
reached the door of the first house in the village. "This is old Mrs.
Hobart's place," he said. "She'll give us something hot to drink."

Charity, half unconsciously, found herself getting out of the
buggy and following him in at the open door. They entered a decent kitchen with a fire crackling in the stove. An old woman with
a kindly face was setting out cups and saucers on the table. She
looked up and nodded as they came in, and Mr. Royall advanced
to the stove, clapping his numb hands together.

"Well, Mrs. Hobart, you got any breakfast for this young lady?
You can see she's cold and hungry."

Mrs. Hobart smiled on Charity and took a tin coffee-pot from
the fire. "My, you do look pretty mean," she said compassionately.

Charity reddened, and sat down at the table. A feeling of complete passiveness had once more come over her, and she was conscious only of the pleasant animal sensations of warmth and rest.

Mrs. Hobart put bread and milk on the table, and then went out of the house: Charity saw her leading the horse away to the barn across the yard. She did not come back, and Mr. Royall and Charity sat alone at the table with the smoking coffee between them. He poured out a cup for her, and put a piece of bread in the saucer, and she began to eat.

As the warmth of the coffee flowed through her veins her thoughts cleared and she began to feel like a living being again; but the return to life was so painful that the food choked in her throat and she sat staring down at the table in silent anguish.

After a while Mr. Royall pushed back his chair. "Now, then," he said, "if you're a mind to go along——" She did not move, and he continued: "We can pick up the noon train for Nettleton if you say so."

The words sent the blood rushing to her face, and she raised her startled eyes to his. He was standing on the other side of the table looking at her kindly and gravely; and suddenly she understood what he was going to say. She continued to sit motionless, a leaden weight upon her lips.

"You and me have spoke some hard things to each other in our time, Charity; and there's no good that I can see in any more talking now. But I'll never feel any way but one about you; and if you say so we'll drive down in time to catch that train, and go straight to the minister's house; and when you come back home you'll come as Mrs. Royall."

His voice had the grave persuasive accent that had moved his hearers at the Home Week festival; she had a sense of depths of mournful tolerance under that easy tone. Her whole body began to tremble with the dread of her own weakness.

"Oh, I can't——" she burst out desperately.

"Can't what?"

She herself did not know: she was not sure if she was rejecting what he offered, or already struggling against the temptation of taking what she no longer had a right to. She stood up, shaking and bewildered, and began to speak:

"I know I ain't been fair to you always; but I want to be

now. . . . I want you to know . . . I want . . ." Her voice failed her
and she stopped.

Mr. Royall leaned against the wall. He was paler than usual,
but his face was composed and kindly and her agitation did not
appear to perturb him.

"What's all this about wanting?" he said as she paused. "Do
you know what you really want? I'll tell you. You want to be took
home and took care of. And I guess that's all there is to say."

"No . . . it's not all. . . ."

"Ain't it?" He looked at his watch. "Well, I'll tell you another
thing. All *I* want is to know if you'll marry me. If there was anything else, I'd tell you so; but there ain't. Come to my age, a man
knows the things that matter and the things that don't; that's
about the only good turn life does us."

His tone was so strong and resolute that it was like a supporting arm about her. She felt her resistance melting, her strength
slipping away from her as he spoke.

"Don't cry, Charity," he exclaimed in a shaken voice. She
looked up, startled at his emotion, and their eyes met.

"See here," he said gently, "old Dan's come a long distance, and
we've got to let him take it easy the rest of the way. . . ."

He picked up the cloak that had slipped to her chair and laid it
about her shoulders. She followed him out of the house, and they
walked across the yard to the shed, where the horse was tied. Mr.
Royall unblanketed him and led him out into the road. Charity
got into the buggy and he drew the cover about her and shook out
the reins with a cluck. When they reached the end of the village he
turned the horse's head toward Creston.

XVIII

They began to jog down the winding road to the valley at old
Dan's languid pace. Charity felt herself sinking into deeper depths
of weariness, and as they descended through the bare woods there
were moments when she lost the exact sense of things, and seemed
to be sitting beside her lover with the leafy arch of summer bending over them. But this illusion was faint and transitory. For the
most part she had only a confused sensation of slipping down a

smooth irresistible current; and she abandoned herself to the feeling as a refuge from the torment of thought.

Mr. Royall seldom spoke, but his silent presence gave her, for the first time, a sense of peace and security. She knew that where he was there would be warmth, rest, silence; and for the moment they were all she wanted. She shut her eyes, and even these things grew dim to her. . . .

In the train, during the short run from Creston to Nettleton, the warmth aroused her, and the consciousness of being under strange eyes gave her a momentary energy. She sat upright, facing Mr. Royall, and stared out of the window at the denuded country. Forty-eight hours earlier, when she had last traversed it, many of the trees still held their leaves; but the high wind of the last two nights had stripped them, and the lines of the landscape were as finely pencilled as in December. A few days of autumn cold had wiped out all trace of the rich fields and languid groves through which she had passed on the Fourth of July; and with the fading of the landscape those fervid hours had faded too. She could no longer believe that she was the being who had lived them; she was someone to whom something irreparable and overwhelming had happened, but the traces of the steps leading up to it had almost vanished.

When the train reached Nettleton and she walked out into the square at Mr. Royall's side the sense of unreality grew more overpowering. The physical strain of the night and day had left no room in her mind for new sensations and she followed Mr. Royall as passively as a tired child. As in a confused dream she presently found herself sitting with him in a pleasant room, at a table with a red and white table-cloth on which hot food and tea were placed. He filled her cup and plate and whenever she lifted her eyes from them she found his resting on her with the same steady tranquil gaze that had reassured and strengthened her when they had faced each other in old Mrs. Hobart's kitchen. As everything else in her consciousness grew more and more confused and immaterial, became more and more like the universal shimmer that dissolves the world to failing eyes, Mr. Royall's presence began to detach itself with rocky firmness from this elusive background. She had always thought of him—when she thought of him at all— as of someone hateful and obstructive, but whom she could outwit and dominate when she chose to make the effort. Only once, on the day of the Old Home Week celebration, while the stray fragments of his address drifted across her troubled mind, had she caught a glimpse of another being, a being so different from the dull-witted enemy with whom she had supposed herself to be living that even through the burning mist of her own dreams he had stood out with startling distinctness. For a moment, then, what he said—and something in his way of saying it—had made her see why he had always struck her as such a lonely man. But the mist of her dreams had hidden him again, and she had forgotten that fugitive impression.

It came back to her now, as they sat at the table, and gave her, through her own immeasurable desolation, a sudden sense of their nearness to each other. But all these feelings were only brief streaks of light in the grey blur of her physical weakness. Through it she was aware that Mr. Royall presently left her sitting by the table in the warm room, and came back after an interval with a carriage from the station—a closed "hack" with sunburnt blue silk blinds—in which they drove together to a house covered with creepers and standing next to a church with a carpet of turf before it. They got out at this house, and the carriage waited while they walked up the path and entered a wainscoted hall and then a room full of books. In this room a clergyman whom Charity had never seen received them pleasantly, and asked them to be seated for a few minutes while witnesses were being summoned.

Charity sat down obediently, and Mr. Royall, his hands behind his back, paced slowly up and down the room. As he turned and faced Charity, she noticed that his lips were twitching a little; but the look in his eyes was grave and calm. Once he paused before her and said timidly: "Your hair's got kinder loose with the wind," and she lifted her hands and tried to smooth back the locks that had escaped from her braid. There was a looking-glass in a carved frame on the wall, but she was ashamed to look at herself in it, and she sat with her hands folded on her knee till the clergyman returned. Then they went out again, along a sort of arcaded passage, and into a low vaulted room with a cross on an altar, and rows of benches. The clergyman, who had left them at the door, presently reappeared before the altar in a surplice, and a lady who was probably his wife, and a man in a blue shirt who had been raking dead leaves on the lawn, came in and sat on one of the benches.

The clergyman opened a book and signed to Charity and Mr. Royall to approach. Mr. Royall advanced a few steps, and Charity followed him as she had followed him to the buggy when they went out of Mrs. Hobart's kitchen; she had the feeling that if she ceased to keep close to him, and do what he told her to do, the world would slip away from beneath her feet.

The clergyman began to read, and on her dazed mind there rose the memory of Mr. Miles, standing the night before in the desolate house of the Mountain, and reading out of the same book words that had the same dread sound of finality:

"I require and charge you both, as ye will answer at the dreadful day of judgment when the secrets of all hearts shall be disclosed, that if either of you know any impediment whereby ye may not be lawfully joined together . . ."

Charity raised her eyes and met Mr. Royall's. They were still looking at her kindly and steadily. "I will!" she heard him say a moment later, after another interval of words that she had failed to catch. She was so busy trying to understand the gestures the clergyman was signalling to her to make that she no longer heard what was being said. After another interval the lady on the bench stood up, and taking her hand put it in Mr. Royall's. It lay enclosed in his strong palm and she felt a ring that was too big for her being slipped onto her thin finger. She understood then that she was married. . . .

Late that afternoon Charity sat alone in a bedroom of the fashionable hotel where she and Harney had vainly sought a table on the Fourth of July. She had never before been in so handsomely furnished a room. The mirror above the dressing-table reflected the high head-board and fluted pillow-slips of the double bed, and a bedspread so spotlessly white that she had hesitated to lay her hat and jacket on it. The humming radiator diffused an atmosphere of drowsy warmth, and through a half-open door she saw the glitter of the nickel taps above twin marble basins.

For a while the long turmoil of the night and day had slipped away from her and she sat with closed eyes, surrendering herself to the spell of warmth and silence. But presently this merciful apathy was succeeded by the sudden acuteness of vision with which sick people sometimes wake out of a heavy sleep. As she opened her eyes they rested on the picture that hung above the bed. It was a large engraving with a dazzling white margin enclosed in a wide frame of bird's-eye maple with an inner scroll of gold. The engraving represented a young man in a boat on a lake overhung with trees. He was leaning over to gather water-lilies for the girl in a light dress who lay among the cushions in the stern. The scene was full of a drowsy midsummer radiance, and Charity averted her eyes from it and, rising from her chair, began to wander restlessly about the room.

It was on the fifth floor, and its broad window of plate glass looked over the roofs of the town. Beyond them stretched a wooded landscape in which the last fires of sunset were picking out a steely gleam. Charity gazed at the gleam with startled eyes. Even through the gathering twilight she recognized the contour of the soft hills encircling it, and the way the meadows sloped to its edge. It was Nettleton Lake that she was looking at.

She stood a long time in the window staring out at the fading water. The sight of it had roused her for the first time to a realization of what she had done. Even the feeling of the ring on her hand had not brought her this sharp sense of the irretrievable. For an instant the old impulse of flight swept through her; but it was only the lift of a broken wing. She heard the door open behind her, and Mr. Royall came in.

He had gone to the barber's to be shaved, and his shaggy grey hair had been trimmed and smoothed. He moved strongly and quickly, squaring his shoulders and carrying his head high, as if he did not want to pass unnoticed.

"What are you doing in the dark?" he called out in a cheerful voice. Charity made no answer. He went up to the window to draw down the blind, and putting his finger on the wall flooded the room with a blaze of light from the central chandelier. In this unfamiliar illumination husband and wife faced each other awkwardly for a moment; then Mr. Royall said: "We'll step down and have some supper, if you say so."

The thought of food filled her with repugnance; but not daring to confess it she smoothed her hair and followed him to the lift.

An hour later, coming out of the glare of the dining-room, she waited in the marble-panelled hall while Mr. Royall, before the brass lattice of one of the corner counters, selected a cigar and bought an evening paper. Men were lounging in rocking chairs under the blazing chandeliers, travellers coming and going, bells ringing, porters shuffling by with luggage. Over Mr. Royall's shoulder, as he leaned against the counter, a girl with her hair puffed high smirked and nodded at a dapper drummer who was getting his key at the desk across the hall.

Charity stood among these cross-currents of life as motionless and inert as if she had been one of the tables screwed to the marble floor. All her soul was gathered up into one sick sense of coming doom, and she watched Mr. Royall in fascinated terror while he pinched the cigars in successive boxes and unfolded his evening paper with a steady hand.

Presently he turned and joined her. "You go right along up to bed—I'm going to sit down here and have my smoke," he said. He spoke as easily and naturally as if they had been an old couple, long used to each other's ways, and her contracted heart gave a flutter of relief. She followed him to the lift, and he put her in and enjoined the buttoned and braided boy to show her to her room.

She groped her way in through the darkness, forgetting where the electric button was, and not knowing how to manipulate it. But a white autumn moon had risen, and the illuminated sky put a pale light in the room. By it she undressed, and after folding up the ruffled pillow-slips crept timidly under the spotless counterpane. She had never felt such smooth sheets or such light warm blankets; but the softness of the bed did not soothe her. She lay there trembling with a fear that ran through her veins like ice. "What have I done? Oh, what have I done?" she whispered, shuddering to her pillow; and pressing her face against it to shut out the pale landscape beyond the window she lay in the darkness straining her ears, and shaking at every footstep that approached. . . .

Suddenly she sat up and pressed her hands against her frightened heart. A faint sound had told her that someone was in the room; but she must have slept in the interval, for she had heard no one enter. The moon was setting beyond the opposite roofs, and in the darkness, outlined against the grey square of the window, she saw a figure seated in the rocking-chair. The figure did not move: it was sunk deep in the chair, with bowed head and folded arms, and she saw that it was Mr. Royall who sat there. He had not undressed, but had taken the blanket from the foot of the bed and laid it across his knees. Trembling and holding her breath she watched him, fearing that he had been roused by her movement; but he did not stir, and she concluded that he wished her to think he was asleep.

As she continued to watch him ineffable relief stole slowly over her, relaxing her strained nerves and exhausted body. He knew, then . . . he knew . . . it was because he knew that he had married her, and that he sat there in the darkness to show her she was safe with him. A stir of something deeper than she had ever felt in thinking of him flitted through her tired brain, and cautiously, noiselessly, she let her head sink on the pillow. . . .

When she woke the room was full of morning light, and her first glance showed her that she was alone in it. She got up and dressed, and as she was fastening her dress the door opened, and Mr. Royall came in. He looked old and tired in the bright daylight, but his face wore the same expression of grave friendliness that had reassured her on the Mountain. It was as if all the dark spirits had gone out of him.

They went downstairs to the dining-room for breakfast, and after breakfast he told her he had some insurance business to attend to. "I guess while I'm doing it you'd better step out and buy yourself whatever you need." He smiled, and added with an embarrassed laugh: "You know I always wanted you to beat all the other girls." He drew something from his pocket, and pushed it across the table to her; and she saw that he had given her two twenty-dollar bills. "If it ain't enough there's more where that come from—I want you to beat 'em all hollow," he repeated.

She flushed and tried to stammer out her thanks, but he had pushed back his chair and was leading the way out of the dining-room. In the hall he paused a minute to say that if it suited her they would take the three o'clock train back to North Dormer; then he took his hat and coat from the rack and went out.

A few minutes later Charity went out too. She had watched to see in what direction he was going, and she took the opposite way and walked quickly down the main street to the brick building on the corner of Lake Avenue. There she paused to look cautiously up and down the thoroughfare, and then climbed the brass-bound stairs to Dr. Merkle's door. The same bushy-headed mulatto girl admitted her, and after the same interval of waiting in the red plush parlor she was once more summoned to Dr. Merkle's office. The doctor received her without surprise, and led her into the inner plush sanctuary.

"I thought you'd be back, but you've come a mite too soon: I told you to be patient and not fret," she observed, after a pause of penetrating scrutiny.

Charity drew the money from her breast. "I've come to get my blue brooch," she said, flushing.

"Your brooch?" Dr. Merkle appeared not to remember. "My, yes—I get so many things of that kind. Well, my dear, you'll have to wait while I get it out of the safe. I don't leave valuables like that laying round like the noospaper."

She disappeared for a moment, and returned with a bit of twisted-up tissue paper from which she unwrapped the brooch.

Charity, as she looked at it, felt a stir of warmth at her heart. She held out an eager hand.

"Have you got the change?" she asked a little breathlessly, laying one of the twenty-dollar bills on the table.

"Change? What'd I want to have change for? I only see two twenties there," Dr. Merkle answered brightly.

Charity paused, disconcerted. "I thought . . . you said it was five dollars a visit. . . ."

"For *you*, as a favour—I did. But how about the responsibility—*and* the insurance? I don't s'pose you ever thought of that? This pin's worth a hundred dollars easy. If it had got lost or stole, where'd I been when you come to claim it?"

Charity remained silent, puzzled and half-convinced by the argument, and Dr. Merkle promptly followed up her advantage. "I didn't ask you for your brooch, my dear. I'd a good deal ruther folks paid me my regular charge than have 'em put me to all this trouble."

She paused, and Charity, seized with a desperate longing to escape, rose to her feet and held out one of the bills.

"Will you take that?" she asked.

"No, I won't take that, my dear; but I'll take it with its mate, and hand you over a signed receipt if you don't trust me."

"Oh, but I can't—it's all I've got," Charity exclaimed.

Dr. Merkle looked up at her pleasantly from the plush sofa. "It seems you got married yesterday, up to the 'Piscopal church; I heard all about the wedding from the minister's chore-man. It would be a pity, wouldn't it, to let Mr. Royall know you had an account running here? I just put it to you as your own mother might."

Anger flamed up in Charity, and for an instant she thought of abandoning the brooch and letting Dr. Merkle do her worst. But how could she leave her only treasure with that evil woman? She wanted it for her baby: she meant it, in some mysterious way, to be a link between Harney's child and its unknown father. Trembling and hating herself while she did it, she laid Mr. Royall's money on the table, and catching up the brooch fled out of the room and the house. . . .

In the street she stood still, dazed by this last adventure. But the brooch lay in her bosom like a talisman, and she felt a secret lightness of heart. It gave her strength, after a moment, to walk on slowly in the direction of the post office, and go in through the swinging doors. At one of the windows she bought a sheet of letter-paper, an envelope and a stamp; then she sat down at a table and dipped the rusty post office pen in ink. She had come there possessed with a fear which had haunted her ever since she had felt Mr. Royall's ring on her finger: the fear that Harney might, after all, free himself and come back to her. It was a possibility which had never occurred to her during the dreadful hours after she had received his letter; only when the decisive step she had taken made longing turn to apprehension did such a contingency seem conceivable. She addressed the envelope, and on the sheet of paper she wrote:

I'm married to Mr. Royall. I'll always remember you.

CHARITY.

The last words were not in the least what she had meant to write; they had flowed from her pen irresistibly. She had not had the strength to complete her sacrifice; but, after all, what did it matter? Now that there was no chance of ever seeing Harney again, why should she not tell him the truth?

When she had put the letter in the box she went out into the busy sunlit street and began to walk to the hotel. Behind the plate-glass windows of the department stores she noticed the tempting display of dresses and dress-materials that had fired her imagination on the day when she and Harney had looked in at them together. They reminded her of Mr. Royall's injunction to go out and buy all she needed. She looked down at her shabby dress, and wondered what she should say when he saw her coming back empty-handed. As she drew near the hotel she saw him waiting on the doorstep, and her heart began to beat with apprehension.

He nodded and waved his hand at her approach, and they walked through the hall and went upstairs to collect their possessions, so that Mr. Royall might give up the key of the room when they went down again for their midday dinner. In the bedroom, while she was thrusting back into the satchel the few things she had brought away with her, she suddenly felt that his eyes were on her and that he was going to speak. She stood still, her half-folded night-gown in her hand, while the blood rushed up to her drawn cheeks.

"Well, did you rig yourself out handsomely? I haven't seen any bundles round," he said jocosely.

"Oh, I'd rather let Ally Hawes make the few things I want," she answered.

"That so?" He looked at her thoughtfully for a moment and his eye-brows projected in a scowl. Then his face grew friendly again. "Well, I wanted you to go back looking stylisher than any of them; but I guess you're right. You're a good girl, Charity."

Their eyes met, and something rose in his that she had never seen there: a look that made her feel ashamed and yet secure.

"I guess you're good, too," she said, shyly and quickly. He smiled without answering, and they went out of the room together and dropped down to the hall in the glittering lift.

Late that evening, in the cold autumn moonlight, they drove up to the door of the red house.

THE HOUSE OF MIRTH

I

Selden paused in surprise. In the afternoon rush of the Grand Central Station[1] his eyes had been refreshed by the sight of Miss Lily Bart.

It was a Monday in early September, and he was returning to his work from a hurried dip into the country; but what was Miss Bart doing in town at that season? If she had appeared to be catching a train, he might have inferred that he had come on her in the act of transition between one and another of the country-houses which disputed her presence[2] after the close of the Newport season,[3] but her desultory air perplexed him. She stood apart from the crowd, letting it drift by her to the platform or the street, and wearing an air of irresolution which might, as he surmised, be the mask of a very definite purpose. It struck him at once that she was waiting for some one, but he hardly knew why the idea arrested him. There was nothing new about Lily Bart, yet he could never see her without a faint movement of interest: it was characteristic of her that she always roused speculation, that her simplest acts seemed the result of far-reaching intentions.

An impulse of curiosity made him turn out of his direct line to the door, and stroll past her. He knew that if she did not wish to be seen she would contrive to elude him; and it amused him to think of putting her skill to the test.

"Mr. Selden—what good luck!"

She came forward smiling, eager almost, in her resolve to intercept him. One or two persons, in brushing past them, lingered to look; for Miss Bart was a figure to arrest even the suburban traveller rushing to his last train.

Selden had never seen her more radiant. Her vivid head, relieved against the dull tints of the crowd, made her more conspicuous than in a ball-room, and under her dark hat and veil she regained the girlish smoothness, the purity of tint, that she was beginning to lose after eleven years[4] of late hours and indefatigable dancing. Was it really eleven years, Selden found himself wondering, and had she indeed reached the nine-and-twentieth birthday with which her rivals credited her?

"What luck!" she repeated. "How nice of you to come to my rescue!" He responded joyfully that to do so was his mission in life, and asked what form the rescue was to take.

"Oh, almost any—even to sitting on a bench and talking to me. One sits out a cotillion—why not sit out a train? It isn't a bit hotter here than in Mrs. Van Osburgh's conservatory—and some of the women are not a bit uglier."

She broke off, laughing, to explain that she had come up to town from Tuxedo, on her way to the Gus Trenors' at Bellomont, and had missed the three-fifteen train to Rhinebeck.

"And there isn't another till half-past five." She consulted the little jewelled watch among her laces. "Just two hours to wait. And I don't know what to do with myself. My maid came up this morning to do some shopping for me, and was to go on to Bellomont at one o'clock, and my aunt's house is closed, and I don't know a soul in town." She glanced plaintively about the station. "It is hotter than Mrs. Van Osburgh's, after all. If you can spare the time, do take me somewhere for a breath of air."

He declared himself entirely at her disposal: the adventure struck him as diverting. As a spectator, he had always enjoyed Lily Bart; and his course lay so far out of her orbit that it amused him to be drawn for a moment into the sudden intimacy which her proposal implied.

"Shall we go over to Sherry's[5] for a cup of tea?"

She smiled assentingly, and then made a slight grimace.

"So many people come up to town on a Monday—one is sure to meet a lot of bores. I'm as old as the hills, of course, and it ought not to make any difference; but if *I'm* old enough, you're not," she objected gaily. "I'm dying for tea—but isn't there a quieter place?"

He answered her smile, which rested on him vividly. Her discretions interested him almost as much as her imprudences: he was so sure that both were part of the same carefully-elaborated plan. In judging Miss Bart, he had always made use of the "argument from design."

"The resources of New York are rather meagre," he said; "but I'll find a hansom first, and then we'll invent something."

He led her through the throng of returning holiday makers, past sallow-faced girls in preposterous hats, and flat-chested women struggling with paper bundles and palm-leaf fans. Was it possible that she belonged to the same race? The dinginess, the crudity of this average section of womanhood made him feel how highly specialized she was.

A rapid shower had cooled the air, and clouds still hung refreshingly over the moist street.

"How delicious! Let us walk a little," she said as they emerged from the station.

They turned into Madison Avenue and began to stroll northward. As she moved beside him, with her long light step, Selden was conscious of taking a luxurious pleasure in her nearness: in the modelling of her little ear, the crisp upward wave of her hair—was it ever so slightly brightened by art?—and the thick planting of her straight black lashes. Everything about her was at once vigorous and exquisite, at once strong and fine. He had a confused sense that she must have cost a great deal to make, that a great many dull and ugly people must, in some mysterious way, have been sacrificed to produce her. He was aware that the qualities distinguishing her from the herd of her sex were chiefly external: as though a fine glaze of beauty and fastidiousness had been applied to vulgar clay. Yet the analogy left him unsatisfied, for a coarse texture will not take a high finish; and was it not possible that the material was fine, but that circumstance had fashioned it into a futile shape?

As he reached this point in his speculations the sun came out, and her lifted parasol cut off his enjoyment. A moment or two later she paused with a sigh.

"Oh, dear, I'm so hot and thirsty—and what a hideous place New York is!" She looked despairingly up and down the dreary thoroughfare. "Other cities put on their best clothes in summer, but New York seems to sit in its shirt-sleeves." Her eyes wandered down one of the side-streets. "Some one has had the humanity to plant a few trees over there. Let us go into the shade."

"I am glad my street meets with your approval," said Selden as they turned the comer.

"Your street? Do you live here?"

She glanced with interest along the new brick and limestone house-fronts, fantastically varied in obedience to the American craving for novelty, but fresh and inviting with their awnings and flower-boxes.

"Ah, yes—to be sure: *The Benedick*. What a nice-looking building! I don't think I've ever seen it before." She looked across at the flat-house with its marble porch and pseudo-Georgian façade. "Which are your windows? Those with the awnings down?"

"On the top floor—yes."

"And that nice little balcony is yours? How cool it looks up there!"

He paused a moment. "Come up and see," he suggested. "I can give you a cup of tea in no time—and you won't meet any bores."

Her colour deepened—she still had the art of blushing at the right time—but she took the suggestion as lightly as it was made.

"Why not? It's too tempting—I'll take the risk," she declared.

"Oh, I'm not dangerous," he said in the same key. In truth, he had never liked her as well as at that moment. He knew she had accepted without afterthought: he could never be a factor in her calculations, and there was a surprise, a refreshment almost, in the spontaneity of her consent.

On the threshold he paused a moment, feeling for his latch-key.

"There's no one here; but I have a servant who is supposed to come in the mornings, and it's just possible he may have put out the tea-things and provided some cake."

He ushered her into a slip of a hall hung with old prints. She noticed the letters and notes heaped on the table among his gloves and sticks; then she found herself in a small library, dark but cheerful, with its walls of books, a pleasantly faded Turkey rug, a littered desk, and, as he had foretold, a tea-tray on a low table near the window. A breeze had sprung up, swaying inward the muslin curtains, and bringing a fresh scent of mignonette and petunias from the flower-box on the balcony.

Lily sank with a sigh into one of the shabby leather chairs.

"How delicious to have a place like this all to one's self! What a miserable thing it is to be a woman." She leaned back in a luxury of discontent.

Selden was rummaging in a cupboard for the cake.

"Even women," he said, "have been known to enjoy the privileges of a flat."

"Oh, governesses—or widows. But not girls—not poor, miserable, marriageable girls!"

"I even know a girl who lives in a flat."

She sat up in surprise. "You do?"

"I do," he assured her, emerging from the cupboard with the sought-for cake.

"Oh, I know—you mean Gerty Farish." She smiled a little unkindly. "But I said *marriageable*—and besides, she has a horrid little place, and no maid, and such queer things to eat. Her cook does the washing and the food tastes of soap. I should hate that, you know."

"You shouldn't dine with her on wash-days," said Selden, cutting the cake.

They both laughed, and he knelt by the table to light the lamp under the kettle, while she measured out the tea into a little teapot of green glaze. As he watched her hand, polished as a bit of old ivory, with its slender pink nails, and the sapphire bracelet slipping over her wrist, he was struck with the irony of suggesting to her such a life as his cousin Gertrude Farish had chosen. She was so evidently the victim of the civilization which had produced her, that the links of her bracelet seemed like manacles chaining her to her fate.

She seemed to read his thought. "It was horrid of me to say that of Gerty," she said with charming compunction. "I forgot she was your cousin. But we're so different, you know: she likes being good, and I like being happy. And besides, she is free and I am not. If I were, I daresay I could manage to be happy even in her flat. It must be pure bliss to arrange the furniture just as one likes, and give all the horrors to the ash-man. If I could only do over my aunt's drawing-room I know I should be a better woman."

"Is it so very bad?" he asked sympathetically.

She smiled at him across the tea-pot which she was holding up to be filled.

"That shows how seldom you come there. Why don't you come oftener?"

"When I do come, it's not to look at Mrs. Peniston's furniture."

"Nonsense," she said. "You don't come at all—and yet we get on so well when we meet."

"Perhaps that's the reason," he answered promptly. "I'm afraid I haven't any cream, you know—shall you mind a slice of lemon instead?"

"I shall like it better." She waited while he cut the lemon and dropped a thin disk into her cup. "But that is not the reason," she insisted.

"The reason for what?"

"For your never coming." She leaned forward with a shade of perplexity in her charming eyes. "I wish I knew—I wish I could make you out. Of course I know there are men who don't like me—one can tell that at a glance. And there are others who are afraid of me: they think I want to marry them." She smiled up at him frankly. "But I don't think you dislike me—and you can't possibly think I want to marry you."

"No—I absolve you of that," he agreed.

"Well, then—?"

He had carried his cup to the fireplace, and stood leaning against the chimney-piece and looking down on her with an air of indolent amusement. The provocation in her eyes increased his amusement—he had not supposed she would waste her powder on such small game; but perhaps she was only keeping her hand in; or perhaps a girl of her type had no conversation but of the personal kind. At any rate, she was amazingly pretty, and he had asked her to tea and must live up to his obligations.

"Well, then," he said with a plunge, "perhaps *that's* the reason."

"What?"

"The fact that you don't want to marry me. Perhaps I don't regard it as such a strong inducement to go and see you." He felt a slight shiver down his spine as he ventured this, but her laugh reassured him.

"Dear Mr. Selden, that wasn't worthy of you. It's stupid of you to make love to me, and it isn't like you to be stupid." She leaned back, sipping her tea with an air so enchantingly judicial that, if they had been in her aunt's drawing-room, he might almost have tried to disprove her deduction.

"Don't you see," she continued, "that there are men enough to say pleasant things to me, and that what I want is a friend who won't be afraid to say disagreeable ones when I need them? Sometimes I have fancied you might be that friend—I don't know why, except that you are neither a prig nor a bounder, and that I shouldn't have to pretend with you or be on my guard against you." Her voice had dropped to a note of seriousness, and she sat gazing up at him with the troubled gravity of a child.

"You don't know how much I need such a friend," she said. "My aunt is full of copy-book axioms,[6] but they were all meant to apply to conduct in the early fifties. I always feel that to live up to them would include wearing book-muslin with gigot sleeves[7] And the other women—my best friends—well, they use me or abuse me; but they don't care a straw what happens to me. I've been about too long—people are getting tired of me; they are beginning to say I ought to marry."

There was a moment's pause, during which Selden meditated one or two replies calculated to add a momentary zest to the situation; but he rejected them in favour of the simple question: "Well, why don't you?"

She coloured and laughed. "Ah, I see you *are* a friend after all, and that is one of the disagreeable things I was asking for."

"It wasn't meant to be disagreeable," he returned amicably. "Isn't marriage your vocation? Isn't it what you're all brought up for?"

She sighed. "I suppose so. What else is there?"

"Exactly. And so why not take the plunge and have it over?"

She shrugged her shoulders. "You speak as if I ought to marry the first man who came along."

"I didn't mean to imply that you are as hard put to it as that. But there must be some one with the requisite qualifications."

She shook her head wearily. "I threw away one or two good chances when I first came out—I suppose every girl does; and you know I am horribly poor—and very expensive. I must have a great deal of money."

Selden had turned to reach for a cigarette-box on the mantelpiece.

"What's become of Dillworth?" he asked.

"Oh, his mother was frightened—she was afraid I should have all the family jewels reset. And she wanted me to promise that I wouldn't do over the drawing-room."

"The very thing you are marrying for!"

"Exactly. So she packed him off to India."

"Hard luck—but you can do better than Dillworth."

He offered the box, and she took out three or four cigarettes, putting one between her lips and slipping the others into a little gold case attached to her long pearl chain.

"Have I time? Just a whiff, then." She leaned forward, holding the tip of her cigarette to his. As she did so, he noted, with a purely impersonal enjoyment, how evenly the black lashes were set in her smooth white lids, and how the purplish shade beneath them melted into the pure pallour of the cheek.

She began to saunter about the room, examining the book-shelves between the puffs of her cigarette-smoke. Some of the volumes had the ripe tints of good tooling and old morocco, and her eyes lingered on them caressingly, not with the appreciation of the expert, but with the pleasure in agreeable tones and textures that was one of her inmost susceptibilities. Suddenly her expression changed from desultory enjoyment to active conjecture, and she turned to Selden with a question.

"You collect, don't you—you know about first editions and things?"

"As much as a man may who has no money to spend. Now and then I pick up something in the rubbish heap; and I go and look on at the big sales."

She had again addressed herself to the shelves, but her eyes now swept them inattentively, and he saw that she was preoccupied with a new idea.

"And Americana—do you collect Americana?"[8]

Selden stared and laughed.

"No, that's rather out of my line. I'm not really a collector, you see; I simply like to have good editions of the books I am fond of."

She made a slight grimace. "And Americana are horribly dull, I suppose?"

"I should fancy so—except to the historian. But your real collector values a thing for its rarity. I don't suppose the buyers of

Americana sit up reading them all night—old Jefferson Gryce certainly didn't."

She was listening with keen attention. "And yet they fetch fabulous prices, don't they? It seems so odd to want to pay a lot for an ugly badly-printed book that one is never going to read! And I suppose most of the owners of Americana are not historians either?"

"No; very few of the historians can afford to buy them. They have to use those in the public libraries or in private collections. It seems to be the mere rarity that attracts the average collector."

He had seated himself on an arm of the chair near which she was standing, and she continued to question him, asking which were the rarest volumes, whether the Jefferson Gryce collection was really considered the finest in the world, and what was the largest price ever fetched by a single volume.

It was so pleasant to sit there looking up at her, as she lifted now one book and then another from the shelves, fluttering the pages between her fingers, while her drooping profile was outlined against the warm background of old bindings, that he talked on without pausing to wonder at her sudden interest in so unsuggestive a subject. But he could never be long with her without trying to find a reason for what she was doing, and as she replaced his first edition of La Bruyère[9] and turned away from the bookcases, he began to ask himself what she had been driving at. Her next question was not of a nature to enlighten him. She paused before him with a smile which seemed at once designed to admit him to her familiarity, and to remind him of the restrictions it imposed.

"Don't you ever mind," she asked suddenly, "not being rich enough to buy all the books you want?"

He followed her glance about the room, with its worn furniture and shabby walls.

"Don't I just? Do you take me for a saint on a pillar?"

"And having to work—do you mind that?"

"Oh, the work itself is not so bad—I'm rather fond of the law."

"No; but the being tied down: the routine—don't you ever want to get away, to see new places and people?"

"Horribly—especially when I see all my friends rushing to the steamer."

She drew a sympathetic breath. "But do you mind enough—to marry to get out of it?"

Selden broke into a laugh. "God forbid!" he declared.

She rose with a sigh, tossing her cigarette into the grate.

"Ah, there's the difference—a girl must, a man may if he chooses." She surveyed him critically. "Your coat's a little shabby—but who cares? It doesn't keep people from asking you to dine. If I were shabby no one would have me: a woman is asked out as much for her clothes as for herself. The clothes are the background, the frame, if you like: they don't make success, but they are a part of it. Who wants a dingy woman? We are expected to be pretty and well-dressed till we drop—and if we can't keep it up alone, we have to go into partnership."

Selden glanced at her with amusement: it was impossible, even with her lovely eyes imploring him, to take a sentimental view of her case.

"Ah, well, there must be plenty of capital on the lookout for such an investment. Perhaps you'll meet your fate to-night at the Trenors'."

She returned his look interrogatively.

"I thought you might be going there—oh, not in that capacity! But there are to be a lot of your set—Gwen Van Osburgh, the Wetheralls, Lady Cressida Raith—and the George Dorsets."

She paused a moment before the last name, and shot a query through her lashes; but he remained imperturbable.

"Mrs. Trenor asked me; but I can't get away till the end of the week; and those big parties bore me."

"Ah, so they do me," she exclaimed.

"Then why go?"

"It's part of the business—you forget! And besides, if I didn't, I should be playing bézique[10] with my aunt at Richfield Springs."

"That's almost as bad as marrying Dillworth," he agreed, and they both laughed for pure pleasure in their sudden intimacy.

She glanced at the clock.

"Dear me! I must be off. It's after five."

She paused before the mantelpiece, studying herself in the mirror while she adjusted her veil. The attitude revealed the long slope of her slender sides, which gave a kind of wild-wood grace to her outline—as though she were a captured dryad[11] subdued to the conventions of the drawing-room; and Selden reflected that it was the same streak of sylvan freedom in her nature that lent such savour to her artificiality.

He followed her across the room to the entrance-hall; but on the threshold she held out her hand with a gesture of leave-taking.

"It's been delightful; and now you will have to return my visit."

"But don't you want me to see you to the station?"

"No; good bye here, please."

She let her hand lie in his a moment, smiling up at him adorably.

"Good bye, then—and good luck at Bellomont!" he said, opening the door for her.

On the landing she paused to look about her. There were a thousand chances to one against her meeting anybody, but one could never tell, and she always paid for her rare indiscretions by a violent reaction of prudence. There was no one in sight, however, but a char-woman who was scrubbing the stairs. Her own stout person and its surrounding implements took up so much room that Lily, to pass her, had to gather up her skirts and brush against the wall. As she did so, the woman paused in her work and looked up curiously, resting her clenched red fists on the wet cloth she had just drawn from her pail. She had a broad sallow face, slightly pitted with small-pox, and thin straw-coloured hair through which her scalp shone unpleasantly.

"I beg your pardon," said Lily, intending by her politeness to convey a criticism of the other's manner.

The woman, without answering, pushed her pail aside, and continued to stare as Miss Bart swept by with a murmur of silken linings. Lily felt herself flushing under the look. What did the creature suppose? Could one never do the simplest, the most harmless thing, without subjecting one's self to some odious conjecture? Half way down the next flight, she smiled to think that a char-woman's stare should so perturb her. The poor thing was probably dazzled by such an unwonted apparition. But *were* such apparitions unwonted on Selden's stairs? Miss Bart was not familiar with the moral code of bachelors' flat-houses, and her colour rose again as it occurred to her that the woman's persistent gaze implied a groping among past associations. But she put aside the thought with a smile at her own fears, and hastened downward, wondering if she should find a cab short of Fifth Avenue.

Under the Georgian porch she paused again, scanning the street for a hansom. None was in sight, but as she reached the sidewalk she ran against a small glossy-looking man with a gardenia in his coat, who raised his hat with a surprised exclamation.

"Miss Bart? Well—of all people! This *is* luck," he declared; and she caught a twinkle of amused curiosity between his screwed-up lids.

"Oh, Mr. Rosedale—how are you?" she said, perceiving that the irrepressible annoyance on her face was reflected in the sudden intimacy of his smile.

Mr. Rosedale stood scanning her with interest and approval. He was a plump rosy man of the blond Jewish type, with smart London clothes fitting him like upholstery, and small sidelong eyes which gave him the air of appraising people as if they were bric-a-brac. He glanced up interrogatively at the porch of the Benedick.

"Been up to town for a little shopping, I suppose?" he said, in a tone which had the familiarity of a touch.

Miss Bart shrank from it slightly, and then flung herself into precipitate explanations.

"Yes—I came up to see my dress-maker. I am just on my way to catch the train to the Trenors'."

"Ah—your dress-maker; just so," he said blandly. "I didn't know there were any dress-makers in the Benedick."

"The Benedick?" She looked gently puzzled. "Is that the name of this building?"

"Yes, that's the name: I believe it's an old word for bachelor, isn't it? I happen to own the building—that's the way I know. His smile deepened as he added with increasing assurance: "But you must let me take you to the station. The Trenors are at Bellomont, of course? You've barely time to catch the five-forty. The dress-maker kept you waiting, I suppose."

Lily stiffened under the pleasantry.

"Oh, thanks," she stammered; and at that moment her eye caught a hansom drifting down Madison Avenue, and she hailed it with a desperate gesture.

"You're very kind; but I couldn't think of troubling you," she said, extending her hand to Mr. Rosedale; and heedless of his protestations, she sprang into the rescuing vehicle, and called out a breathless order to the driver.

II

In the hansom she leaned back with a sigh.

Why must a girl pay so dearly for her last escape from routine? Why could one never do a natural thing without having to screen it behind a structure of artifice? She had yielded to a passing impulse in going to Lawrence Selden's rooms, and it was so seldom that she could allow herself the luxury of an impulse! This one, at any rate, was going to cost her rather more than she could afford. She was vexed to see that, in spite of so many years of vigilance, she had blundered twice within five minutes. That stupid story about her dress-maker was bad enough—it would have been so simple to tell Rosedale that she had been taking tea with Selden! The mere statement of the fact would have rendered it innocuous. But, after having let herself be surprised in a falsehood, it was doubly stupid to snub the witness of her discomfiture. If she had had the presence of mind to let Rosedale drive her to the station, the concession might have purchased his silence. He had his race's accuracy in the appraisal of values, and to be seen walking down the platform at the crowded afternoon hour in the company of Miss Lily Bart would have been money in his pocket, as he might himself have phrased it. He knew, of course, that there would be a large house-party at Bellomont, and the possibility of being taken for one of Mrs. Trenor's guests was doubtless included in his calculations. Mr. Rosedale was still at a stage in his social ascent when it was of importance to produce such impressions.

The provoking part was that Lily knew all this—knew how easy it would have been to silence him on the spot, and how difficult it might be to do so afterward. Mr. Simon Rosedale was a man who made it his business to know everything about every one, whose idea of showing himself to be at home in society was to display an inconvenient familiarity with the habits of those with whom he wished to be thought intimate. Lily was sure that within twenty-four hours the story of her visiting her dress-maker

at the Benedick would be in active circulation among Mr. Rosedale's acquaintances. The worst of it was that she had always
snubbed and ignored him. On his first appearance—when her improvident cousin, Jack Stepney, had obtained for him (in return
for favours too easily guessed) a card to one of the vast impersonal
Van Osburgh "crushes"—Rosedale, with that mixture of artistic
sensibility and business astuteness which characterizes his race,
had instantly gravitated toward Miss Bart. She understood his
motives, for her own course was guided by as nice calculations.
Training and experience had taught her to be hospitable to new-
comers, since the most unpromising might be useful later on, and
there were plenty of available *oubliettes*[12] to swallow them if they
were not. But some intuitive repugnance, getting the better of
years of social discipline, had made her push Mr. Rosedale into
his *oubliette* without a trial. He had left behind only the ripple of
amusement which his speedy despatch had caused among her
friends; and though later (to shift the metaphor) he reappeared
lower down the stream, it was only in fleeting glimpses, with long
submergences between.

Hitherto Lily had been undisturbed by scruples. In her little set
Mr. Rosedale had been pronounced "impossible," and Jack Stepney roundly snubbed for his attempt to pay his debts in dinner in-
vitations. Even Mrs. Trenor, whose taste for variety had led her
into some hazardous experiments, resisted Jack's attempts to disguise Mr. Rosedale as a novelty, and declared that he was the
same little Jew who had been served up and rejected at the social
board a dozen times within her memory; and while Judy Trenor
was obdurate there was small chance of Mr. Rosedale's penetrating beyond the outer limbo of the Van Osburgh crushes. Jack gave
up the contest with a laughing "You'll see," and, sticking man-
fully to his guns, showed himself with Rosedale at the fashionable
restaurants, in company with the personally vivid if socially obscure ladies who are available for such purposes. But the attempt
had hitherto been vain, and as Rosedale undoubtedly paid for the
dinners, the laugh remained with his debtor.

Mr. Rosedale, it will be seen, was thus far not a factor to be
feared—unless one put one's self in his power. And this was precisely what Miss Bart had done. Her clumsy fib had let him see

that she had something to conceal; and she was sure he had a score to settle with her. Something in his smile told her he had not forgotten. She turned from the thought with a little shiver, but it hung on her all the way to the station, and dogged her down the platform with the persistency of Mr. Rosedale himself.

She had just time to take her seat before the train started; but having arranged herself in her corner with the instinctive feeling for effect which never forsook her, she glanced about in the hope of seeing some other member of the Trenors' party. She wanted to get away from herself, and conversation was the only means of escape that she knew.

Her search was rewarded by the discovery of a very blond young man with a soft reddish beard, who, at the other end of the carriage, appeared to be dissembling himself behind an unfolded newspaper. Lily's eye brightened, and a faint smile relaxed the drawn lines of her mouth. She had known that Mr. Percy Gryce was to be at Bellomont, but she had not counted on the luck of having him to herself in the train; and the fact banished all perturbing thoughts of Mr. Rosedale. Perhaps, after all, the day was to end more favourably than it had begun.

She began to cut the pages of a novel,[13] tranquilly studying her prey through downcast lashes while she organized a method of attack. Something in his attitude of conscious absorption told her that he was aware of her presence: no one had ever been quite so engrossed in an evening paper! She guessed that he was too shy to come up to her, and that she would have to devise some means of approach which should not appear to be an advance on her part. It amused her to think that anyone as rich as Mr. Percy Gryce should be shy; but she was gifted with treasures of indulgence for such idiosyncrasies, and besides, his timidity might serve her purpose better than too much assurance. She had the art of giving self-confidence to the embarrassed, but she was not equally sure of being able to embarrass the self-confident.

She waited till the train had emerged from the tunnel and was racing between the ragged edges of the northern suburbs. Then, as it lowered its speed near Yonkers, she rose from her seat and drifted slowly down the carriage. As she passed Mr. Gryce, the train gave a lurch, and he was aware of a slender hand gripping

the back of his chair. He rose with a start, his ingenuous face looking as though it had been dipped in crimson: even the reddish tint
in his beard seemed to deepen.

The train swayed again, almost flinging Miss Bart into his arms.
She steadied herself with a laugh and drew back; but he was enveloped in the scent of her dress, and his shoulder had felt her
fugitive touch.

"Oh, Mr. Gryce, is it you? I'm so sorry—I was trying to find the
porter and get some tea."

She held out her hand as the train resumed its level rush, and
they stood exchanging a few words in the aisle. Yes—he was going to Bellomont. He had heard she was to be of the party—he
blushed again as he admitted it. And was he to be there for a
whole week? How delightful!

But at this point one or two belated passengers from the last
station forced their way into the carriage, and Lily had to retreat
to her seat.

"The chair next to mine is empty—do take it," she said over her
shoulder; and Mr. Gryce, with considerable embarrassment, succeeded in effecting an exchange which enabled him to transport
himself and his bags to her side.

"Ah—and here is the porter, and perhaps we can have some
tea."

She signalled to that official, and in a moment, with the ease
that seemed to attend the fulfilment of all her wishes, a little table
had been set up between the seats, and she had helped Mr. Gryce
to bestow his encumbering properties beneath it.

When the tea came he watched her in silent fascination while
her hands flitted above the tray, looking miraculously fine and
slender in contrast to the coarse china and lumpy bread. It seemed
wonderful to him that anyone should perform with such careless
ease the difficult task of making tea in public in a lurching train.
He would never have dared to order it for himself, lest he should
attract the notice of his fellow-passengers; but, secure in the shelter of her conspicuousness, he sipped the inky draught with a delicious sense of exhilaration.

Lily, with the flavour of Selden's caraven tea[14] on her lips, had
no great fancy to drown it in the railway brew which seemed such
nectar to her companion; but, rightly judging that one of the

charms of tea is the fact of drinking it together, she proceeded to give the last touch to Mr. Gryce's enjoyment by smiling at him across her lifted cup.

"Is it quite right—I haven't made it too strong?" she asked solicitously; and he replied with conviction that he had never tasted better tea.

"I daresay it is true," she reflected; and her imagination was fired by the thought that Mr. Gryce, who might have sounded the depths of the most complex self-indulgence, was perhaps actually taking his first journey alone with a pretty woman.

It struck her as providential that she should be the instrument of his initiation. Some girls would not have known how to manage him. They would have over-emphasized the novelty of the adventure, trying to make him feel in it the zest of an escapade. But Lily's methods were more delicate. She remembered that her cousin Jack Stepney had once defined Mr. Gryce as the young man who had promised his mother never to go out in the rain without his overshoes; and acting on this hint, she resolved to impart a gently domestic air to the scene, in the hope that her companion, instead of feeling that he was doing something reckless or unusual, would merely be led to dwell on the advantage of always having a companion to make one's tea in the train.

But in spite of her efforts, conversation flagged after the tray had been removed, and she was driven to take a fresh measurement of Mr. Gryce's limitations. It was not, after all, opportunity but imagination that he lacked: he had a mental palate which would never learn to distinguish between railway tea and nectar. There was, however, one topic she could rely on: one spring that she had only to touch to set his simple machinery in motion. She had refrained from touching it because it was a last resource, and she had relied on other arts to stimulate other sensations; but as a settled look of dulness began to creep over his candid features, she saw that extreme measures were necessary.

"And how," she said, leaning forward, "are you getting on with your Americana?"

His eye became a degree less opaque: it was as though an incipient film had been removed from it, and she felt the pride of a skilful operator.

"I've got a few new things," he said, suffused with pleasure, but lowering his voice as though he feared his fellow-passengers might be in league to despoil him.

She returned a sympathetic enquiry, and gradually he was drawn on to talk of his latest purchases. It was the one subject which enabled him to forget himself, or allowed him, rather, to remember himself without constraint, because he was at home in it, and could assert a superiority that there were few to dispute. Hardly any of his acquaintances cared for Americana, or knew anything about them; and the consciousness of this ignorance threw Mr. Gryce's knowledge into agreeable relief. The only difficulty was to introduce the topic and to keep it to the front; most people showed no desire to have their ignorance dispelled, and Mr. Gryce was like a merchant whose warehouses are crammed with an unmarketable commodity.

But Miss Bart, it appeared, really did want to know about Americana; and moreover, she was already sufficiently informed to make the task of farther instruction as easy as it was agreeable. She questioned him intelligently, she heard him submissively; and, prepared for the look of lassitude which usually crept over his listeners' faces, he grew eloquent under her receptive gaze. The "points" she had had the presence of mind to glean from Selden, in anticipation of this very contingency, were serving her to such good purpose that she began to think her visit to him had been the luckiest incident of the day. She had once more shown her talent for profiting by the unexpected, and dangerous theories as to the advisability of yielding to impulse were germinating under the surface of smiling attention which she continued to present to her companion.

Mr. Gryce's sensations, if less definite, were equally agreeable. He felt the confused titillation with which the lower organisms welcome the gratification of their needs, and all his senses floundered in a vague well-being, through which Miss Bart's personality was dimly but pleasantly perceptible.

Mr. Gryce's interest in Americana had not originated with himself: it was impossible to think of him as evolving any taste of his own. An uncle had left him a collection already noted among bibliophiles; the existence of the collection was the only fact that had ever shed glory on the name of Gryce, and the nephew took as much pride in his inheritance as though it had been his own work.

Indeed, he gradually came to regard it as such, and to feel a sense of personal complacency when he chanced on any reference to the Gryce Americana. Anxious as he was to avoid personal notice, he took, in the printed mention of his name, a pleasure so exquisite and excessive that it seemed a compensation for his shrinking from publicity.

To enjoy the sensation as often as possible, he subscribed to all the reviews dealing with book-collecting in general, and American history in particular, and as allusions to his library abounded in the pages of these journals, which formed his only reading, he came to regard himself as figuring prominently in the public eye, and to enjoy the thought of the interest which would be excited if the persons he met in the street, or sat among in travelling, were suddenly to be told that he was the possessor of the Gryce Americana.

Most timidities have such secret compensations, and Miss Bart was discerning enough to know that the inner vanity is generally in proportion to the outer self-deprecation. With a more confident person she would not have dared to dwell so long on one topic, or to show such exaggerated interest in it; but she had rightly guessed that Mr. Gryce's egoism was a thirsty soil, requiring constant nurture from without. Miss Bart had the gift of following an undercurrent of thought while she appeared to be sailing on the surface of conversation; and in this case her mental excursion took the form of a rapid survey of Mr. Percy Gryce's future as combined with her own. The Gryces were from Albany, and but lately introduced to the metropolis, where the mother and son had come, after old Jefferson Gryce's death, to take possession of his house in Madison Avenue—an appalling house, all brown stone without and black walnut within, with the Gryce library in a fire-proof annex that looked like a mausoleum. Lily, however, knew all about them: young Mr. Gryce's arrival had fluttered the maternal breasts of New York, and when a girl has no mother to palpitate for her she must needs be on the alert for herself. Lily, therefore, had not only contrived to put herself in the young man's way, but had made the acquaintance of Mrs. Gryce, a monumental woman with the voice of a pulpit orator and a mind preoccupied with the iniquities of her servants, who came sometimes to sit with Mrs. Peniston and learn from that lady how she managed to prevent the kitchen-maid's smuggling groceries out of the house. Mrs. Gryce had a kind of impersonal benevolence: cases of individual need she regarded with suspicion, but she subscribed to Institutions when their annual reports showed an impressive surplus. Her domestic duties were manifold, for they extended from furtive inspections of the servants' bedrooms to unannounced descents to the cellar; but she had never allowed herself many pleasures. Once, however, she had had a special edition of the Sarum Rule[15] printed in rubric[16] and presented to every clergyman in the diocese; and the gilt album in which their letters of thanks were pasted formed the chief ornament of her drawing-room table.

Percy had been bought up in the principles which so excellent a woman was sure to inculcate. Every form of prudence and suspicion had been grafted on a nature originally reluctant and cautious, with the result that it would have seemed hardly needful for Mrs. Gryce to extract his promise about the overshoes, so little likely was he to hazard himself abroad in the rain. After attaining his majority, and coming into the fortune which the late Mr. Gryce had made out of a patent device for excluding fresh air from hotels, the young man continued to live with his mother in Albany; but on Jefferson Gryce's death, when another large property passed into her son's hands, Mrs. Gryce thought that what she called his "interests" demanded his presence in New York. She accordingly installed herself in the Madison Avenue house, and Percy, whose sense of duty was not inferior to his mother's, spent all his week days in the handsome Broad Street office where a batch of pale men on small salaries had grown grey in the management of the Gryce estate, and where he was initiated with becoming reverence into every detail of the art of accumulation.

As far as Lily could learn, this had hitherto been Mr. Gryce's only occupation, and she might have been pardoned for thinking it not too hard a task to interest a young man who had been kept on such low diet. At any rate, she felt herself so completely in command of the situation that she yielded to a sense of security in which all fear of Mr. Rosedale, and of the difficulties on which that fear was contingent, vanished beyond the edge of thought.

The stopping of the train at Garrisons would not have distracted her from these thoughts, had she not caught a sudden look of distress in her companion's eye. His seat faced toward the door, and she guessed that he had been perturbed by the approach of an acquaintance; a fact confirmed by the turning of heads and general sense of commotion which her own entrance into a railway-carriage was apt to produce.

She knew the symptoms at once, and was not surprised to be hailed by the high notes of a pretty woman, who entered the train accompanied by a maid, a bull-terrier, and a footman staggering under a load of bags and dressing-cases.

"Oh, Lily—are you going to Bellomont? Then you can't let me have your seat, I suppose? But I *must* have a seat in this carriage— porter, you must find me a place at once. Can't some one be put somewhere else? I want to be with my friends. Oh, how do you do, Mr. Gryce? Do please make him understand that I must have a seat next to you and Lily."

Mrs. George Dorset, regardless of the mild efforts of a traveller with a carpet-bag, who was doing his best to make room for her by getting out of the train, stood in the middle of the aisle, diffusing about her that general sense of exasperation which a pretty woman on her travels not infrequently creates.

She was smaller and thinner than Lily Bart, with a restless pliability of pose, as if she could have been crumpled up and run through a ring, like the sinuous draperies she affected. Her small pale face seemed the mere setting of a pair of dark exaggerated eyes, of which the visionary gaze contrasted curiously with her self-assertive tone and gestures; so that, as one of her friends observed, she was like a disembodied spirit who took up a great deal of room.

Having finally discovered that the seat adjoining Miss Bart's was at her disposal, she possessed herself of it with a farther displacement of her surroundings, explaining meanwhile that she had come across from Mount Kisco in her motor-car that morning, and had been kicking her heels for an hour at Garrisons, without even the alleviation of a cigarette, her brute of a husband having neglected to replenish her case before they parted that morning.

"And at this hour of the day I don't suppose you've a single one left, have you, Lily?" she plaintively concluded.

Miss Bart caught the startled glance of Mr. Percy Gryce, whose own lips were never defiled by tobacco.

"What an absurd question, Bertha!" she exclaimed, blushing at the thought of the store she had laid in at Lawrence Selden's.

"Why, don't you smoke? Since when have you given it up? What—you never—And you don't either, Mr. Gryce? Ah, of course—how stupid of me—I understand."

And Mrs. Dorset leaned back against her travelling cushions with a smile which made Lily wish there had been no vacant seat beside her own.

THE REEF

XXIII

The next day was Darrow's last at Givré and, foreseeing that the afternoon and evening would have to be given to the family, he had asked Anna to devote an early hour to the final consideration of their plans. He was to meet her in the brown sitting-room at ten, and they were to walk down to the river and talk over their future in the little pavilion abutting on the wall of the park.

It was just a week since his arrival at Givré, and Anna wished, before he left, to return to the place where they had sat on their first afternoon together. Her sensitiveness to the appeal of inanimate things, to the colour and texture of whatever wove itself into the substance of her emotion, made her want to hear Darrow's voice, and to feel his eyes on her, in the spot where bliss had first flowed into her heart.

That bliss, in the interval, had wound itself into every fold of her being. Passing, in the first days, from a high shy tenderness to the rush of a secret surrender, it had gradually widened and deepened, to flow on in redoubled beauty. She thought she now knew exactly how and why she loved Darrow, and she could see her whole sky reflected in the deep and tranquil current of her love.

Early the next day, in her sitting-room, she was glancing through the letters which it was Effie's morning privilege to carry up to her. Effie meanwhile circled inquisitively about the room, where there was always something new to engage her infant fancy; and Anna, looking up, saw her suddenly arrested before a photograph of Darrow which, the day before, had taken its place on the writing-table.

Anna held out her arms with a faint blush. "You do like him, don't you, dear?"

"Oh, most awfully, dearest," Effie, against her breast, leaned back to assure her with a limpid look. "And so do Granny and Owen—and I *do* think Sophy does too," she added, after a moment's earnest pondering.

"I hope so," Anna laughed. She checked the impulse to continue: "Has she talked to you about him, that you're so sure?" She did not know what had made the question spring to her lips, but she was glad she had closed them before pronouncing it. Nothing could have been more distasteful to her than to clear up such obscurities by turning on them the tiny flame of her daughter's observation. And what, after all, now that Owen's happiness was secured, did it matter if there were certain reserves in Darrow's approval of his marriage?

A knock on the door made Anna glance at the clock. "There's Nurse to carry you off."

"It's Sophy's knock," the little girl answered, jumping down to open the door; and Miss Viner in fact stood on the threshold.

"Come in," Anna said with a smile, instantly remarking how pale she looked.

"May Effie go out for a turn with Nurse?" the girl asked. "I should like to speak to you a moment."

"Of course. This ought to be *your* holiday, as yesterday was Effie's. Run off, dear," she added, stooping to kiss the little girl.

When the door had closed she turned back to Sophy Viner with a look that sought her confidence. "I'm so glad you came, my dear. We've got so many things to talk about, just you and I together."

The confused intercourse of the last days had, in fact, left little time for any speech with Sophy but such as related to her marriage and the means of overcoming Madame de Chantelle's opposition to it. Anna had exacted of Owen that no one, not even Sophy Viner, should be given a hint of her own projects till all contingent questions had been disposed of. She had felt, from the outset, a secret reluctance to intrude her securer happiness on the doubts and fears of the young pair.

From the sofa-corner to which she had dropped back she pointed to Darrow's chair. "Come and sit by me, dear. I wanted to see you alone. There's so much to say that I hardly know where to begin."

She leaned forward, her hands clasped on the arms of the sofa, her eyes bent smilingly on Sophy's. As she did so, she noticed that the girl's unusual pallor was partly due to the slight veil of powder on her face. The discovery was distinctly disagreeable. Anna had never before noticed, on Sophy's part, any recourse to cosmetics, and, much as she wished to think herself exempt from old-fashioned prejudices, she suddenly became aware that she did not like her daughter's governess to have a powdered face. Then she reflected that the girl who sat opposite her was no longer Effie's governess, but her own future daughter-in-law; and she wondered whether Miss Viner had chosen this odd way of celebrating her independence, and whether, as Mrs. Owen Leath, she would present to the world a bedizened countenance. This idea was scarcely less distasteful than the other, and for a moment Anna continued to consider her without speaking. Then, in a flash, the truth came to her: Miss Viner had powdered her face because Miss Viner had been crying.

Anna leaned forward impulsively. "My dear child, what's the matter?" She saw the girl's blood rush up under the white mask, and hastened on: "Please don't be afraid to tell me. I do so want you to feel that you can trust me as Owen does. And you know you mustn't mind if, just at first, Madame de Chantelle occasionally relapses."

She spoke eagerly, persuasively, almost on a note of pleading. She had, in truth, so many reasons for wanting Sophy to like her: her love for Owen, her solicitude for Effie, and her own sense of the girl's fine mettle. She had always felt a romantic and almost humble admiration for those members of her sex who, from force of will, or the constraint of circumstances, had plunged into the conflict from which fate had so persistently excluded her. There were even moments when she fancied herself vaguely to blame for her immunity, and felt that she ought somehow to have affronted the perils and hardships which refused to come to her. And now, as she sat looking at Sophy Viner, so small, so slight, so visibly defenceless and undone, she still felt, through all the superiority of her worldly advantages and her seeming maturity, the same odd sense of ignorance and inexperience. She could not have said what there was in the girl's manner and expression to give her this feeling, but she was reminded, as she looked at Sophy Viner, of the other girls she had known in her youth, the girls who seemed possessed of a secret she had missed. Yes, Sophy Viner had their look—almost the obscurely menacing look of Kitty Mayne[1] . . . Anna, with an inward smile, brushed aside the image of this forgotten rival. But she had felt, deep down, a twinge of the old pain, and she was sorry that, even for the flash of a thought, Owen's betrothed should have reminded her of so different a woman . . .

She laid her hand on the girl's. "When his grandmother sees how happy Owen is she'll be quite happy herself. If it's only that, don't be distressed. Just trust Owen—and the future."

Sophy Viner, with an almost imperceptible recoil of her whole slight person, had drawn her hand from under the palm enclosing it.

"That's what I wanted to talk to you about—the future."

"Of course! We've all so many plans to make—and to fit into each other's. Please let's begin with yours."

The girl paused a moment, her hands clasped on the arms of her chair, her lids dropped under Anna's gaze; then she said: "I should like to make no plans at all . . . just yet . . ."

"No plans?"

"No—I should like to go away . . . my friends the Farlows would let me go to them . . ." Her voice grew firmer and she lifted her eyes to add: "I should like to leave today, if you don't mind."

Anna listened with a rising wonder.

"You want to leave Givré at once?" She gave the idea a moment's swift consideration. "You prefer to be with your friends till your marriage? I understand that—but surely you needn't rush off today? There are so many details to discuss; and before long, you know, I shall be going away too."

"Yes, I know." The girl was evidently trying to steady her voice. "But I should like to wait a few days—to have a little more time to myself."

Anna continued to consider her kindly. It was evident that she did not care to say why she wished to leave Givré so suddenly, but her disturbed face and shaken voice betrayed a more pressing motive than the natural desire to spend the weeks before her marriage under her old friends' roof. Since she had made no response to the allusion to Madame de Chantelle, Anna could but conjecture that she had had a passing disagreement with Owen; and if this were so, random interference might do more harm than good.

"My dear child, if you really want to go at once I sha'n't, of course, urge you to stay. I suppose you have spoken to Owen?"

"No. Not yet . . ."

Anna threw an astonished glance at her. "You mean to say you haven't told him?"

"I wanted to tell you first. I thought I ought to, on account of Effie." Her look cleared as she put forth this reason.

"Oh, Effie—!" Anna's smile brushed away the scruple. "Owen has a right to ask that you should consider him before you think of his sister . . . Of course you shall do just as you wish," she went on, after another thoughtful interval.

"Oh, thank you," Sophy Viner murmured and rose to her feet.

Anna rose also, vaguely seeking for some word that should break down the girl's resistance. "You'll tell Owen at once?" she finally asked.

Miss Viner, instead of replying, stood before her in manifest uncertainty, and as she did so there was a light tap on the door, and Owen Leath walked into the room.

Anna's first glance told her that his face was unclouded. He met her greeting with his happiest smile and turned to lift Sophy's hand to his lips. The perception that he was utterly unconscious of any cause for Miss Viner's agitation came to his step-mother with a sharp thrill of surprise.

"Darrow's looking for you," he said to her. "He asked me to remind you that you'd promised to go for a walk with him."

Anna glanced at the clock. "I'll go down presently." She waited and looked again at Sophy Viner, whose troubled eyes seemed to commit their message to her. "You'd better tell Owen, my dear."

Owen's look also turned on the girl. "Tell me what? Why, what's happened?"

Anna summoned a laugh to ease the vague tension of the moment. "Don't look so startled! Nothing, except that Sophy proposes to desert us for a while for the Farlows."

Owen's brow cleared. "I was afraid she'd run off before long." He glanced at Anna. "Do please keep her here as long as you can!"

Sophy intervened: "Mrs. Leath's already given me leave to go."

"Already? To go when?"

"Today," said Sophy in a low tone, her eyes on Anna's.

"Today? Why on earth should you go today?" Owen dropped

back a step or two, flushing and paling under his bewildered frown. His eyes seemed to search the girl more closely. "Something's happened." He too looked at his step-mother. "I suppose she must have told you what it is?"

Anna was struck by the suddenness and vehemence of his appeal. It was as though some smouldering apprehension had lain close under the surface of his security.

"She's told me nothing except that she wishes to be with her friends. It's quite natural that she should want to go to them."

Owen visibly controlled himself. "Of course—quite natural." He spoke to Sophy. "But why didn't you tell me so? Why did you come first to my step-mother?"

Anna intervened with her calm smile. "That seems to me quite natural, too. Sophy was considerate enough to tell me first because of Effie."

He weighed it. "Very well, then: that's quite natural, as you say. And of course she must do exactly as she pleases." He still kept his eyes on the girl. "Tomorrow," he abruptly announced, "I shall go up to Paris to see you."

"Oh, no—no!" she protested.

Owen turned back to Anna. "*Now* do you say that nothing's happened?"

Under the influence of his agitation Anna felt a vague tightening of the heart. She seemed to herself like some one in a dark room about whom unseen presences are groping.

"If it's anything that Sophy wishes to tell you, no doubt she'll do so. I'm going down now, and I'll leave you here to talk it over by yourselves."

As she moved to the door the girl caught up with her. "But there's nothing to tell: why should there be? I've explained that I simply want to be quiet." Her look seemed to detain Mrs. Leath.

Owen broke in: "Is that why I mayn't go up tomorrow?"

"Not tomorrow!"

"Then when may I?"

"Later . . . in a little while . . . a few days . . ."

"In how many days?"

"Owen!" his step-mother interposed; but he seemed no longer aware of her. "If you go away today, the day that our engagement's made known, it's only fair," he persisted, "that you should tell me when I am to see you."

Sophy's eyes wavered between the two and dropped down wearily. "It's you who are not fair—when I've said I wanted to be quiet."

"But why should my coming disturb you? I'm not asking now to come tomorrow. I only ask you not to leave without telling me when I'm to see you."

"Owen, I don't understand you!" his step-mother exclaimed.

"You don't understand my asking for some explanation, some assurance, when I'm left in this way, without a word, without a sign? All I ask her to tell me is when she'll see me."

Anna turned back to Sophy Viner, who stood straight and tremulous between the two.

"After all, my dear, he's not unreasonable!"

"I'll write—I'll write," the girl repeated.

"*What* will you write?" he pressed her vehemently.

"Owen," Anna exclaimed, "you *are* unreasonable!"

He turned from Sophy to his step-mother. "I only want her to say what she means: that she's going to write to break off our engagement. Isn't that what you're going away for?"

Anna felt the contagion of his excitement. She looked at Sophy, who stood motionless, her lips set, her whole face drawn to a silent fixity of resistance.

"You ought to speak, my dear—you ought to answer him."

"I only ask him to wait—"

"Yes," Owen broke in, "and you won't say how long!"

Both instinctively addressed themselves to Anna, who stood, nearly as shaken as themselves, between the double shock of their struggle. She looked again from Sophy's inscrutable eyes to Owen's stormy features; then she said: "What can I do, when there's clearly something between you that I don't know about?"

"Oh, if it *were* between us! Can't you see it's outside of us—outside of her, dragging at her, dragging her away from me?" Owen wheeled round again upon his step-mother.

Anna turned from him to the girl. "Is it true that you want to break your engagement? If you do, you ought to tell him now."

Owen burst into a laugh. "She doesn't dare to—she's afraid I'll guess the reason!"

A faint sound escaped from Sophy's lips, but she kept them close on whatever answer she had ready.

"If she doesn't wish to marry you, why should she be afraid to have you know the reason?"

"She's afraid to have *you* know it—not me!"

"To have *me* know it?"

He laughed again, and Anna, at his laugh, felt a sudden rush of indignation.

"Owen, you must explain what you mean!"

He looked at her hard before answering; then: "Ask Darrow!" he said.

"Owen—Owen!" Sophy Viner murmured.

XXIV

Anna stood looking from one to the other. It had become apparent to her in a flash that Owen's retort, though it startled Sophy, did not take her by surprise; and the discovery shot its light along dark distances of fear.

The immediate inference was that Owen had guessed the reason of Darrow's disapproval of his marriage, or that, at least, he suspected Sophy Viner of knowing and dreading it. This confirmation of her own obscure doubt sent a tremor of alarm through Anna. For a moment she felt like exclaiming: "All this is really no business of mine, and I refuse to have you mix me up in it—" but her secret fear held her fast.

Sophy Viner was the first to speak.

"I should like to go now," she said in a low voice, taking a few steps toward the door.

Her tone woke Anna to the sense of her own share in the situation. "I quite agree with you, my dear, that it's useless to carry on this discussion. But since Mr. Darrow's name has been brought into it, for reasons which I fail to guess, I want to tell you that you're both mistaken if you think he's not in sympathy with your marriage. If that's what Owen means to imply, the idea's a complete delusion."

She spoke the words deliberately and incisively, as if hoping that the sound of their utterance would stifle the whisper in her bosom.

Sophy's only answer was a vague murmur, and a movement that brought her nearer to the door; but before she could reach it Owen had placed himself in her way.

"I don't mean to imply what you think," he said, addressing his step-mother but keeping his eyes on the girl. "I don't say Darrow doesn't like our marriage; I say it's Sophy who's hated it since Darrow's been here!"

He brought out the charge in a tone of forced composure, but his lips were white and he grasped the door-knob to hide the tremor of his hand.

Anna's anger surged up with her fears. "You're absurd, Owen! I don't know why I listen to you. Why should Sophy dislike Mr. Darrow, and if she does, why should that have anything to do with her wishing to break her engagement?"

"I don't say she dislikes him! I don't say she likes him; I don't know what it is they say to each other when they're shut up together alone."

"Shut up together alone?" Anna stared. Owen seemed like a man in delirium; such an exhibition was degrading to them all. But he pushed on without seeing her look.

"Yes—the first evening she came, in the study; the next morning, early, in the park; yesterday, again, in the spring-house, when you were at the lodge with the doctor . . . I don't know what they say to each other, but they've taken every chance they could to say it . . . and to say it when they thought that no one saw them."

Anna longed to silence him, but no words came to her. It was as though all her confused apprehensions had suddenly taken definite shape. There was "something"—yes, there was "something" . . . Darrow's reticences and evasions had been more than a figment of her doubts.

The next instant brought a recoil of pride. She turned indignantly on her step-son.

"I don't half understand what you've been saying; but what you seem to hint is so preposterous, and so insulting both to Sophy and to me, that I see no reason why we should listen to you any longer."

Though her tone steadied Owen, she perceived at once that it would not deflect him from his purpose. He spoke less vehemently, but with all the more precision.

"How can it be preposterous, since it's true? Or insulting, since I don't know, any more than *you*, the meaning of what I've been seeing? If you'll be patient with me I'll try to put it quietly. What I mean is that Sophy has completely changed since she met Darrow here, and that, having noticed the change, I'm hardly to blame for having tried to find out its cause."

Anna made an effort to answer him with the same, composure. "You're to blame, at any rate, for so recklessly assuming that you *have* found it out. You seem to forget that, till they met here, Sophy and Mr. Darrow hardly knew each other."

"If so, it's all the stranger that they've been so often closeted together!"

"Owen, Owen—" the girl sighed out.

He turned his haggard face to her. "Can I help it, if I've seen and known what I wasn't meant to? For God's sake give me a reason—any reason I can decently make out with! Is it my fault if, the day after you arrived, when I came back late through the garden, the curtains of the study hadn't been drawn, and I saw you there alone with Darrow?"

Anna laughed impatiently. "Really, Owen, if you make it a grievance that two people who are staying in the same house should be seen talking together—!"

"They were not talking. That's the point—"

"Not talking? How do you know? You could hardly hear them from the garden!"

"No; but I could see. *He* was sitting at my desk, with his face in his hands. *She* was standing in the window, looking away from him . . ."

He waited, as if for Sophy Viner's answer; but still she neither stirred nor spoke.

"That was the first time," he went on; "and the second was the next morning in the park. It was natural enough, their meeting there. Sophy had gone out with Effie, and Effie ran back to look for me. She told me she'd left Sophy and Darrow in the path that leads to the river, and presently we saw them ahead of us. They didn't see us at first, because they were standing looking at each other; and this time they were not speaking either. We came up close before they heard us, and all that time they never spoke, or stopped looking at each other. After that I began to wonder; and so I watched them."

"Oh, Owen!"

"Oh, I only had to wait. Yesterday, when I motored you and the doctor back from the lodge, I saw Sophy coming out of the spring-house. I supposed she'd taken shelter from the rain, and when you got out of the motor I strolled back down the avenue to meet her. But she'd disappeared—she must have taken a short cut and come into the house by the side door. I don't know why I went on to the spring-house; I suppose it was what you'd call spying. I went up the steps and found the room empty; but two chairs had been moved out from the wall and were standing near the table; and one of the Chinese screens that lie on it had dropped to the floor."

Anna sounded a faint note of irony. "Really? Sophy'd gone there for shelter, and she dropped a screen and moved a chair?"

"I said two chairs—"

"Two? What damning evidence—of I don't know what!"

"Simply of the fact that Darrow'd been there with her. As I looked out of the window I saw him close by, walking away. He must have turned the corner of the spring-house just as I got to the door."

There was another silence, during which Anna paused, not only to collect her own words but to wait for Sophy Viner's; then, as the girl made no sign, she turned to her.

"I've absolutely nothing to say to all this; but perhaps you'd like me to wait and hear your answer?"

Sophy raised her head with a quick flash of colour. "I've no answer either—except that Owen must be mad."

In the interval since she had last spoken she seemed to have regained her self-control, and her voice rang clear, with a cold edge of anger.

Anna looked at her step-son. He had grown extremely pale, and his hand fell from the door with a discouraged gesture. "That's all, then? You won't give me any reason?"

"I didn't suppose it was necessary to give you or anyone else a reason for talking with a friend of Mrs. Leath's under Mrs. Leath's own roof."

Owen hardly seemed to feel the retort: he kept his dogged stare on her face.

"I won't ask for one, then. I'll only ask you to give me your assurance that your talks with Darrow have had nothing to do with your suddenly deciding to leave Givré."

She hesitated, not so much with the air of weighing her answer as of questioning his right to exact any. "I give you my assurance; and now I should like to go," she said.

As she turned away, Anna intervened. "My dear, I think you ought to speak."

The girl drew herself up with a faint laugh. "To him—or to *you?*"

"To him."

She stiffened. "I've said all there is to say."

Anna drew back, her eyes on her step-son. He had left the threshold and was advancing toward Sophy Viner with a motion of desperate appeal; but as he did so there was a knock on the door. A moment's silence fell on the three; then Anna said: "Come in!"

Darrow came into the room. Seeing the three together, he looked rapidly from one to the other; then he turned to Anna with a smile.

"I came up to see if you were ready; but please send me off if I'm not wanted."

His look, his voice, the simple sense of his presence, restored Anna's shaken balance. By Owen's side he looked so strong, so urbane, so experienced, that the lad's passionate charges dwindled to mere boyish vapourings. A moment ago she had dreaded Darrow's coming; now she was glad that he was there.

She turned to him with sudden decision. "Come in, please; I want you to hear what Owen has been saying."

She caught a murmur from Sophy Viner, but disregarded it. An illuminating impulse urged her on. She, habitually so aware of her own lack of penetration, her small skill in reading hidden motives and detecting secret signals, now felt herself mysteriously inspired. She addressed herself to Sophy Viner. "It's much better for you both that this absurd question should be cleared up now." Then, turning to Darrow, she continued: "For some reason that I don't pretend to guess, Owen has taken it into his head that you've influenced Miss Viner to break her engagement."

She spoke slowly and deliberately, because she wished to give time and to gain it; time for Darrow and Sophy to receive the full impact of what she was saying, and time to observe its full effect on them. She had said to herself: "If there's nothing between them, they'll look at each other; if there is something, they won't"; and as she ceased to speak she felt as if all her life were in her eyes.

Sophy, after a start of protest, remained motionless, her gaze on the ground. Darrow, his face grown grave, glanced slowly from Owen Leath to Anna. With his eyes on the latter he asked: "Has Miss Viner broken her engagement?"

A moment's silence followed his question; then the girl looked up and said: "Yes!"

Owen, as she spoke, uttered a smothered exclamation and walked out of the room. She continued to stand in the same place, without appearing to notice his departure, and without vouchsafing an additional word of explanation; then, before Anna could find a cry to detain her, she too turned and went out.

"For God's sake, what's happened?" Darrow asked; but Anna, with a drop of the heart, was saying to herself that he and Sophy Viner had not looked at each other.

XXV

Anna stood in the middle of the room, her eyes on the door. Darrow's questioning gaze was still on her, and she said to herself with a quick-drawn breath: "If only he doesn't come near me!"

It seemed to her that she had been suddenly endowed with the fatal gift of reading the secret sense of every seemingly spontaneous look and movement, and that in his least gesture of affection she would detect a cold design.

For a moment longer he continued to look at her enquiringly; then he turned away and took up his habitual stand by the mantel-piece. She drew a deep breath of relief.

"Won't you please explain?" he said.

"I can't explain: I don't know. I didn't even know—till she told you—that she really meant to break her engagement. All I know is that she came to me just now and said she wished to leave Givré today; and that Owen, when he heard of it—for she hadn't told him—at once accused her of going away with the secret intention of throwing him over."

"And you think it's a definite break?" She perceived, as she spoke, that his brow had cleared.

"How should I know? Perhaps you can tell me."

"I?" She fancied his face clouded again, but he did not move from his tranquil attitude.

"As I told you," she went on, "Owen has worked himself up to imagining that for some mysterious reason you've influenced Sophy against him."

Darrow still visibly wondered. "It must indeed be a mysterious reason! He knows how slightly I know Miss Viner. Why should he imagine anything so wildly improbable?"

"I don't know that either."

"But he must have hinted at some reason."

"No: he admits he doesn't know your reason. He simply says that Sophy's manner to him has changed since she came back to Givré and that he's seen you together several times—in the park, the spring-house, I don't know where—talking alone in a way that seemed confidential—almost secret; and he draws the preposterous conclusion that you've used your influence to turn her against him."

"My influence? What kind of influence?"

"He doesn't say."

Darrow again seemed to turn over the facts she gave him. His face remained grave, but without the least trace of discomposure. "And what does Miss Viner say?"

"She says it's perfectly natural that she should occasionally talk to my friends when she's under my roof—and refuses to give him any other explanation."

"That at least is perfectly natural!"

Anna felt her cheeks flush as she answered: "Yes—but there *is* something—"

"Something—?"

"Some reason for her sudden decision to break her engagement. I can understand Owen's feeling, sorry as I am for his way of showing it. The girl owes him some sort of explanation, and as long as she refuses to give it his imagination is sure to run wild."

"She would have given it, no doubt, if he'd asked it in a different tone."

"I don't defend Owen's tone—but she knew what it was before she accepted him. She knows he's excitable and undisciplined."

"Well, she's been disciplining him a little—probably the best thing that could happen. Why not let the matter rest there?"

"Leave Owen with the idea that you *have* been the cause of the break?"

He met the question with his easy smile. "Oh, as to that—leave him with any idea of me he chooses! But leave him, at any rate, free."

"Free?" she echoed in surprise.

"Simply let things be. You've surely done all you could for him and Miss Viner. If they don't hit it off it's their own affair. What possible motive can you have for trying to interfere now?"

Her gaze widened to a deeper wonder. "Why—naturally, what he says of you!"

"I don't care a straw what he says of me! In such a situation a boy in love will snatch at the most far-fetched reason rather than face the mortifying fact that the lady may simply be tired of him."

"You don't quite understand Owen. Things go deep with him, and last long. It took him a long time to recover from his other unlucky love affair. He's romantic and extravagant: he can't live on the interest of his feelings. He worships Sophy and she seemed to be fond of him. If she's changed it's been very sudden. And if they part like this, angrily and inarticulately, it will hurt him horribly—hurt his very soul. But that, as you say, is between the two. What concerns me is his associating you with their quarrel. Owen's like my own son—if you'd seen him when I first came here you'd know why. We were like two prisoners who talk to each other by tapping on the wall. He's never forgotten it, nor I. Whether he breaks with Sophy, or whether they make it up, I can't let him think you had anything to do with it."

She raised her eyes entreatingly to Darrow's, and read in them the forbearance of the man resigned to the discussion of non-existent problems.

"I'll do whatever you want me to," he said; "but I don't yet know what it is."

His smile seemed to charge her with inconsequence, and the prick to her pride made her continue: "After all, it's not so unnatural that Owen, knowing you and Sophy to be almost strangers, should wonder what you were saying to each other when he saw you talking together."

She felt a warning tremor as she spoke, as though some instinct deeper than reason surged up in defence of its treasure. But Darrow's face was unstirred save by the flit of his half-amused smile.

"Well, my dear—and couldn't you have told him?"

"I?" she faltered out through her blush.

"You seem to forget, one and all of you, the position you put me in when I came down here: your appeal to me to see Owen through, your assurance to him that I would, Madame de Chantelle's attempt to win me over; and most of all, my own sense of the fact you've just recalled to me: the importance, for both of us, that Owen should like me. It seemed to me that the first thing to do was to get as much light as I could on the whole situation; and the obvious way of doing it was to try to know Miss Viner better. Of course I've talked with her alone—I've talked with her as often as I could. I've tried my best to find out if you were right in encouraging Owen to marry her."

She listened with a growing sense of reassurance, struggling to separate the abstract sense of his words from the persuasion in which his eyes and voice enveloped them.

"I see—I do see," she murmured.

"You must see, also, that I could hardly say this to Owen without offending him still more, and perhaps increasing the breach between Miss Viner and himself. What sort of figure should I cut if I told him I'd been trying to find out if he'd made a proper choice? In any case, it's none of my business to offer an explanation of what she justly says doesn't need one. If she declines to speak, it's obviously on the ground that Owen's insinuations are absurd; and that surely pledges me to silence."

"Yes, yes! I see," Anna repeated. "But I don't want you to explain anything to Owen."

"You haven't yet told me what you do want."

She hesitated, conscious of the difficulty of justifying her request; then: "I want you to speak to Sophy," she said.

Darrow broke into an incredulous laugh. "Considering what my previous attempts have resulted in—!"

She raised her eyes quickly. "They haven't, at least, resulted in your liking her less, in your thinking less well of her than you've told me?"

She fancied he frowned a little. "I wonder why you go back to that?"

"I want to be sure—I owe it to Owen. Won't you tell me the exact impression she's produced on you?"

"I have told you—I like Miss Viner."

"Do you still believe she's in love with Owen?"

"There was nothing in our short talks to throw any particular light on that."

"You still believe, though, that there's no reason why he shouldn't marry her?"

Again he betrayed a restrained impatience. "How can I answer that without knowing her reasons for breaking with him?"

"That's just what I want you to find out from her."

"And why in the world should she tell me?"

"Because, whatever grievance she has against Owen, she can certainly have none against me. She can't want to have Owen connect me in his mind with this wretched quarrel; and she must see that he will until he's convinced you've had no share in it."

Darrow's elbow dropped from the mantel-piece and he took a restless step or two across the room. Then he halted before her.

"Why can't you tell her this yourself?"

"Don't you see?"

He eyed her intently, and she pressed on: "You must have guessed that Owen's jealous of you."

"Jealous of me?" The blood flew up under his brown skin.

"Blind with it—what else would drive him to this folly? And I can't have her think me jealous too! I've said all I could, short of making her think so; and she's refused a word more to either of us. Our only chance now is that she should listen to you—that you should make her see the harm her silence may do."

Darrow uttered a protesting exclamation. "It's all too preposterous—what you suggest! I can't, at any rate, appeal to her on such a ground as that!"

Anna laid her hand on his arm. "Appeal to her on the ground

that I'm almost Owen's mother, and that any estrangement between you and him would kill me. She knows what he is—she'll
understand. Tell her to say anything, do anything, she wishes; but
not to go away without speaking, not to leave that between us
when she goes!"

She drew back a step and lifted her face to his, trying to look
into his eyes more deeply than she had ever looked; but before she
could discern what they expressed he had taken hold of her hands
and bent his head to kiss them.

"You'll see her? You'll see her?" she entreated; and he answered: "I'll do anything in the world you want me to."

XXVI

Darrow waited alone in the sitting-room. No place could have been
more distasteful as the scene of the talk that lay before him; but he
had acceded to Anna's suggestion that it would seem more natural
for her to summon Sophy Viner than for him to go in search of her.
As his troubled pacings carried him back and forth a relentless hand
seemed to be tearing away all the tender fibres of association that
bound him to the peaceful room. Here, in this very place, he had
drunk his deepest draughts of happiness, had had his lips at the
fountain-head of its overflowing rivers; but now that source was
poisoned and he would taste no more of an untainted cup.

For a moment he felt an actual physical anguish; then his nerves
hardened for the coming struggle. He had no notion of what
awaited him; but after the first instinctive recoil he had seen in a
flash the urgent need of another word with Sophy Viner. He had
been insincere in letting Anna think that he had consented to speak
because she asked it. In reality he had been feverishly casting about
for the pretext she had given him; and for some reason this trivial
hypocrisy weighed on him more than all his heavy burden of deceit.

At length he heard a step behind him and Sophy Viner entered.
When she saw him she paused on the threshold and half drew back.

"I was told that Mrs. Leath had sent for me."

"Mrs. Leath *did* send for you. She'll be here presently; but I
asked her to let me see you first."

He spoke very gently, and there was no insincerity in his gentleness. He was profoundly moved by the change in the girl's appearance. At sight of him she had forced a smile; but it lit up her wretchedness like a candle-flame held to a dead face.

She made no reply, and Darrow went on: "You must understand my wanting to speak to you, after what I was told just now."

She interposed, with a gesture of protest: "I'm not responsible for Owen's ravings!"

"Of course—." He broke off and they stood facing each other. She lifted a hand and pushed back her loose lock with the gesture that was burnt into his memory; then she looked about her and dropped into the nearest chair.

"Well, you've got what you wanted," she said.

"What do you mean by what I wanted?"

"My engagement's broken—you heard me say so."

"Why do you say that's what I wanted? All I wished, from the beginning, was to advise you, to help you as best I could—"

"That's what you've done," she rejoined. "You've convinced me that it's best I shouldn't marry him."

Darrow broke into a despairing laugh. "At the very moment when you'd convinced me to the contrary!"

"Had I?" Her smile flickered up. "Well, I really believed it till you showed me . . . warned me . . ."

"Warned you?"

"That I'd be miserable if I married a man I didn't love."

"Don't you love him?"

She made no answer, and Darrow started up and walked away to the other end of the room. He stopped before the writing-table, where his photograph, well-dressed, handsome, self-sufficient— the portrait of a man of the world, confident of his ability to deal adequately with the most delicate situations—offered its huge fatuity to his gaze. He turned back to her. "It's rather hard on Owen, isn't it, that you should have waited until now to tell him?"

She reflected a moment before answering. "I told him as soon as I knew."

"Knew that you couldn't marry him?"

"Knew that I could never live here with him." She looked about the room, as though the very walls must speak for her.

For a moment Darrow continued to search her face perplexedly; then their eyes met in a long disastrous gaze.

"Yes—" she said, and stood up.

Below the window they heard Effie whistling for her dogs, and then, from the terrace, her mother calling her.

"There—*that* for instance," Sophy Viner said.

Darrow broke out: "It's I who ought to go!"

She kept her small pale smile. "What good would that do any of us—now?"

He covered his face with his hands. "Good God!" he groaned. "How could I tell?"

"You couldn't tell. We neither of us could." She seemed to turn the problem over critically. "After all, it might have been *you* instead of me!"

He took another distracted turn about the room and coming back to her sat down in a chair at her side. A mocking hand seemed to dash the words from his lips. There was nothing on earth that he could say to her that wasn't foolish or cruel or contemptible . . .

"My dear," he began at last, "oughtn't you, at any rate, to try?"

Her gaze grew grave. "Try to forget you?"

He flushed to the forehead. "I meant, try to give Owen more time; to give him a chance. He's madly in love with you; all the good that's in him is in your hands. His step-mother felt that from the first. And she thought—she believed—"

"She thought I could make him happy. Would she think so now?"

"Now . . . ? I don't say now, But later? Time modifies . . . rubs out . . . more quickly than you think. Go away, but let him hope . . . I'm going too—*we're* going—" he stumbled on the plural—"in a few weeks: going for a long time, probably. What you're thinking of now may never happen. We may not all be here together again for years."

She heard him out in silence, her hands clasped on her knee, her eyes bent on them. "For me," she said, "you'll always be here."

"Don't say that—oh, don't! Things change . . . people change . . . You'll see!"

"You don't understand. I don't want anything to change. I don't want to forget—to rub out. At first I imagined I did; but that was a foolish mistake. As soon as I saw you again I knew it . . . It's not being here with you that I'm afraid of—in the sense you think.

It's being here, or anywhere, with Owen." She stood up and bent her tragic smile on him. "I want to keep you all to myself."

The only words that came to him were futile denunciations of his folly; but the sense of their futility checked them on his lips. "Poor child—you poor child!" he heard himself vainly repeating.

Suddenly he felt the strong reaction of reality and its impetus brought him to his feet. "Whatever happens, I intend to go—to go for good," he exclaimed. "I want you to understand that. Oh, don't be afraid—I'll find a reason, But it's perfectly clear that I must go."

She uttered a protesting cry. "Go away? You? Don't you see that that would tell everything—drag everybody into the horror?"

He found no answer, and her voice dropped back to its calmer note. "What good would your going do? Do you suppose it would change anything for me?" She looked at him with a musing wistfulness. "I wonder what your feeling for me was? It seems queer that I've never really known—I suppose we *don't* know much about that kind of feeling. Is it like taking a drink when you're thirsty? . . . I used to feel as if all of me was in the palm of your hand . . ."

He bowed his humbled head, but she went on almost exultantly: "Don't for a minute think I'm sorry! It was worth every penny it cost. My mistake was in being ashamed, just at first, of its having cost such a lot. I tried to carry it off as a joke—to talk of it to myself as an 'adventure.' I'd always wanted adventures, and you'd given me one, and I tried to take your attitude about it, to 'play the game' and convince myself that I hadn't risked any more on it than you. Then, when I met you again, I suddenly saw that I *had* risked more, but that I'd won more, too—such worlds! I'd been trying all the while to put everything I could between us; now I want to sweep everything away. I'd been trying to forget how you looked; now I want to remember you always. I'd been trying not to hear your voice; now I never want to hear any other. I've made my choice—that's all: I've had you and I mean to keep you." Her face was shining like her eyes. "To keep you hidden away here," she ended, and put her hand upon her breast.

After she had left him, Darrow continued to sit motionless, staring back into their past. Hitherto it had lingered on the edge of his mind in a vague pink blur, like one of the little rose-leaf clouds that a setting sun drops from its disc. Now it was a huge looming darkness, through which his eyes vainly strained. The whole episode was still obscure to him, save where here and there, as they talked, some phrase or gesture or intonation of the girl's had lit up a little spot in the night.

She had said: "I wonder what your feeling for me was?" and he found himself wondering too . . . He remembered distinctly enough that he had not meant the perilous passion—even in its most transient form—to play a part in their relation. In that respect his attitude had been above reproach. She was an unusually original and attractive creature, to whom he had wanted to give a few days of harmless pleasuring, and who was alert and expert enough to understand his intention and spare him the boredom of hesitations and misinterpretations. That had been his first impression, and her subsequent demeanour had justified it. She had been, from the outset, just the frank and easy comrade he had expected to find her. Was it he, then, who, in the sequel, had grown impatient of the bounds he had set himself? Was it his wounded vanity that, seeking balm for its hurt, yearned to dip deeper into the healing pool of her compassion? In his confused memory of the situation he seemed not to have been guiltless of such yearnings . . . Yet for the first few days the experiment had been perfectly successful. Her enjoyment had been unclouded and his pleasure in it undisturbed. It was very gradually—he seemed to see—that a shade of lassitude had crept over their intercourse. Perhaps it was because, when her light chatter about people failed, he found she had no other fund to draw on, or perhaps simply because of the sweetness of her laugh, or of the charm of the gesture with which, one day in the woods of Marly, she had tossed off her hat and tilted back her head at the call of a cuckoo; or because, whenever he looked at her unexpectedly, he found that she was looking at him and did not want him to know it; or perhaps, in varying degrees, because of all these things, that there had come a moment when no word seemed to fly high enough or dive deep enough to utter the sense of well-being each gave to the other, and the natural substitute for speech had been a kiss.

The kiss, at all events, had come at the precise moment to save their venture from disaster. They had reached the point when her amazing reminiscences had begun to flag, when her future had been exhaustively discussed, her theatrical prospects minutely studied, her quarrel with Mrs. Murrett retold with the last amplification of detail, and when, perhaps conscious of her exhausted resources and his dwindling interest, she had committed the fatal error of saying that she could see he was unhappy, and entreating him to tell her why . . .

From the brink of estranging confidences, and from the risk of unfavourable comparisons, his gesture had snatched her back to safety; and as soon as he had kissed her he felt that she would never bore him again. She was one of the elemental creatures whose emotion is all in their pulses, and who become inexpressive or sentimental when they try to turn sensation into speech. His caress had restored her to her natural place in the scheme of things, and Darrow felt as if he had clasped a tree and a nymph[2] had bloomed from it . . .

The mere fact of not having to listen to her any longer added immensely to her charm. She continued, of course, to talk to him, but it didn't matter, because he no longer made any effort to follow her words, but let her voice run on as a musical undercurrent to his thoughts. She hadn't a drop of poetry in her, but she had some of the qualities that create it in others; and in moments of heat the imagination does not always feel the difference . . .

Lying beside her in the shade, Darrow felt her presence as a part of the charmed stillness of the summer woods, as the element of vague well-being that suffused his senses and lulled to sleep the ache of wounded pride. All he asked of her, as yet, was a touch on the hand or on the lips—and that she should let him go on lying there through the long warm hours, while a black-bird's song throbbed like a fountain, and the summer wind stirred in the trees, and close by, between the nearest branches and the brim of his tilted hat, a slight white figure gathered up all the floating threads of joy . . .

He recalled, too, having noticed, as he lay staring at a break in the tree-tops, a stream of mare's-tails[3] coming up the sky. He had said to himself: "It will rain tomorrow," and the thought had made the air seem warmer and the sun more vivid on her hair . . . Perhaps if the mare's-tails had not come up the sky their adventure might have had no sequel. But the cloud brought rain, and next morning he looked out of his window into a cold grey blur. They had planned an all-day excursion down the Seine,[4] to the two Andelys and Rouen, and now, with the long hours on their hands, they were both a little at a loss . . . There was the Louvre,[5] of course, and the Luxembourg;[6] but when he had tried looking at pictures with her she had first so persistently admired the worst things, and then so frankly lapsed into indifference, that he had no wish to repeat the experiment. So they went out, aimlessly, and took a cold wet walk, turning at length into the deserted arcades of the Palais Royal,[7] and finally drifting into one of its equally deserted restaurants, where they lunched alone and somewhat dolefully, served by a wan old waiter with the look of a castaway who has given up watching for a sail . . . It was odd how the waiter's face came back to him . . .

Perhaps but for the rain it might never have happened; but what was the use of thinking of that now? He tried to turn his thoughts to more urgent issues; but, by a strange perversity of association, every detail of the day was forcing itself on his mind with an insistence from which there was no escape. Reluctantly he relived the long wet walk back to the hotel, after a tedious hour at a cinematograph show[8] on the Boulevard. It was still raining when they withdrew from this stale spectacle, but she had obstinately refused to take a cab, had even, on the way, insisted on loitering under the dripping awnings of shop-windows and poking into draughty passages, and finally, when they had nearly reached their destination, had gone so far as to suggest that they should turn back to hunt up some show she had heard of in a theatre at the Batignolles. But at that he had somewhat irritably protested: he remembered that, for the first time, they were both rather irritable, and vaguely disposed to resist one another's suggestions. His feet were wet, and he was tired of walking, and sick of the smell of stuffy unaired theatres, and he had said he must really get back to write some letters—and so they had kept on to the hotel . . .

THE AGE OF INNOCENCE

XXX

That evening when Archer came down before dinner he found the drawing-room empty.

He and May were dining alone, all the family engagements having been postponed since Mrs. Manson Mingott's illness; and as May was the more punctual of the two he was surprised that she had not preceded him. He knew that she was at home, for while he dressed he had heard her moving about in her room;[1] and he wondered what had delayed her.

He had fallen into the way of dwelling on such conjectures as a means of tying his thoughts fast to reality. Sometimes he felt as if he had found the clue to his father-in-law's absorption in trifles; perhaps even Mr. Welland, long ago, had had escapes and visions, and had conjured up all the hosts of domesticity to defend himself against them.

When May appeared he thought she looked tired. She had put on the low-necked and tightly-laced dinner-dress which the Mingott ceremonial exacted on the most informal occasions, and had built her fair hair into its usual accumulated coils; and her face, in contrast, was wan and almost faded. But she shone on him with her usual tenderness, and her eyes had kept the blue dazzle of the day before.

"What became of you, dear?" she asked. "I was waiting at Granny's, and Ellen came alone, and said she had dropped you on the way because you had to rush off on business. There's nothing wrong?"

"Only some letters I'd forgotten, and wanted to get off before dinner."

"Ah—" she said; and a moment afterward: "I'm sorry you didn't come to Granny's—unless the letters were urgent."

"They were," he rejoined, surprised at her insistence. "Besides, I don't see why I should have gone to your grandmother's. I didn't know you were there."

She turned and moved to the looking-glass above the mantel-piece. As she stood there, lifting her long arm to fasten a puff that had slipped from its place in her intricate hair, Archer was struck by something languid and inelastic in her attitude, and wondered if the deadly monotony of their lives had laid its weight on her also. Then he remembered that, as he had left the house that morning, she had called over the stairs that she would meet him at her grandmother's so that they might drive home together. He had called back a cheery "Yes!" and then, absorbed in other visions, had forgotten his promise. Now he was smitten with compunction, yet irritated that so trifling an omission should be stored up against him after nearly two years of marriage. He was weary of living in a perpetual tepid honeymoon, without the temperature of passion yet with all its exactions. If May had spoken out her grievances (he suspected her of many) he might have laughed them away; but she was trained to conceal imaginary wounds under a Spartan[2] smile.

To disguise his own annoyance he asked how her grandmother was, and she answered that Mrs. Mingott was still improving, but had been rather disturbed by the last news about the Beauforts.

"What news?"

"It seems they're going to stay in New York. I believe he's going into an insurance business, or something. They're looking about for a small house."

The preposterousness of the case was beyond discussion, and they went in to dinner. During dinner their talk moved in its usual limited circle; but Archer noticed that his wife made no allusion to Madame Olenska, nor to old Catherine's reception of her. He was thankful for the fact, yet felt it to be vaguely ominous.

They went up to the library for coffee, and Archer lit a cigar and took down a volume of Michelet.[3] He had taken to history in the evenings since May had shown a tendency to ask him to read aloud whenever she saw him with a volume of poetry: not that he disliked the sound of his own voice, but because he could always

foresee her comments on what he read. In the days of their engagement she had simply (as he now perceived) echoed what he
told her; but since he had ceased to provide her with opinions she
had begun to hazard her own, with results destructive to his enjoyment of the works commented on.

Seeing that he had chosen history she fetched her workbasket,
drew up an armchair to the green-shaded student lamp, and uncovered a cushion she was embroidering for his sofa. She was not
a clever needle-woman; her large capable hands were made for
riding, rowing and open-air activities; but since other wives embroidered cushions for their husbands she did not wish to omit
this last link in her devotion.

She was so placed that Archer, by merely raising his eyes, could
see her bent above her work-frame, her ruffled elbow-sleeves slipping back from her firm round arms, the betrothal sapphire[4] shining on her left hand above her broad gold wedding-ring, and the
right hand slowly and laboriously stabbing the canvas. As she sat
thus, the lamplight full on her clear brow, he said to himself with
a secret dismay that he would always know the thoughts behind
it, that never, in all the years to come, would she surprise him by
an unexpected mood, by a new idea, a weakness, a cruelty or an
emotion. She had spent her poetry and romance on their short
courting: the function was exhausted because the need was past.
Now she was simply ripening into a copy of her mother, and mysteriously, by the very process, trying to turn him into a Mr. Welland. He laid down his book and stood up impatiently; and at
once she raised her head.

"What's the matter?"

"The room is stifling: I want a little air."

He had insisted that the library curtains should draw backward
and forward on a rod, so that they might be closed in the evening,
instead of remaining nailed to a gilt cornice, and immovably
looped up over layers of lace, as in the drawing-room; and he
pulled them back and pushed up the sash, leaning out into the icy
night. The mere fact of not looking at May, seated beside his
table, under his lamp, the fact of seeing other houses, roofs, chimneys, of getting the sense of other lives outside his own, other
cities beyond New York, and a whole world beyond his world,
cleared his brain and made it easier to breathe.

After he had leaned out into the darkness for a few minutes he heard her say: "Newland! Do shut the window. You'll catch your death."

He pulled the sash down and turned back. "Catch my death!" he echoed; and he felt like adding: "But I've caught it already. I *am* dead—I've been dead for months and months."

And suddenly the play of the word flashed up a wild suggestion. What if it were *she* who was dead! If she were going to die—to die soon—and leave him free! The sensation of standing there, in that warm familiar room, and looking at her, and wishing her dead, was so strange, so fascinating and overmastering, that its enormity did not immediately strike him. He simply felt that chance had given him a new possibility to which his sick soul might cling. Yes, May might die—people did: young people, healthy people like herself: she might die, and set him suddenly free.

She glanced up, and he saw by her widening eyes that there must be something strange in his own.

"Newland! Are you ill?"

He shook his head and turned toward his arm-chair. She bent over her work-frame, and as he passed he laid his hand on her hair. "Poor May!" he said.

"Poor? Why poor?" she echoed with a strained laugh.

"Because I shall never be able to open a window without worrying you," he rejoined, laughing also.

For a moment she was silent; then she said very low, her head bowed over her work: "I shall never worry if you're happy."

"Ah, my dear; and I shall never be happy unless I can open the windows!"

"In *this* weather?" she remonstrated; and with a sigh he buried his head in his book.

Six or seven days passed. Archer heard nothing from Madame Olenska, and became aware that her name would not be mentioned in his presence by any member of the family. He did not try to see her; to do so while she was at old Catherine's guarded bedside would have been almost impossible. In the uncertainty of the situation he let himself drift, conscious, somewhere below the surface of his thoughts, of a resolve which had come to him when he had leaned out from his library window into the icy night. The strength of that resolve made it easy to wait and make no sign.

Then one day May told him that Mrs. Manson Mingott had asked to see him. There was nothing surprising in the request, for the old lady was steadily recovering, and she had always openly declared that she preferred Archer to any of her other grandsons-in-law. May gave the message with evident pleasure: she was proud of old Catherine's appreciation of her husband.

There was a moment's pause, and then Archer felt it incumbent on him to say: "All right. Shall we go together this afternoon?"

His wife's face brightened, but she instantly answered: "Oh, you'd much better go alone. It bores Granny to see the same people too often."

Archer's heart was beating violently when he rang old Mrs. Mingott's bell. He had wanted above all things to go alone, for he felt sure the visit would give him the chance of saying a word in private to the Countess Olenska. He had determined to wait till the chance presented itself naturally; and here it was, and here he was on the doorstep. Behind the door, behind the curtains of the yellow damask room next to the hall, she was surely awaiting him; in another moment he should see her, and be able to speak to her before she led him to the sick-room.

He wanted only to put one question: after that his course would be clear. What he wished to ask was simply the date of her return to Washington; and that question she could hardly refuse to answer.

But in the yellow sitting-room it was the mulatto maid who waited. Her white teeth shining like a keyboard, she pushed back the sliding doors and ushered him into old Catherine's presence.

The old woman sat in a vast throne-like arm-chair near her bed. Beside her was a mahogany stand bearing a cast bronze lamp with an engraved globe, over which a green paper shade had been balanced. There was not a book or a newspaper in reach, nor any evidence of feminine employment: conversation had always been Mrs. Mingott's sole pursuit, and she would have scorned to feign an interest in fancywork.

Archer saw no trace of the slight distortion left by her stroke. She merely looked paler, with darker shadows in the folds and recesses of her obesity; and, in the fluted mob-cap tied by a starched bow between her first two chins, and the muslin kerchief crossed over her billowing purple dressing-gown, she seemed like some shrewd and kindly ancestress of her own who might have yielded too freely to the pleasures of the table.

She held out one of the little hands that nestled in a hollow of her huge lap like pet animals, and called to the maid: "Don't let in any one else. If my daughters call, say I'm asleep."

The maid disappeared, and the old lady turned to her grandson.

"My dear, am I perfectly hideous?" she asked gaily, launching out one hand in search of the folds of muslin on her inaccessible bosom. "My daughters tell me it doesn't matter at my age—as if hideousness didn't matter all the more the harder it gets to conceal!"

"My dear, you're handsomer than ever!" Archer rejoined in the same tone; and she threw back her head and laughed.

"Ah, but not as handsome as Ellen!" she jerked out, twinkling at him maliciously; and before he could answer she added: "Was she so awfully handsome the day you drove her up from the ferry?"

He laughed, and she continued: "Was it because you told her so that she had to put you out on the way? In my youth young men didn't desert pretty women unless they were made to!" She gave another chuckle, and interrupted it to say almost querulously: "It's a pity she didn't marry you; I always told her so. It would have spared me all this worry. But who ever thought of sparing their grandmother worry?"

Archer wondered if her illness had blurred her faculties; but suddenly she broke out: "Well, it's settled, anyhow: she's going to stay with me, whatever the rest of the family say! She hadn't been here five minutes before I'd have gone down on my knees to keep her—if only, for the last twenty years, I'd been able to see where the floor was!"

Archer listened in silence, and she went on: "They'd talked me over, as no doubt you know: persuaded me, Lovell, and Letterblair, and Augusta Welland, and all the rest of them, that I must hold out and cut off her allowance, till she was made to see that it was her duty to go back to Olenski. They thought they'd convinced me when the secretary, or whatever he was, came out with the last proposals: handsome proposals I confess they were. After all, marriage is marriage, and money's money—both useful things in their way . . . and I didn't know what to answer—" She broke off and drew a long breath, as if speaking had become an effort. "But the minute I laid eyes on her, I said: 'You sweet bird, you! Shut you up in that cage again? Never!' And now it's settled that she's to stay here and nurse her Granny as long as there's a Granny to nurse. It's not a gay prospect, but she doesn't mind; and of course I've told Letterblair that she's to be given her proper allowance."

The young man heard her with veins aglow; but in his confusion of mind he hardly knew whether her news brought joy or pain. He had so definitely decided on the course he meant to pursue that for the moment he could not readjust his thoughts. But gradually there stole over him the delicious sense of difficulties deferred and opportunities miraculously provided. If Ellen had consented to come and live with her grandmother it must surely be because she had recognised the impossibility of giving him up. This was her answer to his final appeal of the other day: if she would not take the extreme step he had urged, she had at last yielded to half-measures. He sank back into thought with the involuntary relief of a man who has been ready to risk everything, and suddenly tastes the dangerous sweetness of security.

"She couldn't have gone back—it was impossible!" he exclaimed.

"Ah, my dear, I always knew you were on her side; and that's why I sent for you today, and why I said to your pretty wife, when she proposed to come with you: 'No, my dear, I'm pining to see Newland, and I don't want anybody to share our transports.' For you see, my dear—" she drew her head back as far as its tethering chins permitted, and looked him full in the eyes—"you see, we shall have a fight yet. The family don't want her here, and they'll say it's because I've been ill, because I'm a weak old woman, that she's persuaded me. I'm not well enough yet to fight them one by one, and you've got to do it for me."

"I?" he stammered.

"You. Why not?" she jerked back at him, her round eyes suddenly as sharp as pen-knives. Her hand fluttered from its chair-arm and lit on his with a clutch of little pale nails like bird-claws. "Why not?" she searchingly repeated.

Archer, under the exposure of her gaze, had recovered his self-possession.

"Oh, I don't count—I'm too insignificant."

"Well, you're Letterblair's partner, ain't you? You've got to get at them through Letterblair. Unless you've got a reason," she insisted.

"Oh, my dear, I back you to hold your own against them all without my help; but you shall have it if you need it," he reassured her.

"Then we're safe!" she sighed; and smiling on him with all her ancient cunning she added, as she settled her head among the cushions: "I always knew you'd back us up, because they never quote you when they talk about its being her duty to go home."

He winced a little at her terrifying perspicacity, and longed to ask: "And May—do they quote her?" But he judged it safer to turn the question.

"And Madame Olenska? When am I to see her?" he said.

The old lady chuckled, crumpled her lids, and went through the pantomime of archness. "Not today. One at a time, please. Madame Olenska's gone out."

He flushed with disappointment, and she went on: "She's gone out, my child: gone in my carriage to see Regina Beaufort."

She paused for this announcement to produce its effect. "That's what she's reduced me to already. The day after she got here she put on her best bonnet, and told me, as cool as a cucumber, that she was going to call on Regina Beaufort. 'I don't know her; who is she?' says I. 'She's your grand-niece, and a most unhappy woman,' she says. 'She's the wife of a scoundrel,' I answered. 'Well,' she says, 'and so am I, and yet all my family want me to go back to him.' Well, that floored me, and I let her go; and finally one day she said it was raining too hard to go out on foot, and she wanted me to lend her my carriage. 'What for?' I asked her; and she said: 'To go and see cousin Regina'—*cousin!* Now, my dear, I looked out of the window, and saw it wasn't raining a drop; but I understood her, and I let her have the carriage. . . . After all, Regina's a brave woman, and so is she; and I've always liked courage above everything."

Archer bent down and pressed his lips on the little hand that still lay on his.

"Eh—eh—eh! Whose hand did you think you were kissing, young man—your wife's, I hope?" the old lady snapped out with her mocking cackle; and as he rose to go she called out after him: "Give her her Granny's love; but you'd better not say anything about our talk."

XXXI

Archer had been stunned by old Catherine's news. It was only natural that Madame Olenska should have hastened from Washington in response to her grandmother's summons; but that she should have decided to remain under her roof—especially now that Mrs. Mingott had almost regained her health—was less easy to explain.

Archer was sure that Madame Olenska's decision had not been influenced by the change in her financial situation. He knew the exact figure of the small income which her husband had allowed her at their separation. Without the addition of her grandmother's allowance it was hardly enough to live on, in any sense known to the Mingott vocabulary; and now that Medora Manson, who shared her life, had been ruined, such a pittance would barely keep the two women clothed and fed. Yet Archer was convinced that Madame Olenska had not accepted her grandmother's offer from interested motives.

She had the heedless generosity and the spasmodic extravagance of persons used to large fortunes, and indifferent to money; but she could go without many things which her relations considered indispensable, and Mrs. Lovell Mingott and Mrs. Welland had often been heard to deplore that any one who had enjoyed the cosmopolitan luxuries of Count Olenska's establishments should care so little about "how things were done." Moreover, as Archer knew, several months had passed since her allowance had been cut off; yet in the interval she had made no effort to regain her grandmother's favour. Therefore if she had changed her course it must be for a different reason.

He did not have far to seek for that reason. On the way from the ferry she had told him that he and she must remain apart; but she had said it with her head on his breast. He knew that there was no calculated coquetry in her words; she was fighting her fate as he had fought his, and clinging desperately to her resolve that they should not break faith with the people who trusted them. But during the ten days which had elapsed since her return to New York she had perhaps guessed from his silence, and from the fact of his making no attempt to see her, that he was meditating a decisive step, a step from which there was no turning back. At the thought, a sudden fear of her own weakness might have seized her, and she might have felt that, after all, it was better to accept the compromise usual in such cases, and follow the line of least resistance.

An hour earlier, when he had rung Mrs. Mingott's bell, Archer had fancied that his path was clear before him. He had meant to have a word alone with Madame Olenska, and failing that, to learn from her grandmother on what day, and by which train, she was returning to Washington. In that train he intended to join her, and travel with her to Washington, or as much farther as she was willing to go. His own fancy inclined to Japan. At any rate she would understand at once that, wherever she went, he was going. He meant to leave a note for May that should cut off any other alternative.

He had fancied himself not only nerved for this plunge but eager to take it; yet his first feeling on hearing that the course of events was changed had been one of relief. Now, however, as he waked home from Mrs. Mingott's, he was conscious of a growing distaste for what lay before him. There was nothing unknown or unfamiliar in the path he was presumably to tread; but when he had trodden it before it was as a free man, who was accountable to no one for his actions, and could lend himself with an amused detachment to the game of precautions and prevarications, concealments and compliances, that the part required. This procedure was called "protecting a woman's honour"; and the best fiction, combined with the after-dinner talk of his elders, had long since initiated him into every detail of its code.

Now he saw the matter in a new light, and his part in it seemed singularly diminished. It was, in fact, that which, with a secret fatuity, he had watched Mrs. Thorley Rushworth[5] play toward a fond and unperceiving husband: a smiling, bantering, humouring, watchful and incessant lie. A lie by day, a lie by night, a lie in every touch and every look; a lie in every caress and every quarrel; a lie in every word and in every silence.

It was easier, and less dastardly on the whole, for a wife to play such a part toward her husband. A woman's standard of truthfulness was tacitly held to be lower: she was the subject creature, and versed in the arts of the enslaved. Then she could always plead moods and nerves, and the right not to be held too strictly to account; and even in the most strait-laced societies the laugh was always against the husband.

But in Archer's little world no one laughed at a wife deceived, and a certain measure of contempt was attached to men who continued their philandering after marriage. In the rotation of crops there was a recognised season for wild oats; but they were not to be sown more than once.

Archer had always shared this view: in his heart he thought Lefferts[6] despicable. But to love Ellen Olenska was not to become a man like Lefferts: for the first time Archer found himself face to face with the dread argument of the individual case. Ellen Olenska was like no other woman, he was like no other man: their situation, therefore, resembled no one else's, and they were answerable to no tribunal but that of their own judgment.

Yes, but in ten minutes more he would be mounting his own doorstep; and there were May, and habit, and honour, and all the old decencies that he and his people had always believed in . . .

At his corner he hesitated, and then walked on down Fifth Avenue.

Ahead of him, in the winter night, loomed a big unlit house. As he drew near he thought how often he had seen it blazing with lights, its steps awninged[7] and carpeted, and carriages waiting in double line to draw up at the curbstone. It was in the conservatory that stretched its dead-black bulk down the side street that he had taken his first kiss from May; it was under the myriad candles of the ball-room that he had seen her appear, tall and silver-shining as a young Diana.[8]

Now the house was as dark as the grave, except for a faint flare of gas in the basement, and a light in one upstairs room where the blind had not been lowered. As Archer reached the corner he saw that the carriage standing at the door was Mrs. Manson Mingott's. What an opportunity for Sillerton Jackson, if he should chance to pass! Archer had been greatly moved by old Catherine's account of Madame Olenska's attitude toward Mrs. Beaufort; it made the righteous reprobation of New York seem like a passing by on the other side. But he knew well enough what construction the clubs and drawing-rooms would put on Ellen Olenska's visits to her cousin.

He paused and looked up at the lighted window. No doubt the two women were sitting together in that room: Beaufort had probably sought consolation elsewhere. There were even rumours that he had left New York with Fanny Ring;[9] but Mrs. Beaufort's attitude made the report seem improbable.

Archer had the nocturnal perspective of Fifth Avenue almost to himself. At that hour most people were indoors, dressing for dinner; and he was secretly glad that Ellen's exit was likely to be unobserved. As the thought passed through his mind the door opened, and she came out. Behind her was a faint light, such as might have been carried down the stairs to show her the way. She turned to say a word to some one; then the door closed, and she came down the steps.

"Ellen," he said in a low voice, as she reached the pavement.

She stopped with a slight start, and just then he saw two young men of fashionable cut approaching. There was a familiar air about their overcoats and the way their smart silk mufflers were folded over their white ties; and he wondered how youths of their quality happened to be dining out so early. Then he remembered that the Reggie Chiverses, whose house was a few doors above, were taking a large party that evening to see Adelaide Neilson[10] in *Romeo and Juliet,* and guessed that the two were of the number. They passed under a lamp, and he recognized Lawrence Lefferts and a young Chivers.

A mean desire not to have Madame Olenska seen at the Beaufort's door vanished as he felt the penetrating warmth of her hand.

"I shall see you now—we shall be together," he broke out, hardly knowing what he said.

"Ah," she answered, "Granny has told you?"

While he watched her he was aware that Lefferts and Chivers, on reaching the farther side of the street corner, had discreetly

struck away across Fifth Avenue. It was the kind of masculine solidarity that he himself often practiced; now he sickened at their
connivance. Did she really imagine that he and she could live like
this? And if not, what else did she imagine?

"Tomorrow I must see you—somewhere where we can be
alone," he said, in a voice that sounded almost angry to his own
ears.

She wavered, and moved toward the carriage.

"But I shall be at Granny's—for the present that is," she added,
as if conscious that her change of plans required some explanation.

"Somewhere where we can be alone," he insisted.

She gave a faint laugh that grated on him.

"In New York? But there are no churches . . . no monuments."

"There's the Art Museum—in the Park," he explained, as she
looked puzzled. "At half-past two. I shall be at the door . . ."

She turned away without answering and got quickly into the
carriage. As it drove off she leaned forward, and he thought she
waved her hand in the obscurity. He stared after her in a turmoil
of contradictory feelings. It seemed to him that he had been
speaking not to the woman he loved but to another, a woman he
was indebted to for pleasures already wearied of: it was hateful to
find himself the prisoner of this hackneyed vocabulary.

"She'll come!" he said to himself, almost contemptuously.

Avoiding the popular "Wolfe collection," whose anecdotic[11] can-
vases filled one of the main galleries of the queer wilderness of
cast-iron and encaustic tiles[12] known as the Metropolitan Museum, they had wandered down a passage to the room where the
"Cesnola antiquities"[13] mouldered in unvisited loneliness.

They had this melancholy retreat to themselves, and seated on
the divan enclosing the central steam-radiator, they were staring
silently at the glass cabinets mounted in ebonised wood which
contained the recovered fragments of Ilium.

"It's odd," Madame Olenska said, "I never came here before."

"Ah, well—. Some day, I suppose, it will be a great Museum."

"Yes," she assented absently.

She stood up and wandered across the room. Archer, remaining
seated, watched the light movements of her figure, so girlish even

under its heavy furs, the cleverly planted heron wing in her fur cap, and the way a dark curl lay like a flattened vine spiral on each cheek above the ear. His mind, as always when they first met, was wholly absorbed in the delicious details that made her herself and no other. Presently he rose and approached the case before which she stood. Its glass shelves were crowded with small broken objects—hardly recognisable domestic utensils, ornaments and personal trifles—made of glass, of clay, of discoloured bronze and other time-blurred substances.

"It seems cruel," she said, "that after a while nothing matters . . . any more than these little things, that used to be necessary and important to forgotten people, and now have to be guessed at under a magnifying glass and labelled: 'Use unknown.'"

"Yes; but meanwhile—"

"Ah, meanwhile—"

As she stood there, in her long sealskin coat, her hands thrust in a small round muff, her veil drawn down like a transparent mask to the tip of her nose, and the bunch of violets he had brought her stirring with her quickly-taken breath, it seemed incredible that this pure harmony of line and colour should ever suffer the stupid law of change.

"Meanwhile everything matters—that concerns you," he said.

She looked at him thoughtfully, and turned back to the divan. He sat down beside her and waited; but suddenly he heard a step echoing far off down the empty rooms, and felt the pressure of the minutes.

"What is it you wanted to tell me?" she asked, as if she had received the same warning.

"What I wanted to tell you?" he rejoined. "Why, that I believe you came to New York because you were afraid."

"Afraid?"

"Of my coming to Washington."

She looked down at her muff, and he saw her hands stir in it uneasily.

"Well—?"

"Well—yes," she said.

"You *were* afraid? You knew—?"

"Yes: I knew . . ."

"Well, then?" he insisted.

"Well, then: this is better isn't it?" she returned with a long questioning sigh.

"Better—?"

"We shall hurt others less. Isn't it, after all, what you always wanted?"

"To have you here, you mean—in reach and yet out of reach? To meet you in this way, on the sly? It's the very reverse of what I want. I told you the other day what I wanted."

She hesitated. "And you still think this—worse?"

"A thousand times!" He paused. "It would be easy to lie to you; but the truth is I think it detestable."

"Oh, so do I!" she cried with a deep breath of relief.

He sprang up impatiently. "Well, then—it's my turn to ask: what is it, in God's name, that you think better?"

She hung her head and continued to clasp and unclasp her hands in her muff. The step drew nearer, and a guardian in a braided cap walked listlessly through the room like a ghost stalking through a necropolis. They fixed their eyes simultaneously on the case opposite them, and when the official figure had vanished down a vista of mummies and sarcophagi Archer spoke again.

"What do you think better?"

Instead of answering she murmured: "I promised Granny to stay with her because it seemed to me that here I should be safer."

"From me?"

She bent her head slightly, without looking at him.

"Safer from loving me?"

Her profile did not stir, but he saw a tear overflow on her lashes and hang in a mesh of her veil.

"Safer from doing irreparable harm. Don't let us be like all the others!" she protested.

"What others? I don't profess to be different from my kind. I'm consumed by the same wants and the same longings."

She glanced at him with a kind of terror, and he saw a faint colour steal into her cheeks.

"Shall I—once come to you; and then go home?" she suddenly hazarded in a low clear voice.

The blood rushed to the young man's forehead. "Dearest!" he said, without moving. It seemed as if he held his heart in his hands, like a full cup that the least motion might overbrim.

Then her last phrase struck his ear and his face clouded. "Go home? What do you mean by going home?"

"Home to my husband."

"And you expect me to say yes to that?"

She raised her troubled eyes to his. "What else is there? I can't stay here and lie to the people who've been good to me."

"But that's the very reason why I ask you to come away!"

"And destroy their lives, when they've helped me to remake mine?"

Archer sprang to his feet and stood looking down on her in inarticulate despair. It would have been easy to say: "Yes, come; come once." He knew the power she would put in his hands if she consented; there would be no difficulty then in persuading her not to go back to her husband.

But something silenced the word on his lips. A sort of passionate honesty in her made it inconceivable that he should try to draw her into that familiar trap. "If I were to let her come," he said to himself, "I should have to let her go again." And that was not to be imagined.

But he saw the shadow of the lashes on her wet cheek, and wavered.

"After all," he began again, "we have lives of our own. . . . There's no use attempting the impossible. You're so unprejudiced about some things, so used, as you say, to looking at the Gorgon,[14] that I don't know why you're afraid to face our case, and see it as it really is—unless you think the sacrifice is not worth making."

She stood up also, her lips tightening under a rapid frown.

"Call it that, then—I must go," she said, drawing her little watch from her bosom.

She turned away, and he followed and caught her by the wrist. "Well, then: come to me once," he said, his head turning suddenly at the thought of losing her; and for a second or two they looked at each other almost like enemies.

"When?" he insisted. "Tomorrow?"

She hesitated. "The day after."

"Dearest—!" he said again.

She had disengaged her wrist; but for a moment they continued to hold each other's eyes, and he saw that her face, which had grown very pale, was flooded with a deep inner radiance. His heart beat with awe: he felt that he had never before beheld love visible.

"Oh, I shall be late—good-bye. No, don't come any farther than this," she cried, walking hurriedly away down the long room, as if the reflected radiance in his eyes had frightened her. When she reached the door she turned for a moment to wave a quick farewell.

Archer walked home alone. Darkness was falling when he let himself into his house, and he looked about at the familiar objects in the hall as if he viewed them from the other side of the grave.

The parlour-maid, hearing his step, ran up the stairs to light the gas on the upper landing.

"Is Mrs. Archer in?"

"No, sir; Mrs. Archer went out in the carriage after luncheon, and hasn't come back."

With a sense of relief he entered the library and flung himself down in his armchair. The parlour-maid followed, bringing the student lamp and shaking some coals onto the dying fire. When she left he continued to sit motionless, his elbows on his knees, his chin on his clasped hands, his eyes fixed on the red grate.

He sat there without conscious thoughts, without sense of the lapse of time, in a deep and grave amazement that seemed to suspend life rather than quicken it. "This was what had to be, then . . . this was what had to be," he kept repeating to himself, as if he hung in the clutch of doom. What he had dreamed of had been so different that there was a mortal chill in his rapture.

The door opened and May came in.

"I'm dreadfully late—you weren't worried, were you?" she asked, laying her hand on his shoulder with one of her rare caresses.

He looked up astonished. "Is it late?"

"After seven. I believe you've been asleep!" She laughed, and drawing out her hat pins tossed her velvet hat on the sofa. She looked paler than usual, but sparkling with an unwonted animation.

"I went to see Granny, and just as I was going away Ellen came in from a walk; so I stayed and had a long talk with her. It was ages since we'd had a real talk. . . ." She had dropped into her usual armchair, facing his, and was running her fingers through her rumpled hair. He fancied she expected him to speak.

"A really good talk," she went on, smiling with what seemed to Archer an unnatural vividness. "She was so dear—just like the old Ellen. I'm afraid I haven't been fair to her lately. I've sometimes thought—"

Archer stood up and leaned against the mantel-piece, out of the radius of the lamp.

"Yes, you've thought—?" he echoed as she paused.

"Well, perhaps I haven't judged her fairly. She's so different—at least on the surface. She takes up such odd people—she seems to like to make herself conspicuous. I suppose it's the life she's led in that fast European society; no doubt we seem dreadfully dull to her. But I don't want to judge her unfairly."

She paused again, a little breathless with the unwonted length of her speech, and sat with her lips slightly parted and a deep blush on her cheeks.

Archer, as he looked at her, was reminded of the glow which had suffused her face in the Mission Garden at St. Augustine. He became aware of the same obscure effort in her, the same reaching out toward something beyond the usual range of her vision.

"She hates Ellen," he thought, "and she's trying to overcome the feeling, and to get me to help her to overcome it."

The thought moved him, and for a moment he was on the point of breaking the silence between them, and throwing himself on her mercy.

"You understand, don't you," she went on, "why the family have sometimes been annoyed? We all did what we could for her at first; but she never seemed to understand. And now this idea of going to see Mrs. Beaufort, of going there in Granny's carriage! I'm afraid she's quite alienated the van der Luydens . . ."

"Ah," said Archer with an impatient laugh. The open door had closed between them again.

"It's time to dress; we're dining out, aren't we?" he asked, moving from the fire.

She rose also, but lingered near the hearth. As he walked past her she moved forward impulsively, as though to detain him: their eyes met, and he saw that hers were of the same swimming blue as when he had left her to drive to Jersey City.

She flung her arms about his neck and pressed her cheek to his.

"You haven't kissed me today," she said in a whisper; and he felt her tremble in his arms.

PART III

LETTERS

Writing for whatever purpose was Edith Wharton's passion, but her clarity and verve came through in even the smallest of her writerly aims. In their edition of her letters, R. W. B. Lewis and Nancy Lewis note that Wharton often wrote a dozen letters a day (they tell the story of her returning from a short trip to find sixty-five letters, only three days' mail, awaiting her). The Lewises drew on more than four thousand extant Wharton letters for the book; those that appear here show the author's intelligent yet always personal ways of communicating with her friends; and one group of the letters traces the painful affair between Edith Wharton and Morton Fullerton.

TO EDWARD L. BURLINGAME

Thusis [Switzerland], July 30, 1894

Dear Mr. Burlingame,

I meant to thank you long before this for your long & helpful criticism of my last story. I appreciate greatly your giving so much time & thought to so trifling a subject, when you have so much to occupy you & what you say will be of great help to me in the future. If Messrs. Scribners still want to publish a volume of my stories, however, I should rather have another six months in which to prepare it, but I haven't a sufficient number ready now for the autumn—

Meanwhile I send you by this mail a little article which should have gone to you before now. It is an account of some rather remarkable terra-cottas which I found last spring in a small place in Tuscany— The article speaks for itself,[1] I will therefore only add that I was so fully persuaded of the importance of the terra-cottas that I determined to have them photographed by Alinari at my own expense, on the chance that Scribner's or one of the other magazines would like to publish an illustrated account of them. Professor Ridolfi's verdict, which I quote in my article, so completely confirms my judgement that I think the subject cannot fail to be of interest to the public, especially as the terra-cottas are *entirely unknown,* even Miss Paget[2] (Vernon Lee) who has lived so long in Italy & devoted so much time to the study of Tuscan art, never having heard of them or of San Vivaldo.

I do not enclose Professor Ridolfi's letter, as I quote it so fully in my article, but will send it to you with pleasure if you wish to see it.

I send you Alinari's photographs with the article. If you do not care to publish the latter, will you kindly keep it & the photographs until you hear from me, as I fear they may be lost if you return them while we are on our wanderings.

Yours sincerely
Edith Wharton

The superior of the monastery, who kindly gave me permission to have the terra-cottas photographed, assured me that they had never been photographed before, except one or two, which were photographed by an amateur living in the neighborhood. I saw these photos which were absolutely worthless—Alinari had never even heard of the place.

Ms:FL

TO EDWARD L. BURLINGAME

Newport, Rhode Island, December 14, 1895

Dear Mr. Burlingame,

Since I last wrote you over a year ago, I have been very ill, & am not yet allowed to do any real work. But I have been scribbling a little & I have sent you a few pages which I hope you may like.

Pray don't trouble yourself to answer this,—I only write it because it is such a distress to me to send such a waif[3] instead of the volume that Messers. Scribner were once kind enough to ask for, that I cannot do so without a word of explanation. And I still hope to get well & have the volume ready next year.

Yours sincerely
Edith Wharton

Ms:FL

TO SARA NORTON

884 Park Avenue, February 28 [1901]

Dear Sally,

I was so sorry not to see you again! We are so "far from today" up in this suburb that I think it a special compliment when my friends try to find me as perseveringly as you did— Yes, I should be delighted to see Mr. Harrison.[4] Do give him a letter, but with the proviso that we *may* not be here; for we had rather bad news of Teddy's mother yesterday & unless she improves we may have to sail in a fortnight.

Still, I hope he will take the chance of finding us.

I believe my play[5] is really "going through," but I don't look forward to the result with any enthusiasm.

I am much more interested in my Italian novel, to which I return with fresh ardour after every temporary estrangement. I wish I could get some one else to write it for me, though!

The little vol. of stories will be out in two or three weeks & you shall have your copy more promptly than last time, I hope.

Affly Yrs—Edith or Pussy as you please.

Ms.BL

TO SARA NORTON

Lenox Mass., November 25 [1901]

Dear Sally

So charmed am I with Mr. Santyana—the volume of him[6] that I may not keep—that I am going to ask you to get me two copies of the same. The sonnets are fine—full of ideas, of imagery, of expression. Some of the single lines are beautiful. But why doesn't he keep to sonnets? He ought to shun the lyric & the ode. Taken altogether—idea & execution—I like the Death of the Metaphysician best—I send back the little book with a faint scratch here

& there to show you the detached things that struck me. A little India-rubber will restore the pages to their first state, & this is the nearest approach to talking over a book together.

Affectionately Yrs,
    Edith

Please put this *a* in the Santyana on page 1.
Will you send the two copies here this week—or, if later than Dec. 1*st*, then to 884 Park Ave? Don't be in any haste about getting them. One can wait for anything so good.

Ms:BL

TO ANNIE ADAMS FIELDS

Somerset Hotel, Tuesday afternoon [Summer 1902]

My dear Mrs. Fields,
    I have just received your kind invitation for Friday, & I am going to reply by making a proposal which I trust you will think a pardonable one under the circumstances. My husband is going out on a bicycling expedition that afternoon & Mr. Updike[7] & I were planning to go & see Mr. Le Moyne; so that I hope perhaps you will let me bring Mr. Updike instead of my husband, & thus not miss the pleasure of seeing you & Miss Jewett.[8] Mr. Updike assures me that you will allow him to act as a substitute, & my husband begs me to say, with his kindest regards, how sorry *he* is to give any one else an opportunity he would so greatly have enjoyed himself!
    With many thanks for your kind thought,

Sincerely yours
    Edith Wharton

Ms:HL

TO WILLIAM CRARY BROWNELL

The Mount, Lenox, Mass, September 12, 1902

Dear Mr. Brownell,

Many thanks for the cheque for $2,191 81/100, which, even to the 81 cents, is welcome to an author in the last throes of house-building—

I am glad to see the new House Decoration[9] has made a good start, but not surprised to find that the G.I. is not being fought for at the railway-stalls— The wonder to me is that the Valley should have reached such heights. I am charmed with the 1 vol. Edition, for which I was just about to write & thank you when your letter came. By the way, I am going to send you a long letter which Mr. James wrote me the other day about the "Valley."[10] You will see there is a personal note in it, so don't circulate it please, beyond Mr. Scribner & Mr. Burlingame. The letter was a great surprise to me, as I never send Mr. James my books, & should not have expected him to be in the least interested in "The Valley."

I rec'd your note of Aug. 14th about Es War,[11] but didn't answer it, as you said you were going off on a holiday (which was a good one, I hope,) & the matter was not urgent. With regard to leave to translate, would it not be better if the request were to come from the Messrs. Scribner? They might mention to Sudermann that the translation will be made under the supervision of the translator of "Es Lebe" (in which character only I am likely to have any identity to him), & that I will write a short introduction to it. Then, as to the play, I am still engaged in trying to find out whether Mrs. Campbell had any right to give me the publishing right. My lawyer has again put the question to hers, & I hope for an answer this week. (It's no use asking her.) The play is ready for you now, but Norman Hapgood[12] who was here the other day, was so pleased with my translation that he carried it off for a few days in order to write an article on it. If I hear it is all right about the copyright I can send it to you next week. I enclose herewith the "Translator's Note."

Yrs Sincerely
    E. Wharton

Don't ask me what I think of the Wings of the Dove[13]—

Ms.FL

TO SARA NORTON

Hotel Bristol, Florence, March 17, [1903]

Dearest Sally

I wept mentally (for I never do physically!) over your poor dear letter, which has just come. How well I know those bitter times, when great trials & small inconveniences pile themselves together on the tired body & strained nerves, & how often have I experienced the fact that when one goes on board ship exhausted & praying for rest, one has a rough voyage & exasperating landing! What you went through, however, surpasses anything I ever heard of, & I hope some of the passengers will say an earnest word to the Dominion Line.

Don't speak of the disappointment of our leaving Rome before you came. There were so many moments when we did the kind of thing that I know you would have enjoyed, & that would have been delicious to talk of afterward. It is part of our friendship that we should never see anything of each other!

I am glad you had sunshine for that heavenly journey from Naples to Rome. It is one of the loveliest bits of Italy— How I wish you had been with us since we left Rome—at Viterbo, Montefiascone, Orvieto, & the delicious villas near Siena! We did not reach here till last night, & Miss Paget (Vernon Lee) has such a prodigious list of villas for me to see near here, & is taking so much trouble to arrange expeditions for us, that I think we shall have to stay here longer than I expected—perhaps ten days.

We had on our little trip as far as Siena a young couple whom I think you will like—the Willie Bucklers. He is Harry White's stepbrother, & she English, a niece of Froude & Max Müller. I mention them because they seem to be great friends of your brother's, so you will probably see them, as they have gone back to Rome. Do be careful about colds, by the way, in Rome. Teddy & I went from one to another, in spite of the heavenly weather; & did not recover till we left. The place must be full of influenza germs. Don't go to the villa Borghese (the Museum) without overshoes or cork-soled boots, for the floors are glacial.

When you are a little better, & have leisure to write, will you give me your advice on the following question. Miss Paget (whom you wd like, I know) is very anxious to go to America, for the quaintest of reasons—"to visit the out of the way parts of New England." She cannot afford to go without paying her expenses, which she proposes to do by lecturing—she would lecture on aesthetics, "Art & Life," & that kind of thing, & I think she would do it well, judging from her books. She does not want to "lecture to fashionable women in bonnets," with a list of millionaire patronesses, for which I respect her; but would like a college audience, men or girls—Bryn Mawr, Radcliffe, Harvard & so on. Her idea is to go to America next August, say, & she must be back before Xmas. If she could do her New England in August & Sept, & lecture in Oct & Nov, it would fit very well. In Boston I should say she might give one or two lectures to a general public too. Now I don't want you to do anything about this but tell me from whom I could get *practical* advice for her. Would Barrett Wendell[14] be a good person, & do you know his address in England?—I am sure he would not mind my bothering him—

Miss Paget has been so kind to me that I should like to do what I can, & I believe her lectures wd be decidedly worth hearing—

I can't say how sorry I am that yr father has had the influenza again.

Don't write till you feel like it—

Yr affte
    E.W

Mitou[15] sends you his best love—

Ms.BL

TO SARA (SALLY) NORTON

The Mount, Lenox, Mass, June 5, 1903

Dear Sally

Your letter glowing with the reflection of the National Gallery
came yesterday, & made me feel more acutely than ever the contrast between the old & the new, between the stored beauty & tradition & amenity over there, & the crassness here. My first few
weeks in America are always miserable, because the tastes I am
cursed with are all of a kind that cannot be gratified here, & I am
not enough in sympathy with our "gros public" to make up for
the lack on the aesthetic side. One's friends are delightful; but *we*
are none of us Americans, we don't think or feel as the Americans
do, we are the wretched exotics produced in a European glass-
house, the most déplacé & useless class on earth! All of which
outburst is due to my first sight of American streets, my first hearing of American voices, & the wild, disheveled backwoods look
of everything when one first comes home! You see in my heart of
hearts, a heart never unbosomed, I feel in America as you say you
do in England—out of sympathy with everything. And in England
I like it *all*—institutions, traditions, mannerisms, conservatisms,
everything but the women's clothes, & the having to go to church
every Sunday.

We arrived safely & comfortably, after a long slow crossing
on the best steamer I ever was on, & came at once to Lenox. It is
very pleasant to be taking one's ease in one's own house, but out
of doors the scene is depressing. There has been an appalling
drought of nine weeks or more, & never has this fresh showery
country looked so unlike itself. The dust is indescribable, the grass
parched & brown, flowers & vegetables stunted, & still no promise of rain! You may fancy how our poor place looks, still in the
rough, with all its bald patches emphasized. In addition, our good
gardener has failed us, we know not why, whether from drink or
some other demoralization, but after spending a great deal of
money on the place all winter there are no results, & we have
been obliged to get a new man. This has been a great blow, as we

can't afford to do much more this year— I try to console myself by writing about Italian gardens instead of looking at my own.

Two days after we landed my niece Beatrix was taken ill with appendicitis. It was a slight attack, & the operation was successfully performed two days ago, but it is a great trial, as she & her mother were going abroad next week, & had rented their house at Bar Harbour, dismissed servants, &c. I expect to have her here as soon as she can be moved, & I doubt if they can sail before August.

Yes, I got your little note about the writing-case, & I am so glad it was right. I am glad also that you are missing this ugly burnt-up June, which wd depress you as it does me. When you write again do tell me how your ear is since the treatment in Paris. I am wonderfully well, & still look on Salsomaggiore[16] as a kind of Lourdes.[17]

The dear dogs were so glad to see us. Miza looks younger than ever, but old Jules is very rheumatic.

Thanks again for your letter, dear Sally—

    Affly Yrs   E.W.

I am so delighted that you think the Maison du Péché as re-markable as I do. It is so full of beauty & feeling, so profoundly moving, so unlike the average French novel in every way.

Ms:BL

TO WILLIAM CRARY BROWNELL

The Mount, Lenox, Mass, June 25 [1904]

Dear Mr. Brownell,

I return the reviews[18] with many thanks. I have never before been discouraged by criticism, because when the critics have found fault with me I have usually abounded in their sense, & seen, as I thought, a way of doing better the next time; but the continued cry that I am an echo of Mr. James[19] (whose books of the last ten years I can't read, much as I delight in the man), & the assumption that the people I write about are not "real" because they are not navvies & char-women, makes me feel rather hopeless. I write about what I see, what I happen to be nearest to, which is surely better than doing cowboys de chic. . . . But this is not business. As to yr. letter of June 23, it fills me with compunction. Of course the understanding was that, on our return to Italy, I should get, or take, photos to complete the Backgrounds.[20] But the bad weather in Italy made it impossible for us to go there, on my husband's account, & I should of course have written you that I couldn't get the photos, since they are not of a kind that one can order from a distance.

I am *very* sorry, & make my excuses to you all— Now what shall we do? I have another article, "March in Italy," which is nearly done, & which will make the book of the requisite length, I think—but if you want photos we are at a stand-still.

It is more than likely that we may go to Italy in the winter, for though my husband is so much better, he seems to be so only because we had no cold weather—still, that will not be decided till his Dr. comes home in September—Meanwhile I must leave it to you to decide whether the book shall be put off on the chance of my being able to get photos on the spot next winter (& also do still another article) or whether you want to give up the pictures—

I might get some photos for Italian Backgrounds (the article) but for Splügen impossible!

I am glad Mrs. Brownell is improving at the Pier, & I still hope for a Sunday from you later on—

My hand is all right, thanks—

Yrs Guiltily
    E. Wharton

Wouldn't it have helped "The Descent" to put in the two new stories?

Ms.FL

TO CHARLES SCRIBNER

The Mount, Lenox, Mass, November 11, 1905

Dear Mr. Scribner,

It is a very beautiful thought to me that 80,000 people should want to read "The House of Mirth," & if the number should ascend to 100,000 I fear my pleasure would exceed the bounds of decency.

Seriously, I am of course immensely interested & amused by all these "returns," & very grateful to you for sending them to me.— And by the way, I hope you got that photograph I sent you about ten days ago, with my eyes down, *trying to look modest?!* The photographer swore he would send it off punctually, but I have had my doubts, as he hasn't sent me one yet. It was to go direct to Mr. Chapin.

I shall be in town for one day next week—Friday, the 17th—& if by any chance you should want to see me about anything, will you send a line to 23 E. 33d St?—I am going to see Miss Marbury[21] about dramatizing the H. of M., as I am having so many bids for it.

Thanks again for your letter.

Sincerely Yrs
    Edith Wharton

Ms:FL

TO DR. MORGAN DIX

The Mount, Lenox, Mass, December 5 [1905]

Dear Dr. Dix,

You would have to write in a very different strain to keep me even twenty-four hours from answering your letter;[22] & I must begin by telling you how touched I am that you would have found time to send it, & how proud—yes, quite inordinately so!—that

you should have thought my novel worthy of such careful reading
& close analysis.—

Few things could have pleased me more than the special form
which your commendation has taken; for, lightly as I think of my
own equipment, I could not do anything if I did not think seriously
of my trade; & the more I have considered it, the more has it
seemed to me valuable & interesting only in so far as it is "a criticism of life."—It almost seems to me that bad & good fiction (using the words in their ethical sense) might be defined as the kind
which treats of life trivially & superficially, & that which probes
deep enough to get at the relation with the eternal laws; & the novelist who has this feeling is so often discouraged by the comments of
readers & critics who think a book "unpleasant" because it deals
with unpleasant conditions, that it is a high solace & encouragement to come upon the recognition of one's motive. No novel
worth anything can be anything but a novel "with a purpose," & if
anyone who cared for the moral issue did not see in my work that I
care for it, I should have no one to blame but myself—or at least my
inadequate means of rendering my effects.

Social conditions as they are just now in our new world, where
the sudden possession of money has come without inherited obligations, or any traditional sense of solidarity between the classes, is a
vast & absorbing field for the novelist, & I wish a great master
could arise to deal with it—but perhaps I may have a chance to talk
of these things with you, for I do not mean to be again in New York
without making a very determined effort to see you & Mrs. Dix.

We never stay long now, because the cold weather is bad for my
husband, but we shall be in our house during January, & perhaps
we can persuade you & Mrs. Dix to come & dine some night
alone so that we may have an unrestrained talk.

I remember with pride your illusion to my little story, "The
Reckoning"—& it has always been a great pleasure to me that, in
your busy & beneficent life, you have found time to follow with
such sympathy what I have tried to do. Believe me, dear Dr. Dix,

Ever sincerely Yrs,
    Edith Wharton

Ms: Archives of Trinity Church Parish.

TO W. MORTON FULLERTON

The Mount, Lenox, Mass, October 15 [1907]

Dear Mr. Fullerton,

We are so pleased that you have not forgotten your promise to look us up—especially as dear H. J., in a letter received last week, sceptically prophesied:—"You won't see Fullerton."

We shall be delighted to see you here when you have pronounced your discours at Bryn Mawr[23] (& do please bring me a copy of it, won't you?), & you will find a good train leaving New York at   , & another in the afternoon at   .[24] I don't know, on second thought, why I call either good, for the train service between here & town has been execrable this last year; but at any rate, they are best we have, & the morning one is not likely to be more than half an hour late!

We shall hope for you, then, either on Friday evening, or on Saturday morning, & your "few hours" will, I trust, be elastic enough to extend over Sunday, as I want to show you some of our mountain land-scapes, & have time for some good talks too?

I am so glad you are going to talk about dear James at Bryn Mawr.

Yours sincerely
    Edith Wharton

I enclose time-table.

TO ROBERT GRANT

The Mount, Lenox, Mass, November 19 [1907]

Dear Mr. Grant,

It is very good of you to take time to write me such an interesting & really helpful analysis of my book[25]—but before thanking you for it, I must throw in a parenthesis to say that I have never yet learned what became of the copy originally meant for you. I rec'd my "advance" copies just before going away on a motor-trip of a week, & they were laid out (but that sounds too mortuary!) with the addresses of the privileged recipients attached, to be sent immediately, but when I got your note on my return the butler (who is the family forwarding agent) said that no volume had been found addressed to Judge Grant! My only solution is that someone staying in the house may have carried it off—but I am very anxious to know how *you* knew it was not lost in the mail? I don't think I can wait till we meet to hear that!!—

I am very much pleased that you like the construction of the book, & I more than agree with you that I haven't been able to keep the characters from being, so to speak, mere *building-material*. The fact is that I am beginning to see exactly where my weakest point is.—I conceive my subjects like a man—that is, rather more architectonically & dramatically than most women—& then execute them like a woman; or rather, I sacrifice, to my desire for construction & breadth, the small incidental effects that women have always excelled in, the episodical characterization, I mean. The worst of it is that this fault is congenital, & not the result of an ambition to do big things. As soon as I look at a subject from the novel-angle I see it in its relation to a larger whole, in all its remotest connotations; & I can't help trying to take them in, at the cost of the smaller realism that I arrive at, I think better in my short stories. This is the reason why I have always obscurely felt that I didn't know how to write a novel. I feel it more clearly after each attempt, because it is in such sharp contrast to the sense of authority with which I take hold of a short story. I think it ought to be a warning to stop; but, alas, I see things more & more from the novel-angle, so that I'm enclosed in a vicious circle from which I suspect silence to be the only escape.

I am very glad, though, that you *do* feel a structural unity in the thing, for some people have criticized the book for the lack of this very thing, & that rather discouraged me. After all, one knows one's weak points so well, that it's rather bewildering to have the critics overlook them & invent others that (one is fairly sure) don't exist—or exist in a less measure.

Your letter is very illuminating, & I am very grateful to you for taking the trouble to write it. It will be a real help to me when I try again.

I am sorry to hear you have reached a "blind alley" in your book. What a hateful trade it is! But suddenly a door will open for you in the blank wall.

I am delighted to hear that your young athlete is safe & sound, & Teddy will rejoice in the New York paper's characterization of him. He (the pronoun refers to Teddy) is off shooting now, & comes back only four or five days before we sail.

Thanks again, dear Mr. Grant. Yrs ever sincerely Edith Wharton

Ms:BL

TO W. MORTON FULLERTON

53 Rue de Varenne, Late February, 1908

Mon ami, Don't let me drag you out at such an early hour to-morrow! What I want to speak to you about will keep till Saturday . . .

Unless, indeed, I can be of use in carrying you to your Ministère, & we can talk en route? I shall have the motor here at 10,30, at any rate, as I have des courses à faire.

We ought to start for the Bréau[26] at about 10 o'c on Saturday.

Thursday eve'g—I have found in Emerson (from Euripides, I suppose) just the phrase for you—& *me*. "The moment my eyes fell on him I was content."[27]

Ms:UT

TO W. MORTON FULLERTON

53 Rue de Varenne, Early March, 1908

Dear, Remember, please, how impatient & anxious I shall be to know the sequel of the Bell letter[28] . . .

——Do you know what I was thinking last night, when you asked me, & I couldn't tell you?—Only that the way you've spent your emotional life, while I've—bien malgré moi—hoarded mine, is what puts the great gulf between us, & sets us not only on op-posite shores, but at hopelessly distant points of our respective shores . . . Do you see what I mean?

And I'm so afraid that the treasures I long to unpack for you, that have come to me in magic ships from enchanted islands, are only, to you, the old familiar red calico & beads of the clever trader, who has had dealings in every latitude, & knows just what to carry in the hold to please the simple native—I'm so afraid of this, that often & often I stuff my shining treasures back into their box, lest I should see you smiling at them!

Well! And if you do? It's *your* loss, after all! And if you can't come into the room without my feeling all over me a ripple of flame, & if, wherever you touch me, a heart beats under your touch, & if, when you hold me, & I don't speak, it's because all the words in me seem to have become throbbing pulses, & all my thoughts are a great golden blur—why should I be afraid of your smiling at me, when I can turn the beads & calico back into such beauty—?

Ms:UT

TO W. MORTON FULLERTON

53 Rue de Varenne, Early April, 1908

Cher aimé, Of the extent of which I have been tiresome & "im-possible," & not-worth-giving-another-thought-to, I am perfectly, & oh so penitently aware—n'en doutez pas! I "walk dreadfully il-lumined," believe me.

On the practical side, as to yr particular suggestion, I'm not as stupid as you think. In my case it would not be "the least risk," but possibly the greatest to follow your plan, even if I could—as assuredly I should—finally overcome my reluctance.[29]

At least believe that I am unhappy, more than I can say, about it all. At first—yes—I hesitated, because I thought it, for you, not very real; & I'm so proud! And then, when I *did* believe it was real for you, that letter you wrote a few weeks ago paralyzed me—then, when everything would have been easy! I mean when you said "réfléchissez," to me whose curse it has always been to do so too much & too long! It drove me straight back into my numb dumb former self, the self that never believed in its chance of having any warm personal life, like other, luckier people. There you have the whole story— And now when you "make a sign" I'll answer—whenever you make it. Only arrange somehow beforehand—

I'm not worthy to write to or to think about; my only merit is that I'm unsparingly honest. But that's not a charm, alas!—

I'll let you know the moment I am free. It might be Monday or Wed.—(If your sister[30] comes on Tuesday). Could you, on your side, tell me when *you* are likely to be? Next Friday, Sat, Sunday, are absolutely mine, en tout cas.

I beg instant cremation for this—

Would you send me that letter you spoke of today, & hadn't with you? When you tell me about yourself, & your situation, & your difficulties—only then do I feel a tenderness in your liking, a something that may go on living a quiet life in you long after the glory has departed from your poor

E

Ms:UT

TO W. MORTON FULLERTON

53 Rue de Varenne, May 20, 1908

I am mad about you Dear Heart and sick at the thought of our parting and the days of separation and longing that are to follow. It is a wonderful world that you have created for me, Morton dear, but how I am to adjust it to the *other* world is difficult to conceive. Perhaps when I am once more on land my mental vision may be clearer—at present, in the whole universe I see but one thing, am conscious of but one thing, you, and our love for each other.

Ms:UT

TO W. MORTON FULLERTON

The Mount, June 19, 1908

When I sent you, eight days ago, that desperate word: "Don't write me again!" I didn't guess that you were already acting on it! Not a line from you in nine days—since your letter of June 2d. Eleven days at least must have passed without your feeling the impulse to write . . .

You know I never wanted you to write unless *you* wanted to! And I always understood it would not go on for long. But this is so sudden that I almost fear you are ill, or that something has happened to trouble you.

Think! You have not even answered *my first letter,* my letter from the steamer, which must have reached you on the 10th; & five steamers have come in, that might have brought an answer to it.—Don't think I didn't mean what I said when I last wrote, or what I reiterated to you so often before we said goodbye: that I don't want from you a sign, a gesture, that is not voluntary, spontaneous—irrepressible!—

No—I am still of that mind. Only, as I said, this is so unbelievably sudden. My reason, even—my reason much more than my *feeling*—tells me it must be some accident that has kept you silent; & then my anxiety begins its conjectures.

Send a word, dear, to reassure me. And if it's not *that,* but the other alternative, surely you're not afraid to say so?—My last letter will have shown you how I have foreseen, how I have accepted, such a contingency. Do you suppose I have ever, for a moment, ceased to see the thousand reasons *why* it was inevitable, & likely to be not far distant?

Allons donc! You shall see what I am made of—only don't be afraid to trust me to the utmost of my lucidity and my philosophy!

—But no! I don't ask you to say anything that might be painful to you. Simply write: "Chère camarade, I am well—things are well with me"; & I shall understand, & accept—& think of you as you would like a friend to think.—Above all, don't see any hidden reproach in this. There is nothing in it but tenderness and understanding.

I am well, and the week since I wrote last has managed to get itself lived. And the novel goes on. And people come and go.—I can't tell you more now, but another time, perhaps—

And now & always I am yr so affectionate E.

Ms:UT

TO W. MORTON FULLERTON

The Mount, August 26, 1908

Dear, won't you tell me soon the meaning of this silence?

At first I thought it might mean that your sentimental mood had cooled, & that you feared to let me see the change; & I wrote, nearly a month ago, to tell you how natural I should think such a change on your part, & how I hoped that our friendship—so dear to me!—might survive it.—It would have been easy, after that letter, to send a friendly: "Yes, chère amie—" surely, having known me so well all those months, you could have trusted to my understanding it?

But the silence continues! It was not *that* you wanted? For a time I fancied you were too busy & happy to think of writing—perhaps even to glance at my letters when they came. But even so—there are degrees in the lapse from such intimacy as ours into complete silence & oblivion; & if the inclination to write had died out, must not you, who are so sensitive & imaginative, have asked yourself to what conjectures you were leaving me, & how I should suffer at being so abruptly & inexplicably cut off from all news of you?

I re-read your letters the other day, & I will not believe that the man who wrote them did not feel them, & did not know enough of the woman to whom they were written to trust to her love & courage, rather than leave her to this aching uncertainty.

What has brought about such a change? Oh, no matter what it is—*only tell me!*

I could take my life up again courageously if I only understood; for whatever those months were to you, to me they were a great gift, a wonderful enrichment; & still I rejoice & give thanks for them! You woke me from a long lethargy, a dull acquiescence in conventional restrictions, a needless self-effacement. If I were awkward & inarticulate it was because, literally, all one side of me was asleep.

I remember, that night we went to the "Figlia di Iorio," that in the scene in the cave, where the Figlia sends him back to his mother (I forget all their names), & as he goes he turns & kisses her, & *then she can't let him go*—I remember you turned to me & said laughing: "That's something you don't know anything about."

Well! I *did* know, soon afterward; & if I still remained inexpressive, unwilling, "always drawing away," as you said, it was because I discovered in myself such possibilities of feeling on that side that I feared, if I let you love me too much, I might lose courage when the time came to go away!—Surely you saw this, & understood how I dreaded to be to you, *even for an instant,* the "donna non più giovane" who clings & encumbers—how, situated as I was, I thought I could best show my love by refraining— & abstaining? You saw it was all because I loved you?

And when you spoke of your uncertain future, your longing to break away & do the work you really like, didn't you see how my heart *broke* with the thought that, if I had been younger & prettier, everything might have been different—that we might have had together, at least for a short time, a life of exquisite collaborations—a life in which your gifts would have had full scope, & you would have been able to do the distinguished & beautiful things that you ought to do?—Now, I hope, your future has after all arranged itself happily, just as you despaired,—but remember that *those were my thoughts* when you were calling me "conventional" . . .

I never expected to tell you this; but under the weight of this silence I don't know what to say or leave unsaid. After nearly a month my frank tender of friendship remains unanswered. If that was not what you wished, what *is* then your feeling for me? My reason rejects the idea that a man like you, who has felt a warm sympathy for a woman like me, can suddenly, from one day to another, without any act or word on her part, lose even a friendly regard for her, & discard the mere outward signs of consideration by which friendship speaks. And so I am almost driven to conclude that your silence has another meaning, which I have not guessed. If any feeling subsists under it, may these words reach it, & tell you what I felt in silence when we were together!

Yes, dear, I loved you then, & I love you now, as you then wished me to; only I have learned that one must put all the happiness one can into each moment, & I will never again love you "sadly," since that displeases you.

You see I am once more assuming that you *do* care what I feel, in spite of this mystery! How can it be that the sympathy between two people like ourselves, so many-sided, so steeped in imagination, should end from one day to another like a mere "passade"—end by my passing, within a few weeks, utterly out of your memory? By all that I know you are, by all I am myself conscious of being, I declare that I am unable to believe it!

You told me once I should write better for this experience of loving. I felt it to be so, & I came home so fired by the desire that my work should please you! But this incomprehensible silence, the sense of your utter indifference to everything that concerns me, has stunned me. It has come so suddenly . . .

This is the last time I shall write you, dear, unless the strange spell is broken. And my last word is one of tenderness for the friend I love—for the lover I worshipped.

Goodbye, dear.

Oh, I don't want my letters back, dearest! I said that in my other letter only to make it easier for you if you were seeking a transition—

Do you suppose I care what becomes of them if you don't care?

Is it really to my dear friend—*to Henry's friend*[31]—to "dearest Morton"—that I have written this?

Ms:UT

TO W. MORTON FULLERTON

Palace Hotel, Rome, June 19 [1912]

Cher Ami— I found your letter late yesterday eve'g, on returning from Benedict's cave in the heights above Subiaco, where I
thought of you (with a more special thought) when the monk who
showed us about the monastery of St. Scholastica showed us the
Lactantius[32] wh. was the second book printed in Italy, & printed
in that very place, as you doubtless knew, O Bibliophile.

I am glad you are off to Luxembourg, & hope you will find
your solitude there as deep & well-defended as Benedict's[33] must
have been in that dark cliff above the gorge of the Anio.—

You see I am not at the ends of the Earth yet, but I seem to be
tending thither, for we start for Naples tomorrow whence, after
saluting the Rodds at Posillipo, we expect to cross to Sicily for a
few days. After that, I don't know, but it will probably be our
southern most étape, for Walter[34] is not well, & I disapprove even
of the Sicilian expedition, much as it tempts me! The good hotels
there are all closed at this season, & the frittura mista (& even
mystica) is precarious diet for an invalid.—Otherwise all goes well.

Rome is cool, delightful & beautiful—or would be, but for the
horrible, pervasive, unescapable, blinding, glaring Victor Emanuel
monument, which obliterates the Capitol, crushes St. Peter's, & is
visible in every direction as far off as Soracte.[35] I had no idea it
was such a National Disaster.

I wish I cd tell you of half the wonders & beauties that I've
seen—but you wd howl for mercy if I began!—

You got my p.c. I hope, saying that I'd decided not to send you
the Reef chapters for the present?—

Savourez your holiday to the utmost, & *finish the book*.

Yrs Ever
    E.W

I haven't *any* photo. Appleton may reproduce any of the published ones if he can find one. Give him yours!—

P.S.

I reopen to say that your letter of the 17th has just come, & that I am grinning broadly at your summing up of yourself as a "coeur simple."[36] Ah, Dieu, non!—

I'm glad you're really off. The concierge will have nothing heavier than this to forward to you (from me, at least!) as I am decidedly *not* sending you the last chapters yet.

Send me a line rue de V. when you have time. Since writing this morning I've decided to turn north at once, as it's rather too hot for more southern explorations, & I shall drop my companion at Plombières for the cure in a few days & then go off somewhere to a solitude with Anna[37] to finish the Reef.

TO SARA NORTON

Stocks, Tring, September 2, 1914

Dear Sally,

I hardly know with what feelings I sit down & write to you in this still & lonely place where I had dreamed of being so happy with my friends, & of seeing you among them!

I am all alone here, & without the heart to ask any one to join me. I feel as if this immense burden of horror could best be borne alone for the present.—I left Paris only six days ago, having stayed on there a month to organize & raise funds for a paying work-room for the poor unemployed women in our quarter. It was the first one to be opened in Paris (except some "soupes populaires"), & the consequence was that people were very generous, & after I had collected enough money to carry it on for three or four months, & seen orders pouring in from all sides, I decided to leave it in the very capable hands of the young woman who founded it with me, & come over here for a few weeks' rest. My servants & luggage were all here, & I had been picnicking in the rue de V. with a bonne à tout faire & a maid; & I thought it seemed foolish not to enjoy Stocks for a while. I left, therefore, on the 27th, & the very next day came the dreadful news of the German advance & the probable siege of Paris,[38] & I felt like a deserter! It was a perfect thunderbolt. I was seeing every day people in touch with the different ministries, & everyone thought the war would be fought out in Belgium & on the northern border. You can understand how I feel—as if my co-workers must think I had planned my flight when I said I was going off for three or four weeks.

My first idea was to try to go back at once, but I hear that General Joffre may order all "bouches inutiles" out of Paris, & as foreigners would certainly come under that head I am waiting for the next developments. Today is intolerable—the anniversary of Sedan, & the Germans within 68 miles of Paris!—

The "atrocities" one hears of *are true*. I know of many, alas, too well authenticated. Spread it abroad as much as you can. It should be known that it is to America's interest to help stem this hideous flood of savagery by opinion if it may not be by action. No civilized race can remain neutral in feeling now.

All this time I am not asking about you—but you know I want to hear, & that I hope that your homecoming was peaceful, & that you have been able to help your poor sister-in-law.

How are you? Has Ashfield done you good? Send me all your news here, for this address is safest.

    Yours affly
      E.W.

I stopped at Rye to see H.J., & found him momentarily unwell—a digestive "crise"—but looking far better than when I last saw him nearly a year ago. The gain is immense.

    Ms:BL

TO HENRY JAMES

53 Rue de Varenne, March 11, [1915]

Cherest Maître,

Your letter of the 5th, which I found here on my return last night, demands such moving incidents that the chronicle I have to send this time is not à la hauteur. The second trip was like all sequels—except that it certainly wasn't a mistake! But it *was* less high in colour than the first adventure, & resulted in several disappointments, as well as in some interesting moments—indeed, once within the military zone *every* moment is interesting.

We left 5 days ago & went straight to Verdun in a bitter rain, dropping bundles of shirts & boxes of fresh eggs & bags of oranges at the various ambulances I told you of. At Verdun we looked up our médecin en chef, who had promised to take us to see an ambulance on the first line, in the Hauts de Meuse; but, alas, it has been moved nearer to Les Eparges where there was such hard fighting that we couldn't be allowed to go. However, thanks to a lucky laissez passer, we *did* get, with him & the Director of the Service de Santé of that region, to an ambulance on the Meuse, within about 7 Kms of Les Eparges—a hamlet plunged to the eaves in mud, where beds had been rigged up in two or three little houses, a primitive operating-room installed, &c. Picture this all under a white winter sky, driving great flurries of snow across the mud-&-cinder-coloured landscape, with the steel-cold Meuse winding between beaten poplars—Cook standing with Her in a knot of mud-coated military motors & artillery horses, soldiers coming & going, cavalrymen riding up with messages, poor bandaged creatures in rag-bag clothes leaning in doorways, & always, over & above us, the boom, boom, boom of the guns on the grey heights to the east. It was Winter War to the fullest, just in that little insignificant corner of the immense affair!—And those big summing-up impressions meet one at every turn. I shall never forget the 15 mile run from Verdun to that particular ambulance, across a snow-covered rolling country sweeping up to the white sky, with no one in sight but now & then a

cavalry patrol with a blown cloak struggling along against the
wind.—

Then we went to another village on the west bank of the
Meuse, where there is a colony of *1500* "éclopés" waiting to pick
up strength enough to be shipped on to the next dépôt d'éclopés
in the rear. Here also the church—a big dreary disaffected one—is
full to the doors, but it is not a hospital but a human stable. The
poor devils sleep on straw, in queer little compartments made of
plaited straw screens, in each of which compartments a dozen or
so are crammed, in their trench clothes (no undressing possible)—
with nothing that I could see to be thankful for but the fact that
they were out of the mud, & in a sort of fetid stable-heat. It was
awful—& the Directeur du Service de Santé was so complacent!

In other places, of course, we saw things better done—but for a
Horror-of-War picture, that one won't soon be superseded. At
least I hope not!

I had everywhere le meilleur accueil from the Drs & Service de
Santé, & came back with a long list of wants. We had hoped to get
back to Nancy & Gerbéviller, but at Ligny en Barrois we came
across a sulky commandant who kept us waiting 4 hours & then
refused the permit—so we had to turn back to Châlons! We got
there at about 7 p. m., on the coldest day imaginable, "only to
learn" that *every* hotel, even to the lowest of the "garnis," was absolutely full. We applied for a permit to go on to Epernay (20
Kms), but were politely éconduits, as motors can't circulate in the
war zone après le tombée de la nuit. We went back to the hotel
where we were known, & the land-lady told us she had two
rooms, requisitioned by the Grand Quartier Général, which had
not been called for that night, & which we might get. In the
restaurant, where we went to dine before making our appeal to
the Quartier Général, we met our friend Jean Louis Vaudoyer,[39]
who is attached to the Q. G.—He gave us little hope, but said we
could go & try! So after dinner we got into the motor again &
went through the pitch black icy streets to the Hôtel de Ville,
where I sent in my papers & my appeal. A polite officer came out
& was désolé—but it was against the rules! I tried to harrow him,
but in vain. Finally he suggested giving us a permit to go back to
Paris—a 7 hours' run on a dark night, with the strong probability

of being turned back at the first railway crossing, as experience had convinced us that hardly any of the sentinels can read!!—We went back to the motor, & Vaudoyer very kindly suggested that we might camp for the night in a little flat he has in a maison bourgeoise, which he uses only in the day time—*if* we found the landlady still up, or could wake her! He couldn't go with us, as he was on duty, & it was past the hour (9:30) when one is allowed to be in the streets. And as we stood in the pitch blackness of the deserted street, & he whispered: "C'est au no. 9, rue de l'Arquebuse—si l'on vous arrête, le mot est 'Jéna,'" I suddenly refused to believe that *any* of it was true, or happening to *me,* or that a nice boy who dines with me & sends me chocolates for Nouvel An, was whispering a *pass-word* to me, & adding: "Quand vous le dites au chauffeur, prenez garde qu'une sentinelle ne vous entende pas"—It was no use trying to keep up the pretense of reality any longer!

Luckily his rooms *were* real, & the landlady was awake, & made fires—but Cook slept in the motor, wrapped in Red Cross dressing-gowns & pillowed on gauze pads!—And so we got through the night—& yesterday morning, when we left for Paris, we understood why Châlons was so crowded, for the cannon was crashing uninterruptedly, & seemingly much nearer than usual, & troops were streaming through the town in the direction of Suippes in a long unbroken train—the biggest lot of them we had yet seen.

We lunched at Meaux, & went to see the Bishop, who took us over his hospital, & a splendid dépôt d'éclopés he has organized with library, games, douches, & all kinds of blessings—& here I am again & must go back to work instead of telling you more adventures. I hope to get off again in 10 days—but one can't be sure of permits nowadays.

Your devoted
    Edith

No, no, you must keep the £6 for English needs—bless you!

Ms:BL

TO BERNARD BERENSON

Fontainbleau, September 4, 1917

Dearest B.B.,

Oh, do you really, *really* think—or better still—feel all that about "Summer"?—It's such a wonderful sensation to find, when one comes out from behind the "haute lisse" frame of the story-teller, that one's picture lives to other eyes as well as to one's own—the picture so blindly woven from the back of the frame!

I was beginning to think there must be a resemblance to nature from the shy & frightened letters I've been getting from the few old friends in Boston to whom I feel bound, in friendliness, to send a copy. D'autre part, their official organ, the Transcript, has a really understanding & honest article, over a column of close type, saying the book "will have reverberations both loud & long."

I'm so particularly glad you like old man Royall. Of course, *he's* the book!.—And, oh, how it does agreeably titillate the author's vanity to have his pet phrases quoted to him!* Non, c'est trop beau . . . Bless you.

Well, we're really off for the Maghreb. I start on the 15th, & Walter picks me up a day later at Madrid. It will be a ventre à terre trip, as he has so many big jobs on his hands in Paris; but never mind, I'll just "poser les jalons" for a good long giro later with you & Mary.

It's so queer to be going to a country that has next to no books about it!—Just a few twaddling "journals" by military explorers, no good at all—& one fairly good vol. by Aubin, wh. takes in only a small bit. I wrote to Chevrillon for a list, & this is the result.—

I'm seeing here a great deal of a very agreeable Cte Gilbert de Voisins (whom I knew before the war) whom you must meet some day. He has just married the divorced (& much maltreated) wife of Pierre Louys, a sister of Mme. H. de Régnier, a nice but not thrilling person.[40] Gilbert de V. is a grandson of Taglioni, & his mother was an English Ralli. It makes the queerest mixture, but a very pleasant one.

I suppose I shall be back in Paris about Oct 25th. When are you coming? By that time I look forward to be—more or less—"living like a lady again," having coalesced most of the "oeuvres" with the Red Cross.—Whereof I send you the accompanying picture—a speaking likeness—from New York!

Much love to you both. I'll write from Mauretania.

Yrs affly
   Edith W

*You see I'm getting a little confused about my sex! A form of megalomania—

PART IV

NONFICTION

Perhaps nowhere else in the array of Edith Wharton's excellent writing does her versatility become so clear as in her hundreds of nonfiction essays. In Wharton's travel writing, including the excerpts here, which date from 1902 and 1908, it is obvious why she was much in demand for this kind of work. Before Wharton was a well-known novelist, she was an acute observer of the exotic: Americans who could purchase the magazines that carried her work were not always themselves travelers. Traveling the ocean by ship was still deemed more frightening than romantic. But for Wharton, who crossed the Atlantic some sixty times, travel was exhilarating—and also, according to biographer Shari Benstock, gave her the leisure to write. Working on a portable lapboard, she used the long days at sea, as well as her travel in Europe by train, carriage, or car, to outline new projects or to complete those in progress.

As several of the excerpts reprinted here show, Wharton wrote often about Italy and its art. Once she had purchased her own auto, she enjoyed Paris and the South of France. Descriptions are her forte, and her accounts are immensely satisfying to the avid armchair traveler. But as she made the transition from travel narratives—essays and books that were in great demand—to writing about World War I, her ability both to describe and to persuade seems to have gathered particular strength.

Despite the relatively calm prose of her essays about the war, Wharton was almost frenetically involved in war relief—especially of the Belgian orphans and in providing a livelihood for Frenchwomen who had no incomes. As Alan Price states in his study of Wharton and World War I, Wharton had fewer than twenty-four hours' notice from the Belgian government before sixty young girls arrived to be cared for. Within days, five hundred more children arrived, and then another two hundred refugees who were aged and infirm. Known as a miracle worker, Edith Wharton yet visited the Front, often endangering herself and her companions—and, of course, wrote about her visits. The war essays included here were originally published in *Scribner's Magazine* in 1915.

From
A MIDSUMMER WEEK'S DREAM: AUGUST IN ITALY[1]

Early the next morning we set out for Colico, at the head of the Lake of Como, and thence took train for Sondrio, the chief town of the Valtelline. The lake, where we had to wait for our train, lay in unnatural loveliness beneath a breathless sky, the furrowed peaks bathed in subtle colour-gradations of which, at other seasons, the atmosphere gives no hint. At Sondrio we found all the dreariness of a modern Italian town with wide unshaded streets; but taking carriage in the afternoon for Madonna di Tirano we were soon in the land of romance again. The Valtelline, through which we drove, is one vast fruit and vegetable garden of extraordinary fertility. The *gran turco* (as the maize is called) grows in jungles taller than a man, and the grapes and melons have the exaggerated size and bloom of their counterfeits in a Dutch fruit-piece. The rich dullness of this foreground was relieved by the noble lines of the hills, and the air cooled by the rush of the Adda, which followed the windings of our road, and by a glimpse of snow-peaks at the head of the valley. The villages were uninteresting, but we passed a low-lying deserted church, a charming bit of seventeenth-century decay, with peeling stucco ornaments, and weeds growing from the florid vases of the pediment; and far off, on a lonely wooded height, there was a tantalizing glimpse of another church, a Renaissance building rich with encrusted marbles: one of the nameless uncatalogued treasures in which Italy still abounds.

Toward sunset we reached Madonna di Tirano, the great pilgrimage church of the Valtelline. With its adjoining monastery it stands alone in poplar-shaded meadows a mile or more from the town of Tirano. The marble church, a late fifteenth-century building by Battagio (the architect of the Incoronata of Lodi), has the peculiar charm of that transitional period when individuality of detail was merged, but not yet lost, in the newly-recovered sense of unity. From the columns of the porch, with their Verona-like arabesques, to the bronze Saint Michael poised like a Mercury on the cupola, the whole building combines the charm and naïveté of the earlier tradition with the dignity of a studied whole. The interior, if less homogeneous, is, in the French sense, even more "amusing." Owing, doubtless, to the remote situation of the church, it has escaped the unifying hand of the improver, and presents three centuries of conflicting decorative treatment, ranging from the marble chapel of the Madonna, so suggestive, in its clear-edged reliefs, of the work of Omodeo at Pavia, to the barocco carvings of the organ and the eighteenth-century *grisailles* beneath the choir-gallery.

The neighbouring monastery of Saint Michael has been turned into an inn without farther change than that of substituting tourists for monks in the whitewashed cells around the cloisters. The old building is a dusty labyrinth of court-yards, loggias and pigeon-haunted upper galleries, which it needs but little imagination to people with cowled figures gliding to lauds or benediction; and the refectory where we supped is still hung with portraits of cardinals, monsignori, and lady abbesses holding little ferret-like dogs.

The next day we drove across the rich meadows to Tirano, one of those unhistoried and unconsidered Italian towns which hold in reserve for the observant eye a treasure of quiet impressions. It is difficult to name any special "effect": the hurried sight-seer may discover only dull streets and featureless house-fronts. But the place has a fine quality of age and aloofness. The featureless houses are "palaces," long-fronted and escutcheoned, with glimpses of arcaded courts, and of gardens where maize and dahlias smother the broken statues and choked fountains, and where grapes ripen on the peeling stucco walls. Here and there one comes on a frivolous rococo church, subdued by time to delicious harmony with its surroundings; on a fountain in a quiet square, or a wrought-iron balcony projecting romantically from a shuttered façade; or on one or another of the hundred characteristic details which go to make up the *mise en scène* of the average Italian town. It is precisely in places like Tirano, where there are no salient beauties to fix the eye, that one appreciates the value of these details, that one realizes what may be called the negative strength of the Italian artistic sense. Where the Italian builder could not be grand, he could always abstain from being mean and trivial; and this artistic abnegation gives to many a dull little town like Tirano an architectural dignity which our great cities lack.

II

The return to secular life was made two days later, when we left our monastery and set out to drive across the Aprica pass to Edolo. Retracing for a mile or two the way toward Sondrio, we took a turn to the left and began to mount the hills through forests of beech and chestnut. With each bend of the road the views down the Valtelline toward Sondrio and Como grew wider and more beautiful. No one who has not looked out on such a prospect in the early light of an August morning can appreciate the poetic truth of Claude's interpretation of nature: we seemed to be moving through a gallery hung with his pictures.[2] There was the same expanse of billowy forest, the same silver winding of a river through infinite gradations of distance, the same aerial line of hills melting into illimitable sky.

As we neared the top of the pass the air freshened, and pines and open meadows replaced the forest. We lunched at a little hotel in a bare meadow, among a crowd of Italians enjoying the *villeggiatura* in their shrill gregarious fashion; then we began the descent to Edolo in the Val Camonica.

The scenery changed rapidly as we drove on. There was no longer any great extent of landscape, as on the other side of the pass, but a succession of small park-like views: rounded clumps of trees interspersed with mossy glades, water-falls surmounted by old mills, *campanili* rising above the villages hidden in foliage. On these smooth grassy terraces, under the walnut boughs, one expected at each turn to come upon some pastoral of Giorgione's, or on one of Banifazio's sumptuous picnics. The scenery has a studied beauty in which velvet robes and caparisoned palfreys would not be out of place, and even the villages might have been "brushed in" by an artist skilled in effects and not afraid to improve upon reality.

It was after sunset when we reached Edolo, a dull town splendidly placed at the head of the Val Camonica, beneath the ice-peaks of the Adamello. The Oglio, a loud stream voluble of the glaciers, rushes through the drowsy streets as though impatient to be gone; and we were not sorry, the next morning, to follow its lead and continue our way down the valley.

III

The Val Camonica, which extends from the Adamello group to the head of the lake of Iseo, is a smaller and more picturesque reproduction of the Valtelline. Vines and maize again fringed our way; but the mountains were closer, the villages more frequent and more picturesque.

We had read in the invaluable guide-book of Gsell-Fels a vague allusion to an interesting church among these mountains, but we could learn nothing of it at Edolo, and only by persistent enquiries along the road did we finally hear that there *was* a church with "sculptures" in the hill-village of Cerveno, high above the reach of carriages. We left the high-road at the point indicated, and drove in a light country carriole up the stony mule-path, between vines and orchards, till the track grew too rough for wheels; then we continued the ascent on foot. As we approached the cluster of miserable hovels which had been pointed out to us we felt sure we had been misled. Not even in Italy, the land of unsuspected treasures, could one hope to find a church with "sculptures" in a poverty-stricken village on this remote mountain! Cerveno does not even show any signs of past prosperity. It has plainly never been more than it now is—the humblest of *paesi*, huddled away in an unvisited fold of the Alps. The peasants whom we met still insisted that the church we sought was close at hand; but the higher we mounted the lower our anticipations fell.

Then suddenly, at the end of a long stony lane, we came on an imposing doorway. The church to which it belonged stood on a higher ledge of the hill, and the door led into a vaulted ascent, with shallow flights of steps broken by platforms or landings—a small but yet impressive imitation of the Bernini staircase in the Vatican. As we mounted we found that each landing opened into a dimly-lit chapel with grated doors, through which we discerned terra-cotta groups representing the scenes of the Passion. The staircase was in fact a Sacred Way like the more famous one of Varallo; but there was distinct originality in placing the chapels on each side of the long flight of steps leading to the church, instead of scattering them on an open hill-side, according to the traditional plan common to all the other sacred mountains of northern Italy.

The dilettante will always allow for the heightening of emotion that attends any unexpected artistic "find"; but, setting this subjective impression aside, the Via Crucis of Cerveno remains in my memory as among the best examples of its kind—excepting always the remarkable terra-cottas of San Vivaldo in Tuscany. At Cerveno, as at Varallo, the groups are marked by unusual vivacity and expressiveness. The main lines of the composition are conventional, and the chief personages—Christ and the Apostles, the Virgin and the other holy characters—are modelled on traditional types; but the minor figures, evidently taken from life, are rendered with frank realism and with extraordinary truth of expression and gesture. Just such types—the dwarf, the beggar, the hunchback, the brawny waggoner or ploughman—had met us in every village on the way to Cerveno. As in all the hill-regions where the goitre is prevalent, the most villanous [sic] characters in the drama are depicted with a hideous bag of flesh beneath the chin; and Signorelli could not have conceived more bestial leering cruelty than that in some of the faces which press about the dying Christ. The scenes follow the usual order of the sacred story, without marked departure from the conventional grouping; but there is unusual pathos in the Descent from the Cross, where the light from the roof of the chapel falls with tragic intensity on the face of a Magdalen full of suave Lombard beauty.

Hardly less surprising than this remarkable stairway is the church to which it leads. The walls are hung with devotional pictures set in the faded gilding of rich old frames, the altar-fronts are remarkable examples of sixteenth-century wood-carving, and the high altar is surmounted by an elaborate tabernacle, also of carved wood, painted and gilt, that in itself repays the effort of the climb to Cerveno. This tabernacle is a complicated architectural composition—like one of the fantastic designs of Fontana or Bib-

biena—thronged with tiny saints and doctors, angels and *putti*,
akin to the little people of the Neapolitan *presepii:* a celestial company fluttering

Si come schiera d'api che s'infiora[3]

around the divine group which surmounts the shrine.

This prodigality of wood-carving, surprising as it is in so remote and humble a church, is yet characteristic of the region
about Brescia and Bergamo. Lamberti of Brescia, the sculptor of
the famous frame of Romanino's Madonna in the church of San
Francesco, was one of the greatest wood-carvers of the Italian
Renaissance; and every church and chapel in the country through
which we were travelling bore witness to the continued practice of
the art in some graceful frame or altar-front, some saint or angel
rudely but expressively modelled. . . .

IV

The sun lay heavy on Iseo; and the railway journey thence to Brescia left in our brains a golden dazzle of heat. It was refreshing, on
reaching Brescia, to enter the streets of the old town, where the
roofs almost meet and there is always a blessed strip of shade to
walk in. The cities in Italy are much cooler than the country. It is
in August that one understands the wisdom of the old builders,
who made the streets so narrow, and built dim draughty arcades
around the open squares. In Brescia the effects of light and shade
thus produced were almost Oriental in their sharp-edged intensity; the rough stucco surfaces gilded with vivid sunlight bringing
out the depths of contrasting shade, and the women with black
veils over their heads slipping along under the mysterious bal-
conies and porticoes like flitting fragments of the shadow.

Brescia is at all times a delightful place to linger in. Its chief possessions—the bronze Victory, and that room in the Martinengo
palace where Moretto, in his happiest mood, depicted the ladies
of the line under arches of trellis-work backed by views of the
family villas—make it noteworthy even among Italian cities; and
it has, besides, its beautiful town-hall, its picture-gallery, and the

curious court-yards painted in perspective that are so characteristic of the place. But in summer there is a strong temptation to sit and think of these things rather than to go and see them. In the court-yard of the hotel, where a fountain tinkles refreshingly, and the unbleached awnings flap in the breeze of the electric fans, it is pleasant to feel that the Victory and the pictures are close at hand, like old friends waiting on one's inclination; but if one ventures forth, let it be rather to the churches than to the galleries. Only at this season can one appreciate the atmosphere of the churches: that chill which cuts the sunshine like a knife as one steps across the dusky threshold. When we entered the cathedral its vast aisles were empty, but far off, in the dimness of the pillared choir, we heard a drone of intoning canons that freshened the air like the sound of a water-fall in a forest. Thence we wandered on to San Francesco, empty too, where, in the sun-spangled dimness, the great Romanino throned behind the high altar. The sacristan drew back the curtain before the picture, and as it was revealed to us in all its sun-bathed glory he exclaimed with sudden wonder, as though he had never seen it before: *"È stupendo! È stupendo!"* Perhaps he vaguely felt, as we did, that Romanino, to be appreciated, must be seen in just that light, a projection of the suave and radiant atmosphere in which his own creations move. Certainly no Romanino of the great public galleries arrests the imagination like the Madonna of San Francesco; and in its presence one thinks with a pang of all the beautiful objects uprooted from their native soil to adorn the herbarium of the art-collector.

From
PARIS TO POITIERS[1]

Spring again, and the long white road unrolling itself southward from Paris. How could one resist the call?

We answered it on the blandest of late March mornings, all April in the air, and the Seine fringing itself with a mist of yellowish willows as we rose over it, climbing the hill to Ville d'Avray. Spring comes soberly, inaudibly as it were, in these temperate European lands, where the grass holds its green all winter, and the foliage of ivy, laurel, holly, and countless other evergreen shrubs, links the lifeless to the living months. But the mere act of climbing that southern road above the Seine meadows seemed as definite as the turning of a leaf—the passing from a black-and-white page to one illuminated. And every day now would turn a brighter page for us.

Goethe has a charming verse, descriptive, it is supposed, of his first meeting with Christiane Vulpius: "Aimlessly I strayed through the wood, *having it in my mind to see nothing.*"[2]

Such, precisely, was our state of mind on that first day's run. We were simply pushing south toward the Berry, through a more or less familiar country, and the real journey was to begin for us on the morrow, with the run from Châteauroux to Poitiers. But we reckoned without our France! It is easy enough, glancing down the long page of the Guide Continental, to slip by such names as Versailles, Rambouillet, Chartres and Valençay, in one's dash for the objective point; but there is no slipping by them in the motor, they lurk there in one's path, throwing out great loops of persuasion, arresting one's flight, complicating one's impressions, oppressing, bewildering one with the renewed, half-forgotten sense of the hoarded richness of France.

Versailles first, unfolding the pillared expanse of its north façade to vast empty perspectives of radiating avenues; then Rambouillet, low in a damp little park, with statues along green canals, and a look, this moist March weather, of being somewhat below sea-level; then Maintenon, its rich red-purple walls and delicate stone ornament reflected in the moat dividing it from the village street. Both Rambouillet and Maintenon are characteristically French in their way of keeping company with their villages. Rambouillet, indeed, is slightly screened by a tall gate, a wall and trees; but Maintenon's warm red turrets look across the moat, straight into the windows of the opposite houses, with the simple familiarity of a time when class distinctions were too fixed to need emphasising.

Our third château, Valençay—which, for comparison's sake, one may couple with the others though it lies far south of Blois—Valençay bears itself with greater aloofness, bidding the town "keep its distance" down the hill on which the great house lifts its heavy angle-towers and flattened domes. A huge cliff-like wall, enclosing the whole southern flank of the hill, supports the terraced gardens before the château, which to the north is divided from the road by a vast *cour d'honneur* with a monumental grille and gateway. The impression is grander yet less noble.

But France is never long content to repeat her effects; and between Maintenon and Valençay she puts Chartres and Blois. Ah, these grey old cathedral towns with their narrow clean streets widening to a central *place*—at Chartres a beautiful oval, like the market-place in an eighteenth-century print—with their clipped lime-walks, high garden walls, Balzacian gables looking out on sunless lanes under the flanks of the granite giant! Save in the church itself, how frugally all the effects are produced—with how sober a use of greys and blacks, and pale high lights, as in some Van der Meer interior; yet how intense a suggestion of thrifty compact traditional life one gets from the low house-fronts, the barred gates, the glimpses of clean bare courts, the calm yet quick faces in the doorways! From these faces again one gets the same impression of remarkable effects produced by the discreetest means. The French physiognomy if not vividly beautiful is vividly intelligent; but the long practice of manners has so veiled its keenness with refinement as to produce a blending of vivacity and good temper nowhere else to be matched. And in looking at it one feels once more, as one so often feels in trying to estimate French architecture or the French landscape, how much of her total effect France achieves by elimination. If marked beauty be absent from the French face, how much more is marked dulness, marked brutality, the lumpishness of the clumsily made and the unfinished! As a mere piece of workmanship, of finish, the French provincial face—the peasant's face, even—often has the same kind of interest as a work of art.

One gets, after repeated visits to the "show" towns of France, to feel these minor characteristics, the incidental graces of the foreground, almost to the exclusion of the great official spectacle in the centre of the picture; so that while the first image of Bourges or Chartres is that of a cathedral surrounded by a blur, later memories of the same places present a vividly individual town, with doorways, street-corners, faces intensely remembered, and in the centre a great cloudy Gothic splendour.

At Chartres the cloudy splendour is shot through with such effulgence of colour that its vision, evoked by memory, seems to beat with a fiery life of its own, as though red blood ran in its stone veins. It is this suffusion of heat and radiance that chiefly, to the untechnical, distinguishes it from the other great Gothic interiors. In all the rest, colour, if it exists at all, burns in scattered unquiet patches, between wastes of shadowy grey stone and the wan pallor of later painted glass; but at Chartres those quivering waves of unearthly red and blue flow into and repeat each other in rivers of light, from their source in the great western rose, down the length of the vast aisles and clerestory, till they are gathered up at last into the mystical heart of the apse.

A short afternoon's run carried us through dullish country from Chartres to Blois, which we reached at the fortunate hour when sunset burnishes the great curves of the Loire and lays a plum-coloured bloom on the state roofs overlapping, scale-like, the slope below the castle. There are few finer *roof-views* than this from the wall at Blois: the blue sweep of gables and ridge-lines billowing up here and there into a church tower with its *clocheton* mailed in slate, or breaking to let through the glimpse of a carved façade, or the blossoming depths of a hanging garden; but perhaps only the eye subdued to tin housetops and iron chimney-pots can feel the full poetry of old roofs.

Coming back to the Berry six weeks earlier than on our last

year's visit, we saw how much its wide landscape needs the relief and modelling given by the varied foliage of May. Between bare woods and scarcely budded hedges the great meadows looked bleak and monotonous; and only the village gardens hung out a visible promise of spring. But in the sheltered enclosure at Nohant, spring seemed much nearer; at hand already in clumps of snow-drops and violets loosening the soil, in young red leaves on the rose-standards, and the twitter of birds in the heavy black-fruited ivy of the grave-yard wall.

IN ARGONNE[1]

I

The permission to visit a few ambulances and evacuation hospitals behind the lines gave me, at the end of February,[2] my first sight of War.

Paris is no longer included in the military zone, either in fact or in appearance. Though it is still manifestly under the war-cloud, its air of reviving activity produces the illusion that the menace which casts that cloud is far off not only in distance but in time. Paris, a few months ago so alive to the nearness of the enemy, seems to have grown completely oblivious of that nearness; and it is startling, not more than twenty miles from the gates, to pass from such an atmosphere of workaday security to the imminent sense of War.

Going eastward, one begins to feel the change just beyond Meaux. Between that quiet episcopal city and the hill-town of Montmirail, some forty miles farther east, there are no sensational evidences of the great conflict of September—only, here and there, in an unploughed field, or among the fresh brown furrows, a little mound with a wooden cross and a wreath on it. Nevertheless, one begins to perceive, by certain negative signs, that one is already in another world. On the cold February day when we turned out of Meaux and took the road to the Argonne, the change was chiefly shown by the curious absence of life in the villages through which we passed. Now and then a lonely ploughman and his team stood out against the sky, or a child and an old woman looked from a doorway; but many of the fields were fallow and most of the doorways empty. We passed a few carts driven by peasants, a stray wood-cutter in a copse, a road-mender hammering at his stones; but already the "civilian motor" had disappeared, and all the dust-coloured cars dashing past us were marked with the Red Cross or the number of an army division. At every bridge and railway-crossing a sentinel, standing in the middle of the road with lifted rifle, stopped the motor and examined our papers. In this negative sphere there was hardly any other tangible proof of military rule; but with the descent of the first hill beyond Montmirail there came the positive feeling: *This is war!*

Along the white road rippling away east-ward over the dimpled country the army motors were pouring by in endless lines, broken now and then by the dark mass of a tramping regiment or the clatter of a train of artillery. In the intervals between these waves of military traffic we had the road to ourselves, except for the flashing past of despatch-bearers on motor-cycles and of hideously hooting little motors carrying goggled officers in goat-skins and woollen helmets.

The villages along the road all seemed empty—not figuratively but literally empty. None of them has suffered from the German invasion, save by the destruction, here and there, of a single house on which some random malice has wreaked itself; but since the general flight in September all have remained abandoned, or are provisionally occupied by troops, and the rich country between Montmirail and Châlons is a desert.

The first sight of Châlons is extraordinarily exhilarating. The old town lying so pleasantly between canal and river is the Headquarters of an army—not of a corps or of a division, but of a whole army—and the network of grey provincial streets about the Romanesque towers of Notre Dame rustles with the movement of war. The square before the principal hotel—the incomparably named "Haute Mère-Dieu"—is as vivid a sight as any scene of modern war can be. Rows of grey motor-lorries and omnibuses do not lend themselves to as happy groupings as a detachment of cavalry, and spitting and spurting motor-cycles and "torpedo" racers are no substitute for the glitter of helmets and the curvetting of chargers;[3] but once the eye has adapted itself to the ugly lines and the neutral tints of the new warfare, the scene in that crowded clattering square becomes positively brilliant. It is a vision of one of the central functions of a great war, in all its concentrated energy, without the saddening suggestions of what, on the distant periphery, that energy is daily and hourly resulting in. Yet even here such suggestions are never long out of sight; for one cannot pass through Châlons without meeting, on their way from the station, a long line of "éclopés"—the unwounded but battered, shattered, frost-bitten, deafened and half-paralyzed wreckage of the awful struggle. These poor wretches, in their thousands, are daily shipped back from the front to rest and be restored; and it is a grim sight to watch them limping by, and to meet the dazed stare of eyes that have seen what one dare not picture.

If one could think away the "éclopés" in the streets and the wounded in the hospitals, Châlons would be an invigorating spectacle. When we drove up to the hotel even the grey motors and the sober uniforms seemed to sparkle under the cold sky. The continual coming and going of alert and busy messengers, the riding up of officers (for some still ride!), the arrival of much-decorated military personages in luxurious motors, the hurrying to and fro of orderlies, the perpetual depleting and refilling of the long rows of grey vans across the square, the movements of Red Cross ambulances and the passing of detachments for the front, all these are sights that the pacific stranger could forever gape at. And in the hotel, what a clatter of swords, what a piling up of fur coats and haversacks, what a grouping of bronzed energetic heads about the packed tables in the restaurant! It is not easy for civilians to get to Châlons, and almost every table is occupied by officers and soldiers—for, once off duty, there seems to be no rank distinction in this happy democratic army, and the simple private, if he chooses to treat himself to the excellent fare of the Haute Mère-Dieu, has as good a right to it as his colonel.

The scene in the restaurant is inexhaustibly interesting. The mere attempt to puzzle out the different uniforms is absorbing. A week's experience near the front convinces me that no two uniforms in the French army are alike either in colour or in cut. Within the last two years the question of colour has greatly preoccupied the French military authorities, who have been seeking an invisible blue; and the range of their experiments is proved by the extraordinary variety of shades of blue, ranging from a sort of greyish robin's-egg to the darkest navy, in which the army is clothed. The result attained is the conviction that no blue is really inconspicuous, and that some of the harsh new slaty tints are no less striking than the deeper shades they have superseded. But to this scale of experimental blues, other colours must be added: the poppy-red of the Spahis' tunics,[4] and various other less familiar colours—grey, and a certain greenish khaki—the use of which is due to the fact that the cloth supply has given out and that all available materials are employed. As for the differences in cut, the uniforms vary from the old tight tunic to the loose belted jacket copied from the English, and the emblems of the various arms and ranks embroidered on these diversified habits add a new element of perplexity. The aviator's wings, the motorist's wheel, and many of the newer symbols, are easily recognizable—but there are all the other arms, and the doctors and the stretcher-bearers, the sappers[5] and miners, and heaven knows how many more ramifications of this great host which is really all the nation.

The main interest of the scene, however, is that it shows almost as many types as uniforms, and that almost all the types are so good. One begins to understand (if one has failed to before) why the French say of themselves: *"La France est une nation guerrière."*[6] War is the greatest of paradoxes: the most senseless and disheartening of human retrogressions, and yet the stimulant of qualities of soul which, in every race, can seemingly find no other means of renewal. Everything depends, therefore, on the category of impulses that war excites in a people. Looking at the faces at Châlons, one sees at once in which sense the French are "une nation guerrière." It is not too much to say that war has given beauty to faces that were interesting, humorous, acute, malicious, a hundred vivid and expressive things, but last and least of all beautiful. Almost all the faces about these crowded tables—young or old, plain or handsome, distinguished or average—have the same look of quiet authority: it is as though all "nervosity," fussiness, little personal oddities, meannesses and vulgarities, had been burnt away in a great flame of self-dedication. It is a wonderful example of the rapidity with which purpose models the human countenance. More than half of these men were probably doing dull or useless or unimportant things till the first of last August; now each one of them, however small his job, is sharing in a great task, and knows it, and has been made over by knowing it.

Our road on leaving Châlons continued to run northeastward toward the hills of the Argonne.

We passed through more deserted villages, with soldiers lounging in the doors where old women should have sat with their
distaffs, soldiers watering their horses in the village pond, soldiers
cooking over gypsy fires in the farm-yards. In the patches of
woodland along the road we came upon more soldiers, cutting
down pine saplings, chopping them into even lengths and loading
them on hand-carts, with the green boughs piled on top. We soon
saw to what use they were put, for at every cross-road or railway
bridge a warm sentry-box of mud and straw and plaited pine-
branches was plastered against a bank or tucked like a swallow's
nest into a sheltered corner. A little farther on we began to come
more and more frequently on big colonies of "Seventy-fives."
Drawn up nose to nose, usually against a curtain of woodland, in
a field at some distance from the road, and always attended by a
cumbrous drove of motor-vans, they looked like giant gazelles
feeding among elephants; and the stables of woven pine-boughs
which stood near by might have been the huge huts of their herds-
men.

The country between Marne and Meuse is one of the regions on
which German fury spent itself most bestially during the abominable September days. Half way between Châlons and Sainte
Menehould we came on the first evidence of the invasion: the lamentable ruins of the village of Auve. These pleasant villages of the
Aisne, with their one long street, their half-timbered houses and
high-roofed granaries with espaliered gable-ends, are all much of
one pattern, and one can easily picture what Auve must have been
as it looked out, in the blue September weather, above the ripening pears of its gardens to the crops in the valley and the large
landscape beyond. Now it is a mere waste of rubble and cinders,
not one threshold distinguishable from another. We saw many
other ruined villages after Auve, but this was the first, and perhaps for that reason one had there, most hauntingly, the vision of
all the separate terrors, anguishes, uprootings and rendings apart
involved in the destruction of the obscurest of human communities. The photographs on the walls, the twigs of withered box
above the crucifixes, the old wedding-dresses in brass-clamped
trunks, the bundles of letters laboriously written and as painfully
deciphered, all the thousand and one bits of the past that give
meaning and continuity to the present—of all that accumulated

warmth nothing was left but a brick-heap and some twisted stove-pipes!

As we ran on toward Sainte Menehould the names on our map showed us that, just beyond the parallel range of hills six or seven miles to the north, the two armies lay interlocked. But we heard no cannon yet, and the first visible evidence of the nearness of the struggle was the encounter, at a bend of the road, of a long line of grey-coated figures tramping toward us between the bayonets of their captors. They were a sturdy lot, this fresh "bag" from the hills, of a fine fighting age, and much less famished and war-worn than one could have wished. Their broad blond faces were meaningless, guarded, but neither defiant nor unhappy: they seemed none too sorry for their fate.

Our pass from the General Head-quarters carried us to Sainte Menehould on the edge of the Argonne, where we had to apply to the Head-quarters of the division for a farther extension. The Staff are lodged in a house considerably the worse for German occupancy, where offices have been improvised by means of wooden hoardings, and where, sitting in a bare passage on a frayed demask sofa surmounted by theatrical posters and faced by a bed with a plum-coloured counterpane, we listened for a while to the jingle of telephones, the rat-tat of typewriters, the steady hum of dictation and the coming and going of hurried despatch-bearers and orderlies. The extension to the permit was presently delivered with the courteous request that we should push on to Verdun as fast as possible, as civilian motors were not wanted on the road that afternoon; and this request, coupled with the evident stir of activity at Head-quarters, gave us the impression that there must be a good deal happening beyond the low line of hills to the north. How much there was we were soon to know.

We left Sainte Menehould at about eleven, and before twelve o'clock we were nearing a large village on a ridge from which the land swept away to right and left in ample reaches. The first glimpse of the outlying houses showed nothing unusual; but presently the main street turned and dipped downward, and below and beyond us lay a long stretch of ruins: the calcined remains of Clermont-en-Argonne, destroyed by the Germans on the 4th of September. The free and lofty situation of the little town—for it was really a good deal more than a village—makes its present state the more lamentable. One can see it from so far off, and through the torn traceries of its ruined church the eye travels over so lovely a stretch of country! No doubt its beauty enriched the joy of wrecking it.

At the farther end of what was once the main street another small knot of houses has survived. Chief among them is the Hospice for old men, where Sister Gabrielle Rosnet, when the authorities of Clermont took to their heels, stayed behind to defend her charges, and where, ever since, she has nursed an undiminishing stream of wounded from the eastern front. We found Sœur Rosnet, with her Sisters, preparing the midday meal of her patients in the little kitchen of the Hospice: the kitchen which is also her dining-room and private office. She insisted on our finding time to share the *filet* and fried potatoes that were just being taken off the stove, and while we lunched she told us the story of the invasion—of the Hospice doors broken down "à coups de crosse" and the grey officers bursting in with revolvers, and finding her there before them, in the big vaulted vestibule, "alone with my old men and my Sisters." Sœur Gabrielle Rosnet is a small round active woman, with a shrewd and ruddy face of the type that looks out calmly from the dark background of certain Flemish pictures. Her blue eyes are full of warmth and humour, and she puts as much gaiety as wrath into her tale. She does not spare epithets in talking of "ces satanés Allemands"—these Sisters and nurses of the front have seen sights to dry up the last drop of sentimental pity—but through all the horror of those fierce September days, with Clermont blazing about her and the helpless remnant of its inhabitants under the perpetual threat of massacre, she retained her sense of the little inevitable absurdities of life, such as her not knowing how to address the officer in command "because he was so tall that I couldn't see up to his shoulder-straps."—"*Et ils étaient tous comme ça,*"[7] she added, a sort of reluctant admiration in her eyes.

A subordinate "good Sister" had just cleared the table and poured out our coffee when a woman came in to say, in a matter-of-fact tone, that there was hard fighting going on across the valley. She added calmly, as she dipped our plates into a tub, that an obus[8] had just fallen a mile or two off, and that if we liked we could see the fighting from a garden over the way. It did not take us long to reach that garden! Sœur Gabrielle showed the way, bouncing up the stairs of a house across the street, and flying at her heels we came out on a grassy terrace full of soldiers.

The cannon were booming without a pause, and seemingly so near that it was bewildering to look out across empty fields at a hillside that seemed like any other. But luckily somebody had a field-glass, and with its help a little corner of the battle of Vauquois was suddenly brought close to us—the rush of French infantry up the slopes, the feathery drift of French gun-smoke lower down, and, high up, on the wooded crest along the sky, the red lightnings and white puffs of the German artillery. Rap, rap, rap, went the answering guns, as the troops swept up and disappeared into the fire-tongued wood; and we stood there dumbfounded at the accident of having stumbled on this visible episode of the great subterranean struggle.

Though Sœur Rosnet had seen too many such sights to be much moved, she was all of a lively curiosity, and stood beside us, squarely planted in the mud, holding the field-glass to her eyes, or passing it laughingly about among the soldiers. But as we turned to go she said: "They've sent us word to be ready for another four hundred to-night"; and the twinkle died out of her good eyes.

Her expectations were to be dreadfully surpassed; for, as we learned a fortnight later from a three column *communiqué*, the scene we had assisted at was no less than the first act of the successful assault on the high-perched village of Vauquois, a point of the first importance to the Germans, since it masked their operations to the north of Varennes and commanded the railway by which, since September, they have been revictualling and reinforcing their army in the Argonne. Vauquois had been taken by them at the end of September and, thanks to its strong position on a rocky spur, had been almost impregnably fortified; but the attack we looked on at from the garden of Clermont, on Sunday, February 28th, carried the victorious French troops to the top of the ridge, and made them masters of a part of the village. Driven from it again that night, they were to retake it after a five days' struggle of exceptional violence and prodigal heroism, and are now securely established there in a position described as "of vital importance to the operations." "But what it cost!" Sœur Gabrielle said, when we saw her again a few days later.

II

The time had come to remember our promise and hurry away from Clermont; but a few miles farther our attention was arrested by the sight of the Red Cross over a village house. The house was little more than a hovel, the village—Blercourt it was called—a mere hamlet of scattered cottages and cow-stables: a place so easily overlooked that it seemed likely our supplies might be needed there.

An orderly went to find the *médecin-chef,* and we waded after him through the mud to one after another of the cottages in which, with admirable ingenuity, he had managed to create out of next to nothing the indispensable requirements of a second-line ambulance: sterilizing and disinfecting appliances, a bandage-room, a pharmacy, a well-filled wood-shed, and a clean kitchen in which "tisanes" were brewing over a cheerful fire. A detachment of cavalry was quartered in the village, which the trampling of hoofs had turned into a great morass, and as we picked our way from cottage to cottage in the doctor's wake he told us of the expedients to which he had been put to secure even the few hovels into which his patients were crowded. It was a complaint we were often to hear repeated along this line of the front, where troops and wounded are packed in thousands into villages meant to house four or five hundred; and we admired the skill and devotion with which he had dealt with the difficulty, and managed to lodge his patients decently.

We came back to the high-road, and he asked us if we should like to see the church. It was about three o'clock, and in the low porch the curé was ringing the bell for vespers. We pushed open the inner doors and went in. The church was without aisles, and down the nave stood four rows of wooden cots with brown blankets. In almost every one lay a soldier—the doctor's "worst cases"—few of them wounded, the greater number stricken with fever, bronchitis, frost-bite, pleurisy, or some other form of trench-sickness too severe to permit of their being carried farther from the front. One or two heads turned on the pillows as we entered, but for the most part the men did not move.

The curé, meanwhile, passing around to the sacristy, had come out before the altar in his vestments, followed by a little white acolyte. A handful of women, probably the only "civil" inhabitants left, and some of the soldiers we had seen about the village, had entered the church and stood together between the rows of cots; and the service began. It was a sunless afternoon, and the picture was all in monastic shades of black and white and ashen grey: the sick under their earth-coloured blankets, their livid faces against the pillows, the black dresses of the women (they seemed all to be in mourning) and the silver haze floating out from the little acolyte's censer. The only light in the scene—the candle-gleams on the altar, and their reflection in the embroideries of the curé's chasuble—were like a faint streak of sunset on the winter dusk.

For a while the long Latin cadences sounded on through the church; but presently the curé took up in French the Canticle of the Sacred Heart, composed during the war of 1870, and the little congregation joined their trembling voices in the refrain:

> "Sauvez, sauvez la France,
> Ne l'abandonnez pas!"[9]

The reiterated appeal rose in a sob above the rows of bodies in the nave: *"Sauvez, sauvez la France,"* the women wailed it near the altar, the soldiers took it up from the door in stronger tones; but the bodies in the cots never stirred, and more and more, as the day faded, the church looked like a quiet grave-yard in a battle-field.

After we had left Sainte Menehould the sense of the nearness and all-pervadingness of the war became even more vivid. Every road branching away to our left was a finger touching a red wound: Varennes, le Four de Paris, le Bois de la Grurie, were not more than eight or ten miles to the north. Along our own road the stream of motor-vans and the trains of ammunition grew longer and more frequent. Once we passed a long line of "Seventy-fives" going single file up a hillside, farther on we watched a big detachment of artillery galloping across a stretch of open country. The movement of supplies was continuous, and every village through which we passed swarmed with soldiers busy loading or unloading the big vans, or clustered about the commissariat motors while hams and quarters of beef were handed out. As we approached Verdun the cannonade had grown louder again; and when we reached the walls of the town and passed under the iron teeth of the portcullis we felt ourselves in one of the last outposts of a mighty line of defense. The desolation of Verdun is as impressive as the feverish activity of Châlons. The civil population was evacuated in September, and only a small percentage have returned. Nine-tenths of the shops are closed, and as the troops are nearly all in the trenches there is hardly any movement in the streets.

The first duty of the traveller who has successfully passed the challenge of the sentinel at the gates is to climb the steep hill to the citadel at the top of the town. Here the military authorities inspect one's papers, and deliver a "permis de séjour" which must be verified by the police before lodgings can be obtained. We found the principal hotel much less crowded than the Haute Mère-Dieu at Châlons, though many of the officers of the garrison mess there. The whole atmosphere of the place was different: silent, concentrated, passive. To the chance observer, Verdun appears to live only in its hospitals; and of these there are fourteen within the walls alone. As darkness fell, the streets became completely deserted, and the cannonade seemed to grow nearer and more incessant. That first night the hush was so intense that every reverberation from the dark hills beyond the walls brought out in the mind its separate vision of destruction; and then, just as the strained imagination could bear no more, the thunder ceased. A moment later, in a court below my windows, a pigeon began to coo; and all night long the two sounds strangely alternated . . .

On entering the gates, the first sight to attract us had been a colony of roughly-built bungalows scattered over the miry slopes of a little park adjoining the railway station, and surmounted by the sign: "Evacuation Hospital No. 6." The next morning we went to visit it. A part of the station buildings has been adapted to hospital use, and among them a great roofless hall, which the surgeon in charge has covered in with canvas and divided down its length into a double row of tents. Each tent contains two wooden cots, scrupulously clean and raised high above the floor; and the immense ward is warmed by a row of stoves down the central passage. In the bungalows across the road are beds for the patients who are to be kept for a time before being transferred to the hospitals in the town. In one bungalow an operating-room has been installed, in another are the bathing arrangements for the newcomers from the trenches. Every possible device for the relief of the wounded has been carefully thought out and intelligently applied by the surgeon in charge and the *infirmière major* who indefatigably seconds him. Evacuation Hospital No. 6 sprang up in an hour, almost, on the dreadful August day when four thousand wounded lay on stretchers between the railway station and the gate of the little park across the way; and it has gradually grown into the model of what such a hospital may become in skilful and devoted hands.

Verdun has other excellent hospitals for the care of the severely wounded who cannot be sent farther from the front. Among them St. Nicolas, in a big airy building on the Meuse, is an example of a great French Military Hospital at its best; but I visited few others, for the main object of my journey was to get to some of the second-line ambulances beyond the town. The first we went to was in a small village to the north of Verdun, not far from the enemy's lines at Cosenvoye, and was fairly representative of all the others. The dreary muddy village was crammed with troops, and the ambulance had been installed at haphazard in such houses as the military authorities could spare. The arrangements were primitive but clean, and even the dentist had set up his apparatus in one of the rooms. The men lay on mattresses or in wooden cots, and the rooms were heated by stoves. The great need, here as everywhere, was for blankets and clean underclothing; for the wounded are brought in from the front encrusted with frozen mud, and usually without having washed or changed for weeks. There are no women nurses in these second-line ambulances, but all the army doctors we saw seemed intelligent, and anxious to do the best they could for their men in conditions of unusual hardship. The principal obstacle in their way is the over-crowded state of the villages. Thousands of soldiers are camped in all of them, in hygienic conditions that would be bad enough for men in health; and there is also a great need for light diet, since the hospital commissariat of the front apparently supplies no invalid foods, and men burning with fever have to be fed on meat and vegetables.

In the afternoon we started out again in a snow-storm, over a desolate rolling country to the south of Verdun. The wind blew fiercely across the whitened slopes, and no one was in sight but the sentries marching up and down the railway lines, and an occasional cavalryman patrolling the lonely road. Nothing can exceed the mournfulness of this depopulated land: we might have been wandering over the wilds of Poland. We ran some twenty miles down the steel-grey Meuse to a village about four miles west of Les Eparges, the spot where, for weeks past, a desperate struggle had been going on. There must have been a lull in the fighting that day, for the cannon had ceased; but the scene at the point where we left the motor gave us the sense of being on the very edge of the conflict. The long straggling village lay on the river, and the trampling of cavalry and the hauling of guns had turned the land about it into a mud-flat. Before the primitive cottage where the doctor's office had been installed were the motors of the surgeon and the medical inspector who had accompanied us. Near by stood the usual flock of grey motor-vans, and all about was the coming and going of cavalry remounts, the riding up of officers, the unloading of supplies, the incessant activity of mud-splashed sergeants and men.

The main ambulance was in a grange, of which the two stories had been partitioned off into wards. Under the cobwebby rafters the men lay in rows on clean pallets, and big stoves made the rooms dry and warm. But the great superiority of this ambulance was its nearness to a canal-boat which had been fitted up with hot douches. The boat was spotlessly clean, and each cabin was shut off by a gay curtain of red-flowered chintz. Those curtains must do almost as much as the hot water to make over the *morale* of the men: they were the most comforting sight of the day.

Farther north, and on the other bank of the Meuse, lies another large village which has been turned into a colony of éclopés. Fifteen hundred sick or exhausted men are housed there—and there are no hot douches or chintz curtains to cheer them! We were taken first to the church, a large featureless building at the head of the street. In the doorway our passage was obstructed by a mountain of damp straw which a gang of hostler-soldiers were pitchforking out of the aisles. The interior of the church was dim and suffocating. Between the pillars hung screens of plaited straw, forming little enclosures in each of which about a dozen sick men lay on more straw, without mattresses or blankets. No beds, no tables, no chairs, no washing appliances—in their muddy clothes, as they come from the front, they are bedded down on the stone floor like cattle till they are well enough to go back to their job. It was a pitiful contrast to the little church at Blercourt, with the altar lights twinkling above the clean beds; and one wondered if, even so near the front, it had to be. "The African village, we call it," one of our companions said with a laugh: but the African village has blue sky over it, and a clear stream runs between its mud huts.

We had been told at Sainte Menehould that, for military reasons, we must follow a more southerly direction on our return to Châlons; and when we left Verdun we took the road to Bar-le-Duc. It runs southwest over beautiful broken country, untouched by war except for the fact that its villages, like all the others in this region, are either deserted or occupied by troops. As we left Verdun behind us the sound of the cannon grew fainter and died out, and we had the feeling that we were gradually passing beyond the flaming boundaries into a more normal world; but suddenly, at a cross-road, a sign-post snatched us back to war: *St. Mihiel, 18 Kilomètres.* St. Mihiel, the danger-spot of the region, the weak joint in the armour! There it lay, up that harmless-looking bye-road, not much more than ten miles away—a ten minutes' dash would have brought us into the thick of the grey coats and spiked helmets! The shadow of that sign-post followed us for miles, darkening the landscape like the shadow from a racing storm-cloud.

Bar-le-Duc seemed unaware of the cloud. The charming old town was in its normal state of provincial apathy: few soldiers were about, and here at last civilian life again predominated. After a few days on the edge of the war, in that intermediate region under its solemn spell, there is something strangely lowering to the mood in the first sight of a busy unconscious community. One looks instinctively, in the eyes of the passers by, for a reflection of that other vision, and feels diminished by contact with people going so indifferently about their business.

A little way beyond Bar-le-Duc we came on another phase of the war-vision, for our route lay exactly in the track of the August invasion, and between Bar-le-Duc and Vitry-le-François the high-road is lined with ruined towns. The first we came to was Laimont, a large village wiped out as if a cyclone had beheaded it; then comes Revigny, a town of over two thousand inhabitants, less completely levelled because its houses were more solidly built, but a spectacle of more tragic desolation, with its wide streets winding between scorched and contorted fragments of masonry, bits of shop-fronts, handsome doorways, the colonnaded court of a public building. A few miles farther lies the most piteous of the group: the village of Heiltz-le-Maurupt, once pleasantly set in gardens and orchards, now an ugly waste like the others, and with a little church so stripped and wounded and dishonoured that it lies there by the roadside like a human victim.

In this part of the country, which is one of many cross-roads, we began to have unexpected difficulty in finding our way, for the names and distances on the mile-stones have all been effaced, the sign-posts thrown down and the enamelled plaques on the houses at the entrance to the villages removed. One report has it that this precaution was taken by the inhabitants at the approach of the invading army, another that the Germans themselves demolished the sign-posts and plastered over the mile-stones in order to paint on them misleading and encouraging distances. The result is extremely bewildering, for, all the villages being either in ruins or uninhabited, there is no one to question but the soldiers one meets, and their answer is almost invariably: "We don't know—we don't belong here." One is in luck if one comes across a sentinel who knows the name of the village he is guarding.

It was the strangest of sensations to find ourselves in a chartless wilderness within sixty or seventy miles of Paris, and to wander, as we did, for hours across a high heathery waste, with wide blue distances to north and south, and in all the scene not a landmark by means of which we could make a guess at our whereabouts. One of our haphazard turns at last brought us into a muddy byeroad with long lines of "Seventy-fives" ranged along its banks like grey ant-eaters in some monstrous menagerie. A little farther on we came to a bemired village swarming with artillery and cavalry, and found ourselves in the thick of an encampment just on the move. It seems improbable that we were meant to be there, for our arrival caused such surprise that no sentry remembered to challenge us, and obsequiously saluting *sous-officiers* instantly cleared a way for the motor. So, by a happy accident, we caught one more war-picture, all of vehement movement, as we passed out of the zone of war.

We were still very distinctly in it on returning to Châlons, which, if it had seemed packed on our previous visit, was now quivering and cracking with fresh crowds. The stir about the fountain, in the square before the Haute Mère-Dieu, was more melodramatic than ever. Every one was in a hurry, every one booted and mud-splashed, and spurred or sworded or despatch-bagged, or somehow labelled as a member of the huge military beehive. The privilege of telephoning and telegraphing being denied to civilians in the war-zone, it was ominous to arrive at nightfall on such a crowded scene, and we were not surprised to be told that there was not a room left at the Haute Mère-Dieu, and that even the sofas in the reading-room had been let for the night. At every other inn in the town we met with the same answer; and finally we decided to ask permission to go on as far as Epernay, about twelve miles off. At Head-quarters we were told that our request could not be granted. No motors are allowed to circulate after night-fall in the zone of war, and the officer charged with the distribution of motor-permits pointed out that, even if an exception were made in our favour, we should probably be turned back by the first sentinel we met, only to find ourselves unable to re-enter Châlons without another permit! This alternative was so alarming that we began to think ourselves relatively lucky to be on the right side of the gates; and we went back to the Haute Mère-Dieu to squeeze into a crowded corner of the restaurant for dinner. The hope that some one might have suddenly left the hotel in the interval was not realized; but after dinner we learned from the landlady that she had certain rooms permanently reserved for the use of the Staff, and that, as these rooms had not yet been calling for that evening, we might possibly be allowed to occupy them for the night.

At Châlons the Head-quarters are in the Prefecture, a coldly handsome building of the eighteenth century, and there, in a majestic stone vestibule, beneath the gilded ramp of a great festival staircase, we waited in anxious suspense, among the orderlies and *estafettes*,[10] while our unusual request was considered. The result of the deliberation was an expression of regret: nothing could be done for us, as officers might at any moment arrive from the Gen-

eral Head-quarters and require the rooms. It was then past nine
o'clock, and bitterly cold—and we began to wonder. Finally the
polite officer who had been charged to dismiss us, moved to compassion at our plight, offered to give us a *laissez-passer* back to
Paris. But Paris was about a hundred and twenty-five miles off,
the night was dark, the cold was piercing—and at every cross-
road and railway crossing a sentinel would have to be convinced
of our right to go farther. We remembered the warning given us
earlier in the evening, and, declining the offer, went out again into
the cold. And just then chance took pity on us. In the restaurant
we had run across a friend attached to the Staff, and now, meeting him again in the depth of our difficulty, we were told of lodgings to be found near by. He could not take us there, for it was
past the hour when he had a right to be out, or we either, for that
matter, since curfew sounds at nine at Châlons. But he told us
how to find our way through the maze of little unlit streets about
the Cathedral; standing there beside the motor, in the icy darkness
of the deserted square, and whispering hastily, as he turned to
leave us: "You ought not to be out so late; but the word tonight is
Jéna. When you give it to the chauffeur, be sure no sentinel overhears you." With that he was up the wide steps, the glass doors
had closed on him, and I stood there in the pitch-black night, suddenly unable to believe that I was I, or Châlons Châlons, or that a
young man who in Paris drops in to dine with me and talk over
new books and plays, had been whispering a password in my ear
to carry me unchallenged to a house a few streets away! The sense
of unreality produced by that one word was so overwhelming that
for a blissful moment the whole fabric of what I had been experi-
encing, the whole huge and oppressive and unescapable fact of the
war, slipped away like a torn cobweb, and I seemed to see behind
it the reassuring face of things as they used to be.

The next morning dispelled that vision. We woke to a noise of
guns closer and more incessant than even the first night's cannonade at Verdun; and when we went out into the streets it seemed as
if, overnight, a new army had sprung out of the ground. Waylaid
at one corner after another by the long tide of troops streaming
out through the town to he northern suburbs, we saw in turn all
the various divisions of the unfolding frieze: first the infantry and
artillery, the sappers and miners, the endless trains of guns and

ammunition, then the long line of grey supply-waggons, and finally the stretcher-bearers following the Red Cross ambulances. All the story of a day's warfare was written in the spectacle of that endless silent flow to the front: and we were to read it again, a few days later, in the terse announcement of "renewed activity" about Suippes, and of the bloody strip of ground gained between Perthes and Beauséjour.

From
IN LORRAINE AND
THE VOSGES[1]

This afternoon, on the road to Gerbéviller, we were again in the track of the September invasion. Over all the slopes now cool with spring foliage the battle rocked backward and forward during those burning autumn days; and every mile of the struggle has left its ghastly traces. The fields are full of wooden crosses which the ploughshare makes a circuit to avoid; many of the villages have been partly wrecked, and here and there an isolated ruin marks the nucleus of a fiercer struggle. But the landscape, in its first sweet leafiness, is so alive with ploughing and sowing and all the natural tasks of spring, that the war scars seem like traces of a long-past woe; and it was not till a bend of the road brought us in sight of Gerbéviller that we breathed again the choking air of present horror.

Gerbéviller, stretched out at ease on its slopes above the Meurthe, must have been a happy place to live in. The streets slanted up between scattered houses in gardens to the great Louis XIV château above the town and the church that balanced it. So much one can reconstruct from the first glimpse across the valley; but when one enters the town all perspective is lost in chaos. Gerbéviller has taken to herself the title of "the martyr town"; an honour to which many sister victims might dispute her claim! But as a sensational image of havoc it seems improbable that any can surpass her. Her ruins seem to have been simultaneously vomited up from the depths and hurled down from the skies, as though she had perished in some monstrous clash of earthquake and tornado; and it fills one with a cold despair to know that this double destruction was no accident of nature but a piously planned and methodically executed human deed. From the opposite heights the poor little garden-girt town was shelled like a steel fortress; then, when the

Germans entered, a fire was built in every house, and at the nicely-timed right moment one of the explosive tabloids which the fearless Teuton carries about for his land-*Lusitanias* was tossed on each hearth. It was all so well done that one wonders—almost apologetically for German thoroughness—that any of the human rats escaped from their holes; but some did, and were neatly spitted on lurking bayonets.

One old woman, hearing her son's death-cry, rashly looked out of her door. A bullet instantly laid her low among her phloxes and lilies; and there, in her little garden, her dead body was dishonoured. It seemed singularly appropriate, in such a scene, to read above a blackened doorway the sign: "Monuments Funèbres," and to observe that the house the doorway once belonged to had formed the angle of a lane called "La Ruelle des Orphelines."

At one end of the main street of Gerbéviller there once stood a charming house, of the sober old Lorraine pattern, with low door, deep roof and ample gables: it was in the garden of this house that my pink peonies were picked for me by its owner, Mr. Liégeay, a former mayor of Gerbéviller, who witnessed all the horrors of the invasion.

Mr. Liégeay is now living in a neighbour's cellar, his own being fully occupied by the débris of his charming house. He told us the story of the three days of the German occupation; how he and his wife and niece, and the niece's babies, took to their cellar while the Germans set the house on fire, and how, peering through a door into the stable-yard, they saw that the soldiers suspected they were within and were trying to get at them. Luckily the incendiaries had heaped wood and straw all round the outside of the house, and the blaze was so hot that they could not reach the door. Between the arch of the doorway and the door itself was a half-moon opening; and Mr. Liégeay and his family, during three days and three nights, broke up all the barrels in the cellar and threw the bits out through the opening to feed the fire in the yard.

Finally, on the third day, when they began to be afraid that the ruins of the house would fall in on them, they made a dash for safety. The house was on the edge of the town, and the women and children managed to get away into the country; but Mr. Liégeay was surprised in his garden by a German soldier. He made a rush for the high wall of the adjoining cemetery, and scrambling over it slipped down between the wall and a big granite cross. The cross was covered with the hideous wire and glass wreaths dear to French mourners; and with these opportune mementoes Mr. Liégeay roofed himself in, lying wedged in his narrow hiding-place from three in the afternoon till night, and listening to the voices of the soldiers who were hunting for him among the grave-stones. Luckily it was their last day at Gerbéviller, and the German retreat saved his life.

Even in Gerbéviller we saw no worse scene of destruction than the particular spot in which the ex-mayor stood while he told his story. He looked about him at the heaps of blackened brick and contorted iron. "This was my dining-room," he said. "There was some good old panelling on the walls, and some fine prints that had been a wedding-present to my grand-father." He led us into another black pit. "This was our sitting-room: you see what a view we had." He sighed, and added philosophically: "I suppose we were too well off. I even had an electric light out there on the terrace, to read my paper by on summer evenings. Yes, we were too well off . . ." That was all.

Meanwhile all the town had been red with horror—flame and shot and tortures unnameable; and at the other end of the long street, a woman, a Sister of Charity, had held her own like Sœur Gabrielle at Clermont-en-Argonne, gathering her flock of old men and children about her and interposing her short stout figure be-tween them and the fury of the Germans. We found her in her Hospice, a ruddy, indomitable woman who related with a quiet indignation more thrilling than invective the hideous details of the bloody three days; but that already belongs to the past, and at present she is much more concerned with the task of clothing and feeding Gerbéviller. For two thirds of the population have already "come home"—that is what they call the return to this desert! "You see," Sœur Julie explained, "there are the crops to sow, the gardens to tend. They had to come back. The government is building wooden shelters for them; and people will surely send us beds and linen." (Of course they would, one felt as one listened!) "Heavy boots, too—boots for field-labourers. We want them for women as well as men—like these." Sœur Julie, smiling, turned up a hob-nailed sole. "I have directed all the work on our Hospice farm myself. All the women are working in the fields—we must take the place of the men." . . .

May 17th.

Today we started with an intenser sense of adventure. Hitherto we had always been told beforehand where we were going and how much we were to be allowed to see; but now we were being launched into the unknown. Beyond a certain point all was conjecture—we knew only that what happened after that would depend on the good-will of a Colonel of Chasseurs-à-pied whom we were to go a long way to find, up into the folds of the mountains on our southeast horizon.

We picked up a staff-officer at Head-quarters and flew on to a battered town on the edge of the hills. From there we wound up through a narrowing valley, under wooded cliffs, to a little settlement where the Colonel of the Brigade was to be found. There was a short conference between the Colonel and our staff-officer, and then we annexed a Captain of Chasseurs and spun away again. Our road lay through a town so exposed that our companion from Head-quarters suggested the advisability of avoiding it; but our guide hadn't the heart to inflict such a disappointment on his new acquaintances. "Oh, we won't stop the motor—we'll just dash through," he said indulgently; and in the excess of his indulgence he even permitted us to dash slowly.

Oh, that poor town—when we reached it, along a road ploughed with fresh obus-holes, I didn't want to stop the motor; I wanted to hurry on and blot the picture from my memory! It was doubly sad to look at because of the fact that it wasn't *quite dead;* faint spasms of life still quivered through it. A few children played in the ravaged streets; a few pale mothers watched them from cellar doorways. "They oughtn't to be here," our guide explained; "but about a hundred and fifty begged so hard to stay that the General gave them leave. The officer in command has an eye on them, and whenever he gives the signal they dive down into their burrows. He says they are perfectly obedient. It was he who asked that they might stay . . ."

Up and up into the hills. The vision of human pain and ruin was

lost in beauty. We were among the firs, and the air was full of
balm. The mossy banks gave out a scent of rain, and little water-
falls from the heights set the branches trembling over secret pools.
At each turn of the road, forest, and always more forest, climbing
with us as we climbed, and dropping away from us to narrow valleys that converged on slate-blue distances. At one of these turns
we overtook a company of soldiers, spade on shoulder and bags
of tools across their backs—"trench-workers" swinging up to the
heights to which we were bound. Life must be a better thing in
this crystal air than in the mud-welter of the Argonne and the fogs
of the North; and these men's faces were fresh with wind and
weather.

Higher still . . . and presently a halt on a ridge, in another
"black village," this time almost a town! The soldiers gathered
round us as the motor stopped—throngs of chasseurs-à-pied in
faded, trench-stained uniforms—for few visitors climb to this
point, and their pleasure at the sight of new faces was presently
expressed in a large *"Vive l'Amérique!"* scrawled on the door of
the car. *L'Amérique* was glad and proud to be there, and instantly
conscious of breathing an air saturated with courage and the
dogged determination to endure. The men were all reservists: that
is to say, mostly married, and all beyond the first fighting age. For
many months there has not been much active work along this
front, no great adventure to rouse the blood and wing the imagination: it has just been month after month of monotonous watching and holding on. And the soldiers' faces showed it: there was
no light of heady enterprise in their eyes, but the look of men who
knew their job, had thought it over, and were there to hold their
bit of France till the day of victory or extermination.

Meanwhile, they had made the best of the situation and turned
their quarters into a forest colony that would enchant any normal
boy. Their village architecture was more elaborate than any we
had yet seen. In the Colonel's "dugout" a long table decked with
lilacs and tulips was spread for tea. In other cheery catacombs we
found neat rows of bunks, mess-tables, sizzling sauce-pans over
kitchen-fires. Everywhere were endless ingenuities in the way of
camp-furniture and household decoration. Farther down the road
a path between fir-boughs led to a hidden hospital, a marvel of

underground compactness. While we chatted with the surgeon a soldier came in from the trenches: an elderly, bearded man, with a good average civilian face—the kind that one runs against by hundreds in any French crowd. He had a scalp-wound which had just been dressed, and was very pale. The Colonel stopped to ask a few questions, and then, turning to him, said: "Feeling rather better now?"

"Yes, sir."

"Good. In a day or two you'll be thinking about going back to the trenches, eh?"

"I'm going now, sir." It was said quite simply, and received in the same way. "Oh, all right," the Colonel merely rejoined; but he laid his hand on the man's shoulder as we went out.

Our next visit was to a sod-thatched hut, "At the sign of the Ambulant Artisans," where two or three soldiers were modelling and chiselling all kinds of trinkets from the aluminium of enemy shells. One of the ambulant artisans were just finishing a ring with beautifully modelled fauns' heads, another offered me a "Pickelhaube" small enough for Mustard-seed's wear, but complete in every detail, and inlaid with the bronze eagle from an Imperial pfennig. There are many such ring-smiths among the privates at the front, and the severe, somewhat archaic design of their rings is a proof of the sureness of French taste; but the two we visited happened to be Paris jewellers, for whom "artisan" was really too modest a pseudonym. Officers and men were evidently proud of their work, and as they stood hammering away in their cramped smithy, a red gleam lighting up the intentness of their faces, they seemed to be beating out the cheerful rhythm of "I too will something make, and joy in the making . . ."

Up the hillside, in deeper shadow, was another little structure; a wooden shed with an open gable sheltering an altar with candles and flowers. Here mass is said by one of the conscript priests of the regiment, while his congregation kneel between the fir-trunks, giving life to the old metaphor of the cathedral-forest. Near by was the grave-yard, where day by day these quiet elderly men lay their comrades, the *pères de famille* who don't go back. The care of this woodland cemetery is left entirely to the soldiers, and they have spent treasures of piety on the inscriptions and decorations of the graves. Fresh flowers are brought up from the valleys to cover them, and when some favourite comrade goes, the men scorning ephemeral tributes, club together to buy a monstrous indestructible wreath with emblazoned streamers. It was near the end of the afternoon, and many soldiers were strolling along the paths between the graves. "It's their favourite walk at this hour," the Colonel said. He stopped to look down on a grave smothered in beady tokens, the grave of the last pal to fall. "He was mentioned in the Order of the Day," the Colonel explained; and the group of soldiers standing near looked at us proudly, as if sharing their comrade's honour, and wanting to be sure that we understood the reason of their pride . . .

"And now," said our Captain of Chasseurs, "that you've seen the second-line trenches, what do you say to taking a look at the first?"

We followed him to a point higher up the hill, where we plunged into a deep ditch of red earth—the "bowel" leading to the first lines. It climbed still higher, under the wet firs, and then, turning, dipped over the edge and began to wind in sharp loops down the other side of the ridge. Down we scrambled, single file, our chins on a level with the top of the passage, the close green covert above us. The "bowel" went twisting down more and more sharply into a deep ravine; and presently, at a bend, we came to a fir-thatched outlook, where a soldier stood with his back to us, his eye glued to a peep-hole in the wattled wall. Another turn, and another outlook; but here it was the iron-rimmed eye of the mitrailleuse[2] that stared across the ravine. By this time we were within a hundred yards or so of the German lines, hidden, like ours, on the other side of the narrowing hollow; and as we stole down and down, the hush and secrecy of the scene, and the sense of that imminent lurking hatred only a few branch-lengths away, seemed to fill the silence with mysterious pulsations. Suddenly a sharp noise broke on them: the rap of a rifle-shot against a tree-trunk a few yards ahead.

"Ah, the sharp-shooter," said our guide. "No more talking, please—he's over there, in a tree somewhere, and whenever he hears voices he fires. Some day we shall spot his tree."

We went on in silence to a point where a few soldiers were sitting on a ledge of rock in a widening of the "bowel." They looked as quiet as if they had been waiting for their bocks before a Boulevard café.

"Not beyond, please," said the officer, holding me back; and I stopped.

Here we were, then, actually and literally in the first lines! The knowledge made one's heart tick a little; but, except for another shot or two from our arboreal listener, and the motionless intentness of the soldier's back at the peep-hole, there was nothing to show that we were not a dozen miles away.

Perhaps the thought occurred to our Captain of Chasseurs; for just as I was turning back he said with his friendliest twinkle: "Do you want awfully to go a little farther? Well, then, come on."

We went past the soldiers sitting on the ledge and stole down and down, to where the trees ended at the bottom of the ravine. The sharp-shooter had stopped firing, and nothing disturbed the leafy silence but an intermittent drip of rain. We were at the end of the burrow, and the Captain signed to me that I might take a cautious peep round its corner. I looked out and saw a strip of intensely green meadow just under me, and a wooded cliff rising abruptly on its other side. That was all. The wooded cliff swarmed with "them," and a few steps would have carried us across the interval; yet all about us was silence, and the peace of the forest. Again, for a minute, I had the sense of an all-pervading, invisible power of evil, a saturation of the whole landscape with some hidden vitriol of hate. Then the reaction of unbelief set in, and I felt myself in a harmless ordinary glen, like a million others on an untroubled earth. We turned and began to climb again, loop by loop, up the "bowel"—we passed the lolling soldiers, the silent mitrailleuse, we came again to the watcher at his peep-hole. He heard us, let the officer pass, and turned his head with a little sign of understanding.

"Do you want to look down?"

He moved a step away from his window. The look-out projected over the ravine, raking its depths; and here, with one's eye to the leaf-lashed hole, one saw at last . . . saw, at the bottom of the harmless glen, half way between cliff and cliff, a grey uniform huddled in a dead heap. "He's been there for days; they can't fetch him away," said the watcher, regluing his eye to the hole; and it was almost a relief to find it was after all a tangible enemy hidden over there across the meadow . . .

The sun had set when we got back to our starting-point in the underground village. The chasseurs-à-pied were lounging along the roadside and standing in gossiping groups about the motor. It was long since they had seen faces from the other life, the life they had left nearly a year earlier and had not been allowed to go back to for a day; and under all their jokes and good-humour their farewell had a tinge of wistfulness. But one felt that this fugitive reminder of a world they had put behind them would pass like a dream, and their minds revert without effort to the one reality: the business of holding their bit of France.

It is hard to say why this sense of the French soldier's single-mindedness is so strong in all who have had even a glimpse of the front; perhaps it is gathered less from what the men say than from the look in their eyes. Even while they are accepting cigarettes and exchanging trench-jokes, the look is there; and when one comes on them unaware it is there also. In the dusk of the forest that look followed us down the mountain; and as we skirted the edge of the ravine between the armies, we felt that on the far side of that dividing line were the men who had made the war, and on the near side the men who had been made by it.

Explanatory Notes

SOULS BELATED

1. *Je n'en vois pas la nécessité!:* I don't see the need for it!
2. *tout d'une pièce:* All of a piece.
3. *"Civis Romanus sum":* "I am a Roman citizen," a claim which provided safe passage even in barbaric lands (Cicero, *In Verrem*, II.v).
4. Doucet draperies: Jacques Doucet (1853–1929), Paris designer, famous for his gowns.
5. Latude: French officer Henri Masers de Latude (1725–1805) was imprisoned three times for plotting to poison the mistress of Louis XV (after escapes from the Bastille).
6. *noyade:* Flood.
7. a Bradshaw: *Bradshaw's Monthly Railway Guide,* a series of timetables begun in 1839 by printer George Bradshaw.

THE MUSE'S TRAGEDY

1. "And did I once see Shelley plain?": "Ah, did you once see Shelley plain" is the opening line of Robert Browning's poem "Memorabilia" (*Men and Women,* 1855).
2. *Pour comprendre il faut aimer:* To understand one must love.
3. Egeria: Nymph said to have advised the legendary Roman king Numa Pompilius.
4. Tithonus: In Greek mythology, Tithonus asked for immortality but did not mention eternal youth. Growing older, he prayed for death but was instead changed into a cicada.
5. *Il faut de l'adresse pour aimer:* It takes skill to love (Blaise Pascal, *Discours sur les passions de l'amour,* 1652–1653).

6. *Lucile:* Book-length verse romance published in 1860 by Edward Bulwer-Lytton, writing as Owen Meredith.
7. *il avait pris son pli:* He was set in his ways.

FRIENDS

1. Venus: The beauty of *Venus de Milo,* and similar statues.
2. Olympian ire: The large passions (including anger) of the Greek gods who made their home on Mount Olympus.

THE HERMIT AND THE WILD WOMAN

1. swallowtails: Fork-tailed flags.
2. the Desert Fathers: The earliest monks of the Middle Eastern deserts (second century A.D. onward).
3. hodden: Coarse woolen cloth.
4. Zosimus: Legendary story of a fifth-century penitent (Mary) who lived as a hermit in the desert beyond the River Jordan. The monk Zosimus met her by chance and promised to return to give her Holy Communion. When he came back, she had died; he buried her.
5. Landsknechts: German mercenaries, sixteenth century.
6. *Angelus Domini nuntiavit Mariae:* "The Angel of the Lord declared unto Mary," a prayer said three times daily to commemorate the Annunciation.
7. a mouth of Dives: See Luke 16:19–31.
8. *Nones:* The ninth hour of the canonical day.
9. *carduus benedictus:* A kind of thistle.
10. *Veni, sancte spiritus:* "Come, Holy Spirit," a song sequence sung at Mass every day during Pentecost.
11. *Salve Regina:* "Hail, Queen of Mercy," a Catholic hymn to the Virgin Mary.

HIS FATHER'S SON

1. Laura: The beloved in Petrarch's famous sonnet sequence.
2. Petrarch: Francesco Petrarca (1304–1374), Italian scholar and poet who popularized the sonnet form of *abbaabba* and a variable sestet.
3. Latmian night: In Greek myth, the Moon visited Endymion, a handsome shepherd, and chastely admired his beauty as he slept.

AFTERWARD

1. *signalement:* Description.

THE EYES

1. *vertige de l'abîme:* Vertigo, dizziness.
2. *bêtise:* Stupidity.
3. Cherubino: Amorous pageboy in Mozart's opera *The Marriage of Figaro,* 1786.
4. Gautier's axiom: "Nothing is truly beautiful unless it is useless" (Théophile Gautier, preface to his *Mademoiselle de Maupin,* 1835).

THE LETTERS

1. *cabinet de lecture:* Reading room.
2. *mention:* Distinction.
3. *bonne:* Housemaid.
4. *blanchisseuse:* Laundress.

XINGU

1. *Robert Elsmere:* novel (1888), by Mary Augusta Ward (Mrs. Humphrey Ward).
2. *manière noire:* Mezzotint, introduced to England in the 1600s by Ruprecht of Pfalz (1619–1682).
3. *The Data of Ethics:* Herbert Spencer's 1879 essay.
4. *Canst thou draw out leviathan with a hook?:* See Job 41:1.
5. Karl Marx: Karl Heinrich Marx (1818–1883), German philosopher and socialist, who promulgated the theory with Friedrich Engels that class struggle has been the chief agent of historical change.
6. Professor Bergson: Henri Bergson (1859–1941), French philosopher whose concepts about the duration of time and the creation of comedy influenced twentieth-century modernism.
7. *Confessions of St. Augustine:* Self-revealing writings by the Roman monk (died A.D. 604) who began the conversion of the English to Christianity.
8. "Mendelism": The theory of genetic influence formulated by Gregor Mendel (1822–1884), an Austrian monk and botanist.

9. Wordsworth: William Wordsworth (1770–1850), English poet, best known of the Romantics, Poet Laureate 1843–1850.
10. Verlaine: Paul Verlaine (1844–1896), French poet whose writing was considered "modern."

COMING HOME

1. *La joie fait peur:* Joy is terrifying.
2. *café complet:* Coffee, milk, rolls, butter.

WRITING A WAR STORY

1. Mr. Bergson's: Henri Bergson (1859–1941), French philosopher.
2. Mélisande: Scene in Debussy's opera *Pelléas et Mélisande* (1902).
3. Florence Nightingale: Known as "the Lady with the Lamp," Nightingale (1820–1910) was the English nurse who organized nurse's training programs and reformed hospital procedures.

NOVELS
SUMMER

1. way-train: One that makes intermediate stops en route to a destination.
2. Washington Irving: American writer (1783–1859).
3. Fitz-Greene Halleck: American poet (1790–1867).
4. Minerva: Roman goddess of wisdom and the arts.
5. "The Lamplighter": Best-selling novel in 1854 by Maria Susanna Cummins (1827–1866) about a rebellious heroine who learns to repress her spirit.
6. "Uncle Tom's Cabin": Abolitionist novel (1852) by Harriet Beecher Stowe (1811–1896), the most widely read book throughout the world during the nineteenth century, next to the Bible.
7. "Opening a Chestnut Burr": A popular sentimental novel (1874), heavily Christian, by Edward Payson Roe (1838–1888), who resigned his ministry after this book's success to become a novelist.
8. Longfellow: Henry Wadsworth Longfellow (1807–1882), American poet popular for his somewhat moralistic poems.
9. traveller's joy: A climbing vine that bears white flowers. Crimson Rambler: A climbing rose.

10. Daniel Webster: Webster (1782–1852) was a famous American statesman, lawyer, and orator whose speeches were published throughout his lifetime.

11. the Creston Almshouse: The poorhouse, a care facility for people without income.

12. Bancroft's History: George Bancroft (1800–1891), a United States historian, published *A History of the United States* in ten volumes from 1834 to 1874.

13. high stock: A broad scarf worn around the neck.

14. "The Surrender of Burgoyne": John Burgoyne (1722–1792) was the British general who surrendered to the Americans at Saratoga in 1777. The etching is probably based on an 1824 painting by John Trumbull (1756–1843).

15. torpedoes: Small fireworks that explode when thrown against a hard surface.

16. the Merry Widow: The English name of Franz Lehár's operetta *Die Lustige Witwe* (1905), which bequeathed both songs and hairstyles to the public.

17. unintelligible words: The waitress and Harney were speaking French.

18. Knights of Pythias: Members of a secret philanthropic fraternal society, whose costumes were a part of their ritual.

19. "Home, Sweet Home": John Payne (1791–1852) wrote the lyrics for the music of Sir Henry Bishop (1786–1855); the song was used in the opera *Clari, or the Maid of Milan* (1823).

20. "Auld Lang Syne": Scottish song by poet Robert Burns often sung on New Year's Eve, to commemorate the past; "auld" is Scottish pronunciation for "old."

THE HOUSE OF MIRTH

1. Grand Central Station: One of two enormous railway stations in midtown Manhattan. It was begun in 1903 but not completed until 1913.

2. disputed her presence: Tried to get Miss Lily Bart to come visit.

3. Newport: Wealthy New Yorkers summered in Newport, Rhode Island, calling their lavish residences there "cottages."

4. eleven years: The time since Lily had made her debut as a marriageable young woman of New York's upper class. Most debutantes were eighteen, and were married within two or three years of their coming out.

5. Sherry's: Stylish New York restaurant on Fifth Avenue.
6. copy-book axioms: Commonplace; children's writing workbooks contained moral pronouncements.
7. book-muslin with gigot sleeves: A thin white fabric that was used to cover books, made up with puffy leg-of-mutton sleeves (not a fashionable style at this time).
8. Americana: Rare objects from early United States settlement history.
9. Jean de la Bruyère (1645–1696), French writer known for his *Characters of Theophrastus,* partly a loose translation from the Greek philosopher, partly his ironic portraits of his own time.
10. bézique: A card game somewhat like pinochle.
11. dryad: A deity or nymph of the woods.
12. *oubliettes:* Compartments that might be overlooked, forgotten.
13. cut the pages: Books were printed on large sheets of paper that were folded and sewn, so the reader needed to cut the edges to create pages.
14. caraven tea: Imported; i.e., in earlier times, brought by caravan.
15. Sarum Rule: The classic Christian liturgy in Latin.
16. rubric: Written or inscribed in red.

THE REEF

1. Kitty Mayne: One of Darrow's early (and lower-class) lovers, probably the reason Anna had ended their first engagement.
2. nymph: According to mythology, a lesser class of goddess—always beautiful women—inhabiting the sea, woods, or trees.
3. mare's-tails: The cirrus cloud that resembles a horse's tail.
4. down the Seine: The French river that flows northwest through Paris to the English Channel; Rouen and the Andelys are en route.
5. the Louvre: Since 1793, a world-famous national museum and gallery in Paris; built originally as a palace.
6. the Luxembourg: Famous Paris public gardens filled with statuary and lush plantings.
7. Palais Royal: The royal palace.
8. cinematograph show: Early (soundless) motion pictures.

THE AGE OF INNOCENCE

1. her room: It was customary within this social class for husband and wife to have separate bedrooms and, sometimes, separate sitting rooms.

2. Spartan: Pertaining to the people of ancient Sparta, who were brave, disciplined, and frugal.

3. Michelet: That Archer chose to read from Jules Michelet (1798–1874), historian of the French Revolution, suggests his own rebellious mood.

4. betrothal sapphire: May's engagement ring from Newland; the diamond was rarely used.

5. Mrs. Thorley Rushworth: Archer's early lover was a married woman.

6. Lefferts: Larry Lefferts, one such philanderer, disguised his behavior by setting himself up as a paragon of both virtue and fashion.

7. awninged: For parties and receptions, portable canvas awnings were installed over entrance stairs so that visitors were protected from the weather.

8. Diana: Ancient Roman goddess of the moon and of the hunt, protectress of women.

9. Fanny Ring: Julius Beaufort's mistress.

10. Adelaide Neilson: An operatic star of the time.

11. anecdotic: Pictures that consisted of scenes based on well-known stories.

12. encaustic tiles: Tiles decorated with burned-in colors.

13. "Cesnola antiquities": Priceless objects from the Cesnola excavation.

14. the Gorgon: Any of three sister monsters—Medusa, Stheno, and Euryale—who had snakes for hair, wings, and eyes that turned anyone looking at them to stone.

LETTERS

1. Wharton's visit to the San Vinaldo monastery in the hills southwest of Florence, Italy, prompted an essay ("A Tuscan Shrine," which *Scribner's Magazine* published late in 1894). Convinced that some of the terra-cottas within the chapels (which were reputed to be imitations of seventeenth-century works) were originals from the fifteenth or sixteenth century, Wharton had Signor Alinari, a famous photographer, make photos, which she showed to Professor Enrico Ridolfi, director of the Royal Museum in Florence. His opinion confirmed Wharton's judgment: the works are now attributed to Giovanni della Robbia.

2. Violet Paget (1856–1935), art critic and novelist, wrote under the name Vernon Lee.

3. "The Valley of Childish Things, and Other Emblems," included in *The Collected Short Stories of Edith Wharton,* vol. 1 (New York: Charles Scribner's Sons, 1968), pp. 58–63.

4. Probably J. B. Harrison, friend of Charles Eliot Norton.

5. Wharton's *The Man of Genius,* a drama of manners, was never finished.

6. *Sonnets and Other Verses* by George Santayana (1863–1952) appeared in 1894; the book includes "On the Death of a Metaphysician."

7. Daniel Berkeley Updike, a Boston friend of Teddy's and founder of the Merrymount Press in that city.

8. Sarah Orne Jewett (1849–1909), the author of the seminal *The Country of the Pointed Firs* (1896) and many other volumes, often visited her close friend Annie Fields in Boston when she traveled from her Maine home. Fields (1834–1915), the widow of Boston publisher James T. Fields, was herself influential in the worlds of literature and publishing.

9. A reprinting of *The Decoration of Houses,* Wharton's first book, which she wrote with Ogden Codman, Jr.; the book was first published by Scribner's in 1897.

10. In an August 17, 1902, letter, Henry James (1843–1916) praised Wharton's novel *The Valley of Decision,* and urged her to write about "the American subject."

11. *Es War,* a novel by Hermann Sudermann (1857–1928), published in 1897. Wharton had just translated Sudermann's play *Es Lebe das Leben.*

12. Norman Hapgood (1868–1937) had recently published his critical study *The Stage in America.*

13. Scribner's had also published Henry James's great novel in his late manner, *The Wings of the Dove.*

14. Barrett Wendell taught English at Harvard and was influential in the United States.

15. Mitou was Wharton's Pekingese.

16. Salsomaggiore ("Salso") is a health resort in north-central Italy, where Wharton sometimes went for her asthma.

17. Lourdes, a shrine in southwest France, known for curative powers.

18. Reviews of Wharton's third book of stories, *The Descent of Man* (1904).

19. Mr. James is her friend Henry James, with whose work hers was often compared.

20. Scribner's was planning to publish a book of her essays, titled *Italian Backgrounds.*

21. Elisabeth Marbury (1856–1933) was one of the first successful author's agents.

22. Morgan Dix (1827–1908), rector of Trinity Church in New York, wrote to Wharton on December 1, 1905, about her "terrible but just arraignment of the social misconduct" of her day.

23. Morton Fullerton (1865–1952) was lecturing on Henry James's oeuvre, prompted by the appearance of James's New York edition (the novels with the author's new preface to each).

24. Rather than listing times, Wharton enclosed the timetable.

25. Scribner's published Wharton's *The Fruit of the Tree* October 19, 1907, in an edition of fifty thousand copies.

26. Le Bréau was the home of Walter and Matilda Gay; the latter was the child of William Travers, a friend of Wharton's family in New York. Walter Gay was a painter of some note.

27. A reference to the captive Iole's comment when she first saw Hercules (from Emerson's essay "Character").

28. As part of the warfare over control of the London *Times,* Alfred Harmsworth wrote an unsigned letter to the London *Observer* that told readers the position of Moberly Bell. Morton Fullerton was a correspondent for the *Times.*

29. The plan was for Wharton and Fullerton to go away together for a night and a day.

30. Katherine Fullerton (later Gerould) (1879–1944) was an adopted child and Fullerton's cousin, not his sister. According to her, they had become engaged in 1907, when he spoke at Bryn Mawr, where she was a lecturer in English.

31. It was Henry James who had introduced the two.

32. The Lactantius refers to the writing of Lucius Caelius Firmianus Lactantius, Christian author and apologist of the third century.

33. Saint Benedict, sixth-century Italian monk, founder of the Benedictine order. His sister was Saint Scholastica.

34. Walter Berry (1852–1927) was a lifelong friend whom Wharton could have loved. Successful as a Washington lawyer, Berry was descended from the Van Rensselaer family and often signed his name Walter V. R. Berry.

35. The Victor Emmanuel monument, begun in 1885, was unveiled in 1911.

36. "Coeur simple" refers to the great short story "A Simple Heart" in Gustave Flaubert's (1821–1880) 1877 book, *Three Tales.* Fullerton is hardly a simple man, or a poor one.

37. Anna Bahlmann (1853–1916) was nineteen when she began caring for Wharton when she was a child, in 1872. She remained with her as "finishing governess," then as secretary and companion until her death in 1916.

38. Wharton did not exaggerate. By September 1, a million German soldiers were in France and within an hour's drive of Paris. On September 2, the French government left Paris to headquarter in Bordeaux.

39. Jean-Louis Vaudoyer (1883–1962), a young French writer and friend of Marcel Proust's, was a frequent visitor at Wharton's Paris home.

40. Pierre Louÿs (1870–1925), author of such erotic works as *Les Chansons de Bilitis* (1894), who had married the daughter of Cuban-French poet José María de Heredia. Another daughter was married to symbolist poet Henri de Régnier (1864–1936).

NONFICTION

A MIDSUMMER WEEK'S DREAM: AUGUST IN ITALY

1. Originally published in *Scribner's Magazine* 32:2 (August 1902), 212–22; reprinted in Wharton's *Italian Backgrounds*.

2. Claude's interpretation: Claude Lorrain (1600–1682), French landscape painter with a studio in Rome after 1627 (actual name, Claude Gellee or Gelee).

3. *"Si come schiera d'api che s'infiora"*: "Just like a swarm of bees that, at one moment, enter the flower," Dante Alighieri, *The Divine Comedy*.

PARIS TO POITIERS

1. Originally published in the *Atlantic* 101 (January 1908), 3–9; reprinted in Wharton's *A Motor-Flight Through France*.

2. Goethe: Johann Wolfgang von Goethe (1749–1832) married Christiane Vulpius, who had been a member of his household, in 1806.

IN ARGONNE

1. Originally published in *Scribner's Magazine* 57 (June 1915), 651–60; reprinted in Wharton's *Fighting France, from Dunkerque to Belfort*.

2. February: World War I had been declared August 3, 1914; during 1915, Edith Wharton made four trips to the Front, traveling in her own auto. As both her essays and her letters express, her trips were dangerous, though at the time she may not have understood how dangerous.

3. curvetting of chargers: Leaping of horses.

4. Spahis' tunics: The Algerian cavalry who served in the French army

were derived from Turkish spahis, who served with the Algerians in the nineteenth century.

5. sappers: Military engineers.
6. *"La France est une nation guerrière."*: "France is a warlike nation."
7. *"Et ils étaient tous comme ça"*: "And they were all like that."
8. obus: An artillery shell.
9. *"Sauvez, sauvez la France, / Ne l'abandonnez pas!"*: "Save, save France, / Do not abandon her!"
10. *estafettes*: Couriers.

IN LORRAINE AND THE VOSGES

1. Originally published in *Scribner's Magazine* 58 (October 1915), 430–42; reprinted in Wharton's *Fighting France, from Dunkerque to Belfort*.
2. *mitrailleuse*: Machine gun.

Selected Bibliography

PRIMARY WORKS

NOVELS AND NOVELLAS

The Touchstone. New York: Scribner's, 1900.
The Valley of Decision. 2 vols. New York: Scribner's, 1902.
Sanctuary. New York: Scribner's, 1903.
The House of Mirth. New York: Scribner's, 1905.
The Fruit of the Tree. New York: Scribner's, 1907.
Madame de Treymes. New York: Scribner's, 1907.
Ethan Frome. New York: Scribner's, 1911.
The Reef. New York: Appleton, 1912.
The Custom of the Country. New York: Scribner's, 1913.
Bunner Sisters, in *Xingu and Other Stories*. New York: Scribner's, 1916.
Summer. New York: Appleton, 1917.
The Marne. New York: Appleton, 1918.
The Age of Innocence. New York: Appleton, 1920.
The Glimpses of the Moon. New York: Appleton, 1922.
A Son at the Front. New York: Scribner's, 1923.
Old New York: False Dawn, The Old Maid, The Spark, New Year's Day. New York: Appleton, 1924.
The Mother's Recompense. New York: Appleton, 1925.
Twilight Sleep. New York: Appleton, 1927.
The Children. New York: Appleton, 1928.
Hudson River Bracketed. New York: Appleton, 1929.
The Gods Arrive. New York: Appleton, 1932.
The Buccaneers. New York: Appleton-Century, 1938.

Fast and Loose, a Novelette by David Olivieri, Viola Hopkins
    Winner, ed. Charlottesville: University Press of Virginia, 1977
    (Wharton's first long fiction, written at fourteen).
The Buccaneers: A Novel by Edith Wharton, completed by Mar-
    ion Mainwaring. New York: Viking Penguin, 1993.

SHORT STORY COLLECTIONS

The Greater Inclination. New York: Scribner's, 1899.
Crucial Instances. New York: Scribner's, 1901.
The Descent of Man and Other Stories. New York: Scribner's,
    1904.
The Hermit and the Wild Woman and Other Stories. New York:
    Scribner's, 1908.
Tales of Men and Ghosts. New York: Scribner's, 1910.
Xingu and Other Stories. New York: Scribner's, 1916.
Here and Beyond. New York: Appleton, 1926.
Certain People. New York: Appleton, 1930.
Human Nature. New York: Appleton, 1933.
The World Over. New York: Appleton-Century, 1936.
Ghosts. New York: Appleton-Century, 1937.
The Collected Short Stories of Edith Wharton, 2 vols. R. W. B.
    Lewis, ed. New York: Scribner's, 1968.

POETRY, TRAVEL WRITING,
MEMOIR, NONFICTION

Verses. Newport, R.I.: C. E. Hammett, 1878.
The Decoration of Houses (with Ogden Codman, Jr.). New York:
    Scribner's, 1897.
Italian Villas and Their Gardens. New York: Century, 1904.
Italian Backgrounds. New York: Scribner's, 1905.
A Motor-Flight through France. New York: Scribner's, 1908.
Artemis to Actaeon and Other Verse. New York: Scribner's, 1909.
Fighting France, from Dunkerque to Belfort. New York: Scrib-
    ner's, 1915.
The Book of the Homeless (editor). New York: Scribner's, 1916.

French Ways and Their Meaning. New York: Appleton, 1919.
In Morocco. New York: Scribner's, 1920.
The Writing of Fiction. New York: Scribner's, 1925.
Twelve Poems. London: The Medici Society, 1926.
A Backward Glance. New York: Appleton-Century, 1934.

SECONDARY WORKS
BOOKS

Ammons, Elizabeth. *Conflicting Stories: American Women Writers at the Turn into the Twentieth Century.* New York: Oxford University Press, 1992.

———. *Edith Wharton's Argument with America.* Athens: University of Georgia Press, 1980.

Auchincloss, Louis. *Edith Wharton.* Minneapolis: University of Minnesota Press, 1961.

Bauer, Dale M. *Edith Wharton's Brave New Politics.* Madison: University of Wisconsin Press, 1994.

Bell, Millicent, ed. *The Cambridge Companion to Edith Wharton.* New York: Cambridge University Press, 1995.

Benstock, Shari. *No Gifts from Chance: A Biography of Edith Wharton.* New York: Scribner's, 1994.

———. *Women of the Left Bank: Paris, 1900–1940.* Austin: University of Texas Press, 1986.

Carpenter, Lynette, and Wendy K. Kolmar, eds. *Haunting the House of Fiction: Feminist Perspectives on Ghost Stories by American Women.* Knoxville: University of Tennessee Press, 1991.

Colquitt, Clare, Susan Goodman, and Candace Waid, eds. *A Forward Glance, New Essays on Edith Wharton.* Newark: University of Delaware Press, 1999.

Dwight, Eleanor. *Edith Wharton: An Extraordinary Life.* New York: Henry A. Abrams, 1994.

Erlich, Gloria C. *The Sexual Education of Edith Wharton.* Berkeley: University of California Press, 1992.

Fedorko, Kathy A. *Gender and the Gothic in the Fiction of Edith Wharton.* Tuscaloosa: University of Alabama Press, 1995.

Fryer, Judith. *Felicitous Space: The Imaginative Structures of Edith Wharton and Willa Cather*. Chapel Hill: University of North Carolina Press, 1986.

Gallagher, Jean. *The World Wars Through the Female Gaze*. Carbondale: Southern Illinois University Press, 1998.

Goodman, Susan. *Edith Wharton's Inner Circle*. Austin: University of Texas Press, 1994.

———. *Edith Wharton's Women: Friends and Rivals*. Hanover, NH: University Press of New England, 1990.

Hadley, Kathy Miller. *In the Interstices of the Tale: Edith Wharton's Narrative Strategies*. New York: Peter Lang, 1993.

Hoeller, Hildegard. *Edith Wharton's Dialogue with Realism and Sentimental Fiction*. Gainesville: University Press of Florida, 2000.

Holbrook, David. *Edith Wharton and the Unsatisfactory Man*. New York: St. Martin's, 1991.

Joslin, Katherine. *Edith Wharton*. New York: St. Martin's, 1991.

Joslin, Katherine, and Alan Price, eds. *"Wretched Exotic": Essays on Edith Wharton in Europe*. New York: Peter Lang, 1993.

Lewis, R. W. B. *Edith Wharton: A Biography*. New York: Harper & Row, 1975.

Lewis, R. W. B., and Nancy Lewis, eds., *The Letters of Edith Wharton*. New York: Scribner's, 1988.

McDowell, Margaret. *Edith Wharton*. Boston: Twayne, 1976, 1990.

Moddelmog, William E. *Reconstructing Authority, American Fiction in the Province of the Law, 1880–1920*. Iowa City: University of Iowa Press, 2000.

Nevius, Blake. *Edith Wharton: A Study of Her Fiction*. Berkeley: University of California Press, 1961.

Preston, Claire. *Edith Wharton's Social Register*. New York: St. Martin's Press, 2000.

Price, Alan. *The End of the Age of Innocence: Edith Wharton and the First World War*. New York: St. Martin's Press, 1996.

Singley, Carol J. *Edith Wharton: Matters of Mind and Spirit*. New York: Cambridge University Press, 1995.

Tintner, Adeline R. *Edith Wharton in Context, Essays on Intertextuality*. Tuscaloosa: University of Alabama Press, 1999.

Tuttleton, James W., Kristin O. Lauer, and Margaret P. Murray, eds. *Edith Wharton: The Contemporary Reviews*. New York: Cambridge University Press, 1992.

Wagner-Martin, Linda. *The Age of Innocence: A Novel of Ironic Nostalgia*. New York: Twayne, 1996.

———. *The House of Mirth: A Novel of Admonition*. Boston: Twayne, 1990.

Waid, Candace. *Edith Wharton's Letters from the Underworld*. Chapel Hill: University of North Carolina Press, 1991.

White, Barbara A. *Edith Wharton: A Study of the Short Fiction*. Boston: Twayne, 1991.

Wolff, Cynthia Griffin. *A Feast of Words: The Triumph of Edith Wharton*. New York: Oxford University Press, 1977.

Wright, Sarah Bird, ed. *Edith Wharton: A to Z*. New York: Facts on File, 1998.

———, ed. *Edith Wharton Abroad, Selected Travel Writings, 1888–1920*. New York: St. Martin's Press, 1995.

SECONDARY SOURCES

ESSAYS

Bendixen, Alfred. "New Directions in Wharton Criticism: A Bibliographic Essay," *Edith Wharton Review* 10 (1993), 20–24; and see Ibid., 2 (1985), 3 (1986), 5 (1988), 7 (1990) et al.

Campbell, Donna M. "Edith Wharton and the 'Authoresses': The Critique of Local Color in Wharton's Early Fiction," *Studies in American Fiction* 22 (1994), 169–83.

Colquitt, Clare. "Unpacking Her Treasures: Edith Wharton's 'Mysterious Correspondence' with Morton Fullerton," *Library Chronicle of the University of Texas* 31 (1985), 73–107.

Dimock, Wai-chee. "Debasing Exchange: Edith Wharton's *The House of Mirth*," *PMLA* 100 (1985), 783–92.

Gooder, Jean. "Unlocking Edith Wharton: An Introduction to *The Reef*," *Cambridge Quarterly* (UK) 15:1 (1986), 33–52.

Gribben, Alan. "'The Heart Is Insatiable': A Selection from Edith Wharton's Letters to Morton Fullerton, 1907–1915," *Library Chronicle of the University of Texas* 31 (1985), 7–18.

Inness, Sherrie A. "Nature, Culture, and Sexual Economics in Edith Wharton's *The Reef*," *American Literary Realism* 26 (1993), 76–90.

Jirousek, Lori. "Haunting Hysteria: Wharton, Freeman and the Ghosts of Masculinity," *American Literary Realism* 32:1 (1999), 51–68.

Miller, D. Quentin. "'A Barrier of Words': The Tension between Narrative Voice and Vision in the Writings of Edith Wharton," *American Literary Realism* 27 (1994), 11–22.

Preston, Claire. "Ladies Prefer Bonds: Edith Wharton, Theodore Dreiser, and the Money Novel," *Soft Canons, American Women Writers and Masculine Tradition,* Karen L. Kilcup, ed. Iowa City: University of Iowa Press, 1999, 184–201.

Price, Alan. "The Composition of Edith Wharton's *The Age of Innocence*," *Yale University Library Gazette* 55 (1980), 22–30.

Robinson, Lillian S. "The Traffic in Women: A Cultural Critique of *The House of Mirth*," *Case Studies in Contemporary Criticism: "The House of Mirth,"* Shari Benstock, ed. New York: St. Martin's Press, Bedford, 1994, 340–58.

Schriber, Mary Suzanne. "Edith Wharton and Travel Writing as Self-Discovery," *American Literature* 59 (1987), 257–67.

Sensibar, Judith. "Edith Wharton Reads the Bachelor Type: Her Critique of Modernism's Representative Man," *American Literature* 60 (1988), 575–90.

Sullivan, Ellie Ragland. "The Daughter's Dilemma: Psychoanalytic Interpretation and Edith Wharton's *The House of Mirth*," *Casebook,* Benstock, 464–81.

Wagner-Martin, Linda. "Prospects for the Study of Edith Wharton," *Prospects for the Study of American Literature,* Richard Kopley, ed. New York: New York University Press, 1997, 201–18.

Wegener, Frederick. "Edith Wharton and the Difficult Writing of *The Writing of Fiction*," *Modern Language Studies* 25:2 (Spring 1995), 60–79.

Werlock, Abby H. P. "Whitman, Wharton, and the Sexuality in *Summer*," *Speaking the Other Self: New Essays on American Women Writers,* Jeanne Campbell Reesman, ed. Athens: University of Georgia Press, 1997, 246–62.

FOR THE BEST IN PAPERBACKS, LOOK FOR THE

In every corner of the world, on every subject under the sun, Penguin represents quality and variety—the very best in publishing today.

For complete information about books available from Penguin—including Penguin Classics, Penguin Compass, and Puffins—and how to order them, write to us at the appropriate address below. Please note that for copyright reasons the selection of books varies from country to country.

In the United States: Please write to *Penguin Group (USA), P.O. Box 12289 Dept. B, Newark, New Jersey 07101-5289* or call 1-800-788-6262.

In the United Kingdom: Please write to *Dept. EP, Penguin Books Ltd, Bath Road, Harmondsworth, West Drayton, Middlesex UB7 0DA.*

In Canada: Please write to *Penguin Books Canada Ltd, 10 Alcorn Avenue, Suite 300, Toronto, Ontario M4V 3B2.*

In Australia: Please write to *Penguin Books Australia Ltd, P.O. Box 257, Ringwood, Victoria 3134.*

In New Zealand: Please write to *Penguin Books (NZ) Ltd, Private Bag 102902, North Shore Mail Centre, Auckland 10.*

In India: Please write to *Penguin Books India Pvt Ltd, 11 Panchsheel Shopping Centre, Panchsheel Park, New Delhi 110 017.*

In the Netherlands: Please write to *Penguin Books Netherlands bv, Postbus 3507, NL-1001 AH Amsterdam.*

In Germany: Please write to *Penguin Books Deutschland GmbH, Metzlerstrasse 26, 60594 Frankfurt am Main.*

In Spain: Please write to *Penguin Books S. A., Bravo Murillo 19, 1° B, 28015 Madrid.*

In Italy: Please write to *Penguin Italia s.r.l., Via Benedetto Croce 2, 20094 Corsico, Milano.*

In France: Please write to *Penguin France, Le Carré Wilson, 62 rue Benjamin Baillaud, 31500 Toulouse.*

In Japan: Please write to *Penguin Books Japan Ltd, Kaneko Building, 2-3-25 Koraku, Bunkyo-Ku, Tokyo 112.*

In South Africa: Please write to *Penguin Books South Africa (Pty) Ltd, Private Bag X14, Parkview, 2122 Johannesburg.*